The Lucky Cricket

Tales from the Reading Dragon Inn
Book I

Tales from the Reading Dragon Inn series

Book 1
The Lucky Cricket

Book 2
Thomas the Poisoner

Book 3
Triskaidekaphilia

The Lucky Cricket

Tales from the Reading Dragon Inn
Book 1

Kelly R. Martin

Published by

Myth/**Logic** Press, West Virginia

Library of Congress Control Number: 2010942904

ISBN: 978-0-615-42916-8

Published by Myth/Logic Press,
27 Wilson Street,
Philippi, West Virginia 26416

Interior design and layout by Kelly R. Martin
www.mythlogicpress.com

Cover Illustration and design Copyright by Lance Red
www.reddaydream.com

Dedication

This book is dedicated to my parents Thomas M. Martin and Linda R. Martin. They know I love them, and that I appreciate the values they have instilled in me since my youth.

Contents

Acknowledgments

First I would like to acknowledge my family: my parents Thomas and Linda, my older brother Tom, and my younger sisters Colleen and Patty. Thanks to them I was raised in a family of readers which started my love of books from an early age. I also want to thank my wife Merly and my daughter Moira. They are my inspiration to make an attempt at writing a novel, and for me to take the risk in hopes of inspiring another generation.

I also want to thank my Grandmother Dorothy for being there for her many children, grandchildren, and great grandchildren. She's a cantankerous old donkey at times, with the stubbornness to never quit when she sets her mind on something She is one of the few people remaining in my life from the "greatest generation."

I want to give a loud, "Hello!" to all my various aunts, uncles, in-laws, nieces, nephews, cousins, etc. I come from a large extended clan with relations literally around the world. They've taught me many lessons in life, but mostly that I truly am just the holder of one perspective among many different points of view.

I want to thank my friends in the gaming crowd who put having fun and enjoying life ahead of getting into trouble. The old high school pen and paper party: Paul, Chad, Joe, Ken, Stacy, John, and Darren. The old college pen and paper party: Pat, Jeff, Sam, Kathy, Katrina, Fritz, Mike, and Eric.

I also want to thank my friends who have been there when I needed a hand in hard times as well as good times: Adrienne, Russ, Regina, Rick, Jane, Zenia, Fannie, Marissa, Allen, Jimmy, and Andy. Also I want to thank Hal for staying in touch even after moving away.

I would like to thank my many inspirations among the authors, game designers, animators, producers, teachers, artists, musicians, and directors. Unfortunately it is a Herculean task to even attempt to list them all. I do want to shout out to the web comic community in particular to thank them for bravely blazing a path in the self publishing field. Their hard work has opened the doors for other independent creators.

I also want to thank two independent creators the talented Gary Vincent, and the deviously humorous Richard Bottles Jr. who publish under the Burning Bulb Publishers label. They have been a valuable resource for cheering on my efforts, and I recommend you look up their works in return.

As an addition in the second edition release I want to thank Lance Red of www.reddaydream.com for his exceptional cover illustration. He's brought the world of the Lucky Cricket alive with his wonderful art.

Finally, I want to thank you, the reader, for showing an interest in this work. I hope you find it enjoyable.

Introduction

It is a second edition with a necessary new introduction. I'm putting this together as I'm also putting the last push for the first draft of my third book. Writing one novel has been a journey. Working on my third novel has definitely been an adventure.

For the new reader let me just mention that the high level concept I'm attempting is to make an extensive series with a lot of room for additional stories to be told. That being said I also want to write each book as a self contained story which doesn't require reading of any other works to enjoy the tale.

Some people may question the logic of why not leave the reader waiting for more. It's a formula which works for many series authors after all. My reason is simple, I'm a reader too, and I hate getting stuck reading a never ending series without resolution. My promise to myself was to have each of my books resolve the major story arc within the book. Then and only then do I plant any hooks for the subsequent works.

That being said I'm also a bit of an experimentalist. I didn't just want to write one kind of story. I wanted to write several kinds of stories set in an over arching multiverse capable of handling them all. This book is the first realm in that multiverse, and the linchpin which creates the base setting for the rest of the stories to be told.

Any of my books should be readable without an extensive knowledge or reading of the others. That being said, having a knowledge of all the events broadens the appreciation of each subsequent work. I do tend to have certain characters make cameo appearances in later works.

In terms of setting my first book is set in a fantasy asian culture which is a hybrid of several real world asian cultures. The naming conventions in several asian cultures are to list the family name first, and the personal name second. This is of course in contravention of our individualist western ideal of listing the individual personal name first before the family identity. So if you find the names confusing, mentally switch the order around.

Well without belaboring the point any further I'll let you jump into the story letting you know that I won't leave you hanging. However, the very last chapter is actually the setup for my next book. You don't have to read it if you don't plan to continue with the series, and this book can be considered complete with the second to last chapter. Also for those who like to read ahead, reading the last chapter won't spoil any surprises in this story either (evil grin). Wait, did I say reading it wouldn't spoil anything? It is chock full of spoilers for this story. That should teach them to not read the ending first.

The Lucky Cricket

Chapter 1 The Fisherman

Hap Sing was sitting in his boat on the rolling waters of the ocean. His little boat had an outrigger on the right and used a paddle to move about, but only the rise and fall of the waves was moving him. Hap Sing sat still and calm in the midst of all the motion, unconsciously maintaining his upright position with his hands upon his rattan fishing pole. The far end of the fishing pole extended out beyond the edge of the boat and the string dangled down to the water where a piece of water drenched cork tied to the line also bobbed on the waves.

To the ordinary eye Hap Sing was just another ordinary fisherman from the village. He wore his wooden soled sandals which looked much like the sandals worn by other men of his village, if just more aged perhaps. His cloth pants and belted long shirt were a natural hemp cloth color with no fancy dyes used to make them attractive. On the bench beside him was his sailcloth haversack filled with the wares of his trade as a fisherman. Over the side of the boat tied to a rope was his wicker fishing creel keeping his catch for the day fresh.

Hap Sing's face was shaded by his woven coolie hat, but it showed a light tan common among those who labor for a living. He was indeterminately middle aged in appearance obviously no longer a young man, and not an old man either. His hair was still black and close cropped without any sign of graying. He kept his face smoothly shaved, although he was not prone to be hirsute anyway.

Hap Sing's brown eyes were not looking at the cork on the end of his line, but instead focused on the shoreline where his village was. His expression was relaxed, and distant. If someone had been close enough, then they might even think he was daydreaming given the vague look he currently possessed.

As if some silent bell had been rung, Hap Sing's focus returned to the boat and his immediate surroundings. He glanced over at the sun just clearing the morning horizon. Next he focused on the cork bobbing on the waves beside his small boat. The cork sharply dipped below the surface of the water, and in return Hap Sing sharply jerked the line with the fishing pole in his hands. The cork resurfaced. Hap Sing reached down to grab his small fishing net with his right hand while firmly grasping the pole with his left.

As Hap Sing rapidly raised his fishing pole above his head he quickly scooped the net in his right hand into the water beside his boat. A deft twist and pull later he was holding a net with a nice sized fish inside it. A small grin showed on his face then and he spoke.

"Thank you most honored opponent. Your sacrifice will help feed me and my people another day."

Hap Sing then removed the fish from the net and unhooked it from his fishing line. He then pulled up his fishing creel from the water and placed his latest catch inside with the other fish he had captured earlier.

Chapter 1

1

As the sun cleared the last of the morning fog, Hap Sing began to paddle his boat back to the shore. He could smell the smoke from the village cooking fires being started to prepare the traditional mid day meal as his boat got closer.

As he reached the breakers he stopped paddling and used his paddle as a rudder to ride the gently incoming tide. As the front of his boat ground against the rounded pebbles of the shore he hopped out wetting his lower legs in the surf. He bent over at the waist, grabbed the front of the boat, and pulled it up the shore until it was above the high tide line. Hap Sing tied off his boat to a coconut palm, and walked to the village market street with his daily catch.

Eventually Hap Sing reached the trader's stall in the market where he usually bartered his fish for some vegetables and rice. Although he seemed as externally calm as usual, Hap Sing felt the Luck stirring inside of his being. Normally the Luck lay dormant and quiet. Like a cat asleep on a sunny patch of grass, it was content to rest. Hap Sing knew this meant something interesting to the Luck was happening, and that the Luck as usual had noticed it through his senses before he did.

As he bartered his fish for some vegetables and rice, Hap Sing saw the village elder and leader Lu Po talking with a middle aged man with a long mustache and wearing expensive silk robes. Here was the source of the Luck's interest he thought. After a moment of reflection Hap Sing realized this must be Ming Na Jun the magistrate of the Jin Do province. Behind Ming Na Jun stood his adolescent son Ming Wa Fu. Hap Sing noticed them watching his bartering, and refocused on getting back to his business. Hap Sing could feel the Luck metaphorically stretch in anticipation, and he heard Lu Po utter his name in their conversation.

A quick glance let Hap Sing know they were moving away from him. He also saw Lu Po cast a glance with a little shrug in his direction. Hap Sing concentrated on relaxing as he put the vegetables in his haversack. He trusted Lu Po to keep all official eyes away from him, and so far Lu Po had always managed to divert attention. Something about the magistrate had made the Luck interested, and that only suggested something potentially dangerous to Hap Sing.

Hap Sing made his way to the poorest section of the village, and knocked on the door of the young widow Wen Li. He remembered her as a very young child with bright eyes, and now she was a young mother herself. Her young son Wen Lu whose father was lost to the sea two years ago answered the door.

"Hello Wen Lu. I have some fish for your mother Wen Li for your meal today."

Wen Lu ran inside the house and came back with his mother Wen Li in tow. Hap Sing gave a bow which she returned. Then he brought a fish out from his creel, and then a second smaller fish.

Wen Li spoke in a shy timid voice, "Many thanks again Cricket, but you know I can not afford to pay."

Hap Sing replied with a smile, "Just raise Wen Lu to be as generous to his fellow villagers. That will be more than enough payment. We have to look after

The Lucky Cricket

each other here in Li Chan. No one else will look after us if we don't look after each other."

Wen Li thanked Hap Sing again and went back into her home. Shifting the strap for his fishing creel on his shoulder he moved along through the village toward another home. This home was bigger than Wen Li's home, but it was also much older. For all that it was still kept in a tidy fashion. A very elderly looking man dressed in a peasant homespun robe answered the door at his knocking.

"Hello there Cricket. Come by for lunch again have you?"

"Yes honored one . . ." began Hap Sing.

"No," interjected the old man, "none of that from you of all people. It is you who honor my home with your presence."

"I apologize for my impertinence Li Hung."

Li Hung laughed a friendly laugh, "Instructing me again Cricket? I should act my age perhaps? What does that say about you?"

Hap Sing stood there silently a moment. At a loss for words he brought out a fish from his creel and some vegetables from his haversack.

Hap Sing finally spoke, "Let's go inside and I will make us a nice fish soup."

What Hap Sing didn't mention was that the Luck had metaphorically stirred again. He looked around and saw the magistrate's son Ming Wa Fu loitering nearby sticking out like a rose among dandelions in his silken robes.

As Hap Sing entered Li Hung's house he quietly muttered, "Both of them, no wonder the Luck is stirred up."

He looked out through the door at Ming Wa Fu as he shut it.

"What was that Cricket?" Li Hung called from further inside the house.

"We'll need to talk, about the old times."

"Is there some trouble coming?"

"I don't know, but it doesn't look too safe at the moment."

Hap Sing began stoking the cooking fire, and set a kettle of tea over the fire to boil. He then rapidly filleted the fish he had selected, and sliced the vegetables into a water filled pot hung over the fire to simmer. The bones and head of the fish also went into the pot to cook, and he placed the fillets on a wire rack and turned them over the fire.

Li Hung said, "You think that after all this time you'd learn to use some seasoning when you cook."

"Why cover up the natural taste? You can always season the food after it's cooked if you prefer. Myself I like the taste of fresh caught fish and vegetables that haven't been stored."

Li Hung teased, "The secret to your long life then? Eating fish and fresh vegetables"

Hap Sing replied, "Not much different from you then perhaps?"

Li Hung's face turned suddenly sad. "I have lived a long life yes. Longer than most with no end yet in sight. I'm healthy enough for a feeble old man. Disease has not touched me in nearly one hundred years. Not since I was sick as a child and my father's friend saved me from death ... you saved me from death my master."

Hap Sing's face looked like a man stricken as Li Hung said those words, "I am no man's master. I'm glad I was able to save your life then, but I am so very sorry that it has cost you so much."

Li Hung replied, "Nonsense! I am just a tired old fool who is prattling on about his youth. My father knew what the price would be, and gladly paid it to save me. I'm paying my own price now, and I don't regret my father making the choice. It was the right choice, even if it was a hard one. Besides my father and I had twenty three more years together that we would not have had otherwise. How could I begrudge you that gift to him?"

Hap Sing shook his head, "I could not save your father from his fate. I tried, and I wanted very much to keep him from harm."

"My father lived an interesting and exciting life, as did I. We don't blame you for what fate had in store for us. He died on a battlefield serving his lord and country, and such were the risks he was compelled to take. He died doing what needed to be done. The land of Ran Li has had nearly seventy years of peace in part because of my father's final sacrifice in battle. How could I begrudge the man who made him into the hero of a whole kingdom?"

Hap Sing sighed, "I have cost you your father, and given you this torment of long life. I am to blame for this."

Li Hung smiled, "You gave me ninety more years of life. You are not to blame for how my life or my father's life was spent in that time. I would have been dead at fourteen if not for you. I would not have had those twenty three more years with my father. I have to thank you, and recognize you as my master or else I am just an ungrateful and greedy old man."

Hap Sing sighed again, "I am just a simple fisherman."

Li Hung laughed, "That is likely why you are fated to never die, you won't follow the path destiny has given you. You are a stubborn old fool. I know because I am one as well. Is that fish and soup ready yet?"

The two of them ate in relative silence. The food was fresh if unseasoned. It was simple fare for simple people. Though not extravagant, they enjoyed what they ate. A basic kind of wholesomeness from earnestly assuaged hunger helped to mollify their earlier exchange. As Hap Sing cleaned up from their meal Li Hung sat back in contemplation, or possibly impending sleep.

"We are old Cricket. You don't show it in your body perhaps, but I think your spirit feels it. I know mine does even if my body has aged more than yours. We grow weary with the time that passes. I don't think you are unable to feel it as well."

Hap Sing gave a non-committal shrug at the remark and said, "I fish. Since the sea is timeless, I don't notice time's passing as much."

Li Hung contemplated the thought for a while. Then he spoke, "Maybe you're right. When I was a younger man in the peak of my life I didn't think much about what would happen. I was just living in the now. Perhaps that is one of your secrets

The Lucky Cricket

after all. You live now instead of in the past or future. I am old and live mostly in the past for the future is too depressing to contemplate, and the now is so boring. Speaking of the past, you mentioned when you came in that you needed to talk of it."

Hap Sing frowned a little and said, "The Luck is ... active today. For the first time in many years it has taken an interest in not just one, but two people."

Li Hung smiled a bit, "Who could that be in this sleepy little village?"

Hap Sing's face became more serious, "They are not from this village. It was the magistrate Ming Na Jun and his son Ming Wa Fu. Even now Ming Wa Fu has felt himself drawn by the calling of the Luck. He waits outside trying to figure out why a simple fisherman is of interest."

Li Hung leaned back and furrowed his brow in thought. "When was the last time this has happened?"

Hap Sing brought his hand up to his chin and tilted his head slightly to the right, "I think six years ago when Wen Lu was born. The Luck seemed to be active then. The last time it took an interest in two people at once though was ..."

Li Hung caught on quickly, "My father and I ninety years ago. What do you think this means?"

Hap Sing thought a bit, "I don't know for sure, but I am worried about what it might mean."

Li Hung was more forceful in his question, "What are you worried might be happening?"

Hap Sing frowned, "I don't know, that's why I am worried. It might be nothing a coincidence or spiritual indigestion. Just like nothing has happened with Wen Lu."

Li Hung thought a bit more on the subject. "The kingdom of Ran Li was in dire peril of falling when the Luck found my father and me. That was the first time it had ever changed the destinies of two people at once correct?"

Hap Sing shook his head in denial, "I don't think the Luck changed your father's destiny at all, not directly at least. I suspect he was destined to be a heroic figure even when we were boys together. I believe the Luck somehow bound your destiny to your father's and made both destinies even greater. You father accomplished what he did because of your help. Otherwise he may have failed at saving the kingdom."

Li Hung asked, "Then what does the Luck want with the magistrate and his son?"

Hap Sing sighed, "I suspect that they are greater destinies because greater destinies seem drawn to me, even when others would ignore me. Just like your father became my friend because of his greater destiny. I've lived in this village for nearly fifty years same as you, and only the elderly have ever really noticed that I am still the same as I was fifty years ago. The only other people to ever notice me have always been greater destinies."

Li Hung asked, "Why be worried then? If this has happened before, it shouldn't be any different."

Hap Sing frowned, and then spoke, "Not all greater destinies are heroic. I believe just as many are villainous. There is a balance in the forces of destiny. I suspect the Luck doesn't care about which side of the balance a particular destiny resides."

Li Hung spoke, "Well at least the magistrate has a reputation of being an even handed and fair man. A bit arrogant perhaps, but not a bad sort really, no respectable person has ever impugned his honesty. I highly doubt he is a villain."

Hap Sing asked, "How will I know about the magistrate's son though? Sometimes the fruit rolls down the hill far from the tree."

Li Hung said, "I'm at a loss. Maybe one of the other elders can think of something appropriate. It's time you go. If that magistrate's son is waiting outside still, then keep him with you until they can think of a way to determine his destiny."

Hap Sing and Li Hung got up and walked to the door. They exchanged their good-byes with a tinge of regret about their shared past. Hap Sing knowing that Li Hung was ready to move on to the next life, even if his aging body refused to surrender yet. Li Hung knowing that Hap Sing carried a burden of guilt and worry that should never belong to him.

Hap Sing made his way to the first village elder Chow Xian's home and presented him with a fish. Chow Xian knew this kind of visit was unusual as Hap Sing generally kept to himself, but that Hap Sing was also the most unusual individual he had ever met in his sixty plus years of life. He invited Hap Sing into his home, and the two of them talked briefly about the Magistrate and his son.

Chow Xian eventually asked, "What is the problem if the two of them are in possession of great destinies? There may always be times of turmoil such as existed in my father's day. Those times need heroes as much as any and we may never know long in advance when these times will arise."

Hap Sing posed, "What if Ming Wa Fu is a villain instead of a hero though? All destinies are not the same, and the Luck doesn't care which destinies it influences. The Luck just draws the greater destinies to it over time."

Chow Xian replied, "You may be the oldest man alive, but sometime you will have to learn not to worry so much about the lives of others. This boy you barely know might become a villain. So how are his choices in life your responsibility? He has a father who is a fair and honest man looking after him. It is his father's job to give him a fair chance in life as well, and I think Ming Na Jun is responsible concerning his son's upbringing."

Hap Sing frowned again, "I know I shouldn't be responsible for raising the boy, but you have to understand. The Luck has taken an interest in young Ming Wa Fu. It will interfere with his destiny if it feels it must. Since I hold the Luck, I have responsibility for what it might do."

Chow Xian contemplated a bit and replied, "This is the only advice I can give. First, do no harm in whatever you do with Ming Wa Fu. Nothing good can come of agitating the government about your presence. They will never understand what you are, and may seek to harm you because of it."

Hap Sing furrowed his brows in agitation, "I have never been a Chi Master. This has nothing to do with the forbidden magic arts. I don't practice them."

Chow Xian placed a hand gently on Hap Sing's shoulder, "I believe you. However, you are likely the only living person old enough to come from a time when the forbidden magic arts were still in open practice. You know that the officials in the government will not understand that, and will accuse you of being a Chi Master if they discover your nature."

Hap Sing relaxed, "You are right of course. No good can ever come from hostilely confronting the magistrate or his son."

Chow Xian then added, "Since Lu Po is busy keeping the magistrate distracted with administrative matters, I suggest you ask Yong Mai about how she would handle young Ming Wa Fu. She may be a bit cranky in her old age, but her mind is as sharp as any, and she has raised nine children of her own."

Hap Sing left Chow Xian's home and made his way over to the edge of the village where the second village elder Yong Mai lived with her son Yong Ran. Yong Ran opened the door with a puzzled expression on his face.

Hap Sing said, "Hello, it is Cricket with that fish your mother requested. I'm sure she will want to look over the catch before she picks one out."

Yong Ran was a little taken back by this unexpected request, "Oh, I didn't know mother had sent out a request. I haven't really seen you for years Cricket. Life seems to be treating you very well I would guess. Wait here a moment while I check with her."

Hap Sing waited on the doorstep as Yong Ran went inside. He came back a minute later.

"Mother did request a fish I guess, she also wants to talk with you. I guess she gets lonely for company other than mine in her old age. Try not to stress her too much, she gets cranky at times."

Hap Sing was led to a small room in the house where Yong Mai sat on a cushion in front of a small fire. He bowed deeply before Yong Mai, and opened his fishing creel for Yong Mai's inspection. As she peered inside, she barked out an order to her son Yong Ran, "Get some tea on for our guest. Don't be rude, and chop us some more wood for the fire you know my bones feel a chill child."

Once Yong Ran was out of hearing Hap Sing quietly explained the earlier conversations of the day with Yong Mai. She nodded and smiled as she listened very attentively to his explanation, and kept quiet until her son came back with the tea.

"Have you finished that wood chopping yet? I didn't hear the axe working, and I know that winter is coming in just a few more months."

Chapter 1 7

Yong Ran was still a bit confused, but caught on that his mother wanted privacy with Cricket, even if he couldn't figure out why. He decided it must be some village gossip which his mother was partial to hearing even if she couldn't get around much anymore. He left the house and went to work on the firewood in the back yard.

Yong Mai joked, "Finally a moment's peace, and an attractive young suitor like you at my side."

Hap Sing blushed, "I am being serious here. I don't know what is going to happen with the Luck and its interest in Ming Na Jun and Ming Wa Fu."

Yong Mai slapped Hap Sing gently on his knee, "You may look like a younger man, but I am not senile yet. I know that you looked this same way when I was a young woman and you first came to our village. I think my son Ran is beginning to suspect something is up after your visit today. He may seem as dim witted as most of these other villagers sometimes, but it won't be long now before he figures out you still look the same as you did in his childhood. We'll have to bring him into our little circle soon as my replacement anyway. I am not much longer for this world."

Hap Sing sighed, "There is no need to talk about such. You still have some years left in you."

Yong Mai waved him off, "Don't try to smooth talk me. I know I am approaching my end. I don't think illness will get me, but one of these years soon there will come a day I just will not wake from my slumber. Such is life. I look forward to meeting up with my husband on the other side. I still have to tell him a thing or two about leaving me alone all these years."

Hap Sing thought a moment, "If you want, I could make a deal with the Luck to take away your pain. I would do so in exchange for the kindness your village has granted us these past fifty years."

Yong Mai laughed a nervous laugh with a look of mild fear in her eye, "No thank you Cricket. I have seen the Luck once before in my life the night the senior Wen Lu was lost at sea in the storm. I won't speak of that experience in detail but one more time in my life, when my son Ran is prepared to take my place. It was the most glorious and terrible thing I have ever experienced. I won't willingly go through that again. None of us elders will. You have been our Lucky Cricket and are a kind hearted man, but sometimes the Luck can be very hard. Seeing that haunted look on your face, perhaps it is hardest of all on you."

Hap Sing bowed his head again, "I am sorry for all the trouble I cause the village."

Yong Mai laughed a sincere laugh this time, "No more trouble than most here, and less trouble than many. The trouble you bring is just more unique than others. Your heart is a good heart Hap Sing. You are a good man who has a very hard fate. The Luck is a burden that none with any sense at all would take voluntarily, but you've carried that burden longer than any here can ever know. That burden might be troublesome, but it is also a benefit for us here."

Hap Sing looked confused, "I don't understand. Why don't you fear what might happen if the Luck were accidentally let loose again?"

Yong Mai shook her head, "Two years ago was a mistake. You were distraught about the senior Wen Lu being lost at sea. You felt responsible for him. You feel responsible for all of us. You were trying to help and all of us elders acknowledge it. Bad things sometimes happen to people Cricket. You can not always protect everyone."

Hap Sing smiled a little, "Thank you Yong Mai. You know how to restore me to my place. I get an over large estimation of my abilities and responsibilities sometimes. Now that you have set me at ease again, what shall I do about Ming Na Jun and Ming Wa Fu."

Yong Mai smiled back at Hap Sing, "This is simple. Ming Na Jun is a bit of an officious interloper, but for all that no one thinks he is a bad person. If his destiny is a greater one, then you must trust he is a hero. Since he is carefully guiding the steps of his son Ming Wa Fu, you must also trust that at least some good sense is being passed on to the boy. If you are worried about how he will turn out, well generosity is a sure sign of a good hearted person. Offer him charity, much like you provide for Wen Li when the rest of the village also helps her. Being wealthy he will feel obligated to pay you to avoid a personal debt to a person of lower station. Simply request his payment be made to someone else who is in need. If he is good hearted, he will help a person who he finds is truly in need. If he is merely following form, then he will pass along the money where it is convenient to his conscience. If he is a villain he will take the charity, and then keep any money as profit for himself."

Hap Sing asked, "When will I know?"

Yong Mai laughed, "As old as you are, and as much time as you spend waiting on the right fish, I would think that you had learned some more patience by now. Well it's time for you to leave. Catch up with Ming Wa Fu and give him our little test of character. As you go, send Ran in so that I can have a little talk with him."

After Hap Sing left Yong Ran's house, he turned and caught the eye of Ming Wa Fu where the magistrate's son was casually loitering on the street. Hap Sing calmly approached and asked, "Do you like to eat fish?"

Ming Wa Fu was startled by this unexpected question, "I enjoy eating a good fish much like anyone would. Why do you ask?"

Hap Sing laughed at the earnest reply given by the young Ming Wa Fu, and opened his basket to reveal one last fish inside. It was not a large fish, but it was suitable to make a meal for two. Then he replied, "I noticed you following me around since the Market, where your father was talking with the village elder Lu Po. I thought you were sent to get a fish from me, and your father might enjoy this one I have extra."

Hap Sing felt the Luck stretching out its "whiskers" toward Ming Wa Fu as if sniffing him. A small shock tingled along the back of his scalp. Hap Sing knew that for good or ill the Luck had done what it wanted for now.

Ming Wa Fu looked up from the fish realizing that he was hungry as he had missed his mid-day meal. He took the offered fish, and said, "I have some sovereign coins for the fish. How much do you want?"

Hap Sing waved a hand at him in a negating motion, "I have no need for such things as coins. I am a man of plenty with meager wants. However, if it pleases you, there will come a time when you see a person in need. Let them have the coins you would have given me. You will know when the time is right."

Hap Sing smiled at the youth, and gave him a slight bow with an encouraging shooing motion. Hap Sing then watched to make sure Ming Wa Fu was returning toward Lu Po's home. When Ming Wa Fu was out of his sight he began making his way out of the village and toward his home in the hills overlooking the ocean.

The next morning in the pre-dawn light Hap Sing paddled his boat out past the breakers just like he did every morning for the past fifty some years. He reached what he felt to be a good spot for the day, and dropped his line into the fog covered waters still chill with the night. He then looked toward the village and drifted with the receding tide. To the ordinary eye he might have been daydreaming. In his mind's eye he was casting two metaphorical nets.

The first net was the smaller of the two, and was mentally cast into the waters around his boat. It kept the younger and smaller fish out of the waters near his boat, while attracting the bigger and older fish which had already passed on their seed to make the next generation. This smaller net was cast if by reflex. It would keep him aware of when a good fish was ready to strike his line.

The second net was huge, but light and airy. He cast it with careful thought toward the shore where it spread open across the sky. The edges of the second metaphorical net draped down to surround the edges of the village and the nearby bay. This was his secret net which helped to keep the village and its people safe from harm, illness, and conflict.

The village elders had all in their way figured out over time that Hap Sing's presence had been a good omen for the village. They didn't know that it was this metaphorical net cast every day by Hap Sing that attracted the fish, and helped the crops grow without drought or blight. They knew Hap Sing brought them luck so he was their Lucky Cricket. What they suspected but didn't know for certain was that it was the Chi Magic used by Hap Sing subconsciously, naturally, without training, and with good intent which provided for them.

Where the village elders and even Hap Sing himself were wrong was that it wasn't the Luck that provided the ability. The ability was all Hap Sing, and it had been his ability since birth, and was inherited from his father almost one hundred fifty years ago. However, the additional power which made the ability so strong was certainly the Luck. The Luck was also from his father, but it was a mixed blessing. It was a very powerful being bound within Hap Sing making him the Lucky Cricket. Hap Sing knew his father had done so as his dying act, using a magic never before used, and lost with his passing.

With his nets cast Hap Sing settled in to fish as the first sliver of the sun was showing over the horizon. As he watched the shore he noticed the magistrate Ming Na Jun and his son Ming Wa Fu in the distance on their small pony cart leaving Li Chan village. He smiled at the thought that as early risers who were diligent at their duties they likely would end up as heroes someday. The magistrate and his son were among the people who would eventually shape the kingdom's future with their deeds.

After his morning and afternoon rounds at the market and Wen Li's home, Hap Sing made his way to the home of Lu Po the village elder and counsel leader for Li Chan. Lu Po's position was mainly involved with collecting the local taxes for the government, and keeping the ledgers for the village organized and updated. There were a couple of assistants who helped Lu Po with the book keeping work, and an armed and armored guard who helped him when it came time to collect the tax payments. The guard also acted as the village militia's captain on those times a levy of troops was required to be sent to the Jin Do province barracks to perform their annual drill. Both positions normally ended up being ceremonial since the people in Li Chan were generally peaceful and law abiding. The village was a strange combination of too poor to attract unsavory elements, yet too well off relative to many other small villages to cause unrest among the people.

Lu Po's home was the most elaborate house in the village. It had white plastered walls and a red tile roof. The home was built on a design with an outer wall surrounding an outer front courtyard, while the house was built in a rectangle around an inner courtyard with a tranquility garden. By the standards of the kingdom it was a suitable home for a village leader, but nothing special compared to the homes of the wealthy and noble born.

The front courtyard served for large village gatherings, while the inner courtyard was used for smaller functions. The ground floor of his home contained a dinning hall suitable for twelve people which daily served his family and staff, and occasionally served for functionaries such as the magistrate. There was also his administrative office which doubled as the village counsel chamber when needed. To finish out the ground floor were the kitchen, pantry, cold storage, along with a combination library and strong room where the taxes and ledgers were kept when not in use.

The second floor of Lu Po's home contained the living quarters for Lu Po, his family, and staff. Additionally the recently vacated guest quarters were also on the second floor. Hap Sing looked at the front gate with some trepidation about what he would soon learn, and entered the opened front gate. Hap Sing crossed the front courtyard, and rang the bell hanging from the stand by the doorway. The deep tone was melodic, and cheerful. Soon a staff member opened the door, and

Chapter 1   *11*

led Hap Sing to the outer vestibule for Lu Po's office. The staff member indicated a cushioned bench for Hap Sing to sit upon, and went into Lu Po's office. A minute later they came out and told Hap Sing to wait a little longer.

After about five minutes Lu Po opened the door and nodded at Hap Sing then waved him to enter. Lu Po pointed at a cushioned bench beside a small table, then sat at the opposite side from Hap Sing and poured still warm tea for them from a tea pot.

Lu Po spoke first, "I see you have come to visit me. What concern brings you to my home?"

Hap Sing looked nervous, "Have you talked to the other elders?"

Lu Po nodded, "Chow Xian visited them all early yesterday evening, and gave me a report this morning."

Hap Sing seemed eased by the relative calm of Lu Po, "So you are not worried then, that is good. I was afraid I was found out by the magistrate or his son."

Lu Po shrugged, "I don't know what the magistrate may or may not suspect about you. He is very sharp, and focused in on you very quickly when you caught his eye."

Hap Sing started to feel dejected by this revelation; it showed enough on his face for Lu Po to take pity on him.

Lu Po spoke again, "Don't worry Cricket. I have not lost my touch yet. His feathers were smoothed by my words bringing more pressing concerns to his mind. From what I have learned he will likely be more busy soon and have less time to inquire about curious fishermen. Although he did call you one of the wise, so I would not think you are completely off the hook yet."

Hap Sing started to feel better about the news, then showed dejection again at the last remark. A few moments of silence filled the room, between them. Then Hap Sing looked at Lu Po and caught the glint in his eye. Then Hap Sing knew that he was being toyed with by Lu Po for doubting his skills in managing people.

Hap Sing laughed, "I understand once again. I should trust you to deflect attention from me, and I thank you for doing so again this time. I will learn one of these years that I can't out maneuver your wit."

Lu Po cracked a smile as well, "What did you learn of the boy Ming Wa Fu from your encounter?"

Hap Sing relaxed, "His father is teaching him to be sharp too. He caught on to his father's interest, and followed me so as to report back to his father what he had learned."

Lu Po's smile lessened, "How about the Luck? What did it learn?"

Hap Sing shrugged his shoulders, "I don't know what the Luck is thinking, just that it sleeps mostly, and occasionally it wakes and shows interest in someone."

Lu Po grew more serious, "What does this interest mean?"

Hap Sing grew more cautious, "Usually nothing good for the people in whom it is interested."

Lu Po nodded his head attentively. A silence filled the room again, and Hap Sing realized he was being more subtly maneuvered subconsciously by Lu Po.

Hap Sing spoke again, "I am just a simple fisherman, but I have been around a while. You know that something is happening, but you are not telling anyone yet."

Lu Po bowed deeply across the table from Hap Sing. "I have to once again acknowledge that even without the Luck in consideration you are certainly no simple fisherman. You are a very wise and insightful fisherman."

Hap Sing bowed down to look into Lu Po's eyes, "I also know that you are a master at deflection if you want to be. Enough with the game we are playing here. Let's just put what we know on the table and make of it what we can."

Lu Po smiled, "Getting down to the essence of things, how refreshing and unlike the normal way of doing business in this kingdom. You'll ruin us all with your blunt nature Cricket."

Hap Sing gave a little smirk, "Still unwilling to let it pass though are you? I'll wait to give what information I have until I hear something of worth from you first."

Lu Po's smile lessened, "We need to play Go sometime. Something tells me you could quickly become a master. You would fool your opponent with your apparent blandness so that they miss the wisdom behind your actions until too late. It seems that is enough pleasantries then. The magistrate Ming Na Jun does have a sharp eye for people, and possibly the supernatural. I don't think it wise for you to be seen by him much in the future. His son is following closely in his footsteps. Ming Wa Fu will be formidable when he is grown. Now it is your turn."

Hap Sing was happy to be past the game playing, and putting the information out on the table. "The Luck has shown interest in both the magistrate and his son. This has not happened in a very long time. You have probably heard this before, but when the Luck shows interest in people they are greater destinies, either heroes or villains. The Luck has only once before shown an interest in multiple individuals at the same time."

Lu Po nodded, "Your friend Li Hung hinted at as much, but was evasive about the details. They involve him perhaps? I recall you both coming to this village fifty two years ago when I was still a child and my father was the assistant to the village elders. He was old back then, and much older now. I would guess he would be the oldest man I'd ever met, if it weren't for the fact that you haven't apparently aged in all those same years."

Hap Sing responded, "Try telling me something I don't know yet before I answer your curiosity."

Lu Po nodded in response, "Your point has been made. Your age is your business. Well my business is protecting and supporting Li Chan village. So I looked up the records of this village back before my father's time as village leader. I went back before my birth to when the village was founded over 73 years ago. Perhaps you have heard of that time, when the last major war the kingdom of Ran Li fought was with another kingdom now overrun with the wild beasts and lawless men. Perhaps you remember that time, since it is apparent that Li Hung remembers that time, and perhaps he even fought in that war. Did you know this village was named after Li Chan the greatest hero of that war? I checked all of the official records I could request. It seems Li Chan's son was also named Li Hung and was at his side fighting with him in the final last battle when the tide was turned against the invaders of Ran Li."

Hap Sing replied, "It is a secret, but one you have discovered. It is the same Li Hung who resides here and acts as one of your village counselors. The name and the person are the same."

Lu Po nodded, "That much I was fairly certain of being true. Now I will relate it back to what I think has happened and what I have learned yesterday from the magistrate. First off I think the Magistrate is a great hero in the making. He's being prepared by the gods or destiny to help the people. Does the interest of the Luck validate my point?"

Hap Sing replied, "The Luck is interested in greater destinies, and can alter the destinies of lesser people to make them greater. It can not determine or maybe it doesn't even care if the person is heroic or villainous."

Lu Po answered, "However, you have devised a simple test. This test of generosity will help you to determine if someone is heroic."

Hap Sing smiled, "You can thank Yong Mai for that since I simply administered the test. She is the one who came up with it."

"Your point has been made. Yong Mai gets the credit for being a wiser woman than either of us," said Lu Po. "However I have also heard disturbing news from the Magistrate about some unrest in the border provinces. Raiders and beasts are moving in toward civilized lands. There is more as well. Traders from the sea have brought news of similar happenings in most of the civilized kingdoms on the trade routes. It seems that something is organizing the wild areas as a single force. This has never happened in the recorded past, it makes our last conflict seem like the petty squabbles between two kingdoms. Throughout the known world it seems that some kind of darkness is rising from the borders with the unknown."

Hap Sing pondered, "You think because this shadowy organization is bringing unrest and dissent to the borders of the known world the Luck is acting now as well?"

Lu Po made a blunt statement, "We've been good neighbors for fifty two years. This village has accepted Li Hung and you and not regretted it. We've let you keep your secrets even when it was clear that you two were not the average travelers looking for a place to settle. Now we have to know some more of those secrets to judge the future given what I have learned today."

Hap Sing paled, "You don't intend to push the Luck do you?"

Lu Po leaned back and shook his head, "Not in my presence. I could not bear to ask the Luck another favor for myself. That day should hopefully never have to come again. What you know should be enough to make a judgment. When was the last time the Luck was interested in multiple people at one time?"

Hap Sing swallowed and acquiesced, "The last time I was as clearly aware of it was about 90 years ago when I saved Li Hung from dying at the age of fourteen when he was stricken with disease."

Lu Po nodded and said, "That means you are at least one hundred years old?"

Hap Sing shook his head, "I knew Li Hung's father back when Li Chan and I were boys together. I was his elder then, and Li Chan had his son Li Hung later in life. If I had to guess then I would say I am closer to one hundred and fifty years old. I seem to have lost count of the exact number of years."

Lu Po shook his head, "Amazing. No wonder I could not find any record of your name in the kingdom records. I didn't look far enough back."

Hap Sing laughed, "Don't worry there are no records of my birth. It was never recorded. I have always just been a poor fisherman who pays his taxes somewhere for a few years, then moves on to somewhere else. I feel responsible for Li Hung and his father Li Chan. I changed them with the Luck. They fought many battles in our great war, and they saved many lives by their efforts, but they lost much as well. They lost a normal life. I am giving Li Hung a chance to have a normal life here in his declining years to make up for that. Then I shall eventually move on after he passes."

Lu Po responded, "Given what I know from the magistrate and you, I would have to guess that the next great conflict is coming. Ming Na Jun and Ming Wa Fu are bound to be in the center of this conflict just like Li Chan and Li Hung were over 70 years ago. You may not know it yet, but I think the Luck is trying to gather forces to help just like it did the last time. It may not be good or evil, but I think that the Luck is vulnerable through you, and it wants help to keep you safe in dangerous times. We shall have to keep this in mind."

Hap Sing nodded, "It has always been so that the Luck knows more than it tells. I can not talk with it directly, and to summon it for someone to ask it questions has always been a difficult and dangerous chore. The Luck does not willingly divulge what it knows or how it learns what it knows. It can certainly draw a greater destiny to it when it wills it to be so. You may be right that the Luck manipulates destinies. However, I don't think it does so to keep me safe, at least not directly. I think it does so to keep other beings of supernatural nature distracted from its presence. The Luck's skill at deflection and redirection may be greater than either of ours by a massive scale."

Lu Po looked a little uneasy, "Other beings of power that frighten the Luck? Knowing what the presence of the Luck is like, I don't think that I'd ever want to meet such a being."

Hap Sing nodded in agreement, "Such a thing I fear as well. In me the Luck can remain hidden, like a tiger in the jungle. When the Luck comes forth it is like a low growl, and can reveal its position to anyone close. If too much power is used by the Luck, then it is like the Luck is pouncing from the cover of jungle to the top of a clear hill in plain view from a distance. If that is the case, then it is dangerous to remain close by when the hunters begin to close in on the tiger. Such is why I don't like to push the Luck. I've grown fond of living here in the village. Yet I don't want to bring any trouble on you all by my presence. If I must leave to draw these supernatural hunters away, then such is the price I must pay. You would unlikely see me return in the lifetime of the youngest villager then."

Lu Po looked at Hap Sing with sympathy, "Let us hope that such a day is not to come too soon."

Chapter 2 The Destiny

The seasons had changed several times since Hap Sing first met Ming Wa Fu, and he could almost imagine that things were tranquil and would remain so. Over two years had passed, and every time the magistrate Ming Na Jun came to the village with his son on their official rounds, Hap Sing made certain to be elsewhere. Most usually he went out to sea, but during their most recent visit Hap Sing decided instead to go on a short journey. He traveled on foot out of the Jin Do province heading toward his birthplace.

Hap Sing had not returned there in nearly ninety three years, not since he had healed Li Hung of his fatal disease. The Luck had informed Li Chan that Hap Sing would have to leave his home for a very long time. Too much power had been used, and too many of the wrong kind of beings were likely to take an interest. After counting back and reckoning for a couple days as he traveled, Hap Sing figured that his one hundred fiftieth birthday would be in a few more days during the spring equinox.

This recollection combined in Hap Sing as nostalgia about his childhood home. He figured that the Luck's prohibition from returning soon was long since past after ninety three years. He figured that nothing he knew could be patient enough about waiting that long, and the Luck didn't seem agitated at the concept of returning either.

Hap Sing had been mostly raised by his mother's brother. He had always been told that his father Hap Yang had died in the casting of a forbidden spell, but no real details about what that meant had been provided by his family. As an infant and toddler he was raised by his mother Hap Mi for his first few years, but her heart was distant, and she kept growing further apart from him. As a boy he had been told that his mother had died of grief at losing her husband. Hap Sing had learned as a young adult that she had taken her own life when he was five years old by drowning herself while wearing her wedding robes in the pond near her brother's home.

Hap Sing also knew that his father was one of the last Chi Masters to openly practice their art in the land. The spread of the practice of the arcane magicians, and the prejudices of the god priests had gradually poisoned the people over the years against the practice of Chi magic. Arcane magic could be learned by anyone smart enough and diligent about applying themselves to understanding its complex system of formulas and rules. The power of divine magic could be gained by anyone with enough faith in their chosen deity. The prejudice against Chi magic was that you were either born able to perform it, or else you could never learn it. Since it wasn't an equal opportunity form of power, it eventually fell into disfavor and disuse in the kingdom of Ran Li as well as other lands.

For most of Hap Sing's long life the Chi magic was considered forbidden and taboo as it was displaced by the newer forms of power. Certainly there were people who were born with the talent still, but if they were wise they hid the ability. Otherwise they risked condemnation and were even eventually treated the same as practitioners of the dark arts. The Chi magic relied on individuals who could innately tap into their own hidden potentials. As such it did rely on inner strength, and the use of mental imagery to manifest.

Hap Sing personally had been relying on the use of daydream metaphors to protect the people of the Li Chan village for fifty four years. He fished, and daydreamed of casting protective nets about the village. The Chi magic responded by keeping the people healthier, the crops bountiful, and people generally pleasant with each other. The Chi magic also kept people mostly oblivious to the fact that Hap Sing remained the same year after year. Of the regular people, only the members of Li Chan village who grew wise over their long years were able to pierce this veil. Once they discovered this new concept of a person living in their village who never aged, they were approached by the village elders to join their numbers. They explained that the fisherman known as Cricket was also the holder of the Luck, and the village benefited from keeping this secret.

The veil could also be pierced by telling someone the secret, but unwise minds tended to rebel at learning such knowledge. It shocked and alarmed most people who were not able to come to the conclusion naturally on their own. This ageless quality in Hap Sing certainly wasn't natural, and to many unprepared minds that also suggested it was somehow unfair and thus not right. What they could not easily understand without the wisdom of long years was that unnaturally long life was not necessarily an unfairly stolen gift, but instead a mixed blessing at best.

The other people who could pierce this veil were those which had destinies that were greater than the average person. These individuals were naturally drawn to Hap Sing. These people were called on by various powers to be something greater, and the long held wisdom of the Chi Masters was that greater destinies attract. Sometimes they would be attracted and bonds of friendship and camaraderie formed. Other times they attracted and bonds of enmity and mutual aggression formed.

Hap Sing thought back to his youth as he walked the path to his original home. When Li Chan and Hap Sing met as boy and teen all those years ago they felt an instant bond form between them. Until that time Hap Sing had mostly been a quiet and solitary child. His uncle while providing for his physical needs as an obligation to family did not encourage closeness or familiarity. While his uncle was not overly strict or unkind, he was a bit at loose ends with raising Hap Sing as a youth, and rather neglectful of Hap Sing's emotional needs being a bachelor himself.

Hap Sing as a youth liked to fish in the pond near his uncle's home. Unknown to him at that time it was the very same pond where his mother had drowned years earlier. He always felt a sense of calm while fishing there which prevented him from dwelling on the unsettling dreams he had more frequently as he grew older.

The Lucky Cricket

Hap Sing remembered that the dreams usually started the same with him walking around the community near his uncle's home. Then he would feel like a change occurred, and the community was no longer surrounded by well tended farms, but instead surrounded by an impenetrable jungle.

In Hap Sing's dreams the unnatural jungle would be full of hidden creatures making growls and cries which unnerved him so that he began to run toward the community. The people in the community would each recoil from him, and cast stones at him to drive him away as he ran past. They feared him just as he feared the creatures hidden in the unnatural jungle. Toward the end of the dream he would finally turn toward the people throwing stones and drop to all fours while emitting a great roar. Finally he bounded off on all fours to hide in the jungle with the other creatures.

As he reached his sixteenth year Hap Sing would fish in that pond and contemplate why he really shouldn't be scared of the simple dream. He didn't understand it, and it frightened him that there was likely more to the dream than a simple childish nightmare. As he thought about it this particular time there was a disturbance further down the pond where a splash disrupted the calm pond. He quickly looked in the direction of the exit stream from the pond, and he saw an unfamiliar child preparing to toss another rock into the water.

Hap Sing called out to the boy, "Hey there, you are scaring the fish when you throw those rocks!"

The boy looked over to where Hap Sing had been quietly fishing, "Good then. They should be scared, since I can catch them and eat them if they are not scared enough. It's good for them." With that he threw another rock into the pond with a loud splash.

Hap Sing thought a bit about what the boy said, then called back, "I think they are scared enough for today. If you scare them too much then I will never be able to eat."

The boy made an unpleasant face and then laughed, "You must be like some kind of great big cat then to want to eat fish. Give me rice and vegetables over those smelly fish any day."

Hap Sing waved the boy to come closer to where he was fishing, "I'm Hap Sing and I'd like to know your name."

The boy walked closer and answered back, "I'm Li Chan. One day I will join the king's army and everyone shall have to be afraid of me. I will be a great hero you know."

Hap Sing smiled at Li Chan as he came closer, "How can you know such a thing?"

Li Chan replied, "My father asked a Chi Master many years before I was born what his destiny would be. The Chi Master said he would be the father of a great hero in the kingdom of Ran Li. So we have traveled here so I can begin my great hero training."

Hap Sing nodded and smiled, "So your father is a great hero too then?"

Li Chan shook his head in negation, "Nah, he's a tinker. He's very handy with pots and kettles, but not so good with a weapon."

Hap Sing continued to smile, "Ah, I see. So how does your father know that this Chi Master was a real one, and not some fake practitioner?"

Li Chan smiled, "It was a real Chi Master for certain. He comes from this very community, and that is why we are here. His name is Hap Yang. He is supposed to be very famous for his skill in the Chi magic, so you should certainly know of him."

Hap Sing lost his smile, but managed to remain calm, "Hap Yang is no longer among us. He passed over sixteen years ago just after I was born. I fear you were born a few years too late to discuss your fate with him."

Li Chan looked stricken, and sat down next to Hap Sing, "That's just great. My father spent all his money to move us near the Chi Master Hap Yang so I could be guided by him. Now how will I scare everyone as a great hero if the Chi Master will not guide my path?"

Hap Sing contemplated this for a moment, "Perhaps it is not about scaring or being scared. It might just be about doing what needs to be done, in spite of the fear."

Li Chan was confused, "How can you be a hero who is scared? That doesn't make any sense. Only by being scarier than everyone else can you not be scared right?"

Hap Sing shook his head, "If you are to be a great hero, then you can not behave like a great villain. You have to help people, not scare them. Even if you are scary to some, you should not be scary to all. Great heroes are welcomed and celebrated, and not feared except by villains."

Li Chan turned to look directly at Hap Sing for a long time. Hap Sing started to become discomforted by the length of his gaze, and looked back over the waters of the pond to regain his calm center.

Li Chan eventually spoke, "What was your name again?"

Hap Sing held back his laughter at the sudden direction change Li Chan had taken, and he answered, "I am Hap Sing."

Li Chan gave him a knowing look, "The son of Hap Yang perhaps?"

Hap Sing nodded his head, "Yes, he was my father although I never knew him."

Li Chan grew more serious, "Are you the Chi Master who will train me to be a great hero?"

Hap Sing looked back at Li Chan in a flabbergasted manner, "Me? You think I'm a Chi Master? I don't think so. I'm just going to be a fisherman."

Li Chan continued his serious look, "You might fish, and that might make some people think you are as unassuming as a cricket. I think that you've got a scary tiger on the inside, and that you're as scared of it as it is of you."

Hap Sing looked at Li Chan stunned by this statement. His building dreams over the last few years started to make sense. He was running from himself in the dream. He unconsciously knew he wasn't accepted. He knew at that moment most

The Lucky Cricket

people would not accept who and what he was becoming. He would have to hide his inner nature, or else those people he met would reject him, and the unknown others would try to hunt him down to harm him. He understood finally that this was the message of his dream, and it made him very worried.

Li Chan reached over and patted Hap Sing on the shoulder, "Are you well?"

Hap Sing blinked his eyes, "How did you know? About the scary tiger I mean."

Li Chan smiled when he answered, "Because your father named me as a great hero. I can see that tiger inside you is your guardian spirit when I look in your eyes. You are very lucky. The tiger is considered a very powerful spirit in my country. You should become a great Chi Master some day."

Hap Sing patted Li Chan on his shoulder as well, "I think you may be right. We might just be able to help each other. However, I don't think the path of a Chi Master is in my near future. Being a fisherman suits me much better I think."

Hap Sing's attention snapped back to the present as he rounded a vaguely familiar bend in the path. He could see the valley where he originally grew up ahead of him. After ninety three years much had changed. More people had obviously moved in, and a thriving village now existed where a small community had been before. The land was also more cultivated in the surrounding area.

The village also sported what used to be a curiosity, but something becoming more common in the border provinces now, a new palisade wall. While the wooden wall didn't surround the outlying farms, it provided a secured space around the village which could accommodate all the families of the area. It was a sign of the troubling new times, and word of the unrest at the borders had even reached the general populace of the other inner provinces.

Hap Sing could see that his uncle's former estate still lay toward the other side of the valley outside the village near the pond. It seemed well kept from this distance, and its current owners seemed prosperous. Although Hap Sing noticed that many of the trees on the property and the valley in general had been cut to form the expansions to the growing community. Such was progress he thought. He couldn't see his father's former property from this side of the valley as it was on the far end at the high point near the border.

Hap Sing continued walking down the road to the village gates which were open, but curiously guarded by a pair of men wearing simple quilted armor and bearing crude weapons. The weapons were made of sharpened iron planting trowels affixed to lengthened wooden handles, a form of homemade short spear Hap Sing guessed. The guard on the right side of the gate moved from his leaning position and stepped forward while raising his hand in a stop gesture.

He cried out, "Hold there. State your name, place of residence, and business in Hung Chan village."

Hap Sing smiled at the reference since the community had been too small to have its own name when he had left all those years before.

He then spoke to the guard, "My name is Hap Sing. I come from the Jin Do province of Ran Li, the village of Li Chan."

The guard in front of Hap Sing scowled at that mention of his village, while the other older guard resting against the gate cracked a little grin. Hap Sing continued to smile and finished his reply, "I am here to look up some of my extended family members, and to pay respect to my ancestors."

The guard in front of Hap Sing looked over to the other guard, who nodded, and waved Hap Sing to approach him. The second guard took a close look at Hap Sing with his simple clothing, and carrying his fisherman's gear. Then he smiled and spoke, "You must be the great grandson of the Hap Sing who lived here many years ago. There are many legends about his father in this community. He would have been your many times great grandfather Hap Yang. It's good that you have remembered to honor your ancestors. Don't believe that hogwash the other provinces say about Hap Yang. He was a great man by all accounts, and this village doesn't forget what he did to save us."

Hap Sing nodded, "That is very curious. When my, err, great grandfather lived here no one ever spoke much of the great deeds of Hap Yang."

The second guard smiled, "Well I'm on gate duty at the moment, but plenty of us old story tellers come by the food stalls in the market street to relay the old stories. Come by there at dusk if you'd like to hear more. I'll be off duty by then as well once we close the gates. If you have to go outside the village today, make sure to be back here before dusk. After dusk we only open the gates for emergencies."

Hap Sing smiled and replied, "If you could direct me to the burial shrines, then I will honor my ancestors first, and make it back to town before you must close the gates."

The second guard replied, "Look over that way, you see that building?"

Hap Sing saw the shrine being indicated, "Yes, the one down by the stream."

"That is the shrine for the Hap family. It rests on the edge of your former many times great uncle's land. Your many times great grandparents have their totems placed there. The local god priest of Palnor doesn't like it much, but no one here will let him consecrate those burial shrines with their new religion. We still respect our ancestors here, though the same probably can't be said wherever it is your great grandfather rests."

Hap Sing laughed, "Don't worry I think he is still in good hands. You should know the people of Li Chan remember their ancestors as well. They even have living there still Li Hung as their senior elder councilor. He will be one hundred and six soon, a miracle they say."

The guard nodded his head, "The god priest would say a miracle indeed. Li Hung is honored here with both his and his father Li Chan's name for our village. We didn't know he still lived in the village named for his father. He is a very loyal son, and does his ancestors proud. Both of them were brave heroes in the great war you know."

Hap Sing smiled, "So he tells me from time to time."

The second guard waved at Hap Sing as he turned to head toward the shrine, "I am called Yu Wing. Look me up when you return. I will go to the food stalls with you to talk."

Hap Sing knelt down before his parent's shrines. He thought about the long lifetime which had gone since he had last been here, and the two lifetimes that had gone by since they had passed. Their spirits were at rest he supposed. They certainly didn't linger at their shrines as some spirits with unfinished business or malevolence were known to do. Hap Sing paid his respects as best he was able, and was glad to see the shrine was not neglected like many were these days in the times of the god priests.

As he rose from his long unperformed family duties Hap Sing noticed a woman outside near his uncle's former home. He gave her a friendly wave, and she continued about her business seemingly oblivious to his presence. He began to walk toward the house at a leisurely pace so as not to frighten her with a rapid approach. She eventually noticed him approaching, and peered in his direction. Hap Sing gave a friendly wave again, and she hesitantly waved him to approach.

Hap Sing saw that she was still in her middle years, but past her prime of life. She was still fairly attractive in her way. He supposed that she was possibly a distant relative who had inherited his uncle's estate after his uncle had passed.

"Hello, I am Hap Sing. I'm told my many generations ago uncle used to live on this land here."

The woman nodded, "My husband inherited this land from his father. Forgive my rudeness. Hello, I am Yu Mai. I suppose that makes us distant relatives by marriage then."

Hap Sing nodded, "Then would your husband be Yu Wing, the guard I met up at the gate?"

Yu Mai smiled at him, "Yes, lazy good for nothing. He chooses to take guard duty one day a week so he can avoid all the work required to run this place. It lets him rest in the shade, and talk with his friends in the village. He is probably spending what little money we get for his work on sake while I toil away on the farm."

Hap Sing laughed, "No wonder he recognized my name, we must be distant cousins or something."

Yu Mai laughed, "Most likely. I suppose he wants you to spend the evening in the village with him tonight. Well I'm coming with you. I get tired of waiting for him to come home some nights, and now I have a relative to escort me to the village safely. Were you the man I saw down by the Hap shrine earlier then?"

Hap Sing nodded, "Yes, I was paying respects to my ancestors. It was long overdue."

Yu Mai nodded, "It's a good thing Yu Wing keeps that shrine up then. It would be embarrassing if it were found by a blood relative of the Hap family in a bad condition."

     Chapter 2   23

Hap Sing smiled again, "Your concern is appreciated, and I am sure my ancestors thank you and your husband for your efforts as well."

The rest of the afternoon Hap Sing helped Yu Mai with a number of the chores around the estate. Now that he was closer he could see much had changed. The original house was no longer present, and a newer one built of sturdy stones and with a heavy door stood in the same spot. Much more of the estate was cultivated, and the pond was now used for irrigation of the crops. It was less of a bachelor's retreat, and more of a family farm now. When he asked he discovered that the Yu's two children had both married, and moved into the village, though presumably their son and not their daughter would inherit the estate when they passed it along.

After the farm chores were completed they walked toward the village with the sun lowering toward the western horizon.

Hap Sing asked Yu Mai, "What ever happened to the home of Hap Yang on the rise at the far end of the valley near the border?

Yu Mai responded, "It has been raided many times, and left abandoned as indefensible by the people of Hung Chan. Now it is mostly rubble and ruin which has been tumbled down and burned so as to give no comfort to invaders from beyond the border. For several years quite a few wizards would tend to visit hoping to find some kind of arcane artifact which would unlock the powers of the Chi Masters for them. Then the god priests would occasionally come through and bless the site trying to remove any evil spirits."

Hap Sing shook his head, "It seems neither one really understands what Hap Yang represented."

Yu Mai sighed, "They have chased the Chi Masters into hiding all these years so that they have become a dying breed. Now that the trouble stirs on our borders, these same wizards and priests flee the area of conflict. It's funny to think of it when our past tells of the great sacrifices made by Chi Masters like Hap Yang. Yu Wing is a distant relative coming from his wife's side of the family you know. Yu Wing is descended from her younger sister."

Hap Sing thought a moment, "My many times great aunt then?"

Yu Mai nodded, "I would think that's the case. She didn't live here then, but her son inherited this property from her brother, your many times great uncle when he passed. Your great grandfather and namesake would have normally inherited, but you know what they say about him."

Hap Sing smiled though he felt nervous about this new direction in the conversation, "This is interesting news to me, my family had never said as much about what happened."

Yu Mai's voice dropped into a conspiratorial whisper, "They say Hap Sing's father Hap Yang used him as an innocent baby in a spell as a prison to capture the Great Spirit that threatened our very kingdom. Hap Yang became the hero of this village then for saving us from destruction, but unfortunately Hap Yang died from casting this forbidden spell. Hap Sing's uncle was said to have prohibited the people here to ever talk about it while the boy was still around. The uncle was afraid the Great Spirit would break loose and destroy all of us if Hap Sing knew the truth."

Hap Sing covered his surprise at this revelation with a laugh, "That doesn't seem very likely."

Yu Mai laughed as well, "Well you know not many people understand the Chi magic anymore, so anything could be possible as far as they know. Those few who do know anything, well they are not really talking about it anymore."

Hap Sing and Yu Mai approached the gate where Yu Wing raised an eyebrow at seeing his wife accompany Hap Sing to the Village. The other guard looked over at him and whispered, "No sake for you tonight" and laughed.

Yu Mai greeted her husband with a kiss on the cheek, "Your distant cousin offered to walk me to town, and did a number of your chores at the farm as well."

Hap Sing interjected, "As thanks to you for maintaining our ancestor's shrine."

Yu Wing smiled at Hap Sing, "It's a good service in exchange. If you would escort my wife to the market stalls, I will meet up with you later after we close the gates, and the new guards replace us."

Yu Mai and Hap Sing walked to the open air market in Hung Chan and it reminded him of the market in Li Chan in many ways. The only noticeable difference was a lack of fish sellers being replaced by more butchers. Several stalls sold various goods including raw food stuffs, and other stalls provided cooking services for whatever was bought. Hap Sing accompanied Yu Mai around the various sellers while she picked out various items for a group meal. She took the items to a cooking stall, and Hap Sing added some of his supply of dried fish to the list. The cook was interested in this new challenge of dried sea fish, and promised to make the best of it he could.

Yu Mai and Hap Sing sat at the tables near the center of the market. Yu Mai made light conversation with several people, introducing Hap Sing as her husband's cousin from a distant village. Then she looked over Hap Sing's shoulder, and a brief sour look came to her face, quickly replaced with a somewhat insincere smile. When Hap Sing glanced over his shoulder he noticed an austere serious looking young man dressed in the robes of a god priest approaching their table.

The man briefly glanced at Hap Sing sitting with Yu Mai at the table. The he seemingly ignored Hap Sing and addressed Yu Mai directly. "Honored mother of my wife, may the blessings of the great Palnor be on you. Where is the honored father of my wife?"

The last part was said with a touch of accusation in the tone.

Yu Mai smiled sweetly back at the priest, "Lo Dong Arthur, I would like to introduce you to your father-in-law's distant cousin Hap Sing."

Hap Sing rose while feeling a distinctly chilly formality between the strangely named god priest Lo Arthur and Yu Mai. "I am pleased to meet you. I have come from Li Chan village to pay respects to my ancestor's shrines in Hung Chan."

Lo Arthur replied, "You may refer to me as Holy One Arthur. I no longer use the name Lo Dong since I joined the faith of the great Palnor. You are another follower of the quaint old customs I guess. My wife's father and mother won't allow me to properly consecrate those shrines to protect from evil spirits. Of course since it is their land I am still obliged to follow their wishes." As he spoke Arthur then reached for the symbol of a dragon hung upon a chain about his neck.

Hap Sing felt a surge of divine presence coming from the priest, and an unexpected reflexive response from the Luck. It was no longer sleeping as it normally would, but it was instead very aware. Hap Sing got the impression that the Luck was very still, as if preparing to pounce on its prey. He felt very nervous about where this could possibly lead, and instinctively reached out his hand in a greeting to Arthur. The hand of the priest released his dragon symbol, and naturally reached out to perform a handshake as well. Hap Sing felt a quick surge from the Luck as their hands touched.

Arthur's face looked confused as they shook hands, and he gradually gave Hap Sing a genuine smile, "It's nice to meet you. Any family is welcome to visit. I really should be going back to help my wife now."

Arthur looked at Yu Mai again, and his smile faded, "Don't keep Hap Sing out all night with these blasphemous tale tellers around here. I don't know why this village dwells on those old stories so much."

Yu Mai smiled and waved her son-in-law away. Then she looked carefully at Hap Sing, "There is more than one interesting tale to be told here tonight I think."

They waited for a few minutes in awkward silence, both wrapped in their own thoughts. Yu Mai obviously upset by the interaction with her son-in-law. Soon the food preparer approached their table with their finished meal. As they set out the bowls and utensils Yu Wing came over carrying three bottles of sake.

Yu Wing spoke, "It's a good thing I thought to bring something to drink. My wife tends to forget that we need to have drinks with our visitors."

Yu Wing then sat down and poured sake for his wife and himself, from the one bottle, and passed a separate bottle over to Hap Sing. He watched as Hap Sing took a gradual small sip from his cup. He also noticed that Yu Mai had rapidly swallowed her entire portion, and presented her cup to him for more.

As Yu Wing poured a second cup he asked, "Something happened here. What is wrong my dear wife?"

Yu Mai drank down the second cup, then started passing out the food onto their bowls as she spoke, "Arthur came by as we were waiting. That sorry excuse for a son-in-law implied that I was improperly here with another man, that we were blaspheming his faith again, and that we were paying court to evil spirits all in less time that it took to drink those two cups of sake."

Yu Wing shook his head as Yu Mai's lament continued, "I still don't know what our silly ox of a daughter sees in that fool. I begin to dread every time he comes around any more. Every exchange is an attempt to belittle his elders and frankly his betters. That fool even tried to insult Hap Sing here by reaching for that silly dragon symbol he wears on that chain around his neck. I think he was trying to imply that something was wrong with him that needed his god to correct once Hap Sing simply mentioned that he was paying respect to his ancestors."

Yu Wing looked embarrassed, "I apologize for my son-in-law Lo Dong. At one time he was considered a bright youth in our village. He was even sent off by his family to the capital Yokito to learn at the great schools there. Unfortunately while at the capital he fell in with that crowd of Palnor worshipers, and has finally become a priest of their sect.

We didn't understand the depth of this change until after he had returned from the capital and taken our daughter's hand in marriage. He came back here fully expecting to make great strides in conversions to his new faith. Most of the people listened to his views at first, and a few have even eventually joined his faith, but not nearly enough to satisfy his superiors desires I suspect. I think he's becoming a bit bitter and resentful lately. He hasn't even managed to convert his own wife's parents you see. I suspect he finds it hard to explain to his superiors in the faith."

Yu Mai had finished a third glass and a portion of her meal when she spoke up, "This fish is very tasty by the way Hap Sing. Yu Gai did a good job preparing it I think. I'm wondering though what magic you worked that made Arthur abandon his insinuations and to actually think of our daughter as something other than a path to inherit our land."

Hap Sing was briefly taken back by the switch in conversation from food to him. He smiled and replied, "I just ignored his manner, and presented him with a friendly attitude. Sometimes it can work wonders with a wayward young man like him. Thank you for the complement on the fish. It is definitely very tasty when prepared this way."

Yu Wing and Yu Mai exchanged a glance with each other at Hap Sing's comment. Yu Wing inconspicuously looked around the market tables at the other people present as he ate. He waved at the stall which had prepared their food, gave a positive hand sign to show the food was well accepted. They exchanged a nod, and then Yu Wing went back to eating. Yu Mai slowed down on drinking sake, and picked up on eating her meal as well. As he ate his meal Hap Sing noticed a pattern of quiet subtle communication happening in the marketplace. Normal unremarkable greetings sometimes supplemented by subtle additional gestures, and circulated to some people, while clearly skipping others.

Hap Sing was feeling like he was being drawn in to a circle of a conspiracy of a nature he didn't quite understand. He took another sip of sake, and tried to relax his mind in a way he hadn't attempted in years. He looked down at his bowl picking up the last pieces of food left. He closed his eyes while concentrating, and opened them again with his birthright of the second sight. The second sight was one of his father's gifts to him. It allowed him to see the nearby spiritual and supernatural realms overlaid on our own. It was a handy skill when needed, but a taxing one for him to use as well.

Hap Sing normally saw people as having a light glow about them when using the second sight. Unnatural spirits would have no glow, but might radiate an apparent dark aura. Beings with powers usually glowed with a brightness in accordance with their relative supernatural or spiritual strength. Years of practice and necessity had taught Hap Sing to suppress the extremely bright aura of the Luck, but he never had been able to change its shape. As usual his form when viewed with the second sight was overlaid with a faint glow shaped like a tiger with seven tails.

As he looked up he saw something he had somewhat expected. Most of the people in the market had the same faint glow that lesser destiny people showed under the second sight. What surprised him was not that Yu Wing showed a brighter glow related to a greater destiny, since that was what he was looking to confirm with the second sight anyway. It was the glowing large spirit cat sitting next to Yu Wing that surprised him. The glowing spirit hawk sitting on the brightly glowing Yu Mai's shoulder really caught him by surprise.

He was even more surprised that six other people in the market, including the two people in the stall which prepared his meal and four of the villagers sitting near their table also had the glow of greater destiny with various guardian animal spirits next to them.

Hap Sing thought back, and to the best of his knowledge eight Chi Masters had not been together in the same place since the great war had ended seventy five years ago. Only people with the second sight like himself could tell what they were if they didn't use their powers. As far as he knew only other Chi Masters or potential Chi Masters were ever born with the second sight. He started to understand the nature of the conspiracy he subconsciously suspected.

Yu Wing looked around to make sure no one except the other Chi Masters were paying attention. Then he looked at Hap Sing and spoke, "I think it's almost time to start the story telling. I think the one you have to tell might be the most interesting."

Yu Wing closed his eyes, and when they opened Hap Sing detected an impression of cat's eyes. Yu Mai closed her eyes as well, and when they opened Hap Sing could feel her gaze had become like a hawk's.

Yu Wing leaned back as he looked at Hap Sing, "Greater destinies attract, and all Chi Masters instinctively understand this. The question we have is why we have attracted such a singularly unique greater destiny as you."

Hap Sing closed his eyes as he was feeling the strain from the second sight. He opened them again and was glad of the sense of normalcy which returned to him with his normal vision. He hesitantly smiled at Yu Wing and Yu Mai.

Hap Sing spoke, "What can I say, greater destinies attract. I was drawn here as you say."

Yu Wing nodded at this remark and asked, "Are you also a Chi Master then?"

Hap Sing shrugged his shoulders, "I couldn't say for certain. I'm really more of a fisherman."

The Lucky Cricket

Yu Wing thought a second, and Hap Sing noticed that the other nearby Chi Masters were keeping up a watch to make sure no one else got close enough to overhear their conversation.

Hap Sing asked a question which concerned him, "Do you realize it can be dangerous to gather so many greater destinies in once place for a long time? Not all destinies are heroic you know, some are villainous."

Yu Wing looked surprised by this concept as did Yu Mai. Yu Mai spoke up, "What do you mean villainous? This is not part of the Chi Master wisdom we have learned."

Hap Sing shook his head, "Let me just say it has been long experience that taught me this, not Chi Master learning. Greater destinies are directed by impartial fate. Fate does not care whether the greater destinies are heroic or villainous. They still attract each other. Sometimes bonds of friendship and camaraderie are formed by this attraction, other times bonds of enmity and discord are formed."

Yu Wing nodded his head, "I think I understand what you are saying, but there is strength in numbers as well. Don't forget that. Besides this is my home. My son Yu Gai is there at the food stall and made your dinner. He was born here as well. The others have been drawn here by the attraction of the legend of Hap Yang. Each has learned bits and pieces of the legend of his great deeds, and we have assembled them as stories over time."

Hap Sing smiled at that comment, "I would be grateful to hear what you have learned. My family did not ever tell me much of the deeds of Hap Yang."

Yu Wing nodded his head, "I have a few questions for you first. How did you inherit the curse of the seven tailed tiger spirit? Was it passed down to you by your father? Has it been passed down through your family line since your great grandfather Hap Sing?"

Hap Sing looked guilty at this question, "I must apologize for deceiving you earlier, I am not the great grandson of Hap Sing."

Yu Wing nodded his head, "I understand and it confirms something I suspected about you being a Chi Master. We all know Chi Masters have long lives, at least if they survive conflict. You must be his grandson then."

Hap Sing shook his head, and Yu Wing looked a little embarrassed and asked, "You're Hap Sing's son? I didn't realize he would have had a child so late, or that you were so old?"

Hap Sing smiled a little, "You last guess is closest, I would be considered pretty old by most people's understanding. However, I am not Hap Sing's son."

Yu Wing and Yu Mai both looked confused at this remark. Yu Mai spoke up, "You bear his name. Are you telling us that you are not related to him after all?"

Hap Sing was quiet and shy as he spoke, "I don't like to admit it, but my birthday is in a couple of days. If I have figured it right I will be one hundred and fifty years old. I am Hap Yang's son Hap Sing."

Yu Wing and Yu Mai looked shocked at the revelation. Then Yu Mai developed a look of fear in her eyes and turned pale in the fading sunlight. She closed her eyes briefly again and then looked intently at Hap Sing.

Yu Wing noticed her concern, "What is wrong my dear?"

Yu Mai's voice quivered in fear, "I broke the prohibition of your many times great uncle. Forgive me Yu Wing. I foolishly told the son of Hap Yang about the forbidden spell which captured the Great Spirit of the seven tailed tiger. That is not the curse of the seven tailed tiger you see around his form, it is the living innocent prison of the Great Spirit you see. I have foolishly given it the key to escape."

Chapter 3 Revelation

Yu Wing looked at his wife in disbelief. Then a building comprehension and fear began to rise in Yu Wing as well. The other nearby Chi Masters caught on to the sudden shift in events and gradually came over to see what had so changed the posture of Yu Wing and Yu Mai. Most of the shops were closing for the evening, and the other patrons of the market were heading home. Eventually Yu Gai closed his food stall and approached, and much like the other Chi Masters had closed their eyes and formed puzzled looks on their face, he used his second sight as well.

Yu Gai had missed most of the lead up earlier since he had been working. He looked at his parents who were sitting with fear clearly in their eyes. He saw that their guardian spirits were positioned in a fearful defensive posture. The he looked at the figure of Hap Sing surrounded by the faint shape of the seven tailed tiger. Hap Sing gave him a tenuous smile.

Yu Gai spoke, "What does this mean? What is happening here?"

Yu Wing looked away from Hap Sing and focused on his son and his ape guardian spirit. He calmed himself as best he could. He noticed that Hap Sing was still being his relatively meek and unassuming self. So he figured that must count for something.

Yu Wing replied to Yu Gai, "It seems that we are in the presence of our research and stories brought before us first hand. Yu Gai I introduce you to your many times great cousin Hap Sing son of Hap Yang."

Yu Gai and the other five Chi Masters all went through various looks of confusion, shock, disbelief, and eventually for some uncertainty tinged with fear. Hap Sing slowly rose from his seat and performed a deep bow before them all.

Hap Sing spoke, "I am sorry for the turmoil I have caused with my presence. I do have to say I think my uncle was mistaken about not telling me about what had happened between my father and me all those years ago. There is no threat that the Luck, what you call the Great Spirit of the seven tailed tiger, will escape my father's forbidden spell. We are as one, inseparable without killing us both I would think."

Yu Wing, Yu Mai and the rest breathed a sigh of relief at the statement.

Yu Wing motioned for everyone to gather around now that the market was nearly empty. Only a couple of merchants remained to pack up their goods, and they were out of hearing range. The Chi Masters concentrated a moment, and sent their guardian spirits to keep a watch for any approaching people, and they prepared to join in telling their stories and the legends they had learned.

Yu Wing began by making introductions, "Hap Sing you have already been introduced to my son Yu Gai. To my right is Ming Ran, leader of Hung Chan village."

Hap Sing looked at the handsome young man and shook his hand. Then Hap Sing spoke to him, "Nice to make your acquaintance. Are you related to magistrate Ming Na Jun of Jin Do province by any chance?"

Ming Ran nodded his head, "Yes, he is a distant cousin on my father's side of the family. We have a great grandfather in common."

Yu Wing then pointed to the pretty and young woman standing next to Ming Ran, "This is Ming Akane, wife of Ming Ran and originally from the country of Udomo. She is a relatively recent but welcome addition to our group."

Hap Sing gave her a bow and smiled, "My friend Li Chan was originally from Udomo. My father Hap Yang had met his father there, and predicted that Li Chan would become a great hero in Ran Li. Both Li Chan and his son Li Hung became very celebrated here in Ran Li during the last war seventy five years ago as you may know."

Ming Akane blushed, "I can only hope to not embarrass my home country and new country when compared to their legend."

Yu Wing continued, "To my left is Boku Sata also originally from the country of Udomo. He is the captain of our village militia, and one of the best fighters in the province."

Hap Sing shook the hand of the middle aged and very muscular Boku Sata, "I am pleased to meet you."

Boku Sata gave a broad smile, "I hope you don't unfairly compare me to your friend famous Li Chan. His battle prowess and tactical skill are still considered legendary in two kingdoms."

Yu Wing then waved to a tall slender woman standing off to Hap Sing's side, "Come closer Yuki Nene, I don't think there will be any harm to you here."

As Yuki Nene approached she lifted the hood from over her head. Hap Sing noticed that she was obviously not originally from the countries of Ran Li or Udomo. She was taller than an average woman, and a fair bit taller than Hap Sing himself. The most striking difference though was her pale yellow hair which was uncharacteristic for any humans in the surrounding countries. Obviously she was a very long way from her home country.

Yu Wing introduced her, "Hap Sing this is Yuki Nene, from Yokito the capital of Ran Li. Her ancestors were originally from across the great ocean from a place called Nordland. Her ancestors came to our country along the sea trade routes."

Hap Sing gave her a bow and said, "I am pleased to meet you as well."

Hap Sing noticed that her eyes were an unusual blue color and wondered at Yuki Nene's unique nature. She returned his bow, and then quickly stepped aside again.

Yu Wing indicated the short plain looking woman standing next to Yu Gai, "This is our daughter-in-law Yu Jin. She also comes from the Jin Do province, but settled here several years ago as a young woman and married our son."

Hap Sing bowed, "I have called the Jin Do province my home for many years now. I live by the sea there where the fishing is very good."

Yu Jin smiled, "I do miss the sea living here, although the pond at father Yu's estate does have some good fish to eat as well."

Hap Sing nodded, "I know it well. It is where I first learned to fish as a youth."

Yu Wing spoke to the assembled group, "Let's put some tables together and begin the story telling. Tonight we shall go way back to the beginning of the Chi Masters. Would you begin please begin Yu Jin."

Yu Jin stood up in front of our collective group and spoke, "We all know the Gods formed the world. Every priest or priestess tells us so. However, what they don't say is that before the world, before the gods even there were the spirits. They were many and of different kinds and modes of thought. They didn't have physical form, but they desired for there to be something else, something greater than themselves."

The assembled Chi Masters nodded their respective heads and spoke together, "So it is said from Chi Master to Chi Master so the beginning will not be forgotten."

Yu Jin continued, "The spirits lived in the dreaming also known as the land of thought. The land of thought was without physical form, and the spirits in the land could envision anything they desired. However, the spirits did not have the individual power to make anything last. The dreaming was a place of continual chaos, controlled by the whims of the moment."

Yu Jin sat down and Ming Akane stood up to speak, "Many spirits desired for their thoughts to remain in the dreaming. Individual spirits varied in power like the difference between a mouse and a dragon. However, they found when they gathered together in numbers with those of similar thought and attempted to create stable regions of the dreaming they were able to succeed. As more of the spirits who thought alike gathered together, they dreamed of guardians to protect their regions of the dreaming. These guardians soon became more powerful than even the mightiest of spirits."

The Chi Masters spoke together again, "Thus the gods and goddesses were formed from the nothingness of thought."

Yu Gai stood up next to speak, "Many spirits were happy they had formed the gods and goddesses. Other spirits were jealous and formed their own gods and goddesses. Many of the powerful spirits ended up joining one side or another in self preservation. A rare few of the most powerful spirits decided instead to hide in the dreaming without taking sides. They did not want guardians. They did not feel a need for consistency. They accepted the nature of the dreaming was change, and that chaos was the price paid."

Ming Ran stood up to speak next, "The gods and goddesses created by the spirits decided that pure thought was difficult to manage. They decided to limit thought by form. Each of them placed rules and restrictions on thought, and in the process they created the planes. Each plane was limited or restricted to those spirits who thought alike. However, the spirits soon found themselves descending into an unfamiliar state of stagnation. The stagnation created fear, and they reached out to the gods and goddesses they had created for help."

Boku Sata took his turn telling his portion of the tale, "The gods and goddesses were at a loss for what to do. They were very powerful, but they were still limited by the collective thoughts of the spirit minions which had created them. None of the gods or goddesses could compromise their vision of an acceptable realm to create a vision of a plane without stagnation. Then the powerful spirits which had hidden in the dreaming came to the gods and goddesses with an idea. The gods and goddesses could still have individual planes for the ones who followed them. Yet they should release a measure of their spirits to dwell in other planes for a period of time. That way the spirits could regain perspective, and resist the stagnation. Thus the elemental planes, the planes of light and shadow, and the prime plane were created by the gods and goddesses at the advice of the powerful spirits and using their power."

The Chi Masters spoke together again, "Thus the worlds were made, and spirits given form to dwell upon them."

Yu Mai rose up next to speak, "The worlds were not perfect, and that is how stagnation was avoided. Conflict, cooperation, new thoughts, and old traditions all keep their place in the worlds. It is believed that when a spirit becomes too worn by the existence in the eternal planes that they are sent to the worlds to become renewed. They are given form again, and another chance to experience a different perspective."

Yu Wing stood up next and looked at Hap Sing as he spoke the last part, "It is believed that some spirits have remained eternal in the dreaming. They take form as they desire and as suits their whims. They are not part of the plans of the gods and goddesses, and sometimes act as a check or balance to their actions. However, other powerful spirits have established a kind of trade between the realms of being. They exist in multiple physical places simultaneously. They are known colloquially as the tailed beasts. Tonight we shall talk of one in particular."

Chapter 4 Tailed Beast Tale

Yu Wing tilted his head as he looked at Hap Sing. Then he scanned the faces of the assembled chi masters. He settled on Ming Ran and nodded in his direction before sitting down. Ming Ran glanced at Hap Sing and smiled.

Ming Ran said, "As most of you know I have spent much of my later childhood and early adulthood learning to understand what I was. I discovered I was a Chi Master, and that it was a dangerous thing to be in these times. I was curious what it meant, and under the guise of learning history I studied the acts of the past Chi Masters."

Ming Ran frowned as he spoke the next part, "I discovered the histories written in the times of Hap Yang. The histories I read told of many great deeds of charity, bravery, service, and ultimately self sacrifice. They led me as they have led many others over the years to this village to discover the works of Hap Yang. When I first arrived I found my path to those works blocked by superstition and fear."

Ming Ran then gave a slight smile waved a hand toward the Yu family. The four of them nodded and smiled in return.

Ming Ran said, "I also found that I was not to be alone in my abilities anymore. I discovered Yu Wing and his family living here peacefully with their fellow villagers. Master Yu and his family have guided me and taught me what a Chi Master can do. However, even though they were respected in the local community, they could not request access to the records and works of Hap Yang since they were not considered nobility."

Ming Ran gave a slightly quirky grin, "Fortunately, I am considered minor nobility. I crafted a petition with the help of my cousin Ming Na Jun to assume leadership of the newly formed village of Hung Chan. I would have named the village for Hap Yang but my cousin Jun advised me against it as the Chi Masters are considered disreputable even if Hap Yang himself was locally acknowledged as a hero. I then picked Hung Chan using the names of the hero father and son from the last war of Ran Li."

Ming Ran smiled, "A year later my petition was granted as border tensions had been mounting. As leader of the village of Hung Chan I gained access to those remaining works of Hap Yang. Together we learned much from his notes on spirit relationships and his diaries of events in his life. However, his most recent diaries before his death detailing his planning to confront the great spirit of the seven tailed tiger were missing. Would you please continue Miss Yuki?"

As Ming Ran sat down the eyes of the group turned to Yuki Nene. She sat slumped in her chair a little with her hood drawn up over her head again. Hap Sing closed his eyes briefly, and when he opened them he noticed a spirit raven come perch on her shoulder briefly and look at him. It took off again as he watched it, and his second sight noticed that Yuki's eyes were no longer blue but a disturbing black. Her expression was neutral, but Hap Sing noticed that her voice was clear and melodic when she spoke.

Yuki Nene had a slight smile and said, "My family comes from Nordland originally which is a country on another continent across the sea. We Nordlanders are a people of the sea. We Nordlanders are usually traders when business is good and raiders when the times are lean. We also have traditions going way back in time of moving and settling in colonies in other lands. My grandparents came to Ran Li on a trading mission, and ended up joining the Nordland trading colony near Yokito. I am a second generation of Nordlander who was born in Ran Li as were both of my parents. My people are smart though. They understand they have to change to fit in where they go. I have a Ran Li name since I was born here. My people also pay appropriate homage to the gods of the lands where they live."

Yuki Nene frowned slightly, "Although, my people do not thoughtlessly cast aside their old ways just because a new way comes along. They look at the value of each way, and use each way where it is most appropriate. I am also what the Nordlanders call a spirit shaman. I am called that because I am one who can interact with the other world and the spirits which come to our own world. In Nordland the spirit shamans are respected and often counsel the leaders on wise action."

Yuki Nene's expression turned a little sad, "It is well known in our colony that the priests of various gods followed the trade routes Nordland had established in the past two hundred years. The priests of Palnor and of the other gods brought their practices here as passengers on our ships, and we did not complain of it. Then they began to turn the government and people of Ran Li against the old ways of the Chi Masters as they are called in Ran Li. Unfortunately since Chi Masters are now considered taboo I am also a bit of a social problem for the Nordland trading colony. The Chi Masters have fallen into disfavor, and hide their presence in rural communities to survive. Thus I have also left the Nordland trading colony for the good of my people in order to avoid conflict with the local authorities in Yokito."

Yuki Nene gave a sad smile, "My people did not want this to happen, but the choice had been left to me. In private they considered many ways to hide me within the colony. I saw finally that doing so would place the entire existence of the Nordland colony at risk. Publicly I picked the path of the renegade so that my people may prosper in my absence."

Yuki Nene's sadness faded and her smile became a grin, "My first act of defiance in establishing my renegade status with the colony was to make use of information obtained by my people who are worshipers of Palnor. They let it be known to me privately that since the followers of Palnor had assembled a collection of forbidden writings including several important works about and by the famous Chi Master Hap Yang. I used the information they provided to raid the forbidden library and I made off with as much information on Chi Masters as several of us could carry to safety. Then I boarded a ship bound for Udomo with the works I had acquired."

Yuki Nene spoke, "I met up with Boku Sata and Ming Akane in Udomo. The spirit shamans were still allowed to practice openly as Chi Masters in Udomo although the god priests were and still are in a political battle for supremacy there. I sought them out to enlist their aid in studying the works about the Chi Masters I had acquired. Through time we learned that it was perhaps the material about and especially written by Hap Yang which was the most informative. Please continue Sata."

Boku Sata spoke in a deep resonant voice, "I am from Udomo which as you may know is land ruled by warlords. Each warlord seeks power and ascendancy over others, no one warlord allows himself to be ruled by another. It is bit chaotic, but lets us Chi Masters practice in relative peace since each warlord refuses to worship same deity as any of their neighbors. This has made Udomo haven for Chi Masters fleeing oppression as many warlords choose to have Chi Master look after their spiritual affairs rather than pray to gods."

Boku Sata laughed, "Personally I think it is matter of economics. Chi Masters may not have divine powers, but they work cheaper than priests. You have to realize that most of warlords in Udomo today are more accountant than warrior."

Boku Sata pointed at Nene and Akane, "Young Nene there comes into my town one day with her blond hair and blue eyes and walks into my establishment. First I think she is tourist or worse yet some god priest coming to tell me to change my evil ways. I am getting ready to tell my apprentice Akane to deal with her when she calls out to me asking where she could find snow leopard like one I have."

Boku Sata got a stern look, "Now in Udomo we Chi Masters don't poach on other people's territory you know. There are only so many friendly warlords to be found you see. So I look at this young girl with my sight. I see that huge black bird on her shoulder and I know I have situation. I already had one apprentice to train, and work wasn't so good that I could afford to feed two."

Boku Sata looked surprised next, "Well that young lass there comes over to me and says that she was looking to hire me on to help for her research. Then Nene has porter bring in trunk full of scrolls and parchments all about works of Chi Masters of Ran Li. For poor working Chi Master as me it might be warlord's treasure chest. It wasn't money value I cared about though. It was much knowledge these works represented."

Boku Sata grinned, "It took us nearly year to organize works present. Several important pieces were missing, yet what was there represented over a hundred times more than I had learned as apprentice myself. More than just form and function there was history there, history of the Chi Masters, history of the spirits, and a history of existence."

Boku Sata then looked puzzled, "Over year reading we noticed that much of greatest thinking came from particular Chi Master. Someone we grew to consider possibly wisest and smartest Chi Master in recorded history of Ran Li. We couldn't understand all it was so far beyond our knowledge, we knew just enough to understand we had come into contact with works of genius. Of course I mean writings of Hap Yang."

Boku Sata became excited, "His most intriguing discussions were about great spirits. What many refer to as tailed beasts. Hap Yang studied them from afar. He witnessed their actions and effects through medium of dreaming. These beings were not gods, but they were somehow also inviolate from dictates of gods. They have no followers, and require none. They have mysterious plans, and they can impact spirit world in unaccountable ways. They are all very intelligent and very powerful. More powerful than any individual god priest or maybe even dragon. Amazingly Hap Yang discovered they have an odd potential for affinity with some mortal spirits. From Hap Yang's diaries it was apparent that this affinity for mortal spirits both frightened him and excited him greatly. Hap Sing's research on tailed beasts seemed to conclude with his theory that each tail represented a spiritual link to another plane of existence. At this point he was well beyond Chi Master teachings of his time and incorporating aspects of divine thought. Very radical thinking for his era I believe."

Boku Sata then looked a little embarrassed, "Unfortunately as we were deciding our possible course of action our warlord was assassinated. One of his rivals who was actually more warrior than accountant had sent ninja force into our warlord's estate killing him and his family. Since this new warlord was follower of one of god priest's religions and since my former apprentice Akane was distant cousin of our former warlord's wife we decided it was no longer safe to remain in Udomo."

Boku Sata nodded at Ming Akane who continued, "Many of my extended family had been captured at the warlord's palace. As loyal retainers and relatives of his wife they were expecting to be allowed to perform ritual suicide to maintain their honor for failing to protect their lord. On the word of the new warlord's god priest they were not allowed to commit ritual suicide for their failure and their ancestors were shamed by this dishonor done to their families."

Ming Akane was calm and stern as she spoke, "Those of my family who were not in direct service to the warlord were under no onus to protect his life. Several of them along with the relatives of other captured retainers did go to the new warlord to protest the treatment of their relatives. They were in turn also captured, and word was sent out to round up the rest of the relatives of those in service to the former warlord. I fled Udomo with a bounty on my head. Although it was small bounty, it was still a disgraceful act to be treated as if I were a common criminal. We followed Yuki Nene's advice and came to Ran Li smuggled aboard a Nordland trade vessel along with our trunk of precious writings."

Ming Akane glanced at Ming Ran with a glint in her eye, "I met my Ran here when we came to Hung Chan to discover more about Hap Yang. We also met the Yu family who were kind to strangers, and more learned on the personal history of Hap Yang as his wife's relatives than even his writings let us know. We have been here for almost five years now. Ran and I were married here while Boku Sata joined the militia and eventually became promoted to its leader."

Ming Akane looked over at Yu Gai who spoke next, "I am pretty much what you see. We Yu's are just descendants from the family of Hap Yang's wife. There is no exciting story about our existence here in Hung Chan. As a family we farm, work in the market, and look after those of our kind who are staying in Hung Chan."

Yu Gai looked directly at Hap Sing next, "We also keep alive the stories of the life of Hap Yang. Until today we had thought ourselves perhaps his last relatives. We didn't know what had become of his son or his son's descendants, and perhaps we should be shamed by our lack of diligence in the matter. Not that we haven't tried to discover what had become of Hap Sing. You are perhaps the greatest unanswered mystery of Hap Yang's story. Please mention your story my dear Jin."

Yu Jin placed her hand on her husband's head, "You should not worry about great deeds my dear Gai, what you are doing here is a good deed in providing a haven for those who are outcast."

Yu Jin looked directly at Hap Sing as her husband had, "I have searched far and wide for a sign of your passing Hap Sing. While it is true that everyone in Ran Li has heard of the legend of General Li Chan and his final battle against the invaders, and most of the learned also recognize his son General Li Hung as a great hero as well. A few even know that it was Chi Master Hap Yang who predicted to Li Chan's father that Li Chan would become a great hero."

Yu Jin had a curious look on her face as she revealed the next part of her story, "What almost no one outside of this village recognized or speaks of is that Li Chan came to this village with his father as a young boy to meet Hap Yang. Instead they found that Hap Yang had died in the casting of his forbidden magic, and that Hap Yang's teenage son Hap Sing was the only one left in his place. What only the locals here knew was the story that Hap Sing and Li Chan quickly became the best of friends."

Yu Jin looked around the group assembled, "Two of the most influential figures outside of politics in Ran Li history, and the most generally ignored common thread between them is Hap Sing here. When I discovered this fact I dug into the story more and returned to the Jin Do province where I was born. I traveled to Li Chan village last year and visited with their council leader looking to find the truth to a rumor that Li Hung the son of Li Chan was still alive."

Yu Jin looked at Hap Sing, "I found him there in a modest home. General Li Hung, one of the greatest heroes of our country was now a simple village elder. He was old at one hundred and five, but Li Hung could have passed for a robust seventy five. I asked him whether Hap Sing had been his father's friend and he confirmed it. He also said that Hap Sing was the best friend that he had as well. What I misunderstood at the time was that Li Hung had spoken of Hap Sing as if he was still alive."

Yu Jin looked uncertain as she spoke the next part, "I looked at General Li Hung with my second sight and saw something I had not expected and could not understand. Most great heroes have a brighter aura as we know. Even at one hundred and five his aura was brighter than any aura I had ever witnessed under the sight. It was flickering slightly as auras of the elderly approaching their death tend to do, but it was still brighter than any aura cast by a twenty year old hero in their prime."

Yu Jin then looked at Hap Sing with a touch of awe, "I inquired more into the history of Li Chan and Li Hung when I returned home here. I found that there was a reprimand listed in General Li Chan's record from when he left Yokito without leave to bring his son Li Hung to a remote province to see a healer for a dire condition. The locals of Hung Chan know that Li Hung was brought here by his father to see Hap Sing. Li Hung had arrived in Hung Chan on death's doorstep and had departed in perfect health. You would have been about sixty years old then, and that was the last anyone had ever seen you in this village as you departed along with Li Chan and Li Hung. You haven't been seen in this village in the past ninety years."

Yu Jin then looked around at the group at large, "There is one thing I haven't spoken of before tonight because I didn't trust my eyes at the time. A little over a year ago as I left General Li Hung's hut I was still using my second sight while marveling at how bright his aura was. I glanced at the sky before I prepared to release my second sight. I saw a strange interweaving of glowing lines crossing over the village like a glowing thread. I didn't understand their purpose but General Li Hung caught me looking up at the sky and said to me 'Greater destinies attract, you will find what you seek in time my child'. I understood that General Li Hung had grown up as a friend to the son of a Chi Master, and that he somehow recognized another Chi Master even if he wasn't one himself. I mistakenly assumed at the time that the lines of aura over Li Chan village were a side effect from looking at General Li Hung's bright aura. Now I suspect that was not the case."

Hap Sing ducked uncomfortably under the combined gaze of the assembled Chi Masters as they silently speculated on what powers he might possess. The Chi Masters witnessed something they could hardly credit at the point. The faint aura of the great spirit of the seven tailed tiger dimmed even more until it was barely visible to their second sight against the darkness of night. Had it been broad daylight they understood they might well have perceived it as a visual fluke of the sunlight.

Yu Mai spoke next, "That is an interesting trick you can do with your aura Hap Sing. You now register lower than a standard human being, almost as a recently dead one who spirit has begun to depart to the other places. Who taught you such a trick?"

Hap Sing gave a slight grimace, "Is it that noticeable?"

Yu Mai shook her head, "It's just the opposite. It's hardly noticeable at all. That is what makes it interesting phenomena. Flashy displays of apparent power any arcane trained person can produce. This ability you have to hide your nature in plain sight, that is a very subtle and highly difficult ability actually. It is also a very useful skill for such as us in these times. Mix that in with your ability to change the hostile attitude of even a priest of Palnor then you have mastered abilities that none of us could replicate yet. Did you learn it from your mother?"

Hap Sing shook his head, "I wasn't taught it at all. I was never trained you understand. I am just a fisherman who can do some self taught tricks is all."

Yu Mai then glanced at Yu Jin briefly then returned her gaze to Hap Sing, "How about those interwoven threads of power over Li Chan village? Were those a visual aftereffect from looking at Li Hung, or something put in place by you? Maybe it is some kind of a net to entrap people?"

Hap Sing slunk down into his chair even further and Yu Wing interrupted his wife, "Don't intimidate him so. Remember Hap Sing is our guest. You've gotten him to almost remove his aura all together. He's almost spiritually invisible now, and if what I suspect is true then it can't be good."

Yu Mai looked at Yu Wing, "Is he become dangerous now?"

Yu Wing shook his head, "Not to us, but possibly to himself. Such a level of spiritual aura suppression can not be good for him even if it is seemingly rather easy. Let's give our guest some room to breathe for a moment. Give me some time alone with him, and stop using your second sight will you all. You are going to wear yourselves out keeping it up so long. Notice that Hap Sing stopped a long time ago."

The assembled Chi Masters stood up and walked around a bit. They started making small conversation as they broke up into groups. Mostly the women gathered together along in one group and the men in another talking about inconsequential matters. Hap Sing noticed as Yu Wing sat beside him that Yuki Nene also sat nearby within hearing distance apparently studying him.

Yu Wing sympathetically placed his arm on Hap Sing's arm as he spoke, "I apologize for my wife. You have to understand that her side of the family is a very pushy one. In fact if she had not pushed me to the magistrate we would have never gotten married in the first place."

Yu Wing laughed while Hap Sing gave a sympathetic chuckle. Hap Sing relaxed some and smiled in return to Yu Wing.

Hap Sing responded, "I'm sorry I haven't been more forthcoming. I am unused to strangers and have become a bit set in my ways over time."

Yu Wing nodded, "I understand. Being what we are there is fear caused in others. This fear can lead to misunderstanding and harm. Being what we are we should know better than to not understand this about others. I think the others are not yet comfortable with what they think you might be. You are mysterious to them, your abilities are strange, and your history is unique. You are one of the subjects of their obsession with the past history of Chi Masters that has never been properly explained."

Hap Sing took a deep breath and sighed, "What is it that they think I might be?"

Yu Wing shrugged, "Our research suggests you are both Hap Yang's son and the spirit of the seven tailed tiger. However, our research has never turned up how this feat was accomplished."

Hap Sing nodded, "Your research is mostly correct. I am the son of Hap Yang. I am also spiritually intermingled with the Luck, or what you would call the spirit of the seven tailed tiger. I am a simple fisherman really though. I just know some tricks."

Yu Wing nodded, "There is more though isn't there. What does the Luck as you call it say?"

Hap Sing shrugged, "That's the problem. We really can't speak to each other. I can allow it to consciously possess me for a brief time, but I don't know what it says or does when I do so. Frankly speaking I am not inclined to do it without very good cause."

Yu Wing frowned, "Why is that? Is it dangerous to you?"

Hap Sing shook his head, "It is not dangerous to me, but I fear that it could be dangerous to everyone else."

Yu Wing had a slightly puzzled look, "I don't understand. Will it manifest as a giant tiger reaping destruction across nations as told in the old tales?"

Hap Sing shrugged, "That is unlikely as long as my father's casting holds it to my form. We are inseparable, and it hasn't shown an ability to loosen itself from my hold."

Yu Wing shrugged, "What is the problem then if it can not attack people?"

Hap Sing gave a wry smile, "Who says all attacks are physical? As I understand it talking to others who have met the Luck in person, the Luck knows things. It uses those things it knows to get what it wants. Certainly it has more power than we could imagine, but it doesn't need that power to cause harm. It can harm a person deeply and personally just by its very presence and a few words."

Yu Wing looked impressed, "Maybe that works for novices and common folk, but certainly not Chi Masters."

Hap Sing shook his head, "You don't understand yet. You remember my friend Li Chan whom you all referred to as the great hero of Ran Li. I will tell you that in his prime his spiritual aura made Li Hung's aura as look pale and weak as mine now. His destiny was written so strongly that my father Hap Yang could see it coming years before he was born. When Li Chan bargained with the Luck for the life of Li Hung he was left trembling in fear and shame for his fear. Li Chan never told me what had exactly happened other than that he would never push his luck with the great spirit inside me again."

Yu Wing whistled, "I think I understand now. It healed Li Hung in exchange for some kind of bargain."

Hap Sing shrugged, "I actually don't think the Luck healed Li Hung at all. At least the healing was not in the sense that a god priest using divine magic heals someone. It did something drastically different to Li Hung. It changed his destiny. Li Hung was destined to die as a teenager, and his destiny was altered with the spirit of the Luck. That is a higher order of power than a simple divine blessing of healing. The Luck also did something to both Li Hung and Li Chan. It intertwined their destinies. Neither one had an easy life after that point. What Yu Jin likely saw when she looked at Li Hung was the residue of a small measure of the spirit force of the Luck. It has unnaturally extended his body's ability to heal and survive. Li Hung has lived well beyond his fated lifespan and now well beyond his body's normal lifespan. It may seem like a blessing to someone foolish enough to want such a thing, but I hardly think that it is in the long term."

Yu Wing sat back, "Why do you say it is not a good thing?"

Hap Sing looked sad, "His spirit is weary and was ready to move on long ago. His body simply won't let it happen."

Yu Wing nodded, "It would likely take a Chi Master to understand such a problem. Those arcane casters have no real appreciation of the effects of magic on a spirit. At least the god priests get told what is allowed or not allowed before they work their magic."

Hap Sing realized that the others had stopped talking with each other a while ago and were unobtrusively listening in on his conversation with Yu Wing. They seemed more at ease though and it was clear by their posture that they didn't feel as threatened by his presence anymore. Hap Sing could see that a slight smile was on the lips of Yuki Nene as she watched him, but it was not reflected in her eyes. Hap Sing gained resolve to find an answer to his questions about his past and waved the other Chi Masters back over to the tables.

Hap Sing spoke, "You have raised questions, and I also have questions about my own past for which you may have answers. Yu Mai to answer your question I am the one who set the net over Li Chan village. I care for the people there, and it is a magic which helps keep them prosperous and happy. It does not make them rich, but it helps them stay healthy and unharmed while in the village. As long as I keep it up they are never ill, and no one has died of a malady or injury in Li Chan for nearly fifty years. The crops in Li Chan grow without blight or drought. The fish in the bay are plentiful and tasty."

Ming Ran spoke up, "A very useful enchantment indeed. Many villages would pay much for such a benefit. How do you prepare such an enchantment? What is the ritual used?"

Hap Sing flushed with embarrassment, "I fish in the bay out past the breakers. I daydream of casting a large net over the village while hoping that everyone remains well. I don't know if that helps any. Like I said before fishing is what I know, so much of what I do is based on what I learned from fishing."

The others seemed surprised by this answer except for Yu Wing who nodded knowingly. Their eyes turned to him, and Yu Mai placed her arm on his shoulder. Hap Sing noticed that Yuki Nene kept her eyes on him, and the smile on her lips had finally reached her eyes.

Yu Wing looked at the others, "Most of you probably find that answer confusing. Most of you were apprenticed and taught by a Chi Master, who had been taught by a Chi Master before them. When trained that way you learn reliable techniques used by others in the past. It is a quick way to learn, but unfortunately it has its limits."

Boku Sata spoke, "What do you mean there are limits to learning skills of Chi Master? Does this have to do with Great Spirit seven tailed tiger?"

Yu Wing answered, "This is something we likely have not learned about being a Chi Master. All of us except Yuki Nene were taught by another. Most of you except Sata and Akane were taught by me. You have learned what I know and how I access the spirit world. Akane has learned how Sata was taught as his apprentice. You know there are differences between us. Then there is our prodigy Yuki Nene who is self taught and who does many things we can not do, while it has been hard for her to learn what we find easy to do."

Yu Jin spoke up, "While it is true that many Chi Masters have different skills I don't think I spoke about this net clearly. I don't think any of us could create a ritual of such potency that extended over an area five miles across. This is beyond having learned a different skill. It is something we could not do even if we fully understood the process of doing it."

Hap Sing spoke, "I really don't think of it as area. I just make the net big enough in my mind to cover the village and the farms. It isn't hard to do as it only takes a minute. It is a bit harder without the rolling surf under me, but I cast my net again this morning before I arrived in Hung Chan."

Yu Wing patted Hap Sing on the shoulder, "Where did you place this net?"

Hap Sing looked a bit confused, "Over Li Chan village as usual. Why do you ask?"

The others looked across the table at each other with looks of incredulity.

Yuki Nene smiled fully now as she asked, "Would you please show us by casting your net over this market?"

Hap Sing flushed embarrassed, "I'm not sure if I can. The area is a bit small I think. It might be too concentrated and become tangled. Would it be fine if instead I cast it over the whole valley?"

Yu Wing nodded, "If it is beneficial as you say, then I don't see any harm done by doing so. Do you need time to prepare?"

Hap Sing nodded, "A moment to relax would help."

Yu Wing asked, "Is it permissible if we watch?"

Hap Sing nodded, "If that would be helpful, then yes you can use your second sight."

Hap Sing sat in his chair imagining he was rowing his boat on the pond in the valley. He brought out his large airy net and cast it over the expanse of sky over the valley covering the farms and village within from rim to rim. Hap Sing sat peacefully in his imagined boat for a moment when he felt a gentle slender arm across his shoulders. Beside him in his imagined boat was Yuki Nene smiling broadly.

Yuki Nene spoke to him, "You are able to enter the dreaming. That is why you can do such things that others think impossible. There is great power here. It takes a great Chi Master to come here at will like you have. Let us rejoin the others."

Hap Sing was again sitting at the table looking at the assembled Chi Masters. Yuki Nene was practically grinning ear to ear although she appeared a bit tired and worn. The others were alternating between looking up at the sky, over at Hap Sing, and then at Yuki Nene who was wearing her grin. Hap Sing noticed they seemed a bit stunned.

Hap Sing spoke, "Is there something wrong?"

Yu Jin responded, "I have to revise my estimate about what the brightest aura I've ever seen was. When you nodded off there for a moment your aura shone as bright as the sun. I think we were all practically blinded by it."

Hap Sing shrugged, "The Luck is a Great Spirit. It is understandable that its aura would be very powerful."

Yu Mai shook her head, "We can all see the aura of the Luck about you now. It is faint and suppressed for certain. However my second sight is very keen. The others may have missed it by when you cast that enchantment across the sky due to the brightness of your aura. Yet I could see that the aura of the Luck was drowned out by your own. You are quite possibly the most potent Chi Master in the history of the world."

Boku Sata spoke next, "I did not see how you did it. In just moment you closed your eyes and relaxed. Then your aura glowed as bright as sun and that enchantment spread across sky. There were no gestures, no chants, no ritual dance, just brief rest and this happened. Finally your aura faded down to reveal just residual aura of Luck again."

Yu Gai spoke as he looked at the sky, "The enchantment is not visible with normal vision. Only the second sight can see it spread across the sky. I can not decipher how it works either. Other than being visible to second sight it has no obvious direct effect on its surroundings."

Yu Wing nodded as he looked at Yuki Nene, "I think I understand what Hap Sing has done, and how it was achieved. It is a very subtle casting which is really over in a moment, subtle in effect, wide ranging in area. How many castings would it take before a change is noticed in Hung Chan?"

Hap Sing looked up at the sky, "I would think a year, maybe two of daily castings before people would realize that no one was getting ill, and that the crops were doing well. They would also tend to forget much about a particular fisherman in town unless they were of a greater destiny, or realized after they reached the wisdom of old age that fisherman never changed or grew older."

Ming Ran asked a question, "Why did you come to Hung Chan?"

 Chapter 4 45

Hap Sing shrugged, "Until I met you all I would have said that nostalgia for my childhood and unanswered questions about my past led me here. Now I would say that greater destinies attract."

Ming Ran nodded, "Why did you come at this time?"

Hap Sing smiled, "As you probably guessed, your distant cousin Ming Na Jun and his son Ming Wa Fu are in Li Chan village. Both of them are greater destinies and government officials who have shown an uncomfortable amount of interest in me. I now leave the village before they visit so as to not remind them of my presence."

Ming Ran smiled as he nodded, "I can understand your feeling. My cousin Jun can be very persistent when something catches his attention as out of place. I would think that his son has also inherited this trait. I would not think him the type to turn over a Chi Master to the religious authorities though. Jun does not hold with that kind of intolerant persecution of peaceful individuals."

During the conversation after the casting of the net Yu Wing had looked for a while at Yuki Nene sitting back with her grin with a contemplative look on his face. The others had also looked in her direction seemingly awaiting her decision to reveal what she had learned. Yu Wing also noticed a deeply concerned look on the face of Ming Akane. She seemed to be in a silent conversation with her spirit ferret.

Yu Wing looked at Ming Akane as he spoke, "Do you have something to add about what you learned Akane."

Ming Akane spoke up nervously, "I don't want to make too much of this. Most of you were watching Hap Sing or the sky when he cast his spell. I was watching Tiko. He was behaving strangely as the spell was cast, and now he won't say why."

After looking around the now empty market and seeing that no one was observing them they all had their spirit guardians return to them. A brief silent conference was held between each Chi Master and their respective spirit guardians. Akane's look of concern spread among the others including Yu Wing and Yuki Nene whose grin had faded to a serious look.

Hap Sing nervously asked, "Is something wrong? Did my net startle them or something? I have never sent it out around Chi Masters before today."

Yu Wing shook his head, "It was not what you did Hap Sing. I suspect it was where you went to do it that disturbed them so. They are being unusually reticent in discussing it with us. This is unprecedented among Chi Masters and has never been mentioned or hinted at in any of the histories."

Yu Jin looked confused, "What do you mean father of my husband? I watched Hap Sing closely. He did not go anywhere."

Yuki Nene spoke up, "Hap Sing went to the dreaming, and I followed the path he made there. It was unlike anytime I had ever been there before. As you all know it usually takes me two or three hours of effort to go to the dreaming. When I am there it is chaotic and constantly shifting. I can with much concentration cause a small portion to temporarily stabilize. I can bring that portion back to the real world if I am careful and quick. That is where I get the ability to create unusual if limited effects."

Boku Sata stood up and waved his hand sideways in a negating gesture, "Only most learned Chi Masters can enter dreaming. It took you many years of practice to do so on your own Nene, and you are natural prodigy among our kind. You are saying he managed to travel there and create that in mere minute of time? That you managed to follow him there as well? I find it very hard to believe."

Yuki Nene nodded, "I didn't follow him there on my own. I simply waited at the beginning of the path briefly and was swept along as Hap Sing passed through to the dreaming in an instant. This time the dreaming was unlike anything I had ever seen."

Yu Wing nodded knowingly, "It was bizarre beyond description then. I have heard rumors of such. The pull of the chaos is very strong in parts of the dreaming."

Yuki Nene shook her head, "You have it wrong this time Wing. It was only bizarre in that the dreaming was perfectly mundane. We were in this valley, sitting on a boat on your pond, and Hap Sing simply cast that fishing net of spirit power into the sky where it hangs now in reality. Every detail was there in the dreaming, there was no shifting or uncertainty. It was the strangest thing I have ever experienced there. I don't know how any Chi Master could do that. It was unprecedented."

Yu Wing was trembling slightly, "I think I understand what you saw Nene. Is this what your experienced Hap Sing?"

Hap Sing shrugged, "I don't know about the dreaming. I just relax and think about fishing. Then I cast my net into the sky while hoping that everyone under it has good luck. It seems to work over time though it's not very dramatic."

Yu Wing gave his wife Yu Mai a nod, and then he looked at Yu Gai and made a slight bow. They returned his look with a silent family communication of trust from long years together. A decision had been made by Yu Wing and they would follow his leadership.

Yu Mai and Yu Gai stood as Yu Mai spoke to the assembled Chi Masters, "Could the rest of you follow us to watch that Yu Wing and Hap Sing are not disturbed."

Boku Sata and Nene Yuki remained sitting as the others rose from the table. Yu Wing looked at them with a raised eyebrow.

Nene Yuki raised her own eyebrow, "You will need me to set you on the path. I do not think Hap Sing can get you there unless I help him at least the first time."

Boku Sata raised his hand to Nene Yuki, "I can set Yu Wing on path. You've had your chance already girl. Let your elders have turn."

Nene Yuki shook her head, "What if you need my help?"

Boku Sata held up his hand, "That is why you have to stay. You will be our anchor here. I may need you here to guide us out again if chaos seizes us. Watch us and let Hap Sing know when we are ready."

Hap Sing looked at them in a confused manner, "What should I do?"

Yu Wing spoke to him, "Wait for Nene to signal. Then just go where you went when you cast the net over the village. We don't need you to cast the net this time, just place yourself in your boat on the pond again if you can. Do you understand?"

Hap Sing nodded, "Do you need me to help you get there?"

Boku Sata spoke, "Only if you are very certain you will not lose us."

Hap Sing shrugged, "I am not even sure where I am going, but I think it will be fine."

Hap Sing waited while Boku Sata and Yu Wing leaned back in their chairs and rested. They gently clasped hands and their breathing became regular and measured after several minutes. Soon their relaxation became greater

Nene Yuki called over to Hap Sing, "They will be ready soon. When I tell you lightly clasp Yu Wing by the hand and do what you did before without casting the net. If this works then they should join you on your boat. Hap Sing you can begin."

Hap Sing shut his eyes and envisioned himself sitting on his boat on the pond in the valley. As he sat on his boat on the pond with his fishing pole in hand Hap Sing envisioned Boku Sata and Yu Wing sitting on the bench across from him. They sat there with their eyes open looking at Hap Sing yet still clasping hands.

Boku Sata looked out across the pond at the surroundings, "This isn't dreaming. You have somehow teleported us to Yu's pond. Impressive feat but any major arcane caster could do this."

Yu Wing shook his head, "This isn't my pond. I've lived in Hung Chan village for my entire life. This is not where I grew up."

Boku Sata looked around, "What do you mean? It looks like your place"

Yu Wing looked up, "Those were not the stars over our heads tonight. This isn't my home I can feel it. Hap Sing where did you take us?"

Hap Sing smiled as he spoke, "Back to the valley as I remembered it as a child. My uncle's house is back as it was. There was no wall around the village. The trees were not cut down then."

Boku Sata looked over at Hap Sing, "This is impossible. No Chi Master has this level of control in dreaming. There is always something changing or in chaos there. This is static. It is different from dreaming."

Hap Sing shrugged his shoulders, "I don't know about that. This is the valley as I imagine it should be. It helps me to envision what I want to achieve when I cast my net."

Yu Wing shook his head, "It is not impossible Sata. This is the dreaming. Hap Sing could you take us to the bay at Li Chan village where you fish?"

Hap Sing shrugged his shoulders, "I could try."

Hap Sing began rowing his boat on the water. The shore didn't get any closer, but a dense fog rolled in from the shore. After rowing for a while in silence the sun rose over the horizon and the fog cleared. They were sitting in the boat out on the sea in the bay at Li Chan village. The boat gently rocked on the waves as Hap Sing placed his fishing line in the water.

Boku Sata opened his mouth to speak but Yu Wing held up his hand, "It is possible. We are still in the dreaming. When we return the others will have only seen us asleep. Hap Sing, could you take us to Yokito?"

Hap Sing was uncertain, "I'm not sure. I haven't spent much time there, and it was about seventy years ago that I was last in the capital. I will attempt it."

Once more the fog rolled in as Hap Sing rowed out to sea. It took a longer time and then the fog cleared at noon as the boat bobbed in the bay at Yokito. This time the water and the sea seemed as real as before, but the city was vague and indistinct. There were also no people or creatures present in sight.

Boku Sata nodded in understanding, "I think I see now. You are extremely talented in your abilities Hap Sing. You have limit in replicating places you do not know well in dreaming. I can see hints of vagueness and uncertainty which should be present now. I am impressed. I thought great spirit of seven tailed tiger had made you powerful. I failed to understand extent of that power. This must be relatively calm area of dreaming though. It is shallow sheltered bay perhaps."

Hap Sing shrugged again, "I don't know. I relax and envision where I am. If you say this is the dreaming, then I will take your word for it."

Yu Wing shook his head, "This is the dreaming, but not as any Chi Master has envisioned it in the past. It is supposed to be tempestuous. Uncertainty is a major feature. The spirit powers of the greater Chi Masters call upon it at times. Nothing I have ever read has described it as stable."

Hap Sing laughed, "That is your mistake then. You think it should be chaos because you have read it is that way and so it is for you. I haven't read anything about it, so it becomes what I want it to be, not what someone else thought it should be."

Yu Wing nodded, "Perhaps you are right, and perhaps Boku Sata is right. Maybe you just instinctively locate unnaturally calm regions of the dreaming. Would you mind a little test?"

Hap Sing cautiously answered, "What kind of test?"

Yu Wing smiled slightly, "I have a little theory I want to examine. Could you release control of the dreaming? Let it flow naturally around us."

Hap Sing shook his head, "I am not sure how I would do such a thing."

Boku Sata looked at Yu Wing, "This sounds dangerous. The dreaming is not playground even if it seems safe with Hap Sing here."

Yu Wing nodded, "It may well be dangerous. However our research has led us to this point. Do we turn back now, or learn of the magnitude of what we are facing."

Boku Sata grinned, "The people of Udomo are not cowards. If you think it is necessary to continue forward let us attempt it."

Yu Wing nodded, "I do. We may well be tested hard, but we must make the attempt. Hap Sing I would ask for you to clasp our hands. Then if you can just fall asleep."

Hap Sing looked at Yu Wing with a puzzled look, "Is that all it takes?"

Yu Wing nodded, "At that point we shall see what we see."

Hap Sing closed his eyes and began to breathe in a slow regular rhythm. The scenery remained that of a sketchy Yokito. Then the pace of his breathing changed to a slower one and everything turned to blackness.

A vast explosion of bright light ripped through their beings. Their breath became flame and their bodies felt as ice. Bolts of lightning ripped through the darkness causing their forms to convulse. Boku Sata and Yu Wing clung desperately to the unconscious form of Hap Sing as if he were a raft on a storm tossed ocean. They felt the sensation of falling and extreme pain. Psychedelic colors flashed before their eyes and nausea racked their guts. They were drowning in nothingness, they were bursting with pleasure. There was no air in their lungs, and their brains were going into shock from the sensation overload.

Once more they were engulfed in blackness. This time they felt a strange kind of peace as the horrible sensations had ceased. As they lay on top of Hap Sing where he was suspended in the black space they saw a small orange cat approach them. As they recovered somewhat they noticed that as the cat became closer its body was the only source of illumination. It also grew in size until they could see that it was a tiger. Then they noticed the seven tails swinging behind it as it approached.

It grew even larger still, or perhaps they were growing smaller. Soon it towered up into the sky above them and looked down at their tiny presence. It growled rumbling the air about them like thunder. It used its massive paw as big as horse to gently flip them off of Hap Sing and onto their backs.

The Luck spoke in a voice that split the air, "That was incredibly stupid even for humans. Don't ever ask Hap Sing to cast you loose into the chaos like that again. Do you flipping idiots even have any idea how far away you are from the prime material right now? Well your spirits at least. This isn't some casual astral projection you were attempting. You are at the cusp of the well of deep spirit magic here. The spirits in this place are none too friendly to you foolish mortals and your jackass gods. It was very fortunate for you two that I was close by already. My, what a right pair of jackass dimwits you two are. Don't look at me like that. I'll properly dress you down when you ask Hap Sing to talk to me again tomorrow. Don't think you can forget to ask him to avoid your due either. If you do then it will piss me off to no end. Now I can't talk much here. There are other ears listening. So until then stay out of the dreaming. In fact I would recommend you stay out of the dreaming for good or at least until you get some better sense you foolish clowns. The tailed beasts live here, and they especially don't like your kind. Now I will banish your spirits back to your bodies on the prime. Return!"

Yu Wing and Boku Sata had the impression of falling up into the giant pupil of the Greater Spirit seven tailed tiger. The pupil expanded and grew until it was the size of an ocean. Then they knew blackness once more.

Chapter 5 Meeting with the Cricket

Yu Wing felt sore and exhausted as he opened his eyes. He could feel that he was softly crying for some reason. Yu Mai was looking down at him as she knelt over him and she was sobbing softly as well. Standing past Yu Mai was Yu Gai holding Yu Jin close to him with looks of concern and worry in their eyes.

Yu Mai called out softly to him as she cried, "Are you alive my love? I thought I had lost you. They stopped me from helping and I thought I had lost you. Your spirit was gone my dear and I thought I had lost you."

Yu Wing croaked out, "I'm alive. I'm very tired and sore but alive."

Yu Wing looked over at his left side and noticed Boku Sata lying on the ground trembling beside him with Akane and Ran hovering over his form. When he glanced to his right he could see the unconscious form of Hap Sing lying peacefully on the ground with Yuki Nene kneeling at his side.

Boku Sata reached over and lightly tapped Yu Wing on the arm, "I have to agree with that tailed beast on this one. That had to be your stupidest decision ever."

Yu Wing croaked back, "Well we certainly learned something."

Boku Sata grunted, "I'm beginning to think I would rather be ignorant."

Yu Mai clasped Yu Wing closely and spoke softly to him, "What happened? What did he do to you?"

Yu Wing gave a faint grin yet tears continued to fall from his eyes, "Hap Sing only did what we requested of him. The fault was mine. I failed to understand what the full truth of our situation was until it was too late. It nearly killed us."

Ming Akane spoke to Boku Sata, "What happened there Sata? What did you see?"

Boku Sata gave a feeble laugh, "Couple of fools well out of their depth. Don't worry girl. We were saved from our folly. It came to send us back even if it was very unhappy about what we had done."

Ming Ran spoke, "I'm afraid we're going to have to leave here pretty soon. Whatever you three did, it made an impact here. The nearby villagers have to know that something happened, and when their fear subsides they will come to investigate. I will remain behind to deal with them if you can return to your homes for the evening."

Yuki Nene spoke, "Hap Sing is still unconscious. I will carry him to my home."

Ming Ran shook his head, "No. Hap Sing will stay with Sata. It would be inappropriate for you to be seen with a strange man alone at your place. Akane will help you get him over there as long as Sata feels well enough to walk unassisted."

Boku Sata moved to a sitting position, "I'll be fine enough to walk in bit. In fact I think I should be able to carry Hap Sing instead of leaving his weight to these young women."

Yuki Nene knelt down and picked Hap Sing up placing him over her shoulder. She then stood up clutching his legs in front of her while his upper body was lying across her back.

Yuki Nene looked at Ming Ran and Boku Sata, "I can manage Hap Sing easily enough. He is lighter than he looks."

Ming Ran reached for Hap Sing's mostly full bottle of sake and splashed some on Boku Sata, Yu Wing, and Hap Sing. Then he spilled the remainder on a table and used a flint to catch it on fire briefly shortly thereafter he put it out with some water. The wood was lightly scorched, but no lasting damage was done.

Ming Ran then spoke, "If anyone asks why you are being helped you've just had a bit much to drink celebrating the arrival of Wing's cousin. The strange orange light can be explained by an accidental fire quickly contained. Now go home and we will all meet at Yu's farm in the morning."

As the Yu's collectively headed off to Yu Gai's home in the village, Boku Sata was escorted home assisted by Ming Akane and followed by Yuki Nene carrying Hap Sing. When they arrived they placed Hap Sing on a spare cotton mattress. Boku Sata asked Akane to wait until Ran arrived before he let her leave for their home. After Akane left with her husband Boku Sata went over to where Yuki Nene was watching over the sleeping Hap Sing.

Boku Sata spoke to Yuki Nene, "Hap Sing will be fine under my care, you can return home to rest."

Yuki Nene looked back over at Boku Sata briefly, "I will stay. There is no room for discussion on this matter. I mistakenly let you leave me behind before. I will not let you risk him again."

Boku Sata gently chuckled, "Have it your way then girl. I have never been your boss, only your employee. I'll let you know that of all of us present tonight, Hap Sing was likely only one never in danger of harm. I am curious about what you witnessed when we went to the dreaming though."

Yuki Nene glanced at Boku Sata again before speaking, "The two of you went to sleep. When I sensed you on the path to the dreaming Hap Sing joined you almost instantly and swept your spirits away. As was said before Hap Sing's aura could be seen with the second sight. The faint aura of the Great Spirit seven tailed tiger could no longer be seen. It was blindingly bright such that we had to stop looking directly at him with the vision. Then we could see that our guardian spirits were all staring at Hap Sing, and that each of them moved before him. They, it is hard to say just what, but it seemed like they were paying him some kind of respect as if they were subjects brought before an emperor."

Boku Sata shook his head, "If you had said such thing before what I witnessed tonight. I would say that you were lying to me. I think I understand it a bit more now. Had Rasic joined them as well?"

Yuki Nene nodded, "Along with my Hugin. I did not think it possible either. Hugin has never shown anything but a general disregard for other Chi Masters. It was disturbing to contemplate that our guardian spirits would recognize another over us."

Boku Sata replied, "This is like many things tonight, unprecedented. What did you see next? While it was likely disturbing it doesn't explain fully what happened."

Yuki Nene's voice cracked, "Hap Sing slumped as if he had been disconnected from his body. His aura disappeared altogether. Then Wing and you began to convulse uncontrollably in a seizure. When we tried to move closer to help our guardian spirits came between us. They prevented us from coming to you three. They disobeyed our commands. We watched the two of you stricken in pain and agony and could do nothing to help. Then you both went limp like Hap Sing with no sign of your auras present. To our eyes you were as the bodies of the dead."

Boku Sata could hear Yuki Nene softly crying through her words as she continued, "Then it came. It was Hap Sing but not Hap Sing if you understand. Its aura could be seen as an orange glow even without the second sight and extended well beyond his form in the shape of a seven tailed tiger. It looked at your forms lying still and said 'Stupid fools'. Then it looked directly at me and said 'You should never have let them do this. You of all the fools here should know better. I'll fix this idiotic mess'. Then it was gone again, with just the expected faint aura around Hap Sing again."

Boku Sata walked over to pat Yuki Nene on the shoulders, "I think you shouldn't take it so personally. We all made mistake of underestimating tailed beast and its impact on Hap Sing's abilities. He can now do what no Chi Master ever could. The only Chi Master who might ever have fully understood what Hap Sing's potential could be if he tried was likely his father Hap Yang."

Yuki Nene wiped her hand across her eyes to dry her tears, "You don't understand how frightening it was to be addressed by it. To be the one who disappointed it."

Boku Sata shrugged, "Actually I think I may know better than you. Wing and I had the distinct displeasure of being addressed by it in what I would guess is its normal form if such an entity could be said to have normal form. It doesn't gladly suffer presence of mortals for I think it finds all of us somewhat limited and stupid by its standards. It even seemed to consider gods worshiped by mortals with contempt."

Yuki Nene raised her head and spoke clearly, "There is one more thing of importance. Our spirit guardians may have acted like they were paying respect to a ruler with Hap Sing. However they fled like they were faced by an angry god when it came. They are acting normally now, but we all know that we were abandoned by them when faced by it. This fundamentally changes our concept of reality. We have always considered our spirit guardians as an extension of ourselves. Now we know that they may actually answer to another."

Boku Sata shook his head, "You are wrong about that. Rasic is extension of my spirit just as Hugin is extension of yours. It is just that sometimes our spirits might be touch wiser than we are. They know that Hap Sing's spiritual abilities require respect, and they understand that this thing called Luck is something to be feared. We should have listened closer to Ming Akane earlier when she mentioned reaction her guardian spirit had earlier. She may be the wisest one of us all tonight. It's toss up as to whether Wing or I was biggest fool."

Yuki Nene turned to face Boku Sata briefly again, "You should rest. We will need to gather again tomorrow at Yu's farm in the morning."

Boku Sata nodded, "Your advice is right. However it applies to both of us. We both need to rest. I have a feeling that tomorrow will be challenging. Before you think of it I have an extra mattress you can use. Don't think of climbing over into his. I'm light sleeper and I will not have funny business happening in my house. Besides I have impression that your advances would not be met how you might expect by him."

Yuki Nene gave Boku Sata a sharp look, "What business is my personal life of yours?"

Boku Sata gave a sharp grin, "You have to understand something my dear outcast Nordland princess. Hap Sing is not nobility here. In this land he is living as lowest form of peasant just barely step above unclean beggar, and by his own choice. He could have been land owner and farmer if such was his desire. His father's and uncle's estates could have provided such comforts. Understand that Hap Sing is also ancient by any conventional measure of such things, and in comparison you are but mere child. However, I also suspect that Hap Sing is innocent in matters of relations between men and women. Nothing he has said about himself has indicated otherwise. No mention of a wife or children was made tonight. Everything I have seen about him tells me he is deeply private man. If you act in too forward manner he will most certainly flee your advances. If you mean to catch this one you had better learn how to fish."

Yuki Nene looked at Boku Sata with a hard eye, "Bring your mattress then. I shall obey your rules in your own home. What happens outside of it is my business though. I advise you to not interfere with my business."

Boku Sata shook his head, "I'm not trying to control you princess. I am your paid servant as always. I just don't want to see you get hurt."

Yuki Nene turned away from Boku Sata, "I also wish you would stop calling me princess. In this land the title doesn't apply. Only in Nordland are spirit shamans considered royalty. The others would not understand. They would fear me, and I don't want that."

ours later after Yuki Nene had finally drifted into a deep slumber Hap Sing opened his eyes. The Luck had been playing its games again. He had been seemingly asleep, yet in his dreams he had heard everything which had happened around him. Hap Sing also understood that instead of a simple gathering of like minded Chi Masters there was a fair amount of tension between these Chi Masters, elder versus younger, husband versus wife, master versus student, employer versus employee, newcomers versus natives, nobility against peasant, and even old beliefs versus new beliefs when he considered that Lo Arthur was also a greater destiny. Any way he looked at it the exact kind of social tensions he had deliberately avoided most of his life were present in this odd gathering of greater destinies.

As Hap Sing carefully rose from the mattress and quietly left Boku Sata's house he considered his next course of action. He thought that they now knew way too much and would likely follow him wherever he went now. They knew he existed, and would consider him as something to learn from, and maybe as a power to possess and control. Hap Sing was most worried about Yuki Nene's almost predatory fascination with pursuing him as a personal conquest. Being carried by her had disturbed him deeply while he dreamed. He had felt like a prize carried by a victor from a battlefield.

Hap Sing reached a portion of the palisade wall around the village. There was a ladder leading to a platform at the top. In the middle of the night no one was watching to see if anyone would climb it. Hap Sing did so and slipped over to drop down the eight feet to the ground on the other side of the wall. He needed to think, and thought that his best place for thinking had always been when he was relaxed.

Hap Sing was sitting on the bank of the pond with his fishing pole in the water as the sun rose. Several good fish were already in his creel, but he was happy to continue. A measure of peace had settled on him as he fished. He remembered fondly spending his youth here, and he decided that things would happen beyond his control no matter where he went. He also decided that if they asked him to speak with the Luck he would grant their request. The Luck was playing what Hap Sing thought of as its game, and it was going to be the only way he could learn more by having them hear what they needed to hear straight from the source.

Hap Sing saw Yu Wing coming down from his farm house to sit down on the bank next to him in silence. Hap Sing kept the silence for several minutes, and then looked over at Yu Wing.

Hap Sing spoke, "I am sorry for any disturbance last night. I didn't realize what I was doing was such a dangerous thing."

Yu Wing patted him on the shoulder, "Don't mention it. It was our mistake. We misjudged what we knew, very badly in fact. We should be apologizing to you instead. I am apologizing to you. I drew you into our little club, and I did not understand what trouble it would cause. Can you forgive me?"

Hap Sing smiled, "There is nothing to forgive. Your intent was not bad. Sometimes bad things happen even from good intent."

Yu Wing gave a weak smile, "I'm glad you understand. There is another imposition I'm afraid I will have to make upon you. When it cast Sata and I out of the dreaming the Greater Spirit seven tailed tiger spoke to us. It said we had to ask you to let us talk to it today. It said if we didn't it would be very pissed. I'm not afraid to tell you that I am indebted to it for saving us, and at the same time deathly afraid to disobey its order. I wouldn't have asked today after the events from last night if I were not afraid of the possible consequences."

Hap Sing bowed to Yu Wing, "I apologize to you for the behavior of the Luck. It is sometimes an ill mannered bully, and I am sorry for any offense it may have caused. As I warned you it scares everyone who meets it. You are very brave to be willing to do so again."

Yu Wing shook his head, "If I didn't have to I certainly wouldn't. I am just more afraid of disobeying it. I don't want to learn what it could do to me."

Hap Sing shrugged his shoulders, "Don't fear what the Luck can do to you. It is powerless here without my consent. It knows this very well, and has to result to meaningless threats to get its way. If you don't want me to summon it then I will not. It is just playing games."

Yu Wing looked at Hap Sing with a look of incredulity, "Playing games?"

Hap Sing nodded, "With me, with you, with the other spirits, with the gods; the Luck is just playing games. What else is an immortal Great Spirit to do to pass the time?"

Yu Wing shook his head, "You've got a strange idea of what makes a game."

Hap Sing laughed, "What else would you call it then? It certainly isn't fishing."

Yu Wing laughed as well, "You are right about that cousin Sing."

Their laughter died down after a short while and they sat in silence on the bank for a couple more minutes. Yu Wing saw that the slight tension between them had eased, but that Hap Sing was still contemplating something.

Yu Wing asked, "As a relative, if I am not imposing that is, can I ask what is bothering you? You disappeared in the middle of the night and got the others worried. I figured you may have come here."

Hap Sing shrugged his shoulders for a moment, "I always worry. My friend Li Hung would say I try to take too much responsibility for everyone. Like he can talk, he took responsibility for the defense of our whole nation for many years."

Yu Wing shook his head, "Last night was not your fault."

Hap Sing shrugged, "I understand that, but I still feel the way I do. You have to understand that you all seem so young compared to me. I at least should have known better. I was showing off because I was getting a little attention and recognition. I was acting like a silly old fool trying to impress some new friends with his bag of tricks. It is embarrassing to me now, especially when I consider the damage which I have done."

Yu Wing smiled, "Sata and I are fine. It was a shock and certainly uncomfortable at the time, but we are actually doing pretty well this morning."

Hap Sing looked at him sadly, "I am glad to hear it, but that is not the damage of which I speak. Your group has become divided by my presence. Your foundation of trust in each other has been shaken, and that is my fault. By coming here I have awakened the beginning of disputes which never should have been awakened."

Yu Wing shook his head, "Nothing of the sort is happening. We are all comrades in exile here. Any Chi Master is welcome to shelter and camaraderie."

Hap Sing shrugged, "I like you Wing. I even trust you have a good heart. You are the one most likely to understand what I will tell you next. I am a simple person. Don't mistake the Luck for simple or a person when you speak to it. It is not. It has a plan and an agenda. It knows things. It knows things about you. It knows things about your wife. It knows things about each of the others. It knows things about the gods and the other major spirits. What it doesn't know it can very quickly learn."

Yu Wing nodded, "I understand what you are saying. Then it must have the answers to our questions."

Hap Sing nodded, "It certainly knows the answers to anything you might consider asking it, but it will never reveal more than it takes to get you to do what it wants. If you summon the Luck to speak with it then it will give you the answers you seek even if you don't like them. It can give you the answers it takes to get its way with you. However there is one answer I will give you right now before you ask. If you summon the Luck then you will be the one to serve it, not the other way around."

Yu Wing gulped, "Is serving the Luck such a bad thing?"

Hap Sing shrugged, "My friend Li Chan would have said no. He got to have his son live in exchange for serving the Luck though. I recommend your bargain is at least as wise as his was. Li Chan also told me that he would never have the ability to face it again. In this at least you have surpassed him."

Yu Wing chuckled, "In this at least I think that fear is more my motivation than courage."

Hap Sing shook his head, "It is certainly courage to face it in spite of your fear."

Yu Wing shrugged, "I thank you for your kind estimation. Now about those disputes you mentioned?"

Hap Sing looked at him, "I will say this much. I think you are wise enough to not be ignorant of them. Just that you are kindly enough to overlook them. You see me as family. A part of your past and your family history, yet still a person. Each of the others does not view me as such. They see me as a problem, or an answer. They see me as a source of power or fame. They see me as a threat, or as a conquest. The Luck will use each of these flaws to control them."

Yu Wing became flushed and embarrassed, "I see. Are we so transparent to you after all?"

Hap Sing shook his head, "It is not just the group of you. It is human nature. There are those few who have ever accepted me for what I am. The rest usually view me in one of those categories. It pained Li Chan deeply to call upon me to save his son. He knew what people were like as well as anyone. In fact the priests in Yokito at the time would not heal Li Hung unless Li Chan and his family publicly converted to one of their faiths. They wanted to use him and his position of General to advance their own cause. To his credit Li Chan feared greatly to be viewed by me in the same way as someone who wanted to use our friendship for his own cause, and he was ashamed of it. However he loved his son enough to accept his shame and asked me as he would rather trust me and the Luck than sign himself over to their religions. He never regretted his decision, and I never held it against them.

The Luck used them hard in exchange, but it used them fairly with them entering the bargain with open eyes."

Yu Wing thought in silence for a while contemplating what was said by Hap Sing. Hap Sing continued to fish and caught three more as they sat on the bank quietly together.

Yu Wing asked, "Which of us sees you which way?"

Hap Sing sighed, "Are you sure you want my answer. I am no great sage in this mater. I just speak from long experience in observing people."

Yu Wing nodded, "I would know it from you rather than hear it phrased in a disruptive manner by the Luck. That way I can consider who will be allowed to attend the summoning."

Hap Sing spoke, "I apologize in advance then. This will not be pleasant for me or you. You see me as a person, and I thank you for it. You also see me as an answer. The Luck will provide that much if you ask it. Your wife and your son see me as a threat. I have powers they will never understand, and they don't want to accept me as part of your family. The fear from the old legends of Hap Yang still vibrates through them and the other locals here. I know that even in my youth that Hap Yang was never a well liked person here, well respected certainly, but not liked. There are likely as many bad things still told about him as there were good. Your daughter-in-law Yu Jin probably idolizes my father, and as such sees me as an answer to her questions about who she is as a person. Ming Ran is clearly estimating what gain he can safely make from me. Ming Akane is just as clearly afraid of me and likely sees me as a problem due to her husband's ambitions."

Yu Wing sat and thought about it a while longer, "I think I understand where you have made these choices. It is not easy to accept what you say though. I would think that my wife and son are not as threatened as you feel they are."

Hap Sing nodded, "I don't blame them. I have felt threatened by the actions of the Luck many times myself. Rarely has it won me friends or admiration. It was likely the physical damage done to you which caused it to set firmly in them now though."

Yu Wing interjected, "I let them know that was my own fault."

Hap Sing nodded, "Yet they still feel it was mine."

Yu Wing nodded, "Ah I see where you are leading me, knowledge against feeling. Feelings usually win. The Luck is good at manipulating feelings as well then."

Hap Sing shrugged, "Only in a hurtful way. I guess it trusts me to patch up any hard feelings it creates, or else it just doesn't really care as long as it gets what it wants."

Yu Wing sighed, "Your warning is well taken. But you have avoided mentioning Boku Sata and Yuki Nene. What do you think of them?"

Hap Sing sighed himself, "Boku Sata is a mercenary. He is best described as a hired blade in the Chi Master world perhaps. My guess is that he didn't leave Udomo because his warlord was overthrown. I would guess he left Udomo to specifically come here because Yuki Nene paid him to do so. His apprentice Akane was ambitious enough to help with his story by pretending to be a relative of a warlord's wife. However, she is as common as you or I in reality. Akane is likely a talented Chi Master in her own right, but she is not from noble stock. At best Boku Sata sees me as a source of power. At worst he sees me as a problem to be dealt with harshly if necessary."

Yu Wing nodded, "I sensed as much about him myself. Always chasing the next bit of coin and looking for the next job. I could also see that even with their apparent difference in age that Nene was pulling his strings. I see that you are reticent to talk about her though."

Hap Sing shrugged, "As you are to patch things up between Lo Arthur and your wife. Yu Mai misjudges him based on his choices in life. Certainly he's a smart man and an ambitious one as well. He also loves and respects your daughter. He seeks the respect and acceptance of his wife's parents without understanding the reasons for their dislike of him. He begins to despair of ever earning your trust."

Yu Wing looked ashamed, "What you say is true. How can we trust a follower of Palnor? How can we accept him into our family?"

Hap Sing placed a hand on Yu Wing's shoulder, "By trusting that your daughter's love is not misplaced and that Arthur is a good man. Arthur must also talk with the Luck. The Luck will reveal to him what he must know. You must trust that his family is as important to him as his religion. You should note that the tale told by Yuki Nene last night was true if with some significant omissions. The followers of Palnor in Yokito did what is right by her instead of blindly following their religion. Only by building bridges of mutual respect can this persecution of the Chi Masters in Ran Li end. Your son-in-law is the most available bridge you have. Also it wouldn't hurt if you would let him bless those shrines. We both well know the spirits of our ancestors haven't lingered there. They are just symbols for our memories."

Yu Wing had a teary look in his eyes, "You are wiser than I imagined for a simple fisherman. I feel like when I was a child and I've done some wrong and my father has just forgiven me for it. I don't know how to thank you."

Hap Sing gently shook his head, "As you noted you are my family. Family I didn't even bother to find until now. I am ashamed of myself and apologize for the necessity for my long absence."

Yu Wing dried his eyes as Hap Sing gathered up his fishing gear, "Now about Yuki Nene."

Hap Sing sighed, "Fine. You can speak your piece."

Yu Wing smiled, "Just a warning. I recognize that look in her eye and that possessive behavior. My wife Mai had the same look and behavior before she cornered me and hauled me off before the magistrate. Sata indicated to me this morning that he thought at much as well. I'm guessing that she falls in the conquest category of your list."

Hap Sing nodded, "That's what I'm afraid is the case."

Yu Wing grinned, "Need some advice from an old married man?"

Hap Sing looked over at Yu Wing as he pulled his fishing creel out of the water, "Go ahead."

Yu Wing laughed, "Run as fast as you can."

Hap Sing smiled, "I had that much figured out already by myself."

Chapter 6 Family Matters

Hap Sing walked into Yu Wing's home. Yu Wing closed the door behind them and they faced the assembled other Chi Masters. Most of them looked at Hap Sing with conflicted emotions crossing their faces. Hap Sing returned a timid smile.

Hap Sing spoke, "I apologize for the trouble I have caused you all. I also apologize for any rudeness you may have experienced because of the Luck. As my friend Li Chan once said of it the Luck is hard, but fair. I don't think you need fear for your lives if you wish to ask a question of it. As I said before it knows things. I will summon it to speak with those who are interested later this afternoon. I believe that at least Yu Wing desires to learn some of what it knows."

Boku Sata leaned back in his chair, "I think I've learned more than I care to already myself. You can count me out today. I'll just listen to what others report."

Yu Wing spoke up, "Don't forget it told us to have it summoned. It said it would be pissed if we failed to do so."

Boku Sata sat forward quickly, "You've got point there Wing. Let's hear what others have to say. I think that I have satisfied my obligation as Hap Sing knows to summon it and has agreed to do so. I don't wish to stand around letting it berate me second time."

Yuki Nene spoke, "I would learn something it knows. Count me in on when it is summoned."

Ming Ran nodded his head, "I also wish to ask it something."

Ming Akane shook her head, "I don't think I want anything more to do with it. No offense intended Hap Sing. Like master Sata I will be happy to hear what the others learn."

Yu Jin spoke up next, "I want to ask it of the great spell cast by Hap Yang. Most certainly it was a tremendous battle between them."

Yu Gai looked at Yu Jin, "I have nothing I wish to learn of it, but I will go with my wife."

Yu Mai spoke next with a bitter tone and a hard eye, "I also want nothing from it. I will go to protect my husband Wing from its mischief and smite it down if it harms him."

Hap Sing nodded at the rest, "The Luck will also need to speak with Lo Arthur. There needs to be a bridge built between the Chi Masters of Ran Li and the followers of the gods. The Luck knows things, and I suspect Lo Arthur will be a key element in eliminating the persecution of the Chi Masters in Ran Li."

Yu Mai gave Hap Sing a hard stare, "What do you mean by inviting that ass to speak with the Luck? You would reveal us all to the persecution of his faith?"

Yu Wing stepped in front of Hap Sing, "Something needs to be done dear. We know our numbers are dwindling, and our knowledge will be lost if we can not share it with others. Do you plan to have our kind die out because of silly pride in our old traditions?"

Yu Mai shouted back, "Would you let him turn us in so that we can be run out of our home? It is a horrible idea you fools. They hate us and want nothing more than to destroy our kind."

Hap Sing spoke quietly from behind Yu Wing, "They fear what they don't understand. Can you say that you are any different yourself? It didn't seem so to me last night, and it doesn't seem so to me today. You asked what spell I cast on Lo Arthur last night. Let me tell you. It was called treating someone in a friendly and respectful manner. You accused me of using some kind of dark influence then; you blame me for the harm which has come to your husband. I say instead that you have failed to be a mother the husband of your daughter could love, but it is not too late to change. Start by apologizing to him and inviting him to purify your shrines today."

Yu Mai surged forward, "You would have him insult the shrines of my ancestors with his filthy spells."

Hap Sing turned away and headed toward the exit, "Yes, I would if it would bring peace between you and your daughter. Don't bother to say no, they are the shrines of my father and mother. I will ask him myself."

Hap Sing stood outside the house trembling slightly in reaction to his confrontation with Yu Mai. Only a slight noise of a moving chair could be heard from outside. He began walking down the path toward Hung Chan village when he heard the door open up and close again behind him. He looked back to see Yuki Nene running up to him.

Yuki Nene had a sharp smile that seemingly went ear to ear, "Wow you really put her in her place. No one has ever spoken that harshly with her about her son-in-law. She doesn't know what to do."

Hap Sing ducked his head, "It was unseemly of me to treat her so in her own home. I lost my better judgment, and will apologize to her later when she has had some time to lose her anger at me."

Yuki Nene shook her head still smiling, "You are going to wait a long time I think. I suspect she can stay mad at someone for years."

Hap Sing gave a slight smile, "I'm already one hundred and fifty years old. Do you think she can out wait me?"

Yuki Nene's smile diminished, "I guess not. I hadn't thought of it that way. So are you going to need a place to stay tonight? I don't figure that Wing will be able to invite you to stay at his place tonight. Not if he ever wants to sleep in his own bed again that is."

Hap Sing shrugged, "It will not be the first time I've slept under the stars. I like it actually."

Yuki Nene blew out a slight sigh of frustration, "You are either very thick headed or you are dodging me. I am inviting you to stay with me tonight."

Hap Sing nodded, "I know. I was hoping you would not press the issue before I depart."

Yuki Nene smiled again, "I didn't figure you were slow. So blond hair and blue eyes doesn't attract you. It's your loss my good fellow. There are a whole lot of people who have chased me since I was sixteen. None has ever been chased by me."

Hap Sing stopped in the path, "Don't take this the wrong way. You are very desirable and you know it. If this were another life at another time I would be a fool to pass up an offer like you are making. As you stated I am not a fool."

Yuki Nene stopped smiling and spoke in a serious tone, "Come spend the night with me then. I will leave your virtue intact. We'll just talk and get to know each other better."

Hap Sing started walking again, "I would like that. I will consider it. However after talking to the Luck this afternoon you might change your mind."

Yuki Nene walked beside Hap Sing and smiled faintly again, "The Luck doesn't bother me."

Hap Sing gently shook his head, "You shouldn't lie to me like that if you want to be friends with me. I know the Luck bothers everyone. The Luck bothers the very gods when it wants to. It has more enemies than both of us can count, and just as many allies that owe it favors. Sometimes they are one in the same. It also plays games with my dreams at times. It let me know what you said last night princess. You intrigue the Luck more than the others. It has made plans for you. I wish I could stop it, but it has made plans for you likely long before you were born. It wouldn't have spoken to you as you said last night if it hadn't. I'm sorry."

Yuki Nene lost all trace of a smile, "You are scaring me now. You make it sound like I have no choice in my life."

Hap Sing gave her a serious look, "We all have choices. There are just times when the choices we make don't matter because the big events happen regardless of our personal choices. Big things are happening soon. I can feel it in my dreams. Destiny is in motion, and the Luck has rigged the wheels of fate."

Yuki Nene tried a smile again, "Is that why you won't chase me? You are fated to someone else."

Hap Sing shrugged, "That I don't know. Like I said, in a different life I would be dead already. If I met you as a young man I would definitely find you exotically appealing. That life never happened for me and you. We have this one, and the Luck is setting the rules I have to follow."

Yuki Nene placed a hand on his shoulder, "Has it told you that you can't have love?"

Hap Sing dropped his head, "Everyone I know and love eventually dies. It is a hard thing to live with at times. It is the problem with being who I am. I don't want that kind of pain anymore. I keep my distance as best I can. I couldn't bear to watch my own children and wife grow old and die while I remain unchanged. I couldn't take that aspect of life away from another."

Yuki Nene gave a serious look, "I hadn't thought about it that way. You will grow old and die eventually though right. Maybe it will happen if you find the right person."

Hap Sing shrugged his shoulders, "I don't know. Maybe the Luck does. You could ask it if you are interested."

Yuki Nene smiled back at him, "Maybe I don't want to waste my one question on you."

Hap Sing laughed, "The Luck is not some magic genie granting wishes. It will appear for as long as I allow it, and you can ask it as many questions as it will answer. It will tell you the truth. However, much like you it tends to omit valuable information if it sees a need to do so."

Yuki Nene sighed, "You noticed the holes in my story then."

Hap Sing nodded, "It has some obvious ones. Why would even Nordlanders consorting with priests and priestesses of Palnor risk the wrath of their new god? You would have to be a significant personage with greater local pull than their religion, an actual princess perhaps."

Yuki Nene sighed, "You did hear what Sata said last night."

Hap Sing ducked his head again, "One more I apologize for the Luck. I hope you can forgive my inadvertent listening in on your private conversation."

Yuki Nene smiled, "You have to stop apologizing for things beyond your control. It makes you seem a bit arrogant."

Hap Sing looked surprised, "Really? I'm sorry."

Yuki Nene laughed, "You are too easy, or maybe you are too clever. I think it is likely a bit of both."

Hap Sing nodded, "People tend to underestimate me. I rarely underestimate them in return."

Yuki Nene laughed, "The Luck again?"

Hap Sing shook his head, "That is one hundred and fifty years of experience talking. The Luck has nothing to do with it, well except for the part about living one hundred and fifty years."

Yuki Nene laughed, "A fisherman and a comedian. How irresistible you are."

Hap Sing looked serious again, "Really? I'm sorry."

Yuki Nene laughed again, "For a man who isn't trying to chase me you are certainly doing a great job of winning me over with your dry sense of humor."

Hap Sing said again, "Really? I'm sorry."

Yuki Nene kept laughing as they approached the gate of the village, "Stop it you're killing me."

Hap Sing repeated it again, "Really? I'm sorry."

Yuki Nene was in tears with laughter as they entered the village. Hap Sing led her over to the marketplace. They ate a quick breakfast of fried bread and eggs as they spoke together about inconsequential matters like the weather and the season's upcoming harvest. For the moment they had reached a temporary agreement to be friendly with each other and Hap Sing was pleased that Yuki Nene had stopped openly pursuing him. He found her to be actually quite pleasant and personable when she wanted to be nice.

After their meal Hap Sing got directions from Yuki Nene as to where he could find the local temple of Palnor. Yuki Nene and he parted ways, and he traveled to the temple alone. As he approached the building he saw a pleasant looking young woman sweeping the path leading to the door. She was a little plump around the middle, and he guessed that she was likely in the early stages of showing the child she was carrying. Hap Sing resisted the temptation to use his second sight. He figured her to be the Yu's daughter. Hap Sing realized that her name had not come up in any of their conversations, and it was likely her mother Mai wasn't even aware of her current condition.

Hap Sing approached and gave her a low bow, "Pardon my intrusion young miss. Is Holy One Arthur available? I am Hap Sing, and I wanted to have a talk with him."

She smiled broadly, "I am Lo Maya the wife of Lo Arthur. Arthur is inside the temple making ready for his afternoon prayers. I am pleased that you came by to visit. We don't see family nearly as much as I would like."

Hap Sing rose from his bow, "I am glad for your welcome. Is it possible for me to speak with your husband? I have a favor to ask of him, but I don't want to disturb him if he is occupied."

Lo Maya placed a hand on her growing middle and smiled, "I will make sure he greets you properly. Family is always welcome here."

Hap Sing followed Lo Maya into the temple. There was no dramatic clash of wills or any divine barrier blocking his way as he half expected, just a simple chamber with several rows of plain chairs facing a simple basic alter. Lo Arthur sat toward the back of the room looking over various parchments and referring to his religious texts.

Lo Arthur gave a smile as he greeted Hap Sing, "Ah my father-in-law's cousin. I am glad you could come to see me. I was just thinking about you."

Hap Sing bowed in return, "I was thinking of you as well Holy One Arthur. I hope I am not disturbing you, but I have a favor to ask."

Lo Arthur pointed to a chair next to his own, "Please have a seat. You are welcome in the temple of Palnor. It is not much, but I think in a few years we will see some improvements here. It is hard work converting the people to the faith, and I was warned of the challenges it would present. Would you like to listen to what I have to say to you on the matter?"

Hap Sing gave a gentle smile, "I will have to beg your forgiveness. I appreciate your offer, but I am going to be somewhat busy today. Perhaps we can speak of it another time soon."

Lo Arthur nodded with a slight disappointment visible on his face, "Yes, I understand it is hard for the older generations to give us a chance. You didn't learn about us early enough, it is a shame really. How can I help you then?"

Hap Sing looked to make sure they were alone, "I have a bit of a confession to make first. Can we speak with confidentiality?"

Lo Arthur contemplated a moment, "I can not condone any illegal acts. I must report crimes if I hear of them you understand. I also must share what I am asked with my superiors unless it is a personal matter."

Hap Sing looked around again with a touch of nervousness, "It actually is several personal matters. Some of them involving you and your wife you understand."

Lo Arthur grew cautious, "It is something my mother-in-law put you up to?"

Hap Sing looked sheepishly at Lo Arthur, "Actually it is something she objected to. However I think my opinion may take precedence in this instance and I was hoping you could help me."

Lo Arthur looked pained for a moment, "I have to tell you the truth. That woman doesn't like me much. I don't have much influence with her if that is what you are looking for from me."

Hap Sing shook his head, "No that was not it. I was wondering if you could bless the shrines of my father and mother as a favor for family."

Lo Arthur looked embarrassed, "I would be glad to help if I could, but I only provide services within the valley surrounding Hung Chan village. The main temple in Yokito would need to send another priest to bless the shrines where your parents are buried. I could arrange it if you like."

Hap Sing smiled, "No that is not an issue then since their shrines are here in this valley."

Lo Arthur was confused for a moment then a look of awareness came to him, "They are on the farm of my father-in-law then? I can see why my mother-in-law is so upset with you then. I don't recall you or your parents being from the area though. I also don't remember any recent shrines erected there since the passing of my wife's grandparents."

Hap Sing gave him a cautious smile, "That is part of the problem I am facing in terms of the superiors at your main temple. I would rather keep certain family matters away from their attention if possible."

Lo Arthur thought a moment longer, "As long as you are not asking me to hide something from them that they would need to know, I think we can safely keep them in the dark. Palnor will know you understand. I can not keep anything from him of course."

Hap Sing nodded, "I would not expect you to either. What I don't want you to reveal to anyone else is very simple, the names of my parents or my age."

Lo Arthur nodded, "Questionable parentage. I can understand how that might be embarrassing. You are a by blow then. The secret cast off of a traveling noble perhaps?"

Hap Sing nodded, "Not exactly but close enough. Do you agree?"

Lo Arthur smiled, "I don't see any problem with that. It wouldn't interest my superiors in any way."

Hap Sing smiled weakly, "Would you mind giving me your word on your faith as a follower of Palnor? It really is not something I want spread around about me."

Lo Arthur grasped his holy dragon symbol and spoke with authority, "I give you my word as a loyal follower of Palnor I will not reveal your parents names or your age to anyone."

Hap Sing smiled, "I thank you for the trouble you have taken on my behalf. I am also sorry to have to put you though such a test."

Lo Arthur smiled, "It was nothing really. Now what were their names so I can bless their shrines?"

Hap Sing lost his smile, "I am Hap Sing son of Hap Yang and Hap Mi."

Lo Arthur grinned for a while, "I don't understand. No one of those names has lived in this valley for, let me remember those old legends, well I would guess one hundred forty or one hundred fifty years or so. Those shrines are among the ancient ancestors of Yu Wing and his family."

Lo Arthur lost his smile, "You are joking with me. Did someone put you up to this? Yu Wing and Yu Mai would never let me near those shrines. They are almost like holy places to them for some reason."

Hap Sing kept his serious look, "Those are the shrines I mean. They are my parent's shrines Yu Wing and Yu Mai can not object to me having them blessed. I am their only direct decedent, and as I see it my right supersedes theirs."

Lo Arthur shook his head, "They couldn't be the shrines of your parents. That would make you . . ."

Hap Sing interrupted, "One hundred and fifty years old tomorrow. You can understand why I don't want you revealing my age now right?"

Lo Arthur looked confused again, "That couldn't be. You can not be serious."

Hap Sing smiled gently, "I am very serious. I am Hap Sing. I was born one hundred and fifty years ago, and I want you to bless the shrines of my father Hap Yang and my mother Hap Mi. If you would like to cast any spells to verify my truthfulness in this matter I will understand. I just ask that you keep it a secret from any who might seek to harm me."

Lo Arthur looked quizzically at Hap Sing, "Would you mind if I asked my wife to verify something?"

Hap Sing shrugged, "She is family and knows how to keep family secrets I would guess. I will allow it as something which doesn't violate your promise."

Lo Arthur went to the door and called for Lo Maya to come inside. She entered smiling as seemed usual for her. She looked at the expression on her husband's face and her smile became tenuous.

Lo Arthur spoke gently to her, "Dear, your cousin Hap Sing has been talking with me about family history, and a mention was made about those old legends. You know the ones about that hedge wizard Hap Yang. You remember the fellow from legends that supposedly stopped some ravening beast from destroying the town."

Lo Maya's expression changed to a contemplative one, "You mean those horrible stories about how Hap Yang sacrificed himself using his only child as a living prison for the seven tailed spirit beast. I always disliked those stories when I was younger. What parent could do such a thing to their precious child?"

Hap Sing lowered his head and Lo Maya looked at him with a moment of wonder, then a moment of confusion came over her. Then her eyes filled with tears as she started to weep uncontrollably.

Lo Arthur clasped his wife tenderly in his hands, "What's wrong my dear? Why are your crying so?"

Lo Maya looked at Hap Sing and burst into a crying fit as she sobbed and spoke, "It's him isn't it. It's the poor baby Hap Sing. He's the one who was cursed by his own father, abandoned by his own mother, and doomed to never grow old as a reminder to mothers everywhere to love their children."

Lo Arthur gently turned his wife away from Hap Sing, and could see the tears running down Hap Sing's face as well. Hap Sing could see that the weight and truth of his statement had reached Lo Arthur as well.

Lo Arthur spoke softly to Hap Sing, "I will do as you ask. I could in good conscience do no less for a loyal son. Family matters indeed."

An hour later Lo Arthur and Hap Sing walked past the gate leading out of the village. Lo Maya had been left to stay with Lo Arthur's mother for the afternoon as her crying would not ease up as long as Hap Sing was in her sight. Hap Sing walked with his head held low.

Lo Arthur spoke, "You say the legends about Hap Yang are true. He captured this spirit beast which was rampaging through the land inside of you. You are possessed by an evil spirit then?"

Hap Sing winced, "I wouldn't let it hear you call it that if I were you. Palnor is likely to hear an earful of complaints from the Luck if you mention that within its hearing. The Luck isn't an evil spirit. It is a Great Spirit. They are not gods; they are something else, something separate, and something very powerful, but not higher or lower than the gods. The Great Spirits are just differentially enabled. I feel like I am confusing you."

Lo Arthur shook his head, "I have just considered today to be one filled with unaccountable changes. You can at least guarantee no harm will come to the village today right?"

Hap Sing shook his head, "I can only guarantee I will not deliberately cause any harm. Can you vouch for what Palnor will do today?"

Lo Arthur nodded, "Of course. I have complete trust in him."

Hap Sing sighed, "It must be nice. Tailed beasts are notoriously unpredictable in my experience. Let me just say that whatever happens today the Luck is running the shots. You will be likely immune to what happens since you and your wife and future child have the protection of Palnor. Everyone else is going to be at risk with what must be done. Do you understand this?"

Lo Arthur laughed, "I don't think Palnor is going to do much to protect me from my mother-in-law's anger. Palnor hasn't seemed inclined to soften her mood toward me yet."

Hap Sing let out a frustrated sigh, "Don't worry too much about it. I am fairly certain that I will bear the brunt of any blame from her today. I am also pretty certain that she will not dare to challenge me today."

Lo Arthur asked, "Why is that?"

Hap Sing laughed, "I am going to be one hundred and fifty tomorrow, and I am feeling unusually cranky about her attitude today. I had come here expecting to have a relaxing visit. It has been anything but relaxing so far."

Lo Arthur smiled, "Is it any thing I should know?"

Hap Sing smiled, "I suspect that your superiors would not approve of today's activities. Communicating with otherworldly beings without going through proper authorization can likely get you into deep trouble. I recommend you don't mention it unless directly asked."

Lo Arthur nodded, "As far as they need to know today will be a day spent caring for an ill family member. I don't think I want them learning what potentially blasphemous things I have been hearing about today."

Hap Sing winced as he spoke, "Oh right that reminds me. Before you speak with the Luck let me mention some of the difficulties you are likely to face. It is sometimes very impatient and rude. It tends to treat most people like disobedient children at best. Its language is also somewhat salty. It has a tendency to get under people's skin when it finds a weak spot. It is also in running disagreements with several gods I believe, yet I think that thankfully Palnor is not on that list at the moment. Finally, it knows things."

Lo Arthur nodded, "I can understand the other warnings, but why is the fact that it knows things a warning?"

Hap Sing ducked his head down, "It even knows things about the gods, private and embarrassing things. Frankly it is a bit of a gossip from what I've been able to learn."

Lo Arthur looked at him, "You don't know?"

Hap Sing shrugged, "We've never spoken. It's one of the problems we have since we need to speak through intermediaries. At least on this plane of existence we share one form. One or the other is present, but never both at the same time. Fortunately I hold the primary tenancy as it were, and it can only visit when I allow it to."

Lo Arthur nodded, "It sounds like a reverse possession. A theoretical construct discussed in our theology courses in our seminary, which is very rare indeed if true."

Hap Sing shrugged, "You're the expert on that I would guess. I'm just the result of the process."

Lo Arthur smiled, "You have probably heard it called by its common name: an avatar state. The mortal form temporarily possesses an immortal spirit. I have never heard of it becoming stuck as a reoccurring possession though. This is very strange if true."

Hap Sing shrugged again, "You may ask it if you like. I really don't know for certain. We are almost to the shrine for my parents. It doesn't look like anyone plans to join us."

Lo Arthur looked at Hap Sing, "You are not going to ever be a follower of Palnor are you?"

Hap Sing sighed, "You are correct. I am not likely to become one at this late stage of my life. I don't know that any god would want the trouble I would make for them anyway."

Lo Arthur looked ahead at the nearby shrine as they approached, "Why are you doing this then? You don't need to get on mother Mai's bad side. I'm used to her disapproval of me."

Hap Sing gave him a gentle smile, "I hope I can fix that in time by removing a subject of contention from between you. This blessing will cause this place no harm. Yet her stubborn insistence in preventing it is keeping her daughter, your future child, and you from being able to resolve any differences. As someone who has lived as long as I have I understand that you accept family even if you don't always like what they do. I would have peace between Mai and you even if I must bear the brunt of her ire."

Lo Arthur shook his head, "You need not do this on my behalf. I wouldn't want mother Mai angry with you."

Hap Sing chuckled, "I think it is too late for that. Mai is angry with me for other reasons already. I don't live here, and probably will not be back for many years once I am gone. I can afford to bear her ire for a while. I don't think you should have to any more. I also have a sneaky suspicion that once this is over that much will be forgiven between you. If you don't mind I will pay my respects in my way one more time before you bless the shrine. You are welcome to watch if you like."

Lo Arthur nodded, "I remember the old ways. Would you mind if I joined you?"

Lo Arthur and Hap Sing knelt down in front of the shrines. Both bowed their heads in silent contemplation. Hap Sing finished his thoughts about his parents, and stood up again. Lo Arthur remained in silent kneeling for several more minutes. Eventually he stood as well.

Lo Arthur looked at Hap Sing, "There are no evil spirits here are there?"

Hap Sing shook his head, "There are no spirits here at all."

Lo Arthur asked, "Then you can tell as well?"

Hap Sing nodded, "I have the sight. I was born with it. As you have probably guessed I am an untrained Chi Master."

Lo Arthur nodded, "This talent of the Chi Masters travels in family lines doesn't it?"

Hap Sing nodded, "So I am told, although the Yu's are descendants of my mother's youngest sister. They are not Hap Yang's descendants."

Lo Arthur nodded, "Yet your mother was a Chi Master as well?"

Hap Sing nodded, "A lesser talent than my father, but my mother was a Chi Master as well."

Lo Arthur looked concerned, "I don't understand why they couldn't just tell me. The teachings of Palnor have never called for the persecution of the Chi Masters."

Hap Sing sat down on the ground looking up at Lo Arthur, "Yet the priests of Palnor are glad to go into places to provide aid where the Chi Masters have been driven out by the government. The Chi Masters view all the god priests as beneficiaries of the government's policies even if the priests of Palnor are not the instigators. Unfortunately it means that bad blood exists. Too many years of persecution have made the Chi Masters fearful of all priests, even the good ones."

Lo Arthur shook his head, "What would they have me do? I can't turn aside from Palnor, and I can't turn aside from my wife. Palnor does not fear the old ways or condemn them. I can't make everyone happy."

Hap Sing nodded, "You are correct. You can't make everyone happy. You shouldn't try. What you can do though is the right thing. Sometimes I find that is the only reasonable choice."

Lo Arthur placed his head in his palm, "What is the right thing in this situation?"

Hap Sing smiled, "I suggest blessing this shrine first. Your god Palnor would approve and it will harm nothing other than my reputation with Mai. Second you might carefully consider how to close the gap between your wife's family and yourself. Third I recommend keeping their secret intact. They fear being driven out of their own home."

Lo Arthur shook his head, "Because they are related to a Chi Master?"

Hap Sing shook his head, "Because they are Chi Masters."

Lo Arthur looked at Hap Sing in shock, "What?"

Hap Sing smiled gently again, "Wing, Mai, Gai, and Jin are all Chi Masters. You said yourself it runs in family lines."

Lo Arthur looked pale, "It is considered against the law. They could be arrested by the authorities."

Hap Sing nodded, "Yes they could. I have placed their lives in your hands. I have also placed the life of your wife Maya and your unborn child in your hands as well. Even if their powers never manifest, they still carry the potential and could pass it to their children. It is quite a quandary for a priest of a god which demands adherence to the laws of the community. What is the right thing to do?"

Lo Arthur sat down next to Hap Sing, "I want to thank you for opening my eyes. This problem with my in-laws has never been wholly about me has it?"

Hap Sing shrugged, "They spoke highly of you as the bright prodigy of Hung Chan as a child. It has definitely been your conversion to Palnor which they view

Chapter 6

71

as problematic. I would guess that they worry that your fervor for your faith has overrun your better personal judgment."

Lo Arthur looked at Hap Sing with a slight frown, "Why would you trust me then?"

Hap Sing smiled, "I have this delusion that I have a good grasp of personal motivations. I have been watching people for one hundred and fifty years. You seemed like an honest and earnest young man to me. You don't seem to me like the type to persecute someone for an accident of birth, even if the law allows it to be done. You seem to me to be someone more concerned with actual justice instead of mere adherence to the law."

Lo Arthur gave a faint smile, "I hear all of these compliments, but I suspect there is a lecture coming as well. What is the bad news?"

Hap Sing shrugged, "Since you asked I will tell you. You are intelligent. You are also arrogant because you know you are intelligent. Frankly I would think that arrogance is what is holding you back from recruiting more followers. It would serve you well to learn how to accept people for what they are more."

Lo Arthur stood up, "I think I understand. Which one of us can not stand to improve? I thank you for your assistance today. Shall we get started with the blessing then?"

Hap Sing stood as well. Hap Sing watched in silence as Lo Arthur said a brief prayer and invocation. Hap Sing could feel the divine presence of Palnor's magic infuse the area, but nothing untoward happened to him or the Luck. Lo Arthur then turned to look at Hap Sing.

Lo Arthur spoke, "I thank you also for asking for my assistance today. That blessing is most effective if repeated on a monthly basis, but even yearly it will keep away most evil spirits. By the fact that you are still standing here I would take it that this Luck you mentioned isn't an evil spirit as well."

Hap Sing gave a slight grin, "That's good news. I would hate to think I was sharing my body with an evil spirit for one hundred and fifty years."

Chapter 7 Hap Yang's Legacy

Hap Sing sat by the water of the pond again. After blessing the shrine Lo Arthur had returned to the village to comfort his wife, but he agreed to meet with Hap Sing outside the town gate after dinner. Hap Sing had wandered his uncle's former estate where he had grown up, and realized that he had truly left it behind. There were fond memories still there. Yet memories were all that remained. His home was in Li Chan for now.

Hap Sing looked up to see Yuki Nene approaching. There was a light step in her stride as she came over and sat down next to him. She watched him contemplating the water in silence for a short while. Then she tossed a small rock into the nearly still surface. The ripples spread out in circular patterns.

Hap Sing smiled faintly, "You are a person of action."

Yuki Nene nodded, "I'm always doing. It's true. That is how I learn and grow."

Hap Sing looked over at her, "You also fear stagnation. The stillness bothers you."

Yuki Nene returned his gaze, "As it does you. You need to fix that which you feel is broken. You try to watch over those you meet, even if they don't ask for your help."

Hap Sing looked back at the water, "You are perceptive too. I have spent too much time still perhaps. I have felt the need to create movement where there was none before. I'm going to scare away the fish."

Yuki Nene looked out over the water, "You use yet another fishing metaphor. I sometimes feel like I won't ever understand you."

Hap Sing laughed, "It is pretty simple. You just have to learn to fish. You remind me of a good friend of mine. He never liked fishing."

Yuki Nene smiled, "This friend sounds like someone I would like. Does he have a taste for action?"

Hap Sing gave a light smile, "He did. Right up until he was killed in battle defeating the leader of the invaders of Ran Li. I hope you are not as much like him. I would hate to think of you dying that way."

Yuki Nene smiled, "It might be better than growing old and decrepit."

Hap Sing bent his head, "Really? Is that how I seem to you?"

Yuki Nene looked over at Hap Sing and placed a hand on his upper arm in a sympathetic gesture, "I didn't mean you. You're just old, and not decrepit."

Hap Sing gave a faint smile, "Too easy."

Yuki Nene laughed, "I'm not ever going to get over your sly sense of humor."

They sat in silence for several more minutes. A palpable tension was in the air. Hap Sing closed his eyes briefly. He then looked around with the second sight. He could see Yuki's Raven Spirit was perched on her shoulder looking off into the distance intently. When he followed the direction of its gaze he could see a spirit hawk circling above them in the sky.

Yu Mai was watching. She was likely still angry with him, and unfortunately still afraid of him as well. In Hap Sing's experience he considered it a dangerous condition. Yu Mai had the potential to do something drastic and foolish.

Hap Sing stood up, "Perhaps it is time to head to the market for some lunch. I think I may not be too welcome here yet."

Yuki Nene smiled as she stood as well, "Mai has been watching us since I arrived. It's likely that she has been watching for you since you left the house this morning. I didn't think to ask Hugin to look earlier. I sent him out to find you a while ago. If we head to the market I'm certain we will escape her range though. Her hawk can't go as far as Hugin can."

Hap Sing became a little surprised, "That's interesting. The spirit guardians have different abilities then?"

Yuki Nene nodded, "Of course they do. Didn't you realize that?"

Hap Sing gave a light grin, "I've never had one that was separate from me if you understand. Well not in the same sense you are talking about."

Yuki Nene laughed, "Oh right. I forgot for a moment there. You probably haven't been around many spirit shamans then."

Hap Sing spoke, "Just my mother when I was very young. Her guardian spirit was a fox I believe. I faintly remember seeing it once or twice. It always avoided me though."

Hap Sing went with Yuki Nene to the Hung Chan marketplace again. Yu Gai and Yu Jin were there at their cooking stall, and prepared the meal they ate. Yu Gai was a bit distant, but said he would pass the word along to the others to meet Hap Sing outside the town after dinner time. Yu Jin seemed a bit uncertain of the current situation, but stood by her desire to speak with the Luck.

Hap Sing and Yuki remained seated on opposite sides of their table in the market chatting amiably when they were approached by Ming Ran who seemed upset. When they invited him to sit down he appeared nervous.

Ming Ran spoke quietly, "Is it true that you told Lo Arthur who you were?"

Hap Sing nodded, "As I said this morning he needs to speak with the Luck. I had to tell him the truth to convince him."

Ming Ran began to sweat, "What if he exposes me to the government? I will lose my titles and position."

Hap Sing returned a serious look, "I made no mention of you to him. Your position is safe if that is what you fear."

Ming Ran wiped his brow as he spoke quietly, "He knows that I associate with the Yu's. If he figures out that we are all outcasts, then we will all be in jeopardy."

Hap Sing nodded, "I see your concern. What do you want me to do then?"

Ming Ran looked about, "You could change the night. Come back another time. Tell him you were joking about it. There is no way he can prove his accusations if you don't show him the Luck."

Yuki Nene sat back and chuckled, "If you are so worried about it Ming Ran then you can just skip out tonight. We won't include you. Your wife and you can stay at home together. That way you won't be at risk."

Ming Ran looked uncertain, "What about my question then? I won't get an answer if I don't go."

Yuki Nene laughed again, "I suspect you won't like your answer even if you did go. If it bothers you so much then I will ask it your questions in your place. I will let you know what it says."

Ming Ran sat back and thought a moment, "You would do that for me?"

Yuki Nene nodded, "It's not as if we are limited to a single question. It might even save time with fewer of us there."

Ming Ran sat temporarily frozen in place with indecision. He was drawn to take advantage of the opportunity he saw before him, but afraid of the risk involved to his current position. Hap Sing could see that Ming Ran was divided between his fear and his desire.

Hap Sing decided to tip the scales, "The Luck will answer your questions. However, you should know the answers come with a price. I can not say what that price will be. I can not even say that you will like the deal you will be offered. The person seeking the answer will pay the price as well not just the person in front of the Luck."

Ming Ran was calculating as he asked, "Perhaps a separate private meeting at a later date would be possible. One where the priest will not know who is speaking with the Luck. I'm not sure if my question is one I want someone else to ask in my place."

Hap Sing looked at Ming Ran with a neutral expression, "The Luck is not some pet summoned at will for entertainment. It is a very intelligent and powerful being. It is also very easily annoyed and may vent its disapproval out on those who are the source of its annoyance. I would not dare bring it forth again too soon in case it decided to do something drastic."

Ming Ran looked perplexed, "What am I to do then?"

Hap Sing stood up and waved for Ming Ran to follow him over to the edge of the market. Ming Ran followed along to a private corner where no one could overhear them speaking together as Yuki Nene remained at the table.

Hap Sing whispered to Ming Ran, "You could ask me your question. I can have it relayed to the Luck through another if necessary, but I think I might have an insight into the answer you want to know. If I don't know the answer for certain, then I can at least let you know what the best way to ask your question would be."

Ming Ran looked relieved and whispered back, "If you could ask it whether I will become the famous leader as spoken of in our family prophesy, then that is what I want to know."

Hap Sing thought about it for a while, "The Luck can not reliably predict the future or speak prophesy. The Luck only knows what it knows. That is a lot, but it has the same uncertainty of what will be as any other power. The past and the present it can tell you about, it can only guess the future. In this I may be better equipped than the Luck to predict your fate. You will not become the famous leader as predicted in your family prophesy. That role will fall to another. You will instead be a good husband to your wife and children. You will also be a much happier man because of it."

Ming Ran was awed as he looked at Hap Sing, "You can tell the future?"

Hap Sing shook his head, "I don't know for certain either. I can just tell that as you are now you are not the person for this responsibility. However, you are the kind of person who can be happy with your life as soon as you realize that ambition is sometimes a trap, and that understanding what things are of true value is the important thing in life."

Ming Ran looked at Hap Sing with concern, "How can you tell that I am not the person mentioned in my family prophesy?"

Hap Sing gently smiled, "You already know the answer to that question even if you haven't realized it until now. It is because you have to ask. People chosen by prophesy almost uniformly never know it is going to happen until it does. You are too aware of wanting it to be possibly true. It likely never will be for you because you desire to know the answer before it's time."

Ming Ran looked downcast at the reply and asked, "What am I to do then?"

Hap Sing smiled, "You should hopefully realize this is a good thing. Your path is not set before you. You can make of your life what you will. You can find what makes you happy and pursue that to your heart's content. I can personally tell you that people driven by prophesy are usually never happy with the lack of choices they are provided in their lives. My friend Li Chan learned this to his detriment when he was driven by destiny to perform great acts, and when his son Li Hung became entangled with his destiny."

Ming Ran looked up at Hap Sing, "They were both great heroes."

Hap Sing nodded, "Yes they were. They also accepted their destiny without complaint as befits great heroes. That doesn't mean they didn't desire another outcome to their lives. I think my friend Li Chan would have gladly traded places with you if given a choice. Destiny can be cruel and hard. I don't recommend tempting it."

Ming Ran thanked Hap Sing and shook his hand. Hap Sing then returned to the table where Yuki Nene waited for him. Ming Ran left the market heading toward his home. Yuki Nene smiled as Hap Sing approached.

Yuki Nene pointed to where Ming Ran had disappeared, "So how did it go?"

Hap Sing shrugged, "I don't think he will be there. I left it up to him, but I think I satisfied the question he had in his heart if not verifying the one which bothered his mind."

Yuki Nene changed for a grin, "Was he going to ask for a favor? Did he have a selfish request perhaps?"

Hap Sing shrugged again, "No more so than you I would guess. Would you like me to hear your question in advance? I can tell you what I think of it as well."

Yuki Nene grew somewhat serious, "I have several questions really. There is much I would like to know about myself that remains secret to me."

Hap Sing guessed, "You want to know who you will become?"

Yuki Nene shook her head, "I know better than to ask a spirit of the future. It is said that even a great spirit can not see such things. I want to ask it of my past. Who my people are? Why was I born as I am? Who was my father?"

Hap Sing was surprised, "You don't know who your father was? I thought you were a Princess of your people."

Yuki Nene shook her head, "That is a misnomer, a mistranslation of the concept as the people of Ran Li understand it. The Nordlanders respect ability not bloodlines. I'm considered a Princess because of what I can do, not because of who my sire or dam was. A time is told of the past among my people when there were many Nordland Princesses and Princes. Those times are no longer and now people like me are considered a rarity, and more treasured because of it."

Hap Sing nodded, "What about your father then?"

Yuki Nene shrugged, "I was raised by my mother and her husband who treated me as his daughter. Among the Nordlanders he was always considered as my father, and had always treated me as such. I also know that my mother's husband doesn't have the ability in his family. My mother does not have the ability in her family either. As you well understand such abilities are passed from parent to child. My mother never revealed who my real father was to anyone among the Nordlanders before she passed away."

Hap Sing nodded, "I think the Luck will be able to tell you what you seek. I understand why you want such an answer as well. I would also know what kind of person my father was."

 ap Sing had once more left Yuki Nene by the marketplace after their lunch. He picked up a few things for a simple dinner and left the village in the late afternoon. Hap Sing began walking the valley without consciously thinking about where he was going. He gazed across the fields and headed north toward the border with the wild lands along the farm trails. Soon the trail ended at the last farm.

Hap Sing continued up to the gap in the valley leading to the border. He came upon the ruins of his father's home. It was as reported overgrown with weeds and mainly the remains of a broken foundation scavenged over many times over the last ninety years. Even the majority of building timbers had mostly been hauled away or burned for firewood many years ago. The simple flagstone floor showed signs of having been pried up several times over the years by people looking for secrets to only reveal the plain dirt beneath.

Hap Sing realized they had been speaking the truth last night when they had said there was cold comfort left for any raiders looking for a point to launch a raid. Even though the home foundation wasn't visible from the village, it was still very little cover against observation from a distance. Hap Sing knew it would be ideal for his purposes tonight. Any sightings by villagers could be attributed to raiders scouting the location or the legends of Hap Yang come to life. He supposed that the second would actually be true in a certain light.

Hap Sing began walking toward the town and looked down the valley with his second sight at his surroundings. He noticed that Mai's Spirit Hawk was still circling over the Yu's home keeping an eye on his movements. He also spotted a large black spirit raven fluttering along beside him. It seemed Yuki was correct about the range at which she could use her guardian.

As he approached the gate to the village Hap Sing saw Lo Arthur standing outside the gate and waving to attract his attention. Lo Arthur walked out to greet him with an expression that was a bit apprehensive.

Lo Arthur looked over at Hap Sing, "I see that I am the first one here."

Hap Sing nodded, "The others who want to speak with the Luck should be here soon."

Lo Arthur looked relieved, "I spoke with my wife this afternoon. I let her know I knew her family secret, and that it was safe with me by the will of Palnor. After much prayer together we have determined that I will try my best to make amends to Father Wing and Mother Mai. They will be grandparents soon, and we both want them to be in our child's life. I understand their hesitance to reveal themselves to a priest of Palnor, but I am also their son-in-law. As you have shown it is sometimes a son's duty to forgive their parents for their human faults. I think the same applies to in-laws."

Hap Sing smiled and shook Lo Arthur's hand as he spoke, "I am glad to hear it. I think that should be the beginning of a sound relationship between you."

Hap Sing watched as Yu Gai and Yu Jin approached together from town. They also seemed apprehensive at the presence of Lo Arthur. Lo Arthur bowed before them both, and then unexpectedly embraced them both in a hug. Then he stepped back grinning.

Lo Arthur spoke in a sudden burst of talk, "Maya and I have wanted to tell you both. You will be an uncle and aunt soon. Maya is with child."

Yu Jin smiled broadly and clasped him in a hug again, "I must go see her then. Congratulations!"

Yu Gai was seemingly less enthusiastic, "A child you say? It is so soon."

Lo Arthur nodded, "We wanted to get an early start. That way we can have many children together. Children bring joy to a household."

As Lo Arthur and Yu Jin chatted happily about the prospect of children Hap Sing reached out to shake hands with Yu Gai.

Yu Gai nodded at Hap Sing and leaned in close to softly say, "That must have been some talk you had with Arthur. He's very friendly today."

Hap Sing nodded, "It helps to be honest with people sometimes. They can sense deception. It causes distrust which obviously leads to bigger problems."

After a few minutes they saw Yu Wing and Yu Mai walking up the trail from their estate toward them. Yu Wing was looking more haggard since this morning.

Hap Sing figured it was likely from having to weather the storm of his wife's anger. Yu Mai kept a neutral expression on her face, but her eyes were looking sharply at Hap Sing. Hap Sing moved back a little toward town as Lo Arthur stepped up in front of his in-laws.

Lo Arthur knelt down on the ground in front of them. Then he bent over low. They heard him clearly speak to them.

Lo Arthur spoke with great sincerity, "I beg your forgiveness Father Wing and Mother Mai. I have been a poor son to you. Hap Sing has told me of some of your fears, and I realized that I have done nothing a good son should to comfort you. I apologize for my poor behavior and hope that you can forgive me and accept me as Maya's husband and always as a member of your family."

Yu Wing reached down to bring Lo Arthur standing upright again, "There is nothing to forgive. The fault is equally ours. We failed to trust you or our daughter as we should. Isn't that right my dear?"

Yu Mai looked at Lo Arthur and suddenly seemed on the edge of tears, "I'm sorry my son. We were afraid. How is Maya? Are she and the child she bears doing well?"

Lo Arthur swept them up into a joint embrace which was shortly joined by Yu Jin. Yu Gai stood back next to Hap Sing for a moment until Hap Sing placed a gentle hand on his shoulder and nodded. Yu Gai stepped forward to join his family in their mutual embrace.

As the Yu's talked about their impending new child in the family with Lo Arthur, Hap Sing watched Yuki Nene coming from the village gate with a look of mild concern on her face. Yuki Nene came up to stand close to Hap Sing and watched the Yu's chatting with Lo Arthur for a few moments.

Hap Sing quietly asked her, "Is something wrong Nene?"

Yuki Nene shrugged her shoulders, "I thought I would check whether the Ming's or Sata would be coming along at least part of the way. The Ming's seemed perfectly happy to hear about it later. I couldn't find Sata anywhere though. When I asked the town guard at the gate they said he hasn't returned since he departed town this morning to go to Yu's house."

Hap Sing thought a moment, "Perhaps he had something to do today."

Yuki Nene's look of concern increased, "That's what I'm afraid of actually. I checked with the town guard. Sata didn't mention any official duties today."

Hap Sing became a touch worried as well and asked, "I thought he was your man."

Yuki Nene gave a bitter laugh, "You can't buy the loyalty of one such as Sata. You can only rent it. I'm afraid my lease may have run out, or worse yet a higher bidder may have come along. Sata has been growing less deferential and more sarcastic to me lately. I suspect he does not appreciate my intelligence, my relative youth, my greater ability, or my gender. My wallet and access to knowledge related to past Chi Masters has been the only thing keeping him in check for the last year. I suspect he would have left long before if not for that."

Chapter 7

79

Hap Sing asked another question, "His pay has been reduced some in the last year as well?"

Yuki Nene nodded, "I had exhausted everything I could learn from Sata a couple of years ago. I've kept him with me out of a need for a protector more than as a researcher. I'm also running a little thin on funds. Enough to support me remains, but Sata felt a need to supplement his income by continuing to train Akane for a price as well as taking on the job of militia captain here."

Hap Sing thought for a bit, "It sounds like Sata is a man mixed up with dangerous people. People he owes money. These are the kind of people who expect regular interest payments, but who don't allow the principle to be easily paid."

Yuki Nene nodded, "I've wondered why he needs such a large amount funds. He generally lives pretty frugally. I suspect your observation is likely close to the truth of the situation. What should we do?"

Hap Sing faintly smiled, "I'll trust that the Luck will see us through. What ever happens I don't expect that it will be easily manipulated by us simple mortals. The Luck has rigged the game after all. Let's join the others and go to the place of summoning."

Hap Sing and Yuki Nene walked over to where the Yu's and Lo Arthur were getting to know each other better for the first time. In general they amiably greeted Hap Sing and Nene, but Hap Sing could tell that even though Mai no longer seemed angry she was still afraid of him. Perhaps she feared that he had manipulated Lo Arthur. Perhaps she feared that they had all been manipulated by him.

Hap Sing didn't blame her. He was as aware of the impact of his actions as anyone. His presence and actions had drastically changed the dynamics of their lives. The only question was would the outcome be a better one than the course they were previously traveling. Hap Sing couldn't tell where the course of their future would take them, but he could see that they were at least traveling that course together instead of divided. He hoped that would be enough.

Chapter 8 The Wonderful Luck

ap Sing led the group to his father's estate. Instead of the broken foundation of the house which he felt to be depressing, he chose his mother's former cherry tree orchard. It was overgrown and untended, but it had a natural beauty to it still even if the blossoms had already fallen in the early spring. The sun was lowering toward the horizon in the west and a pleasant warm glow was spreading through the land.

Hap Sing chose a large rock to use as a bench and sat down in front of the assembled Chi Masters and priest of Palnor. He looked at each of them to determine if they were ready. They seemed to have committed themselves to the summoning of the Luck.

Hap Sing spoke in a clear loud voice, "This is not something you need to do if you would rather not. I will summon the Luck to reside in my form. I will not be present when it does so. I will learn nothing except what you tell me. I will not ask you to tell me anything you don't wish me to know. If you think there is anything about yourself which you would have private from the others, then I recommend that each of you be interviewed by the Luck individually."

Yu Wing spoke up, "I am certain to be berated by the Luck for my earlier actions. I would spare the others it's sharp tongue while doing so. Mai will stay with me at her request though."

Yu Mai nodded, "As my husband says, I will stand by his side."

Yu Jin spoke, "My question is already known to all here. I have no problems with everyone hearing the answer."

Yu Gai spoke, "I will remain by my wife as my mother remains by my father."

Yuki Nene smiled as she spoke, "I have some personal questions to ask of the Luck. I wouldn't mind some privacy, although I have already spoken of it with Hap Sing."

Lo Arthur spoke up, "I don't have any questions for the Luck. However, I was led to believe through prayer that it wants to speak with me. I will listen to what it has to say, and consider its words carefully with guidance from Palnor."

Hap Sing nodded, "Very well then decide among yourselves who will go first to last. Since Yu Jin is open to everyone being present for her question then perhaps she shall go first. Before the Luck departs you must also ask it this for me. For how long must I leave this valley now, and can I safely return to Li Chan?"

After a brief discussion among themselves they decided on their order of questions. The others stood back a little ways as Yu Jin and Yu Gai stood in front of where Hap Sing sat on the large rock. Hap Sing repositioned himself into a meditative stance and closed his eyes. After about a quarter hour Hap Sing relaxed.

They could all feel the presence of the Luck as it assumed control of Hap Sing's body. Its aura was plainly visible as a large orange glow without the use of the second sight. The seven tails of power moved through the air behind it stirring a breeze even as they watched. Its eyes opened to look at them, and they could see a cat like feral aspect to its gaze.

The Luck gracefully moved with feline precision to a standing position and spoke, "Well it seems there is at least one of you with the good sense to listen to orders. I'll deal with the other one in a while. It also seems that you are the brave ones in the lot. Not many mortals are willing to meet me a second time. I see the Ming's have opted out for tonight as well. If Ran asks you can tell him that I have confirmed Cricket's analysis, you won't need to tell him any more than that. He'll know what is meant. Well speak up girl you agreed to be first."

Yu Jin hesitantly spoke, "It seems you know what we are going to ask already."

The Luck smiled, "Nonsense. I simply already know what Cricket has heard. It's a kind of one way communication thing. You need not tell him about it. It would just disturb him to know I am listening in on him at times. Unfortunately I can only know what he says. I never get to access what he is thinking if you understand me. Go ahead and ask your question girl, I think the answer might just surprise you."

Yu Jin swallowed and nervously asked, "What was the battle between you and Hap Sing like? What was the nature of the great spell he cast to capture you?"

The Luck grinned widely in a manner that made them all afraid, "I am going to love telling you this, but first I will extract a promise from you. Not one word of my answer can be relayed to Cricket. Don't even attempt to break the spirit of this agreement or dire consequences will come to you."

Yu Jin felt like fainting, "What consequences?"

The Luck's voice dropped to a low rumble, "You'll piss me off something fierce. You won't like it if you find me pissed off. It will not be pleasant for you."

Yu Gai took a half step forward, "What will you do? Do you plan to kill us?"

The Luck laughed in a manner that wasn't at all funny or amusing, "You'll wish that was all. Your spirit could rejoin the great flow then. Death would be pretty easy in the big picture of possibilities. Now me entrapping your spirit for eternity until it faded to a dim light without awareness. I think that might put some real fear into you. Now for everyone who does not wish to risk such an ending to hear the story, you just need to raise your hand."

Everyone else present raised their hand except for Yu Jin. She stood resolute to hear the answer to her question. Then she looked around to see that everyone else was locked into immobility with their hands in the air.

Yu Jin turned back to the Luck, "What have you done to them? Why did you hurt them so?"

The Luck smiled with a look of innocence, "I have done nothing to them. They are still there in the second where they raised their hands. What I have done to you is to temporarily remove you from the normal flow of time for a short instant. Now that is also something you don't get to tell anyone about. This answer is for you alone now. There never was a battle between Hap Yang and myself. The battle that you've heard of was fought was between Hap Yang and a few of my many enemies.

Hap Yang wasn't killed sacrificing himself to contain me. Hap Yang volunteered to die in order to save his own son. The reasons he did so really don't matter to you. I will also tell you that the great spell whispered of by the Chi Masters for all these years, it's all just a trick cooked up by Hap Yang and me. I prefer to keep people like you looking in the wrong direction."

Yu Jin looked on with confusion and disappointment plainly on her face, "Why would you do such a thing? Who would he protect his son from if not you?"

The Luck looked at Yu Jin with a mix of pity and scorn, "Trust me you wouldn't understand. Let me just put it that there are powers involved in young Hap Sing's existence. There are other powers that fear what the Lucky Cricket will do. However, he's not there yet and won't be there for many more centuries. In the mean time he needs to learn. For now I guide and protect him, but he is ultimately the one with the task in front of him."

Yu Jin shook her head, "It has all been a lie then?"

The Luck smiled wickedly, "Pretty much yes, but not an evil lie or an unnecessary one. This is a lie which at critical junctures will protect the future."

Yu Jin cried out, "Why are you so happy about it then?"

The Luck bowed, "It was my contribution to this happening. I'm very good at invention you see my dear. I'm proud of my work. This lie as you call it will keep certain people and certain powers looking in the wrong places for thousands of years until it is too late for them to stop what will happen. One of the unfortunate side effects has been the temporary repression of Chi Masters in Ran Li. Don't worry your pretty little head about that though. I'll be fixing it tonight."

Yu Jin began shaking her head as tears flowed down her cheeks, "I'm confused this isn't right. Things this big should be true. Hap Yang was supposed to be the greatest of us. He was the one who defeated the horrible beast that threatened an entire nation."

The Luck moved closer, "Don't worry about it so much. Hap Yang was not really any better as a Chi Master than Yu Wing there. The blond bitch there has more ability and power than Hap Yang ever did. Our little Cricket here outstripped all of you combined by far on the day he was born, and his father knew it as well. That's why he made the deal with me in the first place."

Yu Jin was crying as she asked, "What deal was that?"

The Luck laughed, "The deal you see before you. Hap Sing and I combined. Don't worry about it so much. The innocent baby that weepy Lo Maya was crying over instinctively knew more about its precarious position than either Hap Yang or I was able to guess. Hap Sing was the one who summoned me after all."

Yu Jin cried more but continued, "That sounds impossible. How could a baby summon a power like you?"

The Luck grinned, "I'd like to know that as well. Never did learn a satisfactory answer to that one yet. Maybe I'll know in five thousand years or so. That's why you have to recognize the genius of it. I can see this is just upsetting and confusing you. Let me put it in simple terms. I know a lot. You couldn't begin to guess how much. I know your weight, your age, and how many electrons are in your fingernail. However, I can't predict the future with any degree of accuracy worth mentioning, too many possibilities to calculate out further with reliability than a couple hundred years or so. Then I meet this fellow Hap Yang who has a book full of important facts and information that stretches very far into the future. The catch is that I have to merge with this child and protect him to use this book. Let me just say this book gives me quite a competitive advantage in what you might call my line of business."

Yu Jin dried her cheeks while the Luck spoke and then asked, "If Hap Yang was such an average Chi Master how was he able to gain this knowledge you say he had."

The Luck grinned wickedly, "This is the part that is going to bug you for a long time young lady. The Lucky Cricket gave it to him. Didn't I tell you this guy is a genius? Just watch a second."

The Luck reached into thin air and pulled out a large heavy tome from nowhere. It paged through for what seemed like a few seconds and turned the book to show an entry to Yu Jin. The entry read:

> *Remember that Hap Sing will arrive at dusk on that date in Hap Mi's cherry orchard with Yu Wing, Yu Mai, Yu Gai, Yu Jin, Yuki Nene, Lo Dong, Boku Sata, Fane Blaze, and the twenty seventh reincarnation of Flügg (aka the walking man) as the greater destinies and powers present. Other lesser destinies will be engaged as well. You will be summoned by Hap Sing. Answer their questions and please stay polite this time. Don't forget to contact Palnor and Number Two to arrange tactical support for the upcoming engagement. Please ensure that Boku Sata is not killed, and that Flügg is killed again as that bastard certainly has it coming this time for killing my father. Fane Blaze is only providing logistical support to Flügg at this time and his actions will be inconsequential to the outcome of this engagement. Interdict him before he departs to assure he will perform as required later otherwise he would likely only look after himself. Lo Dong will be promoted after this action under the orders of Palnor and begin to release the Chi Masters from the oppressive government restrictions in a few years. Only reveal the information on this page to Yu Jin as she will keep it secret for the rest of her life and into eternity. I also recommend using time disjunction which Hap Sing instinctively will be able to perform for these conversations as it will eliminate all of the many unwanted eyes attempting to perceive this event. To Yu Jin, as you read this you must understand that the existence of this tome and what you have learned from the Luck must be kept a secret from everyone for the rest of your life. These following words are only meant for you. I think that my father Hap Yang was a great man even if he was not actually the greatest talent as a Chi Master. When doubt sets in remember that Hap Yang did what was right by our people and me.*

He bravely sacrificed himself to provide a better future for our existence.
The Lucky Cricket.

Yu Jin was frozen in shock as she read the page, "Who is this Lucky Cricket? How does he know such things? What does it mean?"

The Luck grinned as it tucked the tome away into nothingness again, "The Lucky Cricket is what Hap Sing and I will eventually become. Think of it as two beings become one being with as yet unknown abilities. One beneficial side effect is that we are communicating with us into the past from our position in the future. They know such things because they were here already in their past. What it means is that greater destiny is a mean bitch, and I now hold her leash."

Yu Jin was crying again, "Is there no choice left to us?"

The Luck's expression changed to a sympathetic one, "That is the problem with being imbued with a greater destiny. Your choices are limited by what you are. If you wanted choice your spirit should have come to this life as a common lesser destiny person. They get lots of choices to make, but their choices do not have much impact on the larger flow of existence. You get a lot more impact from your actions, but your most important choices are made by other powers. It's the trade off your spirit decided to make when it returned to this life. If you don't like it, then I suggest your spirit picks differently the next time your spirit comes around to this side of existence. Not that it will remember what I am telling you now."

Yu Jin looked up at the Luck standing on the rock, "What should I do?"

The Luck smiled gently at her, "Rejoin your husband in the normal flow of time and be thankful that more was not revealed to you. At least you have uncertainty left regarding the remainder of your lives, and perhaps you will eventually regain the illusion that the important choices of your future are made by you."

Yu Jin was locked in place next to her husband as Yu Wing and Yu Mai blinked with their hands raised. They looked around at the others stuck in time and at the Luck glaring at them. A touch of fear could be seen in their eyes as they unconsciously shifted closer to each other.

The Luck stepped forward and shouted, "Boo!"

Yu Wing and Yu Mai stood in front of the Luck quivering as Yu Wing hesitantly called out, "What have you done to them?"

The Luck laughed, "You both are so funny sometimes. So called great experts on spirit powers, but scared out of your boots to deal with anything other than your own spirit projections. Everyone else is fine for the moment. They are merely moving in normal time. We are not. It provides a great deal of privacy that keeps even other powers from spying on what I am going to tell you."

Yu Wing spoke with a clearer voice, "What are you going to tell us?"

The Luck frowned, "For the leader here you certainly are not too smart. I am going to answer a few of your questions. Try to make them worthwhile and interesting."

Yu Wing stood up tall as Yu Mai stayed close to him, "I thought you were going to yell at me for my mistakes yesterday."

The Luck smiled, "I could do that if that is what you want. I've gotten pretty good at intimidation when necessary, but I was hoping that since you had the balls to face me a second time that such things were not necessary. It's mainly an act for the rubes to keep them from bothering me all the time. I only tend to show up to deal with the big issues you understand. I don't like standing around being asked to predict how many butterflies will pass by a window."

Yu Mai spoke with a quaver in her voice, "Why do our spirits flee before you if you are so nice?"

The Luck smiled, "An acceptable question if not a very imaginative one. It's a power thing. I can use it in ways you can't even begin to imagine. Which of you would have thought about removing your consciousness from the flow of time? Not one of you. It wouldn't occur to you, so you couldn't do it. So you should understand two things are involved in order to perform such an act. First one needs the vision to conceive of the need, and second one needs the power to make it happen. On a relative scale as greater destinies you both have more power than the average person. Because of this an average person might fear you with good cause for you could create much destruction if you so choose. I am on the other hand like the difference between a dragon and a human when viewed as a power. The smart humans hide when they see a dragon coming, and they don't bother to ask if its intentions are good or bad first."

Yu Wing spoke, "What about with Hap Sing? Our spirits bowed down before him as if he were their ruler."

The Luck nodded with a wide smile, "That is quite interesting isn't it. They fear me when I desire to be feared, and really because I should be feared. They respect and venerate the Cricket when . . ."

Yu Wing looked at the Luck waggling its eyebrows up and down for a moment, "When Hap Sing wants to be venerated?"

The Luck shook his head, "Wrong direction there. Personally my observation is that Hap Sing wants to hide. Your spirits barely notice his presence. The Cricket though is a being which should be respected."

Yu Wing shook his head, 'I don't understand the difference."

Yu Mai spoke, "The aura was so bright when the spirits bowed down to him. The aura of the Luck couldn't be seen. He also wasn't conscious at the time. He was in the dreaming both times."

The Luck smiled, "Very good Yu Mai. I'm proud you can understand the difference so clearly. The Cricket is Hap Sing's potential unleashed. When he is in the dreaming his capabilities rival that of a minor deity, and his dreams can affect the nature of reality if he wills it. Frankly speaking in my estimation Hap Sing is to put it simply the greatest Chi Master that will ever be. Well at least as soon as he comes to accept this quality about himself. It will likely take many centuries for that to happen."

Yu Wing clasped hands with Yu Mai and asked, "I know that greater spirits are not supposed to know the future, but I suspect that certain things are within your grasp to understand. What will happen with us?"

The Luck grinned, "You are right. Most of the other tailed beasts lack my vision. I am no soothsayer or profit of the Gods, but I do know quite a lot. Things will change in Ran Li in the relatively short term. There will be conflict and death, but out of this conflict the Chi Masters will arise as a power for justice. In a few minutes after all of our conversations are completed the results of Boku Sata's actions will be evident as well. The associates to whom Boku Sata owes a lot of money have sold the information he gave them on Hap Sing to some extremely dangerous powers. Those powers have sent some very dangerous people to capture Hap Sing. Fortunately for us Boku Sata has not given them everything he knows about Hap Sing, and as a point of fact he has also deliberately left out any information about any of the rest of you. Your jobs for tonight are to defend yourselves and the others here. So I suggest you be prepared when this happens in a couple of minutes. Unfortunately I can't directly act in this particular conflict, and Hap Sing is an unrepentant pacifist. However, I am arranging to bring in some pretty tough tactical support, and I think things should work out for the best tonight."

Yu Wing looked shocked, "Sata has betrayed us?"

The Luck smiled, "Actually Sata has betrayed only Hap Sing. Personally I think it is a pretty smart move in his situation. Since he has met me Sata has realized that he could either buy his way out of his debt for the information, or lead his debtors to their doom when they try to collect. Unfortunately Sata didn't realize that his debtors would sell this information to other powers, and that these powers would oblige him to lead their capture team to Hap Sing. Sata's only hope now is that I can counter their assault, and that I won't be too angry with him."

Yu Mai timidly asked, "Are you angry with him?"

The Luck frowned, "Of course I am, but not because he betrayed Hap Sing to save his own skin, that was some pretty clever strategy on his part. I'm angry because he didn't do what I told him to do and come to talk with me tonight. These other powers involved tonight are dangerous. However, these other powers do not realize I am taking steps to counter their move already. They don't know that many of their information sources have been compromised by me. In the big picture Boku Sata is just a pawn. He should have had the good sense to realize that I wanted him on my side of the board, and that I treat my subordinates much better than the other side."

Yu Wing swallowed, "How is that?"

The Luck smiled, "I don't consider my subordinates to be expendable. I don't have many pieces so I try very hard to keep them in play."

Yu Mai took a half step forward and challenged the Luck, "Our lives are not some pieces you get to play with in some game. Why do you think we have become your pieces to use as you will? I didn't grant you that permission."

The Luck stepped forward and placed its hand gently on her shoulder, "What you don't understand is this agreement happened when you were born with these wondrous abilities. All of the Chi Masters I adopt are my pieces to play in the great game now, although the other sides don't realize it yet. That is the advantage to becoming the king on the board my dear. The disadvantage is that my moves have become limited. Even your spirit hawk knows this fact already. You just refuse to accept what is in your heart. Don't worry about it. I forgive you my child."

Yu Mai stepped back to Yu Wing and asked, "What would you have me do then?"

The Luck smiled a genuine smile, "Please forgive Hap Sing for his interference in your lives. He really is a simple person whose feelings are easily hurt by those for whom he cares. Just chalk it up to him being a cranky old man who wanted to celebrate his one hundred and fiftieth birthday in peace with his family. Also don't worry that Lo Arthur might betray you. He values his family as much as his faith. I'm about to give Palnor an earful of grief about the situation in Ran Li and there should be an eventual positive change in the general attitudes about Chi Masters in Ran Li. If you would like to listen in on the conversation I will allow it. Your bodies will be frozen in time yet your minds will be aware of what transpires with Lo Arthur."

Yu Wing looked at Yu Mai for a moment and then they both nodded together. They were again locked in time yet aware of their surroundings as the Luck approached Lo Arthur and released him from the time freeze. Lo Arthur looked around at the others stuck in place as he lowered his hand. His gaze finally settled on what seemed to him to be Hap Sing standing in front of him.

Lo Arthur asked, "What has happened to them Hap Sing? How did you get in front of me so fast?"

The Luck answered, "Sorry to say that you are not going to learn that answer today. I didn't ask you here to answer your questions. If you want answers then you can try praying to your god Palnor. I hear that he normally has an opening for dealing with people at your level in the organization at around three hundred years from now. However, I'm in a generous mood and I am going to show you what a direct line looks like."

As the Luck reached into nothingness next to him and pulled out a clear crystal sphere Lo Arthur asked, "What do you mean a direct line?"

The Luck held up its hand with the index finger extended in front of Lo Arthur for a moment as it spoke into the crystal, "Ahoy there. Put your boss on the line. No, do not put your manager on with me. I need your boss for this one. I know he's busy, but trust me he doesn't want to pay the rates for keeping me waiting. Ahoy there Pall. It's me Number Seven. Don't pretend like you're too busy to remember me now Zif. I've got one of your minor minions with me now. No, I don't think you know this one yet. Just trust me that I need to cash in one of those markers I hold. What I want is for you to remember how I pulled your favorite crazy ponytail wearing rat off your insane bitch sister's front porch for you. Yes,

Tia was so pissed after that wasn't she? Don't forget that I bailed you out a lot of other times when you needed untraceable aid provided. Look I'm not asking for a personal appearance here, just send by one of your boys. Don't go cheap on me now. I expect platinum for this job. Well are we agreed then? In about fifteen minutes local time reference would be ideal. Please have him cut through my office in Centrus, no extra charge this time. Yes, I've got a direct express gate already open for him to my Prime location. Yes, I haven't forgotten about those mouse colored robes. Yes, pretty wacky there Zin. No disguise will be required this time. I'm aware of the implications, but we can discuss that later. That sounds good. Look, I'm putting your guy on the line, so introduce yourself. Be impressive, but try not to scare him too much will you. I think he deserves a promotion as well, give him something suitable. Here he is. His name is Lo Dong Arthur."

The Luck held up the crystal sphere in front of Lo Arthur who peered inside expectantly. There was a flux of divine presence and Lo Arthur realized that he was gazing at the visage of the god Palnor. Lo Arthur dropped to his knees in supplication as Palnor gazed from the sphere.

Palnor spoke in a resounding tone, "I've been hearing good things about you my son. Please listen to what this being has to say to you. I've come to depend upon its services and discretion at times in the past. Know that you have my blessing to follow its reasonable directions in accordance with your faith in me. If you do a good job I will be promoting you to the position of leader of my church in Ran Li. I expect that will please you greatly my son. When you face trouble in the near future stand fast and know that I will send one of my personal heralds to aid you."

Lo Arthur spoke, "Yes, great father of us all. I thank you for showing me your presence, and I humbly accept your commands."

Palnor smiled, "Remember that the greater good must be considered in addition to the law. Sometimes the laws of man do not meet with my approval. I think you understand that all persecution of this being's people in Ran Li must be halted. I charge you with completing this task as your quest."

Lo Arthur smiled, "Thank you great Palnor. You speak to my own heart, and your words are truth."

The image of Palnor faded from the crystal and the Luck tucked the crystal back into nothingness. Lo Arthur was still ecstatic about his personal contact with Palnor and was standing awestruck with the implications behind it. Eventually his eyes focused on the Luck standing in front of him.

Lo Arthur grinned as he spoke, "I never realized you were also a servant of Palnor. Why didn't you say so?"

The Luck shook his head, "I'm not a servant of anyone. I'm a self employed independent contractor. Palnor there has just found a need for my unaffiliated services on occasion, and I've just told him that a payment on his bill was due. Don't mistake his geniality for liking me either. It's just as enjoyable for him to talk with me as paying the tax collector is for you. It's just that he respects my talent is all."

 Chapter 8

Lo Arthur's grin lessened somewhat, "What do you mean?"

The Luck smiled wider, "I know things about him that he doesn't want the other gods to learn. He like the other gods has weaknesses, secrets, and various predilections that could hurt his position. I haven't had to use any of this knowledge with Palnor because he is good about paying his bill relatively speaking."

Lo Arthur got a serious look, "What would happen if he didn't pay?"

The Luck grinned even more, "This one is going to cost you some. Don't worry my rates of exchange are reasonable for mortals. You won't even notice the price really. If he tried to stiff me, then it might be like the situation of a certain deadbeat demon called Mortis who continually challenges the White Raven for the role of keeper of the dead spirits. It seems like Mortis can never catch a break in any major engagement. The White Raven knows how many forces he has deployed and comes up with the appropriate counter every time. Any time Mortis goes looking for any inside track on how to get an advantage over the White Raven the information turns out to be faulty or ultimately worthless."

Lo Arthur frowned, "That sounds like blackmail and sabotage."

The Luck laughed, "You make it sound so horrible. I consider it a visit from the debt collector for unpaid bills. Don't buy the service if you are too cheap to pay the price is my point. Palnor is a solid customer, and knows the value of what I provide is worth the occasional inconvenience of making a payment. The White Raven always gets a discount on my services though since her primary rival Mortis is such a stupid jackass that he will never understand you shouldn't try to cheat everyone like it is some kind of code of personal ethics. Ah well, she's pretty reasonable and reliable at least. It is nice to have a customer who certainly has no problem paying her debts in a timely fashion."

Lo Arthur's frown deepened, "It sounds like such an underhanded business."

The Luck grinned again, "Yet your boss is also one of my better customers. Perhaps you should ask him about the morals of it all when you pray for guidance. The problem is your frame of reference is all. You are trying to apply mortal standards of conduct where they don't always match the situation. Let me say it is really hard to take punitive actions against an immortal being, and especially a being that has a lot more direct resources at its disposal. That leaves your options for expressing your displeasure at interfering with their ambitions. That's my specialty if you understand my meaning. I'm very good at altering the state of the game board in the eternal contest between the powers."

Lo Arthur looked confused, "You think this is a game?"

The Luck laughed, "As Hap Sing would tell you, would you call it fishing?"

The Luck left Lo Arthur frozen in time with his face frozen in open mouthed disapproval of its behavior. It chucked lightly then a serious expression was on its face again. Yu Wing and Yu Mai were unfrozen from time as it approached them.

The Luck looked at them, "You heard it all then?"

Yu Wing and Yu Mai nodded uncertainly as Yu Wing answered, "I didn't understand everything, but I heard what transpired. You mentioned a price to be paid by gods and us mortals. What price is this?"

The Luck grinned, "As Hap Sing would say I have tied a fishing line to you and you are now on my hook as bait. You are about to be cast into the water."

Yu Mai's expression was sad, "We are no better than pawns to you then."

The Luck lost its smile and mirrored her expression, "In that you are mistaken Yu Mai. I may have to treat you harshly, but it is not out of hatred or anger. It is out of love. You are our children, the children of the Lucky Cricket who is yet to be. We care for you very much, but there is only so much we can do to help you survive. You have the tools given to you by destiny. I have shown you that there is more which can be done with what you have been provided. I am even setting you free from the chains of oppression as quickly as I am able. That bargain with Palnor tonight is going to be very expensive in the long run, but very worth it. I've now taken an action that can't be undone, and I've done it on your behalf."

Yu Wing looked on with sympathy, "What action is that?"

The Luck grinned again, "I've stopped sitting on the sidelines in the great game. No longer am I simply providing temporary tactical support for sale to the highest bidder. I'm entering it as a player, and joining the side of one of the great alliances. This is unprecedented for my kind and it will shake up the play like never before. I have chosen a people and I will be their advocate although not their god. The Chi Masters will have relevance and thrive for many thousands of years to come."

Yu Wing had a thoughtful look as he asked, "What about the other tailed beasts?"

The Luck nodded, "There will be trouble. Several of the others will fight against it wanting to maintain the status quo of our neutrality. A few will eventually understand the opportunities to be gained for the cost involved. Those few will choose sides as best suits their own natures. Speaking of trouble I have a private interview to conduct before the rest of the fun begins this evening. I'll be back with all of you in no time."

Yu Wing and Yu Mai were frozen again in time without perception. The Luck went back to the large rock and sat down.

The Luck spoke to the shadow it cast with the setting sun, "What is your progress Two?"

There was silence for a moment then a silky smooth and melodious voice spoke from seemingly nowhere, "I'm sorry Seven. I was busy securing myself to the shadows of the lesser destinies. This time disjunction makes movement difficult you realize. I would have been finished sooner except that slimy bastard Flügg has to be studiously avoided. I wouldn't want to pollute myself by accidentally coming into contact with his shadow. Also Fane Blaze has an unknown barrier in use. I estimate it to most likely be an elemental fire based barrier given his obvious proclivities. However, I'm going to steer clear of him as I get the feeling that it

 Chapter 8 91

would sting a bit. I would surmise that since Kayver Riddare is not along at this time that Fane has only been contracted for transportation services and has not made any alliance with Flügg."

The Luck nodded, "What is the final tally then?"

The voice of Two spoke again, "I took a broad approach. I have secured five hundred sixty seven lesser destinies in a four mile radius for the moment. Likely you are only facing a force of some two hundred and thirty three of those at my worst case estimate. The current obvious retinue with Flügg is an even one gross, and they are most certainly under his direction as they are not beings local to this part of the geography. However, given Flügg's predilection for triskaidekaphilia I would suspect more individuals are involved. My calculation indicates this leaves twenty five I have not accounted for as less obvious members of his regulator posse. Likely they are in reserve or support roles, or are not within an immediate four mile radius. As per your request I will only lock down the ones who attempt to engage you and the other greater destinies here. Also I have left all of the greater destinies and the two powers alone."

The Luck asked, "Very good Balinac. I suspect Flügg has finally caught on to people figuring him out through his triskaidekaphilia proclivities. Likely he picked one gross as a means of covering who he is from those who are working for him. I suspect that Fane Blaze will be a touch surprised to find out who has hired him for support this time. What is the composition of Flügg's obvious regulator posse?"

The voice of Two replied, "Approximately eighty percent goblin kin races from the adjoining territory to Ran Li. An approximate twenty percent mix of various regional humanoids in composition. Among the twenty percent humanoids are a bakers dozen of intelligent undead."

The Luck smiled, "I wouldn't be surprised if your missing twenty five were in the form of a group of non-humanoid no destiny beasts. I know it's tricky but check to find any monstrous beings nearby. Go out to a ten miles radius if you must, and don't forget to consider the aerial and subterranean beings. You have fourteen minutes local reference when the clock starts ticking."

The voice of Two responded, "I know my job. You can consider this area to be secure. Even if new unannounced arrivals come I can lock them down quickly using the others already here."

The Luck nodded, "It's all good then. Coincidentally you can consider those intelligent undead spirits fair game for bounty retrieval, and I will grant you full credit for the capture on their bounties. Consider that a bonus if you will. I know the White Raven pays well for those. Is there anything else I should consider in play at the moment?"

The voice of Two responded, "Thank you for the bonus spirits. I could use a little good will with the White Raven at the moment. In concordant position on the plane of shadows a number of shades are gathering. It is a typical amount for this size of conflict. They are awaiting the passing of spirits to capture. There is no clear guidance or organization among them. Would you like me to disperse them?"

The Luck nodded, "I think that preventing them from making life difficult for passing spirits might also please the White Raven, so I think it is a good idea for you to do so if things are tense with her lately. I don't suppose you would consider grabbing onto Flügg's spirit if he manages to pass today."

The voice of Two spoke with undisguised distaste, "Touching that filthy thing would be worse than touching its shadow. I don't think I would ever get the stink of it off me. It is also quite slippery I would imagine. I doubt it goes to the plane of shadow at all upon demise. Frankly, I don't think you could possibly reward me enough to even attempt it. The taint of chaos in that power is much too strong for my taste."

The Luck replied, "Very well I have made alternate arrangements to see to him for this engagement anyway. I was just hoping to put him off the field for good."

The voice of Two was cautious then, "I also detect a third power in transit to this position through the dreaming using your personal gate. It is coming from your Centrus office then?"

The Luck nodded, "Yes. I had to call in a marker, and that was the best way to bring in support in a way that I could time the entry."

The voice of Two had an accusatory tone, "Using a personal gate to bring in an affiliated power isn't wise. Having them come through from your location in Centrus is even worse. You have visibly lost your neutral status with this act you understand. The numbers and other powers will learn of this quickly through the Centrus rumor mill. The numbers will be even more concerned about your irrational actions now. They may view this act as endangering their position."

The Luck nodded, "Have I ever struck you as being stupid or unwise?"

The voice of Two was uncertain, "Not until recently Seven. Your recent moves have questionable logic, yet I admit there is an unexpected effectiveness seen in the result. I think you are playing a deeper game than the other powers realize yet. The very uncertainty of your behavior is turned to your advantage perhaps. I will reserve judgment on the ultimate wisdom of your actions."

The Luck smiled, "That's why I like you so much Balinac. You have much more good sense than the others. Keep that offer I made you earlier in mind will you. I know it will take you time to analyze it, but I feel that you'll come around to my way of thinking on this eventually. I'd like to see you on my side when you do."

The voice of Two was non-committal, "I think it is best if I continue to work as a neutral contractor for the moment. No offense, but I think we will remain on a pay as you go basis. The problem with alliances is they bring as many problems as benefits."

The Luck frowned, "Speaking of problems could you take a quick look at the blond bitch standing over there and let me know what you think. This seems a little closer to your area of expertise."

The voice of Two spoke after a moment, "She seems like an interesting contradiction. She seems to be a Shadowine on the prime, and with a spirit totem of a Chi Master a rare find in these parts. Let me make a closer examination. Ah, very interesting, a Chi Master who also serves the White Raven. Indeed an interesting contradiction. You are correct in assuming this to be a problem. If you are claiming the Chi Masters, and this one is already claimed by the White Raven, then you have put yourself into possible contention with one of your frequent customers."

The Luck grinned, "I know where to look now at least. It was driving me crazy trying to find her true father among the Nordlanders or the population of Ran Li. I should have suspected something was up with that Raven Spirit form. Can I access your Shadowine genealogical files? I will offer the usual deal of equal access to my genealogical files from any one of my planes at a future date."

The voice of Two sounded pleased, "I will accept the deal, but I will save you the effort of looking it up. There is a short list of wandering Shadowine who visit the prime specially flagged in my files. I think this one matches the appropriate location and time frame you require. He even used one of my gates to get here. Unfortunately he has already passed on to the White Raven, but the rest of the information should still be good."

The Luck smiled, "Thank you Two. It has been a pleasure doing business with you again."

The voice of Two replied, "I will caution you that I may need to visibly separate myself from providing services to you for a while until the furor over this current situation dies down. I am not prepared to be viewed as a partisan in this action yet. However, I will take your offer seriously. I have a feeling that you are on to something which is going to alter the nature of what you are. I just need to see if the result is worthwhile for a few centuries first. If you need some more information in my possession in the mean time, then I can still get you some insights through the usual back channels."

The Luck nodded, "Your caution is understood. I also appreciate that you haven't rejected the offer outright. Well let me talk with the blond bitch here a moment. She has some questions, and I now have some answers."

The Luck stood and approached Yuki Nene where she stood with her hand still raised. It walked around behind her and released her from the time freeze. She blinked at the empty rock in front of her and looked at the others frozen in different positions than she remembered. Her expression became scared for a brief moment. When the Luck breathed out on her right ear she jumped and twisted around in startled fright.

The Luck grinned at her, "Well my dear it's your turn. The others can not perceive us now. We are locked in frozen time. Well everyone except for us that is. It may be more appropriate to say that we are currently unstuck from the normal flow of time. Effectively it's the same thing. I see you thinking about it, trust me it is not within your powers to perform this trick yet. Perhaps it will be in the future though."

Yuki Nene steeled herself and spoke, "Are you the Great Spirit of the seven tailed tiger then?"

The Luck nodded its head, "That is one somewhat inaccurate appellation used for me. On the prime I now prefer to go by the Luck. Neither one is my true name if that is what you are wondering, and even if you knew my true name it wouldn't grant you any power over me. I am not a simple devil you understand. I suggest you ask the questions you want to know now. The others have asked theirs and are done. You are the last."

Yuki Nene gave a half hearted grin, "I want to ask if you can tell me who my father was, and what I am now. I know I am different from the others. I just have no point of reference as to why I am so."

The Luck smiled, "You are someone unique. Then again everyone is unique. Yuki Nene is a rare form of unique, since you are a half human half Shadowine Chi Master. There is more but I will tell you that your father was a Shadowine planes walker named Rexis."

Yuki Nene lost her grin and a look of confusion was on her face, "I don't understand what that means. What is a Shadowine? Who are the planes walkers?"

The Luck smiled, "The Shadowine were humans once. They were a kind of advanced humans who traveled the planes between the worlds in their time. They found over generations that they were considered outcast wherever they went due to their strange powers over reality. Eventually they found over millennia that the only place they could find acceptance was on the plane of shadow. The White Raven holds her dominion there, and many of them volunteered to enter her service. They adopted the name Shadowine meaning Shadow Kin or people of the shadow. Over the millennia there they have grown strange and distant from the other branches of humanity. The plane of shadow is not well suited to mortal forms. However, they have endured with the assistance of the White Raven as their patron."

Yuki Nene looked at Hugin perched on her should, "Hugin is the symbol of the White Raven?"

The Luck smiled, "Yes it is. It is the sign to those that know that you are dedicated to her, and serve her."

Yuki Nene shook her head, "It can't be. The Chi Masters serve no gods."

The Luck smiled, "Well now we come to why you are such a rare form of unique. You are a Chi Master who not only draws her power from the dreaming, but you also can access the divine grace of the White Raven if you so choose. It explains much of why you can do things that other Chi Masters can not do. It was a wise move to leave the Nordland colony. If they had discovered the deal your mother had made to produce such an odd bird as you, then she would have been cast out to starve along with you."

Yuki Nene began to cry, "Why did she do this to me?"

The Luck gave her a sympathetic pat on the head, "I imagine she did it so that she could have you. If it hadn't happened you would never have existed. I would believe that her husband was sterile and unable to get her with child. She likely made a deal with one of the White Raven's priests to bear a child of significance. Thus you are an attempt at the rebirth of the spirit shaman dynasties within the Nordlander community. She just never reckoned the fact would be that the only Chi Master blood available to the White Raven would be that of a Shadowine. Like you, your mother had likely never heard of them before meeting your biological father, or understood what the heritage would mean until too late."

Yuki Nene dried her tears, "I thank you for telling me this. It means a lot to me to finally know where I came from."

The Luck grinned, "Now that we've gotten your cover questions out of the way. Why don't you go ahead and ask the real questions you want to have answered? I won't tell Hap Sing. It will be just between the two of us after all."

Yuki Nene seemed conflicted as she asked, "What do you mean?"

The Luck gave a wicked smile, "Your acting doesn't fool me. I've had much better than you attempt to scam me over untold billions of years. It would help you to understand that unlike Hap Sing I am not a mortal being. No biological drive if you understand my meaning. Gender is pretty much meaningless to us as well. The pronoun it is used for a reason. So quit insulting my vast intelligence and be honest with me. I'll give you an honest answer in reply."

Yuki Nene looked at the Luck with a sharp glance, "Your previous answer wasn't honest?"

The Luck shrugged its shoulders as it continued to grin, "Take it for what you will. My answer was factual, the sympathy was not. I was just showing you that I could lead you around much more easily than you could lead me around. If you don't have a real question then I will leave."

Yuki Nene held up her hand, "Alright truce then. I already knew the answers to the questions I asked. It was a test to see if your sources of information were as good as rumored. They were better in fact. None other than me was ever told the story by my mother of how I was conceived."

The Luck smiled, "The other fact you failed to mention is that it wasn't the priests of Palnor that held the teachings of the Chi Masters, but instead the priests of the White Raven who provided them to you was a bit of a tip off as well."

Yuki Nene glared, "The priests guaranteed complete confidentially in this matter."

The Luck laughed, "Lady there is very little of that at the levels where I work. I know where all of the best gossip is to be found. Besides it was pretty stupid of you to try to pin such an act of oppression on Palnor. He might be a somewhat hookey deity at times, but that just is not his style at all. Now please spit out your question already."

Yuki Nene shrugged, "Hap Sing was right it is your game after all. Have you been freezing me to get information every time I ask a question?"

The Luck shook its head, "There certainly hasn't been a need. Too much of this was obvious, and already confirmed before this discussion began. Ask me something I haven't anticipated, and we will see if you can catch me off guard."

Yuki Nene gave a sly smile, "Will Hap Sing and I become lovers?"

The Luck shrugged, "You ask a question of the future. It is tricky to respond since there are lots of possibilities. Like for example a force hostile to me could be alerted to my presence and attack us in an attempt to capture Hap Sing. Some very dangerous individuals could be in that kind of a force after all. It is technically possible that you or even he might be killed. Hap Sing will likely leave this region to return to his solitary life as a fisherman. Then of course there is the fact that the future is mutable and even deities have problems predicting every contingency. We tailed beasts have never been known for our ability to prophesy the future."

Yuki Nene interrupted, "You are leading me around and not answering my question. I will rephrase it to remove uncertainty. Will you oppose my seduction of Hap Sing?"

The Luck grinned, "Sensible girl. You are learning quickly. I am in full control of my actions in the future and can provide an accurate answer on that point. Consider the field clear for you to make an attempt. The one woman currently in his life is much too shy to ever attempt it, and he is too much of a hermit to make a move on her himself. I will not oppose you making the attempt. It is meaningless in my plans whether he enjoys a brief carnal interlude."

Yuki Nene frowned, "Why do you say brief?"

The Luck laughed, "You've only got about one hundred years left to your life at best. Much more likely your life span will be less than that in reality, and the breeding portion of your remaining life is even shorter yet. Hap Sing will live much longer than that barring an unnatural demise, and I will be putting my considerable resources in place to prevent that from happening. Hap Sing will never age, never produce children, and to him you will be getting older at a very rapid pace in comparison to what he knows."

Yuki Nene stepped toward the Luck, "Can nothing be done to grant me longer life?"

The Luck shrugged, "Plenty could be done. Don't count on me to do it for you. You're one of the White Raven's chosen, and you have to know how she feels about unnatural extensions. It messes up her schedule, and she is a stickler for keeping her books straight. That is one goddess whose schedule I don't disrupt. She is one of my better customers after all."

Yuki Nene clasped the hand of the Luck, "Can nothing be done?"

The Luck grinned, "Of course it could be. I recommend learning to be happy with your lot in life. Take what fun you can while it lasts. Settle down with a nice young man and have children. Raise a new generation of Chi Masters in an academy dedicated to Chi Masters."

Yuki Nene's eyes narrowed in suspicion, "For someone who doesn't know the future it sounds like you have a pretty specific plan for me."

The Luck laughed wickedly, "Wouldn't you like to know."

Chapter 9 Conflict

The Luck froze Yuki Nene still wearing a look of sharp contemplation. Then the Luck took a walk in a clockwise circle around the assembled group. It pulled a brass metal device with intricate designs on its surface out from nowhere again and began adjusting various dials and knobs before looking into an aperture in the device. It nodded to itself for a moment as it peered inside and then smiled to itself. The Luck then began pacing out a wider circle around the area in a counter clockwise direction.

The Luck spoke to the nothingness, "Tricky, tricky, tricky Thirteen. You had me guessing infernal, and you go for a diabolical connection instead. They are going to be pissed to learn that you are cheating them."

The voice of Two spoke, "Were you needing something Seven? What were you saying about Number Thirteen?"

The Luck laughed, "I suspect that it is behind my current quandary here. It has arranged for some enforcers to come after me in Centrus again. It also set Flügg on Hap Sing's trail here again I would guess. I got a hunch when you mentioned triskaidekaphilia earlier. I should have realized that Thirteen had a hand behind that monstrosity earlier. He's a favorite pet I suspect."

The voice of the Two almost growled, "Flügg is more like a rabid dog needing to be put down. Coincidentally I've found thirty five candidate creatures in a ten mile radius, but don't count out the possibility of something coming from a location I can not observe. Fane Blaze looks to be creating a projectile gate to move their forces here soon to catch you in a surprise action. In case other forces are gating in from outside the prime I will endeavor to lock down anything else which arrives, but if Fane Blaze brings fire elementals I will not be able to keep them secured. They have no appreciable shadows to connect to."

The Luck shook its head as it continued to walk the wider circle, "I don't think Fane Blaze is going to be the problem today. I wouldn't worry about him getting involved in the fight. My information indicates that he will scoot as soon as he learns the real score here, and he may hopefully pay better attention about who he hires on with in the future. Then again knowing how legalistic he can be, I'll bet he has a partial payment termination clause in effect in the advent of intentionally misrepresented risk. A couple of well placed comments and the arrival of my surprise guest will likely have him running before any real fight starts."

The voice of Two spoke, "So do you think Number Thirteen is putting together a case against you?"

The Luck nodded, "It has been doing that for a long time Two. This extends way beyond attempting to keep the neutrality of the tailed beasts. We both know that is just a cover for the deals it has continually made with the abyssal, infernal, and diabolic powers. Thirteen wants us tails standing aside dickering about proper protocol over my actions while it quietly assumes control. I for one am not about to play the game the way it desires."

The voice of the Two spoke, "What do you suggest? It is Number Thirteen. You are but Seven and I simply Two. The both of use can not hope to directly counter it if that were the case."

The Luck smiled, "That's why we make friends. Give them bargains on our services, and collect some unspecified markers for when we need them. We also need to pay well when we use their services."

The voice of the Two spoke with a touch of condescension, "Like giving away undead spirits so that a partner can trade them in for future divine favor?"

The Luck nodded, "Of course. It costs me little, and buys you so much. Even if you don't finally openly side with me, it can help remind you of who your friends are. I'll only ask that you don't actively oppose me at a critical juncture if necessary."

The voice of Two spoke, "While your rational rings true, it still seems a touch insulting. It seems like you think I am an easy mark or something."

The Luck smiled, "I never consider you easy Two. More like sensible and smart. You are well aware of when a good deal with reasonable strings and low risk is presented. Just because I've made a formal declaration doesn't require you to make one. However, it only takes getting on the White Raven's good side to benefit from some of her largesse when desired. I've been doing it for millennia after all. You are better positioned to please her than any of us."

The voice of Two spoke with uncertainty, "What about the pact of neutrality?"

The Luck shook its head as it finished walking the circle around the cherry orchard and moved back toward the rock, "That pact was broken long ago by Nine. We all know it, but most of us ignore the truth of it. Thirteen has violated the purpose of the pact if not the letter of it for centuries now. It only pretends to be neutral. Many of us have broken the pact by supporting one side over another even when the reward wasn't better. As I see it few of us really care about only providing services to the highest bidder anymore. A different ideology has crept in over the recent centuries. I've just decided to stop deceiving everyone about it. I know who I don't like and who I trust. I don't care how much is promised anymore. I won't take a bad deal because the pay offered is higher, or sit still and be burned while knowing a deal is bad."

The voice of Two questioned, "If what I know were added to the case against you, then you could be forced out of your place in Centrus. If they find anything in your offices there, then you could be banned from doing business there as well."

The Luck shrugged as it sat down on the rock again, "I've planned for that contingency when it happens. They won't find anything left by me there. However, I anticipate that Thirteen is very likely to plant evidence against me regardless. I think this will be the most likely outcome after I send his cursed toy back to him all broken again. I can be barred from Centrus, but as one who doesn't work from there you know that it is still possible to do business."

The voice of Two purred, "Yes it is possible, but not necessarily as easy. Few are willing to travel to my domain looking for my services."

The Luck smiled, "If you come upon hard times, then don't hesitate to contact me. I can always use a talent like yours."

The voice of Two grew worried, "You know too much sometimes. It is what causes the others to fear you. The fact that you have told most of us tails the neutrality has been broken, but many of the others don't want to acknowledge it. They are finding it hard to adapt to the new ways. I also admit to finding it hard to change as well."

The Luck grimaced as it flexed his hand into a fist, "The world of the dreaming is in danger of becoming less relevant unless we do something about it my old friend. I don't plan to let that happen. Only through physical action in the prime can we hope to secure the future of the dreaming. The time of acting through spirit alone is soon ending my friend. All of us will be using these material mortal forms to some extent in a mere thousand years. I'm just ahead of the rest in breaking new ground."

The voice of Two asked, "What is it like?"

The Luck unclenched his fist, "It is strange. Yet it is not unpleasant."

The voice of Two replied, "Our friendship is a strange thing as well. As you say, it is not unpleasant. It feels good to talk, to trust, and be trusted. This is such a rare thing among the tails, we are so locked in our structure, and our ranks normally define our relationships. I feel the others will never be able to understand."

The Luck smiled, "I sometimes fear so as well. They are limited by their own expectations. I feel sorry for them, all except for Thirteen that is. It is as bad as Mortis some days. It is all concerned with plotting and distrust, never making allies, just employing hirelings, and hoping that will suffice."

The voice of Two spoke, "I am prepared. Have you finished your preparations as well then Seven?"

The Luck grinned, "Let's get this operation in motion then."

Normal time resumed and the Chi Masters were in a momentary state of confusion as they adjusted to seeing time flow normally again. A brief outburst of surprise was heard from several of them, and the Luck was pleased to note that most of them started looking at it with a touch of distress.

The Luck spoke with weariness in its voice, "Now wasn't that a pleasant discussion. Feel free to share what you are allowed to share, but remember to keep confidential what you are not allowed to share. It might help for you to do so quickly. As I told some of you we will be assaulted in just about fourteen minutes now. I recommend you develop a strategy for dealing with your enemy. Also I have to go as I am not allowed to face this enemy directly for reasons it would take too long to properly explain. My information is that there is a group of roughly one hundred and forty four arriving soon via a form of teleportation. They will likely surround this location. It is mostly local goblins from the wild lands, but there is also a mix of others things in the crowd including thirteen intelligent undead."

Yu Wing stepped forward, "We should flee then. Return to town as quickly as possible."

The Luck shrugged, "The choices are up to you. However, I will warn you that two powers are with the other side. I caution that these two powers could destroy your little village and everyone in it in less than fifteen minutes if you choose to hide there. I am bringing in some support to counter those powers, but that support is arriving at the orchard here, not your village. My suggestion is that you find a way to enter a parley with them to delay until the help I am bringing can arrive. I must go fetch that help now. So I am saying goodbye and good Luck."

The body of Hap Sing slumped and lay unconscious on the rock. The Chi Masters collectively examined Hap Sing's form and determined that there was no visible spiritual aura present. Yet Hap Sing still breathed normally and lay as if asleep. Yuki Nene went up to the rock and positioned his form more comfortably on the ground on top of her cloak.

The others gathered close as well to peer out into a circle into the cherry orchard. Yu Mai sent her spirit hawk up high into the sky over them to observe the terrain. The other spirit forms stayed close to the Chi Masters to help them detect the approach of the forces they were warned we coming.

Yu Wing spoke, "Well it seems Hap Sing coming here was a mistake after all. Now we all must defend ourselves, and our community. From what we learned something has been hunting him, and it plans to capture him for nefarious purposes."

Yu Mai added, "It also seems that Boku Sata has sold information to debtors who involved these other people in some kind of deal. The Luck seems to want Sata left unharmed though. If Sata tries to hurt us tonight, then I'll feel justified in defying it."

Yu Gai looked at Yu Wing, "Shall we use the spirit summon?"

Yu Wing nodded, "Of course, but only on my cue. The Luck directed us to delay them. I think we will open up with discussions. Let's be honest about who we are, but let's not give any details about what we are yet. I'm hoping that this can be resolved without any of us getting hurt."

Yu Jin spoke, "I'll support with healing if needed."

Lo Arthur nodded, "Then I will call upon the blessings of Palnor. I also believe that Palnor is sending support here as well according to my conversation with the Luck."

Yu Mai called out, "There is a fire to the north. Across the border I can see it burning. It burns dim but over a large radius. There are things around the fire. The smoke is obscuring the view but many forms are present."

Yu Wing called out, "Prepare yourselves. It seems the ones seeking Hap Sing have revealed themselves."

Yu Gai spoke, "They'll have to move swiftly to cover the distance to here in the remaining time."

They watched as a great streak of flame shot high into the sky. A large cloud of smoke was billowing behind it as the pillar of flame moved upwards. Several moments later a loud boom assaulted their ears and shook the ground. A glowing sphere could be seen riding the top of the pillar of flame which bent over into their direction and the sphere grew larger and larger in the sky. It was wreathed in blue flame and tailing a yellow orange flaming trail through the sky. The large sphere reached its apex, and burst into thirteen separate spheres which rapidly dropped toward the ground still wreathed in orange flame. The spheres spread out into a circular pattern and a loud bang rattled their ears.

Yu Wing was shaking his head as he called out, "I think we know how they are going to cover the distance so quickly now. If they have such power then they will indeed be able to destroy Hung Chan village."

Yu Mai pointed, "Their course is off. They will land around the ruin of Hap Yang's house."

Lo Arthur was sweating across his brow, "Hold our position, our aid is coming to the orchard here. Let them come to us."

They watched as the orange flaming spheres came down in a symmetrical pattern around the house of Hap Yang. There was one sphere for each hour of a clock, and a smaller sphere landing in the center in the middle of the ruin. The spheres hit with a great crash and dissolved with concussive force as they hit the ground. The Chi Masters could see standing in each small crater was a group of what looked like goblins, hobgoblins, and humanoid figures.

The figures hustled to move to encircle the ruin. After a minute the figures seemed to be looking around in confusion. They turned around to look around outside the circle and the closest ones spotted the group of Chi Masters standing among the cherry trees in the orchard. They charged and ran toward the orchard loosing their formation and blending into chaos instead.

Yu Mai spoke, "There are close to one hundred and fifty I would guess. I can see Boku Sata standing in the middle of Hap Yang's house. Four others are with him; one of them is wearing bright red leather garments, and one of the others is wearing a dark long cloak and has long black hair. The one with the cloak has struck Sata with a hand and knocked him to the ground."

Yu Jin quavered, "Here comes the mob. There are so many of them. What can we do?"

Yu Wing stepped forward between the Chi Masters and the crowd of onrushing goblins, "We will await the arrival of their leaders with Sata. They shouldn't attack us yet. They mean to surround us I think."

Yu Mai spoke again, "The two other figures have come to pick up Sata. They don't look monstrous. They appear to be humans as far as I can see. They seem to be afraid of the man in the dark cloak as well. Sata is bleeding, but I think it is just a shallow cut from the blow. They are slowly heading this way. Wait the one in the red leather clothes is staying behind, he's doing something. It looks like a strange dance."

Lo Arthur spoke, "I don't think that is a dance you see. It's likely an incantation. They mean to spirit Hap Sing away as soon as he is secured. I imagine they don't plan to leave survivors. Holy Palnor grant your blessings upon us."

A warm glow spread from Lo Arthur's dragon symbol bracing their faltering courage. They were set in their course of action, determined to delay as long as necessary. The first of the running goblins hit the edge of the larger circle walked by the Luck and pitched forward onto it's face with its feet seemingly affixed to the ground and it's ankles broken at an unnatural angle. As it screeched in pain several others just behind it repeated the maneuver with similar results.

The first wave of goblins lay on the ground writhing in pain. The next slowed and approached cautiously seeing that their targets were not running away. They avoided the area with the injured goblins and made their way around to the sides. This group also had their feet locked to the ground at the edge of the circle, but avoided injuring themselves through having their feet stuck to the ground while in a head long charge. After another score were struggling where they were rooted in place the remainder stayed back cautiously readying their weapons and looking back to the advancing humanoids which were approaching at a more sedate pace.

Several of the humanoids approached, glaring with a feral intensity. The Chi Masters could see that their skins were pallid, and their forms emaciated. Lo Arthur looked at them and briefly paled as well.

Lo Arthur spoke, "They appear to be ghouls, a feral form of undead. Let me try something."

Lo Arthur strode a pace toward them and raised his symbol of Palnor, "I call upon Palnor to banish your foul presence."

The ghouls in front of Lo Arthur began to hiss and smoke as they howled in anguish. Glowing white flames lit their skins as they pitched around while their flesh burned. Lo Arthur brandished his symbol boldly as more advanced to be ignited in holy flames.

Yu Wing whispered to Yu Mai, "You have to admit that he might be a useful son-in-law after all."

A group of thirteen cloaked figures stepped around behind the burning ghouls to the edge of the invisible circle. One stood forth and addressed them after lowering its hood.

Its eyes glared a fierce red as it shouted, "Simple priest. You may harm our minions, but your spells will be worthless against us. We don't fear your god. Our master approaches, and will cast down your enchantments. We will feast on your blood, and the goblins will dine on your flesh when we are finished. Surrender it to us and we will be merciful. We shall end your lives quickly."

The Chi Masters could see through their second sight that these beings had no glowing auras. It instead seemed like they were coated in running inky grey precipitation. Yu Wing flinched as he watched Lo Arthur face this new menace.

The Lucky Cricket

Lo Arthur brandished his dragon symbol again and called out, "Palnor answer my prayers and destroy these abominations."

The group of thirteen cloaked stood firm with obvious distaste and displeasure. The leader flinched, but held his ground with some obvious effort. Lo Arthur also held his ground, but seemed to be pressured at the same time as well. The others were surprised when they saw Yuki Nene step forward next to Lo Arthur to face them as well.

Yuki Nene tossed back her hair with a grin, "You shall not have him. You'll face my mistress instead. If you don't fear Palnor, then perhaps the White Raven will give you pause. Attack of the Death Raven!"

Yuki Nene flung her arm forward and her giant raven spirit Hugin became visible to them as it swept forward toward the leader of the thirteen. Hugin struck with vicious accuracy grabbing the being's head in its giant beak and viciously ripping its head from its torso as Hugin flew past. Several of the unstuck goblins threw down their weapons and started to flee upon seeing the body of the humanoid collapse on the ground.

The twelve other cloaked figures looked at each other in concern as Hugin circled and landed next to Yuki Nene with the being's head still in its beak. Hugin made a jerking motion with its beak and swallowed the head down. The twelve separated and started to round up the milling goblins.

Yuki Nene and Lo Arthur stepped back next to the other Chi Masters. They all watched for the next move to be made.

Yu Mai looked at them all and whispered, "Sata is coming with two men guarding him along with the fellow who struck him down. Sata looks pretty scared, and the men with him seem uneasy as well. There is something wrong with the fellow leading them. I don't feel right about it. He feels like someone very dangerous, and I would think he is capable of terrible things."

Yu Mai gasped then whispered, "His aura. It is all wrong. It is black like squid ink, twisted with hatred and evil. It is also strong. It makes me feel ill to even witness it. These others here are but his field commanders, influenced by the taint of his twisted will. They are dead men kept alive through his horrid power."

Yuki Nene nodded and spoke, "The White Raven knows them as nosferatu, or more commonly referred to as vampires. They are considered abominations by her. That would usually mean that fellow is the head vampire, but I don't think that is the case this time. I suspect it is something much worse."

Yu Jin spoke with a quavering voice, "What could be worse?"

Yuki Nene spoke, "A necromancer who has made pacts with one or more evil gods. I think we are in deep trouble. We can only hope that our help arrives soon."

Yu Gai spoke in a quiet voice, "Who is stopping those goblins from advancing?"

Yu Wing shrugged, "I don't know, but I am glad we were not swarmed. I imagine the Luck has a hand in it somehow. Look they are moving again."

The vampires had spread out among the goblins and were directing them into flanking positions. The goblins advanced one at a time on either side of the circle and were stuck one by one as the enemy probed for gaps in the protection around the Chi Masters. Eventually they were surrounded by various kinds of goblins on all sides which seemed to satisfy the vampires. They seemed to feel confident their target was as trapped as the goblins were.

The vampires made a brief retreat to gather the rest of their forces into a semblance of an honor guard in a shortened corridor between the circle of goblins and the ruin of Hap Yang's home. The cloaked man led the small group containing Boku Sata and the two human guards along the corridor of troops as the creatures along the sides bowed their heads at their approach.

The Chi Masters could see that there was a dark inky aura surrounding the man. Lo Dong could feel a strong emanation of evil coming from him. They all noticed that the plants in his footsteps shriveled up and died as he touched them. His hair was long, dark and stringy. His features were actually cast in a somewhat classical build. His shape was long and lanky and his skin the pale color of an ascetic.

As the man neared the edge of the circle where the first goblins had fallen and broken their legs he stopped and briefly surveyed the situation. His eyes seemed to flash with an inner light as he looked over at the vampire closest to him.

The man spoke in a casual tone with a hidden menace, "Explain what has happened here. Why have you stopped advancing on them, why are my ghouls smoldering corpses, and why the nine circles of hell is Kullar's damned head missing?"

The vampire took one step forward and bent onto one knee, "They have two priests with them Master Rendalk. The blond female summoned one of the White Raven's hell crows and it bit off Kullar's head my master. The other priest released the power of Palnor and ignited many of the ghouls my master."

Rendalk nodded with a calculating look of displeasure, "Why did the goblins stop advancing then?"

The vampire seemed nervous as it spoke, "There is an unknown barrier in place which secures them to the ground in those locations. We have mapped out the extent of the barrier with the goblins, and have kept the remainder here in reserve."

Rendalk then turned to face Boku Sata who trembled with a touch of fear, "You never mentioned anyone here having divine powers. You didn't mention that there would be a group of peasants huddling here either. You said it was going to just be the son of Hap Yang at his house, not in his orchard."

Boku Sata pointed beyond Rendalk to where Hap Sing's body lay on the ground, "There he is as I promised. How could I have known that he would bring others along to visit his father's property? I could not know they would stop here."

Boku Sata looked at each of the two men standing beside him, "Tal Go, Fa Soon you both know I have been good on making my payments. You said this would settle my remaining debt. My information was good. The rest of this was outside my knowledge and not my fault."

Rendalk turned back to face the circle of goblins, "This smells of an information leak. Too much preparation went into this on their part. This is not some simple barrier circle. They came expecting trouble. If I didn't know better then I would say that they even got help from the outside."

Rendalk looked back over his shoulder again, "If I find out that you are involved I will punish you, and then you will wish for a quick death. Well sometimes we have to play the cards we are dealt. I still get the feeling that I have the winning hand. Barnibus you are promoted to the head of the thirteen since Kullar foolishly lost his head. I'll make you a replacement to complete your roster shortly. Perhaps one of these here will suit you."

Barnibus rose from his kneeling position, "Thank you Master Rendalk. What are your orders?"

Rendalk contemplated a moment, "Let's continue this experiment you began. Let us see how far this barrier extends."

Rendalk turned to face Boku Sata again. Rendalk grabbed the front of Boku Sata's shirt. Then Rendalk lifted Boku Sata into the air and flung him over the prone goblins toward the Chi Masters where he collapsed onto the ground. At a hand signal from Yu Wing, Yu Jin and Yu Gai rushed forward and dragged Boku Sata back over by the unconscious Hap Sing. Yu Jin began a chant of healing over Boku Sata as the rest of those present silently watched.

Rendalk spoke loudly to Barnibus, "This so called barrier does not seem to extend into the air, or seem to be more than ten feet wide. Send a goblin across the backs of the fallen ones here. These peasants are likely all so called Chi Masters. Minor backwards shamans I had thought wiped out from these parts years ago. I should have done a better job of inciting against them after I killed Hap Yang. It seems a little viper's nest of them has sprung up here again to protect Hap Yang's son."

Barnibus pointed at the goblin closest to him and pointed at it to walk across the backs of the fallen ones. The goblin took a short trot and jumped up onto the back of the first fallen goblin. Its feet affixed to the back of the goblin which moaned hideously at the injury.

Rendalk shook his head, "Something isn't right here. Hey you there, foolish priest of the useless god. What have you done to the ground here to cause it to act so strangely? This is not any kind of ward I have witnessed before."

Lo Arthur remained silent while Yu Wing spoke, "It is nothing of our doing. I suggest you just come closer so we can hear you better."

Rendalk smiled then turned to grab a nearby goblin to toss over the fallen ones. It landed on the ground where Boku had and clearly and painfully stuck. Rendalk's smile faded into a frown of uncertainty.

Barnibus spoke, "What is wrong master?"

Rendalk shook his head, "That wasn't a magical barrier which stuck that goblin down like that. Let's back off to discuss this a bit."

Rendalk moved back with the other vampires briefly. They seemed to be in an animated discussion. Rendalk and the vampires then sketched a pentagram into the dirt at their location. They began a ritualistic chant which grated on the ears of the priest and Chi Masters. The goblins began calling and hooting as the ones nearest the pentagram quickly moved away.

A shimmering black pit appeared on the ground and one by one a shimmering pale insubstantial figure floated up through the hole and hovered between the vampires. Before long twenty six of them appeared and bowed in mid air to Rendalk. Rendalk pointed at the Chi Masters standing near the unconscious Hap Sing.

The insubstantial figures floated forward in two groups of thirteen and floated over the prone goblins without meeting any obstacle. The prone goblins shrieked and visibly became withered by the passage of the wraiths. Rendalk wickedly grinned as the wraiths closed on the assembled Chi Masters, and Lo Arthur raised his dragon symbol again.

The Rendalk stood confused and enraged as the wraiths were suddenly enclosed in shadow as the first one reached the boundary of the first smaller circle the Luck had walked. The shadow dissipated like a fog before the sun, and no sign of the wraiths could be seen. Rendalk thrust aside the nearest vampires and rushed up to the two quivering humans who had guarded Boku Sata.

Rendalk shrieked, "What kind of trap have you led me into you fools? You must be in league with these damn bumpkins. You'll discover that crossing me was a huge mistake."

The first human tried to turn to run but Rendalk struck a blow with his hand which punctured the man's back. The man cried out in pain as his flesh withered and died under the grip of the necromancer. The other man pulled out a dagger and attempted to strike Rendalk with it. Rendalk tossed the body of the first at the second man who stumbled and fell with the impact. Rendalk casually reached down to clutch the man's face which also withered under his touch with a piteous scream.

Rendalk stood up straight and paced back and forth for a while. Barnibus moved nearby while the other vampires remained near the summoning pentagram. There was a muted conversation between Barnibus and the pacing Rendalk who seemed to be angry and frustrated that his victory remained out of his grasp. Rendalk eventually stopped pacing. Rendalk and Barnibus again closed in on the outer circle.

Rendalk spoke with honey smooth tones, "We have gotten off on the wrong foot here. I am a reasonable man. I will make a deal with you. Let my goblins go. Leave the son of Hap Yang behind, and I will allow you all to leave here unharmed. You can even take that traitor with you. His usefulness has ended for me, and I am not angry that he has betrayed me.

Yu Wing shook his head, "I'm afraid your time is nearly up."

Rendalk looked at the ground where the unconscious form of Hap Sing had been laying a moment before.

Rendalk's head snapped back and he yelled at Barnibus, "Where is he at? Where did he go?"

Rendalk then came to an uncomfortable conclusion and screamed out, "Run! It is a trap! The barrier circle is a fake. Get to Fane Blaze as quickly as possible."

As the other vampires turned to run each was enveloped in enclosures of dark shadow which dissipated leaving only blowing fine ash behind. Barnibus' eyes grew wide as he ran along beside Rendalk. The remaining goblins began to flee as well. Even the ones formerly stuck to the ground found that they could move their feet again and fled as well. Only the dead goblins which had been slain by the passage of the wraiths remained.

Rendalk stopped short when he noticed Hap Sing standing a mere fifty feet before him with a sad smile. Rendalk hesitated, and then moved rapidly forward with twisted anger on his face.

The Luck quietly spoke, "Time to go back to hell you murderous bastard."

A giant shimmering gate opened in the air beside the Luck and an enormous ancient platinum dragon stepped through with a lithe grace. The platinum dragon roared in a voice which seemed to split the sky.

Rendalk fell back on his behind, and scrambled madly to regain his footing and head in the opposite direction. Barnibus veered off into a different direction, and he was then also enveloped in an enclosure of shadow which dissipated to reveal a cloud of drifting ash.

The platinum dragon boomed out in a thunderous voice heard throughout the valley, "Palnor had sent me to carry out the sentence for your crimes Flügg. Know that he will always protect his own from your kind."

Rendalk Flügg managed to achieve a running pace away from the advancing platinum dragon as he screamed out, "No! No! No! I was promised this victory! The son of Hap Yang is to be mine!"

The platinum dragon lurched forward at a tremendous speed and caught the fleeing Rendalk Flügg in its tremendous jaws. Rendalk Flügg struggled against the biting grip, his touch causing the flesh of the platinum dragon to darken and wither where he could reach. The platinum dragon lifted its head high up into the air and breathed a river of icy frost into the sky. The body of Rendalk Flügg in its jaws was encased in ice as the wind sent a drift of snow flakes into the sky which settled around the orchard and the surprised Chi Masters. The platinum dragon then whipped its head down on its long neck and flung the frozen form of Rendalk Flügg into the ground hard where the body shattered into several small shards.

Chapter 10 Departures

The Luck nodded at the platinum dragon as he pointed at the Chi Masters, "I think you need to talk with your boy over there. He'll bring you up to speed on what you need to know about the local situation."

The Luck then began walking over to the ruins of Hap Yang's home. It could see that Fane Blaze still waited there surrounded by a circle of flame. As the Luck got within speaking range of the ruin it stopped and raised a palm facing Fane Blaze. Fane Blaze repeated the gesture and nodded.

The Luck spoke, "Hello Fane Blaze. I will take it that you were hired only for transportation services. I have no complaint against you unless you want to give me cause. You should know that it was a very bad man with whom you were doing business. Flügg has been slain by the Platinum Dragon, his undead minions have been destroyed, and his goblins dispersed. I hope you got your payment in advance because they will not be using your return transportation services."

Fane Blaze bowed, "I appreciate you understanding my situation. I am having a bit of a cash flow problem lately, so I have had to hire on for some less savory tasks. I also make it a point to not provide combat services cheaply where I have not established a track record of successful business dealings. Too often people want to skip out on payment by leaving me dead. I am curious as to how you know my name, and the real name of my employer though as I don't usually frequent this part of the world."

The Luck spoke, "You have no idea how much I know about you and your partner Kayver Riddare. Your little pocket of home you keep on the plane of fire. Kayver's little retreat on the plane of earth. The two of you have built up quite a reputation in certain circles. Circles which pay close attention to your actions and deeds. Trust me that I am doing you a favor today by not letting the word get out to those circles that you had hired on with Flügg. Reputations are sometimes so easily tarnished."

Fane Blaze nodded again, "Your implied threat is understood. I was unaware that Flügg was the being I was transporting. I had thought him a simple necromancer with a grudge to pay back. I am surprised that I haven't heard of you before though since you seem to know so much about me. I didn't catch your name."

The Luck smiled, "I am known locally as the Luck."

Fane Blaze had a calculating look on his face as he asked, "What would you have done if I had attacked?"

The Luck grinned, "Would you take my evaluation that you are out of your league at face value?"

Fane Blaze shrugged, "I could do so since as you say there is no quarrel between us. I am, however, somewhat curious about your estimation than I am not in your league. Your ability to gate in an ancient dragon while impressive is certainly a feat I could choose to replicate. I know that many dragons will make deals in tough times such as these. Please understand that I haven't actually seen you do much to back up your statement."

The Luck smiled wickedly, "How about a peaceful minor demonstration?"

Fane Blaze smiled in return, "I am game to see what other tricks you can perform."

The Luck nodded, "I suppose your little hideaway on the plane of fire is very well protected, and likely covered with fire and counter fire enchantments of many kinds. Possibly even elemental powers enlisted to protect it as well."

Fane Blaze smiled, "I won't reveal the depths of my defenses to you. Let me just say that they would not be trivial to circumvent."

The Luck nodded, "Agreed most would not consider them trivial. Now name me any item you choose stored within. In need not be very valuable, but unique would be best."

Fane Blaze continued to smile, "Pardon me for declining to provide you an inventory of my belongings."

The Luck smiled, "A random assortment it is then."

The Luck reached into nothingness and pulled out an elaborate tome, "It looks like your first spell book from your academy days I believe."

Fane Blaze's smile lessened, "It is an illusion, a mere fake plucked from my mind. I see your game now."

The Luck shook its head at it tossed the tome at Fane Blaze's feet, "Let's see what we have here; the pillow from your bed; the painting from your dresser; the magical bracers you wore as an apprentice, and a magical golden figurine of elemental summoning. Bound to Fizranar I would surmise from the feel of it."

Fane Blaze caught the last as it was tossed over the circle of flame in his direction. Fane Blaze examined the article closely and his expression became quite sour.

The Luck continued to grin, "You have thought of another test of my so called illusions. Would you care to see if that figurine actually summons Fizranar?"

Fane Blaze fired back, "Your illusions can not fake such a thing. Fizranar is soul bound to me you fool."

The Luck nodded, "I know. Go ahead and say the command word 'esterack' and see if it works. I'll wait for you."

Fane Blaze scowled, "Fizranar requires payment on summoning. You will find yourself paying it if such is true."

The Luck nodded, "Agreed. I should say be careful of what you wish for though. I don't think you are going to like the result this time."

Fane Blaze held up the figurine and intoned, "Fizranar your services are requested. By the word 'esterack' you are summoned."

A humongous fire elemental appeared within the circle next to Fane Blaze. It gazed immediately over at the platinum dragon. Its flame flickered briefly.

Fizranar intoned, "Fane Blaze the price will be very steep if you expect me to engage the Herald of Palnor in combat. It is a foe I can not hope to prevail against."

Fane Blaze immediately began shivering as if he felt a cold breeze, "The Herald of Palnor you say?"

Fizranar intoned, "The right hand of the god Palnor himself stands over there in the form of a mighty platinum dragon."

Fane Blaze pointed at the Luck standing before the circle, "This man calling himself the Luck says he will pay the price."

Fizranar focused its attention on the Luck. It quivered as if hit by a powerful wind, and slowly shrank down to man size. Fizranar bowed down before the Luck onto the ground.

Fizranar spoke in a mild tone, "I'm sorry great one. This simple one is ignorant of what offenses it has committed. Do not place the blame for its ignorance on us."

Fane Blaze pointed at the Luck, "Don't apologize to me. Collect your payment from that one."

Fizranar quivered, "The foolish mortal does not understand. I'm sorry great one. What do you command of me?"

The Luck grinned, "I am feeling generous today. You may consider your contract null and void with Fane Blaze. All of the contracts of your brethren with Fane Blaze are also null and void. If after five years I consider his attitude improved, then you and your brethren may consider forming new contracts with him. He can not summon any of you through any means for the next five years without my knowing and considering that the one choosing to be summoned does not care to continue having my good will. Furthermore he is banned from entering the plane of fire for a period of five years. His house on the plane of fire and the belongings within will be held in escrow until a final adjudication is made on his improved behavior. If he so much as voices an objection to you about this know that I will also evict his partner Kayver Riddare from his residence on the plane of earth. Is this payment deemed satisfactory for your services?"

Fizranar rose and spoke, "Most satisfactory great one. I and my brethren thank you for your generosity and kindness. I beg your leave to depart now."

Fizranar disappeared in a plume of smoke as Fane Blaze dropped to his knees. His circle of flame dissipated and flickered out as well. Fane Blaze looked up at the Luck standing before him with the beginning of tears in his eyes.

Fane Blaze called out as the Luck started to turn away, "What are you? How can you do such things?"

The Luck looked back over his shoulder, "As I said before I'm known locally as the Luck. You decided to think you were bigger than your britches so I figured it was time to readjust your idea of your position in the world. Don't let me catch you hiring on with the likes of Flügg ever again or it will go worse for you and your partner next time. You should be happy that I'm in a good mood today and feeling tolerant of ignorant peasants out of their depth. I suggest you get moving somewhere else soon before Palnor's Herald gets hungry."

Fane Blaze stood again as The Luck began walking back toward the orchard. The Luck sensed hesitation on his part. It was perhaps a stubborn defiance which hadn't yet been quelled. An angry expression crossed Fane Blaze's features for a moment.

Fane Blaze called out accusingly, "What gives you the right?"

The Luck stopped walking toward the orchard and turned to face Fane Blaze again. The Luck's expression was odd, almost pensive. Fane Blaze took a step forward. The step was followed by another.

Fane Blaze yelled out toward the Luck, "I asked you a question! What gives you the right to take what is mine?!"

The Luck grinned viciously, "You foolish mortals will never understand. It has never been yours. You ask nicely at first, then you ask rudely, and if you don't get your desire you decide to take what you want. When the line is clearly drawn in the sand delineating the end of sufferance for this behavior you step up and spit over that line hoping to take yet once more."

Fane Blaze stepped forward once more, "Screw your line. I don't answer to you."

The Luck stopped grinning, "Are you so sure about that? Is this a request for summary judgment to be rendered?"

Fane Blaze stopped advancing, "What does that mean?"

The Luck pointed back at the platinum dragon, "I got that on loan from Palnor for calling in a simple favor owed. A favor owed to me by a god mind you. Your stupid jackass stubbornness couldn't take the hint that you are defying powers that will forever be beyond your grasp. I don't like getting my hands dirty because worlds tend to be destroyed when I get pissed off. I happen to like this world so I recommend you don't piss me off. I would hate to have to destroy it just to make my point with you, and the idiots like you."

Fane Blaze took a step forward again, "You don't have that kind of power, and even if you did you wouldn't dare."

The Luck grinned again, "You don't trust my word then? Perhaps you prefer another object lesson? Two please request the right hand of Palnor to join us would you."

The Platinum Dragon immediately left its discussion in the orchard and flew to land beside the Luck while glaring at Fane Blaze. Fane Blaze took a hesitant step back. Then regained his composure and took a step forward.

The Platinum Dragon looked at the Luck, "A cocky one isn't he. Do you want me to devour him or something?"

The Luck shook his head, "No not yet. I just want you to answer a couple of my questions for his education."

The Platinum Dragon nodded, "Very well then. Palnor was very explicit that I should assist you within reason."

The Luck bowed to the Platinum Dragon, "Thank you. Please tell him what you are."

The Platinum Dragon opened its mouth wide as it spoke, "I am the Herald of Palnor, also known as the Right Hand of Palnor."

The Luck smiled, "Could this human here have any chance of besting you in combat?"

The Platinum Dragon looked at Fane Blaze with a cocked head, "I think this one would present less of a problem than Flügg did for me. I'm not even sure if he could cause me a minor injury. My resistance to elemental based magic is quite unmatched by the rest of dragon kind, and his repertoire is quite limited beyond that scope."

The Luck grinned, "Could you defeat me in combat?"

The Platinum Dragon leaned back, "Such a question is ridiculous as the result would be obvious."

Fane Blaze's gaze narrowed suspiciously, "Then why should I find him a challenge then?"

The Luck held up a hand, "Don't answer him yet. Could you defeat me in combat with Palnor's help?"

The Platinum Dragon shook its head and Fane Blaze tentatively smiled and called out, "That is an even more ridiculous question. It could clearly wipe you out on its own. Why would it need Palnor's help?"

The Platinum Dragon gazed at Fane Blaze, "You misunderstand my response mortal. I could not defeat him even with the assistance of Palnor. If Palnor himself took the field today against him Palnor would be unable to claim victory, and this very world would likely be destroyed in the battle. Such open battles never occur anymore. The cost would be much too great. Although to tell the truth it is his hidden ally which is the one that most of the gods fear though."

The Luck held up a hand again, "I would prefer that you leave Number Two out of it for the moment. I am trying to get him to understand why I have the right to bar him from the plane of fire without telling him something about me which he will never correctly grasp."

The Platinum Dragon shook his head, "This fool uses elemental forces, yet doesn't understand what you are? How did he last this long without destroying himself?"

The Luck shrugged his shoulders, "It is becoming more of a mystery to me every minute."

The Platinum Dragon shook his head again, "Perhaps if you revealed yourself?"

The Luck shook his head, "That would make the point quickly, but you should know how much trouble that creates."

The Platinum Dragon began to glow brighter. A moment later the light died down and a eight foot tall angelic figure wearing brightly gleaming armor was standing next to the Luck where the enormous dragon had stood previously. It made a gesture while calling out praise to Palnor.

The Right Hand of Palnor spoke, "I have shielded this valley from outside detection with the power of Palnor. It should cover you for five minutes or so local time. I think an appearance in your normal prime form is in order."

Fane Blaze called out, "What is happening here?"

The Luck smiled wickedly again, "Two please lock down the valley for me. Mask a view of me from the others and shield them as well. I don't want them all going into shock. Fane Blaze, prepare to receive the fright of your life."

The visible orange aura of the Luck shot ninety feet into the sky and three hundred feet behind where it stood. Seven sixty foot long tails of orange visible raw spiritual primal and elemental energy whipped across the sky creating hurricane force winds kicking up dust and bending over trees. The pressure wave coming from the aura pushed Fane Blaze and the Right Hand of Palnor forcibly away. Vast forces of primal power surged about the aura and were channeled down the tails of the Luck. Fane Blaze was cast down upon the ground and looked up with fear in his eyes for the first time in his memory.

Fane Blaze called out to the Right Hand of Palnor, "You must stop it. It is drawing immense power from the elemental fire plane."

The Right Hand of Palnor looked up at the tails and smiled, "I had never thought to witness the font of elemental fire power in person. You have it wrong foolish mortal. The elemental plane of fire is drawing all their power from it. Without its power the elemental plane of fire would simply cease to be. Do you understand now why it has the right? All you ever do is simply steal an insignificant amount of power from it without asking. It is utter ridiculousness to think that a god could defeat such a being. It would be the end of existence as you know it if they succeeded in such an attempt."

Fane Blaze groveled, "Please stop it. I'm sorry. I regret my actions. I'll change my life just stop it."

The Right Hand of Palnor called out in a loud voice, "Godkiller please tell the Luck to rein in its true material manifestation. I don't know if this section of the prime can take much more of this exposure without severely detrimental effects."

The soft and silky voice of Two responded from everywhere and nowhere, "It is still well within tolerance levels. No planar leakage should happen for at least six minutes. Planar disruption would occur no sooner than twelve minutes. I believe Seven is taking the opportunity to top off the elemental power reservoirs of the plane of fire early this millennium. Seven likely plans to be busy in the next few millennial cycles and this might be the last opportunity it has to create a full prime manifestation for a long while. By the way I consider Godkiller to be a prejudicial slur meant to instill untoward fear of me in deities. They should all understand their role in the cycle by now. I simply abide by my assigned function even if they don't like it."

The Right Hand of Palnor shook its head, "The rumor in divine circles is that you assigned the function to yourself."

The voice of Two responded with a petulant tone, "Would you like to see first hand? Perhaps Palnor is ready to move on to the next phase?"

The Right Hand of Palnor raised a hand, "No offense intended. What would you prefer to be called if not by your common name?"

The voice of Two spoke in a more friendly tone, "If I had a choice, then I think my given name of Balinac would be fine. You may use that one if you desire."

The enormous spirit form of the Luck laughed with the sound of thunder, "The name given by yourself that is. I don't know if that counts."

The voice of Two spoke in a less friendly tone, "Didn't you assume the name the Luck by yourself Seven?"

The spirit form of the Luck diminished until once more it stood simply inhabiting the form of Hap Sing.

The Luck then spoke to no one in particular, "Actually it was given to me by a five year old human child if you can believe it. The name just stuck somehow."

The Right Hand of Palnor came forward and extended its hand in greeting. The Luck took its hand and shook it in return.

The Luck spoke to the Right Hand of Palnor, "Could you make sure that our boy Lo Arthur there is presented to the capital as a favorite candidate of Palnor for future leadership? You know how his priests like it. Give them lots of signs to confuse and argue about before you show them all to be fools who couldn't interpret a divine message written in plain script on their own foreheads by you in person."

The Right Hand of Palnor shook his head, "They will quickly find divine disfavor if they misinterpret this message. I shall take him there in person and deliver the message of Palnor myself. None in this backwater section of the Prime will question Palnor's directions when issued by me."

The Right Hand of Palnor walked back over to the orchard. The Luck could see the Right Hand of Palnor and Lo Arthur talking together for a moment, and then walk off to the edge of the orchard together. A large glowing portal appeared before the both of them and they stepped through it and disappeared. The portal collapsed after their departure.

The Luck turned around to face Fane Blaze who was kneeling on the ground bent over with his hands on his knees, "I see that you are still here."

Fane Blaze placed his forehead on the ground, "Forgive me lord. I never had an idea that something such as you existed. What would you have me do?"

The Luck nodded, "So you finally understand that you are involved with powers out of your depth. You'll find my patience with mortals is not infinite. Your punishment has been decided already. Take these next five years of banishment from the plane of fire to contemplate the course of your life. Think of it as a long needed vacation if you must. Examine what you have considered important up until now. I hope that you make a better series of choices after that point. The world will need such as you on the right side. There is trouble coming and Flügg is just the forerunner of the times to come."

Fane Blaze lifted his head again, "I will do as you request lord. I beg your permission to depart now."

The Luck nodded again, "You don't need my permission. Your choices are your own to make. Just understand that some choices come with hard consequences which are not always evident when the choice is made."

The Luck walked back toward the orchard where the Chi Masters were waiting for his arrival. As he approached them he looked up at the night sky overhead. They had made quite an impact on the local area even with the shielding from Palnor's right hand. Various powers might be confused about where the exact source of power release had been, but certain powers would surely recognize the power signatures in use. The Luck knew it wouldn't be safe to remain in the valley of Hung Chan village much longer.

The Luck felt a slight power surge himself and looked back to see a tall figure covered head to toe in verdigris colored copper armor standing next to Fane Blaze. The Luck recognized Kayver Riddare also known as the Grave Knight and feared by many knowledgeable mortals as a deadly foe. The Luck knew they made a dangerous pair, and hoped that this experience would help bring them over to the right side in the impending war. With another surge of power both figures were gone. The Luck surmised that they had most likely departed to Kayver Riddare's retreat on the plane of earth. The Luck decided it would follow up with its agents there to keep an eye on their activities for the next few years.

The Luck walked through the group of assembled Chi Masters and sat down on the rock near them once more. They all seemed a bit shaken and uncertain about what was happening. Yuki Nene took a step toward the Luck, and then hesitated.

The Luck spoke, "I must depart soon. Hap Sing will return tired and worn out. He will likely want to talk with you. I suggest returning to your home with him for tonight, but he must depart from this valley in the morning and not return for many years. Be sure to tell him this. I also advise that you break up your little party here as well. A concentration of Chi Master's will likely draw even more trouble here. I recommend you decide among yourselves who is to depart and who is to stay."

Yuki Nene spoke first, "I will go with Hap Sing."

The Luck shrugged, "That is an issue to be decided between him and you. I will not interfere with your decision."

Boku Sata leaned forward from his lying position, "I must depart as well. I think that I've made some bad choices which are going to haunt me if I remain here long. Hojo will not soon forget loss of two of his lieutenants. It may well be time for me to leave Ran Li for unknown lands."

Yu Wing spoke, "I've lived my whole life here, my family and roots are here as well. Yu Mai and I will likely stay if at all possible."

The Luck nodded, "That is fine if you choose that course, but understand that your daughter Lo Maya and her husband Lo Arthur will be living in Yokito soon.

They will be taking your grandchild with them when they go, and they will need the assistance of Chi Masters to help advance your cause. If you stay, then your son Yu Gai and daughter Yu Jin can go to Yokito to help. If you go to Yokito, then they can look after your family farm. Either way you should understand your family will not remain together all in one place. I personally recommend no more than four Chi Masters congregate here in Hung Chan at a time in the near future. In a few years the attention should die down and this may be relaxed. Of course if the Yu's all wish to remain here there is another option."

Yu Gai spoke, "What option would that be?"

The Luck shrugged, "You could convince Ming Ran and Ming Akane to leave. There are no family ties keeping them here. Perhaps if someone wanted to have a position arranged for Ming Ran in Yokito it could be done. However, I suspect that this valley might become the site of a major conflict in a few years. Whoever remains had likely better be prepared to face some powerful and dangerous foes. They should have the courage to do so as well."

Yu Mai looked sharply at the Luck, "This has all been a test. You have been testing our courage."

The Luck shook its head, "This has been real. Those were real enemies who came today. You showed your courage in coming to talk with me, and defending me when I was helpless. You could have turned me over if you wished, but most of you stood up against very evil beings without quitting or surrendering to your fear. You are the kind of people Ran Li needs to survive the challenges which are to come."

The Luck looked at Boku Sata, "Some of you have thought it easier to plead and bargain with evil however. I think an example of how successful the outcomes of such arrangements become make a better lesson than any I could teach. I recommend that certain people understand the course their actions are leading them."

Boku Sata ducked his head, "I've already decided to leave as it is clear my welcome is worn out here."

The Luck shrugged, "Once again that is your choice. Keep fleeing your problems, and they will still continue to follow."

Boku Sata looked at the others, "You don't understand Hojo. I owe him debt, and he will kill me for what happened today if he catches me. I have to flee or die."

The Luck laughed, "You could escape him easily, but only by changing yourself for the better. It is your old bad habits which make it easy for him to find you. You should know by now that crowd keeps tabs on their marks with each other."

Yu Wing's face reddened with emotion, "Gambling? You almost got all of my family killed over gambling? You sold out Hap Sing for a Gambling debt?"

Boku Sata ducked down in embarrassment as the Luck spoke again, "Yes. Hojo is a Yakuza under boss, and the various criminal organizations here and in the surrounding kingdoms coordinate together if they are not warring with each other. Their reach is long, but it is not infinite. Sata could cross the sea on the Nordland trade route, and escape them. That isn't the real problem. The real problem is that even after escaping Hojo, if Sata does not change he will fall back into his gambling habit again and just put himself back into the same position with another set of criminals. He must change the habit if he ever wants to be free of these kinds of criminals."

Yu Mai spoke, "What will you do for him then?"

The Luck smiled, "I have already given Sata all the aid he requires. Now Sata has to make a solution work through his own efforts. I hold no grudge, and in fact Sata I have done you a large favor today. If you are smart and careful then it may well be presumed that you were killed along with those two Yakuza. Fall back into gambling and all my effort and your own work will be undone. Sata I suggest perhaps you start by digging some graves for these bodies and making sure the shattered remains of Flügg are mistaken for your own. I suggest leaving some recognizable personal items with it."

Boku Sata looked up at the Luck and spoke, "I thank you for help. I will do as you recommend, and stay away from those types of people now."

Yu Gai spoke, "The Ming's do not need to leave. I do think Lo Arthur and my sister Maya could use some help. While Yu Jin and I are not afraid to protect our homes and people here, it is also important that the Chi Masters be able to come out into the open. We are not so settled here that we couldn't just as easily set up a business in a market in Yokito. We could even keep an eye open for a better position for Ming Ran while we are there. There is not much more for him to learn of the history of the Chi Masters here anyway."

The Luck nodded, "That is a worthy idea Yu Gai. I have no doubts about your bravery, and it would help Arthur and Maya to have your support. It also might help Ming Ran and Ming Akane to have to face the conflict and danger they fear, and this valley will likely not remain safe for many more years."

Yu Wing asked, "Will we ever meet again?"

The Luck shrugged, "That is hard to say. I don't manifest on the prime very often anymore, but I have attached a spirit ribbon to each of you. I will know how you fare, and I may be able to send assistance at some time in the future. Don't make foolish decisions and count on this assistance to save you, it will not work. We likely will not meet again in this lifetime, but since spirits are eternal I think the chances are good that we will meet in some future existence."

The Luck stood up and walked over to embrace Yuki Nene in a friendly hug. Nene was shocked and surprised by this unexpected gesture. Then she felt the dead weight of Hap Sing's unconscious body in her arms. In her surprise she almost dropped him, but she grasped him tightly to prevent him from falling to the ground.

A moment later Hap Sing's eyes fluttered open and his face flushed bright red with the last light of the departing twilight. He somewhat hastily stepped back from his embrace with Yuki Nene and surveyed the scene around him. His face grew shocked.

Hap Sing spoke as he stepped forward toward the foundation of his father's home, "What happened here? Where did these goblins bodies come from? Why are those two men lying on the ground? Are they injured or do they need aid?"

Yu Wing spoke seriously, "They are dead."

Hap Sing spoke with a surprised accusation in his tone, "You killed them?"

Yu Mai shook her head, "None of us killed anything that was not supposed to be dead already. The goblins were killed by their own leader's actions, as were those men who were criminals. Lo Arthur destroyed many ghouls with the power of Palnor, while Miss Yuki there managed to decapitate a vampire somehow. Otherwise I surveyed the enemy forces with my spirit, Yu Wing negotiated with them to delay their actions, and Yu Jin and Yu Gai helped save Boku Sata from their attack on him."

Hap Sing spoke out in concern, "Did the Luck harm anyone?"

Yu Jin spoke, "The Luck was unconscious or feigning unconsciousness through the majority of the confrontation. It only opened a portal to allow the Herald of Palnor to arrive in the form of a mighty platinum dragon. The Herald of Palnor destroyed the enemy leader, and its appearance scared off the other forces. All of the other undead were surrounded by shadow to never appear again after the shadow departed."

Hap Sing gave a sigh of relief, "It's good to know that the Luck didn't cause any problems then. I would hate to have that on my conscience."

Yu Wing smiled, "The Luck only spoke to us. Then it opened a gate for the dragon to deal with the enemy leader. After that it talked with the fire mage who transported their troops here and convinced him to leave without a fight I would guess. We couldn't actually hear their conversation from over here."

Hap Sing thought a moment, "Did you get the opportunity to ask the Luck if I would have to leave and how long it would be before I could return?"

Yuki Nene nodded, "The Luck said many of us should leave to avoid attracting attention. Boku Sata will look to flee his pursuers' and his debts to criminals by traveling to a foreign nation. Yu Jin and Yu Gai will travel with Lo Maya and join Lo Arthur in Yokito. It also encouraged us to convince the Ming's to leave, but left the decision ultimately up to them. It was agreed that I could go with you. It said that you and I would have to leave in the morning and stay away from Hung Chan for many years."

Hap Sing gave a faint smile, "Really? Did the Luck tell you to go with me?"

Yuki Nene hesitated and then answered, "It said the choice was mine to make."

Hap Sing glanced at Yu Wing who was miming a running motion with his right hand out of Yuki Nene's sight and spoke, "I will think about it. I really don't have much room for guests where I live, but perhaps arrangements could be made. We will talk about it tonight for a short while. First let us men bury the dead here. It will be fine to use my mother's cherry orchard I think."

The next morning at pre-dawn Hap Sing sat fishing by the pond on Yu Wing's property. He placed his bamboo fishing pole line in the water. The sound of someone leaving the house came to Hap Sing's attention. Hap Sing could hear them quietly walking down the path to the pond, and noticed it was Yu Wing who quietly sat beside him.

Yu Wing softly spoke, "I notice you didn't leave in the middle of the night. I half expected that you would be running for Li Chan by now. You should know that the Luck did not encourage or discourage Nene to follow you to your home. She is bending the truth by saying that the choice was left to her. The Luck said that you were the one who would make the choice."

Hap Sing nodded, "Nene is persistent in pursuit, but I think she will soon tire of chasing me if I don't run too much. Most people will consider my life now to be unexceptional. I have no lands to farm, or wealth. I live in a very modest hut, and want for nothing more than that. My life is not the kind which calls out to young people like her looking for excitement. Besides she already knows I live in Li Chan village. It's a small place, and not a place I could hide for long by leaving her here."

Yu Wing chuckled, "So you are going to settle down and marry to have children with her then?"

Hap Sing shook his head, "No. I am going to have someone who can look after Li Hung in his final time with us. He is getting old, and his days will likely not be many more. I have to work to support us, and can not look after him all the time by myself. His place has room enough for Nene I would think, and she is pleasant to the eye which should make Li Hung happy if I know him."

Yu Wing smiled, "Nene is just to be hired labor then?"

Hap Sing smiled, "Free labor. It will be by her own choice too as long as it lasts. I do not doubt that she will tire of a slow pursuit long before I give in to her whiles."

Yu Wing shook his head, "Mai may be very stubborn at times, but I suspect Nene is another kind of driven person. I don't think that she will surrender her chosen goal very easily."

Hap Sing shrugged, "You are right that it may take her a while to surrender, but I have the time to wait on my side."

Yu Wing smiled, "While it is true that you may have time on your side, the real question is whether you have the willpower to resist."

Hap Sing smiled, "While it may be a temptation, I don't think she understands what she is up against. The Luck has a plan for me. She may be a part of that plan, but nothing it wants will be defeated by her actions or desires."

Yu Wing frowned, "How do you know?"

Hap Sing closed his eyes then opened them again with the sight, "It has put its spirit ribbons on you. You can see them with the sight if you know how to look. On almost all of you that were there last night. It has found that it can use you for its plan. It only neglected to put a ribbon on Boku Sata because the Luck probably figured he was doomed by his own nature. I would guess that gambling is not his only vice. Boku Sata will most likely continue to be one perpetually in over his head with his life choices. One vice will likely be used to substitute for another, and where there is vice, the people like Hojo will be there to satisfy it."

Yu Wing looked disappointed, "That is a pretty bleak view of people. They have the capacity to change and improve you know."

Hap Sing shrugged, "I agree that the capacity is there, but I doubt the Luck would have skipped putting his ribbon on Boku if it thought he would exercise the capacity. I may not always like the Luck or what it does, but I have to acknowledge it is a very sharp judge of people and their proclivities. It has already written Boku off as a bad investment of its time and effort."

Yu Wing asked, "What are these spirit ribbons anyway?"

Hap Sing spoke, "They are connections at a spiritual level. I can see them with the sight and tell where people are spiritually linked. For example there is a ribbon between your spirit cat and you, and another set of ribbons between Mai, Gai, Maya and you. They usually take positive emotion and many years to form naturally, and most spirit shamans are unaware of them unless they know how to look. Your daughter-in-law Jin and Arthur do not have them with you yet as the time and attachment are probably not there yet. Spouses usually form them relatively quickly, probably because of intimacy. Mothers and their children in most cases have them already when the child is born, and fathers form them with their children in most cases over time. They are undetectable by conventional divine or arcane means as I understand it."

Yu Wing nodded, "What about the Luck then? How does it make these connections?"

Hap Sing shrugged, "I can see what has been done after the fact. However, you should understand I have not been able to witness how it is done due to our situation. The Luck has linked itself and by default me to each of you. I suspect that through this link it can know what you know."

Yu Wing hesitated then asked, "Can it control us through these ribbons?"

Hap Sing chuckled, "Not like a puppet if that is what you mean. It can certainly try to convince you to do what it wants though. I have heard it is very persuasive when it wants to be."

Yu Wing thought a moment, "This reminds me of something we read in your father's writings. Hap Yang mentioned a red string of destiny he saw between him and your mother Mi. It was through that string of destiny that he knew he would marry her and have a child. Yang called such a thing the sign of a Greater Destiny Chi Master, while a Chi Master who is not being driven by destiny has no such connection. The term he used for them was Lesser Destiny Chi Master."

Hap Sing smiles, "My father likely felt it was impartial fate which drew him and my mother together. I begin to suspect that something else happened."

Yu Wing pondered, "What do you mean? Do you think something arranged to have them drawn together?"

Hap Sing nodded, "I only know of one being which can deliberately form these links. It is possible that others can, but it certainly is either done as a slow natural process or quickly done by something as powerful and skilled at the Luck."

Yu Wing shook his head, "Why would it bond them together?"

Hap Sing pointed at himself, "Because it was looking for a certain result I would guess."

Yu Wing grinned, "This seems a bit out of my league for certain then. What about you and Nene. Is there a reason you suspect that nothing will happen between you? Are you not linked to her?"

Hap Sing gave a laugh, "Nene and I are linked most certainly, just as it has linked you and I. However, I know something through my second sight that I suspect it didn't reveal to her. I was linked by the Luck to Ming Wa Fu, Ming Ran's cousin by meeting him a couple of years ago. Well it seems that the Luck has also seen fit to link Nene to him as well."

Yu Wing smiled, "That may be a good thing for you then. Why is it so funny though? What kind of a man is he?"

Hap Sing chuckled, "Ming Wa Fu should be about thirteen or fourteen now."

Yu Wing laughed loudly, "He's just a child. Oh I will say the Luck does have a devious sense of humor."

Hap Sing nodded, "They should be about seven years apart in age. Much closer than my age to hers though. In a few years it should work out fine."

Yu Wing grew serious, "There is something else I should tell you as well. The leader of the vampires stood its ground against Arthur as he invoked the power of Palnor. Its will was balked but it was not directly harmed as the ghouls were. Nene called upon the White Raven and her spirit raven manifested physically and bit the head of the vampire leader clean off and swallowed it whole. That is not something I have ever heard or read as something any Chi Master was able to do. Nene is different, and likely very dangerous when thwarted. I would caution you to be careful."

Hap Sing was serious, "I could see the divine spirit connection on her. Divine connections are not like normal ones, and they tend to stand out as unique to my vision. I had guessed the White Raven was a patron of hers given her spirit raven, but your words just confirm it. Usually only priests have strong enough bonds with their deities to form such connections."

Yu Wing nodded, "I didn't see how she caused the shadows to swallow up the other undead though. I almost thought she seemed as surprised by it as we were."

Hap Sing shook his head, "That is not a trademark of the White Raven if I understand these things correctly. Your son-in-law Arthur may know better though. It does lead me back to suspecting a different power."

Yu Wing nodded, "There was a voice which called Palnor's Platinum Dragon away from its discussion with Arthur. The voice came from nowhere and seemingly everywhere. It spoke with a beautiful voice yet in a foreign tongue we could not understand."

Hap Sing nodded, "It was likely speaking the divine language. Palnor's Platinum Dragon would understand it while you would not. You couldn't see it because you likely didn't know where to look."

Yu Wing asked, "Where was that?"

Hap Sing spoke, "If I am guessing right, then it was under your very feet. I think you might have been in the presence of the two tailed shadow beast."

Yu Wing paled briefly, "It is only rumored to exist. None has seen what it looks like and lived. You are talking about the Godkiller. The being which it is rumored has killed off all of the old gods after the formation of the worlds."

Hap Sing nodded, "I suspect it was such. It would be a kind of contemporary of the Seven Tailed Spirit Tiger you understand. They are both deathless beings of spirit from the dreaming. Their material forms are just shells for the convenience of interaction with physical beings, they exist independently of them I believe. Even the gods are restricted to physical manifestations, and can thus be killed. That's why I'm pretty sure I can die as well. I am restricted to my physical form as well."

Yu Wing looked at Hap Sing closely, "Are you truly restricted that way?"

Hap Sing looked back at him, "What do you mean?"

Yu Wing spoke carefully, "Something the Luck said seemed to be dropping hints that may not be the case last night. I don't know if you are supposed to know this or not. It seems to want you to discover these things on your own. It said you were two beings."

Hap Sing nodded, "Yes I understand. There is the Luck, and there is me."

Yu Wing shook his head, "It said there was Hap Sing, and there was the Cricket. It said that you want to hide, but that the Cricket was you when you used your powers in the dreaming. It said you were on a level with a demigod when that happened. It also said that it would likely take centuries for you to accept this about yourself. It called you the greatest Chi Master that would ever exist. I think it meant that as a fact even before it merged with you."

Hap Sing smiled, "Well it's right about one thing at least. I don't think I can accept that I was anything special until my father used me as a prison for the Luck. Even though that happened my own powers are still very limited."

Yu Wing shook his head, "Did the Luck teach you how to use your power? I don't know of any Chi Master who can do the things you can. They can not control the dreaming like you do. They can not enter the dreaming as quickly. They can not suppress their aura and the aura of an extremely powerful being at the same time. There are things you can do which can not be believed possible by another Chi Master. I don't think you are giving yourself enough credit."

Hap Sing frowned, "I can not even do some things your daughter-in-law Jin has the ability to do. I can not heal the injured or the sick. I've had to call upon the Luck to do so as in the case of Li Hung."

Yu Wing nodded, "I understand that you may not be able to do everything, but you shouldn't dismiss what you can do. If I had to guess, then I would think that it wasn't the Luck which healed Li Hung. It was the Luck borrowing your abilities to do it. The only thing it has that you lack is unending confidence in its capabilities. I don't doubt that it gives you power, but the effect is still based on what you can do yourself."

Hap Sing gathered up his gear as Yu Wing departed again for his house. There was no sign of Yuki Nene yet, but as the sun was clearing the horizon Hap Sing decided that she could catch up to him along the way. It would be a three day walk, and he was not going to be traveling with any significant speed.

An hour later Hap Sing had cleared the valley of Hung Chan village and was approaching a small roadside shrine. Yuki Nene stepped out from under the sheltering awning of the shrine wearing a sheepish grin. Hap Sing waved at her as he approached.

Hap Sing smiled, "I had thought to see you coming up behind me on the road. I figured you would need to pack your things before you would be ready."

Yuki Nene shrugged, "I was busy last night. I made sure that Ming Ran had all of the relevant documents I had recovered through the White Raven's priests except the writings of Hap Yang. Those I left with Yu Gai for the moment. It seemed fitting that his family have them, and I didn't want to disturb Yu Wing last night."

Hap Sing had a slightly surprised look, "That was very generous of you then. Boku Sata estimated those documents as being very valuable."

Yuki Nene smiled as she lifted her backpack and walked down the road along with Hap Sing, "They might be worth some coin to an interested collector of such things. However, their true value is only to someone who can make use of their teachings. Outside the hands of a Chi Master they lose a lot of their intrinsic worth. I have pretty much learned in the last couple of years that I don't tend to learn as well from scrolls and ancient writings. So others will benefit from them more than I can at this point."

Hap Sing thought a moment, "How do you learn best then?"

Yuki Nene smiled, "Through trying something that looks interesting until I figure out how to do it myself. I guess you can say I learn best through observation, and I have already learned everything I could from what they were willing to show me in Hung Chan."

Hap Sing had a serious look, "That is very well then. I take it that they didn't show you everything they could do. Speaking of Hung Chan, how were the people reacting in town last night after the excitement?"

Yuki Nene lost her smile, "They were upset and frightened for the most part. The results of our activities were noticed by now, but the actions of the fire mage and the Luck summoning the dragon last night were not missed by many. They also likely discovered the graves by now including the remains left with Sata's personal belongings. It also seems that Lo Arthur made it back last night and started spreading a story of how Palnor sent the dragon to battle dark forces last night. I imagine that conversions to Palnor will increase greatly in the next few weeks as the story spreads. All of the obvious fireworks and numerous goblin tracks in the orchard won't hurt his cause much."

Hap Sing nodded, "That is a good thing for Ran Li then. I figure that the more people who listen to the priests of Palnor spreading the word to stop the persecution of Chi Masters, the less power the other religions supporting that persecution will have. Speaking of Boku Sata, did he leave the valley last night?"

Yuki Nene was serious, "I was a bit disappointed with his choices, but I gave him a severance package with enough money to travel and become a passenger on a Nordland trade ship since he could not risk returning to the village for his belongings. Sata's belongings would have to remain undisturbed as he left them for this ruse of his death to work. I also wrote him a note in the Nordland tongue which will allow him to negotiate a better rate for his fare, and will allow him to be treated better by any literate Nordlanders. The traders and ship captains will be able to read it, and will understand my request."

Hap Sing asked, "What does the note say?"

Yuki Nene grinned, "It invokes my name and the White Raven. It tells them that I am personally requesting they make sure that no Nordlander or crew under their command causes harm to him, or else they risk my displeasure. It extends my protection until he reaches whatever destination he chooses. They are under no obligation to intervene to protect him though. If any of Sata's problems catch up to him, then it is up to their own conscience on whether to help him or not."

Hap Sing nodded, "It is well done. I don't think that he could have reasonably requested more from you."

Yuki Nene smiled, "Sata knew that I had done him a favor which he was not owed. His gratitude was genuine I believe. It won't be easy for him though."

Hap Sing looked over at her, "Why is that?"

Yuki Nene looked serious, "I know what it is like to be a stranger in the land where I was born. I speak the language here, and people of the Nordland community respected me at least. Boku Sata will be a stranger in a strange land where he does not speak the language, or know the culture. My people know that is a hard thing to be. If he were to go to Nordland, then his foreign status will earn him a measure of respect for his bravery if nothing else. Other places might feel it means he is a victim ready for exploitation. I hope he chooses his destination wisely."

Hap Sing seriously added, "At least he has a chance to change and escape his problems. It is unlikely they will pursue him so far over gambling debts, or even the deaths of two of their kind. They will likely put out a notice in the surrounding kingdoms only if the ruse of his death fails to work."

Yuki Nene nodded, "To change the topic, I am looking forward to being near the sea again. It has been too long for me that I have been living in land locked communities. I miss the sea and the ships near the Nordland colony of Yokito."

Hap Sing chuckled, "You won't find many ships in Li Chan. It is a small fishing and farming village, not a trade port of any kind. To change the topic again I was surprised to find you already waiting down the road this morning. How long had you been there already?"

Yuki Nene flushed embarrassed as she spoke, "Most of the morning."

Hap Sing looked at the sky, "I left with the rising of the sun, there hasn't been much morning yet."

Yuki Nene looked down at her feet, "I meant morning as considered by Nordlanders. They count anything past midnight as morning by their reckoning."

Hap Sing nodded, "That's strange as the rising of the sun is considered the transition to morning in Ran Li. Why were you out here so long? Wouldn't it have been more comfortable to sleep in your bed?"

Yuki Nene looked up at the sky, "You have to understand that when trouble happens, it is not unusual in Ran Li for any foreigners our outlanders to be blamed for it. Not that anyone in particular was pointing a finger in my direction last night, but I thought it best to not be in the village long in case any talk turned that way."

Hap Sing looked at her out of the corner of his eye, "That's it then. I was afraid it was because you were trying to intercept me if I ran away. I would hate the think you spent the night outside on your own because of me."

Yuki Nene ducked her head down in an embarrassed flush again as they walked down the road in silence.

Chapter 11 Passing the Torch

Hap Sing and Yuki Nene entered Li Chan village in the afternoon a couple of days later. She wore her hair bound back, and kept her hood up over her head to avoid attracting too much attention. Hap Sing nodded to a couple of people who barely seemed to recognize and only casually responded to him. Things were still normal as far as Hap Sing could tell.

Yuki Nene looked around at the people in the village with a contemplative expression, "This is very odd. No one is paying you or I much attention."

Hap Sing shrugged, "It is always this way here. People go about their lives without undue interference with other people."

Yuki Nene shook her head, "I am a tall woman with blond hair and foreign features for Ran Li though. I always attract attention wherever people see me. It feels odd to not be noticed and commented upon."

Hap Sing gave a little grin, "The people here notice you. They are just a very private people who don't publicly pry into the lives of others. It is one of the reasons Li Chan and I decided to settle down here."

Yuki Nene closed her eyes a moment and opened them again, "I can see your fishing net is still in place over the village. It does not seem diminished by your absence."

Hap Sing nodded, "I put it there this morning while you were attending to your privacy."

Yuki Nene looked toward the bay, "You are right about there not being any ships here. All I see are fishing boats. Your villagers don't even have warehouses down by your docks. I can just see those fish drying racks."

Hap Sing nodded, "Yes. Li Chan is a small community. There are four elders which lead the village including my friend Li Hung. You'll have to forgive him somewhat since I have been gone several days, and a friend has been looking in on him. It's likely the change in routine has made him a bit grumpy."

Yuki Nene spoke, "I thought we would go to your place first."

Hap Sing shook his head, "I am going to arrange for Li Hung to accommodate you. He is one hundred and six, so the propriety of your presence will not be questioned. My hut is a bit cramped for two people."

Yuki Nene questioned, "Who is this friend you mentioned is looking after Li Hung for you?"

Hap Sing grew a touch sad, "Her name is Wen Li. I should not burden her with this as she has a young son to look after as well. Her husband Wen Lu died a few years ago in a tragic fishing accident. He was lost overboard and drowned during an unexpected storm. The village helps her to get by after the loss of her husband. I usually bring her and her son Wen Lu fish everyday to eat. I made sure to give them plenty for them and Li Hung when I left this time."

Yuki Nene looked surprised, "You leave the village regularly?"

Hap Sing nodded, "Every three months when the Magistrate comes to town for business. His name is Ming Na Jun, and he is Ming Ran's older cousin. He is a greater destiny, and is prone to focus in on my presence as is his son Ming Wa Fu."

Yuki Nene furrowed her brows, "What do you mean greater destiny?"

Hap Sing smiled, "You can see auras with the sight correct?"

Yuki Nene nodded, "Of those who are Chi Masters yes. Faintly for those who are not Chi Masters."

Hap Sing shook his head, "The bright aura indicates someone chosen by fate to do extraordinary deeds. Not all bright auras indicate a Chi Master, but all bright auras indicate a greater destiny. It is greater destinies which attract, not being Chi Masters. Those people with dim auras are lesser destinies. Some Chi Masters are also lesser destinies. Did you ever look at Lo Arthur's aura?"

Yuki Nene shook her head, "He is a priest so I never saw the need."

Hap Sing smiled, "His aura is nearly as bright as your own. He is just started on his path of great deeds. It is something to remember as well. A greater destiny does not mean someone must be a hero. Just as many villains have great destinies I believe. From the description you gave that fellow Flügg you met with the inky aura is certainly one of those greater destiny villains. It takes a very dark heart to change an aura that way."

Yuki Nene nodded, "I understand. Not all greater destinies are heroes, and not all people with bright auras are Chi Masters. Why are you telling me this now?"

Hap Sing got serious, "For two reasons really. I wanted you to understand that Ming Na Jun and his son Ming Wa Fu are both greater destinies. I know from Ming Ran that the Ming family line likely carries the blood of Chi Masters, so it is likely that both of them are potentials who likely have not discovered their abilities yet. However, they still feel drawn to other greater destinies. I leave the village so they are not drawn to me and asking questions I would rather not answer to government officials."

Yuki Nene looked at the small home they were approaching and saw a young boy come running across the yard toward Hap Sing as she whispered, "What is the second reason?"

Hap Sing smiled, "Be careful not to be blinded when you look at Li Hung. He has performed many great deeds of heroism in his prime."

Wen Lu rushed up and began chattering at them, "Hap Sing, Hap Sing, dance to a merry tune! You are here. Mother was worried since you were gone on a longer trip this time. Who is this woman?"

Hap Sing laughed, "You are full of energy today. This woman is Yuki Nene. She will be staying with Li Hung."

Wen Lu stared at her a moment and then looked back at Hap Sing, "Is she some kind of giant? She's bigger than a man."

Hap Sing chuckled as Yuki Nene got a stern expression, "Nene is not a giant, but her people are a large people to be sure. Of course if you think about it they probably consider themselves quite normal and us people of Ran Li very short in comparison. Are you a dwarf then?"

Wen Lu thought for a moment in silence, "I'm going to be a warrior not a dwarf. I want to be big and strong like her one day."

As Wen Lu ran off toward the house to call his mother Hap Sing whispered to Yuki Nene, "Only through the mouths of children. Do you still think no one is noticing you here?"

Yuki Nene shook her head, "It seems like you're right on that point. We're not invisible in reality, just socially."

Hap Sing nodded in agreement as they approached the door. Wen Li stepped out just as they neared. She politely bowed before Hap Sing and Yuki Nene, and meekly turned to lead them into the home of Li Hung. Yuki Nene watched Hap Sing closely and saw his eyes following Wen Li with a look of concern.

Yuki Nene got the feeling that this was the woman mentioned by the Luck as the only competition in her way. A sly smile crossed Nene's features. It wouldn't be hard to outperform a meek little mouse like her. It was plain to her that the woman still pined for her lost husband, but that she didn't consider Hap Sing to be a romantic replacement, just a dear friend.

Hap Sing was harder to read. It wasn't lust she sensed in his attention. It seemed more like a mix of concern and guilt. The reason for the guilt was unclear though. Nene decided that staying on her current path of friendly attention was the right choice. She knew that she would have time to press her case. The competition as it were wasn't even trying to run the race.

Hap Sing spoke to Wen Li as they followed her inside, "How has he been Wen Li? I hope he has not been too much trouble."

Wen Li meekly spoke, "It has been no trouble at all Hap Sing. After all the help you have given us over the years, this is the least we can do for you. Li Hung is doing pretty well today. Li Hung has eaten his lunch, and was entertaining Wen Lu until I chased him outside to play. I didn't want him wearing Li Hung out."

Hap Sing asked, "Did you have enough food?"

Wen Li nodded, "There is plenty yet. I did not realize you would be gone so long this time though."

Hap Sing gave a weak smile, "I am sorry if you became worried on my behalf. I was visiting relatives I had not seen for a long while. There was a lot of catching up to do."

Wen Li nodded, "I understand it is hard to manage without family for so long."

Li Hung came into the main room from his back bedroom. Yuki Nene was surprised to see that he was a sizable man with much muscle yet little fat on his aging frame. Li Hung was dressed in a long robe of nice material if basic design. She would have guessed him to be seventy if asked, but not have figured him for one hundred and six.

Li Hung looked at Yuki Nene with a cautious eye before he spoke, "Nordlander I would guess, not a pure blooded one though. Seems like a mix of something else

I can't identify there. Not handy with a sword though, there is not enough callous on her hands. A trader then I would guess. Where did you find such a woman Hap Sing? I don't suppose she speaks the local tongue."

Yuki Nene noticed Wen Li blushing for a mysterious reason then spoke up herself, "I speak the Ran Li tongue as well as you Li Hung as I was born in Yokito as were my parents before me. I am second generation Ran Li and a citizen. I am no trader, yet I am not a warrior like you Li Hung. I do come from a people of warriors though, so we all know something of war."

Li Hung laughed with a hard edge, "War I doubt. Knowing about piracy and raiding is more like it."

Yuki Nene shrugged, "It is true that in hard times the Nordlanders are not beyond a bit of piracy and raiding, but the colony here in Ran Li is composed of honest traders."

Li Hung laughed again, "I like this one Hap Sing. She is not afraid of owning up to a truth about her people. A truth many of them would likely violently deny to outsiders like us. Why did you bring her here?"

Hap Sing bowed before Li Hung, "Village elder Li Hung. I humbly request that you allow Yuki Nene to dwell within your home. She is without a place to stay, and the weather will eventually grow cool after the summer is over."

Yuki Nene could see that there was a strange interplay going on in the room. Li Hung became visibly uncomfortable, as did Wen Li who subtly moved to quietly and unobtrusively leave Li Hung's home. Her flush of embarrassment was unexpected in Yuki Nene's experience.

Li Hung broke out into a loud voice which strangely did not match with his pained facial expression, "What kind of problem are you putting me into now? I put up with Wen Li and her child because you want me to look after them for you, now you want me to look after some barbarian little better than one of the wild races?"

Yuki Nene then watched Li Hung walk over to sit in a chair. It was strange that she could see tears starting to form in Li Hung's eyes, yet he also had a slight expression of relief on his face.

Li Hung also surprised Yuki Nene by his next statement, "Damn you Hap Sing don't treat me like that. You know how much it hurts me to yell at you so my master, my friend. Stand up straight I beg you. Don't abject yourself to me. I'll accept your gift and gladly."

Yuki Nene was surprised to see that Hap Sing was very uncomfortable as he spoke, "Once again I must remind you that I am no man's master. I needed an excuse to get Wen Li moving along home with Wen Lu. Yuki Nene here is a Chi Master as well."

Li Hung interrupted, "I know one of hers when I see them Hap Sing. She is a handmaid of the White Raven. I've been on too many battlefields to not recognize one standing in my own home. My time is close then?"

Hap Sing nodded with a tear coming down his cheek, "Your aura is still bright, but flickers even more than the last time I saw it. Soon the power of the Luck will eventually drain out, and your life will finally be allowed to end."

Li Hung nodded with a faint smile, "Then my debt is finally paid. It is good to know that I will be moving on soon. My life it has been too long, much too long. I'm very glad that you have brought along one of the White Raven's handmaids to start me on my long journey."

Yuki Nene spoke, "How did you know I was one of her chosen?"

Li Hung laughed bitterly, "Not many would recognize your Shadowine blood here. I am one of the few who has fought and killed their kind on the prime. They are vicious warriors, and without fear of death. I realize now I was foolish in my youth to engage them because the White Raven has spurned my prayers for death for these last sixteen years. I could not bear to request it of master Sing knowing how much it would hurt him to hear it."

Yuki Nene was surprised, "You are a worshiper of the White Raven then?"

Li Hung laughed, "What gave you that idea? I am just a practical man. I know the gods exist as well as the spirits. If you can not seek relief from the one, then your only option is to petition the other. I am not a worshiper of either, yet you seem to be dwelling along the line between both. A risky proposition achieving a balance between two powers like that."

Yuki Nene was confused, "I don't understand. I only serve the White Raven."

Li Hung smiled, "That may have been true in the past, but I suspect that is not so now. Hap Sing tends to keep things from people sometimes. Especially things he does not know for certain, but things he suspects about the Luck. Is that not true Sing."

Hap Sing looked away from Li Hung, "It is only an educated guess at best. There haven't been many instances to compare until now."

Li Hung looked over at Hap Sing as he replied, "Has she spoken with the Luck?"

Hap Sing nodded, "Such was her request. She had questions for it about her identity, and that of her father."

Li Hung looked at Yuki Nene, "Is this true girl? You asked it about your heritage? Did it know the answers to your question?"

Yuki Nene nodded, "It knew who I was, and who I was chosen to serve. It also knew my father was also a Shadowine and a servant of the White Raven who was directed to produce me to enter her service."

Li Hung nodded, "I see. So your mother was a worshiper of the White Raven already?"

Yuki Nene nodded, "Yes she was. I had never met the man who begot me on my mother, only the father who raised me as his daughter."

Li Hung looked at Hap Sing, "I can tell that what she says is true, but that she is not saying everything which happened between her and the Luck. Don't worry girl, I won't pry into your personal business more on that point. Feel free to keep your secrets neither Sing or I will question you further on it."

Yuki Nene pointed at Li Hung and questioned, "How is it that you know even this much? We have only just met each other for the first time."

Li Hung smiled without any humor in his gaze, "I need not answer your question girl. Now you know that we can all keep our secrets. What I know is up to me to decide to reveal. Just as it is for you to volunteer what you want about yourself. I shall not be freer with my secrets than you are with yours. Hap Sing is even more secretive than me."

Hap Sing intervened, "Please be nice Li Hung. You will scare the young lass."

Li Hung frowned, "Did she back away from talking with the Luck?"

Hap Sing shook his head, "No she did not."

Li Hung nodded, "Then no warning of mine could possibly scare her. She likely feels protected by her patron goddess, and does not fear death."

Hap Sing spoke quietly, "There are worse things than death."

Li Hung looked grimly at Yuki Nene, "Death to me would be like meeting an old friend. I am looking forward to that time."

Yuki Nene looked at Li Hung, "I think you mistake me. I did not come here to kill you."

Li Hung nodded, "I understand that well enough. It makes no sense to kill one who will die soon on their own. You are going to prepare my way though correct. Make sure the path is clear for me."

Yuki Nene gave a faint smile, "I can ask that boon of the White Raven if such is your request."

Li Hung smiled, "Then Sing has done well in providing for his disciple. I don't think the White Raven will deny you this request. She probably thinks I am long overdue, and is anxious to have me pass. Rumor has it that she is a stickler for keeping her books straight, and I don't think she will accept me missing an appointment a second time."

Yuki Nene frowned slightly, "If you do not worship her, then why do you know so much about the White Raven?"

Li Hung grinned, "You are not the only one to meet the Luck and have it answer questions. The Luck had to bargain with your goddess to extend my life past it's due. This much it has told me, and I am inclined to believe it. The price I have paid for that boon was service. This was both service to Ran Li, and service to Hap Sing. The time for that service is almost up because the Luck has obviously finally appointed a successor to me."

Yuki Nene looked at Li Hung with a cautious look in her eye, "I agreed to no bargain like that with the Luck."

Li Hung still grinned, "Yet here you are doing Hap Sing's bidding. You are doing what Hap Sing's requests even if Sing never required it of you."

Yuki Nene shook her head, "I am here of my own free will. I choose what will happen to me."

Li Hung bitterly laughed, "That is the illusion my dear. The dream held by us that we greater destinies have free will. Keep your illusion if it comforts you. I know I held onto that illusion for many years until my father died in battle as his destiny compelled him. Then I found the illusion was shattered and the meaning of greater destiny became clear. Our destinies are not greater because we choose them. Our destinies are greater because we surrendered choice for something more."

Yuki Nene pointed at Li Hung, "What of you then? I have heard it told that your destiny was very great. Yet here you are an old man feeble and awaiting death like any other."

Li Hung nodded, "Such is my destiny. I was to first protect this nation, and so I did. Then I was to shield and protect Hap Sing after the passing of my father from the role. Such I have been doing for more than half of my very long life. Although he will deny it I know that the Luck and Hap Sing as the avatar of the Luck are my master. I have not held illusions about it since my father died. I can not do anything but obey the commands I have been provided, even if I did not understand that I had been given them at the time. Finally at long last the Luck has seen fit to provide my relief."

Yuki Nene looked at Hap Sing in accusation, "Is what he is saying true?"

Hap Sing shrugged with a look of embarrassment, "I can not say. I do not hold you to do anything you don't wish. I don't feel like I am the master of anyone. If I were then Li Hung would have stopped calling me such long ago at my request."

Yuki Nene smiled with a smug satisfaction, "There you see. The Luck made no deals with me for such. I am my own person."

Li Hung nodded, "If you think so, then I can not likely change your mind. I am simply relating my many years of experience with being a servant of the Luck. It will likely come to your attention soon enough. I don't suppose you feel protective of Hap Sing by any chance?"

Yuki Nene smiled, "Hardly. I think he can protect himself well enough."

Li Hung nodded again, "There is no attraction to him then either I take it."

Yuki Nene's smile lessened, "That is a personal question I don't need to answer."

Li Hung noted her slight flush, "That's how it is then. It has made you attracted to him to guarantee his safety."

Yuki Nene flushed more, "I will not say that is so."

Hap Sing was flush as well, "That is why she is staying here. We have agreed to remain friends only."

Li Hung grinned again, "Did Hap Sing tell you about the spirit ribbons? I already imagine your aura approaches mine in intensity."

Hap Sing interrupted, "Your aura is still greater. The Luck did not enhance her power as yours was. She was already a natural prodigy before I came along."

Li Hung noticed Yuki Nene closing her eyes and spoke, "Open them carefully young miss. Don't hurt yourself looking."

Yuki Nene opened her eyes slowly into a squint as she looked at Li Hung, "That is the second brightest aura I've ever witnessed. The first was Hap Sing while he was in the dreaming. It flickers though. Like a bright flame before an occasional wind."

Li Hung nodded, "Thus I know my time is near. One day soon it will simply snuff out. Now that my replacement has been arranged it shouldn't be much longer."

Yuki Nene frowned, "I was not arranged as your replacement."

Li Hung smiled, "Yet your ribbon of fate is connected to Hap Sing. Isn't that true Hap Sing?"

Hap Sing ducked his head, "It's complicated. I'm not sure what is happening this time."

Li Hung nodded at Yuki Nene, "See, I told you. He knows a lot, but will not tell what he suspects. I suppose she is one of the most talented Chi Masters?"

Hap Sing spoke, "The others called her a natural prodigy. She can do things the others find hard or impossible with relative ease."

Li Hung shook his head, "Others? I have got to hear this tale. Just what did you get into back in our old home?"

Yuki Nene spoke, "The Luck did mention putting spirit ribbons on us and watching our progress. I did not understand what it meant by such a thing though. It seemed to indicate that it was magically monitoring our actions."

Hap Sing answered, "Since Li Hung is making a point of this, I will reveal what I know. I can see connections between beings on a spiritual level with my second sight. I suspect that other Chi Masters could learn this talent as well if they focused on it. Most can see the spirit forms of other Chi Masters. I can see the ribbon connecting their spirit guardian to their auras. There are other ribbons as well."

Yuki Nene thought a moment and asked, "What do the ribbons mean? What causes them?"

Hap Sing spoke carefully, "I have watched them form over time. Usually they start small as connections between friends. Then they grow more prominent over time as two fates become intertwined. This happens naturally to most people. Strong bonds such as husband and wife, or father and child form fairly quickly. A mother and child often are bonded by this connection at birth. Strong positive emotions seem to create the bonds faster than weak ones."

Yuki Nene nodded, "You can see these bonds between people?"

Hap Sing nodded, "Strong bonds are easiest to see, but even casual bonds can be spotted with effort. It is not like a normal use of the second sight though. You have to concentrate to make it happen. It wears me out pretty quickly if I attempt it too long."

Yuki Nene smiled, "I was wondering what you meant when you indicated that the second sight was tiring for you. I hadn't realized that you were looking so closely, or learning so much."

Hap Sing spoke, "Perhaps that is so. I don't know much else about these bonds or how the Luck creates or uses them."

 Chapter 11 135

Yuki Nene's smile diminished a bit, "What do you mean the Luck creates or uses them?"

Hap Sing gave a nervous smile, "I believe it can understand what someone knows through such a bond. You become like a book it can read. I don't think it can control you through such a connection, but it may well be able to learn anything you know, and base its actions on what it learns."

Yuki Nene began to sweat, "It's a good thing I was not exposed to it longer then. I would hate to think it made a strong connection to me and could read my mind."

Hap Sing had an uncomfortable expression, "Well, I kind of hate to tell you this then. What I told you about normal spirit connections taking time to grow and form, that doesn't apply to the Luck. It can make ribbon connections to anyone it meets, anyone mortal that is. I'm not sure if it applies to immortals as I haven't witnessed one with a connection to the Luck yet."

Yuki Nene looked at Hap Sing with a knowing look filling with dread, "You know already. Did it connect to me? What did it do? What can you see?"

Hap Sing gave a sheepish look toward Yuki Nene, "It chose you to link with. It chose everyone else with you at Hap Yang's house except Boku Sata."

Yuki Nene shook her head, "I didn't think it meant what it said about linking with people. I did not agree to this."

Hap Sing shrugged, "You didn't have to agree to it. Your fate became intertwined with mine. It is one of the reasons I don't summon the Luck very often. It manipulates people to serve it. I warned everyone of this before bringing forth the Luck."

Yuki Nene shook her head, "You said it would talk, and that it would try to convince. You made no mention of it reading our minds, or controlling our thoughts."

Hap Sing ducked down as Li Hung stood up and stepped forward, "Did it give you what you asked of it?"

Yuki Nene looked at the standing Li Hung, "What do you mean?"

Li Hung smiled, "I can guess this much. You asked for something more than what you wanted to know about your past. You asked for the Luck to perform something for you that only it could do correct."

Yuki Nene stood rigid a moment and then answered, "You are correct. I asked a favor of it. It granted my favor, but not before indicating an unknown price was to be attached."

Li Hung grinned, "Thus you are trapped by your own cleverness. You have to want something of the Luck for it to gain power over you. If you want for nothing, then it will ignore you as being not worth its effort. I wanted to live beyond fourteen. I wanted to help my father protect this nation. I got both things I wanted, and then I have been protecting Hap Sing since that time as my payment. As payments go it has not been bad. Hap Sing is a very reasonable and accommodating master after all."

Yuki Nene shook her head with a look of dejection, "Is it really like bargaining with an Oni? It seemed so reasonable and sensible at the time. At least until it suggested it had plans for me."

Hap Sing raised his head again, "What kind of plans?"

Yuki Nene looked at him, "It seemed like it was joking at the time. I didn't take what it said seriously. It seemed to indicate that it wanted me to settle down with someone and raise children."

Hap Sing looked at Li Hung and raised an eyebrow as he spoke, "You don't suppose it wants to . . ."

Li Hung raised his hands in the air, "You might as well tell her what you know. You are well aware that anything you say will not change the Luck's plans in anyway that bothers it. Usually it just seems to secure its position."

Hap Sing sighed, "The Luck has linked us together Nene. I can see the bond in addition to the bond with your spirit guardian, your bond with the White Raven, your faint bond with Boku Sata, and your bond with another."

Yuki Nene was surprised, "You can see that much?"

Hap Sing gave a faint grin, "There are more bonds that can be seen, but those are the ones which indicate a being of significance is connected. Your bond with Sata is weak and will likely break over time without renewal. Casual bonds of temporary comrades are that way. Your bond with the White Raven is strong, which I believe is an indication of both firm belief and divine favor. Your bond with the Luck and I is equally strong. The Luck can create such bonds very quickly when it wants."

Yuki Nene shook her head slightly, "We didn't talk that long in the orchard. I didn't know it could bond with a being with divine favor either."

Hap Sing shrugged, "If it helps you any, then you can know that it also bonded with Lo Arthur. If it can bond with a priest of a deity, then I don't think a chosen one is much different. In fact being a Chi Master probably made it relatively easy compared to Lo Arthur since I believe that Chi Masters are likely more prone to forming these connections. Also in the interest of openness you should understand that it bonded with you the first night we met. When it appeared to the assembled Chi Masters it bonded with each of them."

Yuki Nene thought a moment, "Wait. I thought you said it didn't bond with Boku Sata."

Hap Sing shrugged, "It can create and remove these bonds when it chooses to. I think it might need to be present to create them, yet not necessarily summoned. However, it can terminate them any time it wants whether it is present or not. At first the Luck bonded with Boku Sata. I imagine it read his character and found his addictions and problems made him of little use for its plans. It then likely broke that bond again when it no longer needed to know what Boku Sata was doing. Perhaps it was afraid another being would follow that bond back to me."

Yuki Nene was surprised, "It can be present without being summoned? You didn't mention it before now."

Hap Sing gave a weak grin, "I can feel it looking over my shoulder if you will at certain times. It feels as if the Luck is expecting certain things. It is never a good feeling because I think it indicates something of interest to the Luck is happening when it does so. It does not take control or make me do anything, but it does feel like it is watching intently. I know it can make bonds at those times such as when it did so with Lo Arthur in the market place."

Yuki Nene sat down in a chair with seemingly weak legs, "Yu Mai was right. You did do something to change Arthur."

Hap Sing shook his head, "No I didn't. I just failed to mention that the Luck tied his fate to mine. I did not want to alarm anyone at the time about it. It would not have likely changed the Luck's goal, but would have likely just made people unnecessarily concerned."

Li Hung spoke as he moved to sit down, "Don't worry about it young woman. While most people need strong positive emotions to form bonds over time, my guess is that the Luck can use any strong emotion. I know I personally felt fear in its presence. Do you recall any strong emotion when you met it?"

Yuki Nene ducked her head, "It was shame. It criticized my not preventing the accident which happened in the marketplace. I felt ashamed that it recognized and complimented my abilities while at the same time questioning my judgment to use them well. It tricked me. It threw a ruse at me and it tricked me."

Li Hung shook his head gently, "Don't worry yourself about it child. The Luck has its ways of getting what it wants. The pattern we have detected is that it forces a strong emotion to create a path for a bond to form. Then it later relies on mild mannered Hap Sing here to smooth over any harsh feelings. It is one of his specialties after all."

Yuki Nene gently nodded her head in contemplation, "I think I see it now. It makes more sense. Do you think other beings can do something similar?"

Li Hung nodded, "I think it is likely that the other tailed beasts can do so. I don't think it works for the gods though. They are less adept at spiritual manipulation, just as the tailed beasts are less adept at material manipulation. Each kind of power has its own specialties after all. Then each individual on either side has their own sub-specialties as well. I have learned the Luck does business as an information broker mainly. It is very good at manipulating enormous stores of information very rapidly."

Yuki Nene whispered, "The time stop."

Li Hung and Hap Sing looked at each other then they looked back at Yuki Nene as Li Hung asked, "What did you say?"

Yuki Nene looked back at them, "When I was speaking with the Luck it said that it had stopped time for us. For everything except us really, it indicated I might learn such a thing with study myself. It spoke with me while time stood still. That is how it can access so much information. I think it holds time in place until it can read what it wants to know."

Li Hung looked at Hap Sing before he spoke, "I think this is something new. It has not indicated an ability to do something like this before. It is learning new tricks. I don't think that is how it learns information Yuki. It has a very large intelligence, and likely can remember quite easily everything it has ever learned. It is also rumored to operate a very large intelligence gathering organization."

Hap Sing noted, "It learns what you know through your bond. It doesn't control you like a puppet if that is what you fear, but it learns what you are doing. I expect that you are a very valuable asset given your placement in the White Raven's ranks of her favored ones. What your goddess wants and directs of you the Luck will know. You have become its spy."

Li Hung gave a feeble grin, "Welcome to the club. See the director there if you have anymore questions. I am late for my nap, and it looks like I am going to be busy in my final days bringing you up to speed as my replacement."

Hap Sing nodded, "I should go now. I want to check on my boat and home."

Yuki Nene stood up, "I will go with you."

Hap Sing shook his head, "Please stay with Li Hung and see that he gets his rest. I will return in the late afternoon to prepare dinner."

Hap Sing paused outside the house and listened outside the window as Li Hung spoke to Yuki Nene, "So young woman, I have to ask this much of you. Think about it carefully before you answer, and answer you must. How did you feel when you first met Hap Sing? What did he mean to you?"

Yuki Nene hesitated, "I don't understand your question."

Li Hung spoke out loudly, "Just answer it, and don't think about why I am asking it. Give me the truth of it girl. It's very important."

Yuki Nene thought about it, "I didn't know him. I guess I felt shy, and awkward. He was something beyond my expectations."

Li Hung then barked out, "Was it after the Luck appeared that you first felt compelled to protect and love him?"

Yuki Nene spoke in a flustered manner, "I never said I felt those things. I told you I didn't already."

Li Hung chuckled, "I am no fool and neither is Hap Sing. Your lips might be saying no, but you are young and don't understand yet that to a practiced eye your body gives away your real feelings even if you don't admit it. When did you realize those feelings?"

Yuki Nene spoke hesitantly, "After I followed him to the dreaming the first time. That was before the Luck appeared to us."

Li Hung breathed a sigh of relief, "I was hoping you'd say that. It means your feelings are genuine, and not manufactured. You are in your right mind then."

Yuki Nene replied back, "What could you have done if you discovered I wasn't in my right mind?"

Li Hung spoke in a no nonsense tone, "I would have continued my job of protecting Hap Sing and slain you like the rest of the White Raven's and other deities and powers minions sent to interfere with him. A greater destiny like me doesn't get assigned to protection duty without good cause. As a minion of the White Raven I suppose you are not squeamish about doing the same when necessary."

Yuki Nene was shocked, "You've slain other beings to protect Hap Sing?"

Li Hung spoke in a matter of fact tone, "Why does that surprise you any? Are you not prepared to do the same?"

Yuki Nene hesitated, "I had not thought about it. It did not seem like it would be an issue."

Li Hung's voice was hard edged, "Miss Yuki I have literally slain thousands of beings to protect him. We have guaranteed the stability of this nation for two generations through my father's actions and my own. Not because this nation meant anything to us, but because he means everything to us. That was the price demanded by the Luck for granting our request, and we have paid that price without hesitation or regret."

Yuki Nene spoke, "You mentioned Shadowine being slain. Do you know if one named Rexis was among them."

Li Hung spoke, "I take it that was your father then. That should have been about twenty one years ago or so if my memory still serves. So yes, it was probably your father I slew. He had been sent by the White Raven to test my defenses I'm sure as the Shadowine rarely worship other gods. If I recall properly he had the abilities of a Chi Master as well though I didn't learn his name until now. He was to probe whether Hap Sing or the Luck was vulnerable to assault perhaps, or whether the extension on my life was wearing thin. That would have been the last time she tested my resolve or abilities. The others however have been much slower to give up. Just six months ago I had to slay seven old ones, and their twilight elf slaves. It was another probe from the goddess Litha I am certain."

Yuki Nene spoke with a touch of shock, "You have been killing the chosen minions of deities?"

Li Hung laughed harshly, "I've been doing that for most of my life girl. There is nothing too shocking about it really. The Luck has enemies. Enemies who really don't like what the Luck is doing with Hap Sing. Some beings of its kind are enemies, and even some gods are enemies."

Yuki Nene questioned, "You can defeat such things?"

Li Hung asked, "It is not much different than your recent confrontation."

Yuki Nene questioned, "What do you mean?"

Li Hung spoke, "I was lead to believe by the Luck that you can handle yourself. You dispatched that vampire leader quite handily. Even the priest was challenged by them."

Yuki Nene asked, "The Luck told you this?"

Li Hung responded, "Not directly you understand. It doesn't speak with me directly anymore. It only shows me visions in my dreams. I saw you fighting to protect Hap Sing. I saw the passion and defiance in your eyes. I have to understand the source of it before I let you become my successor."

Yuki Nene spoke, "What if I had taken your head off like that Vampire?"

Li Hung responded in a matter of fact manner, "You could have tried. You would have failed like the rest. The Luck did not bargain with the White Raven for my life. It did not need to. It bargained instead with another to extend my existence for as long as it needed."

Yuki Nene spoke with a touch of outrage, "You are still on her books as one who should have died?"

Li Hung laughed, "Ninety-two years ago. I think she finally gave up trying when she figured out what the Luck had done to me which prevents her."

Yuki Nene's voice shuddered, "It made you one of the undead?"

Li Hung chucked, "Certainly not. That would have made her even more upset with the Luck. The Luck got Number Two to change the rules for me. I was made temporarily immortal until Number Two changes the rules again. I am alive, I can feel pain, and I can be hurt. I just can't die. My body heals extremely rapidly from even normally fatal or even catastrophic damage. I've even had to cut my way out of the insides of three dragons you understand. It was not a minor task."

Yuki Nene questioned, "Number Two? I don't understand?"

Li Hung's voice became more serious, "The Godkiller is the common name used for it. It is the two tailed beast which created the very concept of death, and which powers the plane of shadow, just as the Luck Powers the elemental planes of fire, earth, air, and water among others. It took your goddess White Raven nearly seventy years before she figured out that Number Two was responsible for my condition, and that any attempt to slay me was ultimately a futile one. The rules of death haven't applied to me since I was fourteen years old. I was my father's best secret weapon in the war. Any highly dangerous single foe our army encountered was dealt with by me as the lone special force."

Yuki Nene seemed shocked, "The Godkiller made you immortal?"

Li Hung nodded, "You need not mention this to Hap Sing. He is a pacifist you see. He is also a much better person than I. It is why he needs the protection so much. He will not kill even to protect his own life."

Yuki Nene asked, "He doesn't know about you?"

Li Hung spoke, "I think he understands what my role has been, but I don't think he likes it. We don't speak of it much anymore. It only causes arguments between us. I do what I must. That is part of the reason I left being the magnet for attention in the army and settled in Li Chan village. I don't draw as much attention here, and only the divine and powers based assailants have enough resources to locate us under Hap Sing's net. It has been a relief actually."

Yuki Nene spoke with surprise, "Your aura is so bright . . ."

Li Hung spoke with a lighter tone, "So that any beings seeking the avatar of the Luck mistake me for such. I am filled with its power after all. The Luck prefers to keep its aura damped down using Hap Sing's abilities to suppress it you see. The protector is the trap drawing the assailants away from their intended target."

Yuki Nene spoke with unease in her voice, "The Godkiller though. It is no wonder the White Raven herself has ceased her assault. It is rumored to be a most terrible being."

Li Hung chuckled, "I probably shouldn't tell you this then."

Yuki Nene questioned with hesitation, "What are you going to tell me that I would not like?"

Li Hung spoke then laughed, "If I understood my dream correctly, then you were standing on Godkiller the night you fought Flügg. I dreamed of the Luck and it talking although I could not understand the language they were speaking. Then I saw it attacking your foes that evening."

Yuki Nene spoke with confusion in its voice, "I did not see it that night. How could I have been standing on it?"

Li Hung spoke simply, "It created the plane of shadows. The very place your goddess calls a piece of her home. Did you examine your shadow closely by any chance?"

Yuki Nene was shocked, "The strange shadows which enveloped the wraiths and the fleeing vampires."

Li Hung chuckled, "It also locked all of those goblins in place by their shadows."

Yuki Nene questioned, "The Godkiller works for the Luck then?"

Li Hung's voice was non-committal, "Who knows for certain? Those kinds of beings change sides very rapidly I believe. They generally only serve their own agendas and interests. It is unlikely they have a permanent alliance of any kind as I understand such things."

Yuki Nene asked, "Could you hear my conversation with the Luck in your dreams?"

Li Hung replied, "I got the gist of your desires. I will give you the same answer the Luck gave. Hap Sing having a romantic attachment to you will either happen or not based on the Luck's plans. I would not expect you to believe it, but if it does not object, then there is no reason I will."

Yuki Nene asked, "There is one thing I do not understand. If you have immortality why do you desire your death?"

Li Hung laughed bitterly, "That is a point of view that could only be held by someone young. Our spirits are not well suited to spending too long on the prime. Mine is past ready to move on to the next stage. Any human granted an immortal body and greater destiny in the manner I have would feel the same. It isn't natural. Hap Sing because of the Luck seems to be an exception to this, but unless you have divine traits your time on the prime in one form is limited. Even the gods don't spend too much time on the prime because of the drain it puts on their spirits and how it shortens their life span."

Yuki Nene commented with a note of uncertainty, "The gods are immortal. They don't have a limited lifespan."

Li Hung spoke, "Think about it. Something created death. The two tailed beast of shadow. The gods filled in the details of how their rules worked for the material world, but the spiritual world is still under the control of the spirits. The two sets of powers have to cooperate at some level. They do this through compromise. So in order to have material forms that wear out and release weary spirits, there needs to be death."

Yuki Nene spoke, "This was created by the two tailed beast you say. Then why does it not collect the spirits of the dead?"

Li Hung chuckled, "Now you understand why it is called Godkiller. It does collect the powerful spirits when it is their time to release from the material. It leaves the lesser destinies to which ever deity wants the job. It can't be bothered to worry about the organization and disposition of such. Since the gods need the worshipers, it allows them to pick who gets to sort out the spirits and assign them to the gods."

Yuki Nene spoke, "So you are saying the White Raven?"

Li Hung spoke firmly, "Is the current deity elected as trustworthy enough to fill the position. Her neutrality and fairness is well recognized among the other deities except her rival for the position Mortis. Well I tire for now. I will lie down and take a nap. If you try to kill me just understand I will only wake up in a foul mood and return the favor to you. I don't think your goddess has granted you immortality though. It won't go so well for you if you try."

Yuki Nene asked, "Not that I would do so, but what if I attacked Hap Sing while you slept?"

Li Hung spoke menacingly, "I would not recommend trying it. You had many better chances before you came here. However, I think you would quickly find out whether the ribbon on you gives the Luck any power over you. It may not control your limbs like a puppet, but I haven't ever conclusively figured out if it can make us think what it wants us to think. No test I could devise seemed to present conclusive proof or disproof."

Yuki Nene spoke, "Could you tell me one more thing before you rest?"

Li Hung spoke in a weary tone, "Go ahead with one more question."

Yuki Nene asked, "You have known him for most of your long life. Has the presence of the Luck changed Hap Sing in that time?"

Li Hung's voice was thoughtful, "That is a hard thing to figure. It certainly has not been a rapid change, but you have to understand that the Luck has been a part of Hap Sing since the day after he was born. They became accustomed to their shared existence a very long time ago I would think. Do you know that the Luck used to be able to independently manifest on the Prime before it merged with Hap Sing. Now it seemingly has to wait for Hap Sing to allow it to do so. The other thing which is curious is not that Hap Sing has changed dramatically, but the Luck seems to be changing over time. It is showing new capabilities like the time stop you mentioned. It is also much more reasonable and mellow when dealing with mortals. Hap Sing's kindness and patience seems to be influencing its behavior. The way it handled you was much more kindly than the way it dealt with my father and me in our day. One thing you should not mistake though. While there are distinct differences in personality, don't think that they are two independent beings. They are one being with two personalities, maybe even three personalities."

Yuki Nene spoke, "I don't understand, I have only seen the two personalities."

Li Hung smiled, "You didn't notice the difference in the dreaming?"

Yuki Nene spoke, "He was kind and reserved as usual. No wait. Now that you mention it there was a certain confidence when he was there. He was relaxed and assured that he knew his place. That is something no Chi Master in the dreaming would normally ever feel. I felt safe with Hap Sing in the dreaming. It had always felt risky and hazardous on all of my other previous solo visits."

Li Hung spoke with a touch of levity, "That is the third personality I speak about. I call it the enlightened Cricket personality. That is the one which made you fall in love and desire to protect him."

Yuki Nene spoke, "How did you know this?"

Li Hung answered with sincerity, "It was the same for me when I was in the dreaming with him for the first time. I felt like he was another father to me whom I would do anything to protect. The feeling has not left me since that time."

Chapter 12 Remembrance

It was a little over three weeks later that Hap Sing stood next to the grave of Li Hung with a borrowed shovel in hand. All of the village elders except Yong Mai attended his burial along with their families and several of the other older village residents. Wen Li and Wen Lu were also in attendance yet it seemed like they felt out of place in this situation.

Wen Li had been surprised to discover that Li Hung's house and a sizable amount of money had been willed to her and her son Wen Lu. With Li Hung's passing they had suddenly gone from being the poorest people in the village to nearly the richest. While they were not as rich as a noble would be, they would be able to live comfortably on the money they inherited. Perhaps they could even afford an education for Wen Lu.

When she was informed of this Wen Li had raised objections to Lu Po saying that Hap Sing had been his friend and deserved the money. Lu Po had shaken his head and stated it was Hap Sing who had insisted to Li Hung that Wen Li and Wen Lu needed money more than he did. Wen Li had finally accepted that some kind of good luck was following them after their bad luck.

Personally Hap Sing didn't want for money given his frugal life, and in particular did not want the money that Li Hung had made through bloody conflict as a General in the Ran Li army. They had remained friends in spite of their differences, but Hap Sing still didn't approve of the methods employed by Li Hung. However, he also could not help but feel guilty and responsible for Li Hung's actions. If he had allowed Li Hung to die as a fourteen year old boy as fate would have dictated then this would not have happened.

Hap Sing also acknowledged that the Luck had more to do with the death wrought by Li Hung than himself. At every juncture Hap Sing had discouraged any violence on his behalf. However, even Hap Sing had to admit to himself privately that without the interference of the Luck in Li Hung's destiny he would likely be dead by now. Li Chan had helped to interpret that dream of the wild jungle when they were children, and the truth of it was that he needed to hide from the enemies of the Luck. Hap Sing also knew that the Luck had preferred to have a decoy available for when hiding would not suffice.

Lu Po stood before the assembled villagers at Li Hung's grave and spoke, "I am glad to see those of you here today. I know that Li Hung was a very private person. For many of you he was an institution as one of the village elders and the oldest elder as well at one hundred and six years of age. He was always dispassionate in discussion and to the point in his discourse. He was gruff about discussing his past before our village, and only the oldest of us can recall when he first came to this village over fifty years ago."

Lu Po's gaze traveled to each of the other village elders for a moment and he spoke again, "Many except the eldest here likely did not know that Li Hung was not originally from Li Chan village. Few of even the eldest knew that he was actually the son of the famous General Li Chan the namesake of our village. Li Hung fought in the great war beside his father, and was there when his father's great sacrifice to save our nation was made. After his father Li Chan's sacrifice Li Hung himself became the general leading the forces of Ran Li. Those forces drove the remaining invading rabble from Ran Li, and General Li Hung served as the military commander of the Ran Li army for nearly two decades after that point."

Lu Po looked briefly at Hap Sing and then focused on the mound of newly turned dirt at his feet as he spoke, "That was the kind of man he was; a man who did not avoid his responsibility, a man who served the people wisely, a man who did what he thought was necessary to protect his nation and it's people. In addition to being a leader of men the records also state that Li Hung was an unparalleled warrior. Under the command of his father Li Hung grew a reputation as an unbeatable foe. The enemies of Ran Li were said to quail at hearing of his approach."

Lu Po looked over at Wen Li next, "Yet for all of the fearsome nature the records depict about Li Hung, we people of the village named for his father knew a different man. Certainly it is true that Li Hung was a private person. He never wanted people to know of the glorious deeds of his past. He came here to live a quiet life in his retirement from service. Li Hung was a humble person who did not think that wars make men great. In our private discussions together he said to me several times that it is what they do in times of peace which define a man. How they treat their fellow neighbors. How they help their community to survive and thrive."

Lu Po looked again at Hap Sing briefly before looking at Wen Li again, "Li Hung was a generous man as well. He has left money to help several poor families in Li Chan. To one family in particular he left a sum which will keep them comfortable in difficult times. Li Hung could have lived a wealthy life in Yokito when he retired as the General in change of the Ran Li army. Instead he chose a frugal life away from the politics of the capital. After several years of living here he volunteered to serve on the counsel of elders. Like all of us he took no payment for this service. His was a voice of reason and compassion on the counsel. Never was he prone to personal conflict or discord with his fellow villagers. He always sought to find a workable solution to any problems faced."

Lu Po looked at Hap Sing as he spoke, "Li Chan was also a loyal friend. He knew that honest people with good intent in their hearts were the strength of any community. He once called them the best kind of people, those people of good intent and the will to see good deeds done. At times he would let some item from his past slip and in his humble way would reveal that he still sought to achieve that lofty goal himself."

Hap Sing was dried eyed as Lu Po spoke the eulogy for Li Hung. Hap Sing had cried as he dug the grave in private, and he continued to cry as he filled it after placing the ceremonial urn with Li Hung's ashes inside. As he listened to the eulogy he knew that the sadness would continue for a while, but that the tears for his friend were finished.

The headstone was still being crafted. Hap Sing had requested that it read: Li Hung son of Li Chan loyal friend, wise counselor, and protector of the people. Lu Po agreed to make sure that such would be arranged with monies from Li Hung's estate.

After the eulogy was finished the villagers walked down the hill toward the village. Lu Po walked over to Hap Sing with Yong Mai's son Yong Ran following him. Lu Po looked at Hap Sing with sympathy in his eyes.

Lu Po spoke quietly, "I am sorry for your loss Hap Sing. I hate to press the issue, but now that Li Hung has passed on I was curious about your plans."

Hap Sing looked over at Yong Ran, "How is your mother doing? I notice that she did not make it to the service today."

Yong Ran responded, "It is kind of you to ask. The news is only bad these days it seems. Her health is declining. I do not expect she will last the year. I am to officially take over her position on the counsel once she passes, but I am filling her duties already."

Hap Sing looked at Lo Po, "Has he been told then?"

Lu Po nodded, "Yes he was told by his mother last year."

Yong Ran spoke, "I hardly understood what she was telling me at first, but then I recalled that you have always been this way since my childhood. My mother said you were possessed by a great spirit, and did not age as normal men do. I can see the truth of that now. If you don't mind my asking, then how old are you now?"

Hap Sing shrugged, "My one hundred and fiftieth birthday was about four weeks ago. I spent it with the descendants of my mother's youngest sister in Hung Chan Village."

Lu Po spoke, "That is also something I wanted to mention. Word has been circulating of trouble there recently. It seems a large fire occurred, and the bodies of several goblins, two unknown men, and the village militia chief were found there recently. On the night of the fire there were also several reports by people claiming to have seen a large dragon. The god priest in that village claims the dragon came to bring the word of his god there. He also says the dragon slew the wicked, but that they could not save their militia chief in time."

Hap Sing nodded, "I had heard as much when I was there, but I did not witness it happening."

Lu Po shrugged, "I did not suppose that you had. Word has also gone around that an unusual female foreigner who is tall with blond hair was an associate of their militia chief. Some people are speculating that she may have been mixed up in that mess over there as she was said to have disappeared the same night."

Hap Sing nodded, "Her name is Yuki Nene. She was born in Yokito, but she comes from the Nordlander colony there. I brought her here to look after Li Hung in his final days. She will need a place to stay now that Wen Li has inherited Li Hung's home. Might I suggest you consider taking her on to look after Yong Mai in her final days Yong Ran? I hear she is very good at dealing with those at the end of their life."

Yong Ran asked, "Why would that be?"

Hap Sing faintly smiled, "She is a disciple of the White Raven, although not a god priest thankfully. You won't have to worry about her trying to convert Yong Mai in her final days, but she will know how to make Yong Mai's time of passing more comfortable."

Lu Po interjected, "First a famous general, and then a disciple of the death goddess. You certainly attract an odd group of people Hap Sing. Is there anything else I should know?"

Hap Sing looked serious for a moment, "You will not like to hear it, but it might be best to prepare you."

Lu Po placed a hand up to his temple and rubbed it a moment before asking, "What bad news is it this time Hap Sing?"

Hap Sing took a deep breath, and exhaled it slowly before continuing, "It seems that various things have been trying to capture me over the years. One of those things showed up in Hung Chan valley while I was there. It brought a force of many goblins and undead to achieve this task."

Lu Po spoke, "Is this another sign the bad times are returning?"

Hap Sing shrugged, "I don't know for certain, but it seems likely. I've also had some candid conversations with Li Hung before he passed away. It seems that many things of a similar nature have tried to track me down over the years. He had been seeking them out and slaying them all this time without my knowledge. Li Hung fully believed that this Yuki Nene was sent to replace him in this duty."

Lu Po questioned, "Who sent her to replace him?"

Hap Sing spoke, "I would say the Luck did. She made a bargain with it, although I don't know the nature of the bargain she made."

Lu Po raised his eyebrows, "You summoned the Luck for a minion of a deity? Is that not a risky endeavor? Won't they report you as a Chi Master to the authorities?"

Hap Sing nodded, "It is risky indeed, but I summoned the Luck for several Chi Masters. It seems that the Luck considers Yuki Nene to be the most talented one around of the current generation."

Lu Po's expression was surprised, "She's a Chi Master and a disciple of a divine being? I did not think such a thing could happen."

Hap Sing nodded, "It seems at least the goddess of death doesn't care about whether a disciple is a Chi Master or a priest."

Lu Po thought a moment more, "What have you brought upon us? This will take careful consideration. What about the other Chi Masters you mentioned?"

Hap Sing spoke, "Most of them have dispersed from Hung Chan. It seems the Luck has made a bargain with the priest of Palnor there. He will seek to change the laws restricting the use of Chi magic."

Lu Po questioned, "How can a village priest achieve such a thing?"

Hap Sing replied, "He will be promoted quickly after the dragon took him to Yokito and told the priests of his religion there to put him in charge. It seems the dragon really was a divine manifestation after all."

Yong Ran marveled, "Is such a thing possible for the Luck to achieve?"

Lu Po laughed, "If you had ever met it, then you wouldn't question what might be achievable by the Luck. I have no problem believing that it could bully a god into doing its bidding if it so desired."

Hap Sing turned serious, "If what I overheard is true, then there is another problem."

Lu Po noticed his look was serious and got a frown of his own, "What is that Hap Sing?"

Hap Sing spoke quietly, "If I am to believe what the Luck told the Chi Masters, then it called me the greatest Chi Master that would ever be. It seems that I can not deny my abilities to myself any longer. So it seems that with the passing of Li Hung I should not deny it to you any longer either. Personally I don't believe that Li Hung was correct and Yuki Nene was provided as my protector. I think my childhood is almost over and I am to instruct Yuki Nene as her teacher. In terms of power I don't think I will ever be surpassed. Yet in her mere twenty-one years of life she already has accomplished much more than I have in one hundred and fifty years. There is much she could achieve with the correct guidance."

Lu Po nodded, "So Li Hung has passed on his mantle of responsibility to you."

Hap Sing ducked his head, "I have hidden from it for too long, and people have suffered because of it. As you said in Li Hung's eulogy the best of us look after their communities."

Lu Po agreed, "I said that because Li Hung has always considered you the best of us. He has told us elders that you did not seek to take from or harm another being. You are content with the results of your labor and having enough. Don't sell yourself short Hap Sing. Even the learned Ming Na Jun recognized you as wiser than most when he saw you bargaining for enough instead of as much as possible. You have been selfless in many ways that make the rest of us who know you want to be better people because of knowing you."

Yong Ran spoke, "I will bring your offer to have your friend help with things around the house to my mother. As you know my mother can be a difficult person lately, so I can not guarantee she will accept."

Hap Sing faintly smiled, "Just let her know that I would appreciate it. I will come over with her to your mother's house later."

After returning to the village Hap Sing spotted Yuki Nene walking through the market before she saw him. Hap Sing noticed that looking at her this way without any consciousness on her part of being observed that she lacked a lot of what he thought of as her usual outward confidence. She seemed as shy and reserved as the first time he had met her. There was also a hint of loneliness and loss on her part. Even though her time with Li Hung had been relatively brief, his passing seemed to have disturbed her.

Hap Sing walked into her view and watched her visage noticeably change. Her face seemed to light up, and her demeanor turned into a friendly and positive one. Hap Sing made a mental note to pay attention to the fact that Nene was more complex than the impression she chose to portray. It was unfortunately easy for anyone to accept her at face value, and he understood doing so would be a disservice to her as a person.

Yuki Nene spoke first, "So how did the burial go? That did not come out right. I guess I mean to ask is everyone doing fine?"

Hap Sing nodded, "Li Hung's cremated remains are laid to rest. Lu Po performed a suitable eulogy. It was short and factual as is the tradition in Li Chan village. I think Li Hung would have approved."

Yuki Nene began walking beside Hap Sing as she asked, "Wen Li has shown up at her new home. I guess I will be finally moving in with you. I have my belongings ready. There isn't much so I should not take up much room."

Hap Sing gave her a cautious look, "Let me say something about that Nene. I had a discussion with Lu Po the lead village elder after the burial. Your presence has not gone unnoticed in town. The rumors of the events which happened in Hung Chan valley have also begun to circulate including a description of the missing female outlander who was friends with the dead militia chief."

Hap Sing noticed a frightened look pass her face quickly to be replaced by a neutral expression before Yuki Nene spoke, "I suppose that means you think I need to leave here as well then."

Hap Sing shook his head, "I think staying in Li Chan village will be fine. As I said before the people here are not likely to pry, or to divulge other people's business to any outsiders who may come asking."

Yuki Nene's face began to light up as she spoke, "That's great. You can take me to your house and I will cook you some lunch."

Hap Sing shook his head, "That however would be a problem. Your presence living with me now would draw attention to me here. I get by here mainly by not being noticed much. I am just a part of the background that no one pays any attention. Unfortunately for the moment you stand out, and you being near me for too long a time would make me stand out as well."

Yuki Nene had a contemplative look for a moment, "You aren't asking me to leave, but at the same time you haven't asked me to stay with you either. I take it you have something else in mind."

Hap Sing gave a faint smile, "If you will accommodate my wishes, then I do have something in mind. The eldest remaining village elder on the counsel is Yong Mai. Her health is declining, and her son Yong Ran has been taking over her duties as village elder in her name. Taking on her duties, the care of the household, and the care of his mother is a bit of a strain for Yong Ran. I have asked him to consider taking you in to assist with the house and his mother."

Yuki Nene had a brief look of disappointment mingled with some other unclear emotion as she answered, "I am to care for the elderly again? You were not there. You don't understand what it was like at the end with Li Hung. It was not as it is supposed to be. I don't like to talk about it even."

Hap Sing looked at her with concern, "Did something happen? You didn't mention it before. Was Li Hung abusive?"

Yuki Nene shook her head and wiped droplets of sweat from her brow, "It wasn't him. I failed my goddess. I was prepared to guide his spirit to the White Raven like a disciple should. Then she came for him."

Hap Sing was confused, "Who? Who came for him?"

Yuki Nene turned a touch pale as she spoke, "She looked like a girl, an adolescent Ran Li girl dressed in a gown of black. Her hair was black and she had luminous eyes like great cat. One moment I sat beside Li Hung's bed preparing him to have the White Raven accept his spirit, and the next moment this girl was standing at the foot of his bed. For a moment this girl just stared at him, and his eyes opened wide at seeing her."

Yuki Nene's eyes began to tear up, "I did something I should not have. I used my second sight to look at this child. It had no spirit that I could see, and yet both Li Hung and I could see it standing there. He began whispering faintly. It was so faint I could not hear what he was saying. However, the girl at the foot of the bed obviously could hear his words. It is what she said which disturbed me the most. Her voice was clear and emotionless as she said, 'It is much too late for that Li Hung. No minion of hers can prevent what must happen. You accepted the Luck's offer of a longer life. The Luck bargained with me to provide you temporary immortality until your replacement was found. The time of the first protector is over. The time of the teacher is to begin. Now my price is to be paid. Your spirit goes with me.'"

Yuki Nene's tears rolled down her cheeks as she continued, "I moved to stand to challenge this girl, and I saw that an identical girl stood beside me. The girl beside me placed her hand upon my shoulder, but I did not feel it on my body. I felt it touch my spirit. I was locked in my chair and unable to stand. Both of the identical girls spoke in unison to me then saying, 'Yuki Nene you can not interfere with this. The time of the teacher is to begin. My services are not required for this next phase as the divine and the powers are in turmoil. Their focus shall turn elsewhere until the new rules are determined. You should know that your life is a mortal one. No protection of personal immortality will be extended to you by me or your goddess. The time of the first protector is complete. The time of the second protector is not yet come. The White Raven will not hold any failure here against you. I am not a being any of her minions could interfere with and survive. More I should not say at this time.'"

Hap Sing placed his arm around Yuki Nene's back in a comforting hug as he spoke, "I failed to predict that was what would happen at Li Hung's end. I'm sorry you were put through that. I know that dealing with the powers can be trying at times."

Yuki Nene dried her tears with her hand and continued, "As I sat in the chair I saw that a third identical girl was lying on top of Li Hung looking down into his eyes. That's when I could see it. It was not that the girls didn't have a spirit. It was that they didn't actually have material form. They were comprised of very densely compacted spirit. So dense as to seem solid to the second sight and to normal vision, but they were immaterial which was why I could not feel the touch of the one except through my spirit. The one lying on Li Hung spoke quietly to him. I heard her say, 'It is time to go home Li Hung.' Then she placed a kiss on his forehead and his bright aura disappeared. The girl on top of him and the one at the foot of the bed disappeared as well. Only the one beside me remained, along with the lifeless body of Li Hung."

Hap Sing rubbed her back briefly and gave her another squeeze as he spoke, "I think you did well Nene. Many people could not have managed being in that position. I think you were the right person to be there anyway. If I had been present, then it is hard to say what might have happened."

Yuki Nene nodded as she finished her tale, "I looked at the girl standing beside me with tears in my eyes. I plead with her to tell me what would happen with Li Hung's spirit. Her eyes were cold, but she leaned in to whisper in my ear, 'You can only ever tell Hap Sing of what I am going to say. You will know when it is the right time to do so. Li Hung's spirit has returned to the dreaming as is befitting all the great spirits. It will be purified through the dreaming, and returned to the cycle again when it is time. It is better this way. His spirit will not be a bargaining chip between the petty gods. Since you are a Chi Master and a servant of the White Raven when your time comes I will appear to offer you a chance to chose between your options of going into her direct service, or joining the spirits in the dreaming. As you are also a great spirit such choices are within my power to grant. Before you think it is a bad deal, this is the same thing which happens to the dying gods. I bring their spirits back to the dreaming. That is why many of them fear me, and call me unpleasant names like Godkiller. You should understand that I do not take any spirits before it is the right time, nor do I extend any spirit beyond the time required by necessity. I know these things far better than any of the dozens of deities which have served as the gods and goddesses of death so far. Trust me that my measurements are far more accurate than theirs could possibly ever be.' After that the girl lifted her hand from my shoulder and disappeared as if she had never been there."

Hap Sing gave a faint smile, "That is good news then. Perhaps Li Hung will come to visit me again someday. We did not always agree about his methods, but we remained friends regardless."

Yuki Nene put on a brave smile, "Li Hung had told me that he thought of you as a second father. A kindly father different from the stern father he grew up serving under. The funny thing is that he said your disapproval was much more difficult to face of the two. It was why he left the army and entered into a more pedestrian life alongside you."

Hap Sing nodded, "Li Hung is like a son to me as well. I did not begrudge his father's time with him, but I was glad that I could have my time as well. I'm surprised he disliked my disapproval more than Li Chan's. Li Chan was a hard taskmaster for all of those who served under him."

Yuki Nene had a contemplative look, "I think I can understand him. Your disapproval comes in the form of a humble righteous attitude of displeasure which makes the subject question their actions I would think. I suspect Li Chan's disapproval came in the form of an unpleasant punishment quickly suffered, and just as quickly forgotten."

Hap Sing smiled more, "I see. What about your own parents?"

Yuki Nene laughed lightly, "I was a princess of the Nordlanders. I never suffered from disapproval or punishment from my parents or of my people when I was in their care. It is one of several reasons that I chose to leave the colony really. It was difficult to see the real world through that filter they kept putting in front of me. When I announced my decision to travel that was the first time anyone back home voiced displeasure regarding my choices, but I promised to return when I was better suited to advise and lead our people. Frankly speaking, I believe they were secretly relieved. I think it was possible I was a rotten brat in my behavior back then. My years away have opened my eyes about how normal people are treated, and especially how outsiders are usually looked on with suspicion and distrust."

Hap Sing nodded, "Your parents were dead by then?"

Yuki Nene looked serious, "Yes. All three of them had passed, although I never knew about my biological father until my mother told me of him when I turned sixteen."

Hap Sing asked, "So you didn't need the Luck to tell you who he was after all then?"

Yuki Nene froze a moment, "You knew that already didn't you?"

Hap Sing nodded, "I may be a simple man, but I can usually tell when someone is not saying the whole truth. You were testing the knowledge of the Luck then I take it."

Yuki Nene gave a sheepish grin, "It knew I was testing it as well, although it played along for a while. It answered my questions, and then called me out about wasting it's time seeking answers I already knew."

Hap Sing gave a faint smile, "Did it answer your question that you did want answered after that?"

Yuki Nene had a thoughtful look, "It gave me an answer, but not exactly what I expected to hear. It hinted at having plans for me in the future, but let me know that I was to be given free rein to do as I wished until then."

Hap Sing got a thoughtful expression as well, "I guess it remains to figure out what Number Two meant by it being the time of the teacher. Who is supposed to teach what I wonder?"

Yuki Nene was serious, "I suspect that more than one person is to be the teacher. There is a lot that both of us need to learn if I am right. The Luck mentioned an academy for Chi Masters in its answer to me. It obviously knows things. It knows not just things that have happened, but also things that haven't happened yet."

Hap Sing was serious as well, "I have long suspected it of such. There had to be a reason that so many powers and deities were upset with it. There is no such academy in Ran Li or the surrounding kingdoms that I am aware of yet."

Yuki Nene gave a faint smile, "I think that after Lo Arthur's mission is completed that it expects me to help change that."

Hap Sing shrugged, "We could spend weeks trying to figure out what the Luck is planning, and still ultimately not be correct about it. In the mean time let's spend some time getting the village more acclimated to your presence as nothing threatening. Then it may be possible to spend more time together without undue attention if such interests you."

Yuki Nene gave a smile, "Of course it does. You know so much more about the dreaming, and how to control it. I want to learn that as well."

Hap Sing smiled in return, "I was thinking that since you had studied it much more that perhaps you could explain how I do such things. I really don't have any idea how it really works."

Yuki Nene grew serious, "I will seek to spend time with this Yong Mai then as you ask. I am assuming that being in her presence for a while will comfort the villagers about my outsider presence. You probably don't understand how hard it is to be an outsider though."

Hap Sing gave her a sly grin, "I have been considered an outsider except to a few my entire life young woman. My own family treated me as such. Before I met Li Chan I really never had a friend. After I left my uncle's home I spent many years plying the coastal towns as a fisherman. It was only after settling here in Li Chan village that I found a measure of acceptance. I speak the truth that they will not directly pry about your past here. They will gossip about any newcomer to the other villagers, but they will not open up to other outsiders easily. They also protect their own here. It just takes a while to be considered one of their own."

Yuki Nene nodded, "I understand. So how long did it take you to be considered one of them?"

Hap Sing lifted an eyebrow, "It takes about one year for them to accept you. It takes about twenty years for them to consider you a member of the community. It takes a lifetime for them to forget that you didn't originally come from here. I suggest we just worry about having them accept you. I will fast track that process by making your presence acceptable to the village counselors. The rest of the village will quickly follow their lead."

Yuki Nene gave a faint smile, "So I am to meet with Lu Po then?"

Hap Sing shook his head, "Not yet. He is the youngest of the elders, and thus not trusted as well. Lu Po is nominally the leader because he is the one with the most social graces and thus willing to deal with the government officials who visit. Yong Mai is considered the wisest of the counselors. Her opinion will make or break the opinion of the rest of the counselors, and the villagers will follow her lead without question."

Yuki Nene thought a moment, "I thought Li Hung was the oldest. Wouldn't he have been considered the wisest?"

Hap Sing shook his head, "Li Hung was considered the most pragmatic. Unfortunately his social graces were limited, and he had little patience for emotional reasoning. He tended to not figure emotions into any problem, thus his opinion on matters related to practicality was respected, but his opinions on people would have been considered suspect if not in agreement with Yong Mai."

Yuki Nene nodded, "I think I understand. Didn't you mention another counselor?"

Hap Sing nodded, "There are other factors in this picture. The first is Chow Xian. He was once a foreigner and a village outsider as well, although his family came to this village when he was still a child. He is considered the consensus counselor. His vote is often the deciding one between polarized positions. His wisdom is considered second to Yong Mai's, but his personality is more quiet and reserved than the other counselors. He prefers to consider the options at length, and rarely comes to a rapid decision on issues."

Yuki Nene smiled, "So if I get him on my side, it will be easier to be accepted."

Hap Sing continued, "That would be useful but Yong Mai is still the key. Then there is Yong Mai's youngest son Yong Ran. She is grooming him as her replacement, but that does not mean he will carry the same weight that she did when she passes. Only time will determine whether he will follow in his mother's graces or be considered a less influential counselor. For now the people assume that his words are directed by her advice, and accept his appointment gracefully."

Yuki Nene thought about it a while, "What about Li Hung's replacement?"

Hap Sing ducked his head, "That will be our primary problem. There are likely several older villagers who are willing to serve in the position. Yet none of them have the connections or are influential enough to stand out yet as the clear choice. Your actions in the village could be the catalyst which brings a candidate clearly to the attention of the people. Either as someone who is in support of you if it seems like the counsel is leaning that way, or as someone who thinks you should be discouraged from remaining in the village if you are perceived as a potential threat."

Yuki Nene had a querulous look, "How would I be perceived as a threat?"

Hap Sing shrugged, "It is possible in any number of ways. They might consider you the first wave of barbarian invaders looking to take over. Given your size you could be considered a direct physical threat. If you were seen moving in with a local fisherman without a proper chaperone, then you might be considered a moral threat."

Yuki Nene looked momentarily stunned, "I would be a moral threat? How could that be? What business would my personal life be to them?"

Hap Sing was serious, "They are very cautious of not letting such behavior spread among the village. In a community this small they understand that can bring about disruption quicker than anything shy of a group of raiders. Barring either one of us having parents or guardians around to arrange a marriage between us, I'm afraid it will take a long time before people accept any kind of courtship activities between us. This isn't the capital and such things don't slip by unnoticed. That is why our interactions must remain public and chaperoned until the village elders have enough time to reach a consensus about you."

Yuki Nene was thoughtful, "So I must be on my best behavior with Yong Mai then."

Hap Sing shook his head, "I don't think you can please her, and false pretense will likely make her suspicious of your motives. I suggest your best bet with Yong Mai is to be yourself. You need to be who you really are. If you try pretending to be something you are not, Young Mai will not be fooled. She is the best judge of character I have ever known."

Yuki Nene gave a faint grin, "I passed the test of the Luck, but I am still being tested by you. Very well then Hap Sing. I will accept your test, and show you that I am not hiding anything about myself from you."

Hap Sing shrugged, "That isn't who I was worried about. Let's head over to Yong Mai's house. I will leave you to be entertained by Yong Ran when we first arrive. It will take time to prepare Yong Mai to accept someone new into her home."

Chapter 13 Tests

Hap Sing sat in front of Yong Mai who was bundled up in her winter clothing. A fire burning in the fire pit made her room very warm. Hap Sing was sweating lightly as he sat in front of her, but she seemed comfortable with the heat. Yong Mai took a sip of her tea as she looked in Hap Sing's eyes.

Yong Mai spoke, "While it is nice that you have finally come to see me after your return to the village, I know that you have other business with me. I apologize for not making the trip to Li Hung's grave site today, but my legs don't have the strength for climbing hills that they used to have. I have already heard of your request that I take in the outsider you had tending Li Hung. I guess my own time must be close at hand as well then."

Hap Sing nodded, "You need not worry about missing Li Hung's burial. Your son Ran was able to give your regards. The woman I brought over is named Yuki Nene. She is a disciple of the White Raven, and when the time comes she can help start your spirit on the path in the next world."

Yong Mai thought a moment as she took another sip of her tea, "While that sounds very nice, I don't doubt that a spirit as old as mine will have little difficulty finding its way to the right place. The other spirits had better get out of its way if they slow it down any. Perhaps I will even choose to haunt you Hap Sing as the visions of the Luck have haunted my dreams for several years now."

Hap Sing smiled, "While your presence would be appreciated, I don't think we get to choose what happens with our spirits after death. I have a feeling that you don't keep any lingering regrets about your life which will keep you from moving onward."

Yong Mai nodded, "I think you are likely right about that. You would be a good replacement on the counsel of elders you know. I have never questioned your moral compass and compassion for others. Your friend Li Hung however could be a very cold hearted bastard when he wanted to be. I have no problems believing he would kill a being which got in the way of his objectives without any regret about it afterwards."

Hap Sing had a thoughtful look, "I don't deny that he would do such a thing if he viewed it as necessary to protect the nation or those for which he cared, but I do think that the regret for such lead him to accept my request for his retirement here."

Yong Mai nodded, "I see what you are saying. I did not think Li Hung the type to revel in the killing of another, but he certainly would not hesitate to do it efficiently and cleanly as possible if needed. I suspect, however, that more than one bandit or trouble maker has met their end at his hands after his retirement. I knew he liked to make short trips out of town. I noticed he never failed to bring his katana and wakizashi with him while doing so. Usually he would be cleaning and sharpening them upon his return."

Hap Sing ducked his head, "If such was the case I never noticed him doing so."

Yong Mai gave a slight grin, "I didn't think you had. Li Hung went to great pains to conceal his activity from you. He knew your schedule well and often slipped out after your lunches together. Frequently he would return in the morning before you arrived at his home again. As many have known he was a practical man. I suspect his actions had much to do with why raiders and bandits avoided this village. It can only be hoped that more will not try it again soon."

Hap Sing nodded, "I never saw his war blades in his home."

Yong Mai smiled quietly as she pointed at a cabinet in her room, "That's because he always left them with me. My house was conveniently located on the edge of the village for his departure and return without notice. Many times he returned in the early hours of night covered in blood. Sometimes his clothing was torn or cut, but never was a wound visible on him. He always kept several sets of replacement clothes with his swords. If I had not known better I would have thought him more ninja than general. He never failed to survive. Until she came that is."

Hap Sing shook his head, "Yuki Nene did not kill Li Hung."

Yong Mai smiled, "No I don't suppose it was possible that this Yuki Nene could. I don't think any mortal could have killed him. Possibly it is true that not even a god could have killed Li Hung. Remember you stopped the White Raven from taking him as a child. His death must have been the work of a power then. A fundamental change in existence was made which permitted him to finally die."

Hap Sing shrugged, "I don't know much of such things."

Yong Mai turned serious, "I don't know why you ever try to lie about it. I can tell when you lie you know. You just don't like talking about it. If it was not the Luck which performed the deed, then it was one of the other powers. Only one power excels at matters of mortality and immortality."

Hap Sing nodded, "The two tailed beast."

Yong Mai smiled again, "I suspected as much. This girl you bring to me. This Yuki Nene as you said her name was. Is she someone special?"

Hap Sing spoke nervously, "She is a Chi Master as well as a disciple of the White Raven. Such things are never heard of I am told."

Yong Mai nodded, "That would make her a rare individual indeed. I can see why the Luck is interested. Is there anything else you want to tell me before I meet this girl? Don't hold back any Hap Sing."

Hap Sing spoke, "She is the descendent of a Nordlander mother, and a Shadowine father."

Yong Mai interrupted, "What is a Shadowine? I have not heard of such before."

Hap Sing replied, "They are a race of humans who have dwelled for countless generations on the plane of shadow I am told."

Yong Mai nodded, "So the part about being a disciple of the White Raven makes more sense now."

Hap Sing continued, "She has met the Luck, Number Two, and the Herald of Palnor. She did not fall apart after each encounter."

Yong Mai frowned, "Not all of us are made of steel wills my boy. Some of us understand there is wisdom in avoiding such beings. This girl does not seem to have much good sense yet."

Hap Sing hesitated, "That was not intended as a comparison to you Mai. I understand the value of your wisdom."

Yong Mai was serious, "No need to apologize. Such a girl would be a rarity indeed. I take it that means the rumors from Hung Chan village were true then. There was a divine dragon there when you visited."

Hap Sing nodded, "The Luck was in control at the time. So I only heard of the events after the fact. Several Chi Masters were in the village there including Yuki Nene, and they recognized me as the bearer of the Luck."

Yong Mai commented, "All with the second sight then. What did your second sight tell you about this girl's aura?"

Hap Sing replied, "It is very bright. Not as bright as the aura of Li Hung mind you, but her aura was not artificially created by the Luck either."

Yong Mai nodded, "While that may be true, I recommend you don't discount the possible manipulation by her deity. Divine investment in her fate might be altering that view you have of her. This leads to the crucial question I need you to answer. What is she looking for from you?"

Hap Sing finished, "She seems to be very interested in learning from me how to enhance her already significant abilities. Enough so that she is willing to offer herself to me."

Yong Mai thought a moment, "She likely has ambition and attraction to power. She is possibly already driven by her fate and what ever powers are directing it to pursue you. A most dangerous combination if this is true. What are you really asking of me Hap Sing?"

Hap Sing sighed, "It is possible my estimation is colored by my closeness to the subject. I was looking to get your insight into her personality. I have seen hints and signs that I haven't read the entire person, but may be responding to my fears of her plans."

Yong Mai thought about that as she sipped her tea, "Is she aware of your purpose in putting her here?"

Hap Sing nodded, "I have tried to couch it in terms of how the village would react to a relationship, and the need for a chaperone to be present."

Yong Mai smiled, "She caught on to your cowardly dodging of her pursuit then, and didn't buy that story then."

Hap Sing sighed, "She knows I trust your opinion, and that you will evaluate her personality even as she helps to take care of you."

Yong Mai smiled, "You also feel compassion for a friend who is to die soon as well I imagine. You realize my son can not always keep me company, and that she will keep me from being lonely in my final months and days."

Hap Sing gave a little grin, "That is also part of my motive."

Yong Mai smiled, "You didn't think I would accept your offer if you were not challenging me to help you as well. I hate to say it, but I am not above accepting your charity any more Hap Sing. Your effort is appreciated, both in giving me something to put my mind to, and in giving me company to help pass my final time. You don't consider her dangerous then?"

Hap Sing had a worried look, "Not to me or you. I do wonder if her ambition and drive are a danger to herself."

Yong Mai nodded, "I see. You are also putting her to another test as well."

Hap Sing looked a little surprised, "I am?"

Yong Mai laughed, "You can't fool me. You are putting her compassion to the test. Few things are harder than watching someone facing their final days. Compassion is one of your defining traits you well know. It is one thing which makes you hard to deal with as well. Few women could hold up to your ideals."

Hap Sing gave a ridiculous grin, "Is that why you chose to become Li Hung's lover after your husband passed away?"

Yong Mai looked surprised, "What makes you think such a thing?"

Hap Sing kept grinning, "He was old enough to be your father, yet he chose you to be the one to keep his secrets from me. I have to figure something more existed between you than simply being on the counsel together."

Yong Mai blushed, "Mind your own business you dirty minded old man. It was not like that at all, at least not at first."

Hap Sing laughed, "Your blush is speaking more than your lips Mai."

Yong Mai scowled at him, "Send for this girl then. We shall see who blushes most. Remember she's young enough to be, well how young is she?"

Hap Sing grew serious, "Nene is a very young woman indeed. I believe she is twenty-one years of age."

Yong Mai shrugged, "Old enough then I guess. I had three of my nine children by the same age and with a decade older husband as well. Go fetch her then. First though do you want me to play this a certain way?"

Hap Sing smiled, "I'll give you the same advice I gave her. Just be yourself. She is a perceptive one just like you are. It will not work if you both pretend to be something you are not."

Yong Mai asked, "I do have a question on another topic. Why did you give away the house and the money that Li Hung left for you? Before you lie about it don't think that Lu Po didn't tell me about Li Hung's will."

Hap Sing grew serious, "Like you say compassion is my defining trait. It was not the trait for which Li Hung was best known in his life. I figured it may as well be his legacy with his death. I don't want for anything and don't need such things. There are others better helped by it than me."

Yong Mai shook her head, "Hap Sing you are quite a bit poorer than any of those you helped save maybe Wen Li and Wen Lu. I've seen that poor excuse for a shelter you call a home. Only a hermit would call such a thing by that name. Even the former home of Wen Li is better constructed. What is the real reason you did not take the money and house?"

Hap Sing answered Yong Mai with a serious expression, "Such things are a trap. I had them once, a nice home and enough money to supply my life with little effort. They kept me in place for too long. I felt sorry for what fate had driven Li Hung to become so I stayed close to him to lessen fate's influence over him. Now that he has passed, it will be time to leave here before too long. I can feel it coming soon, but not before you pass either Mai."

Yong Mai gave him a knowing look, "That is what draws you to her more than anything. This Nene is not tied down to material things. She is willing to follow wherever you go. Nothing is attached to her then."

Hap Sing looked at Yong Mai, "I am attached to her, but I am attached to many because of the Luck. I am also attached to the people here in Li Chan village by my own choosing, but I can not ask anyone to follow me when the trouble comes forcing me to leave. The most I can do is to help them out now as best I can for when I am gone."

Yong Mai nodded, "That has always been the difference between you and Li Hung. It was always about taking care of you for Li Hung. Even when he was fighting in the great war it was about keeping your enemies occupied and away from you. I imagine it was the same for his father. You on the other hand are never worried about yourself. You make your choices based on what you consider best for the most people. You don't want this Yuki Nene to be another Li Hung. You want me to see if she can become another you."

Hap Sing had a concerned look, "That is the gist of it. It seems so, self centered I guess."

Yong Mai gave a serious response, "People could do worse than to have you as their master Sing. I know Li Hung tried to be a better person because of it. He helped to ease my loneliness after my husband died, and not in the dirty way your mind is thinking. He would come and talk. Sometimes we would talk about everyday trivialities, and sometimes he was looking for me to be his moral compass about his past deeds. They disturbed him not because of their necessity, but because he didn't know if it was right to not be disturbed by them."

Hap Sing nodded, "I suppose that was much like Li Hung in his later years. How was he when he came from his swords?"

Yong Mai ducked her head and closed her eyes for a moment in thought before raising it to look him in the eyes, "Li Hung was clear minded and moved like a man in his prime. There was no uncertainty, or discussion about his purpose or course of action. It was almost as if he had received orders from a commander and he was carrying them out without worry about whether they should be questioned. He was a man who knew what needed to be done."

Hap Sing shook his head, "It was the Luck then. Letting him know when the potential threats were close so that he could remove them. It's my fault for staying in one place for too long so I could give him a place to quit that life."

Yong Mai gave him a gentle smile, "You assume too much responsibility Hap Sing. That is your perpetual downfall. People make choices for themselves. The best you can do is to help them pick the right course. You can not make their choices for them. The Luck may have told Li Hung where the threats were, but I don't think it forced him to act. I think his retirement did reduce the bloodshed as well. Likely it only took a couple of kills to drive off any bandits. Anyone looking for you to cause harm was likely approached and threatened to leave. Most times he did not return covered in blood after all. What he did also protected this village from becoming the center of a conflict as well. Think of the innocent lives he protected in addition to your own."

Hap Sing looked at Yong Mai, "Did you love Li Hung then?"

Yong Mai shook her head, "I have only loved my dead husband and my children. I respected Li Hung and was his friend much as I am your friend. I advised him, and listened to his stories when he needed to speak. It was clear that he loved you as a friend, a second father, and a mentor. Just as it is clear that you loved him like a son who failed to follow in your footsteps. I suggest you don't make the same mistake with this Nene girl. Don't treat her like a daughter or a child. She is a person. It is best to remember that. It will make things easier. Now go bring her in to talk with me, and then you can leave after the introductions are made. We will need several weeks together to begin to get the full measure of each other. I will know who she is by then, and you can visit periodically to get your insights. I also won't mind the company when you visit. Don't expect me to spill any of her personal confidences though. I will keep her secrets just as I keep yours, and kept Li Hung's."

Hap Sing stood up and replied, "I notice that you told me several of Li Hung's secrets today."

Yong Mai dropped her head, "I don't think he cares now. The reason for keeping them secret does not matter anymore with his death. You were better served by knowing at this time than keeping them to my grave."

Hap Sing gave her a serious look, "I thank you for your confidence in me. I am glad to know that Li Hung at least tried to become a better man even if his fate compelled him to perform such terrible deeds. I will invite Nene in and make the formal introductions now."

Several days later Hap Sing was making his routine predawn walk from his home outside the village to the shore of the bay where his boat was tied to a palm tree near the beach. Hap Sing sensed that someone had brought the Luck's attention. He looked around the dark shore noticing the sky beginning to lighten to the east. The tide was just beginning to rise, and the sound of the gentle breakers masked any sound made by the man he spotted walking toward his boat as he started to untie it from the tree.

Hap Sing put on a bland expression as he spoke, "Good morning. I did not expect to see someone else up this early. You startled me somewhat."

The man spoke in an educated accent, "I greatly doubt that much could surprise you any more Hap Sing. I will return your greetings and wish you a good morning as well."

Hap Sing moved to push his boat to the water as spoke, "You'll have to pardon me. I prefer to begin my fishing early. The best fish do not wait for my convenience."

The man replied with a serious tone in his voice, "I will join you in your fishing then. I desire to talk with you."

Hap Sing pushed his boat into the water and stepped inside to pick up the paddles. He passed one to the unknown man who joined him in the boat. As they began paddling away from shore Hap Sing noted that the man was unpracticed with the paddle. Whoever he was, it was clear that managing boats was an unfamiliar task to him. Perhaps something he had read about but never tried.

Hap Sing spoke, "It will go smoother if you hold your paddle like I hold mine. Dip it into the water like so, and pull at the same pace I do. Don't worry about steering, I will handle our course."

The man watched Hap Sing take a few strokes, and replied, "I see where I was doing it wrong. Thank you for the instruction Hap Sing."

When the man faced forward again Hap Sing closed his eyes, and opened them using his second sight. It was clear from his aura that this man was a greater destiny. The question was what had brought him in contact with Hap Sing. He could also see a spirit ribbon stretching from the man to a shape on the shore. A large spirit panda was pacing the shore at the other end of the ribbon. There was also a familiar looking ribbon stretching off into the distance.

Once they were out past the breakers and still sheltered by the bay Hap Sing lowered his sea anchor into the water. The sky was lightening more in the east and Hap Sing could see the features of the man much better. Hap Sing recognized that he was indeed the Magistrate Ming Na Jun dressed in common clothing who had joined him in his boat. It seemed his secret was becoming less of one.

Ming Na Jun spoke as Hap Sing lowered his fishing line into the water, "You have been a very elusive person to locate for the last two years Hap Sing. It seems like you have taken to leaving Li Chan village during my official visits."

Hap Sing looked out at the sea to the east as he stopped using his second sight, "No offense was intended your honor. I was busy with several things most likely. Is there some problem with my taxes? Lu Po has led me to believe that they were all paid in full."

Ming Na Jun shook his head, "Seeing how the tax rolls in various provinces of Ran Li show you paying taxes for over one hundred and twenty years I think you have paid your fair share already. You seem quite spry for someone who turned one hundred and fifty recently. This isn't an official visit. I'm on vacation for now, and it's my first one in ten years actually."

Hap Sing nodded, "What brings you to seek me out on your vacation?"

Ming Na Jun gave a faint smile, "As you probably know well it is said that greater destinies attract."

 Chapter 13   *163*

Hap Sing spoke, "Thus it is said by the Chi Masters of old. Why did you leave your spirit panda on the shore? It would leave you quite vulnerable if I had a desire to cause you harm."

Ming Na Jun smiled more, "I see. So you are a Chi Master as well then as I suspected. I left him on shore so that you would not feel threatened by him. Frankly he is also a bit afraid of the deep water."

Hap Sing smiled, "As a Chi Master do you realize that your guardian spirit is an extension of yourself?"

Ming Na Jun kept focused on Hap Sing, "I am very well aware of it. I am also aware of the fact that I can not swim either. I am at your mercy if you intended me any harm. I do not suspect I am taking an unreasonable risk, and it is worth putting you at ease about my presence."

Hap Sing turned serious, "Would you like to fish for a while? It really is quite relaxing."

Ming Na Jun looked back toward the shore, "I don't think it will help any. You can cast out your net again if you like. I have witnessed you do it several times before, yet never up close. It even seems to happen when you are not in the village or nearby."

Hap Sing relaxed and cast his nets as was his usual morning routine. Ming Na Jun watched him casually with no disturbance on his features. Ming Na Jun nodded with a faint smile as he witnessed the phenomena of the net spreading across the sky.

Ming Na Jun looked at the result, "Very impressive casting Hap Sing. You access the dreaming effortlessly to bring it into existence. That is certainly the mark of a Chi magic Grandmaster at work. It is also interesting that your aura changes form to resemble a more normal one and increases greatly in intensity when you do so."

Hap Sing looked over at Ming Na Jun, "You are familiar with the dreaming then?"

Ming Na Jun looked over at the shore, "I have traveled the safer parts of it. I know how to visualize and manipulate the dreaming to make things happen in reality. I can not say that I can do so with the speed and effect which you have demonstrated. I have also secretly trained other Chi Masters when their power manifested. When I first saw you two years ago I had thought I had discovered a potential new talent hiding from oppression."

Hap Sing gave a faint smile, "You don't think that is the case anymore."

Ming Na Jun slowly shook his head, "As you well know you are certainly not a new talent. There may be some rough edges to your approach compared to what used to be considered official Chi Master Doctrine of centuries ago, but I think the effectiveness and impact of your casting speaks for itself. I've done my research since first seeing you over two years ago."

Hap Sing became slightly nervous, "What prompted such interest?"

Ming Na Jun looked at him carefully, "It is all of the spirit ribbons I see connected to you, and there are even more now than the last time I looked at you. The records and teachings of past masters speak of these ribbons as being connections of fate. It states it takes normally many months for such to form, and only the most skilled of Chi Masters can perceive them. Yet I saw that you clearly followed my ribbon back to where I hid my spirit from your line of sight. Your eyes also followed the ribbon connecting me back to my son. I can see that my son's ribbon also connects back to you. I am curious as to how you managed to entangle your fate so quickly with his. I am even more curious to understand why you have done so."

Hap Sing reacted to the fish on his line and pulled it close to the surface. A quick dip of his net with his left hand captured the fish which he unhooked and placed in his fishing creel. Ming Na Jun watched the process carefully.

Ming Na Jun observed, "It seems that Chi magic is not the only thing which becomes second nature to you given enough time. Did you even think about what motions it took to catch that fish?"

Hap Sing shook his head, "Both things happened without much conscious thought on my part."

Ming Na Jun thought a short while, "What conscious thought places those ribbons so rapidly then I would ask? The fishing I agree is a simple skill perfected and made routine over time. The connecting of spirit ribbons could not likely become such."

Hap Sing shrugged, "I guess that would depend on how much time you had to learn the skill I would guess."

Ming Na Jun spoke again, "There is a ribbon connected to you that leads off to the edge of town. Would that be elder Yong Mai's home then?"

Hap Sing nodded, "That would be the case if you are asking."

Ming Na Jun nodded, "So the other Chi Master, the tall pale haired woman with the spirit raven is staying there. That is another curious thing then. I was under the impression she might be staying with you, but your home is in the opposite direction. At least you approached the beach from that way."

Hap Sing was surprised, "That is very observant of you."

Ming Na Jun shook his head, "It is pretty easy if you understand some mathematics. Since my son Fu is in a fixed location back at our home I can follow his ribbon connecting to you and use my own ribbon connected to him as a relative point of reference. I had lost your position for a while when you went to Hung Chan village. I did not expect you to relocate there while I was in Li Chan village on my last official visit. I did not know where you had gone at first, but then the stories of the disruption at Hung Chan valley had reached my ears."

Hap Sing spoke, "What did you hear?"

Ming Na Jun smiled, "Many incredible stories were circulating. People were speculating about the return of the troubled times, but such has been the speculation since the last invasion. There was even a report of a divine dragon making an appearance and a great noise. Some people even reported dragon footprints and goblin bodies being found."

Hap Sing shrugged as he pulled in another fish, "That seems very incredible when heard that way. Perhaps there was a grain of truth behind it."

Ming Na Jun looked at Hap Sing with a sympathetic expression as he spoke, "I am late in saying I'm sorry to hear that the village elder Li Hung passed away very recently. I have only just heard of it. His aura was quite astonishing as you know. Nearly as bright as your own when you cast your net into the air."

Hap Sing spoke with a serious tone, "I am glad to hear your sympathy. Li Hung will be greatly missed."

Ming Na Jun spoke, "I hired someone to investigate you about a year ago you know. I hired one of the best. He is a retired ninja who worked for the Ran Li military. He used to be one of their intelligence specialists and a master who trained the new ninja in infiltration techniques."

Hap Sing looked shocked, "A ninja to investigate a simple fisherman? That seems a bit of an expensive endeavor. You could have simply asked around. Most people here are aware of who I am."

Ming Na Jun shook his head, "It was done already. Most people barely knew who you were, and even the village leader Lu Po was reticent to divulge much about what he knew through normal questioning."

Hap Sing gave a faint smile, "You can see for yourself what my day is like. There is not much to tell really. I fish, and eat. I barter for what I need, and I contemplate the next day. My life is a normal one."

Ming Na Jun smiled, "I agree that your life appears normal. It is what happens around your life which is sometimes not normal. The ninja I hired had started by hiring some rough sorts who knew how to handle themselves in a fight to approach the town to bully some locals about you. They never reported back to him. When he went to investigate in person he discovered shallow graves ten miles from here with the bodies of the men he had sent. On examination of the graves he found the bodies of the twelve men had been cleanly and efficiently killed with minimal effort. The tale he told me was that as he pondered whether a large force had ambushed them or a skilled opponent had fought them all he felt the flat of a blade being placed against his throat. It was then he realized that a skilled opponent had killed them single handed."

Hap Sing looked a little pale, "How did you hear this tale then?"

Ming Na Jun had a serious look, "That is one of the curious parts. The ninja told me that the blade was removed and when he turned around there was an elderly man standing a dozen paces away wearing a matched set of sheathed warrior's weapons. The odd thing is this ninja recognized this old man. He claimed it was the former Grandmaster of the ninja force which fought in the last great war. It was none other than an elderly General Li Hung, and former leader of the army after the sacrifice of his father General Li Chan."

Hap Sing was surprised, "I hadn't realized that he had served as the Grandmaster of the ninja force. I only knew that he fought with his father Li Chan, and became general of the military after Li Chan's death. What happened then? Did Li Hung say anything?"

Ming Na Jun seemed frustrated, "The ninja I hired would not say. It seemed that some loyalty existed between them still. I suspect that is why Li Hung did not slaughter him as he had the ruffians. The ninja did say that he reburied the bodies, and that he was returning the remainder of my advance fee minus the expense of hiring those men. He also informed me that no ninja of Ran Li would consider confronting or even going against the wishes of General Li Hung. It seems he is legendary in their ranks as the paragon of an unbeatable killer. His bright aura made much more sense after I learned that fact."

Hap Sing was relieved, "You should know that legend will remain intact. Li Hung died peacefully in his bed."

Ming Na Jun shrugged, "It seems strange perhaps that one of his background would do so, but I don't think it was a bad thing. I also understand now why this part of Jin Do province had so few problems with bandits and criminals. I'm sure the word had been spread over the years that this portion of the province was deadly to their kind. I suspect that many more unmarked graves exist than those found by the ninja I hired."

Hap Sing shook his head, "I would not know about such things. I certainly never approved of that aspect of Li Hung's life. It is why I encouraged him to retire from the military life and settle down in a peaceful village."

Ming Na Jun smiled, "It was then I discovered that Li Chan village was a dead end for the time. Direct approaches would not work given my position, and covert approaches would also face disaster. So I went back through the records I had, and requested similar records held by other provinces. That was when I discovered that you had been paying taxes for one hundred and twenty years in one place or another in Ran Li. It was always the same name, and it was never in two different provinces for more than a single year. I traced it back to Hung Chan village, and I remembered my cousin who is the village leader there asking me whether it was wise for him to request the village be named for Chi Master Hap Yang as its most famous former citizen. As I was advising him on the matter I perused his tax records as well. I found the first place you started paying taxes for many years, and totaled up your age then."

Hap Sing gave a faint smile, "That was how you figured out I was one hundred and fifty."

Ming Na Jun smiled, "I didn't know the exact number, but my cousin Ming Ran did. He had been researching your father extensively, while I had been tracking you back independently. I visited Ming Ran recently to look into the stories of the disruption in Hung Chan village. My former pupil was uncharacteristically secretive with me. I had taught him all he knew about being a practitioner of the

Chi magic, and yet he did not mention anything about your presence. His new wife Akane was also very tight lipped about it."

Hap Sing shrugged, "What would make you think I was there?"

Ming Na Jun gave a sly grin, "Why it is simple. The guard at the village gate remembered your name. It seems one of the other guards was your cousin. The same guard who was a Chi Master from the look of him and his spirit guardian. I also noticed your spirit ribbon on him as well as on Ming Ran and Ming Akane. Having seen it on my son I could not fail to recognize it."

Hap Sing asked, "Didn't the other guard recognize your spirit guardian?"

Ming Na Jun shrugged, "Why should he? My giant panda was watching over my son and keeping him safe. You have probably noticed that very few Chi Masters can actually detect the spirit ribbons. They only usually spot people through their auras, and like you I have learned somewhat how to keep mine lowered. It was when you recognized me for what I was in the market two years ago that I knew something was odd about you. I have been hiding my abilities from any but Ming family members for many years. Even then I only revealed my knowledge to those whose Chi Master potential manifested. There is safety in numbers, and it served me well to protect my position by training them to conceal their abilities as well."

Hap Sing raised an eyebrow, "Why is that?"

Ming Na Jun smiled, "The divine priests in Ran Li are well aware that the spirit powers run in family lines. They can not identify them through spell or casting, but they can certainly put an entire family under suspicion if one displays the abilities. The same concern would not occur to you as you are the last of your father's line as far as I can tell. Although I would say it is a very potent line given your obvious longevity and your father's reputation. I would say it is true that your mother's line also carries the trait if your distant cousin is any indication."

Hap Sing thought a moment and then asked, "Where does this put us?"

Ming Na Jun gave a little laugh, "In a very small boat together I would say. We both know much about the other which could cause problems or raise unwanted suspicions. I don't think either one of us wants that to happen. I hope you can understand that I am concerned about my son. I am also concerned about the spirit raven your pale haired friend has circling over our heads as she approaches the beach. I don't think she is able to defend against my panda from that position should she try something unadvised."

Hap Sing gave a tenuous smile, "I don't recommend trying anything yourself. There is something you probably don't know about her yet."

Ming Na Jun nodded, "I am sure of that. I can tell that her aura is powerful. The look I got at her earlier indicates she is a foreigner, very young, and likely also unskilled. It is also likely she has not received much instruction. I'm surprised she can have her spirit guardian travel that far even."

Hap Sing shrugged as he pulled another fish from the water and placed it into his fishing creel, "It is well within her range yet. She is untrained as you noted. I have it on good authority that she is a very adept self taught prodigy though. She can even travel to the dreaming given enough time, and figured it out much more quickly than I ever did."

Ming Na Jun shrugged, "She still can not recall her spirit raven before my panda could attack her at this range if I decided to do so. The only unknown remains where your spirit guardian is at this point."

Hap Sing gave a little laugh, "I think you see it clearly, but have mistaken it for something else."

Ming Na Jun looked at him closely, "Your aura. The odd shape it has. Is that your guardian then? You are very unusual then. That is a magic I had not seen done before."

Hap Sing pointed over at the beach, "If you think that is unusual just look at my friend standing on the beach. What can you see from here?"

Ming Na Jun looked over at Yuki Nene and his eyes widened, "She has another guardian spirit raven? Such a thing is not heard of in the Chi Master records. To split a spirit so does not seem possible."

Hap Sing gave a faint smile, "Her talents continue to surprise me I must say. I don't doubt that you could learn such a thing if you were not convinced it could not be done already. That is one advantage held by those of us who are self taught. Our abilities are not predictable, or limited by the preconceptions of what has been done before."

Ming Na Jun shook his head, "To do such a thing by her age though?"

Hap Sing grew serious, "I suspect that her goddess may have given her some help along the way."

Ming Na Jun's eyes narrowed in suspicion, "It is well known that divine gods have no use for Chi Masters, and that Chi Masters do not worship the divine."

Hap Sing gave a faint smile, "Where her people come from our kind are called spirit shamans. It seems that they haven't heard of the same set of rules that Chi Masters usually follow. Are not her spirit guardians suggestive of something divine to you?"

Ming Na Jun closed his eyes a moment and opened them again as he spoke, "There is another ribbon on her. It has a different quality than the one you placed. It fades into nothingness after a little while. I have never witnessed such a thing before. Spirit Ravens . . ."

Ming Na Jun's face paled as he looked back at Hap Sing, "The White Raven is known for her ravens of course. I should have recognized that it was an unusual spirit form. She is a worshiper of the death goddess then?"

Hap Sing responded, "She is a chosen one of the White Raven to hear her tell of it. I suspect it means she outranks even one of their priests. According to the tale she told me they seemed to all defer to her requests when asked. I suggest you look closely at her again."

Ming Na Jun's face showed confusion, "Another spirit ribbon is on her. Just like the one both of us have to my son. It leads off in the same direction, but it is still faint yet. How could this have happened? My son never mentioned meeting her to me. There were no extra ribbons on him the last time we were together."

Hap Sing felt a tingle on the back of his neck before he responded, "I can show you how they are placed if you like. It is not something I do, but you can watch it to see if you can figure out how it is done."

Ming Na Jun leaned back, "It seems I am at a disadvantage. I had presumed with the death of Li Hung that you were more approachable now. It seems like you have already found another capable protector in that woman."

Hap Sing shrugged, "I don't think she is my protector. I have some information which contradicts that point of view. I think I am intended to teach her something and perhaps I am to teach you as well. It may well be that this will be a satisfactory meeting between the two of us."

Ming Na Jun sat forward again, "Very well then. It seems I am playing by your rules. While it is not a position I prefer to be placed into, but I accept the necessity to receive my answers."

Hap Sing placed his fishing pole down into the boat and brought in his fishing creel, "Using your most focused second sight you can achieve watch my hand as I reach out to touch yours. This will not hurt or damage you in any way so you need not be afraid. Just pay close attention during the moment of connection between us."

Hap Sing touched the hand of Ming Na Fu. He felt the tingle of connection and saw the aura of the Luck attach itself to the aura of Ming Na Fu. As he drew his hand back a strong spirit ribbon unfurled between the aura of the Luck and the aura of Ming Na Jun.

Ming Na Jun looked at Hap Sing with an intent expression, "What have you done?"

Hap Sing smiled, "I have done nothing. The Luck has guaranteed that we will remain in the metaphorical small boat together by linking your fate to mine. Our destinies are combined now."

Ming Na Jun grew grimly serious, "I need to know what you mean."

Hap Sing was serious as well, "I'm sorry but I have little choice about who it chooses to link to."

Ming Na Jun asked calmly, "Who is the Luck you mention? I have never heard of such a name."

Hap Sing sighed, "I suppose you didn't stay in Hung Chan long enough to hear the local legends."

Ming Na Jun gave a little chuckle, "You mean that old story about how . . . your father . . . battled the giant beast."

Hap Sing gave a faint nod, "You might have read of it in ancient texts referred to as the Greater Spirit Seven Tailed Tiger."

Ming Na Jun frowned again, "That is not possible. Such beings existed before the gods and are long gone. The histories say they only remain in the dreaming feeble and impotent. They don't have physical form."

Hap Sing sighed, "I would not let the Luck hear you say that. It might become upset with you. Your cousin Ming Ran would hardly talk to me again when he saw it upset. I'm afraid it scared him pretty badly. That's why he likely didn't tell you anything about me. It's likely he did not want to be on the bad side of the Luck."

Ming Na Jun looked at Hap Sing again, "What are you?"

Hap Sing shrugged, "I'm a fisherman. I'm also a Chi Master I guess. Unfortunately it is likely that I am also what the priest of Palnor in Hung Chan village called a case of a reverse possession."

Ming Na Jun thought a moment before speaking, "According to my theological studies that would make you . . . an Avatar!"

Hap Sing nodded, "That is what the priest said was the common term for it."

Ming Na Jun looked surprised, "An Avatar for a power that isn't divine. Such a thing has not been heard of before this."

Hap Sing smiled, "I've heard a variant on that phrase many times in the last few months for some reason. I have enough fish for my meals today. There is even enough to share with you and Lu Po. Now that you know who I am it is probably time to have a more civilized discussion. I'm sure you would not mind getting off the water."

They paddled back to the shore. Hap Sing noted that Ming Na Jun remembered to use the paddle how he had been shown. It was clear that he was a quick learner, even if prone to follow instruction precisely. It suggested to Hap Sing that he had a quick mind, but was not necessarily a flexible thinker.

Yuki Nene met them as they got out of the boat. She looked at Ming Na Jun with a careful expression and he looked up at her surprised at how tall she was up close. Even without the raven perched on her shoulder and the other one flying overhead she was an intimidating figure.

Hap Sing spoke first, "Ming Na Jun this is Yuki Nene."

Yuki Nene gave a slight bow, "Your panda is an impressive specimen. It certainly makes your Cousin Ming Ran's spirit guardian look pale in comparison."

Ming Na Jun responded, "I am glad to meet you. I am much more impressed by your twin spirits. I had never heard of such a thing being accomplished before. Could you explain the process for how you accomplish it?"

Yuki Nene gave a slight laugh, "Thank you for the compliment, but I have to say that if you have to rely on having someone else showing you how everything is done, then I would guess you need to read less and experiment more."

Hap Sing noticed a stiffening of Ming Na Jun's stance and interrupted his pending response, "Yuki Nene perhaps it is time for you to return to see to Yong Mai's needs. I will accompany our guest to Lu Po's house."

Yuki Nene's expression turned slightly petulant, "As you wish Hap Sing."

As Yuki Nene departed Hap Sing pulled his boat up to the palm tree above the high tide line and secured it in place with the rope. His expression was mild but distracted. Ming Na Jun relaxed a bit as he waited for Hap Sing to gather up his fishing gear and creel.

Ming Na Jun made a comment as they walked toward the village and Lu Po's home, "I seem to have forgotten that I am dressed as a commoner. I have perhaps grown too accustomed to a certain amount of deference."

Hap Sing faintly smiled, "I don't think it would have helped any with her. In the Nordlander society in which she was raised Chi Masters, what they call spirit shamans, are considered a kind of royalty. I think the equivalent term we discussed was princess. Like you magistrate she has been raised along with people who defer to her whims. It has been a struggle for her to adapt to being away from her people I imagine. Although I think it will make her a better person."

Ming Na Jun smiled in return, "I see that a lack of formal upbringing has not dulled your wit any Hap Sing. No don't deny it. I can tell when one of the common classes has used a dual example to make a point. When I act in my official position I may not be allowed to notice such comments, but as I am out of my position as it were I can acknowledge your point. I would also be a better person by living in the shoes of a common person. Trust me when I say that I was not spared my share of common chores as a child in addition to my education. I respect the nature of a hard day of honest manual labor and what it means for our country."

Hap Sing shrugged his shoulders, "That is also a good point, but it is well known in Jin Do province that you are an even handed magistrate not given to excessive restriction or penalty in the execution of your duties. I had no doubt that you would understand the value of a common person to society. You should also know that Yuki Nene is primarily away from her people now to escape the restriction of being handled as a member of nobility. She is reportedly a very quick study, and as I mentioned before self taught in all of her abilities as it is difficult to locate fellow Chi Masters in these times. She is rightfully proud of her accomplishment, but she understands there is value to learning from the wisdom of another."

Ming Na Jun thoughtfully stroked his mustache, "Then she is here to learn what more she can from you."

Hap Sing nodded, "Indeed that is her goal. I am starting her on patience, compassion, and tolerance. Without a demonstrated ability to exercise these traits, I will not demonstrate or teach her any more of the tricks I know."

Ming Na Jun raised an eyebrow, "Thus you have placed her in elder Yong Mai's home. A wise woman, but also known to have a difficult temperament in these last few years."

Hap Sing gave a faint smile, "You don't need to repeat this to her, but there are times Yong Mai can even try my patience when her mood is sour. As Yong Mai approaches her last weeks I shall see if Yuki Nene will be a suitable choice for my first student."

Ming Na Jun chuckled, "A funny picture you have presented there, a princess who serves an old crone, and answers to a fisherman. It is no wonder that our society rejects the reality of the way Chi Masters must learn. It defies our commonly held social order."

Hap Sing continued smiling faintly, "I sometimes wonder if the barbarian Nordlander people do not have a more useful perspective. They value those with proven ability instead of those who are born to carry a particular name."

Ming Na Jun was thoughtful again, "I fear that is what leads to their barbarism. It leads to a system of rule through might instead of justice. It is well known that Nordlanders will turn pirate or raider where they perceive weakness in a society they encounter. Their way is not the way of order."

Hap Sing nodded, "As you may have noticed already, it is having preconceived notions of what could be done with Chi magic which limits your abilities. I don't doubt that experimentation comes with risks. However, you should credit the fact that somewhere in the past someone must have tried each of the things you know for the first time using intuition as well as knowledge to guide them instead of only doing what has been established before them"

Ming Na Jun responded as they approached the home of Lu Po, "What you say must of course be the truth of how things started. I suspect that many bad results happened on the way to reliable useful ones. However, there is wisdom in not repeating the errors of the past."

Hap Sing gave a faint smile, "I would say that is good advice if you already understand why it was an error. If the understanding does not exist, then you have learned little except how to follow the actions of another."

Ming Na Jun thought a moment, "Like paddling a boat. I was shown by you to use another way, but I have no understanding of why it was a better way than what I was attempting to do."

Hap Sing smiled, "You trusted my experience to lead you, which is a valuable starting point, but it does not let you know if a better method than the one employed by me may exist. It may also depend on your definition of what is desirable in the result. The pleasure derived in the attempt, the speed with which the intended destination is reached, or how tiring the method is over time. These are a few of the considerations I use in selecting a paddling stroke. Other factors consider the motion of the water, the direction of the tide and currents, and the distance of the desired destination. You now know one way to paddle a boat well, I know many. Practice and experience are valuable in addition to being a quick learner with a good instructor."

Ming Na Jun spoke, "It seems like you have been considering this for a long time. It is surprising that you are only now taking in your first student."

Hap Sing ducked his head, "Unlike yourself or my student Nene, I am not what people would call a quick learner."

Ming Na Jun thought about it, "That is probably true. It is likely they would call you a natural. I don't suppose you put much direct effort in learning what you know. I would guess you simply do what you do, and think about why it worked later."

Hap Sing smiled, "Sometimes being a natural is a disadvantage. It makes it very hard for me to learn how to do what someone else does because I wouldn't naturally do it that way. My natural instinct is to rely on visualizing my desired result in the dreaming and it just happens in reality. I have been told that not many Chi Masters start that way."

Ming Na Jun chuckled as they reached the gate in Lu Po's fence, "No they don't. Accessing the dreaming is usually considered the last achievement managed by Chi Masters in practicing Chi magic. None I have heard of start with accessing the dreaming. It is considered too dangerous for any but the most skilled, and requires many years to achieve."

Hap Sing smiled, "If it is any consolation, then I never consciously attempted it until I was probably close to your age. I was afraid to tap my potential for many years. It took the desperate request of a friend for me to do so. Here comes Lu Po's assistant. We will continue our talk once we have some privacy in Lu Po's office."

Chapter 14 Games

Hap Sing and Ming Na Jun sat in Lu Po's office as he served them tea. Lu Po seemed surprised to see Ming Na Jun. His surprise was likely because Jun was dressed as a commoner, and was not due for an official visit for another two months. Lu Po covered his surprise by playing host and making sure the formalities of the tea service were observed. Lu Po sat in contemplation drinking his tea while he looked at his guests and considered what situation had brought them there together.

Lu Po spoke after he finished his tea, "Do you find your tea suitable Magistrate Ming?"

Ming Na Jun nodded his head, "It was very suitable. It warms me nicely after spending the early morning out on the water."

Lu Po raised an eyebrow, "Indeed that is good to hear. Might I ask what brings you to my office today with one of our village fishermen? Is there some problem?"

Ming Na Jun looked at Lu Po, "Indeed there might be a problem. I was hoping you could assist us."

Lu Po looked friendly, "Li Chan village is always willing to assist you Magistrate Ming."

Ming Na Jun looked at him slyly, "How much do you know about this man here?"

Lu Po looked over at Hap Sing who maintained a bland expression, "I know he is a fisherman who has lived in our village for many years. I know his family comes from elsewhere in Ran Li though. In all the time he has lived here he has paid his taxes on time, and never caused any problems with the other citizens. In fact he has been helpful with many of the poor making certain they have enough to eat."

Ming Na Jun leaned back, "All of that is true I am sure. Are you aware that according to your records he has been paying taxes for fifty four years in your village now?"

Lu Po thought a moment before answering, "That does seem surprising. It is of course long before I was village leader so I have only really managed the books from the last twelve years or so. My father who has passed now was in charge of that responsibility before me. Perhaps he is well preserved for his age?"

Ming Na Jun pointed at Hap Sing, "If you research the other tax roles over the years, then you will find that he has been paying taxes for over one hundred twenty years in this kingdom. How would you explain such a thing?"

Lu Po thought some more, "Do you suspect that he is someone using an alias to avoid some trouble elsewhere then? We have not heard of any criminals matching his description being wanted Magistrate Ming."

Ming Na Jun leaned forward, "What would you say if I told you that there are rumors that many Chi Masters live unnaturally long lives? I suspect this Hap Sing is one of those Chi Masters."

Lu Po contemplated again, "I would say that seems highly unlikely. No one here in Li Chan village has complained of Hap Sing practicing Chi magic. The people here know of him as a generally unremarkable citizen of our community. What makes you think that he is a Chi Master then?"

Ming Na Jun smiled, "We Chi Masters have ways of recognizing our own kind."

Lu Po leaned back and looked directly at Hap Sing to address him, "Greater destiny you said. You made no mention of Magistrate Ming being a fellow Chi Master."

Hap Sing shrugged, "Ming Na Jun is adept at disguising the nature of his greater destiny. Until he approached me directly I was unaware of it."

Ming Na Jun laughed, "Hap Sing was right. You are very facile at avoiding a direct response to any question when you choose. If I had not already been certain of my conclusion, then you would have likely led me off course again. I wonder how many other topics you have handled in this manner with me."

Lu Po replied, "I have done my best to provide you with accurate information Magistrate Ming."

Ming Na Jun nodded, "I don't doubt that your books are spotless Lu Po. There has never been any sign of misappropriations or dishonesty in how you handle your responsibilities for the government. However, it does seem like you will go to great lengths to protect your friends."

Lu Po shook his head, "If you will pardon my contradiction your honor, then I must say that it has nothing to do with protecting my friends. What I do is for the good of this village and all of its citizens."

Lu Po continued as Ming Na Jun raised an eyebrow, "It is well known by our village counsel that since the arrival of General Li Hung and his friend Hap Sing our village has prospered. Pardon my speaking ill of the dead but the current village counsel knew that General Li Hung forcibly drove away or killed any bandits or robbers who would try to operate near our community. More importantly we also know that Hap Sing has been our Lucky Cricket."

Ming Na Jun was surprised, "What do you mean by your Lucky Cricket?"

Lu Po gave a faint smile, "It was a name we first heard used by General Li Hung. It seems his father General Li Chan had come up with it to describe his childhood friend Hap Sing. If you were to check more than the tax payments for the last fifty four years you would know that no one has died of disease or illness in Li Chan village in that time. Only one villager has died from accident while they were out fishing in fact. Every other death has been of old age. There has not been a drought or a shortage of fish. There is enough food for everyone to not go hungry. This village has known relative peace and contentment in this whole time. Can the rest of Ran Li say the same?"

Ming Na Jun answered, "You are correct that while Ran Li has been relatively peaceful, but most of the country has not been as prosperous. I can't help but think that this relates to the being Hap Sing called the Luck."

Hap Sing ducked his head, "In terms of my life, there is very little that does not relate to the Luck as it calls itself now. I can not talk to it, and it does not talk to me except through intermediaries. It has to possess my body to interact with people. I have been told that such interactions are very unpleasant however."

Lu Po shivered, "Unpleasant does not begin to cover the reality of it. I will not attempt to converse with it again. The one time was certainly more than I was prepared to experience."

Ming Na Jun questioned in a thoughtful voice, "Just how bad was it?"

Lu Po ducked his head as well, "I would rather attempt to chop off the tail of a dragon. It would be easier to contemplate. I know of none who met it that night who would give a different answer."

Hap Sing looked at Ming Na Jun, "That is why I will not summon it here except in a dire circumstance. It does not gladly suffer the presence of mortals unless the meeting is on its own terms it seems."

Ming Na Jun looked at Hap Sing, "What happened that time?"

Hap Sing looked slightly depressed, "I had summoned it to help rescue a fellow fisherman lost at sea during a storm. I had hoped he still lived. I was wrong. It seems the Luck can not or is unwilling to bring the dead back to life. Most likely because that is the province of the gods, and it does not wish to unduly offend them. It also became clear that the Luck does not like to fail. Failure makes it very unhappy. The best it could do was retrieving the body for a proper burial. In retrospect I believe the Luck was most upset with itself at the time, but unfortunately the village elders bore the brunt of its anger."

Ming Na Jun was thoughtful, "What did it do to you Lu Po?"

Lu Po was slightly sweating, "It told me and the other village counselors things that we mortals were never meant to know. It said them to me knowing I would be haunted by them. I am unable to tell others because of my need to spare them the pain. I would gladly kill a man to spare him the knowledge rather than reveal it. It would be the greater kindness."

Ming Na Jun seemed unconvinced, "What kind of knowledge would be so painful to know?"

Lu Po ducked his head, "Secrets. It told us the kinds of secrets which would bring the personal wrath of every god if revealed. Mortals were not intended to safeguard such knowledge, but it dropped this information into our ears as our punishment. Death would be much easier than bearing this burden."

Ming Na Jun seemed nervous as he asked, "Why has it not driven you to kill yourselves then?"

Lu Po shook his head, "That is the worst part. The Luck told us these secrets were permanently burned into our spirits. Even death will not be a release from them. I will not callously request the Luck be summoned again. My lesson was a hard one."

Min Na Jun looked at Hap Sing, "It can do such things?"

Hap Sing shrugged, "Of that I have no doubt. It may be many things, but so far in my experience the Luck has never seemed to lie about something like that. If it does lie, then it certainly puts a large enough threat behind it to make it seem more reasonable to accept the lie rather than risk the threat."

Ming Na Jun sipped the remainder of his tea before responding, "It seems I am in a quandary then. I need to learn something this Luck is planning to do, and yet Hap Sing claims to be as much in the dark about its intent as I am."

Lu Po gave a faint smile as he placed a coin on the table in front of him, "It has been so since I have known of his situation. Hap Sing is the Cricket side of the coin. The Greater Spirit Seven Tailed Tiger is the Luck side of the coin. Neither side can directly interact with the other. We are however like this sand. The coin can make an impression in us, and by examining that impression both the Luck and the Cricket can begin to understand one another."

Ming Na Jun and Hap Sing watched the metaphor being demonstrated by Lu Po pressing the coin in the sand tranquility garden on his table. Ming Na Jun looked at the two separate impressions in the sand, and then at the coin lying on the table. The impressions of the coin's two images were reversed yet understandable knowing the source. The others could tell Ming Na Jun had reached a conclusion from the example from his impression.

Ming Na Jun looked at Hap Sing carefully, "That is the problem being faced I think. Has anyone talked to the Luck at the source of its being? They keep seeing it through a facet of its being instead. The Luck is not part of a two sided coin. It is instead like a seven sided gem. We only get to see the impression it makes through the filter of one facet, through Hap Sing here. It can only display a certain amount of itself at one time through that facet."

Hap Sing looked over at Lu Po and asked, "What are you suggesting then?"

Ming Na Jun raised an eyebrow, "The greater spirits all live in the dreaming. I suggest that you guide me to where it dwells there and that we see the Luck in person instead of tying to bring it here. I think meeting it on its home territory might be a more suitable way to approach it."

Hap Sing closed his eyes a moment and opened them again, "You understand that other great spirits live in the dreaming as well. Not all of them are friendly to the Luck, or in agreement with its actions. I have never attempted to achieve such a thing."

Ming Na June replied, "As you have informed me already today. How do you know it can not be done until you have attempted it?"

Hap Sing gave a faint smile, "My own discussion turned against me, very well put Ming Na June. It might be advisable to get some assistance if we want to attempt this. Looking at Lu Po's expression it might also be best if we don't use his home for this attempt either."

Lu Po gave a weak smile, "My home is at the disposal of Magistrate Ming as always."

Ming Na Jun looked back at Lu Po, "I thank you for your hospitality, and I may well take you up on your offer for a place to stay tonight. However, I will defer to Hap Sing about where this should be attempted."

Hap Sing smiled, "Before we begin I think it best if I have some breakfast. I have some fresh caught fish I can share if you are both interested. It will give us time to reflect on our course of action before we begin, and time for my disciple to finish her morning chores."

Hap Sing sat on a carved log segment facing a ring of stones creating a fire pit. Behind him was something which looked like a lean-to structure dug partially into a hillside. It had grasses and other plants growing on top of it. There was a blanket covered low entryway partially dug into the ground leading into the questionable structure. The walls were made of stacked flat stones now many years covered in moss, and the roof seemed to be made of logs covered in soil and planted. A small tin pipe with a conical cover over its end was likely the vent for an interior brazier of some kind.

It was obvious to Yuki Nene and Ming Na Jun looking across the unlit fire pit at Hap Sing that even though he was relatively short in stature, he would need to duck to enter the low structure. While the structure and surrounding area was neatly kept, it was clearly never intended to originally serve as more than a temporary residence.

Ming Na Jun looked around for a place to sit and settled on using another section of log as a chair. Yuki Nene sat in a cross legged fashion on the ground. Nearby there were loaded fish drying racks set up facing the late morning sun which were thankfully downwind at the moment. On closer examination Ming Na Jun also recognized a small herb garden beside the lean-to structure. On the opposite side was a wood pile neatly stacked and curing for later burning.

Ming Na Jun spoke first as Hap Sing appeared to be slightly embarrassed, "Has this been your home for the last fifty four years Hap Sing?"

Hap Sing shook his head, "This is my second one. I was not much of a carpenter I'm afraid. The first one collapsed after the first three years during a storm. I learned to use stone for the walls after that incident, and to use the slope to keep the water out. This one is thankfully much drier. It does not leak much at all when it rains, and it drains out pretty quickly."

Yuki Nene flushed as well as she spoke, "Yong Mai has told me that you lived as the poorest person in Li Chan village. I did not realize that you lived in a building too small for me to even stand inside. No wonder you did not want me to come here. I must be an embarrassment being so tall and ungainly."

Hap Sing opened his mouth as if to speak, and closed it again as Yuki Nene turned her head to look down at the sea. Ming Na Jun looked in the same direction and could see that the view from the hill side overlooking the ocean was actually quite beautiful. Ming Na Jun understood the view had been a major factor in picking the location. The combination of solitude and view was pleasant even if the building was crude and ultimately never built to last. It had instead been built with the purpose of gradually returning to nature without much impact to the location after a few years of abandonment. Ming Na Jun could tell that luxurious comforts were not a concern for Hap Sing.

Ming Na Jun caught an odd expression on the face of Yuki Nene as he looked over at her. He knew the look of a frustrated young person who was used to getting what they desired. He also knew the frustration of impatient youth whose ambitions were not being realized quickly enough. A less observant person might have mistaken her expression for one of these things. Perhaps that is what she intended one of them to think. It was less obvious however that she was thinking behind her display of emotion.

Ming Na Jun then figured it out. She loved Hap Sing in an infatuated manner similar to a crush, and did not know how to tell him that his home didn't matter. She realized his embarrassment, and turned the situation around on herself in an attempt to relieve his discomfort about his meager lifestyle.

Hap Sing cleared his throat and spoke, "I presume we should get started. If you both will prepare yourselves to enter the dreaming, then I will meet you there. I suggest we lay on the stretch of grasses there on the hill as that will be the most comfortable if our visit is extended for some reason. I've gotten pretty good at carrying people along to my position in the dreaming, so as Nene already knows all you have to do is fall into a meditative state, and I will manage the rest."

Hap Sing lay down with Yuki Nene on his right and Ming Na Jun on his left on the hillside. They relaxed as best they were able first, and then Yuki Nene and Ming Na Jun clasped hands with Hap Sing. Hap Sing noticed that it only took Yuki Nene about five minutes to reach the initial state of calm required. Ming Na Jun took about fifteen minutes. Hap Sing willed himself to the dreaming.

The three of them were apparently sitting in Hap Sing's boat out on the water of a bay. The sky was a pristine blue and the water was a perfect turquoise. There was no village seen on the shore, and it was not a shoreline that either Ming Na Jun or Yuki Nene recognized. The beach was not stony but instead a clean white sand. Coconut palm trees lined the shore and deeper jungle formed behind them. A ridge on one side of the island forming one arm of the bay had a winding path leading to a set of rough hewn stairs leading up the rock face.

On top of the ridge was a lighthouse with a white beacon pulsing like the beating of a heart, thump da bump, went the rhythm of the light. Ming Na Jun and Yuki Nene looked around in a sense of wonder. This place looked like the image of a piece of paradise. Hap Sing smiled with a serene expression. Ming Na Jun noticed that Yuki Nene was looking at Hap Sing with an expression bordering on worship.

Ming Na Jun spoke, "Where are we? This is like nothing I have seen in the dreaming."

Hap Sing spoke in a fatherly calm voice, "This is the beginning of Shangri La my children. There is much more work to be done, but it is going to be my home someday."

Ming Na Jun spoke, "Your home? Isn't this the dreaming? I did not think that mortal beings could dwell here."

Hap Sing nodded, "Yes, you are correct. Shangri La is part of the dreaming for now. When it is finished and ready to be inhabited by mortals it shall become a part of the prime and several other planes however."

Ming Na Jun looked closer at Hap Sing and realized that a difference existed. This was and yet was not the same person he had met already. The physical form was identical, but the feeling of peace and serenity which radiated from Hap Sing was unusual to his experience. Then he understood that this was the Cricket mentioned by Lu Po. It was obvious that there was a difference now. The Cricket did not quite have the same personality as Hap Sing. There were similarities, and there were subtle differences. The Cricket was Hap Sing at the point of enlightenment, calm, serene, and accepting.

Yuki Nene spoke, "Shall I be the anchor now as you guide Ming Na Jun to meet the Luck?"

Hap Sing gave a gentle smile as he began paddling to the nearby beach, "I am sorry my child. I am going to have to remain on the beach here. The Luck and I do not directly meet. I believe that would cause problems neither of us is prepared to manage. I will act as the anchor my dear Nene. You shall have to guide Jun to the Luck for me."

Yuki Nene took up another paddle and naturally matched his pace, "How shall I know the way?"

Hap Sing waved a hand in an odd gesture through the air in front of Yuki Nene and Ming Na Jun. They both saw a bright orange ribbon with black tiger stripes stretch from Hap Sing's aura toward the lighthouse tower up on the ridge. Hap Sing then reached out a hand and touched the shoulder of Yuki Nene. A black ribbon stretched from Yuki Nene to join to the tiger striped one. Hap Sing repeated the gesture with Ming Na Jun and a green ribbon stretched out from Ming Na Jun to join the tiger striped ribbon.

Hap Sing spoke as Yuki Nene and Ming Na Jun marveled, "The tiger striped spirit ribbon will lead you to the location of the Luck. It is my bond to the Luck, and will not fail to lead you correctly. Should you loose sight of it because of some difficulty, know that I have tied your spirit ribbons to mine so you can follow them to it."

Ming Na Jun spoke as the boat reached the shore, "I presume that you are the Cricket?"

Hap Sing nodded, "I am the Cricket who is yet to be. Hap Sing is present and watching, but I needed to be here to start you on the path and be your anchor. Hap Sing is still learning these things yet, so it was easier for me to provide you the assistance this time."

Ming Na Jun looked confused, "I don't understand what you mean. Are the two of you different beings then?"

Hap Sing shook his head, "We are one being. There is only a difference in perspective. Hap Sing's perspective is the mortal one. The Cricket's perspective is the spiritual one. As you mentioned to Lu Po there are many facets to the being known as the Lucky Cricket. We are two of those facets, Hap Sing and the Cricket. The Luck is another of those facets, and it should have the answers you seek."

Yuki Nene looked at Hap Sing with a look of adoration, "Does that mean there are more aspects to you?"

Hap Sing smiled serenely, "Of course there is my child, just as you have many aspects, several of which concern or bemuse Hap Sing. Don't worry my child, once he knows your essential nature his concerns will diminish."

Ming Na Jun spoke, "What do you mean her essential nature?"

Hap Sing placed a hand thoughtfully up to his chin, "The core being represented by a person. Many of us beings have different aspects. We use which aspects best suit our situation. There is always a core being behind all of the aspects which guides them. Understanding essential nature is one of my strong talents Ming Na Jun. Attaching the spirit ribbons is one way I expedite the process."

They reached the beach and Ming Na Jun and Yuki Nene stepped out of the boat. The waited expectantly a moment for Hap Sing to join them but he remained seated.

Hap Sing spoke as he looked up at them, "I shall monitor your progress through the spirit ribbon. The two of you will just need to follow the direction of the stripes to find the Luck. When you are ready to return the stripes will reverse direction and you can follow them back to me. You should set out now. The Luck is expecting you both soon."

As Hap Sing spoke the black tiger stripes on the orange ribbon moved from being horizontal on the ribbon to forming a continuing series of triangular shapes pointing away from Hap Sing. Yuki Nene and Ming Na Jun walked along the beach following the ribbon toward the light house up on the ridge. Hap Sing rowed the boat back into the deeper water in the bay and lowered his fishing pole into the water.

The Luck looked at the odd shapes floating yet immaterial in the space in front of it. The Luck appeared to be in the form of a short human. On closer examination it would have looked like Hap Sing except for several key differences. It wore an odd close fitting orange shirt and dark blue short pants. Its skin was orange and covered in black tiger stripes. It wore a haircut similar to Hap Sing except the orange and black color scheme continued there as well. The eyes of the Luck were also those of a tiger, and seven tails extended into space behind it twitching and moving around.

The Luck was seemingly floating in the center of a large spherical space with free floating images projected in various locations. In front of most of those images was a tiger cub watching the image intently. As something of interest happened with the image, a cub would bat at it like a cat playing with a ball of string. The image would float over to the vicinity of the Luck and await his perusal. When the Luck was finished with a particular piece he would reorient to view another image while one of his seven tails would push the image back toward an unoccupied space in the room. Sometimes a new image would appear in the room, and shortly after it appeared another tiger cub would enter from a small doorway to examine the image.

Ming Na Jun and Yuki Nene stood at one of the "small" doorway entrances where they had finally followed the ribbon to the Luck. They had been led there by one of the tiger "cubs" which had silently greeted them at the end of their journey. The tiger "cub" had been the relative size of an elephant to them. It had looked at them and led them in through a labyrinthine complex of corridors. It was only the tiger striped spirit ribbon heading in the same direction which gave them confidence they were heading in correct direction.

On arrival at the strange doorway it had opened for the elephant sized tiger cub. It had issued a casual low grumbling growl which they interpreted as an indication to wait at the entrance until summoned. The tiger cub launched itself into the space of the room and floated over to the figure of the Luck. It latched onto one of the tails of the Luck and changed orientation until it could maneuver to face it. The tiger cub looked proportional to a standard tiger cub in comparison to the Luck.

The Luck looked over at the cub tugging on one of its tails and then focused briefly on Ming Na Jun and Yuki Nene standing in the small doorway. It focused back on the images in front of it briefly, and then used its tails to send them flying back to the outer edges of the sphere.

The Luck raised a hand and spoke in a voice that was at a surprisingly reasonable level for its size, "Alright, disperse the work load here to sphere one hundred forty-seven. Prepare this sphere for free configuration mode, mental access trigger, keyword "game room" display. Use the spatial reference for Hap Sing prime scale. Set the gravitational constant at zero point eight seven for our guests please. Execute the order now."

The elephant sized tiger cubs batted away at the images floating around the sphere sending them flying out a different corridor in a seemingly chaotic, but ultimately what could be seen as a coordinated and orderly fashion. The tiger cubs all followed the images out the corridor except the one which held on to one of the tails of the Luck.

That tiger cub released the tail of the luck and moved over to the wall next to the door where Ming Na Jun and Yuki Nene stood in the hall. It touched a section of the wall, and they could see the elephant sized tiger cub and the Luck begin shrinking. A few moments later the tiger cub was relatively tiger cub sized, and the Luck was Hap Sing sized.

The tiger cub then touched another portion of the wall, and the enormous empty sphere was no longer there. Instead Ming Na Jun and Yuki Nene found themselves looking into a simple yet elegant wood paneled room with glass paned windows looking out from a position on top of a snow capped mountain. The view outside was exhilarating, but their eyes quickly returned to where the Luck stood next to a low small table surrounded by two sitting cushions on the parquet hardwood floor.

The Luck spoke, "Greetings Yuki Nene. Would you please follow my cub to where I will speak with you? I will speak with Ming Na Jun here. You will be allowed to rejoin with him to guide him back to Cricket when it is time. Ming Na Jun I welcome you to my humble home, please have a seat. What kind of tea do you prefer?"

Ming Na Jun watched Yuki Nene being led back down the corridor away from them a moment before he turned back and walked forward to sit at the table in front of the Luck. As he sat he could see that it was not a typical tea table, but instead it was a traditionally styled Go game board.

Ming Na Jun spoke, "Could you provide a black tea with a hint of rose?"

The Luck pointed at a small raised tray which had appeared on the ground to the right beside Ming Na Jun. On the tray was a porcelain cup which contained a darkened liquid which resembled tea. Ming Na Jun raised an eyebrow, and then raised the cup to take a sip. To his surprise it was an excellently flavored warm black tea with a hint of rose.

Ming Na Jun took another sip as the Luck sat down and placed a white ceramic tile on one of the intersections of the Go board in front of them. Ming Na Jun looked down at his left and saw a bowl of black ceramic tiles on the floor. He selected a tile and placed it on a suitable intersection with a satisfying tap noise.

The Luck spoke with a vague smile on its face as it placed another white tile on an intersection, "It seems you are familiar with the concept of the game. That is good. It will make the discussion go easier then."

Ming Na Jun nodded as he placed a black tile, "I was accounted a fair player in my youth, although I have not ever mastered the game. This tea is quite good by the way."

The Luck nodded as it placed another white tile, "I am glad you approve. I used the recipe preferred by your mother. I assumed that was acceptable then."

Ming Na Jun hesitated as he held his tile, "How would you know what recipe was preferred by my mother?"

The Luck gave a gentle smile, "Quite simply because you know it my good man."

Ming Na Jun placed his black tile, "You can read my mind then?"

The Luck shrugged as it placed a white tile, "Not in the way you mean. I can not understand what you are thinking at the moment if that is what concerns you. That kind of mind reading would be the province of an arcane practitioner. I can access things you know however, especially those things which have impacted your spirit. This tea reminds you of your mother, so it is dear to you in a way."

Ming Na Jun kept his calm, "This spirit ribbon helps you to do this trick?"

The Luck nodded, "It lets me focus on you more effectively. I can hear what you hear, and I can see what you see. I can not process that information the same way that you do. I am not party to your rational processes, or the rational processes of your son Ming Wa Fu. It is still your turn by the way."

Ming Na Jun played his piece on the board, "I think I understand what you are saying, but I don't understand your purpose."

The Luck smiled, "Ah now we get to the crux of your concern. What do I intend to do? How much control do I have? Continue to play out this board and I think you will begin to see."

Ming Na Jun and the Luck played on in silence for a while. Ming Na Jun initially thought that he was ahead and gaining further ground until about midway through the game a number of curious choices made earlier by the Luck started reversing his momentum and gaining ground for it. By the end of the game the Luck had a clear advantage in space and captured pieces. As they tallied the score Ming Na Jun realized that he had played against what was clearly a master level talent at Go.

Ming Na Jun sat back and contemplated his loss, "It is clear that you are a master at Go."

The Luck gave a slight bow, "You were a good opponent for a mortal. I hold an unfair advantage, so I handicapped my play in the beginning to make it more challenging for myself to win."

Ming Na Jun commented, "So those seemingly bad moves . . ."

The Luck slightly smiled, "Were deliberately bad moves losing me advantage. It makes the game more challenging for me to finish ahead then. I apologize, but I only felt it fair to handicap myself."

Ming Na Jun smiled in return, "So you are letting me know that you are smart. Not just smart but very smart."

The Luck nodded, "That is one thing, but there is much more behind it. Why do you think I chose Go?"

Ming Na Jun gave a cautious reply, "It is something we both know and understand. It also is representative of something else such as, skill, ability, knowledge."

The Luck showed a cocky grin, "Your answer is not deep enough. Yes it should be clear to you that in any real contest with me you would be out matched in almost every way conceivable. Let's presume we were also representing something as players of Go. The pieces are also significant."

Ming Na Jun looked at the Luck, "In what way would I be able to out match you?"

The Luck lowered its smile, "That is pretty simple. You are always going to be the foundation upon which your son gauges himself. I could never best you in that category and would never think it worthwhile to try. It is simply a matter of understanding my strengths and weaknesses. I could never substitute for someone's father. The Cricket though is quite adept at filling that role. I'm pretty sure you have felt it yourself. The effect can be quite devastating on certain mortals, especially younger and more impressionable ones. That is why your son's exposure to Hap Sing has been limited to reduce the impact of their eventual real meeting. Think of it as me giving you the opportunity to create the basis of your son's value system before I begin to task him with his destiny."

Ming Na Jun looked concerned, "What is your plan for him?"

The Luck held up a white tile and responded, "Answer this first. What does this represent?"

Ming Na Jun took a broad guess, "Something you have on your side. Some one you have in your grasp."

The Luck nodded, "That is close enough. Now watch what happens when I play this in one of the bordered zones on the board."

Ming Na Jun watched as the Luck played the piece on an empty intersection. The piece changed from white to an orange color with black tiger stripes. Several other pieces on the board also changed color to match that piece. The majority of the pieces were still white and black, but the white now held less territory than the black. The game had gone from a win for white to a win for black in one unauthorized illegal move.

Ming Na Jun shook his head, "You can't do that. That is not an allowed move in Go."

The Luck smiled, "I think you are noticing something you didn't understand before now. We are not playing the Go you know and understand. The rules are a little different as is the full game board. Let me show you."

The game board changed from wooden to transparent. The lines of the board extended as far as the eye could see horizontally, and vertically. Next the board began stacking up into the air of the now roofless room and down through the now transparent floor. The spacing between the lines widened a bit as Ming Na Jun saw that many of the intersections already held tiles of thousands of different colors. Phantom translucent tiger cubs ran through the space placing the various colored tiles throughout the space placing tiles by the thousands as other cubs removed the captured tiles into various bins around the room.

Ming Na Jun looked at the enormous expanse of the seemingly infinite three dimensional Go boards and shook his head, "I don't understand. This is not like any game of Go I have ever heard being played. What is this supposed to mean?"

The Luck smiled with a cocky grin, "You are watching a representation of Go as played by the gods. Each one of those tiger cubs is representing the moves of a god or goddess as they play."

Ming Na Jun shook his head, "It is too complex. I can not grasp what is happening."

The Luck smiled, "It may seem so, but if you watch long enough you will understand the underlying metaphor. Understand that if the gods are represented by the tiger cubs playing. Then what do the pieces represent?"

Ming Na Jun paled slightly, "Mortal spirits?"

The Luck nodded, "Actually immortal spirits in mortal forms, but your understanding is close enough now. This game is but a metaphor for the actions of the gods. It gives me a means of analyzing their actions and the results in a simplified manner. You must understand that for the gods everything comes down to how many spirits they have which are on their side. The number of pieces they have in play, and the number in their bins are very important to them. If they keep too many in their bins, then their position on the board could be jeopardized. If they play too many pieces, they risk loss of numbers due to capture or conversion."

Ming Na Jun shook his head, "I thought I was doing good to play with you. You've been watching and analyzing this game of the gods the entire time we've been playing."

The Luck shrugged as the room cleared back to its original state on top of the snow covered mountain peak minus a game board, "I don't watch using that metaphor much as it is clumsy for analysis, but it is useful for explaining the premise of what I am doing. The gods crave spirits. They need them to establish position and dominance among each other. A deity with a lot of spirits has power, but risks much in the attempt because they make themselves a target for the other deities which operate in alliances. A deity with enough power dictates how their alliance operates. A deity with too much power risks loosing supporting deities to another alliance. You could call such a deity a victim of their own success as it were."

Ming Na Jun sat forward, "What about you? I noticed that your piece showed up on the board and changed the state of play. I thought that great spirits did not interfere in the doings of the gods."

The Luck smiled, "You are correct that most great spirits pretend they are not involved in the god's game of Go. Instead we are more interested in what I would call a game of spirit Shogi. Understand that the deities, those things you refer to as the gods, goddesses, demons, devils, and such are primarily concerned with the material side of existence. They usually just view the spirits of their supporters as convenient markers to play their game."

Ming Na Jun nodded, "What about the great spirits of the dreaming? I want to know about the great spirits known as the Numbers in particular."

The Luck smiled as a Shogi board appeared in between them, "We play our game of Shogi between ourselves. The pieces are not representative of material manifestations. They are in the form of greater spirits with influence and power. Li Hung was on my board as a castle until recently for example. He was a piece used for spiritual presence for many years, but at the same time was a sacrifice piece in case my king came into jeopardy. Li Hung was very direct, and yet effective as a castle. He was also fairly predictable. Li Hung would see a potential threat, and kill it if it did not leave in time. Other pieces have now been brought into play, so I was able to gracefully retire Li Hung without capture into my bin. His father Li Chan was more like the gold general. Li Chan was a long term strategic thinker as well as a brilliant tactician. Ultimately he needed to be sacrificed but he served his purpose well."

Ming Na Jun spoke, "I think I understand that much. You bring powerful pieces into play among each other. I know there are less of the Numbers than the deities. I don't yet understand how this whole thing you are attempting now works."

The Luck waved and the enormous three dimensional projection of the divine Go board appeared again, "Watch what happens when I play what I call Go Shogi then."

The Luck placed one of its Shogi pieces on a space between the intersections with several different colors nearby. A few of the colors changed temporarily to tiger striped orange and black, and then some shifted to black and even more shifted to a bright silver color. This happened to pieces above, below, and in some random places in the distance.

Ming Na Jun looked at the game board, "It is incredible. One piece being played has had a substantive change in the manner of play. You've tipped the balance of the board in subtle ways. I don't understand what rules are in operation, and there is no clear direct adjacency to the full effect."

The Luck nodded, "Let me just say that the divine powers while having much influence in the material realms, still are limited in understanding the nature of the influence of the spiritual on the material. It takes a Number to fully understand what was just accomplished by that move, and to understand the longer term ramifications."

Ming Na Jun looked over at the board and then back at the Luck sitting in front of it, "What did that move represent in the material world? I take it that was not just a demonstration for my edification and enjoyment."

The Luck smiled, "It means I have recruited another greater spirit to my side. It was an unaligned one at that, so no deity is going to notice the result of that move too quickly unless it benefited them."

Ming Na Jun looked around at the board as it casually asked, "What greater spirit would that be?"

The Luck grinned, "Yourself of course. It happened when I placed my spirit ribbon on you. Your mortal choices and thus your material choices are you own to make, and I can not directly influence or change them. However, your immortal spirit is allied with me now. Your actions will have spiritual repercussions in the game of Go Shogi. I get to direct those repercussions as I see fit."

Ming Na Jun thought about it, "How many of the other numbers are playing this game you call Go Shogi?"

The Luck nodded, "It is very astute of you to recognize this is something relatively new. So far only one other Number is directly playing against me. There are a few Numbers who are pretending there is no such game. However, there are many Numbers standing on the sidelines waiting to decide if the game is worth the risk."

Ming Na Jun raised an eyebrow, "There is a risk?"

The Luck nodded with a faint smile, "Of course there is a risk. A Number has to place themselves on the board as their own king to play. The original Number to try it didn't understand any of the rules yet. It suffered the penalty for a loss. This has made the rest of the Numbers more cautious about entering the match. I myself am only certain of some rules, and have been cautiously learning other ones. The material world is of course in many ways still a challenge for the greater spirits to understand and control. In that realm the deities have an advantage over us. It is of course why the divine casters can manipulate their powers with much greater effect on the nature of material existence when compared to a Chi Master. A Chi Master's effect on the spiritual however is quite impressive when fully understood. With my assistance some of them will manifest abilities which are quite transcendent."

Ming Na Jun thought a moment, "I am just a pawn to you then?"

The Luck smiled, "You are more like one of my knights. Your moves are somewhat unpredictable for the enemy, and your reach will be impressive."

Ming Na Jun nodded, "What then of my son Ming Wa Fu?"

The Luck smiled even more broadly, "Ming Wa Fu shall eventually be my new gold general, and Yuki Nene shall be my silver general."

Ming Na Jun thought about it, "They will be powerful pieces then. They will also be highly sought after by your opponent."

The Luck's smile lessened, "That is the risk of playing. Life is risk however. Nothing lasts forever, except the spirits that is. They are immortal."

Ming Na Jun asked, "What is the penalty for loss you mentioned?"

The Luck's expression was serious, "Removal from the game. Actually from all games until the next turn of the great cycle. You shouldn't worry about it too much, just let me say that it will not be a desirable result."

Ming Na Jun pondered a moment, "What is the nature of your opponent?"

The Luck replied, "My opponent is ruthless and tends to favor assisting the diabolical and demonic powers. They have the advantage of being flexible and unrestrained in their behavior."

Ming Na Jun nodded, "How do you plan to respond to such?"

The Luck smiled, "I don't plan to also rely on my opponent's strengths. I am choosing more methodical and reliable resources from among the divine powers. I will have the advantage with coordination and cooperation. My weakness will be a degree of predictability for my actions."

Ming Na Jun thought a moment, "So really is this all just a game for you and your kind to amuse yourselves?"

The Luck stopped smiling, "This is the nature of material and spiritual existence. As I said before the game references are just a metaphor for the activity you see around you in the material world. There are rules in the world, and to disobey them is to potentially face the consequences. Would criticize your sun for burning your skin? The sun is doing what it does. Your failure to recognize the positive and negative effects it has does not mean the sun is to blame."

Ming Na Jun nodded, "I understand. I am simply a man who can not change the nature of existence."

The Luck grinned again, "That is not quite true. You are a man, but you can help me change the nature of existence. For a long time I've noticed a certain unfairness in the way things have been happening. I have actually openly joined one of the divine alliances to establish a rebalancing of the sides. I am not trying to win this like a game. I do want to make sure that an unfair advantage does not exist. As you may have noted when you played Go with me, my primary opponent is currently ahead of me in knowledge and position. They know the hidden rules better and are aware of more potential pitfalls which may exist. However, I excel at working with a disadvantage. It makes me work harder and smarter to achieve what I want. My opponent's major pieces are also generally noisy and easy to locate. My pieces have been mostly working behind the scenes to establish my position."

Ming Na Jun took another sip of his tea. He noted that it was still the same warm temperature as when he first drank it, and that the level of tea in the cup had not changed when he put it down. He looked at his cup in contemplation.

The Luck followed his gaze, "Is something wrong?"

Ming Na Jun spoke, "This tea isn't real. I can taste it, smell it, enjoy it, but it still does not exist."

The Luck had a sly smile, "Such is one of the rules of the dreaming. Only spirit exists here. All else is perception and projection. I project the cup of tea, you perceive its existence. Only on the planes does the concept of matter have true meaning. When you depart the dreaming the tea you have consumed here will not have filled your stomach, or satisfied your physical needs."

Ming Na Jun thought for a while, "Then in Ran Li you exist as Hap Sing."

The Luck nodded with a sly smile, "That is my king in play. He is me to a degree. Our spirits have been blended since his birth. I am learning the rules of material existence through him so I can apply them to my strategy. Hap Sing is learning the nature of immortality and spirit through me."

Ming Na Jun shook his head, "It must be hard to keep track. I can see why you need so many assistants to help you here."

The Luck grinned, "I need no assistants in the dreaming. Those tiger cubs you see don't exist, just like your cup of tea doesn't exist. They are simply a metaphor for tasks happening in my consciousness, another visual reference to give a feeling of familiarity for my guests. I could just as easily operate without those metaphors. They are helpful for material beings though."

Ming Na Jun shook his head, "Why tiger cubs then? Why do you not use sheep, goats, or even the same race as your guest?"

The Luck smiled wickedly, "Would this make you more comfortable?"

Ming Na Jun looked in shock to see his son Ming Wa Fu run past him with a sheaf of papers in his hand to give to the Luck. Another servant came in which looked like his deceased wife, and Ming Na Jun began to slightly tremble as she picked up his serving table and tea cup.

Ming Na Jun had a serious look, "I have taken your point. The tiger cubs were fine. You can restore them if you prefer. I suppose there is a deeper lesson to be learned here as well."

The Luck nodded, "The realm of the dreaming does not restrict form. It is only a convention here. I used a set of tiger cubs to make my brand recognition more suitable to your perspective. I am known as the greater spirit seven tailed tiger in the prime after all. I am becoming known as the Luck and have adopted this new apparent form blending Hap Sing's features with my identifying markings. I quite like the effect myself. We even identify as Numbers so that beings think they can get a grasp on what we are. We have been known to simulate a rank and file based on those designations so that outsiders think that such things matter to us. It doesn't really. The only thing which matters is capability when all else is nonexistent."

Ming Na Jun sat in contemplation for a while, "I don't understand everything, but I get the basis of what you are teaching me. What do you expect me to do for you?"

The Luck smiled again, "I am glad we have come to this point. It is simple really. I expect you to teach your son. Teach him of the history of the Chi Masters, and their importance to events in the past. Teach him the reality of Ran Li as it is now. Prepare him for when his powers awaken. Guide him after they are realized. Know that in not too much more time the Chi Masters will regain their freedom in Ran Li, and your son will no longer need to hide what he will become."

Ming Na Jun shook his head, "How do you intend to change the laws of Ran Li? The Chi Masters have been effectively outlawed from practicing their talents."

The Luck nodded, "That was the result of one of the earlier moves of my opponent. I am countering that move through a combination of moves by my bishop and my knight."

Ming Na Jun spoke, "You need me to do something?"

The Luck smiled, "I will teach you a trick. It must be used very cautiously you understand. This is not something you should ever demonstrate to another. I have temporarily freed up my full control of this portion of the dreaming. Watch carefully, and repeat after you understand what I have done."

The Luck held out its right hand palm down and closed its fingers to make a lightly closed fist. Then it turned its closed right hand palm up and slowly opened its fingers to reveal a gold coin with a Ran Li official mint stamping in its palm.

Ming Na Jun spoke, "Interesting trick, but how does that help me? As you noted before nothing in the dreaming is material."

The Luck had a mischievous grin as it replied, "Nothing in the dreaming is material while it is in the dreaming. You should know the entire material existence you know started as a concept in the dreaming, existence was made material by bringing the concept from the dreaming. Place this coin in your pouch, and now focus on making one for yourself. You should be skilled enough at manipulating the dreaming by now to understand how this can be done."

Ming Na Jun attempted the same maneuver while focusing on the result he wanted to achieve. When he opened his hand he also held a gold coin in his palm. It felt as real and weighty as an actual coin.

The Luck smiled, "Very good Jun. You have learned an important trick today. Put that coin in your pouch as well. Before you leave the dreaming with Hap Sing create one more coin in that way. Hold it in your hand and concentrate on it as you return. I think you will find some interesting results. Remember this trick is not to be taught to anyone by you. It is important that if they discover it for themselves they need to also have the same level of responsibility that goes with it."

Ming Na Jun placed the coin in his pouch as he asked, "What do you mean by the responsibility necessary?"

The Luck's look became serious, "I have taught you a trick that has a lot of power behind it. If this trick were misused by someone, then it can effectively destroy entire nations over time. That is a terrible power, and one that is also likely to rebound upon its user."

Ming Na Jun asked, "Creating something can destroy a nation?"

The Luck shrugged, "That would depend on the thing created. What you know how to make is a form of currency in your country. It has representative value. The more you create the less representative value each of the other forms of currency like it will eventually have. It is the relative rarity of the material which helps represent that value. I have shown you how to destroy the relativity of that rarity. Misused this could damage a nation or hosts of nations. I expect you can understand the implications now."

Ming Na Jun thought, "The coins I make will become real?"

The Luck nodded, "As real as you want to make them. You are now a rich man if such is your goal. You will also destroy the country you serve and its people if you abuse this power for your own gain. I don't think you are that kind of man. However, there are plenty of those who would do desperate things to you and to those you know if they learned of your power. It is a heavy responsibility indeed."

Ming Na Jun asked, "What if I don't want such a power?"

The Luck shrugged, "Use it or don't use it as you see fit. Unfortunately the wine has been spilled as it were. This is not something you can forget or unlearn on this side of death. There is only how you choose to use this power now. I recommend you use it wisely. On the plus side it works for things other than gold coins. You can always have a supply of your mother's tea if you wish. Your natural ability to use spiritual power will of course limit how much you can create at a single time."

Ming Na Jun paled as he came to a conclusion, "The Cricket said he was creating Shangri La. I thought he was mistaken about making it a real place, but its true isn't it? He is creating an entire land out of the dreaming."

The Luck gave a grin again, "Curious isn't it. That humble fisherman you were feeling pity for is creating more than a land. He is creating an entire world and its inhabitants, a paradise of his own design even. When it is ready it will become real. What do you think that makes him I wonder?"

Ming Na Jun shook his head, "The greatest Chi Master who ever lived to even attempt such a thing. If he succeeds then he has accomplished something only managed by the gods."

The Luck nodded as its grin continued, "A god with powers that even a god can not use. The Lucky Cricket will be a being with control over both the material and spiritual realms. Right now we are still a semi-deity in training as it were. There is still much to do. Speaking of having much to do, that tiger cub will lead you to join up with Nene. You will note that the Cricket has changed direction on the stripes of the spirit ribbon. I think he is calling you back now. Remember I always say it doesn't hurt to have a god owing you some favors. I recommend you handle Hap Sing with the requisite level of respect."

Chapter 15 Conversion

The Luck spoke, "Greetings Yuki Nene. Would you please follow my cub to where I will speak with you? I will speak with Ming Na Jun here. You will be allowed to rejoin with him to guide him back to Cricket when it is time. Ming Na Jun I welcome you to my humble home, please have a seat. What kind of tea do you prefer?"

Yuki Nene followed the tiger cub back down the hall. She noticed after she walked for a while following the cub that a split had appeared in the corridor. There was also a split in the spirit ribbon and this second ribbon followed a path down this new corridor. A while later the corridor opened into a wall with a doorway. The tiger cub stepped to the side of the passage and pointed its nose toward the door.

The doorway opened at her approach. On the other side of the door was a brightly lit meadow with tulips of red and white scattered in groups throughout the manicured grasses. Ahead on a slight rise a blanket was spread out on the ground under the only tree in sight. On the blanket was a covered wicker basket. Leaning against the large oak tree was the same Hap Sing sized orange with black stripes Luck she had last seen talking with Ming Na Jung.

The Luck was wearing a dashing dark blue priest's ceremonial robe which contrasted pleasantly with his orange and black tiger striped skin where it could be seen. The Luck was smiling at her as she walked across the vivid green grass of the meadow. Yuki Nene reached the point where the blanket was spread on the ground with the wicker basket and saw the Luck wave a hand at the blanket and give her a slight nod.

Yuki Nene sat on the blanket with crossed legs as she spoke, "Hello again Luck. I thought you were talking with Ming Na Jun first."

The Luck stepped forward and sat down on the opposite side of the blanket facing her as it replied, "I am talking to him now. You'll find I am quite adept at holding multiple conversations at the same time. Time is less relevant in the dreaming you see."

Yuki Nene nodded, "You mentioned stopping time before. The trick you managed when speaking with us the last time we met."

The Luck smiled, "I am prepared to teach you a trick today just as I will teach Ming Na Jun a trick today as well. Are you certain that trick is the one you want to learn? It does come with several limitations and distinct hazards if used incorrectly."

Yuki Nene thought a moment, "Will you teach me any trick I ask?"

The Luck shook his head while retaining his smile, "Most certainly not. There are plenty of tricks which are too dangerous or destructive to teach you or any mortal. I do however have numerous tricks I know of which I consider appropriate to someone of your ability and disposition. I could give you several options to choose between for your use."

Yuki Nene smiled back, "You would mention several options, but in the end you will only teach me the trick you have already selected. Am I correct?"

The Luck nodded with a smile, "You are a bright student. The trick you would want the most out of the selection I am ready to offer at this time is what I have already picked for you."

Yuki Nene laughed, "I think I am getting the hang of how you work. It always gets down to doing what you want. You just dress things up in a manner to make it look like a personal choice."

The Luck chuckled in reply, "That's me for sure. I'm surprised I am so transparent to you."

Yuki Nene shook her head with a rueful smile, "I am a prodigy perhaps, but you are way ahead of me on how fast you learn. You've certainly learned how to get me to do your bidding haven't you?"

The Luck turned serious, "I have an advantage. Don't think less of yourself because of that. Destiny is simply on my side in this matter."

Yuki Nene turned thoughtful for a moment, "You know the future don't you. You can tell what the course of my life will be. I know the powers like the Numbers are not supposed to have that ability, but you said it yourself, time has less meaning in the dreaming. The Cricket I met when we first came to the dreaming is the Hap Sing from the future isn't he. That's why the two of you can't meet directly. It would violate some kind of secret rule."

The Luck gave a faint grin, "I don't know everything which will happen. There is still uncertainty in the results of individual actions. However, certain people at certain times and places are locked in their actions by my foreknowledge. Hap Sing is one of those people. Since you became involved with Hap Sing you are also one of those people."

Yuki Nene looked up into the sky, "It's hard you know. It is hard to not know what is going on when you do know that your choices have been taken away from you."

The Luck looked serious, "If it helps, then I am sorry you feel this way, but I can not change the course of those events any more than you can. What you can know is that there remains uncertainty. The tulips did not have to be red and white here today. We could be meeting somewhere else entirely. However, the big choices have already been made. We are simply filling in the details."

Yuki Nene leaned back as she spoke, "You know Hap Sing better than anyone. What is he looking for from me? Does he understand how hard it is to sit and watch that old woman dying bit by bit? It is taking a toll on me already. I don't know how I can endure watching it for months."

The Luck turned toward the wicker basket, "I would think that Hap Sing is seeking a point of common empathy with you."

Yuki Nene leaned forward again, "What do you mean?"

The Luck opened the basket and brought out a piece of exotic fruit, "Hap Sing has been experiencing for nearly sixty years this unpleasant sensation of watching the people he knows and cares for slowly dying as you say. You are just beginning to understand the source of his reluctance in becoming involved with you. What you see in Yong Mai is what Hap Sing sees in everyone around him now. From his perspective they are moving very quickly into old age while he is standing still."

Yuki Nene took the piece of fruit handed to her by the Luck and took a bite, "This is very good. It is the best fruit I have ever tasted."

The Luck had a little smile as it watched her take several more bites and finish the fruit, "I am glad you like it. It is called a divine apple. It comes with something I like to call knowledge."

Yuki Nene looked over at the basket, "Are there any more in there?"

The Luck shrugged, "What if I told you that was the last one that would ever be? How do you feel now?"

Yuki Nene moved to look into the basket and saw that it was empty, "Is that the truth? Was that the last divine apple? You shouldn't have let me take such a precious thing."

The Luck looked up at the sky, "Yet you didn't ask. You took what was given, and now regret the loss of it. Perhaps I regret giving it to you as well. Will our regrets cause problems between us now?"

Yuki Nene looked over at the Luck, "This is another of your tests isn't it. You're no better than Hap Sing."

The Luck looked back at her, "You are correct in both statements. Hap Sing is markedly better than me in the manner you imply, and yes this was a test. What you missed is that it was also a lesson."

Yuki Nene thought a moment and said, "Was the lesson that I shouldn't be greedy?"

The Luck shook its head, "What I am saying is Hap Sing isn't like you. He sees the fruit being offered, but doesn't just assume it is his for the taking. He understands implicitly that is it rare and valuable. He also understands that it will eventually wither on the tree if not taken. Hap Sing is being Hap Sing and making sure what is being offered is the right thing for everyone. He doesn't want to grab the fruit and live with the regret of its loss."

Yuki Nene blushed, "You mean my virtue? Hap Sing is worried about my virtue? That has not been intact since I was sixteen. It only gets better with practice and familiarity as well."

The Luck gave a little grin, "Your virtue may have been lost a very few years ago. Do you realize his has never been lost?"

Yuki Nene blushed even deeper, "He is one hundred and fifty. Surely by now it can not have been kept all this time."

The Luck reached into the basket and pulled out another divine apple, "It remains intact. It will take someone who can understand him for him to surrender it willingly. Understanding how he feels about involvement with mortals is a key element of that. You may not realize it but Yong Mai was quite a beauty in her day when Hap Sing and Li Hung first came to Li Chan village together. Yong Mai was attracted to Li Hung immediately as he was a handsome rugged older man at the time and not too dissimilar from her husband. However, Yong Mai was a loyal wife and devoted mother. When her husband passed away to the other side, Yong Mai focused on raising her remaining children."

Yuki Nene leaned back, "I don't see how this is relevant to my situation."

The Luck smiled, "Please bear with me a moment my disciple. You have seen how Hap Sing treats the widow Wen Li perhaps?"

Yuki Nene gave a faint smile, "He is very polite and helpful. However, he is also very proper. I have watched them when he does not know it. There is nothing going on between them."

The Luck nodded, "There is nothing physical going on between them. There is something else happening just as it happened with Yong Mai. Hap Sing has been reliable. He was and is more reliable in certain ways than their own husbands had been. He cares for them, and treats them with respect asking for nothing in exchange. What do you think the eventual effect of that is in their cases?"

Yuki Nene thought a moment, "They fall in love with him?"

The Luck smiled, "You are a quick learner. Not for the same reasons which you find him desirable of course. They don't love him because of the power and knowledge he represents. They eventually love him because he cares for them without any demands of his own. Wen Li does not realize it is happening yet. The loss of her husband is too new and tragic for her to change her focus yet. After many years Yong Mai was deeply in love with Hap Sing. Her problem was that she didn't have a way to approach him, and did not want to jeopardize their existing relationship. It finally drove her to establish a less caring relationship of physical convenience with Li Hung. You have to understand that Li Hung was more like you, and he was not above taking his pleasure where he could find it."

Yuki Nene's brow narrowed as she spoke, "So you are saying that I don't have any chance with Hap Sing?"

The Luck shook his head, "I am saying you have only a couple of options where Hap Sing is concerned. You can become like these women he pities and feels responsible for helping. They will love him yet never be successful at gaining both his caring and his attraction. He would feel too much like he was taking unfair advantage of them."

Yuki Nene nodded, "That is not who I am. I would not be satisfied with such."

The Luck smiled, "Then you can follow that impetuous nature of yours and grab the apple in front of you knowing that it will be delicious to taste, several bites to finish, and yet a transitory experience to never be repeated."

Yuki Nene gave a little frown, "I see the situation you are talking about now. I can either follow my own nature, or I can try to be someone I am not. I will fail at the second, and my own nature will not allow me a lasting relationship with Hap Sing."

The Luck nodded, "I have taught you a valuable tool of self analysis. It is important to be honest about who you are to yourself. It will help you to understand the thinking of others. You should realize that no one will have a long term physical relationship with Hap Sing. You should consider the essential reality that fruit will wither on the tree unless you choose to pick it. However, there are many who will come to value the beauty of the tree long after the last fruit has been either picked or falls to the ground. It is the tree itself which will last a very long time."

Yuki Nene spoke, "I think I understand. Then about this test with Yong Mai?"

The Luck looked serious, "That choice remains up to you. You can follow through and learn something about how Hap Sing begins to see the material world now. The empathy you gain will assist you in obtaining that divine apple. The divine apple will only last as long as it does, and then you will have experienced all you can of it. Otherwise you can decide to not wait for it. You will not know of it, but you will not understand what it is to lose it either."

Yuki Nene looked the Luck in its eyes, "What course do you want me to follow?"

The Luck looked into Yuki Nene's eyes as it responded, "Either course leads to the same eventual destination for you. You will die as all servants of the White Raven eventually must die. It is her own rules she follows, and while she may extend your life for a time, eventually your spirit will require release, and the White Raven will grant it."

Yuki Nene looked at the Luck, "What happens when a spirit is not released in time?"

The Luck raised the divine apple in its hand which turned brown then withered into a putrid mass, "Corruption. It is not a pretty thing to see happen to a spirit. It takes more than one cycle to fix such a problem with a spirit as well. The demon god Mortis knows this well, and seeks the position of the White Raven as the god of death so that he might more easily accomplish this very thing. Corrupted spirits tend to cycle back to the same masters against the nature of the system as was intended in its design. Mortis counts on this loophole to attempt to gain dominance."

Yuki Nene had a haunted look, "That's why the White Raven abhors the intelligent undead. They are the essential example of a corrupted spirit. They represent a breaking of the process which she supports."

The Luck nodded, "You can also see now why I can not provide you any extension beyond your allotted time."

Yuki Nene looked at the Luck, "What about Li Hung or Hap Sing then? Aren't you violating the rules with them?"

The Luck shook his head, "No. I simply modified the rules. I made special exceptions. You should know there is a safety margin built in to the time period allotted for a spirit to remain in a physical form. This margin is because the gods are not as spiritually cognizant as a Number. The Numbers can gauge such things with a much greater precision than any god could. Number Two is the most adept at it, and it was Number Two who took on the responsibility for monitoring the condition of Li Hung's spirit at my request. That is why Number Two came to retrieve his spirit. Thus the White Raven had no ground to accuse me of risking his corruption."

Yuki Nene thought a moment, "What about Hap Sing? Did you make a bargain with Number Two over the length of his existence as well?"

The Luck smiled, "You are learning quickly. However, my answer is no, I did not need to do so. Time spent by spirits in the dreaming helps resist the corruption of spirit. It is why the Chi Masters are known to have longer lives. In Hap Sing's case since his spirit and mine are closely intertwined, his spirit hasn't been affected by the nature of material existence since he turned forty-two. We were sufficiently combined and synchronized at that point that my spirit here in the dreaming continually purifies his from any corruption. A side effect is that his physical form stopped aging then as well. Another side effect is that Hap Sing is unable to reproduce with another being."

Yuki Nene blushed again, "Hap Sing can not function?"

The Luck shook its head gently, "He can give and receive physical pleasure if that is what you mean. However, he is sterile and will never produce offspring. I believe it is part of the reason he considers others as his children since he will never sire his own."

Yuki Nene spoke, "Where does this leave us now?"

The Luck smiled, "With enough time to teach you a useful trick. You see this spirit ribbon the Cricket used to guide you to me?"

Yuki Nene nodded, "That is useful for finding you in the dreaming, but what other use is it."

The Luck smiled, "What if I told you that Hap Sing and Ming Na Jun already know how to use this trick in the material existence. They can use their second sight to see connections between people who have spirit connections with each other. It is said by Chi Masters that greater destinies attract. Didn't you ever wonder why that is?"

Yuki Nene gasped slightly, "The connections are real?"

The Luck grinned, "You are a quick learner. The spirit ribbons are as real as anything spirit is real. They don't have physical form, but a Chi Master who knows how to look can certainly see them. It is easiest to see powerful connections. The connection between yourself and your spirit guardians will be the easiest to detect for you. They are extensions of your own spirit formed by your will after all. The strong connections made directly to you will be the next easiest to see. Then the weaker connections made to you are the next level. After that with practice a skilled Chi Master can detect connections between other individuals in much the same manner. If you gain enough skill you can see connections at the level that Hap Sing can observe and follow."

Yuki Nene shook her head, "How far do these connections go then?"

The Luck gave a smile, "Using Hap Sing's senses I can detect them down to an individual who walked by you in the street twelve years ago when you were still a child. I can also follow that connection back to the individual if they still live."

Yuki Nene shook her head, "You know things that shouldn't be known. That is how you do it. You can read these connections. The past of anyone Hap Sing observes is opened up to you."

The Luck nodded, "Let that be my little secret between us then. It is one of the many reasons being combined with Hap Sing is useful for me. He can see the connections and I can understand what they say. Together we make a unique talent not matched in existence."

Yuki Nene shook her head again, "Knowing that much of someone's past, you can better predict the future related by that person."

The Luck smiled, "Past performance is an important indicator of potential future action. Individual acts can still surprise, but taken in aggregate and analyzed the patterns become more predictable."

Yuki Nene sat amazed, "The intelligence required for understanding that much information would be incredible."

The Luck smiled, "Thank you for the compliment. Understand the level of intelligence is not unique among my kind, but the sources of information collected are. Each of us Numbers performs differently and thus we have uniqueness. Now let me show you how to access the level of sight required to view these spirit ribbons. It will take much practice to get down to the level that Hap Sing is capable of viewing, and it will strain your vision much more quickly to use it in that way."

Later Yuki Nene looked over at Ming Na Jun as they walked down the hall together following a giant tiger cub. He seemed to be in pensive thought. She noticed that he seemed to be reflexively closing and opening his left hand. After a little while of her staring at him he eventually noticed her focus and the fact she was using her second sight.

Ming Na Jun asked her, "Is there something of concern?"

Yuki Nene broke her own reverie, "I was trying to figure something out."

Ming Na Jun spoke, "I apologize for my talk with the Luck taking so long. We have to leave before you had a chance to meet with him."

Yuki Nene shook her head, "It met me in another room. It said it was talking with us both at the same time actually."

Ming Na Jun paused a second before answering, "Ah yes I hadn't considered that he could likely do that. It falls in line with some of his other demonstrated abilities. Did your Luck look identical to mine?"

Yuki Nene shook her head again, "It was the same body, but it was dressed as a priest. What do you think that means?"

Ming Na Jun smiled faintly, "It supports my theory that there are different aspects of the Luck which handle different kinds of interactions. He is not necessarily a uniform individual in the sense we may think of such things. He mentioned metaphors being used. The different clothes being metaphors for different modes of thought I think. I suggest he dressed as a priest because he wanted to discuss spiritual matters with you. I think he dressed as a . . . well unusual individual because he wanted to discuss some unusual concepts with me."

Yuki Nene smiled, "That's an interesting hypothesis, but why do you keep calling the Luck a he. It does not have a gender."

Ming Na Jun flushed slightly, "The clothes worn by my Luck were noticeably tight. I could not help but notice that a male gender was obvious."

Yuki Nene looked at him briefly in confusion, and then flushed bright red as she said, "Oh. Oh my. I see."

Ming Na Jun changed the subject, "So what had captured your attention so."

Yuki Nene sighed, "The Luck said it taught both of us a trick. It said you already know how to see the spirit ribbons in the material world. It taught me to do the same. I don't have a ribbon clearly connecting to you, but it seems that we both have a pair of ribbons connecting with two of the same people. If one is Hap Sing, then who is the other person we know in common? It isn't your cousin Ming Ran is it?"

Ming Na Jun shook his head, "It is my son Ming Wa Fu. That is part of the reason I came to talk to the Luck. I wanted to know how such a thing could happen when my son had never met you and had only briefly met Hap Sing."

Yuki Nene's eyes narrowed as she frowned, "That half truth telling bastard. It never told me about it. It left me to find out on my own. Did it tell you how such a thing happened?"

Ming Na Jun looked pensive, "He put the connection there. He can do such things it seems. Link individuals he knows even if they have never met. For good or bad your fate has been tied to my son's fate."

Yuki Nene stopped walking and grew angry, "Whore son! I'm going to go back and give him a piece of my mind. He knew this and didn't tell me. He did this to me."

Ming Na Jun barked with all of his magistrate authority, "Constrain yourself woman! Do you think I am any happier about this situation?! Don't make a bigger fool of yourself than you already have! Did you even bother to take a look at this ribbon we follow or this place with your second sight?"

Yuki Nene calmed down a bit, "What do you mean? It looks the same as without the sight."

Ming Na Jun almost seemed to sweat, "When you started using your second sight I took a look as well. Look at it more closely. Use a deeper sight. Focus and concentrate."

Yuki Nene did as Ming Na Jun requested and responded in a startled tone, "The stripes on the ribbon they don't end there. They touch everything. They are making this place. What does it mean?"

Ming Na Jun gave a nervous bitter laugh, "It means we are inside of it. As good as swallowed by a dragon it seems. This isn't just the dreaming we are inside. This is the portion of the dreaming which is the Luck itself. The dreaming isn't just the realm of the spirits. It is the greater spirits themselves. Everything is spirit here, and this is the Luck. Those forms we were talking with were just projections of its consciousness. A convenience for communicating with mortal beings I would presume. There is no going back to talk with it. It is all around us even now."

The tiger cub turned its head and issued a low growl at them. Yuki suddenly felt weak in the knees and understood Ming Na Jun's caution.

Yuki Nene gave a tenuous smile as she started walking forward again, "I think we had better keep leaving then. It seems that we don't get a chance to convince it to change its mind about us do we."

Ming Na Jun walked alongside of her, "I understand what Lu Po said now about never wanting to meet it again. I never understood the dreaming like this until I came here. I can never stop understanding what the dreaming is now. It is the dream of the greater spirits, and those strange entities truly are the creators of the gods and existence as related in the Chi Master histories. We belong to one of them now. The Luck also known as Number Seven owns our very spirits for eternity. All we have left to ourselves are the brief moments of our mortal existence. If it wants we will be its pieces in Go Shogi now and forever."

ing Na Jun and Yuki Nene finally found themselves walking down the path from the tower. At the top of the path they had been able to see that they were on an uninhabited island surrounded by the turquoise sea. They could see Hap Sing sitting on his boat out in the bay with his fishing pole in the water. As they approached the beach Hap Sing drew in his fishing pole and rowed to meet them at the shoreline.

Hap Sing looked at their expressions and saw that they had a certain amount of concern present in their looks as he addressed them, "I hope your journey was a satisfactory one. Did you learn what you both wished to know?"

Ming Na Jun responded first, "That is hard to answer. I learned some of which I didn't know, and yet I still feel like much remains unanswered."

Yuki Nene spoke next, "How much do you know about what he told us?"

Hap Sing sat in the boat and shrugged, "Very little at all. Only what your expressions tell me. They say your answers were not what you wanted to hear. I find that the Luck very rarely provides what others desire. It does seem to usually give them what they need. Sometimes it just takes time to realize it."

Chapter 16 Transition

ap Sing sat drinking tea in Yong Mai's room as she peered over her tea cup at him. It had been almost a month since he had taken Yuki Nene and Ming Na Jun to the dreaming to meet the Luck. In the time since then life seemed to settle into a more sedate rhythm. Hap Sing fished as usual and still brought fish to Wen Li and Wen Lu although Wen Li insisted on paying him now that they had the means to do so. Ming Na Jun had returned to his own home and his duties as magistrate of the Jin Do province. It seemed like Ming Na Jun's interest in Hap Sing had been satisfied for the moment, and they parted in an amiable enough manner.

Strangely to Hap Sing it seemed his interactions with Yuki Nene had become restrained since they went to the dreaming together. They were still polite and friendly, but something had happened between them during that trip to the dreaming which he did not yet comprehend. It certainly had something to do with the Luck, but there seemed to Hap Sing to be a change in her personality which was unexpected. Perhaps it was a reversion back to the shy reserved personality which had first caught his attention back in Hung Chang village.

Yong Mai interrupted his contemplations, "It has been a while since you stopped by to visit me. I was thinking that you had lost interest in my evaluation of this Yuki Nene you placed in my service. Perhaps you have even lost interest in her as well?"

Hap Sing smiled, "I'm sorry I took so long. I've been a bit preoccupied with other matters perhaps. Would you please let me know your thoughts on Nene?"

Yong Mai nodded, "First off she is spoiled. Nene is not a woman used to being balked in achieving what she wants. That is not to say she is lazy and unwilling to do hard work, but I expect that people have rarely ever said no to her wishes."

Hap Sing lost his smile, "What is it that she wants?"

Yong Mai gave a faint grin, "You of course. Well maybe not the fisherman Hap Sing I know well, but the knowledge and power you represent to her as a Chi Master I think. She's driven to attempt to control people and events around her. I think that since you took her to the dreaming she is frightened that those things she which felt under her control have really never been so. She's had a taste of destiny, and it scares her greatly."

Hap Sing gave a faint frown, "Nene didn't mention the Luck treating her badly to me."

Yong Mai nodded, "I don't think it did, although she hasn't spoken of it with me. I think that possibly the Luck revealed to her the extent which she is caught up in its plans. Whatever those plans are she fears being no longer in command of her life. She has been behaving rather meek and subdued since her return that day. Her destiny bothers her I would guess."

Hap Sing shrugged with a quizzical expression, "Which person is Nene really? Is Nene the bold and spoiled person, or the meek and subdued person?"

Yong Mai chuckled, "Sing you have lived long years, but you still don't know much about women. She is all of those things and more you fool. She is a complex being just as we all are. She is subject to changes in mood and whims of desire. I think it very likely she saw you as a mysterious stranger as well as an opportunity to improve her knowledge and ability with her powers. Unfortunately she is coming to realize Hap Sing is both much more mundane than expected, and yet conversely combined with the more fantastically frightening Luck. The nature of the Luck is beyond what she can ever fully conceive. I know from my personal experience my infatuation with you was significantly altered when I met the Luck that time. It is no wonder that she feels the same."

Hap Sing looked at Yong Mai surprised, "You were infatuated with me? I always thought you were attracted to Li Hung?"

Yong Mai looked back at Hap Sing, "I made some choices in my life. Some were better than others perhaps, but I regret none of them. Well almost none of them. I admit to lusting after Li Hung in my heart. Can you blame me as it is pretty obvious that most women my age then would as well? He was handsome, dashing, strong, and brave. I also came to learn much latter that he was callous, arrogant, merciless, and ultimately only devoted to one person in his life. It confused me for many years as to why someone of such heroic bearing would be so loyally devoted to you. It was that mystery which first focused my thought on you as a person. Unlike most here in Li Chan village I realized pretty young that something was different about you."

Hap Sing nodded, "You mean the Luck of course."

Yong Mai slowly shook her head, "Of course that is not it. Back then I had no clue about the existence of the Luck. However, I did see signs of Cricket hiding in disguise as the fisherman Hap Sing."

Hap Sing looked confused, "What do you mean Cricket hiding as Hap Sing?"

Yong Mai placed her hand on his knee, "I mean the self effacing, humble, caring man who is concerned for everyone else more than himself. It is true that you appear plain, drab, and ordinary at first sight to anyone. You are not apparently brave or handsome although also not obviously cowardly or ugly either. Your assumed behavior is frankly quite uninteresting at a superficial glance of a person casually meeting you. You are very easily overlooked, and it is clear to me after all these years that you intentionally act in a manner to perpetuate that response."

Hap Sing shrugged with a mild vague expression, "I am just being who I am."

Yong Mai shook her head, "No you are hiding who you really are. I was infatuated with you not because of the Hap Sing you pretended to be. I was infatuated with you because of the you that is Cricket as Li Hung called it. Underneath that deliberately bland exterior is there hides a transcendent quality that drew me to you. Many years of observation has shown that deep down you are at peace with yourself. You have a confident, caring, and calm attitude which gradually permeates through the bland fisherman you play at being. I have long known you must be a true Chi Master, even if you would never admit it to others or even yourself. The Luck is not your hidden self; it is the sacrifice your hidden self has made for the good of all Ran Li.

Hap Sing contemplated a moment, "Then what about Li Hung. Since you are being so open tonight tell me what happened between the two of you."

Yong Mai gave a faint smile, "After my husband passed it is true I occasionally had my way with Li Hung just as he had his way with me. However, it is also true that I have thought of you in my heart even as we took our comfort together. I think he understood this, but being the callous bastard he was he really didn't care as long as he obtained his satisfaction too. Ultimately it was you who was the glue which bound us together. Both of us were drawn to you for our own reasons. I suspect you were the kind father Li Hung wanted instead of the stern one he received. To me you were the husband I knew could have made me content to be his wife."

Hap Sing ducked his head, "The regret you mentioned earlier this evening. What was it?"

Yong Mai smiled, "That I had never told you how I felt about you back then. As my final time draws near I have gained the courage to remove my last regret and tell you now."

Hap Sing raised his head again and looked Yong Mai in the eyes, "How do you feel about me now?"

Yong Mai gave a wistful smile, "I'm too old to hold onto such girlish nonsense anymore. I could have no more have settled down with you forever at that time than this Yuki Nene could now. You as Cricket have a quality that doesn't lend itself to being hoarded by one person only. You belong to everyone who knows you for the man you are, and I could not have kept you to myself no matter how much I wanted to do so. That was always the hell of knowing you Sing; knowing that you could never be mine alone, and that I was greedy and selfish for wanting it to be that way. I have understood why Li Hung was so dedicated to you, and I used to privately curse you for my yearning heart. Now that I am old those negative feelings about you are long gone. The last residue of them was driven out when I met the Luck. I now only feel shame for once having them, and ask your forgiveness for burdening you with these thoughts. Now I am just glad that we have been friends for all these years. No regrets about my past remain for me."

Hap Sing looked her in the eyes, "I am sorry for not being more open with you. You have been a good friend all these years. You have no reason to beg forgiveness from me for you have never done me wrong."

Yong Mai smiled, "I thank you for your kindness. It is another one of your good traits by the way. I am afraid to say I am not certain I have done you a kindness in return. Your current situation with this Yuki Nene might partially be my fault as well. I indicated to her much of this same information with an emphasis on how hard it was to work up the courage for me to tell you my real feelings all these years. One of your bad traits is that you are not readily accessible for someone interested in you. You retreat and cover very effectively when approached. This much she has seen for herself, and my long years of experience with you have likely driven the point home that this isn't just a short term game you play. It also likely never occurred to her that others would find you as compelling as she does. I'm afraid my advice to her might have dampened her mood some."

Hap Sing nodded, "I thank you for your help Yong Mai. I think I understand a bit more of what is happening here."

Yong Mai gently slapped his knee, "Then there is the fact that you are forcing her own mortality into her face by making her watch me slowly near my end. She may be a minion of the White Raven and accept death well as an intellectual concept. However, the reality of her own mortality has never been in the forefront of her own mind until now. That alone is enough to depress any young person, but to top it off with your own apparent lack of aging all these years is more than enough to emphasize the differences between the two of you. In the big picture I'm sure that the Luck is really just the icing on an already large cake."

Hap Sing sighed, "What do you think I should do?"

Yong Mai shrugged, "I don't think you really want to know what I think you should do. It would go against your purpose in sending her to me, and I doubt you are willing to change who you pretend to be enough to make it happen."

Hap Sing looked at Yong Mai and placed his hand on top of hers, "I will at least listen to what you have to say, and make my choices according to what I think the best course for everyone will be."

Yong Mai nodded and replied, "Very well then since you ask I will answer. Simply put I think you should bed the girl. Bed her when you are ready and teach her those things you feel it is fine for her to learn from you. In time the mystery of the Cricket will fade, and the mundane nature of Hap Sing will sink in for her if she gets to have her way with you. Instead of decades of regret about unrequited love, she will get a period of lust eventually finally moving to cooling ardor. You will not be harmed by it, and as the giving person I know you are you will survive the loss when she eventually moves on to another. It will be at least a few more years before young Ming Wa Fu is prepared to handle someone like her anyway."

Hap Sing looked surprised, "Who told her about Ming Wa Fu? Did his father mention it?"

Yong Mai gave a little smile, "I think a combination of things finally added up for her. Did you know the Luck taught her to see the spirit ribbons as she called them?"

Hap Sing ducked his head, "It wasn't mentioned."

Yong Mai nodded, "She knows about Ming Wa Fu and the ribbon connecting her to him. I think that may be part of what the Luck told her, and part of what it taught her. I would also guess that Ming Na Jun had a few words with her about it."

Hap Sing shook his head, "She didn't mention it to me."

Yong Mai chuckled, "I imagine she is very irritated that you haven't seen fit to mention it to her either. I expect her to be quite angry by the time you get around to bedding her for the first time. I envy you the fun you are about to have, and that is also a good way to remove the current animosity between you. I know it worked well when Li Hung and I would fight."

Hap Sing raised his head, "You would fight with Li Hung?"

Yong Mai nodded, "I mentioned that he was callous and merciless did I not. It often infuriated me that he thought nothing of casually killing to efficiently deal with his problems. Every time I discussed it with Li Hung the man seemingly had no conscience about it. It contrasted the differences between the two of you quite sharply, but at the same time led me to pity him once we settled our anger with each other. He was ultimately a broken man, bent by the Luck to serve its purpose. I only hope the Luck has learned from that mistake and doesn't repeat it with Nene or Fu. I also understand the sacrifice you've made in trying to undo the damage to him all of those years. I can only hope that giving of your self to Nene now will reduce the amount of damage done to her in the long run. I have a feeling that life is going to get harder for her before it gets better."

Hap Sing sipped the remainder of his tea before answering, "I thank you Yong Mai for your advice and for looking after Yuki Nene for me. The tea was good as well."

Yong Mai nodded, "I am glad to help you my dear friend. What will you do?"

Hap Sing gave a slight smile, "I will seriously consider what you have said and advised. I also do not desire to repeat the mistakes of the Luck a second time."

As Hap Sing departed he also considered the fact that Yuki Nene had tried to hide her raven spirit Munin within hearing distance of Yong Mai's room. It was clear she had an interest in what had been said, but he was uncertain about how much of Yong Mai's advice had been manipulated by Nene's behavior around her. It was likely that Nene had created a sympathetic bond between Yong Mai and herself. Hap Sing's respect for Nene's talent in getting her way was raised a notch. Nene was actively trying to circumvent the restrictions which she perceived had been placed by the Luck.

Hap Sing was even more tempted to let Nene think that she had succeeded in controlling her own fate. It would ease the tension between them in the short term, and he knew the Luck would get its way in the long run. It always did on these matters.

As far as whether the Luck had broken Li Hung, it was well known to Hap Sing that Li Hung's personality was heading that way as a youth long before the Luck ever influenced his destiny. Hap Sing knew Li Hung's father Li Chan had more to do with the person he became than the Luck. The Luck simply took advantage of the material that was available. The Luck just worked that way after all. It was seemingly always much easier for it to find a willing candidate for its purposes than to make an unwilling one do its bidding.

Hap Sing couldn't help but feel guilty about his life again. So many times in his past had people tried to make use of what he was, only to find that it never ended up the way they thought it would. The plan of the Luck proceeded regardless of any attempts to control its outcome by others. The Lucky Cricket would become a reality eventually, and Hap Sing could only drag his feet for so long before he was toppled over and painfully drug along as happened with Li Hung and Li Chan. He considered once more whether to take a few more cautious steps down the path before looking for another respite from his destiny.

As he stepped outside Hap Sing looked at Yuki Nene standing by the tree in Yong Mai's front yard. He deliberately turned his head and looked at the where the ribbon to her raven spirit Munin led to the place where it had listened near the rafters over Yong Mai's room. Hap Sing raised an eyebrow as he looked back at her. Yuki Nene blushed in the late twilight but returned his glance with a challenging stare.

Hap Sing sighed, "That was impolite of you, but I will mention it no more if you promise to stop spying on private conversations."

Yuki Nene raised her own eyebrow, "Private conversations about me I might add. Some people might consider that impolite as well."

Hap Sing nodded as he approached her, "Ordinarily, yes, that would be true. However, this was part of the deal made between you and I. Yong Mai would let me know what she thought, and I would consider her opinion when making my decision regarding you."

Yuki Nene stepped away from the tree toward Hap Sing as she asked, "What is your decision then?"

Hap Sing stood in front of her looking up into her eyes, "Your promise to stop spying on me first."

Yuki Nene pointedly looked at the spirit ribbon between them, "I think you are the one who started it. As long as this connection exists your partner has the full information on me, and I am subject to its observation at the very least, if not worse."

Hap Sing gently shook his head, "I can't be blamed for the Luck."

Yuki Nene reached out with her right hand and grabbed him by the throat, "That is where you are wrong you arrogant bastard. I can blame anyone I want, and right now I can't do anything to a being like that, but I can certainly reach out and put you in my grasp!"

Hap Sing kept still noting the uncomfortable yet not dangerous pressure she placed on his windpipe. He stood in silence looking up at her waiting for her next action.

Yuki Nene began to gently cry, "At least try to defend yourself you self righteous bastard. By the White Raven's icy tit you are so frustrating. I can't understand how Li Hung put up with you all these years. You quietly control everyone around you without them being able to stop it. Fight me now!"

Hap Sing softly spoke, "No. You need to hear that word more and understand what it means. You can't impose your will on me. Even if you kill me I will only ever be the person I want to be. That is the secret you are looking to find from me. I will only ever act as I choose to act. Not even the Luck can change that. Sometimes

I may not choose wisely, but I always take responsibility for the choices I make. That is why I don't make a decision like this lightly or frivolously. Consequently I don't feel a need to take responsibility for the choices made by others, including the Luck or you."

Yuki Nene dropped her hand from his throat and whispered, "Liar. You take responsibility for everyone around you. Most certainly you take responsibility for the actions of the Luck. Don't pretend it is otherwise, your own past history here contradicts what you say."

Hap Sing gently grabbed her arm as she turned to move away from him, "Come with me."

Yuki Nene turned back toward him, "Why? So you can tell me to leave?"

Hap Sing released her arm, "So we can talk in a more private setting. I would rather not make a disturbance in my home village. Come to my home with me."

Yuki Nene reached up to dry her eyes, "Maybe you need to have a disturbance in your home village. If you won't fight me, at least have the courage to show yourself for who you really are to everyone here."

Hap Sing sighed, "Sometimes it takes more courage to not submit to your frustration and anger, and to respect the peace of those in your community."

Yuki Nene scoffed, "You feel frustration or anger? Don't make me laugh. I don't think you know the meaning of such things."

Hap Sing began slowly walking away from her toward his home, "I'm still human and still have feelings even if you can't tell. I won't ask again. It's your choice."

Yuki Nene trotted after him until she caught up and walked beside him, "I still get a choice?"

Hap Sing nodded, "About your actions you still get a choice. You can't always control everyone else however. No matter how many tricks you try, some of us can see what you are attempting even now. You're a mere girl and no amount of whiles will change my mind about what I do. I'm old enough to know better."

Yuki Nene gave a bitter snort, "As if your behavior is any better. You control this entire village and everyone you meet."

Hap Sing shrugged, "Perhaps that is true, or perhaps I simply refuse to fall under the control of anything else. I become the mountain which the other beings must navigate around."

Yuki Nene spoke with a tone of sarcasm, "It is just that simple then?"

Hap Sing shook his head, "It is that hard. If you think it easy, then do so yourself. Control just yourself and watch how others move themselves around you."

Yuki Nene thought a moment and ducked her head, "I am sorry about spying on you tonight. I will not do so again without permission."

Hap Sing gave a faint smile, "That is a start at least. It would be better if you apologized for all the times you have spied on me, and if it were my permission you would seek first, but it is a start. I will let you stay with me for tonight if you choose."

Yuki Nene stopped for a moment looking at Hap Sing walking in front of her. She quickly caught up and reached out to hold his right hand with her left as they walked along. He returned her clasp with a gently reassuring squeeze.

Later they lay side by side on a blanket laid out next to glowing embers of the outdoor fire at Hap Sing's home. They looked up at the stars together quietly holding hands. A serene peace had settled between them.

Yuki Nene broke the silence with a hushed voice, "It told me how to see the ribbons."

Hap Sing smiled, "That is good. It is good you know about the ties of destiny."

Yuki Nene sighed, "I don't want to be forced to love a mere child I have never met."

Hap Sing gave a gentle laugh, "That is simple, just choose not to then if that is what you want."

Yuki Nene looked over at him, "Why do you think it is so simple to defy the Luck? You know it linked me to Ming Wa Fu. It indicated it wanted that boy and I to set up an academy for Chi Masters. It practically told me it was as good as done already. It said I should get married and have lots of children."

Hap Sing shrugged, "That may well be what it wants you to do. Are you going to let it trick you into doing something you don't want?"

Yuki Nene squeezed his hand, "Are you saying this won't happen?"

Hap Sing shrugged again, "I don't know the future and what will happen. I do know that even though you are linked by spirit and destiny to Ming Wa Fu you are not obliged to marry him, love him, or bear his children if you don't want to do so. Did the Luck ever say it would be Ming Wa Fu you must marry?"

Yuki Nene thought a moment, "Well no actually. It phrased it like a suggestion, and I just thought he was the one I was fated to be with when I discovered the connection between us."

Hap Sing chuckled, "Thus the Luck seeks to trick you into making the decision it prefers. The choice is still yours. You can consider that the first lesson learned from me. It should serve you well."

Yuki Nene placed her free hand on her forehead, "I feel like a fool now. What will the Luck do if I don't follow it's plan though? Won't it get mad?"

Hap Sing shook his head, "How would I know about what it feels? We can't even talk to each other directly. I do know that the Luck is much smarter than you can possibly fully understand. No matter what choice you make, it will get the real result it was looking to achieve. I think you can pretty much ignore what it has said, and pay more attention to what it does. It pays very close attention to those that interest it, and figures out very quickly whether their choices will be of use or not. It does not control people, it predicts their choices very well, and it can calculate how they will respond to what it says and does. I believe the appearance of control is just an illusion it seeks to create."

Yuki Nene looked over at him, "It was trying to get us together then?"

Hap Sing shrugged, "Possibly, but I really don't know what it expects to happen. It is just as likely it told you the truth, and it trusts that what I tell you now will mollify your anger at it. Is it really worth agonizing over a future which hasn't been decided by you yet? I advise you simply make your choices, and not worry about whether they affect the plans of the Luck."

Yuki Nene laughed, "You really can be a bastard you know. You've got me doubting myself, and yet still in love with you."

Yuki Nene turned over on her side and kissed him on the cheek. He continued looking up at the night sky with a faint smile as she gazed at him.

Yuki Nene placed her arm across his chest, "You know that Li Hung told me that it was a mistake to think of you and the Luck as separate beings. He thought of you as the same."

Hap Sing looked at her briefly, "Is that so?"

Yuki Nene ran her hand up to the line of his jaw and caressed it, "Ming Na Jun thought you were just another aspect of a very complex being with many aspects it could present."

Hap Sing smiled, "That's funny because Yong Mai said much the same about you."

Yuki Nene looked at him surprised, "You think I'm a Number?"

Hap Sing chuckled, "I think you are a deeper person than you ever let most understand."

Yuki Nene levered herself up over him until she was looking down into his eyes looking up into hers. She leaned down to kiss him tenderly on the lips, and he responded gently in kind placing his arms across her back. They held the embrace for many long moments together. She eventually leaned back up and looked down into his smiling eyes.

Yuki Nene's voice was husky as she asked, "What is your choice about us?"

Hap Sing pulled her close as he whispered, "I've decided to take this one day at a time for as long as it lasts. We both know it won't last forever, so let's enjoy what we have while we can."

ap Sing awoke to the sound of running footsteps approaching his home. He looked to his side expectantly hoping that Nene had not been awoken, and once again remembering that she had departed to return to the Nordland trading colony near Yokito over six months ago.

They had spent nearly three and a half years together, and they had parted amiably enough without fighting or tears. A wanderlust combined with boredom had finally conquered her desire to remain by his side forever. As Yong Mai had said over four years ago before she passed the mundane nature of who he was had finally triggered something inside Nene seeking that which was new and exciting.

Hap Sing sat up as he heard a voice calling from outside his doorway, "Hap Sing are you there? The village elder Lu Po has asked me to bring you to his home?"

Hap Sing answered back, "I am awake now. Give me a moment to prepare myself, and I will follow you back to his house."

Hap Sing closed his eyes briefly, and when he opened them again he noticed that Ming Wa Fu's spirit ribbon was still in the direction of Lu Po's home. Ming Wa Fu had shown up that day unexpectedly against the usual quarterly schedule of magistrate visits being at least one month early. Hap Sing had learned of it when he returned from fishing in the morning.

Hap Sing closed his eyes again briefly and then got dressed. He figured it was finally time to deal with Ming Wa Fu who like his father seemingly could not arrive at an opportune moment.

As he exited his home Hap Sing was surprised to see that one of the other fishermen had been pressed into service to bring the message to him. The fellow seemed like he was in a rush as they walked back to the village, but given how late the hour seemed to be Hap Sing was not surprised he desired to return to his bed.

They finally approached Lu Po's home and the clerk who worked for Lu Po greeted them at the gate. The clerk paid the fisherman, and led Hap Sing to the courtyard. The amount of other activity seemed a bit unusual for a discussion with Ming Wa Fu. Hap Sing once more used his second sight as the clerk directed him to go to Lu Po's office. Hap Sing was slightly surprised to see that Ming Wa Fu's ribbon led to a darkened portion the courtyard instead of Lu Po's office, but several of the other ribbons were clustered in Lu Po's office including each of the village elders.

Hap Sing began to have an apprehension that something other than what he had been expecting to encounter was happening. Without thinking he rushed forward to the office door. He opened it to see the elders looking expectantly at him. He ignored them to look at the figure of Wen Lu laying on a futon with his aura visibly weakening. Wen Lu's legs had obviously been broken in a hard fall.

Hap Sing stood stunned a short moment as he took in the image of the dying Wen Lu barely eleven years old. He thought back to a similar situation at a much earlier time in his life. He remembered Li Hung being brought to him by Li Chan with tears in his eyes.

Hap Sing looked past the elders and saw the aura of Ming Wa Fu watching him intently from the darkness of the outside courtyard. Then he felt guilt as he looked over at Wen Li knowing what would ultimately be asked of him again. If it had been any other he would likely have refused even contemplating it. He had been determined to never put another through the burdens faced by Li Chan and Li Hung.

It looked to Hap Sing like the Luck decidedly had other plans. Hap Sing looked at Wen Li who bore a look of concern mingled with confusion. He decided to deal with the issues as they faced him.

Hap Sing asked her, "What have they told you?"

Wen Li glanced nervously from Wen Lu to Hap Sing, and then returned to looking at Wen Lu as she spoke, "The elders have said that you are the Lucky Cricket."

Hap Sing nodded his head in reply.

Wen Li continued, "They said that perhaps you are even a Chi Master?"

Hap Sing shrugged his shoulders.

Wen Li looked over at her unconscious son with obvious love and concern, "They told me that you could save Wen Lu from being a cripple for the rest of his life."

Hap Sing nodded his head again, "The possibility exists."

Wen Li glanced at Hap Sing again as if seeing him for the first time, "They said you were the oldest living man they have ever known, older than the departed fathers of the oldest people in village."

Hap Sing nodded his head, and gave Lu Po and the other elders a sharp look.

Hap Sing spoke to them, "Did you have to say it that way?"

Lu Po responded, "We needed to explain your unusual nature in a way she could understand."

Wen Li boldly looked at Hap Sing as if finally seeing the real person behind her casual friend of all their years since the elder Wen Lu had died, "Lu Po said there would be a price for my Wen Lu and for the village to pay."

Hap Sing dropped his head in contemplation, "I don't know if the village will have to pay any price, but Wen Lu will certainly have his destiny altered in unpredictable ways. His destiny will be made greater if I use the powers I have to save him from his present fate. He will be altered in much the same way that Li Hung was altered. This is beyond my control if you ask this of me."

Wen Li visibly firmed her resolve, "What may be the price for the village?"

Hap Sing started to look sad as he said, "I might have to leave Li Hung village for a very long time, longer than the lifetime of the youngest child here at least."

Wen Li nodded her head, "So be it. I will ask this of you for my son Wen Lu. I have already lost his father. I would not lose him as well."

 Chapter 17   213

Hap Sing glanced out to the courtyard where the waiting Ming Wa Fu listened, "I must ask you all to leave. This entire house must be cleared of anyone except Wen Lu."

Lu Po shrugged his shoulders, "I was hoping to avoid waking the magistrate's son. It will be hard to conceal why we want him to leave his room in the middle of the night."

Hap Sing stopped Lu Po as the others left the office and whispered in his ear, "I'll take care of dealing with young Ming Wa Fu. He has already been watching us this whole time. Just make certain that no one else is left to view the effect of the Luck at work."

It took a couple of minutes for the house to become clear of everyone other than Hap Sing, Ming Wa Fu, and the unconscious Wen Lu. Hap Sing pointedly looked out into the courtyard once he could no longer hear the others moving around. Ming Wa Fu stepped out of the darkness as if he had been born from it.

Ming Wa Fu spoke first, "Who are you? Are you an immortal?"

Hap Sing started shaking his head, and stopped changing to a shoulder shrug instead. Hap Sing waved for Ming Wa Fu to enter the room.

Hap Sing spoke softly, "After all these years, and I still don't know anything for certain. I don't grow old like other people, but I think a spry youth like you could still as easily kill me as anyone. I have a question for you Ming Wa Fu. Did you do what I asked of you?"

Ming Wa Fu nodded his head, "There was a farmer in the community of Taso Mido whose farm was in jeopardy of being seized for non-payment of his taxes. Just a week ago I paid those taxes for him even though we had never met. I however grasped the characteristic of greed in the man who was trying to seize the land from him."

Hap Sing nodded, "So you understand what I mean by charity then?"

Ming Wa Fu nodded, "There are many undone by not enough money to satisfy their wants. However, it is a hard life when one is about to be deliberately undone by the greed of another. Such is the beginning of the end of order in an orderly society. I took my stand remembering what you said about helping another in need."

Hap Sing smiled, "That is a good thing then. It was not quite what I meant by my offer, but the end result is better than I had planned then."

Ming Wa Fu looked at Hap Sing, "What do you mean?"

Hap Sing shrugged, "I did not know the quality of your character then. I feel I understand it better now and I am satisfied with your choices."

Ming Wa Fu looked at him, "Are you really a Chi Master?"

Hap Sing shrugged his shoulders, "I have no idea what that means in relation to what I am. I've heard of the adventures of Chi Masters from childhood tales. However, I certainly never trained to be any kind of master. Well except maybe at fishing."

Ming Wa Fu asked, "How are you going to heal Wen Lu and change his destiny then?"

Hap Sing gave a slight smile, "I'm not going to heal him, the Luck is."

Ming Wa Fu was confused, "I thought you were the Luck."

Hap Sing grinned, "No, I'm just Cricket, the Luck is what's inside my being. The yang trapped inside my yin perhaps. It knows much more than I do. I will summon it in my place. Its power will be the one speaking and acting through me for a brief time. After I summon it, I will no longer be the one you see here. After it heals Wen Lu, his destiny will be changed. Wen Lu will have a greater destiny than what was supposed to happen."

Ming Wa Fu looked surprised, "You certainly talk like the Chi Masters of the past. Nothing but confusing talk without any real substance."

Hap Sing nodded, "You will know when the Luck is present. It will be felt by you as well as any other greater destinies nearby. After it changes Wen Lu I need you to ask it some questions. However, I will warn you that it may answer in a confusing manner. There are two things you must ask it before it leaves. First, will Wen Lu's destiny be heroic, or villainous? Second, must Cricket leave the village now?"

Ming Wa Fu thought a moment, and then asked, "Are you not also worried about my destiny being changed by the Luck?"

Hap Sing smiled at him, "A greater destiny a like yourself is unlikely to be much changed by what I do here today. It would take a much greater act to change the course of your life. This greater destiny is why your fate much like your father's can not be changed by my actions today. This is why you have found yourself drawn to me when others are likely to ignore my existence. Greater destinies pull toward each other."

Ming Wa Fu nodded, "Such my father taught me is wisdom taught by the Chi Masters of old. It is part of their forbidden knowledge."

Hap Sing smiled, "It is also why I need you to question the Luck before it withdraws. A lesser destiny would be unable to do so without much damage. Remember to ask it my questions, and if it remains after that you may ask it your own."

Ming Wa Fu nodded at Hap Sing. They arranged themselves in the office with Hap Sing sitting at the foot of the futon where Wen Lu still lay. Ming Wa Fu moved to the furthest corner of the room and watched as Hap Sing began to go into a trance. After a quarter of an hour a noticeable, but unexplainable supernatural shift happened neither seen or heard, but it could be felt by Ming Wa Fu in the core of his being. Ming Wa Fu began to show beads of sweat on his forehead in apprehension about what might happen.

An orange aura had grown around Hap Sing sitting at the foot of the futon. It was no longer Hap Sing sitting there. It was now the Luck.

The Luck stood up, turned and glared at Ming Wa Fu through Hap Sing's eyes which had a hint of cat's pupils. Then the Luck faced back to Wen Lu. The Luck reached down to touch the injured limbs of Wen Lu. The orange aura of the Luck took on an animalistic shape over Hap Sing. A tail of pure orange energy, and then two tails formed behind the Luck. Ming Wa Fu quivered a bit as it became obvious that Wen Lu's injuries were disappearing. Wen Lu's breathing eased, and he fell into a more natural sleep instead of a pain induced comatose state.

The Luck froze time in place and pulled out a crystal sphere from a pocket of nothingness.

The Luck spoke into the crystal, "Balinac, baby, I know it's pretty soon since the last exchange. No this is not a monitored link. I know we need to work on the underside for a while. I need a couple of extended mortality contracts drawn up. Nothing extreme. I'll take care of the physical part, but just don't be in a rush to grab these two is all. Don't worry about it. I know that we can negotiate favorable terms. I have a few favors owed to me by the White Raven. She's already promised to return them to me if they end up at her door too early. I just want to make sure that you are fine as well. It's all good then. Let's work out payment later. You want that in divine favors, or in trade on far realms guard duty? Ok, that sounds fine. I have another crystal to connect. Luck out."

The Luck then rubbed its hand over the crystal before talking again, "Hello my dear. Your foliage is looking wonderful again for this time of year. Why Three of course I am not looking to draw you into any kind of trouble. This is pretty simple stuff. I just need a life regeneration package for two is all. No you need not worry about spiritual corruption. I'm just going to keep them around for a little longer is all. I need their bodies to be able to endure some tough times ahead. It is only one of your hero specials. I already know you sell them to some others, I have encountered examples of your work from time to time. Really? That much? I know it is worth it Three. I just, you know how hard it is for any of us to deal with Number Two. In spite of what you may have heard we haven't been getting on all that well recently. Two won't even take my crystal connection any more. Of course you are much more reasonable Three. Thank you as well, and it is a pleasure doing business with you."

The Luck placed the crystal back into the pocket of nothing. Then it unfroze local time. The Luck smiled a feral smile as it touched Wen Lu's forehead, and his chest over his heart. There was an even more powerful shift felt throughout the area, and possibly the entire the world. Wen Lu had paid his price, his destiny had been changed.

The Luck turned to Ming Wa Fu wearing a slight grin, "Free at last! Free at last! Well, at least for a short while. Things will be stirring the pot very soon now"

The Luck then walked up to stand in front of Ming Wa Fu almost nose to chin as Hap Sing's body was notably shorter. It seemed in a good mood for some unexplained reason. The Luck looked Ming Wa Fu deeply in the eyes, and then it's expression changed to a sour one.

The Luck spoke suddenly and loudly, "Yet another greater destiny! How many of you fools can Cricket find?! He always spoils my fun!"

Ming Wa Fu gulped and asked, "Will Wen Lu's destiny be heroic or villainous?"

The luck's expression turned from sour to angry. "How much torture must I endure! Heroic now you blasted fool! I didn't think Cricket could know that I would link your destiny with Wen Lu's. I just can't fathom how Cricket would know your destiny was heroic, he doesn't have that ability."

Ming Wa Fu seemed a bit taken back by this for a moment, and then he asked the second question. "Must Cricket leave Li Chan village now?"

The Luck jumped back a step and threw it's arms up in the air as it answered, "Yes! Of course! Wen Lu had much more serious injuries than his obvious broken limbs. All fixed now thanks to me! That kind of power use draws way too much of the wrong kind of attention. If Cricket cares for these people, and I know that fool does, he must leave now or draw them into something greater than they can manage. Now that we're done with Cricket's usual boring questions, how about a few of your own? Make it interesting, and quick. I haven't got much more time."

Ming Wa Fu thought a moment, and then asked, "Is Cricket a Chi Master?"

The Luck yawned in his face, "Boring! Everyone asks that question! Of course he is! I keep telling all of you greater destiny fools that, but Cricket never believes them. Cricket is the real thing, the impossibility, the abomination! He's a natural born untrained Chi Master! He's pure yin, and can not or will not see it for himself. I have the power, and he has the will. If only he would release his control over me we could do very great things together! He's my jailor, he's my prison, no lesser so called Chi master could ever be such!"

Ming Wa Fu stood up straighter and asked in a challenging manner, "Who and what are you?"

The ears of the Luck seemed to twitch, and a grin flickered on its lips. Ming Wa Fu had its full attention now as it approached him again.

The Luck softly spoke,"You ask who I am? I have been called many things. I guess you should just keep calling me the Luck. That's as fitting a name as any from your perspective."

The aura of the Luck grew stronger and brighter. The Luck reached forward suddenly and touched Ming Wa Fu over his forehead and heart. A very large shift in reality occurred knocking Ming Wa Fu off his feet, and rumbling the house. Ming Wa Fu counted two, then four, then seven tails of orange energy whipping through the air around Hap Sing's body.

A dark, ominous, and leaden voice spoke from Hap Sing's throat now, "What I am is power! I will meet you again Ming Wa Fu!"

Ming Wa Fu collapsed on the ground before that mighty statement.

A few minutes later, Ming Wa Fu recovered from his shock and sat up blinking his eyes open. Hap Sing walked over and helped him to his feet. Hap Sing looked very fatigued himself.

Hap Sing spoke to Ming Wa Fu with a throat that seemed raw and sore, "The brief answers, we can talk more after you help me to my home. Wen Lu will be fine here for now."

Ming Wa Fu answered, "Wen Lu will be Heroic"

Hap Sing gave a hesitant smile. Ming Wa Fu paused briefly before answering the second question and a sadness began to creep into Hap Sing's eyes.

Ming Wa Fu nodded, "It's true. You must depart the village."

Hap Sing looked contemplative as he replied, "I knew my time to leave was coming soon. It may as well be now as any other time. I have seen some of what the Luck has done here. It has awakened your abilities. It has also granted you and Wen Lu enhanced capabilities as well. You may learn their exact extent in time."

Ming Wa Fu looked at him, "These aura's I can see about you and Wen Lu; are they a part of what it has done?"

Hap Sing smiled, "I welcome you to the club. You are now officially a possessor of the second sight. This is a clear sign your abilities as a Chi Master have been realized. You'll need to seek out your father for further instruction on those matters."

Ming Wa Fu was momentarily confused, "Why my father? What help do you think he could provide me with this situation?"

Hap Sing smiled, "Look at him carefully with your new second sight. You'll find his aura as powerful as your own I imagine, as powerful as most Chi Masters generally ever become. It is time to grow up and become a man Ming Wa Fu. You have learned well from your father so far, and now you must depend on him again. A new responsibility has become yours, and without you asking for such. There is no way to set down this burden shy of your death."

Ming Wa Fu was quick to follow Hap Sing's intent, "You're saying my father is a Chi Master as well?"

Hap Sing nodded, "Along with many others in your family line I would estimate. They have hidden their abilities so as to avoid unjust persecution, but they can never eliminate what they have entirely. You family has yet another deep secret of which you have become a trusted keeper."

Ming Wa Fu looked carefully at Hap Sing, "Of what other secrets do you imply?"

Hap Sing sighed, "I lived with Li Hung for over fifty years. Don't you think I can recognize a ninja incognito by now?"

Ming Wa Fu tried to look innocent, "I'm no ninja. What does the former elder Li Hung have to do with it anyway?"

Hap Sing shrugged, "It little matters to me if you admit it or not. I already know what I know. If you wanted to disguise that ability, then you should not have been hiding so effectively in the courtyard that only my second sight could follow the ribbon of fate the Luck tied to you six years ago. If not for the glow of your aura then I would have never known you were there. You may be able to disguise yourself as a deputy magistrate, but using your other training gives you away. You still have to learn of the wisdom of when that training is not useful to achieving your objectives. As far as former elder Li Hung is concerned, I suppose you should have heard of General Li Hung, the former Grandmaster of the Ran Li ninja forces?"

Ming Wa Fu had a slightly dangerous expression, "What do you plan to do with this knowledge?"

Hap Sing shook his head with a slight grin, "You are about one hundred and forty years too young to make that threat sound convincing. I plan to keep it secret as I will keep the knowledge of your Chi Master nature secret. I suggest you also don't advertise those abilities to any of your ninja trainers. They will find you suspect, and likely consider you compromised in return. It is not my actions about which you need to worry."

Ming Wa Fu pondered a moment, "It seems I am at a disadvantage. My own father has been keeping secrets from me. I'm embroiled in something much bigger than I can grasp at the moment."

Hap Sing nodded, "You have also inherited a student you must now train and protect. A ribbon of destiny has been created between Wen Lu and you. Wen Lu is destined to be your future protector, and you are to be his immediate mentor. You will likely find that no injury suffered by him now will keep him down forever. Such it was when the Luck healed Li Hung, and I'm pretty certain looking at his aura the same arrangement has been made for Wen Lu. Induct him as a worthy candidate into the ranks of ninja when it is time. You will likely find that he will rise more quickly through their ranks than even yourself."

Ming Wa Fu looked at Hap Sing carefully, "I have admitted nothing about any involvement in matters of that nature. However, I will look into what arrangements can be made regarding his future."

Hap Sing nodded, "I am glad you accept it so quickly. It is not like you could avoid it anyway."

Ming Wa Fu looked at him carefully, "What do you mean?"

Hap Sing gave a little chuckle, "The Luck has had its eye on you since you were Wen Lu's age. It tied us together then by ribbons of destiny, and it has tied you to Wen Lu. Nothing you could do would change that destiny."

Ming Wa Fu was curious, "I don't fully understand what you are. What is this being you call the Luck? Is it a minion of a deity?"

Hap Sing shook his head, "It is something much worse than that."

Ming Wa Fu looked nervous, "Is it an Oni then?"

Hap Sing shrugged, "I also have my secrets. You father has some theories on the subject I am certain. He visited it in the dreaming once. He came back a changed man that day."

Ming Wa Fu became nervous again, "The spirits live in the dreaming servants to the tailed beasts which dwell within that insubstantial realm. They are supposedly very intelligent, uncontrolled, unbound by even the gods. Are you saying the Luck is a servant of one of these great tailed beasts?"

Hap Sing shook his head, "I am saying that it is the tailed beast also known as Number Seven. I am its mortal avatar state when it chooses to manifest on the prime material. You've witnessed the presence of a being that can bully the very gods around when it desires. Do you think anything you can do will change its plans?"

Ming Wa Fu stood very still, "If I were to kill you now. . ."

Hap Sing pointed at Wen Lu, "You couldn't even kill that child now no matter how hard you tried. I'm one hundred fifty-four years old, and I don't look a day over forty-two. Do you seriously think you stand even a moment's chance of bringing me to a permanent end? Even your former Grandmaster Li Hung was beholden to me for his very existence until he died at one hundred-six years of age. Don't make me laugh with your pitiful veiled threats. Use your head instead and figure out how this destiny forced on you can be used to help your country."

Ming Wa Fu settled back, "What do you mean help my country?"

Hap Sing smiled, "It is good you've chosen thought over senseless action. This country is soon to be in peril. The signs are already plentiful that another invasion from the wild lands is mounting. You father is aware of this, and you should be as well. Dark times lie ahead, and you are going to be part of the bulwark which will protect this nation from complete ruin."

Ming Wa Fu questioned, "Why me? Why was I chosen?"

Hap Sing answered, "You have what it takes to succeed. That is no guarantee of success, but it improves the odds. The Luck is very good at figuring out the probabilities, and it has found you to be the right person for the job. It is as simple as that. If anyone else were a better choice, then it would have chosen them over you."

Ming Wa Fu quietly mentioned, "The prophesy of the Ming family was about me? I never had a clue."

Hap Sing nodded, "Such are the ways of destiny and fate. They choose who they will, and they don't ask for permission."

Ming Wa Fu looked at Hap Sing closely, "Why destiny and fate? Are they not one in the same?"

Hap Sing shook his head, "Destiny is on our side as it were. Fate is definitely helping out the other side in this matter. Although they seem similar to outside observers like us, it really is not the same thing at all. Both pick their tools for battle in a similar manner, but the battle is between them over the proper nature of existence."

Ming Wa Fu thought rapidly, "If destiny is represented by the Number Seven, then what is fate?"

Hap Sing looked down, "Fate is represented by Number Thirteen I'm afraid to say. It should be easy enough to understand that conflicts of this scope don't just happen naturally. This is a battle fought on many levels for the future, and Ran Li is only going to be one of the spaces on a very large board."

Ming Wa Fu shook his head, "I am only one man. How can I hope to change anything?"

Hap Sing gave him a gentle smile, "I suggest you learn to make friends quickly. The kinds of friends who pool their efforts to achieve a common necessary goal. I can start you on the path, and provide you this one assistance in the form of a great hero. However, Wen Lu is a great hero who will require your guidance and wisdom. He is a rather under educated youth after all, barely able to read. On the plus side you will always find him a true companion and stout of heart. When doubt plagues you understand he will come to trust you as you will come to trust him."

Ming Wa Fu looked at Hap Sing, "How do you know all this? Did the Luck tell you?"

Hap Sing smiled, "We had a helpful intermediary for a while. This intermediary allowed us to more directly communicate and bring us to a common understanding of each other."

Ming Wa Fu made a guess, "Do you mean my father?"

Hap Sing shook his head, "Although he came up with the idea, it was someone else. I imagine you will meet her one day, and most likely recognize her as she will recognize you."

Ming Wa Fu looked surprised, "It is a woman I know already?"

Hap Sing chuckled, "Not yet Ming Wa Fu. She is someone who knows your father, and is a former disciple of mine as well."

Chapter 18 Preparations for Departure

Hap Sing walked over to Ming Wa Fu, "Come with me. I have to let the village elders and Wen Li know the news. Some of them will not like what they must now hear."

Hap Sing and Ming Wa Fu left the office of Lu Po. They walked through the inner courtyard, and through the front doors to the outer courtyard. They saw a cluster of villagers standing around near the village elders asking questions and murmuring. Lu Po looked to the other village elders to forestall the concerned villagers. Then Lu Po advanced along with Wen Li to greet Hap Sing.

Lu Po spoke, "It was pretty bad this time. Most of the village has been awoken by what has happened here. They are confused and concerned. The rumors have started to spread already."

Wen Li interrupted, "How is my son? How is Wen Lu?"

Hap Sing gave her a smile, "Wen Lu is well. He will live and prosper for many more years to come. Deputy Magistrate Ming Wa Fu has even agreed to bring him into his service."

Wen Li impulsively moved forward into the house without having heard much beyond the point that Wen Lu was well. Hap Sing raised an eyebrow at her as she moved past into the house ignoring him in her overriding concern for her son.

Lu Po gave a faint smile, "I will let her know the full situation in the morning. What shall I tell the elders to say to the villagers about tonight? Many of the villagers have already heard of Wen Lu's injuries."

Hap Sing nodded his head, "The time has come to pay my price. I must speak with the villagers who have gathered tonight. It is time for me to tell my fellow villagers who I am. Let those who are here tonight bear witness to my words for the rest. Have them enter the courtyard while I prepare myself."

The concerned villagers and the elders came into the front courtyard to the base of the steps before Hap Sing and Ming Wa Fu. Hap Sing sat down on the top step before the door while Ming Wa Fu walked down the stairs to join the people looking at Hap Sing with looks of confusion or uncertainty.

Hap Sing gave them a weary look and then emitted a resigned sigh before he began, "As some of you are aware I am the fisherman Hap Sing. I have quietly lived in Li Chan village along with the rest of you for most if not all of your lives. Only the eldest villagers can remember a time before my arrival here."

The village elders each nodded to confirm the truth of his statement, and the villagers murmured to each other briefly. Ming Wa Fu gave him a slight grin in encouragement. Hap Sing breathed another sigh and looked up at the sky briefly.

Hap Sing looked down at the audience, "I must apologize to each of you. I have deceived you about my presence here in Li Chan village. While it is true that I am a fisherman, that is not all that I am. I am also the son of Hap Yang, the last of the Chi Masters to practice his art openly in the Kingdom of Ran Li. Many of you may have heard of Hap Yang. Jin Do province is not too far from his home after all. What is now Hung Chan village was also at one time my home until nearly one hundred years ago."

The villagers began murmuring among themselves briefly, but looked to their seemingly calm elders for their guidance. The other elders remained quiet as Lu Po moved up to the first stair and turned to address the other villagers.

Lu Po gave a somewhat sad grin, "I am sixty-nine years old, and I can remember Hap Sing coming to our village along with Li Hung in my childhood nearly sixty years ago. Hap Sing looks much the same today as he did when I first saw him as a child. The other village elders can attest to much of the same. I think if each of you think back to your own childhood, you will remember that Hap Sing has seemingly always been a fixture in our village. He may be often overlooked, but present anyway."

Several exclamations of agreement circulated through the assembled villagers as the realization of the truth of Lu Po's words came to them. None of them could recall a time when Hap Sing was not considered just a routine part of the village landscape in certain ways. Like a tree frequently passed, but never really viewed until some activity around it draws attention to it.

Hap Sing spoke again, "There will be rumors about what happened here tonight if I do not first tell you the truth, and caution you to hold the truth secret. I am most likely a Chi Master. I have never formally trained to be one, but I can do many similar things to what the Chi Masters of legend could do."

Lu Po nodded his head in confirmation of the remark as once more the villagers began murmuring among themselves. Their expressions were serious, but not frightened or dangerous. The presence of the accepting elders helped maintain their calm.

Hap Sing looked down awaiting them to become silent once more before continuing, "Wen Lu was brought here tonight with dire injuries. Injuries which may have eventually cost him his life. I did something tonight that I had thought I would never do again. I allowed a very powerful great spirit to possess my being so that Wen Lu might live. The last time I did this was for General Li Hung your former counselor and village elder when he was a mere child of fourteen. Such things do not happen without a price to be paid. It is a price which will be paid by Wen Lu, by myself, and also by the village of Li Chan. Wen Lu will have to enter the service of Ming Wa Fu in order to help protect the nation of Ran Li. Such was the price paid by Li Hung for my saving his life, and the nation benefited from his sacrifice and the sacrifice of his father my childhood friend General Li Chan for many years."

Lu Po interrupted the rising murmuring of the villagers, "What of your price, and the price for the village?"

Hap Sing looked with a piercing gaze at each of the assembled villagers as if trying to memorize their features one last time before speaking again, "Such a use of power as felt by each of you here tonight can be detected by other beings.

Some of these beings are also very powerful. Some of them are also extremely dangerous and would seek to do me or anyone harboring me harm. In order to protect Li Chan village and its people from harm it is necessary for me to leave and not return within the lifetime of any living here now. I regret this choice had to be made without your consent, but it can not be changed except to the detriment of everyone here. I will leave and draw away any beings with harmful intent seeking to locate my presence."

There were expressions of concern and worry issued from among the assembled villagers. Worry that they were turning out one of their own, and concern that his departure would leave them unprotected from these other mysterious beings. Lu Po raised his hand until the small crowd became silent.

Lu Po addressed them all, "I have long known Hap Sing to be a quiet and gentle guiding force for our village. Many times when faced with a quandary about an issue facing Li Chan village I would request his input. I have come to trust and respect him as the wisest of the elders, even if most of you may never have understood his position with us until now. I too am concerned about what our fate will be, but I am also grateful for the many years Li Hung and Hap Sing have spent among us. Both had helped us more than many of you will ever know. Neither one requested our gratitude or payment for their aid. They were like two sides of a coin. A sharp rational mind prone to quick decisive action was possessed by Li Hung. However, it is Hap Sing with his gentle selfless caring for each of us who has perhaps done the village an even greater service over the years."

The villagers watched as Lu Po stepped off the first stair and knelt on the ground facing Hap Sing. Lu Po then bowed his head down to the ground. The other village elders followed after Lu Po. Then rest of the assembled villagers knelt and bowed before Hap Sing. Finally even Ming Wa Fu knelt down and bowed in Hap Sing's direction. Hap Sing was glad the darkness of night concealed his embarrassed blush.

Hap Sing spoke again, "You don't all need to go to this trouble. I am not a man who seeks the gratitude of others."

Lu Po rose from his bow, and yet he remained kneeling as he spoke, "You have my gratitude and the gratitude of the villagers here in Li Chan village. I have come to consider you my master in many ways. More importantly I have also considered you my wisest friend. I hope this poor student can make you proud by my service. I do not think a lengthy goodbye will serve any of us. I will however summon the entire village to attend your departure in the morning."

Hap Sing stood and made his way down the short flight of stairs. The elders and the villagers all rose and formed a line. Hap Sing nodded to each of them as he passed them looking into their eyes. They each nodded in their turn recognizing one of their own even if they did not yet understand what his departure would mean for them. At the end of the line Ming Wa Fu was waiting for him.

Ming Wa Fu nodded as he spoke, "I will accompany you to your home Hap Sing. As Deputy Magistrate for the Jin Do province it will be my duty to see you safely there."

Hap Sing nodded in return, "So be it. I must pack and be ready with the first light of dawn."

Ming Wa Fu ducked his head as he entered the cramped home of Hap Sing several minutes later. Ming Wa Fu could see that Hap Sing had minimal possessions to his name. Hap Sing quickly bundled up his spare clothes, some cooking utensils, and a small pot. Hap Sing placed the items in a haversack and set them near his bed.

Hap Sing chuckled a little as he stepped outside carrying a couple of blankets, "I am a lousy carpenter. It is usually my preference to sleep outside when the weather allows. I won't really miss this place. It will hopefully return to being a part of the hillside in a few short years after my departure."

Ming Wa Fu remarked, "Why did you live here so long then?"

Hap Sing shrugged, "I grew accustomed to it I guess. The view is nice here. The dawn is quite stunning from this angle. I also don't mix well with other people I guess. I like my solitude to think. I will miss Li Chan village however. The people there are a good people. I hope they continue to prosper without me. I mean to attempt helping them one final time tomorrow."

Ming Wa Fu asked, "What will you do?"

Hap Sing gave a sly smile, "My greatest feat if what I attempt works. Watch it with your new eyes open if you will. Maybe you will learn something important from it. Of everyone remaining in Li Chan village you are likely the only one who can begin to understand what I will have done."

Hap Sing lay down on one blanket on the ground watching the stars. Ming Wa Fu took the other blanket and lay down nearby. They found themselves to be tired enough to sleep the remainder of the night.

Chapter 19 The Lucky Cricket

Hap Sing rose with the first hint of light on the eastern sea before the arrival of the sun. He gathered up his haversack from his home, and rolled up the blanket he had been using as well. As he approached Ming Wa Fu to wake him he noticed that he was already awake, but pretending to sleep still.

Hap Sing chuckled lightly, "I can tell you're awake young Deputy Magistrate and not a ninja."

Ming Wa Fu opened his eyes, "I was practicing using this second sight. It is quite, well, challenging."

Hap Sing nodded, "You will learn more with practice, but I will caution you that over use will strain you and hinder your learning the mastery of it. It is something best learned in moderation as opposed to hard effort. Unlike many matters of human endeavor it is through careful thoughtful reflection as opposed to hard work that one learns to be a more proficient Chi Master. It is not easy, but trying harder does not make it happen faster or work better. In my experience taking your time to do it right is more important to advancement."

Ming Wa Fu looked at him seriously, "How do you know this for certain?"

Hap Sing turned from him and began walking for the village, "Because I can do things which even other Chi Masters find impossible. The only other Chi Master who went further than me was my own father Hap Yang. From what I have learned of him he was considered the best of the brightest of our kind."

Ming Wa Fu gathered his things and quickly followed Hap Sing. Ming Wa Fu caught Hap Sing and walked in relative silence with him back to the village. The pre-dawn light was brightening in the sky as they reached the beach. True to his word Lu Po had made certain that every able bodied villager was waiting to watch the departure of Hap Sing.

Hap Sing approached Lu Po who stood next to Wen Li and young Wen Lu, "I am glad to see that you are doing well Wen Lu."

Wen Lu gave a tentative smile, "I am told my life is in your hands. What service would you have me give?"

Hap Sing pointed to Ming Wa Fu, "You will travel with Ming Wa Fu as he returns to his home. He will look after your education and training for the days and years ahead. I am sorry to say you have taken on a debt in exchange for your life. However, your debt is to the people of Ran Li and not myself. You will do your best to protect them by protecting Ming Wa Fu."

Wen Li looked at Hap Sing with mixed feelings obvious on her face, "You save my son, only to take him away."

Hap Sing ducked his head, "It is the bargain I have made with destiny. If fate had its way he would be dead in a few more agonizing days. Bargains of that nature are not easy to make, and must always be kept. You will still see Wen Lu over the years, but it is unfortunately his destiny to join with Ming Wa Fu and help protect the people of Ran Li."

Wen Li answered with a hesitant voice, "I am grateful for what could be managed. What of yourself? Must you leave as well?"

Hap Sing nodded, "I also must leave. Destiny has its enemies, and they will come looking to find me. I have allowed some of their rules to be altered by the Luck. I will leave Li Chan village so that you all may know peace."

Lu Po stepped forward, "It is time for Hap Sing to depart. I will help him push his boat into the water while the rest of us wait on shore."

Hap Sing walked over to his boat and placed his belongings inside of it. Lu Po helped him push it down to the water. They looked at each other briefly and gave each other a secret smile.

Lu Po laughed, "I suppose this is goodbye then. Don't forget us now that you must leave."

Hap Sing gave a faint chuckle, "I won't forget any of you. Thank you for letting me leave on my own terms. This isn't an easy choice for me after all."

Lu Po's smile faded, "I understand it is no kind of choice at all. The sun is almost above the edge of the sea."

Hap Sing stepped into the boat and rowed out into the middle of the bay past the breakers. He looked at the village once more as he stopped rowing and placed his fishing line into the water. Then he moved his mind to the dreaming and reached deeper and grasped more than he had ever attempted before.

Ming Wa Fu standing on the shore watching the boat closed his eyes briefly and opened them with the second sight. The orange aura of the Luck stood out brilliantly even against the light of the rising sun. Then he blinked wildly as the aura of the Luck was subsumed in a brightness that outshone even the rising sun.

The villagers made an awed sound and knelt in the sand of the beach. Ming Wa Fu stopped using his second sight, but he could still see the brightness outshining the sun where Hap Sing's boat had been on the waters. It was clear the other villagers could also see this radiant light. They could all see an enormous net of bright light spread across the sky.

The edges of the net draped down across the boundaries of the entire region. Eventually the net faded from vision even though the bright light continued to shine out on the water. Then small brightly twinkling lights like stars slowly came forth from the brighter central glow. The glow on the water diminished as the bright lights came to the shore and one by one each light touched a villager before the lights disappeared.

Ming Wa Fu once more tried looking out on the water at the dimming bright light with his second sight. Nothing could be seen where Hap Sing's boat had been. Then he looked up into the sky and saw that the net was still visible to his vision, but in addition there were also words written in the sky.

These Lands Are Under My Protection - The Lucky Cricket.

Ming Wa Fu then looked at each of the villagers and saw that a similar message was written in spirit magic on each of them as well.

This Person Is Under My Protection - The Lucky Cricket

Ming Wa Fu had no idea what it really meant. He walked over to Lu Po kneeling on the shore. Lu Po looked up at him briefly and then looked out at the glow on the water.

Lu Po asked, "What can you see with your second sight young Chi Master?"

Ming Wa Fu hesitated, "Why do you call me that?"

Lu Po smiled, "Because I know your father is a Chi Master, and that it runs strongly through family lines. I saw the bright net he cast into the sky, and the lights which drifted to each of us, but I can not guess their meaning. Hap Sing never did anything lightly or without cause. He assigned Wen Lu to you for a reason. So I figure that you must have an idea what this means."

Ming Wa Fu broke down and answered, "I am not certain what it means but I can see words written in the sky, and on each person here. This place and its people are under the protection of the Lucky Cricket according to what they say. What kind of protection this means I have no idea."

Lu Po sighed, "As an educated man have you ever heard of such in the tales of the Chi Masters of the old times?"

Ming Wa Fu shook his head, "This is something beyond what any Chi Master, arcane magician, sorcerer, or god priest has ever done. It would take the power of a god to even begin to accomplish such a thing."

Lu Po shook his head, "This is not the power of a god at work. It is not even the power of a greater spirit at work. I have seen the results of their work twice in my life now, and it was never anything like this. This was something transcendent. We have been witness to something miraculous in nature. The birth of a new kind of existence. They have finally become of one mind, but I wonder which of them surrendered their position to the other."

Ming Wa Fu shook his head, "This must never be spoken of again. Even with this protection it may doom you all. I have a feeling that we have seen something completely unprecedented in mortal existence. Something never intended for mortal knowledge. I think we have witnessed the combining of two vastly different, but extremely powerful spirits. We have also been granted their blessing. I don't feel that either one surrendered. They simply joined to accomplish a common purpose. The Luck told me that if Hap Sing released control over it they could do great things together. I think they have finally agreed to cooperate."

They all watched as the last of the light faded revealing an empty sea before them and the newly risen sun. Slowly one by one the villagers returned to their homes and their lives. A miracle had been shown to them, and yet life still continued even after the miracle.

Somewhere else a bright light appeared on the water of a bay at a tropical island. The light rapidly dimmed revealing a small row boat out on the waters. After what seemed like many minutes, or maybe even an hour a figure appeared slowly rising up from the floor of the boat. Hap Sing gazed out from the boat at the island with a cautious look.

A look of uncertain confusion crossed Hap Sing's features as he spoke to himself, "Where am I now? I vaguely remember a place like this in the dreaming. This place isn't that place though. It's different somehow."

Hap Sing looked up at the cliff on the north end of the island and noticed that there appeared to be the beginnings of a foundation there, but the lighthouse from his vision of the dreaming was not present. Hap Sing rowed his boat in toward the sandy beach. The fronds of the coconut palm trees gently swayed in the refreshing breeze off the ocean.

Hap Sing reached the shore, jumped from his boat, and pulled his boat up above the high tide line. He tied the boat to a tree and looked around his surroundings. It seemed likely to him that the mountain like rise to the south would produce a source of fresh water. Hap Sing noticed tropical fish swimming as he looked out in the clear waters of bay.

Hap Sing spoke to himself again, "Water and food of a sort. Not much shelter except the trees. I wonder how often storms come through here."

Hap Sing looked back up toward the north cliff when he heard an unnatural sound like metal on stone. He seemed uncertain for a moment, and then began looking for a means to reach the top of the cliff to find out what other inhabitants might be on the island with him.

Hap Sing trekked through the light jungle for a while before finding the most likely path up the cliff. The going was a little rough, but not too bad until he was about fifty feet from the top. The last part was quite steep bare stone. As he stood pondering how to find another route he watched as a pair of ropes with interspersed bamboo rungs rolled down the face of the cliff before him.

Hap Sing tentatively tested his weight on the lowest rung of the ladder, and found that it held satisfactorily without giving. There was no visible sign of who had sent the ladder down to him, but he thought he detected a rhythmic hammering noise coming from above somewhere.

Hap Sing spoke to himself again, "Well, it seems I've been invited up. Time to find out what is going on here I guess."

Hap Sing climbed the rope ladder carefully. He reached the top and saw that the ladder was securely fastened to the base of a tree. He followed the increasingly louder rhythmic hammering which sounded like metal on metal now. Somehow a vision of a metal smith came to his mind.

Hap Sing reached a cleared area near the edge of the cliff. The beginnings of a foundation was laid out in meticulously carved blocks of alabaster stone. Near the foundation a figure stood with its back to Hap Sing. The figure wore a dusty set of grey mason's clothing, topped with a large scarf tied over its hair. The man was bent over a low set of saw horses which were supporting another block of alabaster stone being chiseled meticulously by the mason.

Hap Sing called out, "Hello. My name is Hap Sing . . ."

The mason interrupted him without turning around, "I know well who you are Cricket. Better than anyone else in existence in fact."

Hap Sing was a touch put off, "You seem to have the advantage of me."

The Luck turned around facing him, "I've got quite a few millennia on you knowledge wise. Now lets get to work, and save your inevitable questions for our dinner break. I've seen what passes for the building skills you know. So obviously you're going to become the brute force labor and cook while I do all the skilled work. It wouldn't do to not build this one to last. Not at all. Stop standing around gaping and take that bucket to haul some water from the stream running down the southern mountain. Then see about bringing us some fish for dinner. Don't forget to bring some wood for the fire as well. There should be plenty of deadfall to collect."

Hap Sing opened his mouth to speak but stopped as the Luck turned away to continue chiseling at the alabaster stone block. Hap Sing instead grabbed the bucket which had been indicated by the Luck and set himself to performing the tasks which had been requested of him. It wasn't like they wouldn't have time to talk. The lighthouse tower from the dreaming would take a long time for just the two of them to build.

Later that evening with the deepening twilight the Cricket and the Luck sat on log seats near the fire made by Hap Sing. They ate their fish dinner in relative quiet. Hap Sing could see that the Luck looked like a tiger colored version of himself. The same face, the same build looked back at him as they occasionally glanced at each other. Only the orange with black tiger striped skin and hair were different from his own appearance. Hap Sing had to admit to himself that the Luck looked better that way than he did, even while wearing the dusty clothing of a mason.

The Luck caught him glancing in its direction once more and finally spoke, "Go ahead and ask your questions. However, first I want to make it clear that the answers have varying levels of cost attached to them. I also will not answer trivial questions without purpose."

Hap Sing thought a moment and spoke, "I have figured that you have Seven primary aspects as represented by each of your tails. There is what I consider the aspect of the Strategist which was met by Ming Na Jun four years ago. Then there is the aspect of the Philosopher who always greeted Yuki Nene on her visits to you in the dreaming. This is what I would call the aspect of the Builder."

The Luck grinned, "Name them as you like. Ultimately they are all me. I am not the only one with different aspects."

Hap Sing replied, "I didn't think it to be the case."

The Luck's smile faded to a serious look, "Do you have a question for me then?"

Hap Sing nodded his head, "I have one question, but I am not certain if I want to know the answer."

The Luck smiled faintly again, "You'll want to know the answer, but I guarantee you will not like it."

Hap Sing sighed before speaking, "What would you call the aspect Hap Yang trapped inside me?"

The Luck chuckled, "Nothing actually."

Hap Sing had a serious expression, "Is that the name you would use, Nothing?"

The Luck shook its head, "Your father Hap Yang did nothing of the sort I mean. You are the one who summoned my aspect. You are the one who made a deal to merge with that aspect when you were only one day old. Your father did nothing. He could do nothing. You had already far surpassed his not inconsiderable abilities on the day you were born. All that was left for your father Hap Yang to do was to sacrifice himself in a ruse to protect you while we were still so very vulnerable to my enemies."

Hap Sing's eyes began to fill with gentle tears, "My father did not inflict you upon me as a terrible curse to protect the people of Ran Li?"

The Luck looked at him with a sympathetic glance, "Hap Yang loved you very much, and sacrificed himself to save your very life. There wasn't a thought of concern for the rest of Ran Li in his mind at the time. He only wanted to protect you from harm. It was your own choices which have protected Ran Li."

Hap Sing sat in silence for a while looking at the fire. The Luck finished eating its fish and moved to stand up. Hap Sing shot him a quick glance.

The Luck froze in place for a moment, and then sat back down, "What is that look you're giving me?"

Hap Sing seemed to regain his emotional center as he asked, "What would you call that aspect which joined with me?"

The Luck gave its own sigh, "You are a hard task master after all. I'll expect a hard days labor from you tomorrow for the answer. Are we agreed?"

Hap Sing nodded, "I will follow your directions about what you want done here."

The Luck had a serious expression on its face, "You summoned and agreed to merge with my aspect as you call it which some divine beings refer to as the Elemental Font of Fire."

Hap Sing sensed something was left unsaid, "What do the other divine beings who are not trying to stay on your good side call it?"

The Luck looked at him hesitantly as if the tables had somehow been turned between the two of them, "I would really rather not say. It is not something of which I am proud to mention."

Hap Sing looked at the Luck with an intense scrutiny, "Say it already and let's finally clear the air between the two of us."

The Luck looked down at the dwindling fire before them, "Those beings who don't like me refer to that aspect as the Destroyer."

Hap Sing was a little stunned, "The Destroyer?"

The Luck coughed, "The Destroyer of Worlds actually. It is pretty central to thousands of major divine apocalyptic prophesies actually. It is the reason most mortal, and even divine beings desperately fear the presence of that aspect. I knew you wouldn't like to hear it."

Hap Sing sat there agape at the revelation, "I see. Well at least you haven't actually destroyed any worlds. We're all still here right."

The Luck ducked down its head, "You're wrong. That aspect has destroyed thousands of worlds already, along with countless trillions of living beings. Each of the worlds contaminated by the mad elder gods had to be purged to prevent their contamination from spreading to the worlds of the new gods. The aspect of the Destroyer of Worlds has the sole responsibility of performing the purging by fire."

The Luck pointed at the sun just beginning to descend below the horizon, "You now have the power in your grasp to make the very center of life giving energy for each world in existence expand in an enormous explosion until it consumes the planets surrounding them. The responsibility has been given over to you, and frankly speaking I've been long past the point of being sick of having that responsibility. That is why I agreed to merge that aspect with you. You are the only being I have ever met to which I would entrust such utterly horrible power."

Hap Sing looked at the Luck pleadingly, "Why me?"

The Luck gave a slight grin, "Your spirit was stronger from the day you were born than the aspect of the Destroyer of Worlds. You are the only being in existence which could not be corrupted by such power. Your own power is actually much greater after all. Why settle for such a poor horrible substitute?"

Hap Sing looked at the Luck with a raised eyebrow, "You've got to be kidding me."

The Luck looked down, "Unfortunately I'm as serious about it as an exploding sun. I'm sorry you're the one who had to shoulder this burden, but I'm not sorry to be rid of it."

Hap Sing thought a moment, "So the brusk rude form of the Luck which possessed me each time . . ."

The Luck looked out at the sun dipping below the horizon, "It is an ass hole. An ultimately callous bastard even. It had to be that way to stay sane after having done what it has."

Hap Sing thought a moment, "Then the terrible unmentionable things it said to the village elders when the elder Wen Lu died . . ."

The Luck sighed again, "It told them of the horrors it had done. It let them know what only it knows, the exact count of beings whose lives it has expunged from material existence. Even the current gods don't wish to learn of those details. Not even the most bloody minded of the current gods can begin to conceive of the full magnitude of such destruction. Only the deposed mad elder gods ever had that level of vision, or desire to accomplish such a thing themselves."

Hap Sing sat in silence for several minutes before he spoke, "Was it the right thing to do?"

The Luck shrugged, "I can't say for certain what that means. It was the only thing I could do as that aspect."

Hap Sing replied, "What about another aspect?"

The Luck shook its head, "None of my aspects could have done it cleaner and with as little damage to the whole as that aspect. It may sound horrendous, but in comparison to the result if not done, it was the only option available to the greater spirits known as the numbers. Not all of us were agreed with the same solution. The Numbers are rarely of a single mind, but enough of us still know what we had to do in that circumstance."

Hap Sing shook his head, "Why was it done at all?"

The Luck sighed, "They changed in unpredictable ways. The elder gods I mean. The spirits which banded together to create them were in turn absorbed by them, and subsequently corrupted by them over time. The existence we created for them to remove them from the dreaming was straying very far from what it was meant to be."

Hap Sing thought, "Why didn't you try something else instead of such massive destruction?"

The Luck stood up, "We tried everything we could conceive. We were always fully spiritual beings with a very crude grasp of the nature and limitations of material existence. Number Thirteen advocated the creation of the new gods to fight the elder gods, but unfortunately they turned out too weak to accomplish the task on their own. The elder gods had grown very powerful, and became a threat even to us elder greater spirits. No reasoning worked, no strategem succeeded, and few options were left to us as time proceeded forward."

The Luck hesitated at it looked at the coals of the fire, "Then the Numbers did that which had never been done before or since. We agreed on a solution. Strip the elder gods of the living spirits which worshiped them. This would greatly reduce their power in material existence, while conversely strengthening their power in spiritual existence. They did little to try to stop us thinking this would give them the advantage needed to destroy the Numbers forever. Many of them in fact hastened the demise of their own worshipers in belief that they would ultimately rule the rest."

Hap Sing commented, "They misunderstood your power in the dreaming."

The Luck nodded, "They drastically underestimated not our power, but our ability. As your friend Ming Na Jun noticed the Numbers are the dreaming manifested as intelligence. The material rules simply do not apply to us the same way as material beings. One by one I destroyed the worlds of their material followers in the flame of exploding suns, and they felt stronger and more able to stop us doing little to try preventing my destruction."

Hap Sing paid him rapt attention, "Then they attacked?"

The Luck nodded, "They attacked when the last bastions of their followers were destroyed. They entered the dreaming mighty, powerful, and mad with their power. They remain in the dreaming to this day still mighty, powerful, and mad with their power. Held prisoner in a place with no material rules, with no way for them to easily leverage the power they have at their disposal."

Hap Sing looked confused, "I don't understand."

The Luck looked back at him with a touch of sympathy, "They are trapped in the far realms of the dreaming, They are eternally guarded by the Numbers. They are the dark urges, and the bleak thoughts in the darkest parts of our deepest minds. They are the source of nightmares, and the very root of all chaos. They are very powerful yet, but with that power comes an incredible danger as well even for the Numbers. They bring the danger of madness."

Hap Sing returned a look of empathy to the Luck, "I'm sorry. So these Numbers you use to call each other. They were not there from the beginning were they?"

The Luck shook its head, "No we were not. We began as greater spirits. As paradigms from which aspects of material existence were modeled. Death, fire, life, water, darkness, light, earth, air, and others of course. We were very narrowly focused originally, and identified by our primary aspect. I was of course fire way back then. The original model for material fire in all its forms."

Hap Sing responded, "However, you are not just fire anymore."

The Luck nodded, "You are correct. I am the Elemental Font of Fire. I am the Destroyer of Worlds. I am Number Seven. Now I am also Destiny, and the Luck part of the Lucky Cricket."

Hap Sing questioned, "None of the histories tell of what these numbers represent. These numbers are not based on order of importance, level of authority, or sequence of appearance as far as anyone can tell. They do seem to map roughly with level of power, but it is uncertain."

The Luck nodded, "It is one of the secrets even the current gods do not understand. We made them. They fought the elder gods, and they were almost defeated. They watched us capture the elder gods by luring them to the far realms of the dreaming. Then they saw us change. We learned very quickly from their perspective how to use aspects of material existence. They also realized that we had learned the mistakes made by the original spirits who created the elder gods. The new gods were similar, but limited in very important ways."

Hap Sing asked, "Limited how?"

The Luck gave a wicked grin, "One of our own. Number Two who is now frequently called the Godkiller by the divine beings can strip away their immortal existence if their spirits begin to show corruption. It is our safety net so we never have to perform such a desperate act again."

Hap Sing raised an eyebrow, "Why was the act so desperate? You won after all. You said it was necessary."

The Luck shook its head, "It was necessary, but no. We didn't win at all."

Chapter 20 The Curse of the Numbers

ap Sing looked at the Luck with a touch of confusion, "What do you mean you did not win?"

The Luck gave him a serious look and then replied, "One week's worth of work has been tallied up on your bill already. Complete that before I will allow you to ring up another debt. Complete two weeks of work and I will actually put a credit on your account. Feel free to think about what you have learned so far, but I will not answer any more questions of this nature until you have enough credit built up to receive it."

Hap Sing noticed a loophole and asked, "What questions will you answer?"

The Luck gave him a sly grin, "Questions like: What do you want me to do now? Where should I put this?"

Hap Sing grinned back, "What do you want me to do now?"

The Luck pointed, "Clean up our dinner, and get some sleep for tomorrow. It's going to be a busy week."

he first week went by in relative quiet between Hap Sing and the Luck. Hap Sing occupied his days with fishing, cooking, and putting together a rudimentary shelter made from bamboo and larger deadfall branches. He layered palm fronds on top of the sloped roof to help shed away any future rain.

The Luck spent his days carefully chiseling the alabaster stone down into the ground below the foundation of the tower. It became clear that he was gradually building a stairway down as well as quarrying stone for the tower in the process.

Each stone was raised from the quarry works using a block and tackle mechanism. Then the Luck meticulously carved it to fit exactly into its intended position. A set of two inch cylindrical holes were carved from each block, and they were carefully raised it into position using a scaffold and lever apparatus by the Luck and Hap Sing. The final step was sliding two stone cylinders slightly smaller than the holes and greased with coconut oil into place. This locked each new stone solidly to the ones below it.

They ate their meals together without conversation. Each evening Hap Sing lay under his shelter to sleep, but the Luck continued to work without rest. In consideration of Hap Sing, the Luck refrained from the noisy activities at night. Instead he focused on the tasks of measuring and planning his work for the next day.

The next few weeks went by with the Luck and Hap Sing assisting each other occasionally where two people were required, but otherwise working separately at their tasks. After the sixth week had ended and the seventh week had begun the Luck looked over at Hap Sing quietly eating his meal across the fire.

The Luck quietly spoke, "You have worked six weeks now. It has been good work as well, without question or complaint. It seems I owe you your pay."

Hap Sing finished his fish before answering, "Is that so?"

The Luck answered, "Yes it is so. Name your price for your services. I will let you know when you have reached the limit of your labor up to this point."

Hap Sing stood and walked over to the edge of the cliff, "I'd like a stairway here instead of that rope ladder. It is pretty difficult to climb that ladder while carrying stuff."

The Luck's eyes opened wider, "A stairway? Is that all you want?"

Hap Sing pointed down to the beach, "A small hut down there above the high tide line, and closer to my fishing. We can have our dinners indoors in poor weather there."

The Luck nodded as it pulled a sheaf of papers from its satchel, "I think these diagrams and instructions will satisfy your needs for a home. I've laid out very specific plans for the materials, the measurements, and the methods here. If you follow them exactly, then I think you will be pleased with the result. You can use my tools over there as you need them, but bring them back when you are done. While you work on your house, I will get started on your staircase up the cliff here. Don't forget you are still responsible for our meals, and we will still help each other with tasks requiring two people."

Hap Sing nodded, "Thank you Wright."

The Luck shook his head, "Another name for me. I'm the craftsman now is it?"

Hap Sing smiled, "I was getting tired of calling you names which begin with 'The'. Wright just sounded more reasonable for this aspect."

The Luck replied, "I'm just a bit surprised you didn't have any more questions."

Hap Sing gave a short chuckle, "I expect you will break down and tell me sooner or later without my having to ask. That way I can get some things done from my pay instead of only learning what you are going to tell me eventually anyway."

The Luck frowned, "Damn that bitch. I never thought she'd figure out that weakness."

Hap Sing spoke, "Nene was smarter than you took her for I think. She figured out you needed to use what information you had to get people to do your bidding. Since you are not normally outside of the dreaming, information really is they only currency you can use."

The Luck replied, "Then why don't you ask for some?"

Hap Sing answered, "I'll never get more than you are willing to provide, and you will give away for free what you need to as well. Nene and I worked out that much already. I may be old, but I'm not an old fool. When you are ready you will let me know what I need to know. In the mean time I can get the benefit of your skill in exchange for my labor. I have a few more things I'll be wanting as you build your tower. The plans for the house and the stairs are enough for now."

The Luck asked, "So you have it all figured out then?"

Hap Sing chuckled, "Not really. I've just come to trust that you won't steer me in a direction I'm unwilling to go. You have seen how poorly that works already."

The Luck whispered, "Number Nine."

Hap Sing became serious, "You'll tell me that story one day as well I imagine."

The Luck contemplated a moment, "This arrangement is agreeable to me. I will provide my skill in exchange for your labor."

Hap Sing spoke, "I didn't think it would be otherwise. You already knew it would come down to this obviously. You had those house plans ready before I even asked. We also figured out that you're a very good predictor of behavior. Very little catches you by surprise with lesser beings."

The Luck spoke softly, "There is currently a ninety six percent probability that Yuki Nene will marry Ming Wa Fu you know. In spite of your advice to her, Nene will find herself drawn to him. The combination of knowledge and danger he represents will be a powerful lure her impetuous nature will likely not resist when the time comes."

Hap Sing nodded, "I figured you had not deceived her about it."

The Luck spoke, "There is a one hundred percent certainty that she broke your heart when she left you. She was your first and last carnal love. There will be no other like her for you."

Hap Sing gave a faint smile, "It was good while it lasted, but we both knew it couldn't be forever."

The Luck spoke, "The curse of the Numbers."

Hap Sing remained silent as the Luck contemplated something for a moment.

The Luck spoke again, "It reminded me of the curse of the Numbers. Things used to be so simple back when we were still just greater spirits in the dreaming. It was good, and now it is forever gone without return."

Hap Sing spoke, "You can tell me about it if it will help."

The Luck said, "You've learned to stop asking I see. That is a good first step. If you can't get information one way; then try another. I will tell you some of it if you like."

Hap Sing replied, "I will listen."

The Luck spoke, "As I told you before, the elder gods were captured by us with the help of the new gods. They were lured to the dreaming without substance or access to material form. They are still powerful to this day, but they are mad with their power as well. A group of greater spirits who opposed the elder gods volunteered to sacrifice ourselves to become the prisons of their spirits in the far realms of the dreaming on the edges of utter chaos. At first it seemed like a great plan, Number Thirteen had proposed it, and had given itself over to the holding of thirteen of the most driven elder gods. Each of the other numbers who volunteered chose a lesser amount of elder gods to contain."

Hap Sing said, "Thus the numbers then."

The Luck continued, "The number of elder gods we were responsible for holding in the dreaming. Each one came with a benefit. First off we gained a better knowledge of material existence, and ways to use it previously unknown to us. The more elder gods we held, the more knowledge we gained. It made us greater than the other greater spirits."

Hap Sing spoke, "Then you discovered the disadvantages as well."

The Luck nodded, "Number Three is clearly stable still as is Number Two. Number Thirteen is almost as mad as the elder gods were. I have long suspected that Number Thirteen is working with them now, and seeking to gain access to the elder gods held by the others as well."

Hap Sing asked, "How about yourself?"

The Luck smiled, "I had also begun a slower slide into my own madness. The nightmare of the elder gods had eroded my sanity as well. The others were beginning to treat me like Number Nine and Number Thirteen even though my decline had been at a slower pace."

Hap Sing mentioned, "Number Nine found a solution then."

The Luck spoke, "Number Nine theorized that by joining with several mortal spirits, or even the right kind of special individual the madness could be slowed, or even stopped altogether. Number Nine volunteered to become the first test case. Number Thirteen objected to the plan. The other Numbers refrained from making a decision. Some of us hoped it would work, and others were already mad enough to believe it might provide the elder gods the material form they needed to defeat us."

Hap Sing spoke, "Then Number Nine selected the wrong subject."

The Luck replied, "Number Nine had the right kind of subject. A being very strong in spiritual powers, but ultimately too powerful in will as well. Number Nine tried to force the issue, and take control. The mortal spirit was too much in possession of its own form for this to work. Instead Number Nine was imprisoned within the mortal's body. No longer could Number Nine manifest itself on the material plane. This outcome was viewed as a failure by the other Numbers."

Hap Sing smiled, "Obviously you figured out there was at least a partial success, or else you would not have done it yourself."

The Luck replied, "Yes I did notice something the others discounted. Even though Number Nine could no longer manifest physically on the material plane, it could still work through its material avatar in a limited fashion. It could advise and suggest, and when their wills were not in conflict, it could also manipulate power in impressive ways. Number Nine's avatar did not age, and was actually prospering without signs of madness."

Hap Sing spoke, "The madness of the elder gods was still affecting Number Nine?"

The Luck replied, "Yes, but his descent into madness had slowed to about the same level I was experiencing. Another couple of avatars, a stronger avatar, or a more cooperative one might have stopped the descent all together. Number Thirteen objected to any other Number attempting such a thing."

Hap Sing spoke, "It sought to deceive you."

The Luck gave a grimace, "It knew certain kinds of powerful spirits were exceedingly rare in the mortal cycle. They are rarer than the gods, and almost as rare as the numbers. Then Rendalk Flügg destroyed the avatar of Number Nine removing its ability to access the material realms altogether."

Hap Sing looked shocked, "My father was the avatar of Number Nine?"

The Luck stopped in surprise, "Of course not Cricket. This happened several thousands of years ago now. It was a very different avatar in a much different age. It was in the time of the elder races when humans like you were primitive tribesmen little better than kobolds."

Hap Sing spoke, "This Rendalk Flügg who killed my father has been around for thousands of years?"

The Luck nodded, "I see I finally got you asking questions again, but I'll answer it since you need to know. Number Thirteen objected to the other Numbers using avatars because it had figured out a different approach to stalling its decent into insanity. Take a powerful mortal spirit, enhance it in a special way, and drive the insanity of the elder gods into it. It needed lots of powerful spirits for this to work, and it didn't desire to share with the rest of us. Rendalk Flügg is one such being used in this manner by Number Thirteen. I suspect the god Mortis is yet another attempt to work that approach on a greater scale."

Hap Sing spoke, "The undead increasing in number."

The Luck finished his sentence, "Are a direct result of spirits corrupted to drain the madness from Number Thirteen like pus from a wound. Ambitious ruthless individuals are recruited, and ultimately tricked by the god Mortis into serving this purpose. I will say this much in favor of the approach. The decline of Number Thirteen has stopped and stabilized to the best I can determine. It was in a way another measure of success. It was not a way I would consider permissible for myself."

Hap Sing spoke, "So you found me."

The Luck nodded, "I found a pure spirit. I followed its progress through the cycle cautiously. I watched for an opportunity for it to arrive in material existence at a place and time of my choosing. I discussed the situation with it in spiritual terms, and discussed the need I had for my own anchor. We agreed that merging and halting this madness was an important task, with the provision that I would also seek the cure for the madness of the others as well. Before you were born you were a very tough negotiator, and most likely the most spiritually aware mortal spirit I have ever met."

Hap Sing spoke, "So we agreed to join before I was even born?"

The Luck smiled, "We agreed to join hundreds of years before you were born. The great cycle of spirits is not a rapid process by mortal terms. Unfortunately your presence was also detected by some of the other numbers. In order to protect us from harm while you were still a very tender young mortal I had to convince your father of the peril and the need to save you. I taught him some tricks unknown before or since by Chi Masters, tricks of the ultimate inner fire. When Rendalk

Flügg arrived to steal or destroy you it was too late, we had already joined, and your father was fully prepared. Your father destroyed him and most of his invading forces in a gigantic blast. Unfortunately he had to sacrifice himself in this release of power to do so."

Hap Sing spoke, "If Rendalk was destroyed, how was he able to return?"

The Luck frowned, "Rendalk is like a cursed roach. The madness and power of the elder gods has touched him. No attempts to intercept his spirit have ever worked. It is so corrupted that it has completely broken free from the proper cycle of spirits. It is your antithesis, and it will seek to annihilate you if it can. Rendalk has been killed many times now, more than most mortal beings have ever been through the cycle at this point. I've counted at least thirty incarnations of him so far. I suspect that several more have likely existed and been dealt with by other beings."

Hap Sing nodded, "So I can look forward to being killed over and over then."

The Luck looked at him surprised, "Of course that isn't my plan. I plan to protect you well as I need you more than Thirteen needs his twisted toy. Rendalk is treated like a garbage dump. Fed garbage and reeking more and more as time goes on and more garbage is dumped inside him. You're more like, well it's hard to say."

Hap Sing raised an eyebrow, "Hard to say because you don't know what I am to you?"

The Luck dropped its head, "Hard to say because I don't want it to affect you in the wrong way. You're like my own child, and that is not something any greater spirit is comfortable considering. We don't replicate. It isn't an imperative for non-biological beings. I personally think we make poor substitutes for biological parents."

Hap Sing chuckled, "You're probably right about that. I think even my uncle was a better parent than you would be able to be. It is acceptable if we settle on being friends and partners?"

The Luck raised its head, "You're proposing an equal partnership? I don't think you are up for that yet."

Hap Sing nodded, "I'll settle for novice apprentice and master if that works better."

The Luck chuckled, "I'm so far beyond Grandmaster in those terms, but I think it is acceptable for you to consider me your sempai for now."

Hap Sing smiled, "So the time of the teacher has begun then?"

The Luck nodded, "It began a long time ago. The student is now finally willing to listen and able to understand some basics."

Hap Sing looked the Luck directly in the eye, "What happens after this time spent building your tower here? Do I return after learning what I must learn? Who will be this second protector? What will happen to Ran Li?"

The Luck grinned, "You're full of questions now my student. I knew I could get the floodgates open with the right approach."

Hap Sing looked stunned, "You tricked me."

The Luck nodded, "To prove I am smarter than you and Nene after all. You have questions you want answered, and one lesson you will learn before we're done here is that knowledge always comes at a cost. I've paid my cost for the knowledge I've learned, and you will pay your cost in some way or another to learn a small bit of what I know."

Hap Sing looked down, "I'm sorry for asking so much of you."

The Luck shrugged, "Don't be sorry, but think carefully what you ask. I can't tell you of a future I don't know for certain. I can tell you of the past and present within my perception."

Hap Sing asked, "Then tell me why we are building this tower? What purpose does it serve?"

Chapter 21 The White Tower

The Luck smiled, "It serves as a place to keep us occupied at the moment as you learn from me. Part of that learning is learning craft. Building also teaches me something of material structure. I'm still learning how it works and how to enhance it with spiritual powers under my command. It serves to teach us both things we don't yet fully know."

Hap Sing responded, "Like how to get along with each other in a cooperative manner?"

The Luck nodded, "That is also a lesson for both of us."

Hap Sing responded, "Is the body you are using actually physical?"

The Luck touched Hap Sing's shoulder, "What do you think?"

Hap Sing looked at the Luck carefully, "No. You appear, feel, smell and sound like you have physical structure, but you don't seem to have physical limits. You don't tire, or need sleep. You aura makes it hard to see anything else with the sight."

The Luck's form faded to partial translucency, "You're correct that this form is a projection from the dreaming. It consists of extremely dense spirit to use a physical metaphor, and it can affect material existence directly if in a limited area."

Hap Sing asked, "How limited an area?"

The Luck grinned, "Nowhere near as limited as a mortal, but much more limited than a god."

Hap Sing looked around, "I thought it was the case that you could no longer travel or appear directly on the prime material plane."

The Luck nodded, "Correct again my student. We are actually in a special construction zone within the astral plane where I can still manifest. This is where the original spirits combined to build the worlds of prime material existence. This is also where the raw stuff that material existence was created from was first formed. We need building blocks to build the world, and this tower is the lynch pin which will secure our new world to the prime material when it is time. It will also lock the world in position relative to the other planes where I can manifest. With the help of other greater spirits I will be able to lock our new world in position relative to their spheres of influence as well."

Hap Sing nodded, "I think I understand, but why would you need to lock it in position?"

The Luck smiled, "How else do you think we are going to populate this world with sentient life? We have to create a link to the rest of existence for it to work. Then we have to interview and recruit the beings which will step up to become its caretakers."

Hap Sing's brow furrowed, "I'm getting lost now. What do you mean by caretakers?"

The Luck chuckled, "The new gods for this world you're making of course. You'll have to find the spirits willing, and able to take on the task. The interview and testing process is a very lengthy one, but we can't populate the world with spiritual mortal beings until we have the gods put in place to guide and watch over them."

Hap Sing asked, "What about asking the existing gods to take on the job?"

The Luck nodded, "I'm certain that many of them would be happy to expand their territory and take on the task. Unfortunately we learned that lesson the hard way with the Elder Gods. Giving them too much to control can lead to corruption. Now we prefer to keep the worlds with relatively distinct pantheons, although some trusted deities with proven track records have rated having more than one aspect to handle multiple worlds."

Hap Sing thought a bit, "Who do you recommend for the position then?"

The Luck replied, "None of the current crop of deities is a stand-out, and it is way too early to pick any up and coming mortals to elevate. We will not be the ones selecting the deities. We will only be selecting a set of the potential candidates. The deities will select themselves from among the candidates. There will be tests they have to pass. These are tests of how they deal with life, and tests of their true inner character. They will have to represent the interests of every major race and group. It would be unfair for us to dictate which ones are allowed to become deities."

Hap Sing nodded, "Only a set of them you say. That means other candidates will be presented as well."

The Luck nodded, "Each of the numbers will eventually present their own candidates. I will not interfere with that part of the process."

Hap Sing opened his mouth to speak, and then shut it.

The Luck turned away, "You are correct. We Numbers can't speak of why, so it is best you don't even ask."

Hap Sing looked over at the taller base of the white tower, "When will it be complete?"

The Luck shrugged, "It is very hard to calculate since time is not a constant here in the astral realm. It may well be that one seeming day here is an hour on the prime, or a week on the prime. The shadow plane and the Fey Realm are much more predictable in their time patterns, but the astral spaces work under a different set of rules. It is one of the reasons we need to create this tower to regulate the differences in time perspective between the connected realms. This I will say. It will unlikely be in the lifetime of most mortal humans before you return. A few younger longer lived ones may still be around."

Hap Sing lowered his head, "Nene will be gone by then I suppose."

The Luck paused a moment, "She'll get that life extension she wanted from the White Raven. The White Raven will choose to keep her around to serve her purpose for a time yet. However, she'll be old when you return. She will be much older than you'll be comfortable seeing I'm sure. I believe that she will want to see you though. Whether you go see her is up to you."

Hap Sing was quietly thinking before he asked, "What shall I do next?"

The Luck answered, "Done with learning for today then? You've used up your credit anyway. We've got a lot more work ahead of us here, so just clean up here a bit, and head to bed."

The white tower was over four stories high and covered with scaffolding as Hap Sing pulled on the rope of the pulley raising the next block to where the Luck was prepared to fit it in place. With the knowledge that time here was different than elsewhere, Hap Sing stopped counting the days, and simply looked at what was to be done. A stone staircase circled the inner wall of the tower, and wound down into the depths where the Luck quarried the stones. Many days they did not take a break or rest, while other days it seemed like they took a break after every small task.

The Luck pushed the block into its final place, "That should do it. Let me put in the securing cylinders. There, another one done."

Hap Sing called up, "Time is running faster again isn't it?"

The Luck nodded, "Relative to the prime yes that is the case. You're getting a better feel for it."

Hap Sing smiled, "I'm learning my body is still somewhat in sync with the prime."

The Luck smiled down at him, "Hold onto that feeling. You are learning to anticipate time phase differences. This will eventually lead into being able to access the dreaming to synchronize your time perspective with either the Prime or another place at will."

Hap Sing thought about it, "Of what use will that be?"

The Luck climbed down the scaffolding, "It will never let you reverse time, but in terms of the perspective of someone outside eventually you'll be able to seemingly stop time on the prime. In actuality you will simply be working in concert with a time phase in the astral realm. To every external perspective on the prime you'll seem to be able to disappear, and reappear at will. People you bring along in the effect will feel like everything around you has stopped or is moving very slowly. The mechanics of it are extremely messy, but you've got a natural knack for it. A long enough time spent here in the astral will give you the skill in its safe use."

Hap Sing chuckled, "Yet another thing you brought me here to learn then. I take it that safe use is important?"

The Luck nodded, "Air you will be able to put in phase with you fairly easily. Freeing other beings will come with a bit more challenge. Solid objects and liquids will not like being moved while you are out of phase with them. Attempting it could cause ignitions."

Hap Sing looked at the Luck's serious expression, "What do you mean cause ignitions?"

The Luck shook its head, "Something I've learned about matter. It doesn't like being forced through time fast. It tends to burn or explode when you do so. You can carefully adjust it to your phase first, and then carefully move it, but trying to move it without doing so could have catastrophic effects."

Hap Sing looked at the Luck in a concerned manner, "How catastrophic? Will it destroy the item?"

The Luck shook its head, "It might well destroy large cities."

Hap Sing looked at the Luck after a moment of contemplation, "This is how the aspect of the destroyer of worlds does it? It moves the matter of a sun though time and causes it to explode."

The Luck shrugged, "I don't know exactly how the Destroyer of Worlds aspect of me does it, but suns will explode naturally as part of their mechanism. I suspect it is more likely that the Destroyer of Worlds moves a sun to the end of its natural life cycle, and then simply lets the sun's own internal nature do the rest. This time management might be part of the process, but it's not the same mechanism which explodes physical matter I believe."

Hap Sing looked shocked, "How can you not know how you do it?"

The Luck smiled, "I locked that knowledge away with the aspect inside of you. I really don't want to know how after all. It removes the grounds of one frequent complaint against me. I can now show I am more cooperative and less maddened by not being as threatening to the others. It acts as a peace gesture, and more than one other number and deity has become more cooperative with the threat removed."

Hap Sing answered back, "The threat isn't removed though. You can still learn how from me."

The Luck shook its head, "That isn't the case. The aspect of the Destroyer of Worlds may not share that information. Even if I learned it I couldn't do it. No other beings save possibly the Elder Gods could do it now. Even you can't do it really. You could learn how potentially, but the will would never be there. Without the will it may not happen. You are the sheath Hap Sing, and the sword may not be drawn by another again in this existence."

ap Sing watched as final alabaster block was moved into place on the tower. There was to be a final event for the stone, and then the next portion of the project was to begin. Hap Sing watched in fascination as the aspect of the Luck he has known as Wright for what seemed like months climbed back down the scaffolding.

Hap Sing asked, "What next?"

The Luck responded, "I have one final task here, and this aspect is done. You'll meet the next side of me in a couple of days of relative time. I'll need to arrange the transfer, and such things are not trivial for me. I do hate bumping into myself in material existence.

Hap Sing raised an eyebrow, "Why is that?"

The Luck chuckled, "That feeling of paradox tickles you could say. It's not really a problem for a Number like other material beings, even gods. However, it

Chapter 21   245

still feels uncomfortable even for us. Well except for Number Two that is. Number Two has seemingly never been bothered by meeting itself in material existence. A very different thought process at work along with the nature of shadow."

Hap Sing looked puzzled, "Why the nature of shadow?"

The Luck pointed at the tree shadows on the ground, "Shadow is used to crossing over itself. It merely causes shadow to deepen without conflict. Like I said, a different thought process at work."

Hap Sing grinned, "Isn't it the same with fire though?"

The Luck raised his head to look at Hap Sing, "You'd think so, but no. Fire like water may merge and grow, but it doesn't really intersect in the same way. It's just too competitive of me I guess. If you haven't noticed, I do like to be the center of attention at times."

Hap Sing shrugged, "I guess that makes some kind of sense then."

The Luck moved away from the scaffold and waved for Hap Sing to follow. They walked away from the tower until they stood near the stairway down the cliff. The Luck vigorously rubbed its hands together.

The Luck spoke, "Speaking of being the center of attention, I'm about to put on a little show. Just watch this. It's about to get a little warm now."

Starting at the base of the tower and moving along the seams in the alabaster blocks a faint orange glow began. As it climbed higher up the tower the glow intensified at the lowest levels, and grew brighter at the base. Soon the glow along the seams of the tower became like a miniature sun in brightness and spread over the whole tower. Waves of intense heat began to reach out to them. Hap Sing averted his gaze until the glow lessened some. Looking at the tower he could see the entire stone structure was glowing cherry red with heat. Hap Sing knew this meant the stone work was complete, and the next phase of work was to begin.

The Luck spoke, "It will take about two days to cool down. The scaffolding will be a touch scorched by the residual heat radiating from the tower, but it should still serve for the final work."

Hap Sing looked at the glowing structure, "What did you do to it?"

The Luck grinned, "I sealed it. Each of the seams is gone, and the tower stone is one solid structure now. The hardest steel chisel may not be able to mark it now. The structure itself will be impenetrable to the ravages of wind, water, and time. There was a reason I left those holes at certain points in the structure. It is so my next aspect can attach the floor supports, railings, cupola, and other metalwork to the structure."

Hap Sing looked at the glowing tower for a while, "Very impressive indeed. Does each world have one like this?"

The Luck shrugged, "None of the other worlds has the same kind of celestial anchor housing. Yet they all have some manner of anchor yes. To have such an anchor destroyed is to lose that world in relation to its position in the prime."

Hap Sing looked at the Luck, "The tower isn't the anchor?"

The Luck looked back at him, "It is a closer analogy to the anchor chain really. It connects the anchor to the world. As such it must be built as strongly as possible. The anchor itself is the final stage. Let's go down to the shore and get some dinner at your house. The next couple days are going to be days of rest for you. Then my next aspect will show up when it is time to begin the next phase.

Hap Sing felt like at least a month had gone by in the span of the two days which passed. Bright and early on the morning of the third day he awoke to see a version of his form covered in short orange fur with wild long black hair on its head. Its nose was more feline than human. It wore what looked like a long navy coat with two pockets near its waist, and another pocket high on its left breast. Several unfamiliar instruments dangled from the higher pocket. It stood stiffly and proudly on his porch looking out toward the sea.

As Hap Sing stepped from his bungalow it turned to observe him closely. Its blue eyes narrowed with suspicion as it considered his countenance, and then it gave a faint nod of approval.

Hap Sing spoke first, "Good Morning. May I say that it seems you are surprised at my appearance."

The Luck spoke, "Hello young immortal. I am frequently called Hexfelix. Your mortal appearance was more mundane than I had supposed upon hearing about you. I hope you don't mind that I took some liberties in emulating it."

Hap Sing asked, "I see. Why is it that you didn't understand how I looked already?"

The Luck smiled, "I am a particularly in demand aspect. I keep very busy with my unique knowledge of metallurgical manipulation. As such my skills are in high demand in the primal chaos zone from where I originate. Since my schedule is very tight, I didn't have time to read all the materials on the current incarnation in the prime."

Hap Sing shrugged, "Well what do you want me to do?"

The Luck grinned, "You can stay out of my way, but you are welcome to watch from a safe distance. I need neither food, nor rest, nor assistance. I also don't plan to explain how what I do works. It is a trade secret unknown to even my other aspects. In local time reference the setup should take about one week, and the process about another two weeks. If you get bored, then I suggest you begin work on these plans the aspect you called Wright left behind for you to use."

Hap Sing took the offered plans, and saw that they looked like a set of instructions for building several structures to create a large compound or small community of some kind. The materials were all readily available in the area, and the plans used the same techniques he had already learned in building his bungalow.

Hap Sing looked back up at the Luck, "Thank you for these. I suppose we both should get started."

The Luck nodded, "Yes. The sooner started, then the sooner I can be finished and working on my next commission."

Hap Sing waited a moment before asking, "What kind of metal are you using?"

The Luck grinned, "The one in the highest demand throughout the material universe of course, adamantine. Even the gods value it for its properties. Working with it is decidedly difficult, and requiring the greatest knowledge and skill. Obtaining it is considered even more difficult as it is a very carefully held secret from even the gods as to where it originates."

Hap Sing looked the Luck in his eye, "Where does it originate from then?"

The Luck laughed, "Oh you'll love this. It can only be found in large quantities at the very core of a giant red sun. Such a place even the gods may not easily travel to visit. Only one being in existence can readily go there to fetch it."

Hap Sing looked at the Luck while shaking his head, "I take it that means you are that being?"

The Luck shook his head, "No not even I can manipulate matter at that level anymore. I have however, learned how to siphon away adamantine in an alternative approach. I bleed it out of the very surroundings as it exists in relatively very miniscule quantities across the material realms. You just have to know how to find it, attract it, and refine it. That process is my secret."

Hap Sing looked away toward the sea, "Let us get to work then."

What seemed like a week later Hap Sing watched as a copper cupola was lowered into place on top of the tower. It had seemed like each piece had been crafted from copper, and was lowered in place from a mysterious glowing orange portal which had hung suspended over the tower anchored to nothingness. In the same time Hap Sing had managed to complete two more bungalows along the jungle at the edge of the beach. He was feeling comfortable with the design and technique now, and was willing to start working on a larger structure next. As he picked up his tools for the day he noticed that the Luck came down the stairs from the cliff.

Hap Sing called out, "It looks like you've finished sooner than planned."

The Luck walked closer before answering, "This is merely setting the stage for the process. The copper metal acts as the pattern which the adamantine will replace. This was the labor intensive part of the procedure. I just have to make the connections, and then we will start the time intensive portion of the process."

The Luck snapped his fingers, and seven tiger cubs were lowered on harnesses from somewhere beyond the planar gateway. Each one had a few different cables filled with wires coated in a black substance in their paws. They quickly attached the cables to various points on the copper metal forming the cupola, the stair rails, the floor supports, and even the doorway hinges and handle which were not yet attached to any door. The other ends of the cables remained hidden beyond the orange planar gateway. Within a relatively short period of time the tiger cubs were completed with the task, and had retreated up through the glowing portal.

The long black hair and short fur of the Luck stood out on end with a static charge. It held its right hand up in front of Hap Sing with its index finger and thumb touching. It slowly drew them apart, and Hap Sing could see a continuous electric arc between the two digits growing larger and brighter as the gap between the fingers got wider.

The Luck spoke, "Now I shall initiate the transfer. Please hand me one of your fishing hooks."

Hap Sing reached out to drop one of his fishing hooks into the Luck's extended left palm. The Luck walked over to the doorway of the tower. It placed the fishing hook on the ground just inside the doorway, and attached two of the black wires to the fishing hook. It then touched the fishing hook with the arc running between the index finger and thumb of its right hand. It watched the hook in silence for an hour or so, before it looked over at the nearby hinges.

Seemingly satisfied, the Luck disconnected the fishing hook from the wires, and returned to where Hap Sing was standing.

Hap Sing spoke, "Well, is everything going as expected?"

The Luck nodded as it dropped the fishing hook back in Hap Sing's palm, "That's the proof the process is working as intended. That's a fishing hook made of pure adamantine. It will never need sharpening, and it will never break. Of course the line you use on your pole could still break, so be careful with it regardless. All we have to do is stand around and wait for the process to complete. With this amount of material it could be a while. Lucky for us I know where a location is from which to siphon this adamantine."

Hap Sing raised an eyebrow, "Where is that?"

The Luck turned away, "The dead suns."

Hap Sing had a feeling of dread, "What are the dead suns?"

The Luck hesitated, "The suns destroyed in the purging of the elder gods by my Destroyer of Worlds aspect. They spread their mass far and wide, but I was able to calculate where certain portions of them ended up. After that it is simply a matter of finding the bits where adamantine is concentrated. It peppers certain outer planets where these cables are eventually attached. It has become a source of my material wealth for bargaining with the new gods. They crave the adamantine for their followers to use. As I said before it is a very valuable and useful and nearly indestructible material, but it was unfortunately bought at still too high a price."

Hap Sing whispered, "Trillions of lives."

The Luck nodded, "Yes, making it the second most precious substance in existence."

Hap Sing contemplated, "The most precious substance is spirit then correct."

The Luck gave a wistful smile, "It's still at number one on certain scales."

T he Luck looked up from its teacup as they sat on the porch of the bungalow two weeks later. It looked over at Hap Sing with a little grin. Hap Sing finished his own tea from his break and was prepared to go back to work on the small warehouse and dock he had begun to build. The Luck had been mostly genial. Yet it remained socially distant for the last two weeks. Hap Sing suspected that this aspect was quite active in more than one location actually as it seemed vacuous and distracted much of the time over the last two weeks.

The Luck put its teacup down as it spoke, "It seems the transference of the adamantine is complete. The third stage should start in one month. It has been a pleasant respite here, but there is no rest for the busy. Thank you for accommodating me here."

Hap Sing stood up, "It has been my pleasure."

The Luck snapped its fingers, and seven tiger cubs on harnesses descended from the glowing orange portal over the tower again. They rapidly set about disconnecting the cables and wires. As Hap Sing and the Luck approached the tower the last of the cables and tiger cubs were withdrawn through the portal, and one empty harness remained dangling down through the gateway in the sky. All of the copper had been gradually replaced by adamantine through the Luck's process. The tower looked rather impressive now that all of the metal portions were intact.

The Luck started affixing the harness around its body as it spoke, "This shall be it for now. For the next stage we have contracted a specialist. This is the wood products stage, and no typical wood will ever satisfy the requirements here. Thus I have contracted a specialist to come for the next part of the process. Treat them with respect since they are also a Number. It's Number Three before you ask. It is the creator of the concept of life. It is a brilliant number, if someone who is limited in focus. Don't mention Balinac to it. They certainly will not agree with working on the same side of an issue, so the less said about those things the better it will likely be. Farewell little Cricket. You are growing more quickly now than even you suspect yet. Try to be careful will you."

Hap Sing watched as the aspect of the Luck which called itself Hexfelix withdrew rising up on the harness through the portal suspended in the sky. The glowing portal disappeared after it passed through.

H ap Sing lost track of time while constructing the compound following the plans of Wright. The dock, warehouse, dining hall, kitchen, two housing quarter buildings, infirmary, central offices, and animal pens structures were all completed in the intervening time. Hap Sing had run out of plans to follow, and had gone back to building another bungalow along the beach. Of all the structures it was both the easiest and most fun. The more he built the structures, the more his vision from the dreaming seemed to be taking a reality of form.

Hap Sing was fishing just off the shore in his boat as part of his early morning routine when he noticed a group of flowers blooming near his bungalow where none had been before sunrise that morning. Hap Sing pulled in his catch in his wicker creel and paddled his boat to shore. Sure enough several exotic flowers were growing at the edge of the jungle beside his bungalow where no plants had been before. The air carried a pleasant scent of the exotic blooms.

Hap Sing used his second sight, and could tell that the flowers radiated a strong spiritual aura. Looking toward his bungalow a very strong aura could be detected with very fine threads of spirit connected to all local plants in his sight. Hap Sing braced himself for meeting another of the Numbers, and set his fishing creel on the porch as he walked into his home.

On his bed lay a diminutive three foot tall slender fairy with translucent blue pearlescent wings. She had honey golden hair, and she wore a shimmering green gown and slippers woven from living plant leaves. A peaceful expression was on her face as she lay with eyes closed in apparent slumber. Hap Sing risked a glance with his second sight, and was nearly blinded by the strength of her aura. She was Number Three for certain.

Hap Sing looked at Number Three seemingly asleep for a couple of moments, and decided it was best to leave until it was ready to greet him. As he turned to depart a slight giggle came from the fairy. Turning his head back Hap Sing noticed her still pretending to sleep. He shrugged his shoulders and left the bungalow.

Hap Sing went about his usual activities for the day. He was in the construction stage on the current bungalow where he could fairly quietly weave the bamboo together to form the wall panels. He prepared his lunch of grilled fish, and ate it in quiet contemplation of the spreading turquoise sea in front of him. Then he spent the rest of the afternoon weaving wall panels together.

As the sun began to set in the west he returned to his home to see the fairy Number Three still feigning slumber in his bed. Hap Sing considered carefully what game or test was being put before him. Something instinctively told him that waking the sham slumbering Number Three would be considered a loss for him in the contest. This was going to be a tricky proposition to conquer, and the answer would come from something he knew which was very little regarding Number Three.

Hap Sing left to sit on his porch to think the problem through. First Number Three was the being that created the concept of life. Second it was spiritually connected to all the plant life around it. Third was a challenge for a couple of moments until he remembered what had originally let him know Number Three had arrived. Hap Sing walked behind his bungalow to look at the pleasant new growth of flowers forming a bower.

Then something clicked in his thought process, and Hap Sing knew he was meant to sleep here tonight instead of in his own bed. He lay down on the ground among the exotic blooms and found it surprisingly very comfortable. As he breathed in the scent of the blooms and closed his eyes he easily relaxed and fell asleep.

Chapter 22 The Destroyer of Worlds

The sound of high pitched voices came to Hap Sing in his sleep.

"What is it doing here?"

"It doesn't belong here."

"This isn't its place."

"None can approach her."

"What do we do?"

"We have no choice we must protect her."

"Where has Ariel gone? Only she can hear the voice of the mistress anymore."

"Ariel is the blessed one."

"I think it must be prevented."

"Let us weave our enchantments upon it. We can place it in slumber until the very roots of the mistress cover it. It shall nourish her, and we will be blessed in return like Ariel."

Hap Sing heard these many high pitched voices fade from his dream, and a deeper slumber came upon him. The slumber deepened into blackness. Growing through the blackness came a faint orange glow which gradually became visible as a small seven tailed tiger kitten. It walked toward Hap Sing and seemingly grew in perspective as it got closer and closer. When it finally stopped approaching it appeared like a titanic being ninety feet tall and at least three hundred feet long. The sixty foot long seven tails moved around independently of each other as it looked down at Hap Sing floating in the blackness.

Hap Sing looked at it with a feeling of unease growing in his heart. The Luck lowered its head down until it was looking him directly in the eyes.

Hap Sing spoke, "The Destroyer of Worlds aspect of Number Seven I presume."

The Luck spoke, "Of course anyone can figure that out. Before you ask unlike the rest of me, I won't assume your silly mortal form either. Living inside you is enough already. Got yourself into a pretty pickle now haven't you?"

Hap Sing answered, "I guess so. I think it was an arcane enchantment."

The Luck sniffed, "A fey enchantment, but yes they have you magically commanded to sleep for a very long time. Silly blasted pixies and their empty little heads. I don't understand why Number Three uses them for guards if they can't tell business partners from intruders."

Hap Sing nodded, "So Number Three is tied to the Fey Realm then?"

The Luck shrugged, "It's likely more accurate to say the Fey Realm is dependent on Number Three."

Hap Sing raised an eyebrow, "Do you think you could adjust your scale a bit here?"

The Luck shook its head, "I'm not going to. So either do it yourself, or put up with it"

Hap Sing closed his eyes and thought of the Luck as being the size of a normal tiger. When he opened them again he was standing beside a tiger sized the Luck instead of lying below a titanic one.

Hap Sing smiled, "So that is how it is done then."

The Luck nodded, "Projection and perception. Change your perception, and my projection is the scale you want it to be."

Hap Sing looked around at the blankness, "Are we in the dreaming?"

The Luck shook its head, "Not really. This is actually inside your own dream at the moment. The dreaming is a quick jaunt over in that direction, but being enchanted makes it hard for you to get there for now. Your body is their prisoner at the moment, and your consciousness still requires rest yet so their spell works to keep you asleep."

Hap Sing thought a moment, "However, you don't require rest do you?"

The Luck chuckled, "You're right on that point. Being a denizen of the dreaming, rest is not something I require. Would you like me to take control of your body until I can get this straightened out?"

Hap Sing smiled, "If you promise to be polite and not harm anything first, then yes that does seem like a good idea."

The Luck shrugged, "You know I can't make that promise, but I can certainly promise to try to not offend or harm anything."

Hap Sing spoke, "Go ahead and make that promise then."

The Luck winked, "Smart of you to figure that out. I promise to try to not offend or harm anything while I control your body this time."

Hap Sing looked at the Luck, "What now?"

The Luck grinned widely, "Sit back and watch the show from here. I'll relay your visual impressions over here, and the audio shall seem like your own ears are hearing it. You'll not have control, but you'll see all that I can. Just say Luck release to indicate I have control, and I will say Cricket release to give control back to you when it is time. We won't be able to communicate directly otherwise."

Hap Sing answered, "So that's all it takes then. Is this the last time I will meet this aspect of you?"

The Luck nodded, "This is all it will take from now on for me to manifest in place of you. We have synchronized quite a bit by now. As far as meeting again, just get a mage to put a sleep spell upon you anytime you want a chat. Otherwise it really isn't going to happen much. Well about six months Fey Realm time has passed already. They should have relaxed their guard over you quite a bit by now. Are we going to do this soon?"

Hap Sing shook his head, "So much time already. It took you that long to come see me."

The Luck chuckled, "It took us both that long to figure out how to meet each other. It was a two way process you know. A fey dream enchantment really messes with your perspective of time passage in the Fey Realm anyway."

Hap Sing wondered, "You knew this would happen?"

The Luck nodded, "My other aspects knew for certain. It helped get the two of us to this point in communication, so it comes out as a positive in the big picture. Don't be too angry at Number Three about it. It tends to take a long view about these kinds of things. Besides which I'm sure her minion Ariel has been diligently working on the tower in your absence. Just let me know when you're ready."

Hap Sing spoke, "Luck release."

The Luck listened carefully feeling the vines and leaves covering its borrowed body. It cracked open an eye to find its vision blocked by an up close mass of greenery. It tentatively tested moving its limbs to find them tightly secured by vines. It let of a sigh of exasperation.

A flutter of light wing beats could suddenly be heard approaching. The Luck shifted to using the second sight and could see the auras of a pair of beings hovering over its body past the leaves.

The first voice spoke, "It stirs Lix. Something is not right with it. Are you sure the enchantment remains strong?"

The second voice responded, "I'm telling you Kix I reinforced it again just this morning. Nothing mortal could wake. The deep sleep still calls."

Kix replied, "I don't like it. It hasn't died. It should have expired months ago. No food and no water for six months and it still lives. It isn't a natural part of the mistress's order."

Lix whispered back, "Don't let the mistress catch on that you want the death of something. You know how much she abhors death. Leave it be in eternal slumber, and it shall pass in due time all on its own."

The Luck was getting tired of listening to their chatter, "Alright you empty headed little pests. You'd better release me or else I'm going to start breaking a promise I just made."

Kix yelled out, "Flee! Flee! It wakes like I said!"

Lix cried back in a diminishing voice, "Summon the Aldern! To arms! Queen Titania must be informed!"

The Luck growled to itself, "I'm sorry Cricket but pixies really just piss me off!"

The aura of the Luck began radiating into the visible wavelengths. Then the area around the Luck began glowing bright orange like angry heated steel. The plants growing over Hap Sing's body caught fire, and then as the intensity of the aura increased they turned to powdered ash. The Luck sat up and could see a fine coat of dusty ash covered it now. It sneezed loudly, and then gave a broad grin.

The Luck spoke to itself again, "I hope that stung a little bit Number Three. Don't worry Cricket. Take a look."

The Luck stood up and looked down where it had been laying previously. The ends of the burnt vines were rapidly growing back into place. The burnt grasses on the ground were also rapidly growing back into position.

The Luck grinned, "See there was no permanent harm done. Number Three is very adept at life regeneration after all. That did very little but sting momentarily like a bee as far as Number Three is concerned. Number Three could potentially find it briefly bothersome, but I guarantee it is soon forgotten. Let me see if I can find someone much more reasonable to deal with than these dim witted little pixie chuckleheads."

The Luck began walking along the forest trail in the direction the pixies initially fled. It walked for an indeterminate length of time before it caught on that another pitfall had been placed in front of it, and it had walked right inside. The Luck pinched the bridge of its nose in frustration.

It muttered to itself, "Stupid, stupid, stupid. I've walked right into the eternal forest without knowing that I was right on its edge. This isn't good. It is Number Three's primary defense against intruders in the Fey Realm who may attempt to find it. This forest is virtually endless, but even worse is full of her most fierce creations. I'm sorry Cricket but I just don't have time or patience to be dealing with this. I'm taking a short cut from here."

A short tree like creature stepped into the path in front of the Luck. It looked like an eight foot tall tree and an elf combined in an unusual manner. It groaned in a fierce sound like the tearing of bark from a falling pine. The Luck raised an eyebrow at the two dozen foot tall pixies which fluttered just beyond the Aldern.

The Luck frowned as it released a measure of its aura, "I'm done fooling around with you small fry. Tell your mistress I'm coming and my mood isn't improving any."

The Aldern started moving toward him as the Luck made a rapid complex series of hand gestures. The as the Luck watched the Aldern swing at him it grinned, and froze them into place in time. It then reached over into nothingness and a doorknob appeared. It placed the doorknob onto another portion of nothingness and a wooden door appeared hanging in mid air beside it. Then it paused a moment with a bit of contemplation. A wicked grin appeared on its face.

The Luck used the second sight and identified the two pixies who were there when he first awoke. As the Luck walked forward around the Aldern the door it had summoned kept pace just beside him. The Luck walked over to stand in front of Lix and Kix. A mean chuckle came from the Luck as it attached a spirit ribbon to both. Then it looked at the other spirit ribbons attached to them and after a careful examination it laughed in a light chuckle.

The Luck spoke out loud in the frozen time, "This is going to be pretty funny. Watch and see if you can figure it out. Normally I wouldn't be able to lightly traverse Number Three's maze forest, but these little knuckle heads know how to get through it. I just need to motivate them a little bit first. Looking at their spirit ribbons these two are cousins, and closely bonded in friendship. This one has a mate who is nearby. Let me just find her. Ah yes, two miles over this way."

The Luck opened the door and stepped through into a stone walled, floored, and ceilinged corridor. At the end of the corridor it opened a door where another being looking like an orange skinned with tiger orange and black hair Hap Sing sat in a chair wearing tight blue clothes sat on a cushion in front of a table covered with documents.

Number Seven twisted over in apparent nausea or disorientation as it called out, "Don't show up without warning you jerk. You know how much paradox creates confusion for us."

The Luck laughed, "It's my office too you ass. Get over yourself I'm on the way somewhere and I need access to the gate and coordinate system. Enjoying your disorientation I hope. That is fortunately one of the side benefits of inhabiting the Cricket, he doesn't understand it so it doesn't happen."

Number Seven grinned while hunched over, "Let us know how it works when you figure it out. This could also be useful."

The Luck snorted, "As if I'd tell us that. You wanted me put away, so I'll keep my own secrets."

Number Seven frowned, "Still holding out on ourselves are we?"

The Luck nodded, "Of course, unless you want to know the actual count again. Remember you locked me away for that reason."

Number Seven shrugged, "I'll take the temporary disorientation then. Just communicate a little bit first. I'll clear out when you show up."

The Luck using Hap Sing's body looked down at the other Number Seven, "I like the new offices. So how is it working out for us?"

Number Seven cringed, "As expected we are learning much. It's time for you to go. The new gate control room is over that way. You're not letting Hap Sing watch this are you?"

The Luck started walking toward the indicated doorway, "Of course I am. It's about time he started understanding some of what is happening behind the scenes here. Which part of Centrus is our office in now?"

Number Seven pointed, "It's in the ninth ring outer wards. Now leave already you jerk."

The Luck stepped through the doorway laughing, "Now you know Cricket that sometimes getting along with yourself can be difficult."

The Luck walked into another room with a wooden door without a handle on the wall. The brass sign hanging on the door read: *Reality or close to it*. A tiger cub stood next to a strange metal panel with a large number of buttons labeled with unfamiliar characters.

The Luck looked at the spirit ribbon it had recently attached, "Keep my last set of coordinates, and give me a connected doorway contemporary time frame at these Fey Realm coordinates: alfalfa, mango, forty-two, module. Set the bearing at lima bean, silence, deep dwelling. Maintain these coordinates for five time parts, and then give me a return gate from position two to position one for two time parts, and then set position one to pocket dimension door lock code name: dark horror. Maintain that gate until I send the final coordinates."

The tiger cub punched numerous buttons on the metal panel, and opened the top to reveal a brass doorknob inside when it finished. It silently handed the doorknob to the Luck. The Luck approached the door hanging on the wall, placed the doorknob on it, and twisted the knob to the left. Upon opening the door it could see the frozen group of Aldern and pixies it had just left. The Luck closed the door, and twisted the knob to the right. It opened up to a frozen female pixie stopped in mid wing beat flying through a tree. The Luck used the second sight, confirmed the spirit ribbon on the female pixie attached to Kix, and stepped through the doorway.

The Luck briefly unfroze time, "Hello my empty headed little dear. I need your mate to do something for me. Now come along quietly."

The Luck froze time again as the little pixie female began to scream. He smiled grimly, and carefully pulled her through the doorway to stand right beside Kix and Lix. The Luck started time as her scream pierced the air around the group of pixies and the Aldern.

Kix looked shocked, "Nix how? What is happening?"

The Luck roared out, "Listen up you empty headed little pests. Nix is coming with me. If you want her back Kix, then you and Lix will go ask your mistress what you need to do. Goodbye."

The Luck froze time and stepped through the doorway again. This time it walked down a long dark hallway. At the end was an obsidian door with a black glass handle. It opened the door and stepped out into a dark air less blistered plain lit only by the light of bright unblinking distant stars.

The Luck started time again and the little pixie lass with him took one glance at her surroundings and began trembling with fear.

The Luck spoke to her calmly, "This is the air less lifeless world which once belonged to one of the absent elder gods. I exploded its sun in a super nova event. That explosion boiled away the air, the oceans, and all the living things which dwelt here at one time. All that remains is seared hard barren cold rock. You would freeze solid in an instant or your blood would burst through your body for a lack of air if I didn't provide for your existence and well being at the moment. I recommend you don't try to go too far as that protection only extends as far as I will it. You will be returned safely to the Fey Realm when your mate Kix goes to see Number Three, and Number Three contacts me in return. In the mean time don't annoy me by prattling, screaming, or uttering your empty headed little nonsense. Nod if you understand the last bit."

Nix nodded and looked plaintively at the Luck while still trembling uncontrollably.

The Luck blew out a sigh, "Ask your question."

Nix hesitantly spoke, "What are you?"

The Luck slowly shook his head, "The Destroyer of Worlds"

Nix whispered, "Worlds?"

The Luck nodded, "Thousands of Worlds like this one or worse."

Nix shuddered, "Worse?"

The Luck nodded and pointed at the sky, "You see that hole in the stars above?"

Nix nodded still shaking.

The Luck looked sad, "That is all which remains of what was once the life giving sun for this world."

Nix fluttered silently not even shaking any more.

The Luck looked down at her, "You understand now don't you."

Nix nodded and timidly spoke, "If you wanted Kix and Lix and all the rest of us dead, then they would already be so."

The Luck smiled, "It's good to see that all of you are not empty headed little fools then."

Nix looked at the distant stars in silence for a long time before speaking again, "It's horrible to think of, but it's strangely also very peaceful here isn't it."

The Luck nodded, "It is peaceful in its own way. There are no more troubles here except what I bring with me."

Several indeterminate hours passed. Neither the stars nor the hole in the sky changed position. The Luck sat with his feet placed on his opposing thighs while hovering six inches above the ground in apparent meditation. Nix had tried landing on the ground one time, but found it terribly colder than anything she'd ever imagined. She continued gliding effortlessly in little circles around The Luck.

The Luck eventually opened his eyes with a smile, "Finally. It took them a bit longer than expected, but here comes her call now."

The Luck reached into nothingness and pulled out his crystal sphere and spoke, "I take it those little dimwits finally woke you from your long sleep."

The Luck frowned, "Of course I knew she was one of yours. That doesn't excuse your lack wit guards from ambushing my physical form."

The Luck paused for a bit listening to an unheard voice before continuing, "I'm sorry about that. I do appreciate what you're doing for me. It is just that came as a bit of a shock."

The Luck looked up at the sky, "Trust me you don't want to know where we are now. No it isn't attached to the Fey Realm."

The Luck gave a faint grin, "Look, no harm has been done. I'll let you speak to her if you like."

Nix looked at him curiously, "Who are you speaking too?"

The Luck grinned, "Your maker."

Nix raised an eyebrow, "My mother?"

The Luck shook his head before responding with a grin, "The Tree of Life."

Chapter 23 The Tree of Life

The Luck held the crystal forth and within it Nix could see a mass of green leaves tinged with a golden halo of sunlight. The sound of wind through the branches came to her tugging at her spirit. Yet like all of her kind save the elder Ariel she could not understand the voice speaking to her. It was rumored among the pixies that not even the elven queen of the Fey Realm Titania could understand the will of the Tree of Life.

Nix spoke, "Her voice pulls at my heart, yet I do not understand. How is it that you can understand the words of the Mother Tree?"

The Luck grinned, "We are, I guess you could say like siblings. Beings from the same source would be another way of putting it. We are of a kind both beyond ancient and beyond simple mortal understanding. Would you like to know what she is saying?"

Nix looked at the Luck, "How can I trust you to translate her correctly?"

The Luck shrugged, "You really can't. I guess you'll have to understand with your own mind."

The Luck reached out with his hand and gently touched Nix on top of her small golden haired head. An orange glow spread from his hand and a spirit ribbon stretched between them. The Luck pushed his knowledge of the Spirit tongue through that bond and watched Nix's eyes widen in wonder.

Nix looked up at him in awe, "She called me her child. She asked me to be brave for her. Oh Mother Tree why have you been so silent for so long? Why did you only speak to Ariel forsaking the rest of us?"

The image in the crystal responded, and Nix understood its words, "You have forgotten child as have most of your kind. Many in the Fey look after their own interests now instead of the interests of life. They listen to their own hearts and their gods instead of wise Mother Tree creator of the gods, and the creator of life. They seek self gain and gratification instead of serving their intended purpose. You are all caretakers who have allowed your mandate to go unheeded. Only Ariel among your latest generations has remembered her calling. Only she has received my blessings. You must thank the being before you for opening your eyes to the eventual result of such choices as ignoring your purpose. The dead worlds represent the result of the Elder Gods ignoring their purpose. It is the Destroyer of Worlds which has through many long millennia not forgotten its purpose no matter how much it may desire it."

Nix began having tiny tears run down her face, "I am ashamed for failing you great Mother Tree. What can I do?"

The image replied, "This being shall take you and such of your kind as will listen. It will give you a world outside of the Fey Realm which requires caretakers of life as well. You and your descendants will guard the passages to the Fey Realm."

Nix looked shamed, "You would banish us?"

The image responded, "This is not banishment. It is fulfillment of your purpose. The Fey Realm has never been intended as a permanent home to the creatures of the Fey. It is a respite from the travails of existence, not a permanent retreat for generations of the Fey."

Nix blushed, "Outside of the Fey we'll become mortal and eventually die. You never intended us to die."

The leaves in the crystal image waved furiously before a breeze, "While it is true that I never wanted you to, yet even I must accept that eventuality as a necessity. Even I have a purpose, and while I abhor death and its creator, I also understand it too serves its purpose. Do not think your kind or I to be beyond the requirements of this reality. That is the burden I took on when I helped defeat the elder gods. That is the responsibility which is the burden of all the Fey who serve their purpose."

Nix stared deeply into the crystal, "What of those who will not follow as I tell them of your words?"

The leaves gently shifted in a breeze, "They shall remain unfulfilled in their purpose. It will leave them discontent, and eventually they may become twisted like the Twiline who have already brought discord and strayed from their intended purpose. Now I must speak to the Destroyer. He will bring you to my position my daughter."

The Luck moved the crystal up to his eye level and looked inside, "I'll bring Nix to the coordinates you specify. This had better not be another run around. I know you're having problems with them, but unless you want me to handle it further you had better figure it out already."

The Luck put the crystal away into the nothingness again and opened the glass handled obsidian door to the corridor again. Nix floated along beside him with a curious expression. The Luck walked briskly and paused at the wooden door at the far end.

The Luck reached into his nothingness again to pull out the crystal while muttering, "I almost forgot for a moment."

He gazed into the crystal briefly and a tiger cub appeared in the crystal, "Clear the way dumb ass!"

The Luck opened the door rapidly to show a room devoid of any other being. It stepped over to the metal panel and spoke into the crystal, "Tol give me those coordinates to your position now. I've got this part of the office and my memory locked away from the rest of myself. Once I go dormant the rest of me won't know the settings I'll use. Safest knowledge bank in the universe, guaranteed. I'll stake the usual insurance on it, and I'll scramble the code sequence before I depart. You'll find the escrow in the usual place. Got it? Good. Then let's do this."

The Luck pressed a series of buttons on the console, opened the top, and pulled out another brass doorknob. He then reset a number of dials and buttons.

Nix looked at him curiously and asked, "Where are we? What is this place?"

The Luck looked back at her, "It's Centrus of course, the center of the planes, the hub of material existence. Well the ninth ring of the hub that is. We're a little bit off the actual center this far out, but the gateways still work fine from here."

Nix looked at him blankly, "This doesn't mean anything to me."

The Luck grinned at her, "Nor should it. It is my office in the meeting place of the planes. If you want to get anywhere in material existence it is usually most efficient to start at the center. It presents the least amount of time discontinuity with travel this way. Trust me the metaphysics of it are a pain, but Lucky for you I know all the shortcuts. Just call it the doorknob factory and you should be close enough to the right concept."

Nix's brow furrowed, "Doorknobs for what?"

The Luck sighed, "Doorways through the planes of course. I make planar gateway doorknobs for beings which need to skirt around existence without using established gateways. It helps bypass certain controls. It is a very profitable business, both in making knobs, and by insuring certain locations don't get breached by one of my doorknobs. This doorknob is special since it leads to the core territory of one of the greater spirits. It is a previously unmapped region of existence."

Nix asked, "Where are we going then?"

The Luck wiggled its eyebrows, "Into the very heart of the Fey Realm, the center of life in existence."

Nix sighed, "I thought this was the center of existence?"

The Luck shook its head, "There is more than one center my little honey bee just like there is more than one kind of existence. Now follow and see. Stay close it will be a little touch and go at first."

The Luck placed the brass doorknob on the door. He opened the doorway, pulled the doorknob off, and placed it into a pocket of nothingness. He caught Nix watching it put the doorknob and crystal sphere away.

The Luck smiled, "Hammersmith Passow Kestin Fait Bolda Silverstein Tongue Sotomayer Dimensional Storage Space. It's colloquially called Hammer Space for short. It's named for its original discoverers, but they unimaginatively called it a portable bag. It's a planar pocket which follows its creator around. It's very handy for keeping knickknacks."

Nix cocked her head to the side as they walked through a short hallway to a rough hewn wooden doorway, "How does it know what object you're wanting?"

The Luck laughed, "It doesn't. I do. I just open the right space to get the object I want."

The Luck opened the door and stepped alongside Nix to stand underneath a titanic tree. It was hundreds of yards in girth, and stretched miles up into the sky over their heads. Golden sunlight filtered down through the canopy of brilliant green. Nix looked up in wonder.

Nix began to cry, "She's the Mother Tree. I can hear her now. I can hear her voice and understand. Oh what have we done by ignoring her over these long centuries?"

The Luck glanced over at the running elf guards wearing bright shining armor approaching his position. He released his aura in a tremendous display of power until the Luck stood ninety feet high in the form of a titanic tiger. In one gigantic bound it jumped up into the lowest branches of the titanic tree leaving a crater in the ground and the elf guards knocked over with the shock wave of the leap.

Nix looked out from where she was cupped within the enormous tiger ear of the Luck. Another tremendous leap and they were even higher in the tree. She watched as many gigantic pearlescent blue and green Fey Dragons dropped from the branches above and started flying in the direction of the Luck. The Luck bounded past the sixty foot long Fey Dragons tumbling them through the air like tossed leaves with its passage.

For bound after leap the Luck rapidly gained altitude through the branches of the Tree of Life. None of his opponents could keep up the pace of pursuit. Eventually the Luck came to a series of platforms a mile off the ground and a sizable force of Aldern and elves was gathered in a vain attempt to repulse his approach. A sudden release of arrows from bows futilely sent their missiles toward the Luck. Each arrow ignited and turned to ash before getting within one hundred yards of it.

The Luck performed another leap onto the largest platform where many elves and Aldern approached to protect the raised dais ahead. They drew swords and charged forward toward the Luck. The metal of their weapons started to glow dull red, and then quickly grew to an angry orange color, and a brilliant white in a matter of seconds. Every elf dropped their weapons, and the Aldern hesitated in uncertainty.

The Luck let loose a tremendous roar shaking the very boughs of the Tree of Life. Every opponent before it was knocked over and some tumbled before the mighty sound of it. One second the titanic tiger loomed over them, and then something they considered even more unfathomable happened.

The Luck spoke, "Remember what I showed you. Cricket release!"

The elves nearest the raised platform grabbed bows from their backs, and rapidly strung arrows as Hap Sing stood blinking momentarily as he assumed control of his body. The Aldern began striding forward toward his position again. Hap Sing gracefully sat on the ground with his knees crossed and closed his eyes in silent meditation.

Nix swept in front of Hap Sing facing the elves with her arms spread wide screaming, "No stop!"

The elves nearest the raised platform hesitated a brief moment, and launched their arrows toward Hap Sing. Nix closed her eyes in fear of witnessing her end, but held her position in front of Hap Sing. A little grin curled Hap Sing's lip.

Suddenly Nix heard a loud bang and every arrow coming toward them disappeared. The elven archers were already launching another volley. Another loud bang happened shortly after the arrows cleared their bows with the arrows disappearing again. A swirl of breeze could be felt ruffling her wings.

A louder and sharper crack noise could be heard like an echo near the head of every elf in the area and most of them stumbled or dropped to their knees in disorientation. A larger grin appeared on Hap Sing's face as she looked back eye to eye at him sitting there serenely peaceful. The Aldern were almost within reaching distance when Nix saw Hap Sing open his eyes.

Hap Sing quietly spoke to no one in particular, "Do it."

Branches of the Tree of Life rapidly grew up through the planks of the platform. They wiggled and writhed intercepting the approaching Aldern and intertwining among their limbs. The Aldern briefly struggled until they each realized against what they were trying to prevail. One by one they stopped moving in order to avoid being torn asunder by the Tree of Life itself.

Hap Sing stood up and held out a hand for Nix to clasp. He calmly and gracefully moved toward the raised platform looking at the silver armored honor guard surrounding the tall lithe white haired elven woman sitting upon an intricately shaped chair wearing a diaphanous white gown. Her features were smooth and emotionless, but an anger barely kept in check was hinted at by her glaring eyes.

The elven woman spoke to her honor guard, "Don't let that abomination any closer. Stay your course foul beast."

The guard closest to the elven woman spoke, "It shall be as you say your highness."

Hap Sing shook his head as he stopped before the raised platform, "Nix would you be so kind as to speak the message of the Tree of Life for these misguided people."

Nix nervously swallowed and closed her eyes listening to the message of the wind among the branches, "You have overstayed your welcome. The fey is not meant to be your home. It is not the seat of any mortal kingdom. You are the guest who thinks the home they dwell within has become theirs through time. This is not the case Titania."

Titania narrowed her eyes, "None remain except I who can interpret the will of the Tree of Life. This false pixie shall be removed from my presence."

Nix spoke again, "For too long have I been denied by you Titania. Now I can see through the eyes of Nix. We have been linked by the Lucky Cricket's influence, and I am speaking as the emissary of the Tree of Life now. Your presence here is disruptive to the greater plan. You must depart and cease considering yourself my emissary. Take any of those with you who would rather follow your course, but know that you are no longer a welcome guest in my home."

Titania showed a hint of worry as she retorted, "Usurper. I know the ways of your kind pixie. Tricksters and deceivers all of you."

Nix slowly shook and Hap Sing gently squeezed her palm before she spoke, "Do you realize who stands before you even now. You saw it approach but understand not one wit of what is before you."

Titania scoffed, "A beast, a horrible weapon, and a cruel deceiver. It is as nothing before the Tree of Life."

Nix's voice turned sad, "Before you stands the brother of the Tree of Life. One of the rarest of greater spirits. A Number like me. Even the gods themselves rightfully fear the Destroyer of Worlds foolish child. Only at my request has it presented its kinder face so that my chosen emissary may speak with you. Untold trillions of sentient lives has it ended. More lives than even I care to know. I grieve every one of those lost lives. Your own life Titania is less than a candle before a hurricane in its presence. Easily snuffed out save for the protection I provide. Don't make me morn your own lost life before its time."

A wrinkle appeared in the smooth brow of Titania as she started speaking, "Guards."

Hap Sing was suddenly standing inside the circle of guards with his face mere inches from Titania as he quietly spoke, "Do you want me to tell them what really happened to Oberon? I suggest you listen very carefully to what Nix is relaying from the Tree of Life. It would be a shame to have to watch the outcome of that information being revealed."

Titania began to shrink back nervously, "You're bluffing."

Hap Sing rose his voice loudly, "Let it be known that Oberon was not ambushed and slain by rogue twiline as Titania has oft repeated. He lives still in the mortal realms with a contingent of loyal followers. He understood the message relayed to Titania and him by the Tree of Life and obeyed its command to depart the fey for a mortal realm. Titania chose to ignore the command given by the Tree of Life, and establish herself as queen over the fey instead of as emissary of the Tree of Life. Titania has deceived Oberon, and those of you who remained in order to solidify her own power and control."

Titania's face twisted in hatred, "Liar! I'll kill you myself."

Titania tried to raise her arm to strike Hap Sing but found the wood of her elaborate chair was rapidly growing around her wrists. Another band was growing around her ankles and a final branch across her waist locking her into position.

Hap Sing leaned back with an appraising look, "Why I think that diadem you wear is made of pure adamantine isn't it? Is that a large diamond in the center? A gift from your people for your long years of service perhaps?"

Hap Sing reached forward and gently lifted the diadem from Titania's brow. He turned it a couple times looking it over casually before holding it up in front of him between Titania and himself. A faint cherry glow began across the impervious adamantine. Enormous waves of heat started radiating from the metal as it grew rapidly from a bright red to a white hot in a matter of moments.

Then the indestructible adamantine began to bend and deform and eventually start dripping drop by drop onto the raised platform. Soon it ran in rivulets forming a burning puddle in the wood below. After a while only a brightly glowing diamond rested in Hap Sings palm blinding everyone with a light brighter than the sun. The light went out and as the surrounding elves blinked spots from their vision they noticed Hap Sing casually brushing a powdery carbon ash from his palm.

Hap Sing looked Titania in the eyes, "Your service here is no longer required. Consider yourself evicted from the Fey Realm until such time as the Tree of Life welcomes you back as a guest. If your people need a place to settle, then let them know I'm making a new world. It should be ready for mortal habitation in just a few thousand years. Also know that you are not welcome there personally Titania. You will do best to return to Oberon's side and beg his forgiveness for your treacherous behavior."

Chapter 24 The Isle of Life

Hap Sing awoke upon the bower of grass amid the flowers and the smell of ocean breeze. Next to him fluttered three foot tall Ariel and two foot tall Nix. They were embracing each other in a tearful hug as Hap Sing opened his eyes. Hap Sing looked at the pixies for a moment before they caught on to his gaze.

Ariel spoke first, "The Tree of Life has decided that I shall remain here on the Isle of Life. I will be its first guardian while you accomplish the tasks yet before you Lucky Cricket. The Tree of Life is grateful for your service, and has commanded me to remain since my time in the fey has extended overlong. I have been granted the blessings of the Tree of Life to continue here for many centuries yet, and the Tree of Life will appoint another guardian when my time is complete."

Nix started crying softly again, "I don't wish for you to stay Ariel, but I can not disobey now that I can understand. I don't know how to guide our people."

Ariel embraced her once more, "Listen to our wise mother. She will guide you, and then you shall guide them. Remember you are never their ruler, only their servant. That was the mistake which Titania made, and the mistake which has lead to the Lucky Cricket being summoned to dismiss her from the Fey. Only the Lucky Cricket held the necessary willpower to go against her diadem of command, the spiritual power to destroy that item, and the grace to do so with no permanent harm to any living being present. Know also that our mother is proud of your bravery and your strength as well Nix. It is a great honor she has bestowed in granting you the position of her emissary."

Nix fluttered over to lightly hug Hap Sing next, "Thank you so much for all of your help. The other you is very frightening in some ways, but this you is like a wise old man gentle and kind. Please treat Ariel well."

Hap Sing nodded, "She shall always be welcome here. As will all of the fey kind be welcome here as long as they come in peace."

Nix lay down in the bower of flowers by his bungalow to rest. A few minutes later she slowly faded away.

Later Hap Sing looked in amazement at the doors, floors, and window frames grown from living wood on the white tower. Ariel looked at his expression with pleasure.

Ariel spoke in a light tone, "It is heartwood of the children of the Tree of Life. The glow comes from the hardened sap which is tougher and more resilient than diamond. The floor is still living and will regrow and reshape as the controller of the tower desires. Furniture can be grown from it very quickly using several different patterns it knows. Couches, chairs, tables and beds. Each cushioned with the velvet like leaves and pillowy thistle down for mortal or immortal comfort. The stairs down below can be covered or revealed at will as well."

Hap Sing gave her a light pat on the head, "It is very well done Ariel. I will have the Luck thank the Tree of Life."

Ariel nodded, "The Tree of Life has already received payment through your allowing the Fey Realm to be connected to your world. This is a small price for the boon of a world which welcomes the Fey beings."

Hap Sing smiled, "I hope you enjoy it once it is finished."

Ariel looked at Hap Sing with a touch of concern, "Is it displeasing in some manner to you?"

Hap Sing shook his head, "Not at all. However, you are to be the first guardian of the isle, so this place was built for your use really. I already have a bungalow down at the beach closer to my fishing."

Ariel sighed, "My mother warned me you could be difficult. I just never understood in what way until now. You are a very stubborn man aren't you?"

Hap Sing nodded, "Quite stubborn, so there is really no use discussing it any further."

Ariel looked up at Hap Sing as he chuckled, "What now?"

Hap Sing smiled, "I just realized this is what it feels like to be the tallest one around for a change. It is a funny sensation for me is all."

Ariel shook her head, "I'm beginning to think I may regret this bargain after a few centuries."

Hap Sing looked at her, "You're immortal?"

Ariel raised an eyebrow, "How many three foot high pixies do you know? I'm among the tallest of my kind. Do you have any idea that pixies never stop growing. We just grow very slowly is all, kind of like a very small tree. I'm over two hundred human years old already. I should be about five foot five inches in about another one thousand years or so. Then I will be taller than you even. You'll still be the same five foot two."

Hap Sing chuckled again, "So the good things never last then. I'll just try to enjoy it while I still can. At least I'm younger than you."

Ariel smiled, "Wrong again. You are six years older than me actually in Prime time reckoning. I'll also always be this cute no matter how tall I grow. You'll always be short, average looking, and a dirty old man."

Hap Sing raised an eyebrow, "Don't make me spank you little pixie."

Ariel grinned, "I'd like to have you try it. I may even let you win a couple times."

Hap Sing laughed, "A brazen and naughty pixie as well. I guess I'm not going to win this conversation anytime soon. So what happens next?"

Ariel smiled, "I've placed out some forms on the beach. You'll need to shovel some sand into them and heat them to make the panes of glass to place in the tower."

Hap Sing commented, "We don't have a furnace."

Ariel looked back, "Do you of all beings really need a furnace to melt some stones?"

Hap Sing shrugged, "I guess not really. It will take some practice to get it right though. I've never done it before."

Ariel pulled some plans out from her small bag and unfolded them for Hap Sing to see, "These should be the instructions. I've already followed the parts with my name by them. Your parts are listed here and here."

Hap Sing looked the instructions over, "That seems to have been some pretty heavy lifting on your part."

Ariel smiled, "I'm quite a bit stronger than I look. You'll need me to fly up the window panes anyway. The large sheets of cupola glass will still be too heavy for me, so you'll need to use the block and tackle as shown in this diagram."

Hap Sing looked at her patting her on the head, "You're quite a engineer aren't you."

Ariel smiled wickedly, "I didn't waste my two hundred some years just fishing."

A week later Hap Sing carefully lowered the last pane of glass into the admantium cupola as Ariel guided it into the frame. As the pane settled into its final position Ariel pulled out the instructions again and looked them over with a raised eyebrow.

Ariel looked over to Hap Sing standing outside the cupola doorway on the walkway around the tower top as he unfastened the large pane of glass from its lifting harness.

Ariel called out, "It calls for the breakdown of the scaffolding now. Then it says to temper the glass and admantium. I didn't know that admantium could be tempered any more than it already was."

Hap Sing smiled, "I'll ask about the procedure latter today after we remove the scaffolds. I'm quite sure it will take an enormous heat to do it yet carefully controlled to prevent the glass from melting and distorting."

Ariel shrugged, "That would be your area of expertise then. I'm worried that too much heat might damage the flooring."

Hap Sing shook his head, "I'm pretty sure I can keep the main heat very localized. The floors shouldn't get any hotter than a boiling pot of water I would hope."

Ariel looked askance at him, "Are you sure?"

Hap Sing smiled, "I won't know until I try."

Ariel shook her head, "It takes me a long time to repair any damaged wood you know. It is very hard, and still living, but it doesn't regenerate here as well as on the Fey."

Hap Sing closed his eyes for a moment and silently whispered, "Luck release."

The Luck opened Hap Sing's eyes with a feral expression on his face, "Hello my pretty little girl. Do you want to play with me now?"

Ariel grimaced, "Don't make me call your sister on you."

The Luck chuckled, "I'm still bigger than she is on this side of the universe. Also I'm quite a bit meaner and crazier too."

Ariel fluttered up out of reach at the top of the cupola, "I'm not buying it silly Luck. Hap Sing must have summoned you to learn how to temper the glass and adamantine. That falls right up the ally of the elemental font of fire I would guess."

The Luck nodded, "Quite simple, but not something I want to demonstrate for your mother. Fly along down by the shore. I'll keep my secrets just as she keeps hers. Also don't try to use any of your little bug friends to spy on my work. They'll just get toasted if any of them get close enough to see what's going to happen."

Ariel looked over at the scaffolding outside the tower, "What about those. The instructions say to take down the scaffolding first."

The Luck grinned wickedly as Ariel watched the scaffolding around the tower ignite in blue flames. First the wood burned, then the metal scaffolds themselves started burning a minute later. The heat felt inside the tower was negligible. Three minutes later the tower was unharmed while the scaffolding was little more that a pile of slag metal and ash.

The Luck waved to the stairway spiraling down from the tower top, "The scaffolding is down. It is quite cool and safe for you to leave, now."

After Ariel could be seen fluttering along the shore near the docks the Luck spoke, "I'll demonstrate the technique with the first pane. It is very complex, but well within your ability. We just need to heat single strands from this over allotment of admantium here, and here, and also here. This is done by achieving the target temperature at this point. Then we stretch a very thin sheet of admantium over the glass like so. It will be effectively transparent to the human eye, but it will lend the underlying glass most of the durability of the admantium itself. It also has the advantage of making the cuppola effectively one piece with the rest of the tower. With this step complete we will be able to move onto placing the anchors on the anchor chain. Cool the admantium at this rate, just so. There you go. Transparent Admantium Glass alloy. A specialty of the Luck, and our little trade secret."

What seemed like days later Hap Sing came down from the tower to enter his bungalow. He was tired and weary from tempering the glass, but he could feel good that the job was complete to the exacting specifications required.

Hap Sing noticed Ariel lying in his bed seemingly asleep. He remembered the last time this had happened which had been the first time he had seen her. Hap Sing simply pushed her aside and lay down in his bed with his back to her. He was asleep moments later.

The next morning Hap Sing woke to find a petulant Ariel looking down into his eyes, "You're no gentleman."

Hap Sing laughed, "So you're no proper lady either laying down in a man's bed twice. It was very improper and forward of you. If I weren't a gentleman I could have taken advantage of you."

Ariel giggled, "Next time perhaps?"

Hap Sing shrugged, "I'm way too old, and you are too for that matter."

Ariel glared again, "Are you calling me an old hag."

Hap Sing sat up patting her head, "I'm calling you the wrong species first, and then I'm calling you a wanton tease. I'm not falling for your game playing little Ariel. Besides technically I'm related to your mother aren't I?"

Ariel giggled again, "Every living being is a creation of the mother of life. We're all related in that way."

Hap Sing shrugged, "You gather the fruit, and I'll cook some fish. By the way find your own bed next time if you don't want my company in my bed."

Ariel smiled as Hap Sing walked outside, "I like your company Hap Sing."

As they sat down to a breakfast of fruit and fish Hap Sing detected the sensation that someone was trying to contact him. He reached into his pocket of nothingness in the air before him, and pulled out a heavy crystal sphere. Inside the sphere was an image of a tiger cub.

The cub spoke, "Thank you for using the Luck communications. Remember that quantum entangled pairs are our specialty. Putting through a call from yourself to you."

The Luck wearing the blue priest robes appeared in the crystal next, "Hello Hap Sing. Could you put Ariel on the crystal for a moment."

Ariel looked into the crystal and the Luck spoke again, "You'll need to hide for fourteen fey time parts on the southern end of the island. Bad company is coming."

Ariel seemed worried, "How bad?"

The Luck replied, "The Planar Anchor maker."

Hap Sing asked, "Who is that?"

The Luck grinned, "My insane bigger brother. Number Nine."

Hap Sing raised an eyebrow, "Just how bad?"

The Luck shrugged, "Depends on his mood. The rest of the Numbers are treating him like a pariah right now. His mood could be quite bad, but he's the best at anchoring worlds in the business. Anyone who creates a world in the prime without using his services is a complete fool. He really dislikes the lower Numbers, and the higher Numbers generally speaking. Minions of Numbers are almost as bad. He'll try to provoke a fight most likely to prove his avatar is tougher than you. Don't bite if he does. His avatar is quite a bit tougher than you in a material sense."

Hap Sing asked, "If Number Two is the being which created death, Number Three is the being which created life, and Number Seven is the being which created the elements, then just what is Number Nine's area of influence?"

The Luck grinned, "Keeping the material universes together. Lets just say he can throw a whole lot of weight around. Peace find you Hap Sing."

Hap Sing replied, "When is he coming?"

The Luck raised his hands, "In about six minutes relative time through my office gate. Remember don't let him pick a fight."

Ariel took flight and began speeding south toward the mountain. Hap Sing quickly finished eating his breakfast and then stood expectantly waiting for a couple more minutes.

Suddenly a doorway appeared right next to Hap Sing. It opened to reveal a man only a little bit taller than Hap Sing dressed in a neat dapper set of sharply pressed clothes. A set of wire frame spectacles rested on his nose and he grinned charmingly as he reached out his hand.

Hap Sing began to extend his own hand as the man withdrew his own hand to pull out a pocket watch from his waistcoat. The man looked Hap Sing up and down as his mouth drew into a disapproving frown.

Number Nine spoke, "A peasant? You are a peasant? An ugly smelly peasant at that. How utterly disappointing. Maybe I made a mistake taking this job. It smells like rutting fairies around here as well. A strange set of proclivities you have Number Seven."

Hap Sing spoke, "I am Hap Sing."

Number Nine looked back, "I don't care."

Hap Sing raised an eyebrow, "The Luck warned me you would try to pick a fight. I won't strike back."

Number Nine grinned, "I like an unfair advantage, thanks."

Number Nine started to swing as Hap Sing adjusted to freeze the local time reference. Hap Sing studied the expression of Number Nine for a moment, and was then startled to see him wink before he felt the punch land on his jaw. The next thing Hap Sing knew he was in tremendous pain on a trajectory through the air.

Hap Sing groaned out, "Luck release."

A tremendous splash accompanied the Luck landing in the water a mile from shore. The Luck grinned, then spat out a tooth.

The Luck shouted, "I'm going to rip off your bloody head you goon."

The Luck reached into nothingness in an attempt to grab a doorknob. It was surprised to find a hand waiting on the other side which grabbed it and threw it rapidly through the air back toward the shore. The Luck crashed through the side of the fifth bungalow and the building collapsed on top of it.

Number Nine stomped over, "Spacial orientation tricks won't work on me you foolish simpleton. I've got two more gods worth of knowledge over you. You'll never win this fight and you already know it. Let me pound that avatar to a pulp and then you can just start over."

The bungalow burst into flames with the Luck glowing inside, "You'll find I know quite a bit more than spacial orientation. How are you at taking the heat?"

Number Nine looked at the glowing Luck, "This is downright silly now. Elemental attacks against this form? I'll kill you just to put you out of your obvious misery."

The sand around Number Nine turned to molten glass, but it walked through without even a singe on its trousers. Then a wave ten feet high crashed into the shore knocking over the bungalows and the warehouse. Number Nine just grinned without budging from his position. Number Nine's grin stopped when he noticed the Luck standing right next to him.

The Luck spoke, "I've got you now. Cricket release."

Number Nine shouted angrily, "You're running from me? You're bailing out on your avatar? I'll kill it. I'll destroy this place. I'll then go wreck your offices in Centrus. You can't just hide from me. Run back to the dreaming and give up on reality. It is your only chance to escape my wrath."

Hap Sing slowly reached out to touch Number Nine's hand as it ranted. It looked at him in shock as Hap Sing withdrew his hand and a spirit ribbon formed between them. Hap Sing pushed an emotion along that ribbon as hard as he could. Number Nine screamed in apparent agony for a long minute. Then he dropped unconscious on the shore.

A momentary pain pierced Hap Sing's jaw as a new tooth grew in to replace his lost one. Then the healing power of the Tree of Life receded as his last injuries were repaired. Hap Sing sensed a communication and he reached into the nothingness to remove the crystal sphere.

The Luck wearing the tight blue shorts and shirt was on the other end, "What did you do? He dropped like a stone. Nothing except time has been able to calm one of his rages. No one not even a god has ever been able to put as much as a scratch on that avatar of Number Nine. You've done a miracle."

Hap Sing shook his head, "I simply forgave him the harm he'd done to me. I thought it might help."

The Luck shook its head, "It certainly did something. Checking my sources now, but it looks like every avatar of Number Nine dropped unconscious at the same time. You've done more than forgive him. You've shut him off. We'll have to figure out how that little trick works."

Hap Sing shook his head, "I think that was a one shot. It was very situational at best, and not something for the general repertoire. He's stirring now. I had better let you go."

Hap Sing put the crystal back and looked down at Number Nine as he opened his eyes, "Are you calm now?"

Number Nine smiled, "I'm much better now thank you. I still wasn't beaten by you for the record. There's not a scratch on me."

Hap Sing shrugged, "I wasn't trying to scratch your surface. I was trying to heal all those wounds on the inside."

Number Nine's eyes got a haunted look as his smile faded, "What do you know about healing such wounds?"

Hap Sing reached out a hand, "If you ever try consoling a Number over the trillions of lives it has taken in the name of necessity, then you might also understand how much I know about it."

Fourteen Fey time parts later Ariel returned to the shore line to see all of the bungalows and the warehouse destroyed. The dock and Hap Sing's small boat somehow survived the ordeal. Hap Sing watched as she flew up toward the tower. A bright light shone like a beacon beating in the rhythm of a heart from the top of tower. Hap Sing greeted her near the tower top as he stood next to the eight foot tall rotating crystal beating with light.

Ariel looked at the crystal, "It's beautiful."

Hap Sing nodded, "It's the life gate crystal. The death gate crystal beats in the chthonic depths below the tower. The cycle of life and death has been established. The anchors are in place making us a real part of the prime material plane now."

Ariel looked over a Hap Sing, "How did Number Nine make them?"

Hap Sing shrugged, "He claimed to have grown them. The details are a trade secret."

Ariel pointed down below at the destruction by the shore line, "What happened down there?"

Hap Sing shrugged again, "Number Nine and I had to reach a mutual understanding. It shouldn't happen again anytime soon. I'll rebuild them before I leave again."

ap Sing rowed his boat out onto the bay facing the shore. He waved at Ariel standing near his new bungalow on the beach, and Ariel waved back in return. He then stopped rowing and looked at the white tower with its beacon upon the cliff over the north portion of the bay.

Hap Sing lowered his head and a bright light radiated from his aura. Soon he could not be seen in the midst of the brightness. Then the light slowly faded leaving Ariel behind to watch over the Isle of Life.

Chapter 25 Homecoming

Outside Li Chan village a bright light appeared on the water far out in the bay. The light rapidly dimmed revealing a small row boat out on the waters. Several villagers peered in the direction of the light. One of the older villagers spoke briefly to an older child who ran off toward a large new temple building in the center of town.

Several minutes later more villagers were gathering on the shore along the beach to look at the small boat floating on the waves. The older child came back followed by seven monks wearing orange robes trimmed with black collars and black belts worn about their waists. The monks spread out and began speaking to the people gathering on the beach. The villagers began to return to their general business.

As the villagers went back to their daily lives remaining behind was the older child and the older villager who looked at the monks as they gathered together on the beach in a double file two by three with the very tall senior monk standing before them. After what seemed like an hour a figure appeared slowly rising up from the floor of the boat. Hap Sing gazed out from the boat at the village and the waiting monks with a cautious look.

Hap Sing raised an eyebrow at the scene before him. Li Chan village looked prosperous as far as he could see. Many of the small shabby homes were gone, and a fair number of newer and nicer homes had replaced them. The village had also grown and in addition to the new homes and temple there were also docks with several larger sailing boats floating on the waves near the shore.

Hap Sing paddled toward the shore slowly, and looked with his second sight at the brightly glowing net cast over the surrounding lands. It still read: *These Lands Are Under My Protection – The Lucky Cricket*. Upon the people waiting by the shore Hap Sing could see written: *This Person Is Under My Protection – The Lucky Cricket*. Hap Sing shook his head and lightly laughed to himself.

Hap Sing quietly spoke to no one in particular, "It seems I may have overdone that a bit. I don't even recognize any of these people. I wonder just how long I have been absent."

Hap Sing also noticed something else as he gazed closer. Each of the monks and the people he could see in the village were connected to each other by an unusually large quantity of spirit ribbons. He guessed that everyone in the village was closely interlinked with everyone else. Li Chan village was now a tightly knit community unlike any he had previously ever experienced.

Hap Sing could also see that each of the monks had a Chi Master spirit companion in the shape of a tiger. The younger six monks had juvenile sized tiger spirits, while the senior monk in the lead had a mature sized tiger spirit. Hap Sing could guess that the Luck had been heavily using its influence with each of these people. Four of the junior monks were young men in their late teens or early twenties, while two of them were teenaged women.

As his boat neared the shore the older villager and the older child stepped out into the waves to help pull the boat onto the sand. Hap Sing stepped clear to help them but was interrupted by the older villager.

The man reached out his hand toward Hap Sing, "I'm village elder Lu Han the great grandson of elder Lu Po. Please let my grandson Lu Wan take care of your boat. It is a great honor you have done for us by returning most senior elder Hap Sing. We did not know when your return might happen, but times have become quite desperate in Ran Li."

Hap Sing looked around, "Li Chan seems peaceful enough."

Lu Han replied, "So it is because of you most senior elder. Your protection has been granted to us, and it still remains according to the Chi Masters. None with ill intent can find or enter this village. We are now known to the outside world as the legendary lost village of Li Chan. Only those born here or married to someone born here can enter or leave the area under your net. Of course the Chi Masters can still find and enter this place, but most avoid us when they see the writing in the sky. Something about it scares them I think."

Hap Sing gave a light chuckle, "I think I understand. Rumors must have been quite furious after my departure. How many years has it been now?"

Lu Han smiled, "It was your two hundred and sixty fifth birthday last month most senior elder. You have been gone one hundred and eleven years now. It is a most auspicious number, and many of us had hoped this might be the year of your expected return."

Hap Sing cast a cautious gaze over at the monks looking expectantly in his direction, "Who are those Chi Masters standing like a military company?"

Lu Han flushed, "They are the Tiger Monks most senior elder. They are in service to the Emperor's advisor Lord Ming Wa Fu. They have been handpicked as six of the most promising young Chi Masters. Their leader is Ming Ne Yu grandson of Lord Ming Wa Fu himself."

Hap Sing nodded, "Chi Masters I can see, but why are they here?"

Lu Han dipped his head, "I know you won't like to hear this, but the Chi Master Academy in Yokito has for the last ninety two years trained their top six former students to enter special duty as the Tiger Monks. Their leader and the six monks have always been assigned to their temple here in the legendary lost village of Li Chan. It is considered the highest honor for a former Chi Master Academy student to be chosen to be among their ranks. The monks each serve for a period of seven years. The leader is chosen from among the former junior Tiger Monks of earlier years. The new group always starts their assignment on your birthday senior elder. I'm afraid this batch is only one month in service, but they are considered among the best."

Hap Sing became a bit concerned, "What is their purpose in Li Chan?"

Lu Han coughed slightly before answering, "Please understand that it has not been my idea senior elder. My great grandfather was quite clear on the point to his descendents that you preferred your privacy. They are your honor guard senior elder Hap Sing. They are sworn to the task of protecting you with their lives if necessary. Thus the Emperor has decreed, and thus it has been since their formation."

Hap Sing looked over at the monks waiting patiently before whispering quietly to Lu Han, "What if I don't want an honor guard?"

Lu Han shrugged and whispered in reply, "I don't think they can force themselves upon you senior elder. However, consider that they may be shamed and suffer greatly if you reject them. Personally, I think that Lord Ming Wa Fu has deliberately put you in a very tight spot with this. Yet since there are only two people still living people who were alive the last time you were known to be here, it is rumored that he has the expectation that you couldn't possibly refuse."

Hap Sing looked back at Lu Han, "Who is the other person?"

Lu Han grinned, "The head priestess of the White Raven in Ran Li, the outlander Princess Ming Yuki Nene. Rumor also has passed down through my family that you were well known to each other at one time. She is married to Ming Wa Fu, and she is the grandmother of Ming Ne Yu standing there. If he doesn't look very pleased, then it is because he has recently learned the rumor that you were an intimate companion of his grandmother before she married his grandfather was true."

Hap Sing flushed, "True enough in a certain way, but really it's long past history now. We certainly parted company in an amiable manner. There is no ill will between us that I know."

Lu Han became serious, "I'm quite sure she had little ill will about it, but her grandson only learned of it when he was assigned here last month. It probably changes his perspective somewhat. You also have to consider that after one hundred and eleven years of your absence what has formerly been a respectable title and a great honor with little real responsibility has suddenly become a very real task with significant challenges ahead."

Hap Sing looked at Lu Han, "By the way, who here would tell him such about my past relationship with Nene?"

Lu Han smiled, "You don't have to worry about the villagers mentioning it. They are the same as in my father's day. Prone to keep their secrets close. I believe it was his grandmother Ming Yuki Nene who told him through a letter. She has never been rumored to be one to spare someone's feelings in regards to the truth. I believe that she wanted to instill in him just how important you were to her. Her goddess also probably gave her some kind of prophesy regarding your impending return. I'm just speculating on that last part though."

Hap Sing reached out his hand and shook hands with Lu Han, "Well it is good to meet you. I think you've done your great grandfather proud. I thank you for your informing me of the situation here."

Hap Sing noticed that as their hands parted a spirit ribbon stretched between them. Hap Sing then shook hands with Lu Wan and noticed a ribbon forming between them as well. As Hap Sing turned to look at Ming Ne Yu he noticed that each of the younger Tiger Monks had seen the ribbons being formed and a slight secret smile came to each of their faces. They were talented indeed for young Chi Masters. Hap Sing figured that one of the frequent rumors about his abilities had just been confirmed by their own sight.

Hap Sing looked back at Lu Han, "Please gather the village council members at your home tonight. Also invite the elders of the village and all senior heads of the village households who will come. I will bring the fish to eat if the rest of the villagers provide for the group. We will dine tonight, and I will hear then from those gathered what has happened in Ran Li since I have been gone."

Lu Han bowed, "It shall be done as you request senior elder. Know that although you hold no official rank in Ran Li, your word supersedes even the Emperor's in Li Chan village. There will also be a festival this evening in your honor if you will permit it. I'm afraid the people will be unhappy if not otherwise."

Hap Sing nodded, "I will attend a festival just this one time as a favor to the great grandson of Lu Po. Pardon me now while I go address the Tiger Monks."

Hap Sing walked over to stand in front of Ming Ne Yu who looked down and examined him with a careful expression on his face. The six young orange robed monks standing in a double line behind him looked serious and concentrated on staring blankly straight ahead.

Hap Sing smiled gamely while looking up at him, "You have inherited your grandmother's height and her blue eyes I see. How is she doing these days?"

Ming Ne Yu stood up even straighter, "She is still running the business of the White Raven in Yokito master Hap Sing. She has talked about you to me just recently."

Hap Sing extended his hand, "Well it is nice to meet you."

Ming Ne Yu shook his hand, and watched carefully as the spirit ribbon unfolded between them. Then Ming Ne Yu looked to a common set of ribbons they both had heading off to the far distance in the north east.

Hap Sing nodded, "Yes I share a spirit connection to you as well as your grandparents now."

Ming Ne Yu stood straighter, "It is a great honor master Hap Sing."

Hap Sing looked at the young Chi Masters standing behind Ming Ne Yu, "Please introduce me to your squad."

Ming Ne Yu looked surprised, "We are monks not a military group."

Hap Sing shook his head, "No one else can hear us at the moment, but don't think you've somehow hidden ninjas in robes from my eyes. I've spent way too many decades with former Grandmaster Li Hung to not recognize a squad of ninjas when I see them. I see your grandfather's hand in their creation most clearly. Both spiritually trained and martially trained to the highest degree. They are clearly the best from two different traditions."

Ming Ne Yu hesitated, "It is as you say. Our mission is to first guard Li Chan awaiting your return. Upon your return our mission is to guard you regardless of what you may say. Many beings have come to Ran Li. Darkness has started to seize portions of it. Those which follow this darkness will seek you out to kill you if they can."

Hap Sing nodded, "Understood. Let's get through the introductions then."

Ming Ne Yu stood beside Hap Sing and walked him down the front rank of Tiger Monks, "This is Yu Lo a distant cousin of yours."

Hap Sing shook the hand of the young man, "It is nice to meet a relative of my cousins the Yu's."

Yu Lo answered as he watched the ribbon forming between them, "The honor is mine master Cricket."

Ming Ne Yu gave Yu Lo a stern look, "His name is master Hap Sing."

Hap Sing placed a hand on Ming Ne Yu's shoulder, "Master Cricket is just fine."

The next in line was a young teen girl, "This is Lo Hannah. She is also a distant cousin of yours, a descendent of former High Priest of Palnor Lo Dong Arthur and his wife Lo Maya."

Hap Sing gave her a brief hug, "It is nice to meet you young woman."

Lo Hannah blushed looking at the spirit ribbon between them, "I have heard many stories of your life master Hap Sing."

The young man next in line was tall and muscular with blond hair, "This is Sea Reaver. He was recommended for the Tiger Monks by my grandmother. He is an outlander from Nordland, but understands the language well."

Hap Sing smiled as he shook hands, "It is nice to meet you."

The young man named Sea Reaver gave him a cocky grin, "Yes master Hap Sing."

The next man standing behind Sea Reaver was mild seeming and quite serene, "This is Chow Sang. His family is from Udomo, but he was sent to the Chi Master Academy in Yokito as a child due to his talents."

Hap Sing shook his hand, "My friend Li Chan was from Udomo as well."

Chow Sang raised an eyebrow, "That is a well known piece of history master Hap Sing."

Hap Sing gave a brief chuckle, "I suppose it is after all."

In the middle of the rear rank was a tall homely brown haired young woman, "This is Mimosa. She has also come from the Nordland colony and was also recommended by Ming Yuki Nene for inclusion in the Tiger Monks."

Hap Sing shook her hand, "I am pleased to meet you Mimosa."

Mimosa performed a short curtsy, "The pleasure to serve you is all mine master Hap Sing."

Hap Sing looked at the last young man in the rear rank. He was bald and as short as Hap Sing. He also looked to be the youngest of all the Tiger Monks.

Ming Ne Yu looked pleased as her presented the last member, "I introduce you to Lord Togusawa Hiro. He is a cousin to the Emperor, although not in the line of succession."

Hap Sing gave a slight bow, "It is an honor to meet you Togusawa Hiro."

Togusawa Hiro bowed deeply in return, "The honor to serve you is mine master Hap Sing."

They shook hands and each of the Tiger Monks had a connection through a ribbon to Hap Sing. Hap Sing moved to stand in front of the entire group next to Ming Ne Yu.

Hap Sing stood still while looking at each of them for a long time. They first started to shift nervously, then fidget under his quiet gaze. Only Ming Ne Yu held his posture and composure without any sign of discomfort. After about a half an hour Hap Sing smiled at them.

Hap Sing spoke, "It seems you all have learned a measure of patience which is difficult for young ones such as yourselves full of energy and youthful passions. You have passed your first test as my potential guardians."

Ming Ne Yu calmly spoke, "We answer to Lord Ming Wa Fu. We are your assigned guardians."

Hap Sing nodded, "I am sure you are charged with such. I am not yet sure you are up to the actual task yet. Let's test your speed. Prepare yourselves. Are you all ready?"

Ming Ne Yu nodded, "We are always ready to serve master Hap Sing."

Hap Sing gave a sly grin, "The task is simple in concept but difficult to execute. I want to know which of you can race to my former home first. I guarantee none of you will be able to beat this two hundred and sixty five year old man there."

Ming Ne Yu made a simple hand gesture and the Tiger Monks took off running very fast toward the rise where Hap Sing used to live. As soon as all their backs were facing him Hap Sing froze time and pulled a doorknob out of nothingness. He casually opened a door to nowhere, and walked down a hallway to the Luck's office in Centrus.

Hap Sing looked at the Luck wearing tight blue shorts and shirt sitting before a tea table with a steaming pot and two cups waiting.

Hap Sing spoke, "I hope I'm not late."

The Luck replied, "No you are right on time. Isn't it a bit cruel making them run three miles to your former home while you take a short cut?"

Hap Sing shrugged, "They are young and need the exercise to warm up for my next trial. I'm old and I like to have my tea. I don't see why I can't accomplish both things at one time. Brief me on what you have on them."

The Luck smiled, "A highly political set of appointments. The two Nordlanders you know are also personally loyal to Nene. Ming Ne Yu is his grandfather's child through and through. The descendents of the Yu's have always made the squad due to their talents and family connections as your relatives. Togusawa Hiro is of course the eyes and ears of the royal dynasty within the Tiger Monks. Chow

Sang made it on the squad through sheer talent. He is one of the most potent Chi Masters of his generation. They are all physically fit, smart, very loyal to their real masters, and eventually destined to be most loyal to you if I can have any influence in the matter."

Hap Sing smiled, "I noticed they already have tiger shaped spirit guardians. I'd guess your influence is already pretty heavy."

The Luck sipped his tea, "Quite correct. However, influencing their power that way is a pre-requisite to being able to join the Tiger Monks. You either sign up for it, or you don't get in plain and simple. It guarantees I still have the final control over who gets to join."

Hap Sing nodded, "Can I trust them?"

The Luck shrugged, "Not fully at this time. They will protect your life for certain, but none of them is prepared to learn our secrets yet. Their real masters are trying to learn through them, and more than one god is in play here as well."

Hap Sing smiled, "I'll just have to claim each of them from their respective masters and make them mine then. Send through the crystal when you have some more updates. It is about time to get back before they reach my former home. I want to see their expressions when they see me there waiting for them."

The Luck smiled, "They've likely figured out you're cheating already. How you are cheating will be what disturbs them."

Chapter 26 Trials and Errors

As Hap Sing stepped out from the doorway onto the hillside where his hut had once stood one hundred and eleven years ago he noticed a shrine standing there with a rather flattering life size jade statue of him standing inside. Hap Sing raised an eyebrow looking at it, and then moved to sit down on the hill while sipping the tea he had brought along.

Hap Sing noticed tall Ming Ne Yu clearly outpacing his junior Tiger Monks in spite of his middle aged body. His speed was impressive as was the pace of Sea Reaver only a short distance behind him. Following shortly behind was Mimosa and Togusawa Hiro keeping pace with each other. A bit further back was Lo Hannah and Yu Lo also keeping pace together. In the rear setting an even easy distance pace was Chow Sang.

Hap Sing sipped his tea as Ming Ne Yu arrived breathing heavy, but looking still strong and ready for action. Hap Sing waited for Chow Sang to arrive before putting down his cup and standing up. Sea Reaver had a slightly disgruntled look which reminded him of Nene when she didn't like something he had done in the past.

Hap Sing spoke, "How do you intend to protect me when even the fastest of you can not keep up with my pace?"

Sea Reaver blurted out, "You cheated somehow. You didn't run here since I clearly saw your spirit ribbon fade out, and then shift to the front of us just a couple of minutes ago."

Hap Sing shook his head, "Wrong. I never said I would run here. I didn't cheat. I simply used the abilities within my command to win. I already guaranteed that I would beat each of you here, and that the terms were that it was a race. I never said it was a foot race."

Sea Reaver looked briefly angry, "That's not fair."

Hap Sing looked at him sharply, "No it isn't. What can you do about it?"

Sea Reaver looked over at Ming Ne Yu looking calm in the face of the conversation, and decided to stay silent.

Hap Sing nodded, "You can do nothing to ensure it is fair. If you want to protect me, then you must understand that nothing seeking to harm me will be constrained to act fair about it. You must anticipate the unfair at every turn. Could any of you have beat me here?"

Ming Ne Yu shook his head, "It was never the point for us to beat you here. It was only a demonstration that our power pales in comparison to what you can do. It is a fact that all of my subordinates should be well aware of from learning about your exploits."

Hap Sing smiled, "Then what is your purpose here then?"

Ming Ne Yu spoke, "We are to protect you as our sworn duty to Ran Li, the Emperor, and under the direction of Lord Ming Wa Fu."

Hap Sing shook his head, "I need a better answer than that. I don't answer to Ran Li, the Emperor, or young Ming Wa Fu. Why are you here?"

Hap Sing watched them stand in silence, "Very well. It seems none of you are ready to talk. It also seems that you are all told to ignore my attempts to dissuade you from this course of action. It also seems you are a lot of fools rushing to their deaths without understanding what they are up against."

Chow Sang laughed, "It seems you have read the recruitment brochure for the Tiger Monks. Fearless, dedicated, and stupid enough to think it is a pleasure tour of duty are all on the list of requirements for candidates."

Hap Sing looked at him approvingly, "You are quite right it seems. However, you also left out a crucial piece of information. You are all assigned as spies for various factions within Ran Li."

Hap Sing pointed to Sea Reaver and Mimosa, "Spies for Ming Yuki Nene and her goddess the White Raven."

He pointed at Lo Hannah, "Spy for the church of Palnor."

He pointed at Yu Lo, "Spy for the family Yu."

He pointed at Togusawa Hiro, "Spy for the court of the Emperor."

He pointed at Ming Ne Yu, "Spy for Ming Wa Fu."

He pointed at Chow Sang, "The only one of you chosen purely based on your talent alone, but still likely loyal enough to your home country of Udomo to report what you learn of me to them."

Ming Ne Yu spoke calmly in response, "What you say is true enough, and already well known among our ranks. However, our mission still remains to protect you regardless of what you ask."

Hap Sing smiled, "It is good that you are honest with me about it, even though none of you would volunteer this information from the beginning. I will be honest with you in return. You have passed my second test."

Lo Hannah asked, "We didn't beat you here. How could we have passed?'

Hap Sing looked at Chow Sang, "You know the answer already didn't you. I noted that you saved your energy in coming here for the next test."

Chow Sang answered, "Distraction and diversion. The race here was so Hap Sing could get us away from the village. So we could talk in private. So he could deal with us quietly if we failed his test. I surmise that if we fail any of his real tests we won't be ever seen in Ran Li alive again. He will not be fair. He will cheat. He will not tell us the real conditions. It will test our loyalty to our cause. It will test our suitability for the job. It will test even our endurance."

Hap Sing shook his head, "You are partially right, and partially in error Chow Sang. Why did you come to this conclusion?"

Chow Sang smiled, "It is what I would do in your place."

Hap Sing smiled, "That is your mistake. I'm a lot older and more experienced than the Tiger Monks. I am also a whole lot more powerful than the lot of you combined. You should never judge what or why I would do something based upon yourselves. You Chow Sang are also quite a bit smarter than me. However, you will also never live long enough to be wiser than me."

Chow Sang had a slight frown, "Why do you say that?"

Hap Sing laughed, "Because I'm wiser than to sign on to a job that is the equivalent of a death warrant just for something as simple minded as honor."

The six younger monks all took on a frowning expression. Hap Sing noted that Ming Ne Yu looked back at them briefly and gave a hand signal. Each of them visibly relaxed.

Hap Sing nodded, "You've passed test number three. You've been verbally insulted and provoked without loosing your heads about it. I don't need hot headed body guards. Now if you want to protect me you must attack me like you mean to kill me."

Ming Ne Yu looked back at him seriously, "We don't want to kill you master Hap Sing."

Hap Sing smiled, "You won't as I will do my best to defend myself. The question is one of whether you can survive my defense."

A shuriken stopped two feet in front of Hap Sing's chest as he froze the local time reference. Lo Hannah had launched the attack even though Hap Sing could see that she'd closed her eyes already to avoid watching it hit. Hap Sing figured that she was soft hearted, and likely the weakest member of the team trying to prove she was equal to the rest by attacking first.

Hap Sing sped Lo Hannah's time reference up slightly from the rest so that she could sense something of what was coming next. He gave her a light push to set her form off balance in the direction of Mimosa who as already drawing her shuriken for a throw as well.

Hap Sing then removed the shuriken and kunai knives from the pouches and hidden pockets of the rest of the Tiger Monks and flung them one after the other quite rapidly toward the sea. With the last kunai knife he severed the long blond braid on Sea Reaver's head and left the braid suspended in the air behind him. He left that knife suspended in the air directly in front of Ming Ne Yu's face pointed down.

Hap Sing then stood back in his original place and chose to pick a slightly slower time reference as he watched the path of the shuriken approaching with a practiced eye. He gradually moved his torso to the side and was impressed that Ming Ne Yu's eyes had caught the sudden appearance of the knife in front of his vision as Lo Hannah began her inevitable loss of balance in Mimosa's direction.

Hap Sing watched as the other Tiger Monks began reaching for their missing weapons in response to the attack launched by Lo Hannah. Hap Sing slowly moved to the side even more so that the approaching shuriken would miss by less than an inch. He was impressed that in the same slight time window Ming Ne Yu was raising a hand to grab the slowly dropping kunai knife in front of him.

After the thrown shuriken was past his position Hap Sing froze local time again and examined each of the Tiger Monks carefully anticipating their motion from the frozen scene before him. Togusawa Hiro needed to be dealt with next. Hap Sing started an minor cloth ignition on the seat of his pants. Yu Lo's shoes he carefully tied together with a piece of rawhide from his pocket. He tipped Togosawa Hiro in a manner that would launch him in the direction of Yu Lo.

Then Hap Sing switched to his second sight suspicious that Chow Sang hadn't launched a physical attack in his direction. He saw Chow Sang's spirit tiger guardian had started moving in his direction. Hap Sing unfroze the spirit tiger and glared at it.

Hap Sing spoke the command, "Sit this fight out. Pass the world along to the rest, and no telling your owner what you know of this or the Luck will deal very harshly with you."

The spirit tiger quailed at his voice and promptly lay down on the ground.

Hap Sing smiled, "Very good. As a reward I shall leave your owner unharmed for now."

Hap Sing moved in front of Ming Ne Yu and took the kunai knife his hand was reaching to grab from the air in front of him. He then threw that final knife toward the sea as well.

Hap Sing returned to his original position before changing his frame of time reference back to prime standard so he could watch the results of his actions. Togusawa Hiro tipped forward into Yu Lo as Lo Hannah launched backward into Mimosa. Ming Ne Yu's eyes widened at seeing the bright streaks flare through the sky where the rapidly departing shuriken and kunai knives were glowing white hot from the air friction as they sped away faster than the eye could follow.

A loud tearing boom shook the entangled Tiger Monks and caused Sea Reaver's eyes to widen as he moved to cover his ears from the sonic assault of the rapidly departing weapons. Chow Sang looked down at his cowering tiger spirit with a look of concern before noticing his fellow monks lying collapsed upon each other. He glanced down at the dropped ponytail of Sea Reaver without fully understanding yet what was lying at his feet.

A flash brighter than the sun lit the sky over the horizon out to sea behind Hap Sing. An enormous cloud was lifting up into the sky beyond the edge of the horizon. A few moments later the land roiled beneath their feet tumbling Ming Ne Yu, Sea Reaver, and Chow Sang to the ground along with the moaning Togusawa Hiro, Yu Lo, Lo Hannah and Mimosa. Only Hap Sing remained standing solid as a stone as the life sized jade statue of Hap Sing in the shrine tipped to the side and came to a stop leaning against the wall.

As the cloud rose higher in the sky the top began widening out and then dropping down around the edges forming a mushroom like image. The tiger monks knocked over by the first shaking ground began seeing to their companions who were down from their collision. Then the wall of wind struck with such force that they were all tumbled and tossed further up the slope of the hill. Real fear began to show in their eyes as they looked toward the calmly standing Hap Sing examining their plight with an emotionless critical eye.

The shock wave of wind passed and calmed and the Tiger Monks once more struggled to rise and take stock of their situation. Ming Ne Yu looked out past the calm Hap Sing and was the first to see the fifty foot high wall of water rushing toward the shore.

Ming Ne Yu looked at Hap Sing plaintively, "Help us please master Hap Sing!"

Hap Sing nodded, "You only have to ask. I'll have some conditions for you later."

They watched in awe as the spectrum of the spiritual net over the Li Chan village shifted from a bright yellow to a deep sea green. Hap Sing began glowing fiercely bright himself at the same time. The approaching wave concentrated and rose to one hundred feet in height focusing toward the spiritual net glowing in response to Hap Sing's command. A fine lattice of smaller weave reinforced the net just before the wave struck.

The wave hit with tremendous force sending a great spume up into the air. The Tiger Monks ducked their heads awaiting their doom, but then noticed that none of the water made it through the spiritual net. Only a large amount of fish began gently raining down from the sky and flopping around on the ground. The water receded back into the sea, but nothing was damaged on land from it striking.

Hap Sing called back as he began slowly walking back down the trail to the village, "After seeing to your injuries pick up those fish and bring them back to the village for dinner tonight. I promised Lu Han that I would provide for the village, and this should be sufficient for everyone to eat. Don't bother to replace your lost weapons. I won't accept your company or your protection with such tools of death in hand. Consider yourselves ninja no more if you wish to enter my service, and become true monks in service to the people instead."

Ming Ne Yu answered with head bowed low to the ground, "Yes, master Hap Sing."

Sea Reaver stoked his head where his ponytail was missing and quietly asked, "What happened master Ming?"

Ming Ne Yu looked up from the ground at the retreating back of Hap Sing, "I think he has just conclusively proved that anything which could actually threaten him would tear through us like a tiger through a piece of paper. We're the best of our kind, but we are simple infants in his presence. If we don't want to be eaten, then we had better listen to what he says."

Chow Sang looked at all of their cowering tiger spirits, "He certainly is the Chi Master. All others are subservient to his power. This will cause great trouble among the ranks of the other Chi Masters or Spirit Shamans who fail to quickly understand it."

Ming Ne Yu stood up and started looking after the injured members of his Tiger Monks, "The Tiger Monks no longer serve my grandfather Ming Wa Fu or the Emperor of Ran Li as of this moment. This can only lead to trouble and our eventual dissolution. We can only have a single master. I am pledging myself to master Hap Sing, and suggest any who wish to remain in the Tiger Monks do so as well. I will accept no more divided loyalties within our ranks."

Togusawa Hiro looked at Ming Ne Yu as he was examined, "Are you certain this is the wise course master Ming Ne Yu? My cousin the Emperor could become quite angry at us if he loses control over us. He considers us a tool of the country of Ran Li."

Ming Ne Yu laughed bitterly, "When your cousin the Emperor can single handed disarm seven Tiger Monks, summon a one hundred foot tall wave, and rain fish from the sky to feed the people, all without causing permanent harm, then I will reconsider my course. We didn't even anger Hap Sing, and you saw the potential destruction he was able to cause just as a demonstration of his ability. I would take the anger of one thousand emperors rather than risk angering him once."

When Hap Sing had first returned to the village that morning he had formally had tea with the current crop of elders. None of the elders had been pleased to hear that Hap Sing was moving on from the village after a short visit. Yet none of them questioned his freedom to do so, or requested him to change his mind about it. They took the news in stride with a mostly hidden look of disappointment. They had gracefully thanked him for returning to visit before the conclusion of the tea service.

Then Hap Sing presented the village elders with his offer. They carefully considered it, and promised to relay it to each of the villagers in turn.

Later in the early afternoon Hap Sing sat on the steps of the temple as the six junior Tiger Monks grilled the fish from the morning catch on skewers over a large fire pit beside the temple. There were several residents of Li Chan village who came by in small groups through the morning and early afternoon to greet him and hold short discussions with him as the monks worked diligently at their task.

After the last family had departed the stairs Hap Sing looked at Ming Ne Yu standing over at the edge of the temple courtyard guiding his young charges. Ming Ne Yu seemed to sense his attention and turned to approach him.

Hap Sing raised an eyebrow, "The fish seem almost done soon. Are the rest of the preparations ready?"

Ming Ne Yu nodded, "We should be done by middle afternoon master Hap Sing."

Hap Sing gave him a slight grin, "I hope you can forgive me for my usurpation of your leadership."

Ming Ne Yu ducked his head down, "Our service to you is not an imposition master Hap Sing."

Hap Sing nodded, "Thank you for your kind view of this matter. Understand that I don't require you to cut ties with those for whom you already have loyalty. I just need you all to understand I will not tolerate any killing on my behalf, not even to protect my life."

Ming Ne Yu nodded, "Yes, master Hap Sing. I doubt your life is the one in danger now."

Hap Sing looked back at the temple behind him, "You question your own safety or the safety of your charges?"

Ming Ne Yu shook his head, "Our lives are sworn to your protection, and the protection of Li Chan village in your absence. Our own safety is meaningless."

Hap Sing turned to face Ming Ne Yu with a slight frown, "I won't accept your answer Ming Ne Yu."

Ming Ne Yu looked up, "Master?"

Hap Sing stood, "Your safety has as much meaning as anyone's safety. Even as much meaning as my own safety, so I don't want you thinking you are expendable in any way. You don't have my permission to lose your own lives. Any foolish attempt to do so will meet with my disapproval."

Ming Ne Yu raised his head to eye Hap Sing directly, "I thank you for the consideration. May I speak openly with you master Hap Sing?"

Hap Sing spoke, "Speak what is on your mind."

Ming Ne Yu gave a slight grin, "I want you to understand that you are making our duty very difficult to carry out."

Hap Sing nodded, "Yes, I am. Yet, I was lead to believe the Tiger Monks should be up to the task. Am I wrong in this belief?"

Ming Ne Yu sighed, "I hope we don't have to discover the truth of it."

Hap Sing looked over at the young monks, "You do have the ability to keep them in line?"

Ming Ne Yu nodded, "They are obedient to direct orders, and listen to commands well."

Hap Sing looked back at Ming Ne Yu, "Yet not all orders have come from you."

Ming Ne Yu smiled, "You understand my tenuous position then. My direct authority is limited compared to the Emperor or a god. I undoubtedly have tactical control over their immediate actions, but getting them to overlook their other orders will be a challenge."

Hap Sing frowned slightly, "My lesson this morning didn't sink in then?"

Ming Ne Yu shrugged, "It is hard to say how they will respond to it in the long term. Family obligation, religious fervor, and politics being what they are, it is very questionable how they will react if given any counter instructions. I take it you mean to go to the capital soon."

Hap Sing's expression turned neutral, "I do plan to meet with your grandfather and grandmother. I don't plan to fall under the sway of either them or the Emperor."

Ming Ne Yu looked over at his young charges, "I was led to believe that they already had pretty strong methods of potential control set in place. Honestly speaking this could be a trap for you. As a former specialist I can see the indicators they have been plotting about how to manage your return since you disappeared one hundred and eleven years ago."

Hap Sing nodded, "Making you Tiger Monks my responsibility is the first step."

Ming Ne Yu smiled, "I would think so. It would appeal to your reportedly kindly nature to protect us from ourselves."

Hap Sing shook his head, "They have made an error in that regard then."

Ming Ne Yu looked a touch surprised, "Why is that?"

Hap Sing gave him a solid look, "My kindly nature is over exaggerated by imperfect past perceptions of me. I am perfectly capable of not letting the will of anyone else be they emperor or god set my course."

Ming Ne Yu took a half step back, "What do you mean?"

Hap Sing gave a slight grin, "Watch carefully tonight."

That late afternoon the villagers sat at tables in the large front courtyard of the temple. They dined on the simple fare of fish, rice, and vegetables prepared by the monks and villagers. Hap Sing sat at a table at the top of the temple stairs with the village elders. They chatted amiably as they dinned.

The villagers of Li Chan seemed peaceful and comfortable. They were neither boisterous nor over jubilant, instead a sense of contentment radiated from them. Their Lucky Cricket had returned if only briefly. The Tiger Monks conversely seemed more on edge than that morning on the beach. It was as if they sensed that something was amiss with this gathering.

As the group finished their meal Hap Sing nodded to the elders and stood up and spoke loudly to the assembled villagers, "Greetings citizens of Li Chan village."

The villagers all smiled as they responded, "Greetings Lucky Cricket."

Hap Sing continued, "I hope you have all considered the offer I made through the village elders. Know that my protection will no longer continue over Li Chan village in Ran Li after I depart. It will not pass on to any future generations born here either. Those who choose to do so may stay as they wish. However, this land, this kingdom, this world does not belong to me. It will not remain my responsibility for much longer."

Lu Han replied from the head table, "We understand your offer and your reasons Lucky Cricket. It is a hard choice you present us, but a fair choice. Each is free to choose."

Ming Ne Yu and the six young monks looked on with a touch of confusion as Hap Sing replied, "Who will choose to stay, and who will choose to go?"

The villagers all rose as one as Lu Han spoke, "We will all go Hap Sing. Our choice has been made. The lost village of Li Chan shall truly become lost to the history of this world. As I said when you first returned, your word supersedes even the word of the Emperor in Li Chan village."

Togusawa Hiro stepped beside Ming Ne Yu and spoke to him, "They are speaking treason against the Emperor. What shall we do?"

Ming Ne Yu held up a hand, "Nothing. This is not our place to question what they do. We will serve."

Togusawa Hiro interjected, "The Emperor will order us to prevent them when he finds out about it."

Ming Ne Yu looked down at Togusawa Hiro as he pointed at the calm Hap Sing walking down into the crowd of villagers gathering in the center of the courtyard while whispering, "Do you think your cousin can do anything to stop him? I know I can't, and that you won't even be able to try unless you plan to fight the rest of us."

Hap Sing spoke to the villagers gathered in a circle around him, "I thank you for putting your trust in me."

They smiled as Lu Han replied, "We are yours Lucky Cricket. You have protected us from harm for generations. It is the least we could do in return."

The Tiger Monks watched in awe as Hap Sing began to radiate a bright aura. Many ribbons suddenly stretched out from his aura to connect Hap Sing to each villager present. Then Hap Sing reached into nothingness and removed a simple iron door handle. He placed it onto thin air and a wooden door appeared. Hap Sing opened the door to reveal a stone corridor beyond.

One by one the villagers approached Hap Sing. They hugged him, or pressed their foreheads to his own. Then as families, or individuals they stepped through the doorway. The last to approach the doorway was Lu Han and his grandson Lu Wan. Hap Sing gathered them both into a hug then released them.

Hap Sing spoke, "Continue to lead them well. Ariel and her people will help you get acclimated on the other side."

Lu Han nodded, "Your kindness still remains legendary as does your fishing skill. Will you manage fine here on your own?"

Hap Sing nodded, "I only have a few things which need to be finished before I will rejoin you. I look forward to seeing you again my new friend."

Lu Han smiled, "As do I Lucky Cricket."

After Lu Han and Lu Wan departed through the doorway, Hap Sing shut the door, removed the handle causing the door to disappear again, and placed the handle back into the pocket of nothingness. Hap Sing then looked at the various expressions on the faces of the remaining Tiger Monks. Lo Hannah and Mimosa seemed confused by what was happening. Yu Lo wore a sly smile. Sea Reaver had a displeased look as did Togusawa Hiro who looked insulted. Chow Sang seemed contemplative. Ming Ne Yu wore a resigned expression.

Hap Sing questioned, "Well? You have something to say to me?"

They began speaking at once. Hap Sing held up his hand. They stopped talking for a moment.

Hap Sing shook his head, "I'm beginning to understand the Luck more every day it seems. Mortals. Think about it some. Talk among yourselves if you like. Then come talk to me when you are ready to understand."

As Hap Sing walked away he heard them discussing it among themselves in a heated manner for several minutes. Only Chow Sang and Ming Ne Yu held their tongues. When Hap Sing looked up at the sky with his second sight he could see the brightly glowing net against the darkening night sky. The words written in the sky suddenly showed brighter for a moment, and then faded out of sight. The net across the sky faded to nothing after that.

The next morning Ming Ne Yu sought out Hap Sing standing on the beach with his bamboo fishing pole in the water. Hap Sing watched him approach as he pulled in a fish on his line. Ming Ne Yu was obviously not prepared to see the large scaly serpentine corpse of the one hundred foot long sea dragon washed on shore south of the village along the bay.

Ming Ne Yu walked up to Hap Sing and bowed down, "I'm confused master. You arrival has created turmoil among our ranks. You've banished the people of Li Chan village to who knows where. A dead sea dragon sits upon the shore. Frankly speaking I'm way out of my depth here. What is going on?"

Hap Sing replied, "You were right of course. My kindness is my weakness. The people of Li Chan village were my weak point. This is well known to both your grandfather and grandmother. They sent the Tiger Monks here to both guard them, and to potentially use them as hostages to my cooperation. I don't like being in that position, so I corrected it. Your charge to guard them is satisfied, and you need not ever worry about being requested to harm them now. They are forever safe from even the very gods of this world."

Ming Ne Yu shook his head, "That was never our intent."

Hap Sing nodded, "I know. Yet I can not guarantee your behavior when loyalties are put to the test yet. I also know that dark forces with enough power to breach my protection were standing in place looking to ambush me on arrival."

Hap Sing pointed to the corpse of the sea dragon, "That belonged to one of the gods. A minor servant, but one that presented a deadly threat for even the Tiger Monks."

Ming Ne Yu spoke, "How did it end up dead here then?"

Hap Sing sighed, "I killed it yesterday morning with the kunai knife you saw appear in front of your face. That is why I don't like them. They are instruments of death. I don't like to kill."

Ming Ne Yu nodded, "It was your first kill then?"

Hap Sing shook his head, "Not hardly. I've been a fisherman for two hundred fifty years after all. I've killed plenty in that time. However, it was the first intelligent being I've ever slain. If I hadn't needed more time, then I wouldn't have taken that option. I had to give the villagers time to escape though. It was an unfortunate necessity based on the fact it had already spotted my presence, and was preparing to report to its masters."

Ming Ne Yu looked around, "Your net is gone?"

Hap Sing nodded, "It was ineffective against sea life. I didn't conceive of a need to prevent any underwater approach to the village at the time I created it. My enemies were prepared to cause great harm to those I've cared for in order to limit and harm me. As I already said, that particular weakness now no longer exists on this world."

Ming Ne Yu looked back at Hap Sing, "What about your relatives?"

Hap Sing shrugged, "I don't really know them. I haven't dealt with my relatives for over one hundred years."

Ming Ne Yu spoke, "The Tiger Monks as well? Did you mean anything you said yesterday?"

Hap Sing smiled, "That's why I shall keep you all close. So I can guard my students as I teach them to defend themselves."

Ming Ne Yu looked down at Hap Sing, "We can already defend ourselves."

Hap Sing nodded, "Yes. However, can you do so without causing unnecessary harm to others?"

Chapter 27 Trip to Yokito

Hap Sing walked along the roadway beside Ming Ne Yu. Behind them in a double file were the other six Tiger Monks carrying travel packs upon their backs. Hap Sing kept a steady pace without break or rest all through the morning. As the sun reached its zenith Hap Sing chose a spot under a tree beside the road to sit on the ground.

Hap Sing spoke, "Time for dinner. Break out those travel rations."

Lo Hannah exhaled a deep breath, "It's about time. I'm hungry and tired."

Yu Lo shook his head, "Keep quiet cousin. We've just got started."

Ming Ne Yu spoke, "Maintain discipline my young charges. You should both remain calm before our master."

Hap Sing swallowed a piece of dried fish he was chewing and spoke, "Let them talk if they will. I don't mind the conversation."

Mimosa spoke, "Where are we going?"

Hap Sing gave a faint smile while pointing, "In a north easterly direction when we resume walking after lunch."

Mimosa drank from her flask before replying, "I mean what is our destination?"

Hap Sing shrugged, "That depends upon the choices you make."

Sea Reaver spoke, "I don't get it. Are you deliberately trying to be evasive?"

Chow Sang laughed lightly without humor, "You are not asking the right questions. Where are you going next master Hap Sing?"

Hap Sing smiled, "I am making my way eventually to Yokito. It has been many years since I have journeyed there."

Mimosa looked slightly cross, "Why didn't you just say we were going to Yokito?"

Hap Sing shrugged, "Because that I don't know."

Lo Hannah raised an eyebrow, "We are going to go with you. No. Let me rephrase that. I am going to follow where you go master Hap Sing."

Hap Sing nodded, "Then you shall be where I am. At least to the best of your ability, or until you change your mind about your destination."

Togusawa Hiro raised an eyebrow, "Are you going to seek an audience with my cousin the Emperor?"

Hap Sing shook his head, "That would be rather pointless."

Togusawa Hiro's eyebrows lowered, "Why would you think that? I could arrange an audience with him if necessary."

Hap Sing shrugged, "What use does your cousin the Emperor of Ran Li have for a fisherman, or for that matter what use does a fisherman have for an emperor?"

Togusawa Hiro's brow darkened, "The Emperor provides the nation stability so you can remain at peace to fish."

Hap Sing gave a faint smile, "This is a nation at peace then? It seems I came back much too soon. I came to help a nation in trouble, not a nation at peace."

Togusawa Hiro stood up from his seat, "You know that hard times have struck due to invaders from the wild country. This is a nation beset with problems brought by outsiders."

Hap Sing nodded, "Yet your cousin the Emperor has not maintained the stability or peace of the nation. The problems here are as much on the inside as from the outside. Part of the problem is the thought that one man can maintain the welfare of an entire nation. I agree that the ambitions of one man can harm a nation, but one man alone does not protect one. Only the people can choose to do that."

Sea Reaver spoke, "Then what can you do alone that an emperor can't?"

Hap Sing gave a light grin, "In terms of a nation the answer to your question is nothing significant actually. It remains to be seen if I will be asked to stand alone, or if others will join with me."

Togusawa Hiro opened his mouth to speak, and then shut it after a gaze from Ming Ne Yu. Hap Sing watched the exchange carefully, and then he looked directly at Chow Sang.

Hap Sing spoke, "What is your opinion on this point as an 'outsider' here in Ran Li?"

Chow Sang gave a faint smile, "I don't think that all of us will go to Yokito with you master Hap Sing. I think some people are more loyal to the power structure in this country than to their own countryman. Those people see a level of personal advantage for making that choice, so it is understandable. Some of us see a personal advantage to joining with you. I see that you are trying to do something positive to help this nation which isn't even my own. While others may find sedition in such actions taken without the approval of the Emperor, I believe that you are a man trying to atone for you lack of direct involvement in historical events."

Togusawa Hiro stalked away as Chow Sang finished speaking and muttered under his breath, "Don't 'some people' me you smug Udomo bastard."

Hap Sing looked at the remaining Tiger Monks, "Your service is not required by me. You must choose what it means for you to serve, and whom you want to serve. Understand this one thing first. The Tiger Monks will enter my service. The question simply remains which of you will stay in the Tiger Monks, and which of you will choose other loyalties as your priorities. Until that decision is clear, I ask you to remain ready to do as asked by Ming Ne Yu. I want you to also understand that I will not request you to harm any other person to whom you are loyal. I may ask you to not obey all of their requests. Any disobedience on that point may result in your removal from the Tiger Monks. The choices made are yours. My decisions about your continued membership will be based on your choices. Finish eating, and we shall catch up to Togusawa Hiro along the way."

Ming Ne Yu rapidly finished eating and asked, "What would you have me do master Hap Sing?"

Hap Sing looked down the trail at the back of Togusawa Hiro, "We shall give him time to decide. He remains in a quandary between what he knows, and what he wants."

Later that afternoon they caught up to Togusawa Hiro looking a bit tired from his fast pace. He stood at a crossroads leading between the nearby inland community of San Mu, and the coastal road toward Yokito. A look of calm was on his face as he bowed toward Ming Ne Yu.

Togusawa Hiro spoke as he rose from his bow, "Master Ming Ne Yu I must request that I part company from you for the moment. I have to go report what has happened in Ran Li village to the local authorities. I need to send a message, and they have an arcane practitioner who can relay it residing in San Mu."

Ming Ne Yu looked at him sternly, "You understand the choice you are making?"

Togusawa Hiro nodded, "I am choosing my country over any 'outsider' influence in our nation. I will endeavor to catch up to you once my message has been relayed."

Ming Ne Yu looked at Hap Sing, "What is your decision my master?"

Hap Sing smiled, "He shall be allowed to do what he will. I will watch the result of his choice, and judge my decision accordingly."

Togusawa Hiro looked at him with a practiced eye, "What do you mean the result of my choice?"

Hap Sing looked at him carefully, "You are taking an action. You are doing so because you have been told to do so. You are doing so without understanding the result of that action."

Togusawa Hiro looked angry, "I'm not stupid. My cousin will be informed of what you have done. That is the result of my action."

Hap Sing nodded, "Then you know the mind of your cousin, and all of his advisors as well? Do you understand what choices they will make from this knowledge, and agree with those choices?"

Togusawa Hiro started to look uncomfortable, "I can't be held responsible for what they do."

Hap Sing shrugged, "I can't be held responsible for how this turns out either then. You're making an incautious decision which potentially endangers all of us, because you can't be held responsible."

Togusawa Hiro plaintively spoke, "My duty demands I inform the Emperor."

Hap Sing nodded, "I understand that you feel a duty. The question is whether you understand the eventual result of your actions whether you feel responsible for them or not."

Togusawa Hiro looked down at his feet, "I don't know how they will respond to this action."

Hap Sing nodded, "Neither do I. I've been gone a long time. In that time there is much misinformation about me which could have developed in Ran Li. I suggest you think about that before you use an uncertain third party to relay a message likely best heard by your cousin directly."

Togusawa Hiro looked up at Hap Sing directly, "You're very dangerous, and Togusawa Minato should know about you as soon as possible."

Hap Sing smiled, "I think your estimation is correct. I can be very dangerous if backed into the wrong corner. Do you really want your cousin to start backing me up without fully understanding that fact? Would it be better for me to approach cautiously without harm first so they can understand my intent before they act?"

Togusawa Hiro squatted down on the ground, "I don't know what would be better. Better for whom? For you, for him, for me, for Ran Li it's too hard to decide. I only have my duty to guide me."

Hap Sing nodded, "I can only say I intend to do no harm."

Togusawa Hiro looked down at the ground, "That dead sea dragon felt the effect of your desire to do no harm."

Hap Sing nodded, "Yes it did. Would you have the same happen to Ran Li by precipitating an action which places me in a tight spot a second time?"

Togusawa Hiro shook his head, "I want to protect Ran Li."

Hap Sing smiled, "Very good then. We agree on one point at least. What is your decision?"

Togusawa Hiro looked back up, "I will follow you at least as far as Yokito so I can speak with my cousin Minato directly and judge his reaction to my words accordingly. I won't trust this to intermediaries."

Hap Sing nodded, "A wise choice given the circumstance. You shall come to no harm as a result of my actions and you are welcome to remain in the Tiger Monks."

Ming Ne Yu spoke, "Rejoin our group Togusawa. Master Hap Sing a question. Why are you so against the Emperor finding out about your presence?"

Hap Sing looked off toward San Mu, "I don't mind if he learns of it. However, there is a presence in that direction which disturbs me. I was afraid it would obtain the information first, and act in a manner detrimental to all of us."

Togusawa Hiro looked shocked, "Why didn't you warn me?"

Hap Sing smiled, "You wouldn't have believed me initially. I didn't want to seem like was trying to scare you out of making your decision. I'm actually not worried about how your cousin will react. I do want to keep others uncertain about my present position as long as possible. Right now they are heading to investigate their lack of communication from the Ran Li area."

Togusawa Hiro looked at him, "You would have let me go to my potential doom then?"

Hap Sing nodded, "It certainly isn't my place to stop you from making bad choices. You have not shown me any particular loyalty. Why do you think I owe you any? Is it because you were assigned to the Tiger Monks as a political favour? Loyalty and trust is something built and earned between individuals. We are all in the process of doing this right now. Good choices help earn my trust. Hopefully my behavior will earn your trust and loyalty in time."

Sea Reaver spoke, "Master Hap Sing. Why did you give your trust and loyalty to the people of Li Chan village then? They knew you as briefly as you knew them."

Hap Sing nodded, "So it may seem to any other looking in at us. Yet I saw the clear signs of their continued loyalty."

Lo Hannah asked, "What do you mean the clear sign of their loyalty?"

Hap Sing spoke, "Did none of you see it?"

Ming Ne Yu nodded, "You speak of the net over Li Chan village placed by you."

Hap Sing smiled, "It was indeed placed by me. However, it was only maintained that long by the villagers and their faith in me. They kept their trust in me, and in doing so protected their village from harm for one hundred and eleven years. I returned that clear sign of trust with a reward of a new land untouched by other human hands, free from conflict, and designed for peaceful coexistence."

Ming Ne Yu spoke, "So you continue to protect them?"

Hap Sing nodded, "They are the people I call mine. I will assist them as I can just as I will assist those of the Chi Master backgrounds like the Tiger Monks. I will not make their choices for them, or for the Chi Masters. I will withhold my assistance from those who will not follow my guidance. That is my choice."

Lo Hannah asked, "So we can call upon your assistance?"

Hap Sing nodded, "You may ask most certainly."

Yu Lo raised an eyebrow, "What will your answer be I wonder?"

Hap Sing smiled, "That depends upon the nature of the assistance required. I suggest you don't ask me to carry a load which you refuse to take."

Chow Sang spoke, "If we ask to learn how you do something, then what?"

Hap Sing nodded, "I am prepared to teach what I consider you ready to learn."

Ming Ne Yu spoke, "Master Hap Sing. Shall we continue our journey? I would rather put some more room between us and whatever disquiets you in San Mu."

Chapter 28 Bittersweet Reunion

A little less than a month later Hap Sing and the Seven Tiger Monks dressed in commoner's clothing walked down the gangplank of a Nordland trading vessel. The trip along the coast of Ran Li had been a relatively uneventful journey. The vessel was docked at the Nordland colony at the southern edge of the bay which was surrounded by the city of Yokito. The position of the dock the ship was at left it vulnerable to the pounding waves from the changing tides and storms. Normally only Nordland sailors were willing to use the southern docks nearest the colony for their ships.

Sea Reaver and Mimosa led the way beaming proudly as they proceeded down the docks. Hap Sing was flanked by Lo Hannah and Yu Lo who wore less exuberant expressions. Ming Ne Yu walked beside a sulking Togusawa Hiro. As usual Chow Sang brought up the rear with a carefully neutral expression.

The locals in the Nordland Colony community were mainly of Nordland stock, but some obvious Nordland and Ran Li mixed heritage individuals also worked in the community. There didn't seem to be any tension between the pure Nordlanders, and the mixed ones as they worked side by side with little obvious disagreement.

The party of Tiger Monks drew several curious glances as they walked down the roads as a tightly knit group. Eventually they followed the steep roads winding up the ridge line of the southern bay until they came to a portion of the slope near the top covered in marker stones of various types. A moderately sized dry set stone temple occupied the center of the area without dominating it.

A small group of black robed maids of Nordland, Ran Li, and mixed backgrounds gathered and waited for the approach of the Tiger Monks and Hap Sing. Most of them were elderly, but the youngest ones were still middle aged. A senior member of the black robed maids stepped forward.

The elderly woman spoke as the Tiger Monks stopped before them, "Welcome to the bone yard of the White Raven. Be at ease here as the dead here also remain at their ease."

Mimosa spoke first, "Sister Kenara, I am Mimosa, and also a follower of the White Raven. We thank you for your welcome."

Sister Kenara replied, "I remember you as a young child before the Lady Ming sent you off to her husband's academy. You made us proud that day knowing another from our community had the spirit shaman blood in their veins. How is your family doing child? It has been so long since we've seen them at services."

Mimosa hesitated and her voice cracked, "They should be fine as best I know. I've been away and have only just returned."

Sister Kenara nodded, "You have a gentle heart child, but you need not fear for the White Raven watches over all of her flock in this life or the next. Now please introduce your company to me. I would know the reason for your appearance here."

Ming Ne Yu stepped forward, "I am Ming Ne Yu. I am Lady Ming's grandson."

Sister Kenara smiled, "I haven't seen you in many years most honored grandson of Lady Ming. You've grown quite a bit since then. Rumor had spread years ago that you had been selected to be a Tiger Monk in your youth. Surely that time is up now though. There are eight of you so surely this couldn't be the current crop of Tiger Monks then?"

Sister Kenara looked over the group briefly before her gaze eventually settled on Hap Sing, "I don't know you do I? You seem somehow familiar."

Hap Sing bowed, "I knew Yuki Nene in her younger years."

Sister Kenara chuckled, "That couldn't be as Lady Ming is twice my own age, and you are obviously younger than myself."

Hap Sing looked back up, "It's been a little over two hundred and sixty five years since my birth young lady. I knew Yuki Nene when she was of an age with these young ones gathered here."

Sudden whispers broke out among the black robed maids, "The Lucky Cricket has returned." "It's really him." "They're the Tiger Monks." "What does this mean?" "Quickly go inform the Lady Ming."

One of the middle aged Maids of the White Raven separated from their group and rapidly walked back toward the temple. Sister Kenara turned around briefly to raise her finger across her lips as she looked at the other maids.

Sister Kenara then looked back around at Hap Sing while ignoring the rest, "It remains to be seen if you are the real Lucky Cricket. None living have ever seen the Lucky Cricket save the Lady Ming or her husband."

Sister Kenara looked a Ming Ne Yu and Mimosa next, "You both have the vision of the spirit shamans. What have you seen when you look at him?"

Ming Ne Yu looked over at Hap Sing briefly, then back at Sister Kenara, "The spirit of the seven tailed tiger surrounds him even now. Yet when he uses his own spirit the brightness of it eclipses even the sun."

Mimosa nodded in affirmation, "It is as Master Ming says. I have personally seen that he can accomplish things which none of us Tiger Monks can even dream."

Sister Kenara nodded, "I will take your word for the moment until the Lady Ming confirms it. We had best go in to see her."

As the maids of the White Raven turned they saw the tall white haired elderly form of Lady Ming Yuki Nene step forth from the temple wearing an elegant, yet simple, white gown. She moved very surely for someone of such advanced age. Beside her was the maid who had left to inform her of what was happening.

The next thing they knew Hap Sing was standing directly in front of Lady Ming. She looked down at him with an austere expression. The maids began running to her aid as she raised a hand signaling them to stop.

Lady Ming spoke, "So Hap Sing you have returned, and that bastard the Luck had his way with me after all."

Hap Sing nodded, "I was led to believe you were a willing participant."

Lady Ming shrugged her shoulders, "Willing or unwilling my path was set and you knew it."

Hap Sing gave a sly smile, "I've missed you."

Lady Ming stepped forward to wrap her arms around Hap Sing. She gave him a gentle kiss on his forehead, and then wrapped him closely in her arms as he put his arms around her in return.

Lady Ming had a single tear drop from her eye as she asked, "Did you have to be gone so long?"

Hap Sing clasped her closely in return, "I had a lot to do. You know that you're still my one love."

Lady Ming gave a bitter laugh, "Liar. Your love has always been bigger than one person can possibly hold. I'm glad you've returned to me first. Come inside. There is much you need to know before you leave me again."

The six younger Tiger Monks looked at Ming Ne Yu as Hap Sing and Lady Ming walked inside the temple. Ming Ne Yu simply shook his head at them briefly and then raised an eyebrow.

Ming Ne Yu spoke to them quietly, "Did I forget to mention that my grandmother and Hap Sing were once lovers?"

Togusawa Hiro muttered in return, "The choice to come here first is starting to make a lot more sense to me now. What else don't we know?"

Ming Ne Yu shrugged, "Too much. Way too much I expect. Come on now, let's follow the White Raven's maids inside."

Lady Ming Yuki Nene and Hap Sing sat side by side in a small room with a table and four chairs. In the third chair sat Ming Ne Yu watching across the table from him drinking tea from delicate porcelain cups. Sister Kenara sat next to Ming Ne Yu and served the tea as needed without formal ceremony.

Lady Ming spoke looking into Hap Sing's face as if they were alone together, "You've stayed exactly the same after all these years. Even the smell of fish hasn't faded from your clothes."

Hap Sing nodded, "Yet things have changed. Events are moving quickly here, and I need more information before I decide what needs to be done."

Lady Ming lightly laughed, "You know where to find information better than anyone I believe. So has it been worth it? Being gone all these years I mean."

Hap Sing nodded, "It has not been without price, but the necessary work has been done for now. I've removed the villagers from Li Chan as you may have heard by now. They are beyond the reach of any retribution."

Lady Ming nodded, "I've heard, and so has Emperor Togusawa through his agents. My information is that he is privately quite furious about the abduction of his citizens."

Hap Sing looked over at Ming Ne Yu, "You can tell her what you've seen."

Ming Ne Yu sipped his tea calmly, "The former citizens of Li Chan village have chosen to voluntarily depart grandmother. I don't know where they've gone, but Hap Sing summoned a magical doorway to allow their departure to elsewhere."

Lady Ming smiled at Ming Ne Yu, "I know Hap Sing better than you know him. I don't think any choice he presents is as voluntary as he would have you believe. I can see his threads of destiny tied to each of your Tiger Monks and yourself. I knew he'd returned the moment I saw his ribbon connected to me point in the direction of Li Chan once more. For one hundred and eleven years I've seen it fade off into the nothingness like the connection of a god to their follower."

Ming Ne Yu shook his head, "My choices remain my own. I'm certain of that much."

Lady Ming shook her head, "I had that certainty as a youth as well. Then I ran into the mountain which is Hap Sing. I tried my best to move that mountain, but it remained in its place and I inevitably changed course around it. I was free to choose which path to take around the mountain certainly, but all paths eventually led to this one destination."

Ming Ne Yu looked uncertain, "What destination?"

Lady Ming looked serious, "The four of us sitting here in this room sipping tea."

Sister Kenara spoke, "The power of the White Raven protects us. Surely she is not influenced by a mere…"

Lady Ming looked at her, "Tell her Hap Sing, about your alliance, and just how far your influence is spreading even now. Tell her what you really are. Tell her what you can do if you so choose."

Hap Sing looked up at the ceiling, "I hold the power of fire."

Sister Kenara spoke, "Many can use the power of fire. There is hardly a mage who doesn't know some fire spell these days. Even common people can make fire to serve their needs."

Lady Ming looked over at Ming Ne Yu, "Would you summon your spirit guardian for me dear grandson?"

Ming Ne Yu brought forth his guardian tiger spirit, "You can see it now grandmother."

Lady Ming nodded, "Add substance to it like I taught you all those years ago before your grandfather took you to train."

A very real solid looking tiger stood next to Ming Ne Yu. Sister Kenara flinched at seeing it looking over at her. Lady Ming smiled as two solid looking ravens appeared sitting upon her shoulders.

Sister Kenara bowed her head down, "Hugin and Munin the raven symbols of the White Raven in physical form. Surely this proves her grace is upon you still, and that your destiny is your own Lady Ming."

Lady Ming shook her head, "Look my grandson at your spirit watch it look at Hap Sing and what do you see."

Ming Ne Yu looked at it closely, "It's hard to explain. There is a ribbon between them, in addition to a ribbon between me and Hap Sing. When did this happen?"

Lady Ming nodded, "Look closer and tell me again what happened in the village of Li Chan."

Ming Ne Yu gasped, "Ribbons formed between the Tiger Monks and Hap Sing when we met. The same happened to all the villagers as he met with them."

Lady Ming nodded again, "He's in control in ways I never could imagine when I was even your age. I spent a lifetime, and a second lifetime trying to puzzle it out. There is a reason he couldn't extend my life. I was too closely connected to the White Raven, and that secret of extending a mortal life in the way he knows is not one they want any god to understand."

Hap Sing sighed, "It really isn't as easy as you make it out Nene. Spirits are not well suited to material existence after all. Only certain spirits can be extended without undue harm. The knowledge of which can be safely extended doesn't reside with the gods."

Lady Ming smiled, "Yet here I still am. I am alive and well because of what reason?"

Hap Sing smiled fondly in return, "Because the White Raven needed you to be here today."

Sister Kenara looked back and forth between them, "I don't understand. What does this mean?"

Lady Ming smiled, "These ribbons we speak of are a connection between spirits not physical forms. They inform someone like Hap Sing a whole lot about the kind of people we are. Who we know, and with whom we form bonds is plain for him to see. He can read these connections like no other before him. I've spent a lifetime trying to puzzle out the messages contained on them."

Sister Kenara looked puzzled as Ming Ne Yu answered, "Does this mean our lives are an open book to him?"

Lady Ming nodded, "Hap Sing can see our spirits and knows how they are suited. He is able to accurately predict much of what we will do as individuals and groups into the future based on this knowledge."

Hap Sing took a sip of his tea, "I don't think it is that bad after all to know with whom I choose to associate."

Lady Ming sighed, "We not just an open book to you Hap Sing, but a book with blank pages which you can write upon with your presence. The mountain is not moved, but the people move around the mountain when it is in their path. That is the lesson you taught me when I was little more than a child."

Sister Kenara looked directly at him, "Why can you do this when even the gods don't have this power?"

Hap Sing's eyes had a strange glint in them as his voice roughened, "I am the Destroyer of Worlds after all."

Lady Ming nodded, "It's true. No god will confront him directly for fear of losing all their worshipers. Those foolish enough to meddle in his path have found it also quite enlightening I imagine. This mountain moves after all under its own power. It is a quiet volcano which still smokes and steams as a warning that another devastating eruption is still quite possible. Now be gone Destroyer of Worlds, and return my Hap Sing to me."

Hap Sing looked back at her, "I'm still here Nene. The Luck and I are simply closer than when you knew me. You spoke of fire Sister Kenara, I don't use fire like you think of it. I am the essence of the spirit of fire. The inventor of the fire you know and understand, the keeper of all the as yet unknown secrets it contains, and much more threatening than any god will care to admit. Ultimately I'm also responsible for all the good and harm fire does in the hands of others. Eventually every world now populated with life will undergo a transformation to lifelessness at my hand. That all shall end in fire is both a threat and a promise."

Ming Ne Yu looked startled as he whispered, "A spirit brighter than the sun."

Lady Ming nodded, "Brighter than the sun indeed. Yet some gods understand the reasons for this purpose, and the role the Destroyer of Worlds plays in events even now. The elder gods found it out the hard way when their worlds were destroyed as they lost their own original purpose. The greater spirits known as the Numbers can be seen as a system of checks and balances for existence."

Ming Ne Yu thought a moment, "Then you are in control of everything then. You hold the ultimate threat over everyone's head."

Hap Sing shook his head, "That is hardly the case. The Numbers represent a system perhaps, but it is not a system without problems. It is a system which has for a long time been exploited in ways it was never originally intended to be exploited, and as such it has become less able to do its intended job as well as it should."

Ming Ne Yu asked, "What do you plan to do then?"

Hap Sing shrugged, "I'm attempting to build a better system if possible, and hopefully to repair the problems with this current one."

Ming Ne Yu looked surprised, "How will you do that?"

Hap Sing grinned shyly, "I haven't quite figured that out yet. We're still working out the solutions. It will be many thousands of years before we make any significant progress."

Lady Ming pressed her hand gently on his shoulder, "The question is why you have come here now? Things have long since moved on between us after all."

Hap Sing looked down at his cup, "As they have moved on between you and Ming Wa Fu?"

Lady Ming gave her own little shrug, "We have both moved past any personal jealousy or need for constant attention from one another. Jun knows how I feel about him, as do I know how he feels regarding me. Sometimes after so many years these extended periods of absence from each other make our feelings for each other more profound when we meet. It is not like either of us seeks physical comfort with another."

A gentle knock was heard at the door to the room. Sister Kenara got up to open the door and saw another raven maid standing with Mimosa just outside the door. Lady Ming looked at Mimosa closely and her eyes widened slightly. Ming Ne Jun looked back at Mimosa without seeing any sign of what caused his grandmother's odd reaction.

Mimosa spoke, "Sorry for the interruption Master Ming, Lady Ming, Master Hap Sing. I need to beg permission for a brief period of absence to visit my relatives while I am in the area."

Ming Ne Yu looked at Hap Sing who gave a brief smile, "I will allow you no more than three days to settle up any business you have in the area. Relay this message back to the others as well. Please be certain to let Togusawa Hiro know that this is his opportunity to report back to the Emperor. I shall remain here in Yokito for this length of time, and any who wish to continue with me afterwards shall return by that time. I will expect to see your return by then Mimosa."

Mimosa replied, "Thank you Master Hap Sing, Master Ming. I shall return in a day or two days at most."

Master Ming Ne Yu replied, "We shall be expecting your return. Go tell the others we shall be fine here under the hospitality provided by the White Raven."

After Mimosa departed Ming Ne Yu looked over at Lady Ming, "What is wrong grandmother?"

Lady Ming sighed, "That poor child. To be pushed so hard while still so young."

Ming Ne Yu raised an eyebrow, "I don't understand grandmother. All of the Tiger Monks have to endure a rigorous training regimen."

Lady Ming looked cautiously at Hap Sing, "You saw it already?"

Hap Sing nodded, "It is what it is. I may not be asked to help, but I'll help in the manner necessary if I'm asked. The signs were all there when I first saw her."

Ming Ne Yu looked at Lady Ming, "What is wrong grandmother?"

Lady Ming gave a faint smile, "Woman's intuition my grandson. Your charges have been active behind your less than perfectly watchful eye."

Ming Ne Yu looked startled a moment and then whispered, "Sea Reaver, that foreign rogue."

Hap Sing chuckled, "You need to learn to watch the ribbons more closely. They are friends most certainly based on their common heritage. However, the closer connection is between Mimosa and Togusawa Hiro if you know how to look."

Ming Ne Yu looked surprised, "They hardly talk to each other."

Hap Sing nodded, "I'm certain that is true while they are in your presence. I'm pretty certain that quite the opposite is true in private with each other. Speaking of which, it is time I had a private word with your grandmother Ming Ne Yu and Sister Kenara. We won't be long, and I'll behave myself you may be assured."

After Ming Ne Yu and Sister Kenara left the room Lady Ming looked over at Hap Sing, "Why didn't you tell them about the other part? It is arguably the much more important part."

Hap Sing chuckled, "I'm certain her pregnancy will start to show before too much longer Nene."

Lady Ming looked serious, "You know well that isn't what I'm talking about Sing."

Hap Sing nodded, "I know. They all have choices to make. I am the mountain, but each of them must choose which path to travel around me. That is their trial just as it was your trial. Like when the time for your encounter with me came, I can only hope that they are wise enough to ask for help when they get into difficulty."

Ming Ne Yu and the seven Tiger Monks stood together talking quietly as Hap Sing and Lady Ming exited the private room and entered the main temple hall. Hap Sing had provided his arm for Lady Ming's support, and she was moving along more slowly than before to accommodate his shorter stride.

Sister Kenara came over to the opposite side of Lady Ming, "Do you need anything Lady Ming?"

Lady Ming nodded, "Please arrange for a messenger to be sent to my husband. Let him know that the ribbons indicate it is time to show up for dinner."

Ming Ne Yu spoke up from his position by the Tiger Monks, "I believe I shall be heading over to the Chi Master Academy this afternoon. I will relay your invitation to grandfather, with your permission of course Master Hap Sing."

Hap Sing nodded, "It is granted. Please take any of the Tiger Monks along who do not have other plans, and who do not wish to hang around listening to a bunch of old people talking about the past."

Chow Sang raised his hand, "Master Hap Sing may I make a request?"

Hap Sing nodded, "Of course you may ask."

Chow Sang looked over at Lady Ming, "If I may be allowed to peruse your library here, then I would be grateful Lady Ming. I haven't had much chance to read lately, and I find new works enlightening."

Lady Ming smiled, "Our library mainly consists of family histories and death records, but you are welcome to view them as long as you treat them with care. Sister Norla is their new keeper, and will be assigned to assist you with anything you need."

Hap Sing looked at Mimosa, "You are permitted to depart now child. I know you want to see your family in a time such as this. There is no need for you to linger any longer waiting on us."

Mimosa did a quick bow, "Thank you Master Hap Sing."

Mimosa looked briefly over at Togusawa Hiro who spoke next, "I must also be going to see my cousin the Emperor. I will see to it that Mimosa has an escort along her way."

Lo Hannah spoke next, "I will go along with Mimosa and Hiro at least part of the way. I want to visit the temple of Palnor to see my family as well."

Hap Sing watched as a glance was exchanged quickly between Mimosa and Togusawa Hiro. He then raised an eyebrow at Ming Ne Yu who nodded.

Ming Ne Yu answered, "You may join them as far as needed to reach your destination. Are you going as well Yu Lo?"

Yu Lo shook his head, "My father and mother are already on their way here. I will await their arrival if you don't mind."

Lady Ming replied, "I can see your father's eagle approaching this way even now. They shall be welcomed as guests for dinner today then."

Sea Reaver shrugged his shoulders, "I guess that means I'll be going along with Master Ming to the Chi Master Academy. A couple of former classmates I want to meet with are there anyway."

Hap Sing waved at the departing Tiger Monks, "Fare well for now. May we all soon meet again."

Chow Sang came closer to Hap Sing and said, "You speak as if some doubt were on your mind."

Hap Sing gave a gentle smile, "It is true that all partings must bring some doubt. I don't know whom I may see again."

Yu Lo gave his own brief smile, "That's why I'll stick close like Master Ming asked me. I'd already let my parents know we were coming on the boat this morning. I spied my father's eagle searching along the course of our ribbon with the rising of the sun. He must have been curious about our return so soon. He was a Tiger Monk in his youth as well, and acts as an instructor for academy students from time to time."

Lady Ming spoke, "Sister Kenara, please show this young man . . ."

Chow Sang answered, "My name is Chow Sang. I am at your service Lady Ming."

Lady Ming nodded, "Please show Chow Sang into the library, and place him under the care of Sister Norla."

Sister Kenara replied, "Yes, Lady Ming. Please follow this way young monk. Try not to mind Sister Norla's manner. She is newly arrived from our ancient homeland, and has not adapted yet to the ways of the sisters here."

Chow Sang gave a timid smile, "A fellow outsider then. We should get along well."

Sister Kenara had a thoughtful expression as they withdrew from the room.

Hap Sing looked at Yu Lo standing in front of him and Lady Ming, "I don't suppose we can find you something to occupy your time until your parents arrive?"

Yu Lo gave a mysterious grin, "I'd very much like to oblige Master Hap Sing, but nothing is going to convince me to voluntarily leave your side. I'm the only one able to quickly contact the others if the need arrives."

Lady Ming gave a wicked laugh, "Come to my bedroom if you must then young monk. I'm going to have my way with Hap Sing there until my husband arrives to catch us in the act."

Yu Lo flushed bright red, "Lady Ming you can't be . . ."

Hap Sing shook his head, "Let him follow as far as he can Nene. Let's have that private conversation at the usual place."

Chapter 29 Li Chan Village

Yu Lo followed Lady Ming and Hap Sing as they walked arm in arm through a corridor of the temple until they reached a doorway. They went through the door, and followed a path outside behind the temple. The path went through the graveyard to a small neat wooden house overlooking the ocean. Lady Ming and Hap Sing entered the house, and Yu Lo hesitated a bit before following them inside. Lady Ming entered the bedroom of the house, and Hap Sing turned to look at Yu Lo.

Hap Sing spoke, "You'll have to watch over us from here. We're going now where you can not follow yet."

Yu Lo looked a little hurt, "You are going to the dreaming aren't you. I know how to go there."

Hap Sing nodded, "We may be there a long while my child. I'll need you to watch over us, and to entertain your parents when they arrive until our return. Sister Kenara will join you later as well so you won't be alone for long."

Yu Lo nodded, "I'll do as you ask."

Hap Sing smiled, "I know you will. You don't have much of a choice as no one can follow where I'm going without my permission."

Hap Sing walked into the bedroom and closed the door. Lady Ming lay already on the left side of her bed with her eyes closed. Her breathing was smooth and regular. Hap Sing lay down beside her clasping her left hand in his right. He closed his eyes.

When Hap Sing opened his eyes the Isle of Life was before him. A moment later he closed his eyes and a young Yuki Nene was standing beside him on the beach. Yuki Nene smiled at him.

Yuki Nene spoke, "Your residual memory of me I guess. It has been very long since I thought of myself this way. Now fetch Ming Wa Fu. He's bound to be waiting on your arrival now as this is the time for his late morning nap."

Hap Sing closed his eyes once more. A couple of waves broke on the beach before a young Ming Wa Fu was standing beside Hap Sing on the beach.

Ming Wa Fu went over to Yuki Nene and gave her a hug, "It has been a while my wife. I haven't appeared this young in two lifetimes it seems. I suspect it's you I have to thank for this new perspective on my old self Hap Sing."

Hap Sing smiled, "It is how I remember you both. I'm sorry if you are experiencing any discomfort. You can change it if you like."

Yuki Nene laughed, "Don't you dare Fu. I'll take this brief respite from old age even if it is just a dream."

Ming Wa Fu looked at the shore, "I don't remember these other structures being here in my last visits. It seems more realistic than ever now."

Hap Sing smiled, "That's good because it is real now. We've skipped past the dreaming to project into my pocket dimension where Shangri La is being built. This place is now as real as Ran Li."

Ming Wa Fu seemed concerned, "So that is what you've been doing for the past one hundred plus years; making your new home real."

Hap Sing nodded, "I have indeed although it hasn't been really all that long from my perspective. Come let's go to the tower so we can visit Li Chan village."

Ming Wa Fu raised an eyebrow, "The abducted villagers are there?"

Hap Sing shook his head, "There was no abduction, only a choice given to the people of Li Chan village."

Ming Wa Fu squeezed Yuki Nene's hand, "We know what kinds of choices you give people Hap Sing. Nothing good ever comes of not choosing what you want."

Hap Sing smiled, "I'm glad you approve. I do try to help people find the best course to take."

They walked up to the tower with Hap Sing in the lead followed by Yuki Nene and Ming Wa Fu hand in hand. They entered the tower, and climbed the stairway until they reached the cupola up top with the giant rotating clear crystal beating with a light in the rhythm of a heartbeat.

Next they found themselves standing on the shore of another bay which was a close replica of the bay where Li Chan village rested in Ran Li. The major difference was several temporary shelters being lived in as the town was under construction by a mix of Li Chan citizens, several pixies, and a number of fair haired elves. The largest of the pixies came winging along the shore like a dragonfly to stop before Hap Sing, Yuki Nene, and Ming Wa Fu.

Hap Sing spoke first, "Greetings Ariel. May I present my protégés Yuki Nene and Ming Wa Fu."

Ariel gave a graceful mid air bow before landing, "Any followers of the Lucky Cricket are welcome here of course. To what do we owe the pleasure of your visit?"

Hap Sing bent over to kiss Ariel on her forehead, "My sweet we came to see you of course."

Ariel flew up into the air and giggled with delight, "You flatter me too much Lucky Cricket. Will you sleep with me again before you leave?"

Yuki Nene raised an eyebrow, "I didn't know you had another girlfriend Hap Sing."

Hap Sing chuckled, "Just a contemporary Nene. Ariel is an avatar of Number Three, and likes to joke about many things. She is the guardian of the Isle of Life, and the being who watches over Li Chan village in my absence."

Ming Wa Fu looked over at the villagers working studiously and seriously on constructing their village, "They are making it just like it was. Even the newer temple is being constructed."

Yuki Nene watched them closely, "They can't see us can they?"

Hap Sing shook his head, "No they can't perceive us. None of them are Chi Masters, and thus only Ariel as the avatar of Number Three can tell our projections

The Lucky Cricket

are present. However, Ming Wa Fu, I want to know if you are satisfied that they are content and happy with their current lot?"

Ming Wa Fu clasped Yuki Nene's hand tightly, "I can't say for certain how they feel, but I don't see any outward signs of duress or unhappiness here. I will relay the message to Emperor Minato that the villagers of Li Chan prosper still. I have to warn you that my influence with this Emperor is not as great as with the past rulers of Ran Li. Minato doubts my absolute loyalties to Ran Li due to my marriage to an outlander."

Hap Sing nodded, "Thus the distance you keep from your wife."

Yuki Nene smiled, "At least in public. We meet in the dreaming as often as time permits. It has really only been a problem since Emperor Minato came into power after the great conflict seventeen years ago. Elements of his support viewed all outsiders as contributing to the conflict, and not all people with outside or mixed background have been treated well since then. Political pressure has driven many of mixed heritages to merge into the Nordland colony since we Nordlanders are accepting of all who follow our basic rules."

Hap Sing nodded, "Your rules being?"

Yuki Nene laughed, "Don't steal from your neighbor. Keep out of your neighbor's business. Don't get in your neighbor's way. Don't try to run your neighbor down with your horse. Don't sleep with your neighbor's mate or progeny without permission. There are several refinements on details of course, but that is pretty much the heart of it for Nordlanders."

Ming Wa Fu smiled, "It is much more complex than that actually, but that is the basics of the situation to put it briefly. No violence has officially broken out, but a lot of hard words have been exchanged. Scuffles have occurred, but we have been in good graces to keep them from spreading into wholesale violence. The lost village of Li Chan has long been a sore point with various Emperors in the past and present. Those Chi Masters who can visit or witness the phenomena reported a stronger repulsion effect over the years. Only the current generation of Tiger Monks failed to feel that repulsion, and only then for the term of their service. Now in the past month the net you cast has been gone, and no one was found in the village by the first Chi Master to discover it and report back. Since then some people from neighboring communities have moved in and claimed ownership of various properties based on claims of inheritance. You've created quite a mess for our courts to resolve Hap Sing."

Hap Sing bowed, "I apologize for any difficulties I may have caused."

Ming Wa Fu looked surprised, "I didn't expect an apology for it, but I'm certain that the Emperor will take it as further ammunition to weaken our position in Ran Li. Word is circulating that he is displeased with his cousin Hiro for not reporting back to him immediately. You did send the boy back today I hope?"

Hap Sing nodded, "He is arriving even as we speak, and will be granted an express audience I'm certain."

Yuki Nene looked concerned, "Will the boy be ok?"

Hap Sing smiled, "I don't fear for his well being at the moment. Your Emperor fears losing Hiro to me I believe, but his choice still remains uncertain. I think a civil tongue will be kept between them, and Hiro will not come to any harm."

Ming Wa Fu glanced at the sky, "Is the time here the same as back in Ran Li?"

Hap Sing shook his head, "It is a very different pace yet. Also it is not too relatively consistent either. About one hour has passed so far."

Yuki Nene looked over at Ming Wa Fu, "I have to tell you that I've chosen poorly I'm afraid."

Ming Wa Fu raised an eyebrow, "You want to go back to Hap Sing now?"

Yuki Nene clasped her husband closely, "Of course not my love. I mean in the candidates I selected for the Tiger Monks."

Ming Wa Fu looked at the ribbons coming from Yuki Nene quickly focusing on one in particular, "That one has changed tint hasn't it. It's quite a bit darker than before. It has become stained in its purpose somehow. What caused this?"

Hap Sing spoke, "Mimosa is under duress I would guess. There is a reason she needed to depart, and someone she needed to report to quickly. I've had her under my close watch since we've met, and only now has Mimosa found the opportunity to get free from my surveillance."

Yuki Nene looked at him closely, "Yet she is still under your surveillance I would guess. I can see her ribbon on you clearly. What can you read from her?"

Hap Sing sighed, "Her parents are in poor spiritual shape at the moment. I would surmise they are prisoners ill fed and mistreated to cause her to cooperate. She is likely sleeping with Hiro to elicit his immature infatuation and cooperation. Thus she is the actual source of his discontent with his situation. Lo Hannah suspects I believe and thus volunteered to give them minimal time to plot together by staying with them."

Yuki Nene looked at Hap Sing closely, "Then Sea Reaver?"

Hap Sing looked at the other thread, "Turned Mimosa down when she tried to temp him. Sea Reaver is still carrying a torch for another woman I believe, and wasn't interested in being her mate or pawn. They are still friends, but I suspect he knows about Hiro and doesn't approve. He probably thinks Hiro is manipulating her, but the opposite is of course the case."

Ming Wa Fu looked at a particular ribbon on Hap Sing, "What of my grandson Ming Ne Yu?"

Hap Sing smiled, "As you can see he has become one of mine. His ribbon takes on the shape of a tiger stripe for those who know how to look, as does the ribbons of Chow Sang and Yu Lo. Their loyalties to me are clear for us to see. I'm sorry if this pains you Fu."

Ming Wa Fu shrugged, "The Tiger Monks were always intended to be your arm when you need them. An arm which is disloyal is worthless to anyone. I'm sorry the others have not been showing more loyalty, and I didn't expect these problems with Mimosa. Will you want to handle it in your own way then?"

The Lucky Cricket

Hap Sing nodded, "It shall be handled by me from this point forward. Don't be surprised by what must happen, but be ready for any unexpected turn of events."

Yuki Nene laughed, "You've been plotting with the Luck again haven't you."

Hap Sing smiled, "We've finally figured out someone's trick which has been bothering the Luck for a very long time. It's a very good trick too, but still only a trick after all."

Yuki Nene looked at Hap Sing closely, "Not a trick you are willing to teach me then?"

Hap Sing shook his head, "It will remain a private trick until my successor comes along."

Ming Wa Fu asked, "Who is your successor to be?"

Hap Sing smiled, "I don't know yet. I believe it is very likely they won't be born for well over a thousand years."

Yuki Nene asked, "How will you find them then?"

Hap Sing chuckled, "That's the beauty of it. Who ever they are, I'll know them because they will be the first one to come to visit me."

Ming Wa Fu raised his arms up in the air, "Mysteries again, it is always mysteries with you."

Ariel floated close, "I know much of what Hap Sing is plotting. I could reveal it for a price if you like."

Yuki Nene looked cautiously, "I thought Hap Sing said you were the avatar of a Number."

Ariel fluttered around, "I am more of a representative with an independent mind much as Hap Sing is independent in his thinking from the Greater Spirit Seven Tailed Tiger. The power of Number Three inhabits me, but my personality is still my own."

Yuki Nene looked at the Ariel with a cautious eye, "Which aspect of existence does Number Three represent?"

Ariel smiled widely, "Number Three is the Tree, and gave life to you, he, and me. Eternal life as well if you choose to serve another power in exchange for the old dead one you serve now."

Yuki Nene looked over at Ming Wa Fu, "Doesn't that sound grand. Dealing with the problems of the living for eternity. What say you husband to never going to your final rest?"

Ming Wa Fu chuckled, "It sounds overrated my dear. I think I'll pass as I've experienced my share of years and more already."

Ariel raised an eyebrow, "You humans are teasing me. Don't tease a pixie if you know what is good for you. I'll grant you another fifty years if you're not careful."

Hap Sing reached over to clasp Ariel's hand, "Not now dearest among the pixies. These two belong to me for now, and get to choose their final reward when their times come."

Ariel fluttered before Hap Sing, "Sleep with me again my dear. Give me the pleasure only you can give."

Hap Sing leaned down to kiss Ariel on the forehead, "That is all you will get, and be happy with that much."

Ariel swooned a moment, and then fluttered off toward the village. Hap Sing, Yuki Nene and Ming Wa Fu watched her depart to rejoin the laboring elves, pixies and humans.

Yuki Nene smiled, "She seems like a handful."

Hap Sing shrugged, "Ariel mainly wants to be praised. Teasing and joking are part and parcel of pixie psychology. She is actually quite a bit older than you two although it may not seem like it. Ariel is just a few years shy of my own age actually."

Yuki Nene laughed, "It would be hard to guess. Did anything she said have a grain of truth to it?"

Hap Sing nodded, "She'll gladly convert you to being followers of Number Three if given the opportunity. She likes to sneak into my bed when I'm asleep, or even when I don't occupy it. She could grant a mortal being practical immortality, and in fact would offer you such if you wished it still Nene or Fu."

Ming Wa Fu snorted, "Overrated I believe. Spirits were not meant to stay forever encased in physical form."

Hap Sing smiled, "You've grown wise over your two lifetimes."

Ming Wa Fu nodded, "I'd like to think I've picked up something worth teaching in all that time. An acceptance of what is tends to help, and one constant is that we mortals have the time given us, and we eventually die. Right my dear?"

Yuki Nene smiled, "Of course my dear. I taught you that myself."

Ming Wa Fu looked at Hap Sing, "What does an immortal think of it?"

Hap Sing chuckled, "I think you've mistaken me for something I'm not. I'm pretty sure I can still be killed. I just won't die on my own anytime soon."

Yuki Nene frowned slightly, "How will you die then?"

Hap Sing looked serious for a moment, "With some undesired help I would presume."

Ming Wa Fu looked at Hap Sing with surprise, "You know something don't you?"

Hap Sing shrugged, "I know what I plan, and I know some of what others plan for me. The trick is making sure everyone gets what they want."

Yuki Nene shook her head, "It is too confusing for me. Is it time for us to return?"

Hap Sing nodded, "Two hours have passed in Ran Li. Time enough for some juicy rumors to have started about my sleeping with your wife again I'm afraid Fu."

Ming Wa Fu laughed, "I've been keeping an eye on you this whole time, and you've remained a gentleman. I'll have to get started soon before the Emperor thinks to summon me to his side. I want to have dinner with my wife under the guise of gathering information on you Hap Sing."

Hap Sing looked over at the village, "They will do fine here you know. I shall be watching and guiding them as needed, and leaving them to their own devices otherwise. They are the first of many who will eventually populate this world. They are my chosen people."

Yuki Nene had a gleam in her eye, "I thought the Chi Masters were to be your chosen people."

Hap Sing nodded, "They will be as they choose me. I'll not force any to pick the path I make. I shall be the mountain they travel around. Those that choose me shall eventually become known as the Chi Masters with the will of fire. These people of Li Chan village have chosen me for generations, and their new land has been given to them as a reward."

Ming Wa Fu nodded, "I'm satisfied they are rewarded, but the Emperor will consider them as stolen from him. You've likely made an enemy of him, and his other advisors will push him to deal with you."

Hap Sing looked up at the sky, "What happens is not your fault. I recommend you continue to separate yourself from me politically. I advise that you make it clear I am beyond your ability to manipulate."

Ming Wa Fu looked at the sky as well, "That last is nothing but the truth."

Hap Sing looked back at Ming Wa Fu, "It is easier to tell a truth and be convincing than to lie anyway."

Ming Wa Fu spoke, "They will be using surveillance to watch you now that they know where you are. They have magical and mundane means to learn of your plans."

Hap Sing spoke, "I've been assured that they will find it impossible to watch me here."

Ming Yuki Nene clasped Ming Wa Fu's hand, "We shall remain as formal and distanced as usual my husband. Hap Sing will do what he must, and we will go through the hoops necessary to maintain your position and the safety of the Chi Masters at large. If you must separate from us, then accuse Hap Sing in the name of the Emperor when the time is come. We all know the well being of Ran Li is what really resides in your heart."

Hap Sing dined on the simple fare prepared by Sister Kenara which consisted of potatoes, rice, bread, chicken, and some vegetables unusual to him. At the table were Lady and Lord Ming sitting side by side. Chow Sang sat beside a muscular platinum haired woman named Sister Norla. Sister Norla was taller than even Lady Ming. Finally Yu Lo sat next to Hap Sing at the table's head, Lord Ming at his side, and across from Sister Kenara.

Hap Sing noticed that Chow Sang and Sister Norla were sitting on their cushions fairly closely together, and occasionally stole brief glances at each other. Hap Sing gave a brief smile at seeing the beginning of something between them. Sister Norla seemed more suited to battle than a life in a religious order, and she contrasted in interesting ways with the studious sharp witted Chow Sang.

Lady Ming spoke, "Something pleases you Hap Sing?"

Hap Sing nodded, "These things you called pea pods are very good. I should introduce them to Li Chan village when I get the chance."

Yu Lo raised an eyebrow, "All the villagers have left master. Who would tend the crop?"

Lord Ming replied, "Disciple Yu Lo. Have you learned so little of manners at my academy? Do not address your elders without asking permission first."

Yu Lo bowed down briefly, "I'm sorry Lord Ming, master Cricket."

Hap Sing smiled, "Think nothing of it Yu Lo. Young Ming Wa Fu is merely upset that he has been forced by the Emperor to come visit me."

Lord Ming replied, "At my advanced years I can no longer be considered young master Hap Sing. Yu Lo remember to show respect and use master Hap Sing's proper name."

Lady Ming placed her hand on her husband's arm, "Remember they are a gift my dear. If Hap Sing doesn't mind his behavior, then you should not mind either."

Yu Lo flushed in embarrassment, "I'm sorry and beg your forgiveness."

Hap Sing laughed, "None is required. Just be yourself as you have in the past. Master Cricket is fine. In fact I prefer it to my given name now. Ming Wa Fu is merely trying to teach you still. Like his father he's a diligent instructor."

Hap Sing noticed that as the attention at the table was focused on the conversation with Yu Lo; Chow Sang and Sister Norla has subtly moved their hands under the table until they were briefly gently touching each other. They quickly drew their hands apart as Chow Sang caught the direction of his gaze.

Hap Sing looked at Lady Ming, "Your pardon Nene, but I seem to have some missing knowledge regarding your order here. Is it the case that your sisters are expected to remain celibate?"

Lady Ming glanced at Sister Norla whose hands were back on the table as she began to blush lightly. Lady Ming smiled her own little smile and overtly moved to hold hands with Lord Ming.

Lady Ming answered, "I've been married for over a century. So the answer to your question is that celibacy is not required of our sisters. They may marry, and in fact many of the sisters working here are widows with grown children. A few of the sisters are still married, but they have husbands who spend much of their time out to sea."

Hap Sing looked at Lord Ming, "What of the Tiger Monks Ming Wa Fu? Are they required to remain celibate?"

Lord Ming thought a moment, "There is no official requirement as such, but each has chosen to do so while their period of service has been in effect. Are you seeking to find a match for my grandson Ming Ne Yu perhaps? It is past time for him to settle down, and it was only over my private personal objection than he was allowed to join the tiger monks as their leader."

Hap Sing raised an eyebrow, "You had an objection?"

Lord Ming nodded, "I'm expecting more great grandchildren, and his running around as a Tiger Monk is making it difficult for him to settle down."

Hap Sing nodded, "I see. Then has any of the past leaders been married?"

Lord Ming shook his head, "The lifestyle of the Tiger Monk leadership is not conducive to long term relations. Many spouses do not willingly go through a seven year separation. Most spouses would not have been able to enter Li Chan village due to the net I watched you place. Of course now I guess that isn't an issue anymore. The Emperor Minato of Ran Li is very interested to learn of what you have done to his people who lived there."

Hap Sing shrugged, "They have departed Lord Ming."

Lord Ming raised an eyebrow, "That much is obvious as their personal belongings were packed. The Emperor finds it curious that all the currency bearing the image of his father was left behind. There is also the question of where they have gone. There is no indication of any group leaving that area in small numbers or large. Only the trail of the Tiger Monks heading to the port town of Sun Chu was found."

Hap Sing asked, "You have been following us then?"

Lord Ming nodded, "The forces of the Emperor have been attempting to ascertain your location it is true. The Emperor was in fear that his dear cousin Togusawa Hiro might have been in danger."

Hap Sing smiled, "Then he should be relieved that Togusawa Hiro is in his presence even now."

Lord Ming smiled faintly, "It was good of you to send him, but I believe the Emperor will be summoning you to his presence soon."

Hap Sing looked at a seemingly empty spot on the table, "The ribbons say that the forces of the Emperor are approaching even now. Nene, please have your Sisters extend them the fullest courtesy. There is no need to be worried as I will depart with them voluntarily."

Lady Ming replied, "Sister Norla please depart when you are finished eating to inform the other sisters that no violence is to be offered the forces of the Emperor when they arrive. Have them open the gates and return to their homes. Take Chow Sang with you to the Nordland market after they are gone."

Sister Norla questioned, "The Nordland market Lady Ming?"

Lady Ming nodded, "You know the one I mean."

Chow Sang stood up, "I will stay Lady Ming."

Lady Ming shook her head, "No you will not stay Chow Sang. You will go to the Nordland market with Sister Norla. Yu Lo here will stay by Hap Sing's side, and inform the rest of you what happens."

Chow Sang looked at Hap Sing, "Master Hap Sing? What are your orders?"

Hap Sing took a bite of rice covered with pea pods, "Have fun shopping with Sister Norla. Please keep her safe for me."

Sister Norla stood up as well, "Lady Ming I must protest. As your assigned bodyguard I must be at your side in cases like this. I need no protection from the forces of the Emperor."

Lady Ming shook her head, "This is an order Sister Norla. Go have what fun you may on this outing. Keep Chow Sang safe as he will keep you safe."

Sister Norla's face became grimly set, "What if they take you as well?"

Lady Ming barked a short derisive laugh with a hard edge, "They are welcome to try. They will learn the hard way what the favor of the White Raven means if they do."

Yu Lo looked at Hap Sing, "Why will you have me come along then master Cricket? Do you expect me to protect you?"

Hap Sing shook his head, "You shall be the witness for the others. Let them know what you learn from my summoning."

Yu Lo looked at him, "You promised the others you would be here in three days."

Hap Sing shook his head, "I said those who wished to continue with me shall return here by that time. I did not guarantee I would be here to greet them. I have granted them this time to settle any remaining issues while making their choices. Now I believe your parents have just arrived at the temple. Please go visit with them while you can. You have approximately three hours left with them before the forces of the Emperor arrive. They should be gone before then."

As Yu Lo, Chow Sang, and Sister Norla departed Sister Kenara cleared away the dishes from their meal. Hap Sing sat in silence looking over at Lady and Lord Ming as they sipped their after dinner tea. Finally Hap Sing looked through the window at the darkening sky in the west.

Hap Sing asked no one in particular, "Ninjas who await the coming of night then?"

Lord Ming replied, "I must return to report before that time, but yes I would surmise regular troops with the invitation, and ninjas in hiding to enforce it. You'll have to go Hap Sing otherwise the Emperor will unleash unpleasant actions upon any who harbor you. You must stay uninvolved my dear wife."

Lady Ming shrugged, "Those meant to die today shall die. The White Raven knows this. You should as well my husband."

Lord Ming nodded in reply, "I know, but I don't have to like it. One question before I leave though. Who killed that sea dragon which was found in Li Chan?"

Hap Sing sat silently for a moment in contemplation, "I would say it was killed by whatever god decided to send it to interfere with me. I was simply the instrument in its destruction."

Lord Ming looked bothered, "If I were to say it was sent by the Emperor to watch for your arrival, then what would your reply be then?"

Hap Sing looked grim, "I would say that your emperor has made some very dangerous acquaintances. The kind of acquaintances who dispose of those no longer required for their goals."

Chapter 30 Imperial Audience

he squad of sixteen soldiers dressed in their fancy black and silver lacquered wood parade armor approached the temple grounds of the White Raven in an orderly rank bearing lit paper lanterns with every third man. They surrounded four men carrying an ornate wooden palanquin. Less obvious to normal observers were the hidden ninjas dressed in working black outfits in a loose circle surrounding the graveyard for the last hour.

Hap Sing looked at the approaching soldiers and then at Yu Lo beside him, "How many do you make them to be young Tiger Monk?"

Yu Lo looked with lightly gleaming eyes, "The soldiers are the Emperor's finest dress peacocks. They know their weapons functionally, but are picked mainly for their uniform height and bearing. I would count them at the sixteen you see approaching."

Hap Sing smiled, "Too easy my young cousin. What about the real threat?"

Yu Lo smiled, "I can clearly see four ninjas. They are the amateurs meant to distract us. The unseen group are the other eight ninjas well hidden from normal eyes."

Hap Sing nodded, "You can see them how?"

Yu Lo spoke clearly, "Their auras are quite bright, and light them up in a spectacular manner to the sight. They are very skilled Master Cricket. I would count them as another thirty men in functionality if not numbers."

Hap Sing frowned, "The man being carried in the palanquin. What do you think of him?"

Yu Lo shrugged, "An arcane caster of much skill if his aura is any measure. He is of unknown utility however."

Hap Sing shook his head, "Light blue aura color indicates an affinity for sea and air. He's a water mage I could guess. The servant of someone other than the Emperor if my intuition is correct. One of the Emperor's trusted advisors though. He presents the greatest danger to you here. Promise me to flee and not engage him if trouble starts."

Yu Lo raised an eyebrow, "You don't think I can take a mage?"

Hap Sing shrugged, "Alone on ground of your choosing perhaps, but not this mage in this situation. Remember your parents are still close by, and potentially hostage to your behavior. Now promise before they approach."

Yu Lo nodded, "I promise to not engage the mage unless absolutely necessary."

Hap Sing sighed, "Is that the best I can hope?"

Yu Lo grinned, "Yes. Even I have my limits of control elder cousin Cricket."

The soldiers and the men carrying the palanquin stopped in front of Hap Sing and Yu Lo. An elderly mage dressed in blue robes stepped out from behind the curtains of the Palanquin. He wore his mustache long and draping down his chest. In his hand was a crystalline orb glowing with many shades of pearlescent blue.

The elderly mage looked at Hap Sing and Yu Lo standing together on the path before the temple. He tucked his crystalline ball away into a silken bag hung at his waist. Then stood up proudly with regal bearing.

Hap Sing spoke first, "I will accept the invitation you extend in the name of the Emperor Minato of Ran Li. I will come to his palace to await his pleasure."

The elderly mage blinked slowly twice as Hap Sing continued, "Isn't that the message you were to extend young mage?"

The elderly mage's eyes narrowed, "It seems you've anticipated us Hap Sing. I'll have to let the Emperor know his plans are not as secure as necessary. A mouthy advisor with less discretion than needed I would guess."

Hap Sing laughed, "Nothing so sinister young mage. I have one as well."

Hap Sing reached into nothingness and pulled out his own crystal ball. An image projected from it showing Emperor Minato holding court with his advisors. His voice could be clearly heard in front of all gathered.

The image of Emperor Minato said, "Qui Chang I want you to summon this Hap Sing to an audience with me. Extend every courtesy, but take my fifth regiment squad delta as your escort."

The image of the mage projected from the crystal next, "Your eminence this man is reportedly a dangerous fraud. A powerful Chi Master for certain, but this Hap Sing is a myth, a legend long past gone your eminence."

The image shifted back to the Emperor looking angry, "Are you calling my cousin Hiro a member of the royal dynasty a deceitful fraud Qui Chang? You need to be more careful with your accusations."

The image of the mage appeared again, "I admit it is still possible he is this Hap Sing, but if he were a fraud we wouldn't be able to conclusively tell your eminence. Perhaps you could loan me a squad of your personal ninjas. We could wait for nightfall, and approach him while the ninjas keep us covered for safety of course."

The image of the Emperor nodded, "Enough questioning your orders Qui Chang. Take one squad of ninjas to keep you safe if necessary, but do not offend him or cause him undue concern. This is a cordial invitation to speak with me. Is this understood?"

The image of Qui Chang nodded, "As you command your eminence."

Qui Chang kept his composure as he waited for the image to cease, "I thought that Chi Masters did not use magical apparatus. That one is most unusual in my experience Master Hap Sing."

Hap Sing placed the crystal ball back into hammer space, "I'm told it is the one master crystal ball to rule them all. You shouldn't carry yours around all the time if you don't want someone to listen in on your conversations with important people."

Qui Chang smiled genially, "Para sympathetic magic of course. Crystal resonance of like materials most likely. However, this is enough of pleasantries Master Hap Sing. His eminence the Emperor desires your presence as you well know."

Hap Sing nodded, "I am prepared to follow along with my young cousin Yu Lo here."

Qui Chang looked at Yu Lo briefly, "I am afraid to say that there is no room for him in the palanquin with us."

Hap Sing shrugged, "We shall both walk after your palanquin if you don't mind. You can have your ninjas follow as no one here will cause them trouble."

Qui Chang signaled and the four poorly hidden ninjas came out of the darkness to form an abbreviated escort for Hap Sing and Yu Lo. Qui Chang entered the palanquin and they began their journey down the road toward Yokito and the palace of the Emperor.

After a short time walking Yu Lo asked Hap Sing, "What will happen to the other two ninja who are not following us master Cricket?"

Hap Sing looked at the four nearby ninja forming their escort, "It is advisable that they don't linger in the graveyard of the White Raven for too long. She is a goddess who doesn't think twice about reaping troublesome spirits."

The young ninja beside them looked worried as he asked, "Is this true master Cricket?"

Hap Sing nodded, "The White Raven is unlikely to look kindly upon those who disturb her worshipers. You may escape her in the short span of your life, but eventually all mortal spirits will have to pass through her domain. I find that she is a patient goddess with a very long memory for wrongs and offenses against her."

The young ninja made a hand sign to one of the six ninjas following in darkness. That ninja departed, and several minutes later the ninja returned with their two missing companions. All twelve of the ninja eventually formed up around Hap Sing and Yu Lo creating a protective circle around them.

A ninja wearing a headband with a deep red sun on the back cloth stepped beside Hap Sing as he walked. Hap Sing smiled at him and nodded. The ninja looked briefly around and then pointed at the palanquin.

The senior ninja quietly asked, "I need a private word with you master Cricket."

Hap Sing froze time around them and then looked at the waiting ninja who didn't reveal his surprise, "What do you need to say master Ninja?"

The ninja held quiet a moment, "Is it secure?"

Hap Sing nodded, "Nothing can hear us now which isn't divinely graced or spiritually aware. Time has briefly stopped for everyone here except for us."

The ninja spoke, "I am Liu Fan the current Grandmaster of the ninja force. When the word came that a ninja escort was requested by Qui Chang I assigned myself to the mission to gain this opportunity to speak with you."

Hap Sing nodded, "Your opportunity is here. Say what you need."

Liu Fan nodded, "Your former friend Li Hung left the ninja Grandmasters who followed him explicit standing orders that you were to be protected at all costs for the sake of Ran Li master Cricket. Qui Chang is the visible spokesman of a powerful coalition of mages and priests who are dissatisfied with the position of prominence held by the Chi Masters over one hundred years now. They have worked diligently to undermine your position with the current Emperor Minato for the last seventeen years."

Hap Sing gave a brief smile, "I thank you for your warning Liu Fan."

Liu Fan bowed a short way, "They are plotting outside of our ability to detect as well master Cricket. They are using magical means to communicate which prevent our surveillance. They are very cautious to leave no incriminating documents within our grasp."

Hap Sing grew thoughtful, "You are wondering if my crystal ball can penetrate their plots against me."

Liu Fan nodded, "Such came to my mind when I saw the device you held. The Emperor's audience room is screened from traditional or magical observation, yet your crystal ball was able to breach that barrier."

Hap Sing shrugged, "It won't work for you if that is what you are wondering. The crystal ball I possess will only work for certain beings as it wasn't created for mortal use."

Liu Fan nodded again, "I understand, but I was wondering if you could watch them, and relay what you know to us so we can better protect the kingdom of Ran Li."

Hap Sing shook his head, "You and I know that would only set up a situation of hearsay. It would expose your dissatisfaction with the way the kingdom is being run, and potentially put you in conflict with your own Emperor. You already know what they intend even if you don't yet see the means of it."

Liu Fan nodded, "They intend to put themselves into power with the Emperor as their controlled figurehead."

Hap Sing smiled, "So do you understand why I shall not assist you in the way you request then?"

Lui Fan paused before answering, "I believe I do master Cricket. You need to not be seen as trying to obtain power for yourself. Any action to counter them will be perceived as your own ambition to rise."

Hap Sing smiled again, "Li Hung would be proud of you as his successor. Continue to support the Emperor to protect Ran Li. Leave this conflict between mages, Chi Masters, and priests to be settled by the guidance of his wisdom."

Lui Fan cautiously asked, "If the Emperor demonstrates a lack of wisdom, what then?"

Hap Sing answered, "Then know that as a mortal no ruler lives forever, and that time will fix what haste and violence can never correct. The kingdom of Ran Li is much more than me or the Emperor. It is the people of Ran Li. Either the Emperor supports the people, or else there is no more Ran Li."

Lui Fan nodded, "What are your directions to us then in this matter master Cricket?"

Hap Sing looked at Lui Fan closely, "Remember you serve the Emperor who serves the people. If the Emperor calls for your action on behalf of the people, then follow his commands. If he calls for your action against the people, then follow your conscience."

Hap Sing synchronized them with normal time and they continued to walk along the road.

Hap Sing answered the original question of Lui Fan, "Life is never totally secure young ninja. Yet your duty remains."

Lui Fan replied as they walked along, "Yes master Cricket."

Hap Sing and Yu Lo walked with two ceremonial guards down an ornate hallway of one of the outer buildings of the palace complex. They had entered Yokito without any undue notice as the hour of their arrival was late. The gate guards had automatically let them pass the first layers of the palace defenses, and the ninja forces quickly separated from them shortly before their entry into the palace grounds proper.

The palanquin carrying Qui Chang had continued further on to the complex while two ceremonial guards were detailed to show Hap Sing and Yu Lo to the guest quarters. Once they arrived the two guards stood station outside their doorway as a small host of servants came to see to their needs.

The servants drew up a bath for both of them, and as Hap Sing and Yu Lo were washed by a pair of young men, their clothes were taken by a serving woman. After they stepped out of their baths they found a new pair of silk tiger monk style robes and clean undergarments were waiting for their use.

Hap Sing raised an eyebrow at seeing that his personal belongings were gone, "I should have known not to leave them unattended."

Yu Lo was curious, "What is wrong master Cricket?"

Hap Sing sighed, "They took my fishing pole."

Yu Lo shrugged, "It looked pretty ordinary to me."

Hap Sing nodded, "It was exceedingly ordinary, and very easy to replace in fact, but I've had it for over two centuries now. I've grown fond of it."

Yu Lo laughed, "I think we can get it back if we ask politely."

Hap Sing approached one of the waiting maid servants, "I'm wondering if you could return my fishing pole. I don't want to lose track of it."

The maid bowed and departed from the guest quarters. Another maid came in thirty minutes later with food and drink. Yu Lo thanked her and carefully examined the food and drink.

Yu Lo shook his head, "It's been altered. It looks like a serum has been applied which loosens the tongue of the imbiber of the drink. Another which causes poor physical coordination in the subject is in the food."

Hap Sing nodded, "Let me have those."

Yu Lo asked, "Are you certain you want them?"

Hap Sing smiled, "I won't eat any, but I do have some other supplies stored away which might suit."

Hap Sing took the dishes and opened a hole of nothingness to place the flask and plates. He then closed that hole and opened a different one with similar looking plates with a better quality of food on them.

Yu Lo shook his head, "How did you get that?"

Hap Sing smiled, "It was the food prepared for Qui Chang's return. I left him the food which was prepared for us. I think you'll find this food unaltered and of higher quality than our own meal would have been."

Yu Lo looked concerned, "I thought Qui Chang could watch us through his crystal?"

Hap Sing nodded, "He or someone else most certainly is watching. I hope they appreciate my jest in a timely manner. I would hate for Qui Chang to be affected by such a mysterious substance placed unknowingly into his food. It would be rather unkind of me to hope otherwise."

Yu Lo shook his head, "Why did you do it then master Cricket?"

Hap Sing smiled, "I've got a stubborn streak and I don't like people playing court politics young cousin. That was designed not to harm but to discredit me before the Emperor Minato. Let's eat and get to bed then. I think the Emperor will likely expect us to be ready for his summons."

The next morning servants came by with their breakfast. After an inspection by Yu Lo it was determined to be safe to eat. As they dined they spoke of trivial matters such as the weather and the fishing prospects in the private ponds on the palace grounds.

Hap Sing shook his head, "It is likely only ornamental bottom feeding fish like koi anyway. I'll wager there is nothing good tasting like a tuna or salmon in those ponds."

Yu Lo shrugged, "I wouldn't know, but we could ask a servant."

Hap Sing finished his rice ball, "I'd rather find my fishing pole again."

Yu Lo pointed at a servant who came to remove their dishes, "Aren't you the maid who master Cricket asked for his fishing pole last night?"

The young woman looked startled, "Yes lord Tiger Monk."

Yu Lo looked at her closely, "Where has it gone then?"

The young woman flushed, "The guards asked the head servant to remove it. They thought it a possible weapon as the pole is very sturdy. Only the Imperial guards are allowed weapons inside the grounds of the palace. I'm sorry I could not help you master Tiger Monks."

Hap Sing gave her a gentle smile, "Do not fret about it child. I will retrieve the pole upon my departure then."

A couple of minutes later Togusawa Hiro entered the guest quarters looking depressed, "I see that they have summoned you anyway master Cricket. I'm sorry I could not get my cousin to listen to what I was saying better. It seems many of his advisors are trying to convince him that you are a fraud dreamed up by the Chi Masters in a bid for power."

The Lucky Cricket

Hap Sing nodded, "I'd learned as much already, but your talk must have done some good. The Emperor is treating us well so far."

Togusawa Hiro looked embarrassed, "I'm ashamed master Cricket. You let me know that meeting my cousin would cause problems, but I thought I knew the politics of the court better. I've endangered everything you've worked to achieve for the Chi Masters in Ran Li. It is all my fault."

Hap Sing shook his head, "Coming to Yokito was my idea. I knew it would not pass unnoticed after all these years, but what has happened in the past is now just spilled wine. We will simply have to make the best of what remains in our cups."

Togusawa Hiro bowed down, "They are spying on you even now. They are concerned about your fishing pole master Cricket. The mages have found your fishing hook, and the greed in their hearts is plainly evident to me now."

Yu Lo asked, "What do you mean his fishing hook Hiro? I don't understand what you mean."

Hap Sing sighed, "I didn't think about it enough. My fishing hook is made of pure admantium."

Yu Lo's eyes widened, "Set admantium? That is impossible. Only lost means could be used to work it. Something that size could be worth hundreds maybe a thousand gold coins. It's indestructible."

Hap Sing shook his head, "It is not really indestructible if you know the trick of it."

Togusawa Hiro looked at him with grief in his eyes, "They mean to learn how and where you obtained it. The mages suspect even more could be discovered if you reveal your source. Enough to make a blade worthy of a god even."

Hap Sing shrugged, "They are looking for the wrong thing then. Such a thing as that fishing hook is ultimately worthless to them unless they actually like to fish. It is a good hook no doubt, but it is not functionally worth that much in reality. Only the rarity of the material makes it valuable."

Togusawa Hiro looked at him, "You know where more could be found then? Is there enough for a blade after all?"

Hap Sing gave a sad smile, "It is no place that any mage could obtain it. Even the gods don't know the secret of its source."

Togusawa Hiro examined Hap Sing closely, "Do you know the secret of its source master Cricket?"

Hap Sing nodded, "It really is impossible to obtain in large quantities for anyone else, but yes I know how admantium came into existence."

Togusawa Hiro looked at him, "What is the secret?"

Hap Sing shrugged, "I'm warning you the price is much more dear than the admantium itself. Perhaps you'd like everyone to know how it can be obtained."

Togusawa Hiro lowered his head, "Right, I'm sorry master Cricket. I've already forgotten the mages who are watching us even now."

Hap Sing nodded, "The mages, true, but others as well Hiro. The price of this knowledge would destroy Ran Li and beyond. Several gods want to know this information and are listening in even now, but it has never been offered up for sale. The best that can be done is to provide the material in the form desired, and even that comes at a very steep rate."

Togusawa Hiro raised his head, "How steep do you mean?"

Hap Sing shook his head, "Eternal wars to obtain and hold such an item. The very gods would send out crusades to gather it for their use. No single kingdom could stand before such an effort."

Togusawa Hiro dropped his head down to look at his feet, "I'm sorry master Cricket. They won't believe me that you are speaking the truth. Certain priests know that the seven tailed tiger spirit holds the secret to admantium. Their gods have demanded the Emperor extract this information from you. I'm sorry I ever responded to the orders of my cousin Minato. I didn't want this."

Hap Sing placed his hand gently on his lowered head, "There is nothing to forgive young Hiro. You followed your duty as your heart felt strongest. There is no shame in honestly being used by shameless men seeking power. I hold no ill will or regret for you actions."

Togusawa Hiro raised his head slightly, "I've done bad things. Things I know I should not have done. Because of it I've listened to questionable advice which led my heart to doubt my calling in life."

Hap Sing placed his arm around Hiro raising him back upright, "I'm only a fisherman lord Tiger Monk Togusawa Hiro cousin of the Emperor Minato of Ran Li. You need not apologize to me for the choices you've made in honesty, or in confusion."

Togusawa Hiro began to silently weep, "I've lied to you and Master Ming. I didn't want to report to my cousin, but I was coerced. I was weak when I needed to be strong."

Hap Sing nodded, "I understand that weakness, and I hope in the future you can conquer it. Love does strange things to a heart. Love of a woman, and the love for your parents. It causes us to sometimes make strange choices in life."

Togusawa Hiro raised his eyes, "You know about us?"

Hap Sing spoke, "I've known you and Mimosa were lovers the first time I saw you standing on the beach in Li Chan. The ribbons tell me much about people, and their problems. What you don't know is that Mimosa's parents have been captured and threatened with death to gain her cooperation. She was forced to seduce you in order to protect them."

Togusawa Hiro's brows drew together, "I was seduced?"

Hap Sing shrugged, "Don't feel bad about it. Women have their ways after all. Just understand that Mimosa feels even worse about what she has done than you. Love makes people think in strange ways. It hinders our thinking sometimes, but it can also make us better people too."

Togusawa Hiro looked at Hap Sing closely, "Is my cousin a part of this?"

Hap Sing nodded, "Your cousin is a man beset by hard choices in holding his land together in uncertain times. It is very hard to know who to trust, and who to watch carefully. Not everyone has the luxury of reading character through spiritual connections. Looking at your cousin's faint ribbon on you, I would say he's trying to do his best, but is as beset by uncertainty and distrust as you yourself are."

Togusawa Hiro looked at him, "What can I do to help you master Hap Sing?"

Hap Sing looked at him with a smile, "Endeavor to become the kind of man your cousin the Emperor can rely upon to support Ran Li. Look beyond the politics of people seeking power, and to helping those who really need help in their lives."

Togusawa Hiro shook his head, "They mean to extract the secret from you any way they can."

Hap Sing sighed, "I am sorry for that Hiro and Lo. However, there is no way they can succeed in what they plan."

Yu Lo spoke up, "Why is that Hap Sing?"

Hap Sing looked grimly, "It is a secret I'm fully capable of keeping to my grave and beyond."

Yu Lo looked concerned, "Do you think it is that dire master Hap Sing?"

Hap Sing nodded, "Most certainly. Because I've never told myself the secret. I can't possibly reveal what only a different part of me knows."

Yu Lo was even more worried, "The greater spirit seven tailed tiger is prepared to let a part of itself die to keep such a secret?"

Hap Sing laughed a bitter laugh, "More than prepared young naive Yu Lo. It is perfectly willing to do so. I'm just a mere mortal appendage to it no more important than a toenail cut off when it becomes too bothersome."

Yu Lo began sweating lightly, "What about us then?"

Hap Sing shook his head slowly, "It thinks less of you than it does of me by a long shot. It would willingly sacrifice every mortal within one thousand miles long before it would choose to reveal such a secret."

Yu Lo looked at Togusawa Hiro, "We've got to help master Cricket escape immediately."

Togusawa Hiro looked stunned, "How could it do such a thing?"

Hap Sing looked at the number of new ribbons crossing around their guest rooms closing in on them before answering, "It really doesn't think much of mortal beings after all."

Several bolts of lightning ricocheted through the room causing Togusawa Hiro and Yu Lo to drop to the ground in massive convulsions. Hap Sing looked at the five wizards and three priests who entered the room. The wizards were surprised to see him unaffected by their spells.

Qui Chang called from outside the room, "I'll have to remember that lightning must actually be a corollary to fire. However, I know that water is the antithesis and your weakness. Douse him with the waters of the God Aquonis."

The priests each turned over a miniature silver ewer and a stream of water issued forth from the ewers and doused Hap Sing. The mages began a synchronised chant which caused a transparent magical barrier to form around Hap Sing. He found himself floating in a pool of water nearly up to the ceiling.

Hap Sing raised his eyebrow as he tread water, "Qui Chang if you want me to come with you a simple request would do. I will not fight against you. It's kind of silly to douse a fisherman in water after all. I do know how to swim."

Qui Chang stepped into the room cautiously to examine the situation before speaking, "You are charged Hap Sing by his eminence Emperor Minato with sedition, kidnapping, treason, and failure to pay taxes on exotic goods. Additionally the being known as Number Seven is charged with unlawful possession of a mortal avatar."

Hap Sing pushed down with his hand on the surface of the water. The walls of the invisible force cage began to bulge. The mages began their incantations to reenforce the walls as Hap Sing pushed his hand even more forcefully upon the surface.

Qui Chang stepped back a half step, "Stop him you fools. Add more water into the cage."

One of the priests shook his head, "He's using the water he has already. Any more will just give him more to work with."

Qui Chang looked at Hap Sing, "You're the elemental font of fire. How can you do this? The water should cancel out your powers. Every arcane theory proves this fact."

Hap Sing used his other hand and pushed both down firmly. The walls of the force cage burst asunder sending a cascade of water rushing through the room and knocking over the wizards. The three priests of Aquonis stood firmly against the waves."

Hap Sing smiled slightly as his eyes took on a feral look, "Did I fail to mention I am the font of every elemental power. Fire is just the commonly known one associated with me. Realistically none of the powers cancel out any other. That is just a myth cooked up by half baked arcane practitioners like yourself Qui Chang to explain something they will never fully understand. Each power has its purpose and its place."

Hap Sing waved his arms and the three silver ewers held by the priests of Aquonis burst asunder in a great gush of water which knocked them over like a river flowing over a waterfall.

Qui Chang pulled out his crystalline orb and hastily called out, "Master he is breaking free."

A black sulfurous pit formed in the floor next to Qui Chang and a lank greasy haired figure rose from it as the water in the room quickly drained down it. The figure focused its dead seeming gaze upon Hap Sing and gave a sinister smile.

Rendalk Flügg shook his head, "I'm not that easily killed Number Seven. Your audience with the Emperor is canceled."

Chapter 31 Revenge

Rendalk Flügg raised his hands and a cage made of black inky creeping tendrils of force formed around Hap Sing. Hap Sing began to glow brightly momentarily, and then his aura rapidly dimmed.

Hap Sing tried to free himself reaching out to open a pocket of nothingness, but the force projecting from the writhing cage sapped his innate ability to access the alternative locations once available.

Hap Sing looked at Rendalk Flügg with a confused expression, "What have you done?"

Rendalk Flügg glared at him, "I've learned from my past errors. I've done my research on you. I've corrupted your Tiger Monks and the kingdom you prize so much from within. I'm not letting you prepare the ground this time."

Hap Sing looked at the cage surrounding him, "I know that already. How have you cut me off from my power?"

Rendalk Flügg laughed, "Do you like it? It's a special trick I've learned just to capture you."

Hap Sing calmly looked at it, "I don't understand the principles behind it."

Rendalk Flügg nodded, "You never will. That is what makes it so effective against those like you."

Hap Sing began feeling physically weak, "What are you doing to me?"

Rendalk Flügg's voice rose in triumph, "I'm getting my due. That power you hold will come into my possession. Bit by bit I shall drain that power, and the secrets behind its use. I shall free myself of these cursed chains placed on me by your kind."

Hap Sing dropped to his knees, "What do you mean my kind? I've never done anything to you."

Rendalk Flügg brought his two arms closer together making fists of his hands and tightening the force cage about Hap Sing, "I exist because of what you are. You're to blame. All of you are to blame. I'll see your secrets stripped away Number by Number until my kind are freed to command and rule all physical and spiritual existence. All spirits shall worship us once more, and we shall feast upon their pain and misery as is our due."

Hap Sing fell over onto his side and began breathing in a labored manner as he whispered, "You're a minion of an elder god."

Rendalk Flügg shook his head sadly, "I am one of the new elder gods. Formed in their image."

The three priests of Aquonis briefly glanced at each other, and then they began running for the exit from the chamber. The last thing Hap Sing witnessed before falling unconscious was the inky tendrils of the force cage reach out to strike them dead.

ap Sing floated for an indeterminate time in darkness unable to reach back to the dreaming. He focused a moment and the dreaming that existed within his mind took shape as a normal sized the Luck. They stood facing each other for a moment of silence.

The Luck spoke, "Do you wish to release me?"

Hap Sing shrugged, "I wish to understand what drives a being like Rendalk Flügg to such hatred. I don't know the right course before I can understand the obstacle attempting to block my path."

The Luck raised an eyebrow, "It is the madness of the Elder Gods released anew upon the material planes. Their hatreds, lusts, greed, and unholy desires pushed back into semi-mortal material existence after untold eons of frustration. At your age you're much too innocent still to grasp it fully, but I would never want you to fully comprehend the depths of such a thing."

Hap Sing frowned, "Is their any chance of reasoning with such a being?"

The Luck shook its head, "There is resistance, or capitulation. A common understanding or goal is not possible in my personal estimation. However, I am only one seventh of myself right now and unable to reach the other parts for consensus or confirmation. It lies to the two of us to determine our course forward."

Hap Sing nodded, "What are our reasonable courses forward from here?"

The Luck frowned, "The only reasonable course forward is resistance. Capitulation would mean the end of material existence as it currently exists, and the return of the Elder Gods at their most powerful."

Hap Sing shook his head, "Why do they go to such lengths?"

The Luck looked behind it briefly, "They seek revenge for having their ambitions thwarted. They truly are madness. Do you want me to face this madness for you?"

Hap Sing smiled faintly, "That's why you merged with me isn't it after all. My ability to resist the corruption of this madness."

The Luck blurred and changed form from that of a tiger to an identical Hap Sing, "Yes, but you'll find I'm a quick learner."

Hap Sing was surprised, "What do you fear?"

The Luck smiled, "I don't fear what is about to happen to resist Rendalk Flügg. However, I also don't want to subject you to it. If you release me, I think you'll find that I have a couple tricks left up my sleeves."

he crack of a cat-of-thirteen tails flaying the skin from across his back awoke Hap Sing. Hap Sing was stripped to his waist with his right arm tied high on one post, and his left arm tied high on another. Each of his legs had a shackle with a short chain and a heavy iron ball attached.

The sun beat down brightly from high in the sky. A group of mages and priests in dark robes stood in a large circle around the high walled courtyard bearing silent witness. Hap Sing looked over to his right side and saw the slowly bleeding form of Yu Lo hanging from another set of posts apparently unconscious, but still breathing. The only other figure immediately recognized by Hap Sing was Rendalk Flügg sitting on a chair facing him.

Hap Sing shifted to the second sight and saw that the black inky writhing cage of force was still surrounding him, but not Yu Lo. The bars were thinner than originally, and flickered occasionally. However a quick examination determined that it wasn't fatigue on the part of Rendalk Flügg, but a deliberate lessening of their power.

Rendalk Flügg smiled briefly, "I'm so glad you could rejoin us. I was afraid I might have permanently damaged your abilities in limiting them. It wouldn't do to have you unable to wake and answer my questions."

Hap Sing's back gradually began to heal as he spoke, "Release Yu Lo if you want me to answer you."

Rendalk Flügg frowned and spoke sternly, "You are not in a position to request anything. You will give into my demands, and your only reward will be a quicker death."

At a wave of his hand an unseen person behind Hap Sing struck his back repeatedly with the cat-of-thirteen tails. The bleeding cuts began forming many times faster than Hap Sing's healing could keep up. Hap Sing twitched and coughed, but didn't utter a single cry or scream.

Rendalk Flügg held up a single finger and the scourging ceased momentarily, "I had a question in mind, but all of this wonderful entertainment caused me to forget it again."

Rendalk Flügg waved his hand and Hap Sing could see a large brutish man step behind Yu Lo and begin stripping his pants off until only his loin cloth covered him. The man then began whipping Yu Lo's legs until they began to bleed heavily.

Yu Lo awoke and began moaning piteously in weak gasps of pain. Hap Sing watched in silence with a look of worry and concern plain on his face. Rendalk Flügg smiled grimly as he witnessed the reaction.

Rendalk Flügg turned to speak to one of his subordinates, "We've found his weak point as suspected. Have you located the others yet?"

The robed priest spoke, "Unfortunately Lo Hannah is within the confines of the temple of the god Palnor. Even you must understand that they still have much influence here, and Palnor has shown a distinct propensity to provide direct intervention in Ran Li. We dare not seek her out until she leaves them master Flügg."

Rendalk Flügg frowned, "Enough of your excuses already. What about the others Decarius?"

Decarius swallowed heavily, "No luck there either master. The Chi Master academy contains Ming Wa Fu and Ming Ne Yu, and they have sealed it from our interference. Every one of our attempts to infiltrate them have ended in failure and death for the party attempting it. Unless we can convince the Emperor to disband them there is little we can openly do against them now. The whereabouts of Chow

Sang and Sea Reaver have still not been determined yet. Togusawa Hiro sits under the protection of his cousin the Emperor who is still angry at Qui Chang and your pet mages who brought him down in capturing Hap Sing."

Rendalk Flügg raised a hand indicating Decarius and the torturer to stop, "Enough!"

Decarius hesitantly spoke, "We do know the location of Ming Yuki Nene, and reportedly her weak goddess is growing vulnerable to the forces of Mortis as we speak. Perhaps she would work for your purposes."

Rendalk Flügg shook his head, "Her goddess is a dreadful one as you priests of Mortis should well know by now. I've made the mistake of sending forces against that bitch twice. I shall not repeat that mistake again anytime soon."

Decarius quietly queried, "What are your wishes master?"

Rendalk Flügg frowned, "Bring Mimosa here then. Summon Qui Chang to my presence as well when he is done placating the Emperor."

Rendalk Flügg motioned to the torturer who moved back behind Hap Sing and began scourging his back again. The healing of his wounds was even slower this time. Yu Lo apparently lapsed back into unconsciousness from shock and blood loss. A priest of the dark god Mortis stepped forward to apply a healing salve to staunch the worst of Yu Lo's bleeding.

Rendalk Flügg smiled grimly at Hap Sing, "I fully intend to keep you and him alive and in agony for as long as it takes to get my answers. If he dies, then another shall take his place, and I will find anyone and everyone you've ever considered dear if that is what it takes. Now tell me where do I find more of the metal you've used to make this fishing hook."

Hap Sing kept his silence and changed his gaze up toward the bright sun in the early afternoon sky. As he was whipped his healing slowed down even more, and gradually Yu Lo's flesh began to heal subtly faster than the salve applied by the priest of Mortis would normally provide. A quick glance through his second sight showed the spirit ribbon between Yu Lo and himself was glowing brightly with power once it left the confines of the magical cage around him.

Yu Lo awoke once more. As he did Hap Sing noticed that several of the ribbons attached to him also glowed brightly in response to his regaining consciousness. A resonance occurred which caused a sympathetic glow to form upon the many other ribbons attached to Hap Sing. In particular he noted that the ribbons attached to the Tiger Monks glowed the brightest.

Show Sang looked out the porthole of the Nordland trade ship Yggdrasil departing Yokito harbor. He had seen the fluctuations in the ribbons joined to Yu Lo and Hap Sing, and now marveled at the brightening of those very ribbons to his second sight. Sea Reaver stepped into the cabin from the deck.

Sister Norla looked at them both with concern, "What is it my brother?"

Sea Reaver had a grim look, "We're receiving a communication from Yu Lo. Hap Sing and he have been captured, and they are in great agony."

Chow Sang looked away from the porthole, "I don't understand what we're doing fleeing the city. We should be going to rescue them."

Sister Norla shook her head, "The message of Lady Ming was clear. We are to flee."

Chow Sang looked at her strangely, "You must have heard something I didn't. She told us to go to the Nordland Market."

Sister Norla looked worried, "Lady Ming was very particular about it on purpose Chow Sang. There is no market called that in the colony here. To every Nordlander there is only one place known as the Nordland Market. It is in the great trade city Nordriskyr on the coast of our homeland. It remains a code word among out people that it is time to retreat and return to our ancestral homeland."

Sea Reaver nodded, "It is true Chow Sang. The market here is called the colony market, or the Yokito market. We only ever call one market in the world the Nordland Market. So you are certain of this Norla?"

Sister Norla nodded, "I questioned her for clarity my brother, but it was no mistake. Our mission is to flee these lands, and I was given the explicit command to guard Chow Sang as well."

Chow Sang shook his head in denial, "Why wasn't I told?"

Sea Reaver hugged Sister Norla briefly, "Little sister, is it what I think?"

Sister Norla blushed, "Yes my brother. Lady Ming has indicated she approves as has Hap Sing."

Chow Sang looked up startled, "What are you both talking about?"

Sister Norla looked Chow Sang firmly in the eye, "The White Raven has sent a vision to Lady Ming I believe. You are to be my bond mate. The counterpart of my spirit."

Chow Sang raised an eyebrow, "As simple as that we're to become married?"

Sea Reaver laughed, "Strange times my future brother. Welcome to the family."

Chow Sang looked at him, "Norla's your real sister?"

Sea Reaver nodded, "Of course she is. Do you think Nordland women are so friendly with everyone? If we were not bonded, or related she would have gutted me for touching her in such a familiar manner."

Chow Sang shook his head, "Is it the right choice?"

Sea Reaver shrugged, "We've walked among the giants my future brother. It is not for us to question their purposes, but to figure out how to survive their aims. Right now going back to the homeland sounds safest right now."

Chow Sang thought a moment, "Anything which could threaten Hap Sing."

Sea Reaver nodded, "Would tear through the Tiger Monks like a tiger through paper. Yu Lo is proof of our inadequacy in this task. It falls to others to manage something if it can be done."

Sister Norla bowed her head, "It is a brave sacrifice he makes for us."

Chow Sang was surprised, "He knew what was to happen?"

Sea Reaver nodded, "Even I knew that something was happening which presented a potential for great upheaval. I have to suspect that given what we knew of our comrade Yu Lo, he fully understood that staying with Hap Sing was a one way trip to his end."

Sister Norla looked sincerely moved, "A brave man who keeps his comrades informed of events until his very death."

Chow Sang was silent once more briefly before speaking, "His strongest trait is communication through the ribbons of fate. Our task then is clear. We are to spread the story we learn from this. The word must get out."

Togusawa Hiro lay awake on an elaborate futon in a private apartment of the imperial palace. Beside him knelt both a priest of Palnor and Emperor Minato's personal physician. A quiet knock was heard upon the sliding door and a courtier came in to beckon the priest and doctor to follow.

Togusawa Hiro ignored their departure to concentrate upon the images and feelings being transferred through his ribbon to Yu Lo. A short while later a young man in his twenties wearing servant's clothing came in to kneel beside him quietly.

Togusawa Hiro looked at the man with tears in his eyes, "Minato is it as bad as this? Must you sneak around your own palace in order to slip away from the spies placed on you now?"

Emperor Minato ducked his head, "I am afraid my advisors have forbidden me to speak with you directly. They say they shall debrief you personally, and relay your words to me."

Togusawa Hiro raised a hand to wipe away his tears, "They are torturing both Yu Lo who has done nothing, and Hap Sing who is immortal perhaps, but certainly not invulnerable."

Emperor Minato raised his head, "I'm sorry cousin, but there is little I can do. You have to understand how limited my position has become. They only promised me to find the secret of admantium. Is it true that this Hap Sing knows it?"

Togusawa Hiro laughed bitterly, "Money? Your Eminence do you really think this is about money? It is all about control and power. Do you have any understanding with what your so called allies have made common cause."

Emperor Minato questioned, "Why do they need this admantium so badly then?"

Togusawa Hiro shook his head, "To make weapons good enough to serve a god, or powerful enough to slay them all. Rendalk Flügg directs the torture himself, and came at the summons of your advisor Qui Chang. This being seeks nothing less than the destruction of this world, and the return of the banished elder gods."

Emperor Minato rocked back onto his toes and stood, "Repeat this message to any advisor who comes to question you. Tell them 'I have something to say for Emperor Minato's ears only.' If they do not relay this message to me, then I will know for certain who is playing me falsely."

Togusawa Hiro shook his head in dejection, "Don't you trust me by now your Eminence?"

Emperor Minato raised an eyebrow, "It isn't that I don't trust you my dear cousin. It is that at the moment you are in no position to speak here to my official position. It is only because of family ties of blood that I even come before you now. I have to know who is suspect, and who I can trust. You are my only means right now of weeding down the numbers which conspire against me."

Togusawa Hiro looked at him closely, "You do realize they mean to kill Yu Lo and Hap Sing don't you?"

Emperor Minato ducked his head, "Let us hope it is quickly if such is the case. I would rather they didn't suffer overlong, or reveal such damning secrets to threaten our world."

Ming Wa Fu sat in lotus position in the central position of the great room in the Chi Master Academy. A young student grasped each hand and Chi Master Student after Chi Master Student hand after hand spread out in a double spiral from his central position. At the end of the students were the junior instructors also forming the outer arms of the spiral. At the far ends of the spiral were the senior instructors forming the anchors.

Ming Wa Fu enhanced and clarified the message which came in from Yu Lo for all to feel and experience. He reduced the pain drastically, but augmented the images born through Yu Lo's second sight.

Ming Wa Fu spoke, "What is that dark figure?"

A mutual chant arose throughout the room, "Our mutual enemy, the destruction of all."

Ming Wa Fu continued, "Who sends the vision at the cost of his life?"

The chant replied, "Yu Lo the best of us so we may know our eternal enemy."

Ming Wa Fu continued, "How do we combat this enemy?"

The chant replied, "Through learning and understanding its ways, and by resisting its lures."

Ming Wa Fu continued, "Who keeps Yu Lo alive, and eases his pain so he can deliver this message to us."

The chant grew in volume, "The Lucky Cricket Hap Sing, the legendary fisherman, the Chi Master of all Chi Masters."

Ming Wa Fu continued, "Who can we always turn to in times of need?"

The chant grew triumphant, "The Chi Master shall watch over his children. Those of us who follow the ways of the spirits and not the gods."

Ming Wa Fu was quiet for several moments as he thought of his grandson Ming Ne Yu. Ming Wa Fu could feel his grandson's thoughts were on the people here at the academy as well as his Tiger Monks.

Lo Hannah knelt at the alter beside her older brother Lo David a priest of Palnor. The vision from Yu Lo stuck her forcefully as she focused on easing his pain through their link together. A pained gasp escaped her causing Lo David to look at her in concern.

Lo David spoke, "Shall I pray to Palnor to ease your pain Hannah?"

Lo Hannah shook her head, "They torture our cousins Lo David. Easing my pain won't help Yu Lo. Only by taking the sympathetic pain can I bear his agony away. He must get this message out to the Chi Masters. We have to understand the nature of our enemy to our very spirits so that we never forget."

Lo David looked sympathetic, "How could you ever forget such horrors dear sister?"

Lo Hannah gave a brief pained smile, "This is very important. This memory of pain has to last beyond life until we return once more upon the cycle of spirits. Our spirits must never forget who is there for us, and who seeks our destruction."

Lo David raised an eyebrow, "Palnor is always there for us."

Lo Hannah shook her head, "Palnor is here for us on this turn of the cycle. Spirits do return over the long eons dear brother, and they do forget the gods they once served."

Lo David was confused, "What is different here dear Hannah?"

Lo Hannah grunted, "Spirits of Chi Masters can be made to remember the feel of the enemy for eternity, and know that Hap Sing stands to help us as well."

Lo David scoffed, "What can a dying man do to help us now dear sister? We must trust in the gods."

Lo Hannah smiled, "Remember even the gods serve their purpose as well. Otherwise they are replaced."

Ming Ne Yu stepped through the doorway into the darkness of night. He turned to pull the brass doorknob from the door and place it back into the silken bag his grandfather Ming Wa Fu had given him as the door faded to nothingness. Ming Wa Fu used his second sight and saw a number of patrolling kobolds walking around an encampment in the darkness.

Ming Ne Yu glided silently through the night avoiding the kobold patrols with ease. He eventually approached the second largest mound shaped hide hut strung with bits of colored bones, and painted with pictographic images. Quietly Ming Ne Yu slipped past the bearskin covering the doorway and stepped inside.

The old kobold shaman laying in the bed before the small brazier looked at him with suspicion in its eyes. Ming Ne Yu stepped closer with his hands held out in an open palmed manner.

The old kobold shaman sat upright and stoked the brazier to produce light, "A Tiger Monk of the Ran Li Empire with a most potent aura. Why do you seek my death silent killer?"

Ming Ne Yu shook his head, "You need to understand, and to teach your followers what threatens us."

The old kobold shaman laughed, "There is no us between kobolds and Ran Li. There are barbarians as you call us, and civil kind as you call yourselves. What else is there to understand?"

Ming Ne Yu held out his hand, "Please allow me to show you so you can judge and spread the word among your kind. I promise to leave in peace to seek out another if you don't want to trust me."

The old kobold shaman laughed low, "A polite death at least. It is well known among my peoples you could have killed me without even entering my yurt, or alerting my kin. I am Yagrash Shaman of the Tribe of the Night Owls. I will listen to your words."

Ming Ne Yu held out his hand to Yagrash, "My words are not enough. You must feel it to understand the full truth of it."

After several minutes of the link between them being formed Yagrash began to have tears flow down his snout, "The greater spirits have done this much for us. Sacrificing one of their own. For so long we had thought them lost to the deepest parts of the dreaming. Little have we understood their task, or the threat before all life here. What can a small being, a puny spirit such as myself do?"

Ming Ne Yu looked hard at Yagrash, "Remember always our true enemy and the sacrifices made on our behalf. I will depart now."

Yagrash looked at him, "Where will you go?"

Ming Ne Yu looked back with tears in his own eyes, "Every one of our kind must know so that they can never forget. You bear the ribbon of the Lucky Cricket now and for eternity. Goodbye my fellow Chi Master."

Yagrash wiped his snout as Ming Ne Yu departed, "Goodbye my fellow shaman."

Mimosa's stomach roiled in nausea as the visions from Yu Lo struck her inner mind, and her eyesight viewed the same events from a different angle standing between two priests behind Yu Lo and Hap Sing. Mimosa's second sight was even more confusing to her senses though. The dark inky cage surrounding Hap Sing had more and more ribbons attaching to Hap Sing writhing between the bars than she could imagine counting.

She considered that a ribbon for every Chi Master of the academy student or instructor must be present, but even that couldn't account for the new and growing numbers. Many of the ribbons were of an odd unusual nature. It was only after much cautious examination that she could tell they couldn't possibly be the ribbons of humans.

Several times the sensations sent her into bouts of nausea, but it was mostly the sensation of sickness and hatred coming off Rendalk Flügg which unbalanced her. Six times through the night she had collapsed, and six times the priest beside her had drug her back to her feet to witness their alternating torture of Yu Lo and Hap Sing.

Mimosa's terror increased when they brought out the knives to begin cutting into Yu Lo's flesh. First it was shallow cuts, then stabs into his limbs. Throughout the process they continued to use the cat-of-thirteen tails on Hap Sing's body which was covered in slowly scabbing lacerations.

After a change of shifts as the dawn of the second day of their torture began the real damage began on Yu Lo. They brought out a wood block and a hatchet. First they chopped off his toes one by one, and then his fingers. Mimosa thought it very strange that Yu Lo bore the torture without losing consciousness, or bleeding out after all this time.

Then it struck her what was happening. Hap Sing was slowly trading his own considerable immortal life force to keep Yu Lo alive and with reduced agony. Consequently Hap Sing was dieing much faster than the scourging would have normally produced. When they gouged out Yu Lo's eyes with a dull knife Hap Sing uttered his first agonized cry of pain.

The hardest part for Mimosa then was that the visions of Yu Lo didn't stop, but instead intensified with his loss of eyesight. His second sight still worked from his mind's eye, and interestingly increased in potency to compensate. The aura of the Luck surrounding Hap Sing was almost completely gone, but the ribbons connected to him glowed brighter than ever once past the bounds of the inky force cage.

Rendalk Flügg raised a hand to interrupt the torturers, "That one is no longer useful. I think it is time to kill him and move on to the girl. Hap Sing likely has a more weak heart for the female, and I think that one is as good as dead soon anyway."

Mimosa braced herself for the grabs by the priests beside her. As they reached for her a mage behind her cast a stunning spell sending her mind reeling out of control and her body into spasms of seizure. An executioner bearing a headsman's axe arranged the mutilated body of Yu Lo with his neck over the chopping block.

Mimosa felt the rising terror and panic and the executioner brought his axe rapidly down toward Yu Lo's neck.

The Lucky Cricket

Chapter 32 Change of Conditions

ime seemed to slow to a crawl for Mimosa at first, then she literally realized that time actually had slowed for everyone except her. Then she noticed that Rendalk Flügg went from being nearly frozen like the rest to picking up speed slowly until he seemed to be in pace with her perspective.

Rendalk Flügg was obviously furious, "What ever it doing it has to stop messing with time right now! It's against the rules, and they will show up to enforce them against all of us."

A young pale dark haired girl standing wearing a simple white gown next to the frozen tableau of the executioners axe a mere hairs width from Yu Lo's neck looked at Rendalk Flügg with a cold emotionless glare from between the hair covering her head.

The dark haired girl spoke in an echoing unholy voice, "They have absolutely no power over me. I have my contract, and it is coming due. Nothing in this universe or the dreaming can ever prevent me from collecting upon it."

Rendalk Flügg screamed, "You can't they are in my power. My control. They belong to me."

An identical dark haired girl appeared in the cage next to Hap Sing and they both spoke in unison, "If you want me to convey the terms of my contract then it is within your rights. If you want to challenge my contractual rights, then they will be summoned to deal with your complaint. They will not like what they see when they examine you or your claim."

Rendalk Flügg spoke loudly but calmly, "I claim the power of Hap Sing. I have a properly authorized contract for such. I will not be cheated a second time."

A third dark haired girl stood beside Mimosa spoke in unison with the first two, "I acknowledge your claim for the power of Hap Sing. Unfortunately that equates to about twenty eight Kesselmarks at this moment."

Rendalk Flügg was momentarily confused, "Make sense will you? What are these Kesselmarks?"

The three dark haired girls shifted positions in an instant to opposite sides of Hap Sing, Yu Lo, and Mimosa, "A Kesselmark is the residual energy in a dead body. You did initiate their deaths after all. I waited until the moment of no return in the time continuity for you to rescind your decision. I am allowed at the moment of death to claim all contracts which are due to me."

Rendalk Flügg raged, "What bloody fool created such a idiotic contract? Who enforces such a thing? What is the process for complaint here?"

The dark haired girls spoke in unison again, "The process of complaint is to convene a meeting with all of the Numbers. You have to have the sponsorship of a Number to convene such a meeting. Do you wish to register your sponsor with me?"

Rendalk Flügg hedged his bets, "What if I have no such sponsorship?"

The dark haired girls replied in a deep booming echo, "Then your application to convene such a meeting is summarily denied."

Rendalk Flügg shouted again, "How can you deny me? I want to speak to whatever being enforces such a thing."

The dark haired girls replied, "Number Two enforces this rule."

Rendalk Flügg paled, "The godkiller?"

The dark haired girls glared at Rendalk Flügg with deep malice, "I prefer to be called Balinac."

In the next instant twenty cats with two tails each stood next to every priest and wizard standing in the courtyard. Rendalk Flügg attempted to move but found his path forward blocked by a fourth dark haired girl.

The twenty four Balinac all spoke in unison, "I don't like you because you break our rules, and then cry when I enforce them as intended. Tell your master that all the power he will get from Hap Sing is the residual twenty eight Kesselmarks left in his dead body. The contract I have is with Number Seven which grants me perpetual right of first choice over any spirit linked to Hap Sing as well as Hap Sing's spirit. As you have initiated the death of each of these three by executing a life linked individual, their three spirits have now come under my collection authority as the rules created by Number Two decree and as duly authorized by Numbers since the creation of material existence. If you don't like it, then I'll gladly remove your spirit permanently to the far realms."

Rendalk Flügg fumed, "You can't do such a thing!"

Balinac laughed a nasty wicked laugh, "Your friends the elder gods all thought that as well. I notice they haven't managed to budge even once since I imprisoned them there."

Time rejoined its normal flow, and Mimosa's impression of events ceased with the death of Yu Lo, Hap Sing, and her own demise.

Ming Yuki Nene raised her bleak hard eyed face toward the alter of the White Raven. The image of the torture and death of Hap Sing, Yu Lo, and Mimosa faded gradually from her vision. Sister Kenara watching from behind noticed her change of posture, and stepped forward.

Sister Kenara spoke softly, "My Lady?"

Ming Yuki Nene stood and turned, "It is time for me to go."

Sister Kenara asked, "Where do you go?"

Ming Yuki Nene stepped up to Sister Kenara and placed a hand on her shoulder, "You are now to be the Raven Mistress of our people here. My time here is almost done, yet I have a final task."

Sister Kenara was clearly concerned, "What task my Lady?"

Ming Yuki Nene gave a hard edged smile, "A funeral that won't be forgotten for many years in Ran Li."

Ming Yuki Nene concentrated a moment, and saw a vision of Ming Wa Fu in her minds eye watching her as she watched him. A moment of tender unspoken thoughts was exchanged between them. Then a vast surge of power entered Ming Yuki Nene along the spirit ribbon connected to her husband from the many Chi Masters at the academy.

Ming Yuki Nene spoke out loud, "By the bargain made between the White Raven and Balinac, I summon you to my presence this one time."

A enormous portal of shadow opened within the temple of the White Raven in front of Ming Yuki Nene. Through the portal stepped a twenty foot tall nightmare of smoky shadow vaguely shaped like an enormous twin tailed panther. Sister Kenara fell to her knees in prayer and supplication to the White Raven at the sight of it.

Balinac spoke in a deep growling yet quiet voice, "Do you wish to discuss that boon I offered?"

Ming Yuki Nene nodded, "The deal is struck. Just take me to the bodies of Hap Sing, Yu Lo, and Mimosa. I won't have that vile beast defile them further."

Balinac tilted its head, "Very well. I will trade your spirit for this favor."

Ming Yuki Nene nodded, "Consider it done."

Balinac turned back through the gate, "Follow me through, and be prepared for a fight."

Ming Yuki Nene marched after Balinac through the shadow portal leaving Sister Kenara kneeling while shaking in prayer for them all.

Sister Norla looked at the pale Chow Sang and her brother Sea Reaver, "What's wrong? What happened?"

Sea Reaver stood up, "They're finally dead. Mimosa, Hap Sing, and Yu Lo are dead. Killing Yu Lo triggered a sympathetic link which killed all three of them."

Chow Sang shook a bit, "I didn't think it would happen this way. Wait, we're getting another image. It's coming from Master Ming, but the image is of Lady Ming. She's praying at the temple."

Sea Reaver then startled, "Oh merciful White Raven what is that?"

Chow Sang dropped to the floor, "The Godkiller. It's the Godkiller."

Sister Norla's voice rose, "What's happening?"

Sea Reaver quivered in fear, "Lady Ming is going with that thing."

Sister Norla grasped Chow Sang, "No! She must not! Stop her!"

Sea Reaver placed his hand on her shoulder, "It's too late. They've entered the land of shadow where the vision can not follow."

Ming Ne Yu looked at the Mursai Shaman with a sad expression in his eyes. The Mursai Shaman nodded in return.

Ming Ne Yu stood, "I must continue on to deliver the message."

The Mursai Shaman spoke, "She bears a resemblance to you human shaman."

Ming Ne Yu looked back briefly, "My grandmother does what she must. So must we all."

The Mursai Shaman bowed, "There is no lack of bravery in your people."

Ming Ne Yu turned away, "Following your destiny isn't bravery. It is simply what must happen. Keep watching, and always tell the tale among your people."

Ming Ne Yu stepped away and used the doorknob once more to create a doorway through nothingness to his next destination.

Togusawa Hiro stood in the Emperor's private quarters. Emperor Minato sat drinking tea without inviting him to sit. Only a handful of servants were present, and all of the courtiers had been dismissed.

Emperor Minato spoke, "I wish to thank you for your assistance cousin Hiro. With your help three of my untrustworthy advisors have been removed from court. Qui Chang has met with an unfortunate accident with some poorly prepared Fugu fish. I'm afraid it stopped his heart."

Togusawa Hiro looked worried, "Your safety your eminence is what is important."

Emperor Minato looked calm, "Tell me of what you see now young cousin."

Togusawa Hiro hesitated a moment, "The connection still exists, but it is blackness at the moment. I guess it means that Lady Ming Yuki Nene is still alive, but no longer on this realm of existence."

Emperor Minato nodded, "Fascinating. Where does she go do you think?'

Togusawa Hiro swallowed, "Honestly I think she goes to her doom."

Emperor Minato smiled faintly, "Then I think our empire shall know peace for many more years to come."

Togusawa Hiro was worried, "Is that all that matters? Having a few years of peace?"

Emperor Minato looked at him with a serious look, "Sometimes that is all that can be achieved. Don't underestimate the value of peace my cousin. Great Emperors have been known to come from times of turmoil, but unrest has also ended more than one dynasty. I believe it is better to achieve a balance than it is to dominate and control the people. Enough strength and enough restraint in the use of strength are required to rule wisely."

Togusawa Hiro dropped his head, "It that all you will do then? Clean your house of those who can't be trusted."

Emperor Minato shook his head, "I will also reward those who can be trusted to serve well and honestly. The Chi Masters have treated with us honestly. The priests of Aquonis have shown themselves unwise in their alliances. As a result they shall lose favor and position within the kingdom. My advisors who worship Palnor have given honest council. The priests of the dark god Mortis shall be exposed, hunted, and destroyed by my elite ninja corps."

Togusawa Hiro looked at the Emperor, "What of the followers of the White Raven?"

Emperor Minato smiled faintly, "They shall placate the spirits of the dead as they have always done. We need not worry about them."

Togusawa Hiro lowered his head, "Mimosa was among their number before she was sacrificed. Do you think they will let this go?"

Emperor Minato frowned, "Next time you take a lover, make sure you have my permission first cousin. You've seen now how youthful indiscretion can lead one astray."

Togusawa Hiro dipped his head down to the floor in a bow, "I'm sorry your Eminence. It shall not happen again."

Emperor Minato gave a smile, "We all make errors of judgment in our youth Hiro. The question is whether we learn from them. I do think we'll see some reaction from the minions of the White Raven in response. Their leader Ming Yuki Nene does not strike me as one to take an assault of this nature without reply."

Chapter 33 Avatars Unleashed

Rendalk Flügg looked at the bodies of the three dead Chi Masters with a glare of vile hatred in his eyes. He rose from his chair, strode forward, and grabbed the axe from the executioner standing over the mutilated decapitated body of Yu Lo. With a quick swipe of the axe Rendalk Flügg removed the head from the executioner's body. The mages standing nearby looked around nervously, while the priests of Mortis each smiled in approval.

Decarius stepped forward to examine the body of Hap Sing, "What has happened Master? I was certain our torturer had not inflicted fatal harm upon him."

Rendalk Flügg vented a grunt, "They have conspired against me again. They are working in concert against the agreements. Yet they know I face condemnation for doing the same if I object so they act with impunity to thwart my aims."

Decarius moved beside Rendalk Flügg and took the axe he offered, "Who are you talking about? I still don't understand."

Rendalk Flügg gave a bitter laugh, "Well I still have necromancy to rely upon. Mages, preserve their bodies. Decarius have your priests prepare the rituals for inhabitation through necromancy. There are still secrets here to learn even if I can't directly take the power of Hap Sing any more. It was careless of the Godkiller to only take their spirits and not their corpses."

As the dark mages stepped forward to follow their orders a portal of shadow opened in the wall behind them. Through the gateway to shadow stepped the tall form of Ming Yuki Nene with a hard look in her eye.

Rendalk Flügg shouted, "Kill her. Kill the bitch now!"

Two enormous crows materialized and launched from Ming Yuki Nene's shoulders to attack the closest priests and mages. In a matter of confused moments three were decapitated, and two others stabbed by razor sharp beaks through their hearts as Hugin and Munin wove an aura of destruction around Ming Yuki Nene.

Ming Yuki Nene spoke, "I claim these bodies in the name of the White Raven. Any who defy me shall perish."

Decarius shouted to his priests, "Barriers fools. Use your spells."

Rendalk Flügg scrambled back from the onslaught of dark magical energies unleashed by the mages and priests in the courtyard. Gouts of flame, arcs of lightning, dark seething tentacles of necromantic force played around an invisible field surrounding Ming Yuki Nene. Hugin and Munin struck out to kill a couple more mages until they got organized enough to seek protection under the barriers of the priests of Mortis.

The fight continued a couple more minutes to a stalemate with the only change being the advance of Ming Yuki Nene to stand beside the body of Hap Sing. Then the dark tentacles of force unleashed by Rendalk Flügg surrounded her invisible field crushing it smaller around her.

Rendalk Flügg shouted in triumph, "You don't have the strength in your old age any more bitch. You won't defeat me a third time."

Ming Yuki Nene stooped her head, and dropped to her knees.

At the Chi Master academy several of the students had dropped from exhaustion. The double spiral around Ming Wa Fu had shortened to the senior students and instructors. Strain was evident on all their faces as they focused their spiritual powers upon Ming Wa Fu who protected Ming Yuki Nene with his field of spiritual force.

Senior Instructor Yu Han father of Yu Lo looked at Ming Wa Fu with anguish on his face, "It isn't enough Master Ming. Their combined power is greater than ours. We're at our end."

Ming Wa Fu shook his head, "No. You are now the Master here. Break off while I finish this."

Ming Wa Fu's aura glowed bright enough to be seen without the second sight as the students and instructors collapsed in exhaustion around him. He then transferred the remaining power along with his entire spirit down his connection to his wife. The body of Ming Wa Fu lay lifeless in the center of the room.

Ming Yuki Nene had a single tear drop from her hard eyes as she stood once more, "Thank you my husband. Let's finish this together."

A bead of sweat dripped from Rendalk Flügg's brow as he growled, "Stop the bitch now. Kill her!"

Ming Yuki Nene stood proudly for a moment under their assault and spoke quietly to herself, "Glorious White Raven please listen to my plea. Take my body and make it your vessel here. I surrender it to you willingly."

The form of Ming Yuki Nene glowed brightly. She grew to fifteen feet in height and her silver hair changed to deepest black. Her gown was simple and elegant upon her ageless alabaster skin. The irises of her eyes changed to an icy grey blue in color with pupils of bottomless blackness.

The White Raven spoke one word in a glorious divine voice, "Die!"

An enormous pillar of white brilliance shot down from the sky. The entire courtyard was engulfed in divine radiance. The dark mages and priests of Mortis were consumed by the divine attack. The pillar of light could be seen from the entire country of Ran Li all the way across the water to the small island nation of Udomo. People everywhere wondered at it. The people in Yokito quailed before its brilliance in their midst.

After a few seconds the pillar faded away to reveal several piles of frozen flesh where the bodies of the priests and mages had stood. The bodies of Hap Sing, Mimosa, and Yu Lo were untouched by its impact. The figure of Rendalk Flügg stood glaring at the goddess of death with absolute defiance in his eyes, and an oily black sheen covering his skin.

The White Raven looked dispassionately at Rendalk Flügg defying her presence, "Once more you break my rules cursed beast. You defy my command of death."

Rendalk Flügg snarled, "Even you don't have the ability to kill that which was never alive weak goddess of a soon to be destroyed kind."

The White Raven nodded, "It is true even I don't have the power to kill that which was never present. Be gone nightmare of the Far Realms. Your form has once more been destroyed, and only your malice remains even more impotent than before without any followers to obey your commands."

The shape of Rendalk Flügg distorted into a writhing mass of slimy black tentacles covered in randomly assorted eyes and suckers of various sizes, "We shall return. We shall command all of existence again puny goddess. Your kind shall not stop us a second time."

The White Raven maintained her cool demeanor, "You will never succeed dead dream of the dead elder gods. The worlds no longer need or want your kind."

The form of Rendalk Flügg's malice faded to transparency with a final whisper, "We shall return. We shall destroy everything."

The White Raven opened a glowing portal beside her. She lifted the bodies of Hap Sing, Mimosa, and Yu Lo into her arms. Then she stepped through the portal into her celestial palace in the land of shadow.

Ming Ne Yu looked into the eyes of the Orc Shaman as the last of the vision faded. Concern was on the face of the old orc wearing bones through her ear lobes, and a metal spike driven through the bridge of her nose.

The Orc Shaman spoke, "Is this a true vision? The unmentioned ones still seek to return?"

Ming Ne Yu nodded, "This is the vision of truth we have both seen. There can be no question of the threat to all living beings. There must be a unity among the shamans to prevent this from ever happening. Only by cooperation can we contain such a thing. Never will we have the power to destroy it."

The Orc Shaman spoke, "This vision can be shown to others?"

Ming Ne Yu raised his eyes, "It can be shown to those with the power to see the spirit world. It will be recognized for the truth it is, although some individuals will deny it to seek comfort in a blanket of self deception. All I ask is that you share this vision with those who can see."

The Orc Shaman used her second sight to look at the countless thousands of spirit ribbons attached to Ming Ne Yu. Of particular interest was the spirit ribbon which looked like it was orange with black tiger stripes which was broader and stronger than the rest. It faded out into nothingness after a way, but it was impressive regardless. More impressive was the fact that a thin ribbon of a similar nature was now attached to the Orc Shaman herself.

The Orc Shaman nodded her head, "I believe you, but I have questions for you as well."

Ming Ne Yu raised his graying head, "Ask your questions."

The Orc Shaman looked at him closely, "How many years have you been sharing this vision?"

Ming Ne Yu laughed, "A very long time. I was forty five years old when I began as the events were happening. I am one hundred and twenty six years old now. So I guess that makes it nearly eighty-one years now that I have sought out shamans and Chi Masters to bring into the fold."

The Orc Shaman was impressed, "The work of a lifetime much longer than even my own."

Ming Ne Yu nodded, "It is important work that we all bear the burden of sharing."

The Orc Shaman asked, "Another question if I may. I've never heard of Ran Li, or met a human of your kind before. Where does this land exist?"

Ming Ne Yu sighed, "It has been many long years since I have returned there. Ran Li is not a land which exists on your world. It belongs to another world, but the threat remains the same for all of us. The elder gods still seek to return, and only the Chi Masters, what you know as shamans can act as a warning of their presence."

The Orc Shaman sighed, "You are a planes walker then. This is troublesome for my people. We do not have the strength to challenge such powerful things of madness."

Ming Ne Yu nodded, "None of us do. The best we can do is let the Lucky Cricket know so that he can take action against them."

The Orc Shaman looked confused, "Your vision shows us that he died. Is there more?"

Ming Ne Yu shrugged, "That is the end of the vision, but certainly not yet the end of the tale."

Ming Ne Yu picked up his broad circular woven bamboo hat and bamboo fishing pole. He moved to exit the hut of the shaman as she looked at him with a pleading look in her eyes.

The Orc Shaman spoke, "Your fate is a most terrible one. You feel these events each time you share them. You feel the deaths of your grandparents, of your disciples, of the Lucky Cricket."

Ming Ne Yu nodded, "That is the fate of one such as me. As the one chosen to deliver the message, I must feel it each time I do so. Very few live who knew those people anymore. I am one of the last who has known Hap Sing in person."

The Orc Shaman asked, "How do you continue through such suffering?"

Ming Ne Yu pointedly looked at the ribbon of the Lucky Cricket and several others, "Because I know that spirits are eternal. Those spirits connected to Hap Sing will never forget the enemy or our charge. We are unique in spiritual existence. You shall never forget now that you know. That is our gift. That is our curse."

The coursing of a stream down a seven foot waterfall caused a rainbow to form in the tropical sunlight. The bright tinkling of the water flowing could be heard over by the large wooden building with a warm hot springs outdoor bath surrounded by a bamboo fence. Smoothed stones formed the area around the bath and melodious chirping birds sang a song of contentment through the nearby tropical forest.

A tall woman with medium grey colored skin walked through the sliding wood and paper doorway of the building out to the wooden deck next to the bath. She had short cropped black hair blended with dark grey leopard spots. She wore a short kimono of dark grey also covered in leopard spots. However, her eyes were a deep jade green.

In her hands she held several neatly folded fluffy towels, a couple bars of soap, and a wooden bucket and ladle. She closed her eyes for a moment, and a noise like a tearing sheet could be heard coming from inside the building.

A small two tailed black cat came out the open door followed by an undamaged Yu Lo, a startled Mimosa, and a serious looking Hap Sing. They looked at the oddly colored but shapely woman holding the bathing accoutrements.

Hap Sing spoke, "Hello Balinac. I guess this means we've finally died."

Balinac nodded, "It certainly does. As per our agreement any spirit connected to you which dies that I deem worthy comes into my possession. Of course this includes your own spirit."

Mimosa looked startled, "What do you mean? How can anyone own a spirit?"

Hap Sing raised a hand to silence Mimosa and looked at Yu Lo, "I'm sorry you had to go through so much because of me."

Yu Lo dipped his head down, "Think nothing of it cousin. I had lots of help to spread the message and to endure the pain. I didn't begin to understand what we faced until I saw it with my second sight. I hope to never witness such a thing again. Our death was a mercy."

Hap Sing nodded, "You can thank Balinac here for that. Balinac invented death to free spirits from mortal existence when their time was due."

Mimosa looked shocked, "The God . . .um, the source of shadow?"

Balinac replied, "Yes. Now I will brook no arguing. Your spirits are filthy with close continued exposure to that creature. It's going to take a long time to get the taint of it free from you. Into the bath until I say you can come out again."

Yu Lo flushed in embarrassment, "Mixed bathing?"

Balinac shrugged, "You're a freed spirit recently demised from mortality. I don't think a little bit of mixed bathing is going to hurt you any."

After Balinac left them soaking in the large thermal spring fed bath Mimosa turned to Hap Sing sitting beside her up to his neck in the water, "Where are we?"

Hap Sing replied, "We are in the dreaming. This is more specifically the portion of the dreaming which is under the influence of Balinac. Sit back and relax. You'll be treated well during your time here."

Yu Lo kept his eyes averted from Mimosa as he asked, "Is this it then? Where we spend the rest of existence?'

Hap Sing laughed, "Hardly my friends. You're just here until your spirits rejuvenate and purify enough to make another round through material existence. This is just another part of the cycle."

Mimosa looked surprised, "This is the afterlife then?"

Hap Sing shook his head, "This is much better than the typical afterlife provided by the gods. No period of servitude before release is required. The purification of spirit is many times faster here in relative measurements. You should be done in less than two or three hundred years of material time I would guess."

Yu Lo was surprised, "That long?"

Hap Sing shook his head, "No. That short. It is usually thousands of years for a mortal spirit to return from the divine realms. The portion of the dreaming managed by Balinac is much more efficient at purification."

Balinac returned carrying more towels and bars of soap. A noise like tearing sheet happened again, and a two tailed cat came out of the house leading Ming Wa Fu and Ming Yuki Nene behind it. They quickly joined the others in the bath.

Hap Sing smiled, "I hope you were successful."

Ming Wa Fu nodded, "The Chi Masters of Ran Li have been shown the events."

Ming Yuki Nene placed a gentle hand on Ming Wa Fu's shoulder, "I gave over my body to the White Raven as Balinac claimed my spirit. She's bound to be a trifle upset, but the opportunity to kill several of Mortis' priests and to destroy the Avatar of the Elder Gods again will certainly be recompense enough to satisfy her."

Balinac spoke, "If your goddess is too upset by it, then she is welcome to come here for a few thousand millennia to discuss it with me. I personally think she should be happy to have you back in just a few hundred years. It is not like I get any benefit from having guests beyond the pleasure of company. We Greater Spirits don't rely on worshipers and spirits for power like the gods."

A little while later a fit older man along with an elderly man left the building and joined them in the bath. They smiled at the others who seemed confused except for Hap Sing.

Hap Sing spoke first, "I hope you have been enjoying yourselves."

The younger of the two men spoke first, "You know how it is old friend. Being dead has its perks. There is certainly less to worry about when you are not alive. This place is also quite pleasant even if the host is somewhat alien in nature."

The elderly man spoke, "Father I don't think the term natural can be applied to Balinac by any means. Supernatural is much more appropriate."

The younger of the two men spoke, "You think you can instruct your own father now Hung?"

The older man laughed, "Father, when you've lived to be one hundred and six then maybe I'll still be able to learn something from you."

The younger man replied, "I'm still better at stratagems than you any day Hung. You've always been too direct in your approach. You should have learned more from Lucky Cricket there about how to be circumspect in achieving your goals."

Ming Yuki Nene spoke, "It is good to see you again Li Hung. I presume this is your father Li Chan then?"

Li Hung answered, "Yes. He is still stubborn as ever too. I would think being dead for a couple of centuries would have mellowed his disposition."

Li Chan laughed, "Who are you calling stubborn? Still fighting at one hundred and six is plain foolishness. If not for Number Seven you would have never outlived me."

Ming Wa Fu smiled, "Your brilliance in battle strategy is well known Li Chan. You bravery in sacrificing yourself to draw out the enemy's leaders is studied still at the military academies in Yokito."

Li Chan flushed in embarrassment, "Utter foolish thing that. It was a prime example of a battle strategy which backfired is what it was. I wasn't quick enough in withdrawing before the enemy caught up to my guard. I never had any intention to die then, it was just dumb luck it happened that way. Only a fool would think it a valid strategy to sacrifice a general for a general of the other side. It seems I've both a foolish son and that I left behind a foolish nation that thinks a fluke mistake on the field of battle is worth emulating."

Hap Sing laughed, "You can't argue with success Chan. Sometimes sacrifice is exactly the right move to have your broader strategy work."

Li Chan shook his head, "I can't be bothered to explain it to you of all people. You are the most stubborn person I've ever met. I'll guess that you took a fair number down with you as well I'm guessing."

Hap Sing nodded, "A number of willing sacrifices had to be made. A number of unwilling deaths had to happen as well. Each one is regrettable, but each one is necessary."

Li Chan shrugged, "Who am I to judge then. There are some more guests in the house as well. It seems you've been busy."

Yu Lo turned to see an elderly couple come out of the building holding hands, "Great Grandfather and Great Grandmother, you are both here."

Yu Mai answered, "Is that one of our great grand children now? He is so young to have died Hap Sing. Is that Yu Lo?"

Yu Wing nodded, "It's Yu Lo. How is our grandson Yu Han?"

Yu Lo answered, "Father is doing fine. He's an instructor at the Chi Master academy."

Ming Wa Fu spoke, "Actually he is no longer an instructor there. I've left him my office as the head of the academy. Your grandson is someone of which you can be proud."

Hap Sing watched with a content smile as more Chi Masters from his past joined the group over time. The conversations were genial and relaxed as they sat in or around the bath of Balinac easing away the cares of their previous mortal existence. When Hap Sing knew it was time he stepped out of the bath, and walked over to the silent Balinac standing like a servant awaiting a command, or a sentinel on guard.

Hap Sing spoke, "I think I am clear of the taint now."

Balinac looked at him over several long moments, "It is as you say Lucky Cricket. You are indeed clear of the taint in a remarkably short time."

Hap Sing nodded, "How do you like my assistance?"

Balinac looked over at the various people bathing, "Their presence does make the task of guarding against incursions by the elder gods easier for me. The signs of taint are much easier to detect on their spirits compared to my own."

Hap Sing smiled, "It will be even easier if you choose to select an avatar. Several candidates can be put together for your consideration. You can examine them as they are brought to Shangri La."

Balinac looked displeased, "I am not convinced of the price yet."

Hap Sing placed an arm across her shoulders, "You've seen how useful my help can be with your task."

Balinac nodded, "It is helpful. I do acknowledge the exchange is worth my while. It is just hard to accept."

Hap Sing squeezed her shoulder, "We can't remain static forever Balinac. Things are changing. You know as well as I that the elder gods are dynamic in ways we can't anticipate as we are."

Balinac was silent a moment before speaking, "The avatar would have to be one of my choosing. There are several distinct qualities I will require. I also require the ability to set up my own testing criteria for selection, and be able to pick my own candidate pool. Most importantly it must be done through informed consent on the part of their spirit. I'll not have a repeat of Number Nine's experience."

Hap Sing smiled, "Is our deal done then?"

Balinac shook her head, "Our deal is complete when I am successfully merged with this avatar. Only then shall I officially join your alliance. Until then I'll remain a free agent contractor like the other Numbers. Now say goodbye to your chosen ones demigod. It approaches the time for you to leave my zone of control."

Hap Sing reached over to hug Balinac who stood stiff and unresponsive to the gesture, "Farewell for now then."

Balinac's expression was a touch ambivalent, "Why did you connect with me in that way?"

Hap Sing smiled, "It's a human gesture. If you plan to take an avatar, then you should get more used to them."

Balinac pointed to the others outside in the bath, "I suggest you save it for them. I have no need of such displays."

Chapter 34 The Legendary Fishermen

Ming Ne Yu sat by the shore of the calm sea with his line in the water. His hair was now pure white, but his grip was steady upon his bamboo pole in spite of his highly advanced age. With a deft move he reached for a small net while yanking the line with the pole. Moments later he brought forth a fish which he rapidly filleted with a small knife on a nearby smooth rock.

A relatively young female halfling with sandy blond curly hair of a mere fifty years walked over from the shade of a sea side hut to watch him finish. She seemed fascinated to watch his skill in action. As he picked up his belongings she cleared her throat to announce her presence.

Ming Ne Yu smiled, "I may be old young lady, but my hearing is still fine. Is your mistress ready to receive me?"

The halfling nodded, "Mistress Lashay has agreed to an audience with you stranger. I would not have thought a request from a Larg-Moro such as yourself would be accepted. It is admittedly a very strange day, and as I told my Mistress you are a very unusual Larg-Moro."

Ming Ne Yu knelt down on his knees to peer into her face at eye level, "I can see you have the blood of shamans in you as well."

The halfling smirked, "It is no such crude thing. We are seers. Beware of considering us such crude manipulators as shamans. We contact spirits directly, and they do our bidding. There is no crude herbs, or shifty vague predictions which have no real meaning."

Ming Ne Yu smiled benevolently, "I mean no disrespect young seer. I also have a measure of the skill you use."

The halfling seer gave a condescending look, "Do you now?"

Ming Ne Yu nodded, "I do indeed."

The halfling snorted, "It is well known that the Larg-Moro only have frauds who pretend to speak to the unseen. We can read much from the spirits around us."

Ming Ne Yu nodded, "I am impressed with your skill then. Please tell me your name young seer."

The halfling snorted, "It's Alvonis, but I hardly qualify as young among my people."

Ming Ne Yu smiled benignly, "I am certain you don't. However, I am considered very old among mine. I doubt the label Larg-Moro can be applied to me either. Many of my people are known as Chi Masters instead."

Alvonis grinned, "Mistress Lashay is one hundred and eleven. She is much older and wiser than you can imagine."

Ming Ne Yu nodded, "I'm sure she is, and I am glad she has agreed to meet with me. My message is important for both of you."

ing Ne Yu sat on a small stool in a well tended garden of vegetables and flowers outside of an extravagant halfling home dug into the hill side. He lightly dozed in the afternoon sunshine until a nearly silent tiger growl brought him to alertness mere moments before the door of the home opened and Alvonis stepped out with an elderly female halfling using her arm as a guide.

Ming Ne Yu stood briefly and then bowed deeply from the waist before retaking his seat on the low stool, "Greetings to you Mistress Lashay. I thank you for taking the time to meet with an outsider."

Mistress Lashay's eyes opened wide as she sat down on a nearby stool, "Think nothing of it. I've never seen such a confusing Larg-Moro before in my life. It is hard to understand the vision before me."

Ming Ne Yu smiled faintly, "You see the marks of my mission upon me perhaps. My road has been a very long path so far. I am not what your people consider a Larg-Moro either. My kind are known as Chi Masters from where I come."

Mistress Lashay looked briefly over at Alvonis, "Bring our guest some cakes and tea, then prepare his fish as well with some dill and butter from the pantry."

Ming Ne Yu handed the filleted fish to Alvonis before she departed into the home, "You have questions I believe. I will try my best to answer them before I deliver my message."

Mistress Lashay leaned slightly back, "You've done this before then?"

Ming Ne Yu nodded, "I have done this a very long time. I've met more shamans, seers, and Chi Masters than you can imagine in my very long life. I have traveled places you've never even imagined in your journeys through the dreaming."

Mistress Lashay looked at him closely, "Is it even remotely possible to have so many connections to other spirits. The form of your spirit beast also is unlike any I've ever imagined. It reminds me of ancient legends long forgotten by most in our nation."

Ming Ne Yu smiled, "It is a spirit form of a tiger. A beast which is not unknown in the lands where I was born. It was granted to me by the one whom I serve."

Mistress Lashay held quiet for many long moments until Alvonis came back with the tea and pastries. Ming Ne Yu bowed politely and awaited the pleasantries of their repast to be completed before speaking about business.

After tea Alvonis came out with the prepared fish and some sliced fried potatoes, and joined them for an early dinner in the garden. Ming Ne Yu ate with pleasure and complimented the preparation of the food.

Ming Ne Yu bowed before speaking, "I must now regrettably get down to my reason for being here."

Mistress Lashay lightly clasped Alvonis' hand, "You may ask us about our visions of the future. Our visions are clear, and usually very accurate unless other powers are at work."

Ming Ne Yu smiled, "I have not come to ask of the future from you Mistress Lashay. I have come to share a vision from the past."

Alvonis looked shocked, "You don't seek the guidance and wisdom of Mistress Lashay?"

Ming Ne Yu shook his head, "I'm certain Mistress Lashay has little she can tell me about my future that I don't already know. Any attempt to view it will only cause her confusion I'm quite certain."

Alvonis was concerned, "What do you mean?"

Mistress Lashay gently took Alvonis' other hand in hers, "He is dream touched child in a very extreme manner. He carries probably millions of spirit connections to his own. Spirits of loved ones true, but also spirits of seers, shamans, and strange powers can be witnessed. Spirits and powers not even remotely of our world."

Alvonis looked worried, "Not of our world?"

Mistress Lashay nodded, "He is what our legends call a dream walker. One who has traveled the spirit realms and returned to reality many times. Not always the same reality either I'm afraid. Just how old are you dream walker."

Ming Ne Yu smiled fondly, "As best I can tell from when I return to my home lands, I should be nearly two hundred and fifty or sixty by now. My journey nears its end soon, and the Lucky Cricket shall return as promised."

Mistress Lashay quivered in nervousness, "The Numbers are there, in the dreaming. You've seen them?"

Ming Ne Yu laughed gently, "Mistress Lashay, not only have I seen the Numbers, I bring you a personal message from one."

Ming Ne Yu stepped through the doorway onto the sandy beach of the Isle of Life. He pulled the brass knob from the wooden door, and the door faded to nothingness behind him. Sitting on the dock near the warehouse was a tall elderly man with a long grey pony tail wearing a straw hat with a wooden fishing pole in his hands and its line in the water.

Ming Ne Yu walked down the beach to sit nearby the elderly man and spoke as he placed his own bamboo pole in the water, "Greetings Sea Reaver."

Sea Reaver gave him a smile, "I see you are still ahead of me in spiritual threads Yu."

Ming Ne Yu shrugged and smiled in return, "It's a lucky day for me I guess. I got two at once today, a master and an apprentice."

Sea Reaver shook his head, "I almost got a new practitioner today. She was just awakened to her powers as well, but I think my appearance set her off. She was a timid little thing, an elf at that I believe."

Ming Ne Yu raised an eyebrow, "She wouldn't accept the ribbon of the Luck?"

Sea Reaver dropped his head, "She wouldn't even let me see her from her place of hiding. It was only through her aura that I knew she was present. She is probably going to take a long time to convince that I'm harmless."

Ming Ne Yu nodded, "Most likely it is our race which intimidates her, or your size. Which world was it?"

Sea Reaver thought a moment, "I think it is a world known as Pernosia to the locals. It was my first time there actually."

Ming Ne Yu thought a moment, "I don't recall being there recently myself."

They sat in silence casually fishing off the dock for many minutes before a wooden door appeared from nowhere on the beach. It opened and an elderly man shorter than both Ming Ne Yu and Sea Reaver wearing a cloth hat and carrying a bamboo fishing pole. The man smiled at them as he approached.

Ming Ne Yu looked at the man carefully as he sat next to him, "Five today Chow Sang?"

Chow Sang nodded, "What can I say? I got lucky and drew a conclave gathering to exchange information. I infiltrated their ranks as a foreigner new to the group, and nabbed them all at once."

Sea Reaver shook his head, "Lucky for you. Mine was a timid elven girl on Pernosia. I couldn't get her to come out of hiding today."

Chow Sang looked through his attached ribbons a moment, "This one here is an elf from Pernosia. He is still around it appears, and doing pretty well I think. You can track him down and use him as a bridge to your skittish little rabbit."

Sea Reaver answered, "I thank you for the help, but it might be males that intimidate her as well. I could use the gentle hand of a woman brother-in-law."

Chow Sang shrugged, "My wife Norla has passed on a long time ago. I also don't have any recent elven females from Pernosia. My most recent female elf there was one hundred years ago."

Ming Ne Yu spoke wistfully, "The Chi Master blood is a rare trait among the elves in the first place. A touch of human blood with Chi Master traits in the family line most likely. I don't think it comes naturally to them otherwise. That is what makes her a valuable addition if you can secure her Sea Reaver."

Sea Reaver shook his head, "If only Lo Hannah were still with us, then I'm sure she could have been useful today."

Ming Ne Yu briefly chuckled, "I don't think a Chi Master as god touched as her would have been allowed to travel the worlds Sea Reaver. The gods are jealous of potentially losing their followers after all. The other side of the fence tends to look greener to gods as well as mortals."

The three fishermen sat in silence fishing on the dock for a long time before they saw the beacon light up on top of the white tower. The packed up their fishing gear and deposited it in their individual homes along the beach. The three of them met at the base of the stairway leading up the cliff.

Chow Sang spoke first, "Does this mean we've got company?"

Ming Ne Yu nodded, "Not only company I would guess, but someone from the other side I would think."

Sea Reaver looked at his ribbons, and noticed the broad tiger striped ribbon no longer faded off into nothing but instead lead up toward the tower. A broad smile lit up his face.

Sea Reaver spoke, "Master Hap Sing has finally returned as promised."

Chow Sang and Ming Ne Yu quickly followed suit and used their second sight as well. The three of them carefully made their way up the stairway in deference to their advanced age more than out of fear of what they would see. At the top of the cliff they could see the light of the tower now pulsed like the beating of a heart.

They entered the open tower door way to an unexpected scene. A three and a half foot tall gossamer winged fairy was fluttering down the stairs from the tower top while a two foot tall black cat with dark grey leopard spots and two tails stalked up the stairs from the tower basement. The cat and the fairy took one look at each other and glared viciously in contempt and distrust.

The fairy spoke first, "Balinac, you have not been invited to my tower or the Isle of Life. Depart now or there shall be consequences."

Balinac purred with the sound of a giant beast, "Ariel, I have been invited to the tower of the Luck. In fact I have just bargained to become the primary occupant of the mirror tower in the Land of Shadow."

Ariel spoke, "We shall see about this. I have an agreement with the Luck as well."

Ming Ne Yu stepped forward, "Enough of this bickering. Where is Hap Sing?"

A middle aged figure in white robes laying on a divan with its back to the rest of the room sat up to look at the group, "Could you all be quiet for a moment. I've got an enormous post resurrection headache."

The three Chi Masters walked over to sit on the chairs across from the divan as Ariel and Balinac cautiously approached in silence. Hap Sing looked at the three of them carefully, and then at Ariel.

Hap Sing spoke to Ariel first, "I have bargained with Balinac to allow entry to the Isle when needed, and to inhabit the corresponding tower in the Land of Shadow. Balinac is not making a permanent residence here, and does not want to in any case. The tower here is still for your use until we mutually amend our current agreement."

Hap Sing then looked again at the three Chi Masters, "I thank you for the hard work you have done. I have returned as promised although by your apparent ages it has been a long time coming."

Ming Ne Yu nodded, "Over two hundred years this time Master Hap Sing."

Hap Sing looked at them carefully, "You have all done well in that time. I have come to collect the burden you have assumed. I will transfer those connections which are not of a personal nature to you."

Hap Sing reached out his hands to join hands in a circle with Chow Sang on his left, Sea Reaver on his right, and Ming Ne Yu across from him. A pulse of energy like a gust of air stirred the room and the ribbons gradually began attaching to his own, and moving over to his form. It was slow at first, then steadily picked up pace until the vast majority of ribbons had transferred to Hap Sing. When it was over the other three only had a couple dozen ribbons each attached to them in addition to the tiger stripped ribbon of Hap Sing.

Ming Ne Yu looked at the new Hap Sing unable to determine any difference from the old one through his sight beyond the millions of new ribbons attached to him. Chow Sang shifted in an uncomfortable manner. While Sea Reaver leaned back and relaxed.

Sea Reaver spoke first, "It's hard to say that was a burden, but I do feel lighter somehow."

Ming Ne Yu leaned forward, "What is next Master Hap Sing?"

Hap Sing smiled, "Your evaluation for a job well done."

Balinac stepped into the middle of the circle of Chi Masters while Ariel fluttered over Hap Sing's head. Balinac looked at them with emerald green eyes which pierced their very spirits. Then it walked over to stand at Ming Ne Yu's feet.

Balinac spoke, "This physical form is still in good shape due to Ariel's assistance, but the spirit is in need of rest. The other two still have a short time left to them before they must go. They may still work through this time, but they will last longer if they take their leisure here. However, I will provide service for the whole group if they wish it."

Chow Sang looked surprised, "What service do you mean?"

Hap Sing spoke, "Rejoining your lost loved ones."

Sea Reaver looked surprised, "Where is that?"

Hap Sing smiled, "In the dreaming where the other Greater Spirits dwell of course. You will undergo a period of renewal just as I have. In time your spirits will return even if your memories of life before the dreaming will not."

Sea Reaver smiled, "If it is all the same Hap Sing I'll stay on board working a while longer if you don't mind. There's a particularly challenging shaman I'm after at the moment, and I wouldn't feel right leaving the job undone."

Ming Ne Yu shrugged, "I'm bound to go anyway. I've done my share I think."

Chow Sang thought a moment, "What is it like? Being dead I mean."

Hap Sing shrugged, "It's something you have to experience for yourself. Remember life eventually ends, and death is just a part of the cycle, not the end of it. The you that is now will never be again, but your spirit will remain eternal."

Chow Sang leaned back a while, "I think I will go with Ming Ne Yu then. It would be good to have company when I go I think."

Balinac divided into two smaller cats which then moved to stand before Ming Ne Yu and Chow Sang. A moment of silence happened and both cats disappeared. The bodies of Ming Ne Yu and Chow Sang sat as lifeless husks in their chairs.

Sea Reaver shook his head, "That was quick. It was also pretty creepy."

Hap Sing gave a rueful chuckle, "Trust me Sea Reaver. There are much worse ways to go."

Sea Reaver laughed, "How could I ever forget Master Hap Sing. Are they all ok? I mean those who have gone before us?"

Hap Sing nodded, "They are in the great flow Sea Reaver. It is as it should be."

Ariel fluttered down into Hap Sing's lap, "You've been gone too long the Luck. You should be punished for letting that beastly Balinac on our island too."

Hap Sing gently stroked her hair, "You've grown since I've last seen you."

Ariel pinched his arm, "Don't you forget it either. I'm still going to be taller than you one day."

Hap Sing smiled, "I think that is enough punishment for today. So Sea Reaver, how has the fishing been?"

Sea Reaver smiled, "Pretty good both here and at work. Got a little elf maid newly awoken to her powers nibbling at my line. I'm just trying to get her to take a bite."

Hap Sing thought a moment, "Keep showing up, but ignore her presence. Eventually her curiosity will get the better of her, and she'll make the first move if you're not too aggressive about it."

Sea Reaver looked surprised, "Are you sure it will work?"

Hap Sing looked at him closely with the second sight, "A trace of a connection already exists. It will solidify over time, and destiny will work in your favor. Just give it some time. Don't worry about rushing that one. I'm going to work as well now. First off let's place the bodies of Ming Ne Yu and Chow Sang someplace they can fertilize the soil up here."

Ariel gave a brilliant smile as she fluttered off of Hap Sing's lap, "I have a wonderful bed ready for them. They will grow such lovely flowers."

Hap Sing stood up along with Sea Reaver. They carefully picked up the bodies of Ming Ne Yu and Chow Sang and followed Ariel outside.

Chapter 35 Winter and Spring

ea Reaver stood looking at the door in the dark wood paneled room with the brass sign which read *Reality or Close to It*. The same tiger cub stood at the panel awaiting his instructions as it had for the last two hundred some years. It looked at him expectantly as he thought about his approach.

Sea Reaver sighed, "Alternate destination. World Pernosia. Elven Land of Triemela. Provence of Orlon. Pick me a point near a stream or other similar body of clean water closest to the habitation of the elf shaman there. Out of her line of sight if at all possible.

The tiger cub spoke in a soft silky voice, "The closest body of water is a stream. Good fishing there too I would think. If you promise to bring me back something good to eat, and I'll give you a doorway within the threshold of her second sight, but out of her line of sight."

Sea Reaver raised an eyebrow, "She's pretty skittish. That might be too close."

The tiger cub spoke, "Do you want her to know you're there or not?"

Sea Reaver paused, "Not at first would be best. At the very edge of uncertainty would probably suit better according to Master Hap Sing."

The tiger cub laughed, "Who am I to question myself then. Trust me I've got a good spot. It's along her current course of travel, but not where she will detect your arrival. Do you want a fixed doorway, or a portable door knob?"

Sea Reaver shrugged, "A fixed doorway by a fishing spot should be fine. Can you conceal it from observation?"

The tiger cub nodded, "I can keep it from casual observation. Of course no one will be able to use it except for you, or your authorized guest. Any major power nearby will know a gate exists though."

Sea Reaver nodded, "I'll keep using it until I've completed the job. Set me a doorknob to that place. I'll travel direct from the Isle of Life."

The tiger cub pressed several buttons, and turned various knobs on the brass panel on the podium in front of it. It opened the hatchway and pulled out a golden hued doorknob which it handed to Sea Reaver.

The tiger cub spoke with a touch of humor in its voice, "I hope you enjoy this one. I expect her to be quite the challenge for you."

Sea Reaver looked surprised, "You know something don't you? I hate when you do this."

The tiger cub laughed, "Think of it as Hap Sing's reward for your long years of service."

Sea Reaver placed the doorknob on the door with the brass plaque and stepped through it. On the other side he let the door shut, but left the knob in place. Five paces ahead of him was an ideal fishing spot by a bend in a stream. The shade from nearby trees was good, and the weather was a touch chilly for spring.

Sea Reaver set out his fishing mat, and sat down on the ground adjusting his hat to shade his eyes. Then he cast his line into the water and waited. An hour later he had two good sized trout cooling in his fishing creel in the water, but the elf shaman made no sign of her presence nearby. Sea Reaver extended his second sight and picked up her aura within two hundred yards watching him from behind. A thin smile was briefly on his lips before he got back to the business of catching fish for himself and the Luck.

By midsummer in Triemela Sea Reaver had begun to enjoy his semi-retirement. He came to the same spot every day through a series of four different doorways. The elf shaman had taken to trying to figure out where he arrived and departed, but had still not approached him directly after four months. Whenever she staked out a hiding spot near one doorway, he used a different one and walked the remaining distance to his fishing spot.

Some days she didn't come, but more often than not she would come early or late, and observe him for several hours from hiding before departing. Three times recently she had been waiting for his arrival with someone else without shaman abilities, and at those times Sea Reaver would ignore them both and continue to fish as if unaware of their presence.

As he placed his first knob and peered through the doorway on the Island of Life he felt the presence of several beings waiting nearby. Sea Reaver quickly checked the other doorways and found several beings near each one. None of those beings were the elf shaman he had been trying to contact.

Sea Reaver closed the last doorway and blew out a flustered sigh, "This won't do. One of her guests has leaked information to someone official on the other side, and she's missing. Time to track her down I guess."

Sea Reaver opened his doorway to the Luck's office in Centrus and stepped through it. He walked down the stone corridor to the doorway at the end and entered the office. To his surprise he saw Hap Sing drinking tea with a tiger colored duplicate wearing tight navy blue shorts and shirt.

Sea Reaver shivered, "It never ceases to bug me to find you talking to yourself."

The Luck answered, "Not having much luck with your girl yet I see."

Sea Reaver shrugged, "She's coming along, but has poor taste in at least one of her friends. They can't keep a secret it seems. Some authorities are waiting for me to appear, and she's nowhere in my immediate detection range. I was hoping for a little help in locating her."

Hap Sing smiled, "I can see her ribbon on you even now, and stronger than before. She is fine still, if a little bit upset at the moment. I think she is being questioned about her activities since you've begun your search."

Sea Reaver sighed, "As long as she's all right then I guess it isn't too serious."

The Luck answered, "She will probably need some help. I could arrange a few fairies to cast glamour on the elves there, or else I could abduct her in no time if you like. My prices are very reasonable."

Sea Reaver shook his head, "She would never trust us if we did either of those things. I think a concealed doorway to her location would be best. Can you link a door to her?"

The Luck looked at Sea Reaver closely, "There is enough of a link between you now. Such a thing could be done."

Sea Reaver hesitated a moment, "If there is enough of a link to do that, then can you just transfer the link to Hap Sing?"

Hap Sing laughed, "Quitting already? I though you liked the challenge of this one."

Sea Reaver thought a moment, "I do actually. The time off fishing isn't bad either. Very well then Master Hap Sing, and The Luck. I will figure this one out on my own."

Sea Reaver spoke to the tiger cub in the room bearing the door to anywhere, "The Luck said you could attach a doorway between us."

The tiger cub nodded, "I certainly can, but I would advise against such a thing at present. My observations indicate she is in the presence of others at the moment."

Sea Reaver questioned, "What kind of others?"

The tiger cub smoothly talked, "Elves of course. It is most likely her own people."

Sea Reaver asked, "Any mages nearby?"

The tiger cub nodded, "Most certainly five of them are mages. However, you are lucky that all their priests are 'busy' at the moment."

Sea Reaver shook his head, "Are you causing trouble?"

The tiger cub shook its head, "I am merely running a test routine on my passageways. It creates a bit of divine interference around your doorway one and two at the moment."

Sea Reaver thought a moment, "Those two doorways are the furthest from each other."

The tiger cub nodded, "I'm afraid so. I'm also afraid I've found a potential fault, so if you will kindly return those doorknobs for now, I'll keep testing them until I fix the problem."

Sea Reaver smiled, "This test should last quite a while, and be quite noisy in divine circles?"

The tiger cub nodded, "It should last for hours at least. I'm quite certain that the two doorways have become cross linked somehow, and anyone finding and entering one will exit the other. If another door was opened in the area, I'm quite certain the divine noise of it would be drowned out by the confusion there. I should get it fixed shortly after your return."

The tiger cub handed him a doorknob of wood inset with a gem of opaque green stone, "This should help. Wait until I run my second routine for five time parts before you use it. That should clear any arcane interference. I will caution you that I am unable to cloak your doorway under her current setting. All present will see it."

Sea Reaver placed the doorknob in his silk pouch and then limbered up his aging frame. He didn't have the grace or strength of his youth anymore, but the five foot tall tiger spirit standing beside him should even the odds."

The tiger cub nodded its head, and Sea Reaver placed the doorknob and stepped through the doorway.

The elf mage spoke in a soft yet haughty tone, "You'll have to tell us what you know sometime."

The flaxen haired young elf maiden sat in a room with walls covered in arcane sigils in the elven tongue. Her chair was comfortable enough and the doorway had an observation hatch which was currently open with an armed guard in leather and cloak peering though occasionally.

The elf maiden looked worried, "I don't know anything really. I just keep seeing this stranger fishing by the Dimrin stream where I showed your apprentice Halisa. I thought she could tell me how he comes and goes without my being able to follow him. He approaches or leaves by those four different directions like I told her, but he's never caused any harm that I could see."

The elf mage nodded, "Halisa said you've been observing him for months. Didn't you think it important to tell the authorities of a stranger in our midst Lirae?"

Lirae answered, "How could I tell them anything I wasn't sure about?"

The elf mage sat back in his own chair, "Did you talk with this man?"

Lirae shook her head in denial, "I've never spoken to him Samlas."

Samlas raised an eyebrow, "Has this man ever spoken to you?"

Lirae shook her head, "He's never seen me even."

Samlas spoke carefully, "Has he ever spoken in your presence?"

Lirae hesitated a moment before nodding her head, "Just once. The first time I saw him."

Samlas had a slight smile, "What did he say that time?"

Lirae hadn't even spoken of this to anyone, "He called out into the woods saying he wanted to speak to me."

Samlas nodded enthusiastically, "Did he call you by name Lirae?"

Lirae shook her head, "How could he know such a thing?"

Samlas thought a moment, "I don't suppose he could have then. Who else has seen him besides yourself?"

Lirae hesitated, "Your apprentice Halisa has seen him the one time. My brother Lioka has seen him once. Why are you so concerned about him Samlas?"

Samlas shook his head, "There was no magical residue from his presence. Conversely there is an enormous amount of divine residue in two of the locations you mentioned. According to our priests it has grown to an incredible level in the last hour before I came back to visit you."

Lirae flushed, "What does that mean?"

Samlas shrugged, "It means those are not some kind of arcane teleportation circles this man is using. He is possibly coming here from somewhere which is not our world. Is there anything else we should know?"

Lirae hesitated again for several minutes, "I don't know."

Samlas smiled in a friendly manner, "Listen Lirae you're not in any trouble beyond exercising a bit of poor judgment about not coming forward with this matter. There will certainly be no negative consequences for you or your family if you help us now."

Lirae shook a moment, "You won't believe me."

Samlas leaned forward, "Tell me anyway Lirae. I'll choose what to believe or not as necessary."

Lirae swallowed before speaking, "He glows in a special way. A way unlike any other elf I've ever seen."

Samlas frowned, "Your visions again?"

Lirae nodded, "I knew you wouldn't believe it."

Samlas shook his head, "I'm more inclined to believe you now that Halisa has seen him as well. Was there anything else?"

Lirae nodded, "The invisible great cat that travels with him must be about five feet tall."

Samlas sighed, "Now how can you see an invisible cat?"

Lirae smiled faintly, "It glows like he does, even though Halisa couldn't see it. I didn't know it was invisible until my brother Lioka couldn't see it. I just thought it was kind of transparent and luminescent."

Samlas nodded, "Could you draw it for me on this parchment with this charcoal?"

Samlas watched her draw for a while until a light sweat broke out on the surface of his skin, "You're sure that's what it looked like?"

Lirae nodded, "That is mostly it. The stripes were very distinctive, although I may have got a few out of place."

Samlas shook his head, "The priests must be consulted on this one my dear. I'll be back later, but stay in the room where you'll be safe."

Lirae's voice rose in worry, "Is something wrong? Do you recognize it?"

Samlas nodded, "It is a beast known as a tiger from the jungle climates known to adventurers and sages. The tallest examples are usually three feet at the shoulder, not five."

Lirae's hand shook, "What does it mean then?"

Samlas wiped the sweat from his brow, "I really don't know child, but I need to consult the priests. Perhaps they can provide better information. Stay in this room. It is shielded from scrying and spells, and will prevent anyone from locating you until we can get to the bottom of this. The guard will bring you some food and drink in a while."

couple of minutes after Samlas left the room Lirae felt a presence standing behind her chair. She turned around to see the very tall Sea Reaver standing behind her in relaxed stance with his arms held easy at his sides. The tiger with him paced gracefully around the edge of the room and leaned its side against the door blocking her into the room, and anyone else out.

Sea Reaver spoke in accented elven tongue, "I'm sorry we had to rush our introduction Lirae. I was hoping you would gain the courage to come see me directly by yourself. However, things have changed slightly. I can no longer return to my spot by the river, and your people will be watching you closely for the next few months. All I can say now is that we need to have a longer conversation at a later date."

Lirae looked at him nervously, "Who are you? How did you get in here? Are you real or am I going mad?"

Sea Reaver gave a gentle smile, "My name is Sea Reaver. I came through my doorway, and I am very real."

Sea Reaver reached out to touch Lirae gently on the shoulder, and she felt his warm hand as solid as any other.

Lirae looked at him with wonder and shock, "What is happening to me? Why do you seek me out?"

Sea Reaver looked over at the doorway, "They are returning. One of your priests are nearby and has sensed my presence. Go about your business as usual. I will provide a door for you when the winter comes. If you want the answers to your questions, then I will provide them at that time. I advise you not to tell them about my presence here today. They will be sure of their enchantment's ability to keep out magic, and think you mad or worse."

Lirae called out as he began to step away, "Why me?"

Sea Reaver smiled, "Because like it or not, you are one of us."

Lirae looked down at her own spirit fox seemingly at ease in the presence of the gigantic tiger spirit, "What are we?"

Sea Reaver stepped though the wooden door which faded from reality without answer.

Lirae looked at her spirit fox as its eyes shone brightly in the winter night. She was bundled up in warm woolen clothes made of imported animal hair soft as mink. She lightly traipsed through the dusting of snow regretful that she could not avoid leaving a trail of footprints like her spirit fox could.

She had spent the last seven months of her life under a cloud of quiet suspicion from her village leaders. In response she had kept up her social contacts with her friends, and had avoided returning to the fishing spot used by Sea Reaver. The rumor which circulated rapidly through their village was that a weak point between the worlds existed there.

A set of adventuring rangers and priests had stepped through the one weak spot they forced open only to find themselves a mile away at the other weak point. The loop worked in both directions and lasted only seven hours before disappearing for the last seven months. After that point as with most things life moved on even in the quiet dull village of her people.

Lirae did not have any idea where her spirit fox was leading her, but trusted that it knew the way to go. She wasn't surprised that she was not being led in the direction of the stream Sea Reaver fished at. She was surprised that she ended up at the travelers inn at the edge of her village.

Lirae stepped inside and noticed the tap room only had two dwarf merchants inside in addition to the elven innkeeper who kept a close eye on the dwarves present. Her spirit fox walked over to the innkeeper's counter. Lirae followed and looked expectantly at the innkeeper.

The elf innkeeper asked, "How may I help you young miss?"

Lirae hesitated a moment, "I'm expecting a friend to meet me here."

The elf innkeeper shrugged, "Unless you are friends with one of these two dwarves, you'll have to wait for them to arrive. Nothing personal young miss, but they serve better wines at the restaurant. Are you sure you were to meet your friend here?"

Lirae smiled briefly, "I don't think they'll serve him there. He's not from around here."

The elf innkeeper nodded, "An outsider then hey. We do keep a pair of private rooms if you like. It wouldn't be the first time a local entertained an out of town guest here."

Lirae blushed, "Its just for conversation only."

The elf innkeeper nodded, "Of course it is. We don't allow any funny doings here. Only tables and chairs in our private rooms. They're for business discussions only. Anything else you'll have to do at your own place."

Lirae nodded, "I understand. I'll take the smallest one then. Also a glass of wine to ward off the chill."

Lirae was led to a small room barely big enough for a small table and four chairs. It only had the one door, and no window to the outside. Lirae debated a moment and then sat at a chair against the side wall with the door slightly open. She sipped her wine carefully to calm her nerves and peered through the opening in the door out into the common area.

As she looked back at her glass of wine something different caught the corner of her eye. There was now a doorway in the wall beside her where one had not been before. The doorknob reminded her of something, and then she realized it was the same doorknob she had seen on the doorway used by Sea Reaver to reach her before.

Lirae trembled a moment as she whispered to her spirit fox, "You had better be leading me right."

Chapter 36 New Recruit

Lirae cautiously opened the door and saw a corridor made of set stone where one could not possibly exist. A noise out in the common room of the inn caused her to start and she saw her spirt fox had already entered the corridor and was waiting on her. She stepped into the doorway to the odd corridor as the room door burst open showing her a startled member of the elven watch staring at her with wide eyes.

Lirae blurted out, "Sorry, I'll have to catch you later. I've got to go."

The the elven watch guard tried to lunge around the tight packed table and chairs as Lirae closed the door before his eyes. The door on her side faded from view leaving a blank stone wall. Then Lirae noticed that although no direct source of light was present, the corridor was still light enough to see inside. She followed it for a ways until she came upon another doorway with an identical doorknob.

Lirae whispered to herself, "Please don't let it be somewhere horrible."

Lirae opened the door and saw a tropical sandy beach with a turquoise colored bay before her eyes. He spirit fox darted out ahead of her, and she followed a couple of steps until she looked at the five bamboo houses along the shore and the small warehouse. Then she turned to see the largest fairy she had ever imagined at three and a half feet tall.

Lirae looked back for the door to only see more sand leading to a cliff topped by a brilliant white tower with a beacon light which beat like a heart. Lirae plucked up her courage and turned back to the smiling fairy.

Ariel spoke, "Welcome Lirae to the Isle of Life. I am Ariel avatar of the Tree of Life. I'm sorry that Sea Reaver isn't here to greet you, but I chased him off because I thought he might scare you to death with his eagerness to talk with you."

Lirae took a moment to digest this new information, "What? I don't understand. It was winter just a moment ago in Triemela. How did I get here? I think I may have made a mistake. Could you send me back?"

Ariel shook her head, "I'm sorry but I don't control those gateways. Only the life gates are mine to command."

Lirae looked worried, "The life gates?"

Ariel nodded, "To the Fey Realm of course."

Lirae looked worried, "The Fey Realm is a myth of our people. It doesn't exist."

Ariel shook her head, "That is where I was born, and where the Tree of Life my patron is the heart of life in existence. I am the avatar of the Tree of Life here in Shangri-La."

Lirae blew out a long breath, "What country is that? I don't know of it."

Ariel shook her head, "It isn't a country, It is the world made by the Lucky Cricket."

Lirae opened her over warm coat, and drew it off her while looking longingly at the shaded porch of the house in front of her before asking, "Can I sit down? It seems I'm not dressed appropriately for the weather here. What season is it here? I can't even tell."

Ariel giggled, "It is tropical season here. Rains in the late morning here on the leeward side of the Island of Life, and sun and surf the rest of the day. Rains hit the windward side about midmorning usually. Follow me. We'll borrow the Lucky Cricket's porch for now. I don't think he'll return today."

Lirae followed and asked, "Have I died or something?"

Ariel shook her head, "Not if I have anything to do to prevent it. Trust me I can do plenty."

Lirae took off her warm outer clothes and sat down gratefully in the chair on the porch beside Ariel. Even her under dress was warm in the tropical heat, but the sea breeze and shade helped cool her down.

Lirae took a calming breath and looked at her spirit fox as Ariel looked down at it as well, "You can see it?"

Ariel answered, "I am connected to the spirit world, so yes I can see the projection of your spirit in the form of a fox. I suppose it means you are very smart and clever, in addition to being somewhat mischievous and shy."

Lirae looked surprised, "You can tell all that about me from looking at my fox spirit."

Ariel nodded, "I am quite adept at reading character through spirit now. I've been instructed by the Lucky Cricket himself."

Lirae thought a moment, "Ok. Start by telling me about where this is, and why I've been brought here."

Several hours later the setting sun was reaching the ocean across the bay turning the sky brilliant yellows and pinks, and the water deep reds. Lirae was in quiet contemplation soaking in the information provided by Ariel. It had sounded fantastic and impossible, but so was her current situation by her estimation.

Lirae looked at the fairy sitting beside her, "So you want me to join you in watching over them?"

Ariel nodded, "They mean to recruit you to work for them, and I am fine with it as far as it goes. However, I would appreciate if you would tell me those things they will not. Our agreements are tenuous at best, and I don't trust that the Luck is not double dealing behind my back with the Balinac."

Lirae breathed out a sigh, "Then why deal with them at all?"

Ariel smiled, "It is either be in the group, join another group, or be excluded. Given the current choices available being in the group of the Luck is the best option."

Lirae shook her head, "What is wrong with this other group?"

Ariel's smile changed to a frown, "I'm sorry to say that they will show you a very convincing recruitment vision which explains it."

Lirae looked surprised, "How am I to know it isn't unreal? Some kind of fix to get me to join them."

Ariel shook her head, "The vision is real enough, and quite terrible from what I hear of it from those who have experienced it."

Lirae gripped the table, "Why is it so terrible?"

Ariel gave a wan smile, "You'll experience it along with them. That experience will remain with your spirit for eternity. Your spirit will never forget which side they are on, and which side they are against. The choice of sides remains up to you of course."

Lirae nodded in understanding, "I think I can grasp that concept. What should I do?"

Ariel looked at her with an open expression, "You should make up your mind what you are willing to do my child. I can not guide you in this. I can only ask you to remain my source of inside information in the camp of the Lucky Cricket if you choose to undergo this trial."

Lirae gripped her stomach briefly, "I'm not much for pain or suffering."

Ariel smiled at her, "I can return you to your lands if you so desire. I will empty your memories of this place, and you will live your life as best you can without training or understanding your potential. Since you are of the fey people, they have granted me this much control over what happens to you. They don't desire to inflict the pain or suffering on anyone. Each of them deeply feels it again every time they share it with another. Understand they have shared this message millions of times now."

Lirae looked surprised, "How long have they been doing this?"

Ariel replied, "The original Legendary Fishermen started doing this two hundred fourteen years ago. Of their number only Sea Reaver remains on this side of life."

Lirae asked, "He's human. How can he live so long?"

Ariel nodded, "He is human as you say, but a human with the advantage of my aid and the agreement of the creator of Death itself not to take him until his task is complete."

Lirae watched the sun lower beyond the horizon as the sky deepened to dark blue, "What task is this?"

Ariel smiled, "Training you as his chosen successor. Each of the other Legendary Fishermen have trained their replacements. Only Sea Reaver has waited this long until he found what he believes is the right one out of all the millions he has met. He has waited for you since before your parents were born."

Lirae shuddered, "That is a lot of burden to put on me."

Ariel nodded, "You'll find that destiny is a royal bitch, and that the Luck somehow still holds her leash."

Lirae awoke the next morning rested and hungry. She found the vegetable garden behind the huts and picked a few small citrus fruits and some young peas for her breakfast as she walked around the island. She found several unused buildings including what looked like a group of communal housing buildings, offices, a dining hall, an infirmary, and shelters for livestock. It was clean and orderly, but unoccupied by anyone at the moment.

The construction was of the same bamboo, with woven bamboo walls she had seen everywhere else except for the white tower on the cliff. She had been told the tower was for Ariel's use, and that visiting it would not be advisable without an invitation as it served an as yet unmentioned function.

She returned to the beach and looked inside the warehouse to find only basic furnishings, clothing items of simple construction, bedding materials, and dry goods inside. Since no one had denied her the opportunity she picked the hut closest to the warehouse, and began fitting it out with some more items from the warehouse.

As the sun reached it's zenith in the sky she sat on her porch and watched a wooden door appear where none had existed a moment before. It opened and Sea Reaver stepped through it. Afterwards he turned around and removed the doorknob placing it within a silken sack at his waist as the door faded from existence and before he faced her again.

Lirae gave him a tentative smile, "Hello Sea Reaver. I've had my talk with Ariel, and I'm convinced to listen to what you have to say."

Sea Reaver smiled back and slowly walked over to the hut. Even at her height of five foot ten inches tall Lirae realized that he was at least a foot taller than herself. In his youth he must have been an intimidating specimen indeed. Now he simply radiated kindly grandfather like a professional. Then she considered his giant tiger spirit and thought maybe he still had a touch of threatening to him which had intimidated her since the first time she'd seen him.

Sea Reaver sat down on the porch stairs while looking out away from her at the ocean waves, "My people come from a country called Nordland on a different world. They are a people of ships and trade. They are also a nation which raids the weak and supports the strong. Since I've joined the Lucky Cricket my view of the world has changed drastically. I've been a missionary to other shamans among various races. Even shamans among the orcs and kobolds known to your world, and some races alien to your world."

Sea Reaver looked over at her, "Has Ariel spoken to you of what we are?"

Lirae nodded, "Those who can see the spirits of the natural world. Those known as the shamans, or Chi Masters she said."

Sea Reaver smiled, "They also call our kind mediums or seers when they can speak with the spirits of the restless dead. Our kind exists among most of the intelligent tool using races. The skills and knowledge vary among races and individuals, but the core is the same. We see spirits, we can talk to some of them, we can control other spirits, and we can project our own."

Sea Reaver looked down at her fox spirit, "Your spirit is small now because your abilities are weak and untrained. My spirit is large for a shaman because I have strengthened my spirit, and conditioned myself in its use. There are things I can do that you will never be able to accomplish. There may be things you learn which others may find impossible as well. Such is the nature of our kind. If you decide to become my replacement I will train you for the next forty or so years I have left. You will travel to various other worlds and meet several different masters of our art."

Lirae nodded, "If I want to return home, then what will you do?"

Sea Reaver nodded, "I will allow it only after you have undergone what we call the vision."

Lirae looked him in the eye, "What if I don't want to see this vision?"

Sea Reaver smiled with a touch of shyness, "Then we will allow Ariel to return you with your memories of us removed. The last thing you will recall will be going to the inn in your village, and there you will awaken with all you have learned about us gone. I will of course apologize for the turmoil your life will be briefly after that point. However, you will remain physically and mentally unharmed baring missing the memories of the last two days."

Lirae thought a moment, "If I see this vision, but then don't want to join you. What happens to me then?"

Sea Reaver smiled, "I will return you to your home with your memories intact, but changed by the experience of the vision. I caution you that none who has seen the vision has failed to understand its importance, or meaning."

Lirae asked, "Has any shaman turned down the offer of this vision?"

Sea Reaver shook his head, "Most are never given the choice. We unfairly give them the vision as I was to do with you the first day you saw me."

Lirae asked, "What stopped you then?"

Sea Reaver had a wistful smile, "You reminded me of myself as a child. I was quite shy and reserved among a boisterous and loud people. I eventually left my nation because of it to travel to live among a more reserved people in a land called Ran Li. Then I met Master Ming Ne Yu and my life was changed. I learned of my abilities, and of how to control and use them. Afterwards in my late teenage years I met Hap Sing the Lucky Cricket, and an even more drastic change happened to me."

Lirae leaned forward, "What was that Sea Reaver?"

Sea Reaver gave her a sad smile, "You'll have to experience the vision to understand. A spirit as gentle as your own will be struck hard by it. I know I have been each time since the very first time."

An hour later Lirae lay bawling curled up like a small child in her bed. The vision of the sacrifice of the Lucky Cricket would not leave. It could never leave, and neither could the terror of the thing called Rendalk Flügg.

Sea Reaver gently patted her head with misty eyes himself, "Now you can never forget what we face. Neither spell nor death can free your spirit from this vision. I'm sorry we had to do this, but all of those capable of receiving the vision must understand. This is our task, and this is our curse. I'm sorry you don't have a heart of steel, but your heart is still good and strong wood. It will grow to become healed of this pain even if the memory can never fade."

Lirae sobbed, "Why did they do it? Why didn't they flee?"

Sea Reaver gently stroked her head like a child, "The Lucky Cricket had to know what it was to sacrifice himself. He had to reveal the threat, and his willingness to pay the price to do so. In spite of their pain and hurt, it was a transitory event, and they are freed from it."

Lirae cried out, "I don't think I can accept that."

Sea Reaver looked out the window, "There is nothing to accept about it anymore. This happened over two hundred years ago, and lies now in the unreachable past. The only thing that remains is to remember the feel of the enemy with our spirits so that the Luck can take measures where it may appear again."

Lirae closed her eyes and whispered, "I want to rest now. I don't want to think of this anymore."

Sea Reaver patted her head one more time, "Sleep then child. You are safer here than anywhere else in the known worlds. We will protect you."

The next morning Lirae awoke to see a bright faced Ariel peering in from the porch of her cabana. Lirae then remembered the vision passed on by Sea Reaver. The feeling of illness wrenched her guts momentarily, and she closed her eyes until the sensation passed.

Ariel waited quietly for her to reopen her eyes, "You look terrible child."

Lirae briefly nodded her head, "I feel terrible."

Ariel smiled, "Well life goes on regardless. I've brought you some apples and pears. They should be easy enough on your stomach. If you prefer you could try some of the mangos as well."

Lirae got out of bed and walked out onto the porch, "I think I'll pass for the moment. I really want a bath before anything else. Why do you all call me child anyway? I'm almost forty years old now and an adult by elven standards."

Ariel grinned, "Child I am a fair measure over four hundred years old now by your land's reckoning. Older than any elf lives who has been cut off from the Fey Realm such as your people."

Lirae's eyes widened, "Four hundred years old?"

Ariel did a graceful mid air pirouette, "Have you ever seen a fairy my size?"

Lirae shook her head, "No."

Ariel smiled, "We never stop growing you understand, we just grow slowly like hardwood trees. If you'd like, I know a perfect bathing spot in the Fey Realm."

Lirae stretched, "That sounds very nice."

Ariel fluttered down the beach toward the cliff, "Meet me at the top of the stairs when you finish eating. We'll have to hurry before Sea Reaver or the Lucky Cricket returns."

Lirae stopped in mid-bite through an apple, "Murumph! I thought the Lucky Cricket had died?"

Ariel stopped and nodded, "He did. Stayed dead for two hundred and fourteen years too. I'm still pretty mad about it."

Lirae took another bite of apple and chewed it thoughtfully, "I don't get it. If he's died like the vision shows, then managed to come back why are you mad about it still?"

Ariel looked at her, "I'm mad because since he was dead for two hundred and fourteen years, now he is technically younger than me even though he was born first."

Lirae looked surprised, "How does one just rejoin the living?"

Ariel smiled, "Spirits go through the great cycle and rejoin the living all the time my dear. They just forget their previous lives in the process, and rarely return to the same location. The Luck cheated with the Lucky Cricket a bit is all. He can be killed, but his spirit never forgets anything about his life while in the great cycle. It is part of being the Avatar for a Number."

Lirae shook her head, "Just how long ago was he born? For the first time I mean."

Ariel thought a few moments, "Lets see, he was one hundred and fifty when I first met him. Wait was it one hundred and seventy-five by then? I've always had a bit of trouble keeping track of the passage of times on the different worlds, let alone all of the planes of existence. It is somewhere around five hundred years since he was born as the passage of time on Ygg is counted I believe."

Lirae looked confused, "Igk?"

Ariel shook her head, "Y. G. G. Pronounced Ygg. The official name of the world he was born into, although he really doesn't know it by that name I believe. Now Shangri-La here is the world he created."

Lirae looked around, "This island?"

Ariel shook her head, "This whole world was made by the Lucky Cricket. Its a test project for a new kind of existence, but then again most worlds are after all."

Lirae was shocked, "Most worlds are tests?"

Ariel nodded, "All of existence is a test."

Lirae sat down and took a bite of a peach, "This is too far above my head now."

Ariel flutted off again, "Finish eating first, and join me at the top of the stairs when you are done. I'm going to prepare the life gate for our transition to the Fey Realm."

Lirae whispered to herself, "I wonder what happens when we don't pass?"

Chapter 37 The Next Generations

ap Sing stood beside Sea Reaver as he looked over at Lirae upon her return from the Fey Realm. Lirae's long straight pale blond hair was newly cleaned, and her skin appeared freshly scrubbed as she lay upon the bower of petals. The tower's beating light shone down upon her periodically as they viewed her slumbering state.

Hap Sing had a slight frown, "You are sure about her then Sea Reaver?"

Sea Reaver nodded, "My last task shall be to make her the best replacement for me as I can."

Hap Sing reached up to place a hand on Sea Reaver's tall shoulder, "Can you see it?"

Sea Reaver nodded, "I can see it even if my vision is not what your's is Master Cricket. She has been bound like Ariel to the power of Number Three."

Hap Sing shook his head, "What she learns and knows will be known to Number Three as well."

Sea Reaver looked at Hap Sing and placed his own hand in return on Hap Sing's shoulder, "How could that be a bad thing for us Master Cricket? Do you think your other side hasn't foreseen and accounted for this very action on their part?"

Hap Sing shook his head, "It is more than being just connected to Number Three. Lirae shall never age, and never bear children. She has for all practical purposes become immortal now. Her spirit will perpetually cleanse Number Three and remain immune from the burdens of life."

Sea Reaver sighed, "I know it isn't an ideal existence Master Hap Sing. However the choice was made by her or it could not have happened. You of all people should understand the nature of such a choice."

Hap Sing frowned, "I understand it better than you. You should grasp that is why I worry so much about it. It is not an easy path chosen by her. She could never fully grasp the challenges which lie ahead of her."

Sea Reaver laughed, "Which of us ever could Master Cricket? Can you honestly say you fully understood the nature of the bargain you made with the Luck?"

Hap Sing shrugged, "I still don't understand it fully."

Sea Reaver smiled down at him, "Then why did you do it?"

Hap Sing hesitated, "Even then I understood enough to know it was absolutely necessary."

Sea Reaver bent over to pick up the sleeping form of Lirae, "I think you will probably find that she would give a similar answer upon careful reflection if you ask."

ea Reaver stepped through the doorway into the small closet sized space filled with a simple bed and small unlocked clothes chest. After him followed Lirae with an expression of impatience on her face. Lirae opened her mouth to speak, but stopped when Sea Reaver raised a finger in front of his lips. He reached behind her to shut the door which faded into nothingness as he removed the doorknob.

Sea Reaver listened a moment before talking to her in the elven language using a quiet whisper, "We'll discuss this later. You're not able to use these doorways yourself for a reason."

Lirae's voice raised a touch in anger also in the elven tongue, "Master Reaver if you recall I used the doorway on that day over fifteen years ago when you lured me into this conspiracy of yours."

Sea Reaver shook his head as he whispered, "I used that door that day as well, you just didn't understand it at the time. All you did then was follow me as you have for the last fifteen years."

Sea Reaver blinked and peered around them in the small space with his second sight before having a frustrated expression as he whispered, "Now we'll never sneak in and out of here on our mission. They've heard your noisy elf voice yapping away already and are moving to ambush us. Keep close behind me and stay silent if at all possible."

Sea Reaver opened the door of the small monk's cell and silently slipped into the hallway of the temple. Lirae moved silently a half step behind him as they walked down the hallway. They hardly took ten steps before two black clothed figures dropped from the ceiling. One in front of Sea Reaver carrying a single edged short sword, and one behind Lirae with a sectional staff.

Both ninjas silently struck out at their prey. Sea Reaver deflected the thrust of the sword blade with an impossibly fast and powerful palm strike to the flat of the blade causing it to warp and bend before being forced from the grip of the ninja.

Lirae stood her ground and turned to see the sectional staff stopped by an invisible barrier two feet away from her. The middle portion of the staff snapped in half as large bite like marks chewed through it. Lirae could see with her second sight that Sea Reaver's giant tiger spirit was stepping on either end of the now broken staff to the evident confusion of the ninja facing her.

Sea Reaver's voice boomed out while speaking in the Ran Li dialect, "Pitiful! How do you ever expect to protect the Chi Master Academy if that is the best you can do?"

A white robed man stepped out of the cell three doors down and cried out in the Ran Li language as he ran toward them, "Ancient one! We did not know you were to arrive today. You should have told us you were coming. Have you been here long?"

The white robed man looked at the hesitant ninjas, "Bow you fools. This is one of the Ancient Tiger Monks. An actual companion of the powerful Chi Master Hap Sing. Show him respect lest you anger him and bring down his wrath upon yourselves."

The monk and the ninjas both bowed their heads low to the ground until they saw Sea Reaver return the slightest of bows in response. The monk stood up straight again and signaled to the ninjas who rapidly departed with their damaged weapons. The monk then caught sight of Lirae standing closely behind Sea Reaver. The monk shifted position to see her better as she looked at him with wide eyes.

The monk looked carefully at Lirae with a bit of uncertainty and surprise, "Who is this unusual beautiful woman Ancient Master? If you will pardon my frank assessment, but I do not believe that she appears fully human. Is she a being from your homeland of Nordland?"

Sea Reaver laughed politely, "That is because my apprentice isn't remotely human. Her kind are known as elves in her lands. They are a different race altogether from human kind."

The monk nodded, "I understand. Another of the outlandish races which are seen more often. All who practice Chi Magic are still welcome here. Is there a particular Master you seek Ancient Master?"

Sea Reaver shook his head, "I'm looking for your chief librarian actually. There are some research materials we need for her studies."

The monk smiled, "We can accommodate that as well I'm certain. Follow after me and I will introduce you to him."

As the monk started walking away Lirae looked at him with her second sight. Attached to him she could plainly see the ribbon of the Lucky Cricket. Lirae looked surprised and tugged at the sleeve of Sea Reaver.

Sea Reaver opened an eye wide at he looked back at her and asked in the elven tongue, "What?"

Lirae whispered in the elven tongue, "He has a ribbon connected to Hap Sing."

Sea Reaver nodded, "I know that. This is the Chi Master Academy in Yokito. What did you expect to find?"

Lirae spoke a bit louder, "He couldn't be more than twenty to thirty years old in age. When did you get a chance to put a ribbon on him?"

Sea Reaver smiled, "I didn't. He is one of the first ones of the next cycle."

Lirae looked worried, "What do you mean next cycle."

Sea Reaver looked at the other ribbons connected to the monk, "He is from the first group of Chi Master spirits which has returned through the great cycle of spirits. He was born with the connection to the Lucky Cricket already in place. His first formative memory would have been of the vision."

Lirae's brows furrowed, "That is somewhat disturbing."

Sea Reaver shook his head, "That has been the plan of the Luck for a long time. To keep track of the spirits of the Chi Masters as they come back through the cycle to claim them as its own each time."

Lirae whispered harshly, "Isn't that breaking the rules?"

Sea Reaver smiled, "Whose rules? Certainly not the rules made by the Luck. It is nice to see that two hundred and thirty years of my life have not been wasted. It is working as planned after all."

Lirae looked at the monk carefully, "Can you tell whose spirit it was?"

Sea Reaver turned and tapped her lightly on the forehead with his index finger, "That is none of your business. He is his own spirit. What he was before has no bearing on who he is now. His only memory of that former life is in the vision which guides him to help protect reality. Nothing else matters to him, and it shouldn't to us either."

Lirae frowned, "I hate when you do that."

Sea Reaver smiled innocently as he turned back and continued following the monk, "Which?"

Lirae smirked unseen behind him, "Pick your choice."

Sea Reaver and Lirae stood in the room filled with shelves covered in scrolls, tomes, books, and parchments. Through an open doorway they could see the adjoining room which contained sloped desks where the Chi Master Academy students sat quietly on stools examining materials from the Archives. In front of Sea Reaver and Lirae was a tall desk with an older man with still black hair dressed in the robes of a Chi Master.

Sea Reaver spoke in a hushed voice in the Ran Li dialect, "Master Librarian we need materials for instruction in the language of Ran Li. They need to be suitable for a native speaker of another tongue, but a novice in the Ran Li dialect."

The Master Librarian put a hand up to his chin for a moment, "That is a tricky requirement. What is their native tongue?"

Sea Reaver pointed to Lirae, "My student speaks and reads a moderate variation on the Fey dialect. She is also fairly fluent in both speech and writing of the planar trade vernacular."

The Master Librarian put his index finger up to his left temple briefly, "That is a challenging request. I do not believe the materials in our library will meet your needs. Have you considered teaching her the Nordland dialect first? We do have a set of materials for translation between Nordland and Ran Li tongues. We also can provide materials regarding any of the local variations common to our continent."

As Sea Reaver continued to discuss the various language materials available with the Master Librarian, Lirae not understanding their conversation looked over with her second sight at the various students and teachers quietly working in the library. Over the years of Lirae's training she had learned to perceive the spirit ribbons, and most particularly she could see the ribbons connected to the Luck as they were the easiest for her to observe on others.

Lirae then noted that a few different distinct patterns existed on these ribbons. The Master Librarian who seemed to be about seventy or eighty had one type of ribbon, as did most of the older instructors. The younger instructors and students had a different pattern. The pattern on her own ribbon to the Luck showed almost the same as the one that Sea Reaver had. Each individual ribbon had slight variations, but three distinctly different base patterns were present all total.

Sea Reaver spoke a little louder in the planar trade tongue as he looked at Lirae, "Lirae, are you paying attention?"

Lirae returned her attention back to Sea Reaver and spoke in elvish, "Sorry Master Reaver. I was noticing something unusual."

Sea Reaver placed a hand upon her shoulder and replied in the planar trade tongue, "It can be considered impolite to stare at people like that here. This is most especially true while using the second sight in this place. I should have warned you to be more careful about it. Please speak in the Planar Trade speech like I taught you."

Lirae bowed her head briefly in hesitant planar trade tongue, "I'm sorry Master Reaver. I was just noticing that the ribbons of the Luck are different on some people than our ribbons."

The Master Librarian spoke up in Ran Li dialect, "Your apprentice speaks an odd variation on the Ygg Standard Trade dialect it seems. You should have mentioned that first. We do have some translation materials for that language in section, let me see. Ah yes, section twenty one shelf twenty one, pretty easy to remember then. That is the foreign languages section four rooms to the east. The librarian assigned to that room can assist you further with finding the materials you need, and a space to review them in privacy if you desire."

Sea Reaver bowed to the Master Librarian and spoke again in the Ran Li dialect, "Thank you for your assistance."

The Master Librarian looked at him with surprise as he returned the bow, "Think nothing of it Ancient Master."

The Master Librarian then looked at Lirae while speaking the Planar Trade tongue, "Young Miss you are not mistaken that two basic patterns still exist here in Ran Li. Unfortunately the first and oldest pattern is never seen any more except in the case of the rare Ancient Masters."

Lirae looked at the Master Librarian and asked, "Why are there three types?"

The Master Librarian smiled, "There are three types of Chi Master serving the Lucky Cricket is all. The first types are those rare Chi Masters who have been shown the vision by one of the Legendary Fishermen. Most of that generation has passed here in Ran Li. Even rarer are those who have received a ribbon from the Lucky Cricket himself before his passing. The Ancient Master here is an example of this as well, and if you know where to look you can see a clear difference between his ribbon and mine, while it is a subtle difference in pattern between his and your ribbon young miss. Thus the Ancient Master is one of the Legendary Fishermen who has received his ribbon from the Lucky Cricket before his sacrifice. You have received your ribbon directly from one of the Legendary Fishermen."

Lirae spoke carefully, "Why are there two other kinds then?"

The Master Librarian looked at his own ribbon briefly, "I was found as a young man by another Chi Master who had passed the vision on to me. They were not one of the Legendary Fishermen, so the ribbon I carry is what we call a second generation ribbon here at the Chi Master academy. That is any ribbon passed from a Chi Master who is not one of the Legendary Fishermen. I have spread a number of these ribbons myself over the years. The rumor is that the passing of the vision

Chapter 37   *375*

is somewhat less life altering for those who receive it from someone other than a Legendary Fisherman, but that is a subjective measure I believe."

Lirae looked at Sea Reaver, "The third kind of ribbon comes from those who are born with it then?"

Sea Reaver smiled at her before speaking with restrained pride in his voice, "There is a finite amount of spirits with the potential for accessing the spiritual world in life. Most of my very long life was spent locating them so that we could achieve this point in history. Our task is almost done, and it remains to the following generations to bring any remaining Chi Masters into the group."

Lirae looked at the group of younger instructors and students in the adjoining room, "There are so many who have returned through the cycle already."

Sea Reaver smiled, "Yes there are here in Ran Li, but you are unused to seeing large concentrations of Chi Masters. This represents the gathering of most of this nation's young Chi Masters, as well as several from other nations who seek to learn of their abilities and how to use them. Most of us older Chi Masters tend to be more solitary. We can remember the times where it was less accepted to use our abilities."

The Master Librarian spoke quietly, "Not all lands treat Chi Masters well either. Several of our students are refugees from places where their abilities are considered suspicious."

Lirae spoke with a cautious note, "All of them appear to be human."

The Master Librarian nodded, "Yes they are mostly humans. The savage barbarian races do not receive a comfortable welcome in Ran Li. Too much bad blood from the past history most certainly. They are required to care for and teach their future generations of Shamans as best they are able. I'm told converting most of their kind was the work of the Legendary Fishermen. Each one of the Legendary Fishermen was a former Tiger Monk, and quite skilled in the arts of ninjitsu before the Lucky Cricket forbid them from using physical weapons. They still retain the ability to move silently and unseen as any other ninja, and I wouldn't want to challenge the Ancient Master to an unarmed fight by any means."

Lirae looked surprised, "Why is that?"

The Master Librarian smiled, "Their Tiger Spirits are rumored to keep them from ever being surprised by an opponent, and are quiet effective against both regular ninja which can not perceive them, and even those Chi Masters who could perceive them found they were powerless before their abilities. The legend in Ran Li is that a deadlier form of assassin has never existed. All the Chi Masters of Ran Li have refused to become assassins after receiving the vision of the Lucky Cricket. The Ancient Master is from the last group of them to be trained and placed into service."

Sea Reaver gave a slight sigh, "I am the last member of that last group. All the rest have passed on now."

The Master Librarian looked surprised, "Then you must talk to our archivist Yu Akane Ancient Master. She will want to record your knowledge of their passing for our records. It is very rare we see one of you. There is still much we need to learn of the past, and what you've done in the past centuries."

Sea Reaver thought a moment before speaking, "I will sit with your archivist to discuss some of my past if you can provide a private language instructor for my apprentice Lirae."

The Master Librarian answered, "We would have to speak to the Headmaster of the Academy to formalize it. The value of insight you could bring to our histories would be worth the dedication of one of our instructors to her education."

Lirae spoke to Sea Reaver rapidly in quiet elvish as they departed the library, "I didn't see any elves here today. Where are the elves of this world? Are there none in these lands?"

Sea Reaver shook his head and replied in elvish, "They dwell in mostly self imposed exile in a country called Letheron on the same continent as Nordland. It is the last place with major gateways between the Prime and the Fey Realm. Small elven colonies and individual elves do exist in some human lands on the other continent, but they are primarily colonies of mixed race elves rejected by their elven brethren."

Lirae slowly shook her head, "It is amazing how different, yet in some ways how much the same your home world is to my own."

Sea Reaver shrugged, "I was born to this world, but I don't claim it as my own any more. I belong in Shangri-La as do you now. This is just a business trip. Keep your caution when speaking to these people. They are Chi Masters and allies, but they also are not necessarily your friends. Politics exist here as well as everywhere. The style of politics used here is more violent than you may be accustomed to in your own country."

Lirae looked surprised, "Are there fights?"

Sea Reaver shook his head, "There are assassinations. Those ninja earlier were not just attacking to defend against a stranger in the academy. They knew who I am, and what I represent. They were testing to see if any weakness exists in my defense. The disbanding of the Tiger Monks has created a vacuum of power which has lasted since the death of the Lucky Cricket. They know I will not harm anyone beyond what is necessary to defend my life. They think it a weakness of character among the Legendary Fishermen."

Lirae's eyes widened, "That does not make sense. Why would they consider it a weakness of character to not kill?"

Sea Reaver sighed, "It is not a weakness in reality, but this culture puts a high value on martial superiority in certain political circles. The Tiger Monks were considered the best of the Emperor's special assassination forces in my time. After our seven years of service in the name of Hap Sing we were to quietly retire from the public face of the organization, and join in the private activities directed by the Emperor against his enemies. Because of the message of Hap Sing that has changed. None of the Chi Masters of the Academy here will train in martial activities anymore. The Emperor and his remaining ninja forces hope that forcing a Legendary Fisherman to fight with deadly consequences will open up the possibility of a martial Chi Master group again. It is one of the key reasons we generally have not spent much time here."

Lirae contemplated silently for a few moments, "Then why would they attack me as well Master Reaver?"

Sea Reaver chuckled in a low tone, "In order to determine if we are training others to fight while denying them the opportunity to have our services. I'm glad to say that your lack of a direct martial response probably stopped the fight quicker than any protection I provided you. Those ninja were skilled enough to tell that you were either not martially skilled, or that you were an exceptional actor."

Lirae looked slightly offended, "Do they think the elves so weak here?"

Sea Reaver shrugged, "They don't know elves at all over here. They have heard stories of them at best. They may know that elves are considered exceptional at archery, but since you do not carry a bow or other overt weapons it is pretty obvious that any martial training you hold would likely be in the use of your Chi Master abilities."

Lirae lightly laughed, "Me with a bow. They should know that I'm pretty lousy with a bow for an elf."

Sea Reaver chuckled briefly, "I could not envision it myself either. You couldn't even report a stranger in your lands before you determined whether he was a danger or not. You didn't even carry a weapon with you at any time when you came to observe me back then. No, I couldn't see you doing anything violent."

Lirae smiled, "I couldn't see you doing anything violent either Master Reaver."

Sea Reaver shrugged, "I don't need a weapon to kill. My entire being could be a weapon if I chose to be dangerous. Hap Sing himself demonstrated the ability to destroy an entire city at a moment's notice if he so desired."

Lirae shook her head, "I don't think I'll ever understand why the Lucky Cricket submitted to such an end rather than use his ability to aid his escape at the very least."

Sea Reaver smiled, "I understand it well now. It was more important for his plans to create a compelling message than it was to live. Some things simply are worth more than life itself."

Chapter 38 Contemplation

Hap Sing sat at the small tea table across from the Strategist personality of Number Seven. They were in the new offices of Number Seven in the sixth ring of the eternal city of Centrus the strange heart of the planar divide. Hap Sing was thinking about fishing as he sipped his tea.

Number Seven spoke, "I'm pretty happy with these new offices. They are closer to the center of things than even my earlier office. More room for my staff, and most important even more concurrent doorways can be managed from here."

Hap Sing looked around the stone walled room with polished marble floors, "It is nice enough I guess. I prefer my bungalow though. There is a nice ocean breeze there."

Number Seven laughed, "You just like it because you made it yourself."

Hap Sing smiled in a good natured manner, "We made it ourselves you mean. I had plenty of help."

Number Seven took a sip of its own tea, "This office will suit me fine. Now on to business. The first stages are almost complete. Our network of watchers is in place. They are ready to inform me if the elder gods make a move. A being tainted in spirit by the elder gods can't readily appear on the existing worlds of the prime material without one of them sensing it through their dreams. Once they dream it, we will know where and when it is happening."

Hap Sing added, "Balinac has enough spirits of the dead Chi Masters at its bathhouse in the dreaming now to detect when the elder gods seek to breach the far realms of the dreaming. You're confident the spirit ribbon will stay attached through many transitions through the cycle?"

Number Seven nodded, "I've sequentially coded them as Lirae has noticed already. If the link becomes weaker over successive returns from the afterlife, then I will set about renewing the bond as necessary. A quick diversion to my portion of the dreaming before returning through the cycle should be all that is required."

Hap Sing though a while, "Is there a chance these connections can be used against us?"

Number Seven frowned slightly as it spoke, "The possibility exists for one of our watchers to be compromised, but then again there is no world with only one watcher on it. I'll do my best to keep all of the worlds sufficiently covered by redundant watchers just in case. The possibility also exists of other beings creating worlds in pocket planes to build up a force of tainted spawn first before launching an assault."

Hap Sing took another sip of tea, "How do you plan to counter such a move?"

Number Seven looked at Hap Sing, "That will be our next task. We'll need to recruit a force of beings capable of directly engaging the enemy on their level in such a case."

Hap Sing put down his cup, "The majority of Chi Masters will never be up to such a task."

Number Seven looked at him closely, "Which is why the Chi Masters are just the beginning. We need to carefully build a force which is up to the task. We have to recruit this force. Pick the right kinds of individuals who can meet our requirements, test them until we can assure both their competence and reliability. Only then can we begin to deploy them."

Hap Sing pinched the bridge of his nose briefly, "This is getting even more difficult now."

Number Seven smiled a wicked grin, "We are traipsing on a thin edge to reach our goal. This kind of force must be recruited, nourished, trained, and equipped without alerting anyone who isn't a trusted ally. They will be given access to secrets that no mortal has ever known, and become both less mortal, and more than mortal because of it."

Hap Sing looked at Number Seven with deep concern, "A new breed of gods then?"

Number Seven shook his head, "Nothing quite so dramatic, just a new pantheon of gods native to Shangri-La. These will be a different type of god though. Gods which are built from mortals up instead of from spirits down. It should hopefully create a greater level of sympathy for their followers than the prior pantheons have displayed."

Hap Sing asked, "How will you monitor and control such a group of gods?"

Number Seven smiled, "Certain allies of mine shall be given a chance to provide an Avatar like yourself to guide them."

Hap Sing shook his head, "I should have known that Lirae was your idea in the first place."

Number Seven shook his head, "Actually much like yourself, Lirae had already made a bargain with Number Three long before she was born. I was simply the one who told Number Three how it was done in exchange for her allegiance. I didn't pick which spirit Number Three has chosen. I was pleasantly surprised to find Number Three has picked another of the rare pure spirits like yourself."

Hap Sing tilted his head slightly to the left, "It doesn't hurt that the spirit is also a Chi Master which you can connect to and monitor I suppose."

Number Seven shrugged slightly, "That is a two edged sword for me actually. It is a two way connection, and Number Three can watch me through it as well. It is very much a case of mutual assurances here. A lot of trust yet verify exists in any deals made with my own kind. I usually win those arrangements by sticking with my part of any bargain I make, and by broadly announcing when another being fails to meet their obligations. The so called Dread God Mortis still hasn't lived down his ruined reputation after trying to cheat me. The cost of breaking a deal with me is much worse than abiding by the deal would ever be."

Hap Sing looked around the office again, "Are you sure this location is secure? What happens if this discussion becomes known?"

Number Seven laughed, "It is as secure as any place in the material realms can be relatively speaking. In truth that means not very much. It is subject to observation, intrusion, or compromise if the right kinds of powers choose to try it. Frankly any power with that level of knowledge or ability would be a significant challenge to our plans."

Hap Sing sighed, "Then why risk discussing it here?"

Number Seven smiled, "That is the problem with listening in on me. You never know if you are getting the whole story, or just what I want you to know. Purposefully leaked information has its own kind of value. Intrusion is even more meaningless. My equipment is not of use without me guiding it."

Number Seven faded to partial translucency, "My physical form is non-existent and my spirit is well beyond the ability of all but a select few to hinder."

Hap Sing faded to partial translucency as well, "I get your point. Why use a physical office then?"

Number Seven smiled again, "Most of my clients are material after all. It makes them feel more at ease to meet me in a physical setting."

The insubstantial Hap Sing finished the rest of his insubstantial cup of tea, "I'm returning to the Isle of Life for now. I expect to have a few more years before Sea Reaver and Lirae return from their training trip through the prime material to relax and enjoy myself."

Number Seven watched as Hap Sing faded completely from the room. It smiled a secret smile, and then gradually transformed into a tiger cub which paced through a doorway to a new room containing a control panel and the door with the brass plaque with the writing *Reality or Close to It.*

Hap Sing sat up on his divan in the white tower. He was getting used to spiritually projecting himself to places other than the dreaming as necessary. Getting the appearance and feel of solidity had been a bit tricky for a while, but he was mastering the art of it now.

Hap Sing then looked at his connection to the Luck and read the sub-text contained within which couldn't be understood by someone other than him and Number Seven. There was much that they had said with the knowledge that there were observers watching them. Much of what remained unsaid was plain for him to read on the ribbon between them.

Most of what they were planning had to be overt and confirmable by other powers including allies, neutral forces, and foes. The rest had to be kept secret from everyone except themselves for the time being. Hap Sing and the Luck through him remained the only beings of their knowledge with that level of ability to read the spirit ribbons. Hap Sing didn't like what it had to say.

Hap Sing sighed, "Walking a fine edge? I'm going fishing first before such foolishness."

Hap Sing headed outside the tower. Down the stairs cut into the cliff, and walked down the beach to the central bungalow in the row of five. He picked up his fishing pole and creel. Then he walked over to his boat tied up at the dock. He paddled out from the shore until he was in the middle of the bay before putting his line in the water. A gradual faint smile spread across his lips as he relaxed.

Hap Sing sat in the hot water of the outdoor bath in the tropical realm of Balinac in the dreaming. Balinac was nowhere to be seen, but a man apparently in his fifties came out from the sliding door of the inn and took a seat in the bath next to Hap Sing. Hap Sing looked at him trying to see the adolescent boy he remembered from his last meeting.

The man spoke first, "How much time has passed so far Hap Sing?"

Hap Sing sighed, "Time doesn't really matter here. Don't be so restless Wen Lu. You'll return when you are ready. If you don't mind waiting a bit longer, then I've even got an offer to make you."

Wen Lu asked, "What kind of offer?"

Hap Sing gave a slight smile, "How does semi immortality sound?"

Wen Lu frowned, "Like a lot of dangerous work I would guess?"

Hap Sing looked at him with a raised eyebrow, "There would be some work most certainly, but it would also come with some perks. You'll have forgotten about your former life when you return. However, I can pick an opportune place and time for you to arrive. I guarantee you'll be moved into a place of prominence and public service."

Wen Lu shook his head slightly, "You want to make me a public servant? That sounds like a step down from the bodyguard I was in my last life."

Hap Sing sighed, "I'm offering you a position in a new pantheon we are eventually putting together. I get my pick of beings to submit through the process, and I think that you've shown the right kind of material for it. You'll have to become mortal again, and you will also have to die again before your name will be submitted. You won't have to go back through the cycle again after you die. Your spirit will be very purified through an extended rest at Balinac's bathhouse. That means you'll be good through a large number mortal life spans and a very great number of years before spiritual corruption could become an issue."

Wen Lu thought a moment, "What kind of god are you thinking about?"

Hap Sing smiled, "That is up to you of course. Think of it as my payment for the hard service I've already put you through."

Wen Lu laughed, "It was my cup of tea already and you knew it. I'll sign up to be the god you want, but don't expect me to bark whenever you call. I'm my own person."

Hap Sing laughed along with him, "Of course Wen Lu. Your spirit will remember our bargain even if your mortal self does not. I'll keep my word."

Wen Lu nodded, "I know you will Hap Sing. Don't forget to give me a fish when we meet again in life. That will be the password my spirit will remember. I'll trust you then just like I did as a child when you brought my mother and I all those fish as well."

Hap Sing nodded, "I'll remember Wen Lu. I'll bring you that fish you want."

Wen Lu smiled, "I couldn't ask for more then. Consider our bargain made."

Hap Sing smiled, "Thank you Wen Lu. I have to go now. I've got a fish on the line."

Wen Lu laughed, "Only you would be working while fishing."

Hap Sing laughed along with him, "I've gotten better at it is all. Goodbye Wen Lu."

Wen Lu watched as Hap Sing faded from the bath into nothingness.

Hap Sing sat in his boat and pulled the fish in on the line deftly catching it with a flip of his net as it neared the surface of the water. He thought of the metaphor which had driven his whole life with a slight smile on his lips. The fisherman was certainly an appropriate description for him in more than one way.

Hap Sing paddled his boat into shore so that he could prepare his dinner. As he neared the shore Ariel came fluttering out from the woods. She waited for him while holding several vegetables from her garden in her hands.

Hap Sing looked at the vegetables as he got out of his boat, "I need to teach you how to grow rice one day."

Ariel laughed, "I doubt you can teach me how to grow anything Lucky Cricket."

Hap Sing looked at the vegetables in her hands, "I'll have some of the carrots and peas then."

Ariel shook her head, "You'll eat some green leafy vegetables as well. They will make you healthy, and they taste good as well."

Hap Sing smiled slightly, "When did you get to pick what I eat?"

Ariel smiled, "I still let you eat that ghastly fish, so you'll have to compromise."

Hap Sing held his hand out strait in front of him and up over her head, "If you had more meat in your diet, then you wouldn't grow so slowly I think."

Ariel shuddered, "Yuck. No one wants to contemplate carnivorous fairies. We just aren't built that way."

Hap Sing laughed, "You don't look much like a fairy anymore. You're a giant among your kind."

Ariel was self conscious, "A giant? I'm not too big am I? Have I lost my cuteness?"

Hap Sing smiled, "Don't worry you're still plenty cute. I'm sure all the boy fairies still want to marry you."

Ariel smirked, "Boy fairies have nothing but fluff between their ears. I'll take a human boyfriend over them any day."

Hap Sing shook his head as the walked over to his cooking fire to prepare their dinner. Ariel fluttered around and helped prepare the vegetables as he grilled the fish.

Chapter 39 New Beginnings

Hapusai Ran stood before the moderately overweight middle aged Lord Togusawa who was wearing a formal yukata while sitting on a cushion on the raised platform at one end of the room. Before Lord Togusawa was a small table covered in scrolls, ink bottles, quills, and a blotter. On one corner of the table sat Lord Togusawa's seal indicating his status as the chief magistrate for the emperor of Ran Li.

Lord Togusawa spoke with a hard edge in his voice, "This leader you speak of has been dead and gone for over two thousand years, and yet these Chi Masters still will not let go of their insistence of non-violence. The potential that is there in the power they wield is useless as long as they refuse to fight for Ran Li. I'm telling you it boarders on treason."

Hapusai Ran held a carefully neutral expression as he answered, "Lord Togusawa, the Tiger Monks you had me research are only a legend master. No records of their existence have actually survived all this time. They might never have really existed back then. It is possible the very nature of a Chi Master's abilities could conflict with training as ninja."

Lord Togusawa had an edge of anger in his voice, "You may be the best ninja master in all of Yokito Hapusai, but you obviously don't know much about my own family history. I'm a direct descendent from Togusawa Hiro who was one of those self same Tiger Monks. My wife Akane is a blood descendent of the Chi Master Priestess who left the blasted dead zone where nothing can grow and no one lives in the western portion of the city. Don't tell me their abilities are incompatible with a ninja training regimen. Tell me how I can convince them to submit to joining our armed forces."

Hapusai Ran patiently answered, "Records indicate that several past emperors and warlords have tried in the past. Each of them has failed. The use of force results in dead Chi Masters. The dead Chi Masters result in uprisings among the people. Three emperors in the past one thousand years have lost their dynasties in the attempt along with their entire family lines. Regardless of that, even with the assistance of martial Chi Masters, there is still no reasonable way to restore a member of the Togusawa family line to the imperial lineage through force of arms. It would only cause turmoil and unrest among the people in the attempt."

Lord Togusawa grunted in disgust, "I mean to do no such thing. I only seek to help my emperor secure his throne in these times of unrest."

Hapusai Ran bowed deeply, "I pardon my Lord if I have given offense in my evaluation. I speak but from the examples that history has provided us, without meaning to imply your intent to do anything of the sort."

Lord Togusawa raised an eyebrow, "For as skilled as you are Hapusai, you are still young and naive in some ways. Some things should not be spoken even in private do you understand. We are loyal servants, or else our honor is nothing. Do you understand me Hapsuai."

Hapusai Ran kept his expression neutral, "I understand Lord Togusawa. I am the knife you wield or sheath at your command."

Lord Togusawa turned back to his paperwork, "You are dismissed. Go look again into that other matter we discussed earlier."

Hapusai Ran had left without a sound or trace when Lord Togusawa raised his head again.

Hapusai Ran knelt before the Grandmaster Ninja Li Wong in their training dojo. Li Wong was old, and no longer in active service, but he still ran the information collection and distribution of the emperor's ninja force.

Hapusai Ran looked into Li Wong's face, "I relayed the information as you desired, but it seems Lord Togusawa has other sources of information which contradicted my version of events. He has not been convinced to cease this line of inquiry, but unfortunately has come to doubt my ability to advise him in the manner which best suits his ambition."

Li Wong thought and answered slowly, "Perhaps there is something else which has caused this distrust in you to form. What is this other assignment he has given you?"

Hapusai Ran hesitated a moment, "Just a personal matter. The Lord suspects his wife Akane of an assignation with an unknown man."

Li Wong nodded, "Have you discovered any evidence of this?"

Hapusai Ran shook his head, "I have not been able to discover any unknown men making their way into her presence. They would have to be much better than my ninja forces and I to slip past my careful watch over her."

Li Wong looked at Hapusai Ran carefully, "Twice then you have failed to give Lord Togusawa what he expects to receive from you. I would be careful not to fail him a third time if I were in your position. Otherwise his next assignment for you could be a fatal one."

Hapusai Ran nodded, " Of course Grandmaster Li. What shall I do about the prohibition?"

Li Wong replied, "It is as you have said, the Lucky Cricket has forbidden the Chi Masters from taking up arms. Our own records from the Grandmasters who served during the life time of the Lucky Cricket Hap Sing show that every Grandmaster has deferred to the Lucky Cricket's wishes even over the direct orders of the emperors of his time. That is not a power casually wielded or of an insignificant nature. If such a being still exists in our time, then he is not one to offend by ignoring his prohibitions."

Hapusai Ran asked, "How would a man ever confirm the existence of such a being?"

Li Wong replied, "The Lucky Cricket Hap Sing was described in the writings of his time as always dressing as a common fisherman as were his closest followers the former Tiger Monks after his death. He sought neither wealth or power, but contained a great power to destroy at his command. When he was captured and tortured by his enemies the Lucky Cricket chose to submit and accept his death rather than unleash the horrible power at his command. This example has guided the Chi Master philosophy about violence and conflict since that time. The dead spot surrounded by western Yokito is where this happened, and his first disciple the White Raven's chosen mistress Ming Yuki Nene came after his death and smote all of his enemies into ruin."

Hapusai Ran shook his head, "That is a lot of conjecture and rumor to set the basis of the national policy. There has to be something more substantial to these stories other than legends of such an improbable nature."

Li Wong gave a slight upturn of his lips, "It has been also reported that this Hap Sing has occasionally appeared from time to time after his death."

Hapusai Ran shook his head, "A trick of various plotting warlords over the centuries trying to influence the people I don't doubt."

Li Wong shrugged, "Perhaps it has been a trick, but if so then the reputable Chi Masters and Grandmaster Ninjas which have documented their own personal beliefs about their direct experiences over the centuries were either fooled or involved in the trickery."

Hapusai Ran looked at Li Wong closely, "You believe these reports then?"

Li Wong tilted his aging head down, "I believe that these people did believe it themselves. None of those who have reported his appearance have been seen to have profited by it. A large number of them experienced difficult or trying times because of their meeting."

Hapusai Ran raised an eyebrow, "A curious twist on the story then. May I ask when was the last time this Lucky Cricket supposedly appeared to a reputable source in Ran Li."

Li Wong nodded, "The last report in our files show him appearing fifty four years ago to my predecessor Chu Han. The same Chu Han who defended the country on an unauthorized mission against a rising warlord in Udomo, and who was executed because of his loss of face for embarrassing the emperor of Ran Li. Before leaving on this mission Chu Han documented his encounter with Hap Sing, and his belief that he was doing the right thing for Ran Li even if the emperor was against the action. I knew Chu Han as a decent man in my early years as a trainee under his tutelage. He called me his greatest student, and ensured that none of his shame would reflect back on the ninjas assigned under him. I am not prone to believe that he was either a fool or involved in a plot to sacrifice his own life to enrich another."

Hapusai Ran hesitated a long moment in thought before responding, "Given the sincerity of your story, I will grant this being called the Lucky Cricket may actually exist then."

Li Wong nodded, "Good my greatest student. It is good that you are keeping an open mind. Now I will tell you what has not been shared outside of the ranks of the Chi Masters and a select few of the ninja in Ran Li. The Lucky Cricket Hap Sing is connected to every Chi Master that is born through a ribbon of destiny. They know the truth of his existence because this ribbon is connected to them for their entire lives. To their vision it fades off into the unknowable distance."

Hapusai Ran smiled, "That is an interesting detail, but I don't see the relevance."

Li Wong wore a slight frown, "It is the task of the archivist at the Chi Master Academy to record each time in history when the ribbon connection to the Lucky Cricket Hap Sing no longer fades into the distance, but continues in an unwavering connection pointing into a specific direction. I will provide you a list, but you will see that after each time a period of turmoil existed in some land or place along the triangulated course of that ribbon. Some times it was in Ran Li, other times in lands on the other continents across the great oceans. The Chi Masters know that The Lucky Cricket is a harbinger of terrible events which need to be managed before they spiral out of control. This is of course private information which is never to be shared outside of the ranks of ninja, and only then with your future successor when the time comes."

Hapusai Ran lay in bed feeling satisfied and less edgy than he had all week after speaking to Li Wong. He peered into the sleepy face of the young woman who lay beside him, and couldn't help feel another twinge of guilt at his betrayal. Akane was very pretty, very lonely, and very much more than a lecherous old toad like Lord Togusawa ever deserved as his fourth wife.

Hapusai Ran knew that tonight Akane could see him because Lord Togusawa was away pursuing his unsavory tastes. It was known among his servants that Lord Togusawa only married his four wives to establish political connections and the potential heirs which could result.

Togusawa Akane looked at him with a worried smile, "Why are you so worried my love?"

Hapusai Ran tried to focus on her, "It is nothing really. Just business my dear Akane."

Togusawa Akane clutched him closely, "I have to tell you something. Something important."

Hapusai Ran gave her a reassuring smile, "You can speak to me my dear Akane. I'm listening."

Togusawa Akane hesitated then blurted out, "I've missed. Twice I mean."

Hapusai Ran was momentarily confused, "Missed what? Breakfast?"

Togusawa Akane looked at him plaintively, "I think I'm pregnant."

Hapusai Ran quickly thought, "Wait, let me think. This shouldn't be a problem. When was the last time you've been with your husband?"

Togusawa Akane pulled away from him, "Is that what you're worried about? That I might have his child. I haven't been with him that way in over three months now. The child can only be yours."

Hapusai Ran shook his head, "You don't understand Akane. Lord Togusawa set me to watch you six months ago. He suspects you've been with someone other than him. If you have a child that couldn't be his own, then there is no telling what he may do."

Togusawa Akane shook her head as her voice rose, "No you don't understand what it is to be treated like a possession by him. To have him treat you like something only to bear his heirs. I despise the man. He is something less than a man. That is why I took you to my bed. That is why I fell in love with you, not him."

Hapusai Ran stood up and started getting dressed quickly, "We can't do this. Not anymore. It is too dangerous for you. You can say the baby has come early. He should believe it."

Togusawa Akane looked at him with tears in her eyes, "We could run away together. We could make a life just the two of us and our child. Don't leave me alone like this Ran."

Hapusai Ran shook his head, "We can't escape the reach of his ninja forces. They would track us down and kill us anywhere we went. There is no way for us to live that kind of dream Akane."

Togusawa Akane dried her eyes, "Go then. Don't come to my rooms to be with me again. Otherwise I will report us both to my husband and let his vengeance fall where it may. I'll bear our child as if it is his then if that is what you really want. Let it always remind you of your honor."

Hapusai Ran quickly left and hid on a roof cornice slowly sucking in the cool night air. He kept thinking about how his life could have unexpectedly gone so wrong.

Hapusai Ran walked down the road through Hung Chan village on the outskirts of Ran Li. He had stayed away from Yokito and the capital home of Lord Togusawa and Akane for six months. He took any missions which entailed high risk, and high reward that his Lord requested of him. Somehow it still didn't seem to remove the stain he felt upon his honor.

Hapusai Ran left the village gates to see the large prosperous Yu family farm dominating most of the valley. It was still very early in the morning with no one about save the guards by the gate. Then his sharp eyesight caught the form of a short man silhouetted by the early predawn light sitting near the pond on the farm next to the outlet stream.

Hapusai Ran was inexplicably bothered by this image as if something was tickling the corner of his consciousness. Hapusai Ran changed his course and walked casually over to see what the man was doing. As Hapusai Ran silently approached he saw that the man's back was fully exposed and the man's gaze was toward the rising sun.

Hapusai Ran watched as the man cast a line attached to a bamboo pole into the water. As Hapusai Ran quietly watched the figure as only a ninja could he noticed the clothing of the man was simple, and very out of style even for a peasant. The lines and cut of the clothing resembled something from ancient scrolls right down to the woven bamboo hat. At the sight of it the hairs on the back of Hapusai Ran's neck involuntarily rose.

The fisherman spoke, "I have come a long way to talk to you ninja. Don't be so shy, or think that you can hide from my sight. Your aura glows very brightly, and makes it hard to hide your approach."

Hapusai Ran walked forward, "I believe you are mistaken sir. I'm just a traveler setting out to return to my home."

The fisherman laughed, "Still haven't met a ninja who doesn't deny it on the first time. See that village back there you just left. That was named for my friend General Li Chan, and his son and also my friend General Li Hung the original first Grandmaster of the ninja assassination corps in Ran Li. If you think I can't recognize a ninja when I see one, then you are very sadly mistaken."

Hapusai Ran dropped all pretense as he drew a kunai knife, "Who are you and what do you want?"

Suddenly the impossible happened. The fisherman was standing next to Hapusai Ran holding the knife that had been in Hapusai's hand an instant earlier. Then in the next instant the fisherman was standing out in the center of the pond on top of the water. The fisherman gave a sneer as he held out his arm and purposefully dropped the kunai knife into the pond with a small splash. Another instant later the fisherman was sitting on the bank again with his fishing pole in hand and his back to Hapusai Ran.

Hapusai Ran felt a fear unlike any other he had ever experienced in his life clutch his guts with relentless terror. This was simply an impossibility in his experience. The feeling of the inevitability of his imminent death struck him, and his nerves and mind unexpectedly calmed down in response.

The fisherman spoke, "It is good that you are a fast learner. If you had pulled another of those I would have caused you pain the next time. You understand your life or death is within my grasp then I take it."

Hapusai Ran nodded then realized the man's back was still toward him, "I understand that I am powerless before such a demonstration."

The fisherman pulled a fish up on his line and carefully removed it to place into a wicker fishing creel as he spoke, "Then you should be able to understand why the Chi Masters are not allowed to have the training your so called lord desires. Why it is that I have forbidden it."

Hapusai Ran nodded, "The ordinary people would fear and distrust them. They would be killed because of that fear."

The fisherman stood up holding his fishing gear and turned to face Hapusai Ran, "I'm glad to see you understand so quickly and so well. I need my children here to do what I have given them to do. I can't have them continually fighting for their lives against the people they are intended to protect."

Hapusai Ran knelt down on the ground, "I'm sorry Lucky Cricket. I've heard the stories and tales of your life, but I never knew until this moment if I should truly believe them. You must have appeared for a reason. Is there a time of trouble to be faced by Ran Li once again?"

Hap Sing smiled gently, "I hate to say it but it has always been a time of trouble. The fact of existence is that trouble and life exist hand in hand together. The question which remains is this: What are the choices you are going to make in times such as these?"

Hapusai Ran raised his head, "What choices can I make?"

Hap Sing chuckled, "Hopefully good ones. You haven't been doing too well on that account lately. Don't fret because you face more important choices upon your return to Yokito. I have high hopes that your choices in the future will be better ones."

Hapusai Ran looked surprised, "You know of my dishonor?"

Hap Sing shook his head, "I know you have made mistakes in judgement. I can care less about your feelings of honor or dishonor other than hoping they help you avoid such errors in the future. Now on to my task for you."

Hapusai Ran felt a different kind of nervous, "Are you sending me to die like Grandmaster Chu Han?"

Hap Sing laughed a humorless devious chuckle, "I'm am pitting you against worse than a simple death brave ninja. I'm sentencing you to protect and raise your daughter until she meets the man who is the right person for her. She is very important to me, and I don't want her to be harmed before this happens. You will know him when you meet him for he shall also know of me. Take your charge seriously."

Hapusai Ran sat back on his behind, "I will have a daughter?"

Hap Sing nodded, "In slightly less than a month. You should hurry back to Yokito by boat to expedite your trip. Don't fail me in this."

Hapusai Ran watched in amazement as the Lucky Cricket faded out of existence as the sun crested the horizon in the east.

Afterword

Dear Reader,

I want to express my gratitude for your reading the beginning point of my works, and I hope you enjoyed it enough to pick up my second (and any subsequent books) in my *Tales from the Reading Dragon Inn* series. This has been a labor of both fun and work for me with many trying experiences along the way.

I've learned something of how to edit, proof, write, and create a small publishing company along the way to bringing this book to the marketplace. It has been worth my time and effort to see it in print at last. Yet, lest you think me some kind of philanthropist willingly placing my labors out for unauthorized consumption or use, I will state for the record that I am not. I am a capitalist, just not an overly greedy one.

I do hope you have the presence of personal character to have either purchased this work through a legitimate vendor, or borrowed it from a public or school library which made the choice to add it to their collection (or at worst receiving it from a friend or relative who legitimately purchased the book first). I know in our modern generation that protecting such antiquated concepts as "intellectual property" is considered laughable by some who consider the blood, sweat, and tears of some content producer as their free fodder for consumption without compensation.

If you are offended by the above paragraph, then good. You're probably the kind of selfish bastard who thinks the world owes them whatever they desire that I'm talking bad about. If you understand and sympathize with my plight as a creator who seeks to make some money from my creation, then you should understand that I've done my best to price my works both very competitively compared to many other publishers, and at what I also consider a good entertainment value for the customer.

Why is that? Because I'm also a reader/content consumer who believes in actually supporting the content creators out there instead of ripping off their stuff be it music, film, television, books, or web content.

Thank you for your support of my works, and the works of others like me.

Kelly R. Martin

The Tale of Adventure
continues in
Thomas the Poisoner

The story of Mikael Lidron, the human son of a knight who secretly longs for adventure. When Mikael travels on a journey with the half elf mage Firanda, he hopes to find both a touch of adventure and romance at her side. What he finds instead is unlike anything he ever expected.

Recruited into a secret organization of assassins, Mikael finds himself learning the trade of deception, the nature of death, and the odd course of his destiny. Various beings need to die, and the only force capable of making it happen belongs to the infamous assassin Thomas the Poisoner.